Here's what people are saying about Blood Moon:

In-your-face thrills. Forget morality. Forget redemption. Hide it from your children, and by all means, don't let your wife know you're reading it. She's always suspected you. This will convince her.
—*Queer Biz*

In the gay genre, *Blood Moon* does for the novel what Danielle Steele and John Grisham have been publishing in the straight world for years.
—*Frank Fenton*

Blood Moon is a novel about passion, betrayal, and murder among the very rich and powerful, some of whom just happen to be gay. It's about the false gods of power, wealth, and physical beauty. It's an epic tale about depravity in the glittery, glamorous, and sometimes tawdry world of South Florida
—*Glenn Moore*

A gut punch to the psyche—a masterpiece of power, pacing, and form. If only I could be Buck Brooke!
—*Ford Dutton*

This is an epic without rules or morality—like no other novel I've read. Dazzling like quicksilver. Luscious, intimate…and definitely on the cutting edge.
—*Gab*

A fireball from the time capsule of the pre-AIDS 70s. It will blow your mind or something else. Tell your friends, but keep it from your lover. It will give him too many ideas.
—*Munich Found*

A torrential new novel like the flooding of a riverbank. A poignant, spellbinding saga of a university class that went on to fabulous wealth, fame, and glory, except for those who took tragic and sometimes psychotic detours.
—*La Movida*

This book is loaded with cinematic images. Read *Blood Moon* at your own risk, and don't come looking for Oz or the ruby slippers.
—*James Stafford*

At center stage is the handsome, charismatic Buck Brooke III, a 27-year-old crusading newspaper reporter who's a member of that very rare breed of man who can voluptuously satisfy both women and men. He's notorious for ruining whomever he beds for all other sexual partners.
—*Pink Tri*

Power, money, and sex—not necessarily in that order—drive the characters in this siren song of the flesh.
—*What's New in Fiction*

Mesmerizing and brilliantly crafted, *Blood Moon* reads like *Dynasty* on steroids. A compelling psycho-sexual adventure of three beautiful men meeting on the fast road to hell.
—*Kathryn Cobb*

Blood Moon is a brilliant, thought-provoking, and neurotic thriller that's among the best in its genre.
--*Mississippi Rex*

If *Blood Moon* is ever made into a movie, it deserves nothing less than "knock your socks off" stars—it's that good.
—*Between the Sheets.*

A psycho-sexual *tour de force*. *Blood Moon* has kinetic power and the kind of razor-sharp images that mark you for life.
—*Night Reader*

BLOOD MOON

A novel about power, money, sex, brutality, love, religion, and obsession.

by Darwin Porter

The Georgia Literary Association
New York City, 2002

Also by Darwin Porter:

Rhinestone Country
Hollywood's Silent Closet
Midnight in Savannah
Razzle-Dazzle
Butterflies in Heat
Venus
Marika
and many of the *Frommer Guides* to Europe and
The Caribbean

The Georgia Literary Association
75 Saint Marks Place
Staten Island, NY 10301-1606
See our website at www.georgialit.com
or contact us at georgialit@aol.com

Photos by Russell Maynor
Design by SylvesterQ.com, Graphics by Jennings Studio NYC

For Danforth Prince

The Georgia Literary Association was established in Wilkes County, Georgia, in 1997, and relocated to New York City several years later. Aware of the distinguished literary history of Georgia, it's dedicated to the promotion of worthwhile reading that might not be endorsed by larger, more conservative publishing companies. With the re-release of one of our organization's best-sellers, *Blood Moon,* we'll continue to showcase the fine, diverse, and sometimes controversial entertainment coming out of the Deep South. For more information, see our website at www.georgialit.com.

"Imaginative entertainment for the 21st-century sensibility."

About the Author:

Darwin Porter, one of the most prolific writers in publishing today, once lived in South Florida, where much of this novel takes place. A former bureau chief based in Key West for the *Miami Herald*, he's the co-author of more than 600 editions of the *Frommer* travel guides to destinations that include most of Europe, the Caribbean, the Carolinas, and Georgia. When not traveling, which is rare, he lives in New York City.

Apart from his travel writing, he specializes in sagas, many of them brutal, all of them artful, showcasing some aspect of the social history of America during the 20th century. One reviewer defined Porter's literary niche as "set midway between intense one-handed eroticism and the literary canons of D.H. Lawrence and E.M. Forster."

His plots are not for the prudish, the squeamish, or the faint-hearted. His work is ballsy, edgy, satirical, charming, seminal, and funny. Occasionally his moral code, as shown by the behavior of his characters, is a bit untidy. Invariably, we receive as many letters denouncing him--especially from the Far Right--as we get in praise of his highly creative vision. But despite this (and perhaps because of it), we always find his work interesting, and at times, fascinating.

Film entrepreneur Eugene Raymond has stated, "Darwin Porter's work is characterized by an articulate obsession with the almost supernatural power of physical beauty. On the subject of beauty, male or female, Porter believes that extreme moralists are wrong: To be enraptured by physical beauty isn't so much the worship of a 'false god' as it's to a large extent hard-wired in the human brain. How far can physical beauty take you? *Blood Moon* says very far indeed. Try the Oval Office. Or Hollywood stardom. Even obscene wealth and world power."

Porter's other recent works have included *Rhinestone Country*, a homoerotic treatment of the country-western music industry and closeted lives south of the Mason-Dixon line, and *Hollywood's Silent Closet*. Based on interviews with eyewitnesses during the final years of their lives, *Hollywood's Silent Closet* presents a steamy but accurate portrait, set between 1919 and 1926, of the gossipy world of pre-Talkie Hollywood, which had a lot to be silent about, and where many of the sins were never depicted on the screen. A "brilliant primer" (*Gay London Times)* for the *Who's Who* of early filmmaking.

These, and other fine titles by Darwin Porter, are brought to you by the Georgia Literary Association.

Prologue (1977)

The wail of an ambulance sounded in Buck's ears, reminding him that it had been a night of sirens. "What a pack of bastards," he groaned in disgust as he fought his way through a milling throng of protesters.

At the edge of People's Park, the glow of a bonfire—a mock funeral for porn—roared like a furnace. Cheering the flames of burning books, high-stepping, short-skirted majorettes, the "Collins Girls," led a school band through its brassy sounds.

He wasn't part of the burst of ecstasy that surged through the crowds. Even in the midst of such strong moral crusaders, he could smell the air, heavy with the fumes of marijuana.

Some of the characters who'd answered Sister Rose's call to arms had made him recoil. By far, though, most of the demonstrators were the evangelist's "normal majority," good church-going people who felt betrayed by the moral drift of much of the country. But the rally also drew the fanatics of the far right, the Ku Klux Klan and the American Nazi Party.

A shouting, occasionally chanting group, some singing gospel hymns, formed a tight circle around a mountain of burning books and magazines. Guarding the print-fed flames, a dozen uniformed men carried a blood-red banner with black letters. *Firefighters For Christ.*

The police had cordoned off the bonfire but, as the crowds surged closer, the cops desperately fought to hold them back. The heat intensified, making Buck's face sting. Smoldering white-hot sparks shot out, sending streaks into the night. As flaming liquid rain showered down, several women screamed.

Appalled by the spectacle, he broke through the phalanx in time to watch the shapely legs of a *Playboy* centerfold catch flame and disintegrate.

The implication of the book-burning filled him with an ominous dread. He hadn't heard of a bonfire like this since the Nazis condemned books to the flames in 1933, and even then, it was a scene evoking the Middle Ages.

Before the pile of print could burn down, firemen tossed more books into the flaming mass. Turning from it, he stared defiantly into the enraptured faces of the spectators, their gleeful eyes paying no attention to him, as they reflected a spellbound joy. He felt trapped, the reluctant participant in some ancient tribal rite of exorcism.

Deep in its third hour, Sister Rose's moral crusade through the town of Okeechobee's "Combat Zone" of pornography and prostitution had erupted in violence. He was anxious to be at the core of the action.

Cutting a path through the crowds, he raced back to the main drag, The Strip, as a police helicopter hovered over his head. At a shop only twenty yards away, a gang of hardhats tossed bricks into a plate-glass window of a store advertising its wares as adult material. Once the glass was smashed, the men skirted over the jagged edges, climbing through the display window, seizing pornography from the shelves, and tossing it into baskets to feed the flames of the bonfire in the park.

All along the ten-block Strip, protesters confronting counter-protesters were caught in the mélée. A squad of policemen charged at combatants fighting in the middle of the street. The cops threw tear gas into the crowds, but some young men lobbed the canisters back. Choking on their own gas, the police, facing a barrage of raining rocks, fell back for cover.

Buck stood far out of the way, yet near enough to watch the police regroup to charge again. Their faces protected by plexiglass shields, they'd become more aggressive. Both protesters and counter-protesters were clubbed, as nightsticks flailed wildly. Rocks and bottles sailed through the air. Advocates of non-violence reverted to self-defense. Middle-aged women ran screaming, some of them falling back against the broken shards of glass left by the hardhats. More tear-gas canisters came crashing down. Mace burned unprotected skin.

Gangs roamed the streets, setting random fires in trash cans. Sirens wailed. Smoke bellowed from a movie theater as fire engines pulled in.

For no reason at all, a burly woman in a Salvation Army uniform came up behind Buck, getting a stranglehold on his neck and shouting incoherently in his ear. His eyes smarting from the gas, he broke her hold, escaping her noose. The coins in her collection bucket scattered on the pavement below. Her eyes were crazed.

He ducked out of the way, just as rebellious prostitutes in a "hot bed" hotel overhead dropped water-filled balloons into the crowd who would deny them a living.

In saffron robes, a bedraggled crew of shaven-headed Hare Krishna disciples stood forlornly on the sidewalk, stoically facing the taunts of punks. When one of the punks spat in the young man's face, he didn't resist.

Imitating the Nazis, the punks were clad in brown shirts. Cheering them on in their attack was a band of determined-faced National Socialist League members, both men and women, carrying swastikas and a large metal eagle which wavered precariously over the heads of the Hare Krishna.

Buck slipped through the crowd forming around them for a closer look, the better to write an eyewitness account for tomorrow's *Examiner.*

Out of the same hotel from which the balloons were tossed, a skinny, sleazily dressed prostitute—a girl no more than fifteen—fled onto the street. Spotting her, the brown shirts broke from the Hare Krishna and chased after the teenager. She ran screaming into an alleyway off The Strip.

In mob frenzy, the National Socialist League members rushed to see what their own punks would do to the girl. Buck headed for the alley too, just in time to see one of the brown shirts deliver several chopping strokes to the girl's head. Small rivulets of blood cascaded down her temple. Squirming hysterically, the girl cried out in pain and fear, as more blows rained down.

With no regard for his own safety, Buck—outnumbered in a dark alley and surrounded by a pack of Nazis—lunged forward, grabbing one of the punks by his brown shirt, yanking him back and slugging him in the face. As he ducked the man's retaliatory blow, a huge black blur descended upon him. Out of the corner of his eye, he had a glimmer of the big bronze eagle.

The blow to his skull resounded like a sickening, dull thud. In moments, piercing shock waves electrified his body.

As the world grew faint, fainter, a whirlwind of images spun in his mind. On The Strip, the sounds of bullets fired into the air ricocheted in his head. He welcomed the all-encompassing blackness, the spinning, staggering fall into oblivion.

***

He found himself wandering in a state, almost dreamlike, where the mind travels in the astral world, floating between semiconsciousness and reality.

Everything was viewed like a startling confrontation with a distorting mirror—shattering, overwhelming.

In the mirror, he confronted Medusa's face—intense, savage. Then the image became his own, only to revert to Medusa again, her serpentine headdress coiled to strike him at any moment.

Would he, as in mythology, turn to stone, or would he live to slay her as Perseus had done?

As he asked that question, he struggled for control of his mind. It was still foggy, and he found himself drifting back to where all this had begun.

There were no shadows then, no blur.

The way he remembered it, the sun was shining.

Chapter One

The old news tower dominated the southern skyline of Okeechobee. When thirty-year-old Buck Brooke I, already a millionaire, had arrived here in the 1920s and saw spread before him a town of flat one- and two-story buildings on the edge of a mangrove swamp, he'd conceived of the idea of a news tower rising majestically over the merging city like an exclamation point.

Coral colored, it soared like a Romanesque campanile, modeled after the Leaning Tower of Pisa. The news tower didn't lean, except in its archly conservative view of the day's events. In fact, Buck I came to be known as a symbolic bedfellow of President Coolidge.

When Buck I ran out of white marble, he'd ordered his architect to substitute inexpensive ceramic tiles from Cuba and, in years to come, he would view that fact as one of the wrong decisions of his life. "It was the beginning of compromise," he would tell his son, Buck II. "If you begin with one compromise, the second one is waiting at the door."

Local residents had predicted the belfry would collapse when hit by its first hurricane. They were wrong. It rode out the storm of 1927 and went on to withstand more assaults, both from nature and the public.

Before 1937, three men had leaped to their deaths from its oyster-shell balcony before it was closed to the public.

In time, other skyscrapers would rise to pierce the landscape and, in spite of that competition, the tower defiantly stood—still the tallest building in the city, still the symbol of Okeechobee, and now with tourists buying picture postcards of its likeness from vendors nearby.

Its worst attack came in September of 1969 when Hurricane Rose swept over Okeechobee, a disaster unprecedented since Donna unleashed her fury way back in 1960. The blast from Rose claimed thirteen lives and left hundreds more homeless among those who lived in trailer camps and poorly constructed little frame houses on the marshy swamplands of the city.

The tower bravely stood, but hundreds of its Cuban tiles were sent hurtling into the devastating winds, becoming deadly missiles. When the storm had passed and city building inspectors surveyed the tower, they warned that it was structurally weak and might not withstand another blow like Rose.

To the press the following day, Sister Rose, the evangelist, protested furiously, claiming the hurricane bearing her name was an attempt on the part of the U.S. government to embarrass her and discredit her charismatic Christian movement. The Weather Bureau responded by saying the name, Rose, was selected at random from a list prepared years before. It had been time to name a hurricane after a woman, since the last big blow was called Quentin and had been even more destructive.

Sister Rose had not been convinced and, in her fury, she'd set about to stir up an even greater storm than nature's death-dealing blow.

***

The soggy heat came right through his T-shirt as Buck Brooke III, the third in line of the Brooke newspaper dynasty, eased his six-foot frame into the back seat of his Fleetwood sedan. He was fresh from jogging. No window separated the rear and front seats. He'd had it removed. Such a separation didn't strike him as very democratic, and he was also too news-oriented to keep many secrets. He would prefer to ride up in the front seat with the driver, except for one reason. He always read his morning rival, The Okeechobee News, along with The Miami Herald and The New York Times. For that, he needed all the room in the back seat available to him.

He leaned back, finding the most comfortable spot. At twenty-seven, nearly the same age as old Buck I was when he'd first arrived in town in the 1920s, Buck No. Three was already one of America's youngest and most dynamic publishers. His critics labeled him a 1970s breed of muckraker. He preferred to call his relentless, diligent digging for truth honest reporting. The day he'd taken control of the failing, ultra-conservative *Examiner* from his octogenarian grandfather, Buck I, he'd told his editors, "We're gonna raise some hell!"

At first, few took him seriously, perhaps because of his youth, inexperience, and his reputation as a sexual athlete. In the past few months, he'd managed to raise the ire of the conservative community, as a dramatic shift in his newspaper's readership had come about.

Passing the causeway-linked islands that lay in the blue-green bay, he pressed a button on his left, lowering the window to let the fresh sea breeze blow through his light sand-colored hair.

Sucking the clean air deep into his gut, he leaned forward to reach for his phone. Between work and play, he hadn't been getting much sleep lately. Yet he was still exceptionally handsome, lean, muscular and, as an ex-Marine, no longer able to pose for a poster advertising the purity of the all-American boy, an image that had plagued him through his college days.

A stubble of blond-red beard appeared like golden flecks on his strong jaws, the only feature about his appearance that made him look solid and reliable. Certainly not his eyes. Flecked with white, his piercing blue eyes always seemed to be searching. It was a fierce, hungry look he had as he stalked the city like a hunter, seeking a story, excitement, a partner for the night—but mostly a story, and the subject didn't matter. He was a "scoop artist," often accused of journalistic excess. He preferred to think he "outreported" his rivals. He didn't believe in secrets, particularly if those closeted facts had to do with the public's business and right to know. He'd read *All the President's Men* three times.

Hurriedly, he made two calls, one to postpone a karate lesson scheduled for that afternoon, another to delay an interview and photography session with a national magazine that was flirting with the idea of naming him, "The Sexiest Man in America," perhaps even "The Sexiest Man Alive!" He didn't exactly picture himself as a pin-up, and he wanted to be taken more seriously, maybe even winning a Pulitzer Prize one day. But his public relations department had convinced him that inviting this kind of publicity would only increase circulation of the *Examiner*.

He wasn't so sure, but he finally gave in. What the hell! It was the 70s after all. If dropping trou before a photographer would make his paper stronger, he'd do it. After all, it was a national family magazine, and they surely didn't plan to photograph his dick. No doubt he'd be asked to wear the skimpiest and most revealing of swimwear but not show "the full monty," as the British say. Here in Florida and certainly on his private island he went nude or practically nude half the time anyway.

The reason he had to postpone these sessions was that he'd received a sudden and unexpected dinner invitation.

The meeting had been long overdue, and he dreaded it. But the time had come to meet Okeechobee's most famous, controversial, and glamorous resident. The celebrated evangelist herself, Rose Phillips, had invited him "for a little bread and wine in the name of Jesus" at her bayfront mansion.

With pride, he took in his newspaper tower rising from the horizon, glistening in the bright early morning sun. Stripped of many of its tiles, it was still a mighty fine sight, and he felt honored to occupy a penthouse office in it.

Even now, after more than eighteen months as publisher of the *Examiner*, he still couldn't believe at times that he was in charge, and only so recently after leaving the Marine Corps. He was always reminded that he got that post by an accident. If his father, Buck II, along with his wife, Margaret, hadn't died in the crash of a private plane near Tampa in 1967, Buck III might still be a copyboy.

When Buck I's doctors had insisted that he—America's last Citizen Kane, as they called him—step down, the old man had done so reluctantly. With no enthusiasm, he turned over the *Examiner* to his grandson and, within weeks, had accused his heir of "destroying my life's work." That accusation stung Buck III. He wanted his grandfather to like him. He loved the old man, and it was with great pain that he watched him advance rapidly toward senility

Their differences were political.

Buck III's driver pulled into the no-parking zone at the main entrance to the *Examiner*, and in a moment Buck had leaped from the sedan, disappearing behind the wrought-iron grillwork. He knew his grandfather would age another year if he could see his heir going to work in shorts. Buck III cared little for formalities. He'd have plenty of time later to shower and dress in a suit.

Stepping into the precincts of the *Examiner* always brought back memories, many of them painful.

From copy boy to telephone dictationist to ad salesman, he'd run the gamut of jobs on the paper. When he'd gotten serious as a reporter and had started to write about slum housing and the problem of guns and their connection to random violence, he'd watched in dismay as those stories were killed.

In frustration, he'd quit the *Examiner* and joined the Marine Corps. Old Buck had approved of that, as he'd found containing young Buck too difficult. "The corps will make a man out of you." Now, after being away from Okeechobee for several years, Buck III was back and in total charge. He knew he'd been placed at the helm only because of his grandfather's declining health, and not because the old man had any great faith in him as a publisher. The thought saddened him.

Sighing, he stepped into the elevator. Brushing aside thoughts of old Buck, he headed for the publisher's suite. He had a gut feeling. This was not to be a typical news day. Some big, hot story was about to break.

***

Going up in a baroque birdcage elevator, he stepped out in time to encounter one of his city reporters, Susan Howard, both of them refugees from the University of Okeechobee's class of '71. As the daughter of Jim Howard, one of the country's best known criminal lawyers, and Ingrid, one of America's leading female columnists, Susan's news sources ranged from a retired Secretary of State, whom she'd once dated in spite of the age difference, to a feminist *cause célèbre* who'd killed a man to avenge her rape.

On seeing Buck in shorts, her vivacious green eyes flashed and she let out a soft whistle. She tossed back her long auburn hair, which revealed her aristocratically pale complexion and the white expanse of her throat. She'd been named after the late actress Susan Hayward, to which, amazingly, she bore a striking resemblance. Half of her mail was still addressed Hayward instead of Howard. "My, what a fine pair of legs!" she said.

"Tacky, tacky," he said. "But if you like looking at them so much, why won't you go out with me?"

She placed her hand on the waist of her beautifully toned and well-shaped body. "What? So I'd be accused of using you to advance my career? No way!"

He smiled and stood for a long moment, watching her as she made her way across the city room. As she did, he remembered when, as editor of the university newspaper, *The Okeechobee Hurricane*, he'd presented her at the football stadium with an orchid and a kiss when her classmates had voted her "Hurricane Honey of the Year."

He'd always liked her and was sorry about the breakup of her marriage to Gene Robinson, who'd been the university's champion tennis player.

Buck had never dated Susan because his best friend, Robert Dante, preferred to keep him on a tight leash. He often resented Robert's hawk-eying his every move but to keep a best friend as devoted as Robert you had to make compromises, and he was prepared to make them. He'd been lonely too long to turn down love, particularly love as powerful as Robert's. Maybe it wasn't the type of love Buck truly wanted and desired, but, what the hell, he wasn't saying no.

He'd never had many friends except for Robert. A lot of people, both men and women, were attracted to him but nothing lasting ever came of it. Before his marriage to Susan, Gene Robinson had been his closest friend. Or at least one of his two closest friends. Robert and Gene used to compete for that best friend label. Buck agonized a lot back then over how to spend his evenings. Would he go out with Gene for a night on the town, or else stay home with Robert? Robert didn't like to go out much. When Gene started dating Susan, the problem was solved for him. He happily spent more time with Robert, even though he missed Gene something awful.

Gene had become involved in a sex scandal with a little girl which had led to his divorce from Susan. After that incident, Buck had never seen Gene again. Buck suspected that Gene might have called him, but Robert screened all his calls and had claimed that there had never been a message from Gene.

Buck felt ashamed about how he'd let Gene fend for himself and hadn't stood by him. He'd deserted Gene, and that's what Robert had demanded. If Buck had it to do over again, he would not have listened to Robert and would have helped Gene through his ordeal.

Sweating and feeling like he smelled like a football locker room, Buck headed for the private quarters of the tower, where in the 1930s old Buck had been known for auditioning some of the editors who worked on the women's page.

Robert would be there waiting for him.

***

Even when Susan was writing seriously about a subject, one not related to sex such as her University of Okeechobee series, much of her mail still brought up that marriage to Gene Robinson. It was an image that had stuck in the public mind. Their marriage had even made the frontpage of the *Examiner*. Every now and then she still went to the morgue to gaze at her wedding pictures snapped by the paparazzi. Back then they had been Florida's golden couple. The luminously handsome tennis star "with the great legs" marrying the university beauty queen "with the great legs." Even though it was the 70s, their whole romance carried the aura of the 50s with it, evoking prom nights and pink carnations.

After Gene's arrest, and while she was still his wife, she'd been left alone at home to receive the offers pouring in. They were lurid. The most modest proposal came from *Playgirl* who wanted him to pose nude for the centerfold. At the bottom of the offer, a photo editor had written this notation: "We can even go for a shot fully erect, although I hear in his case we'll have to extend it to a three-page spread. Is this true? Or just a rumor?"

The first thing Susan spotted was a pile of mail on her desk. A lot of people objected to her three-part series on her former alma mater. Many readers—former classmates—chastised her for being so cruel to the school that had received her with open arms and honored her with so many awards, even acknowledging her beauty.

Some of the letters she'd read in yesterday's pile were embarrassing. "If you'd been a proper wife to Gene Robinson and hadn't spent all your time in beauty parlors, he wouldn't have exposed himself to that little girl."

One gay male reader, having nothing to do with her article, wrote in: "Gene Robinson can expose himself to me any day. The spin is, he's hung like a horse."

Even her female classmates back in college had been open in expressing their jealousy over her snaring Gene. He was the most desirable "catch" on campus with the exception of Buck himself. The gay men at the university and the horny young women were about evenly divided in the debate over who was hotter: Gene or Buck. They were definitely the pin-up boys of the class of '71. Buck was constantly photographed without his shirt jogging around the campus in too tight shorts that showed an endowment larger than that of the university's.

Gene was equally pursued, especially by the almost all-gay staff of the university's picture magazine Tempo. One student photographer, Leroy Fitzgerald, finally got the "shot" he wanted: a frontal nude view of Gene snapped while he was showering after winning a tennis match. She'd heard that copies of that picture lined the walls of some gay fraternity houses.

Curiously enough, Gene didn't seem embarrassed about this exposure of his privates at all. If anything, he took perverse delight in this notoriety. Perhaps that should have been her first clue about the streak of exhibitionism in him. But she'd been too blind to see.

That exhibitionism didn't extend into their private lives. If anything, after her marriage he was extremely modest around their apartment. Once when it had been too long between sexual encounters, she'd gone into the bathroom where she'd heard him showering. Hoping to entice him, she'd pulled off her clothes and stepped into the stall with him. He'd been horrified at her action. "You fucking whore!" he'd screamed at her. "Get the hell out of here. There are some things men like to do in private."

She'd been brutally rejected and had fled to her mother's house, until Ingrid had finally counseled her to go back and make the marriage work. "It's just a period of adjustment."

That period of adjustment seemed to stretch on forever until she felt at times she'd never adjust to him. Deep into the third month of her marriage, she came to fully realize that he regarded women either as sluts or madonnas. He clearly wanted her to play the role of madonna. As long as she was the dutiful wife, the perfectly groomed playmate, the meal preparation artist, the toilet scrubber, the grocery shopper, he adored her and often brought her fresh flowers. The moment she wanted sex, she was the "whore of Babylon." He often compared her unfavorably to Sister Rose, demanding she use the evangelist as her role model instead of some "whorish Hollywood trash like Jane Fonda."

"When I married you," he had told her, "I didn't want Marilyn Monroe. I wanted someone like Donna Reed."

"But even she played a whore in *From Here to Eternity*," Susan had protested.

He'd slapped her face real hard that afternoon and stormed out of the house. Never before had he struck her. She feared this was the beginning of a violent streak in their marriage and she wasn't going to tolerate it. She wanted to rush home again to Ingrid, who had a long background in writing about domestic violence, but she decided to stick it out, learning to solve her problems by herself.

The marriage hadn't gotten better—if anything, it had worsened. The night before what turned out to be the last big game of his career had been the worst. When he'd stormed out of the house that night, he hadn't come back at all. She didn't know where he'd spent the night. She suspected he'd gone off with Buck that evening, although she could never be sure. Gene didn't come home the next morning, the day of the big game.

By five o'clock on the same day, after he'd lost one of the big matches of his career, a call had come in from Jim, her father. Gene had been arrested for exposing himself to that little girl. Jim was willing to take on Gene's case, but Susan had talked him out of it. She greatly regretted her decision today. Back then she'd wanted revenge. Even though she didn't have the perfect marriage, she had had the image of the perfect marriage. The subsequent humiliation of Gene and the public exposure of her imperfect marriage caused her even today to feel a sense of shame. Gene's case had never come to trial. After all the publicity, the girl's mother dropped the charges. The mother, it seemed, was not a paragon of virtue herself. As the case gained more attention, the mother didn't want her own background investigated. The evidence was that the little girl had seen men exposed before, often as they made love to her mother. The mother still had a strong case against Gene, but her lawyers finally told her to drop it.

Like Buck, Gene was an orphan, his parents dying of cancer within three years of each other. Susan had been equally amazed that Biff, the Police Chief of Okeechobee, in spite of the bad publicity, gave Gene a position as a police officer, but the chief always liked grand plays like that. He appeared understanding and generous to a fallen hero, and, although criticized in some quarters, he won renewed respect from voters for his act of kindness.

After the awful hot smelly afternoon of Gene's arrest, nothing was ever the same again for Susan—not that it had been that good before. She'd known other men following her divorce from Gene. But with none of them had she been able to capture the excitement she felt when she'd first gotten to know Gene and his best friend Buck. They were both golden boys who had thrilled her. Like the rest of the university, she couldn't decide which one to go for, as she found both men immensely appealing and very sexy. She'd finally settled for Gene because Buck seemed to have an implacable guardian at the palace door, Robert Dante.

She'd heard the usual rumors about Robert and Buck, but she'd also known that Buck was dating her rival beauty queen, Pamela Collins, who was Pamela Harrison back then before her subsequent marriage to the present mayoral candidate, Barry. One day Pamela confided to her, "There's no way in hell that Buck can be gay. I'm walking bow-legged."

Susan wasn't sure. She'd even heard rumors about Buck and Gene, although she felt that this was just gay gossip. The gays wanted to include Buck and Gene as one of them whether they actually were gay or not. But who knew what went on behind closed doors with Buck and Gene, or with Buck and Robert?

In time she'd turned her sights away from both men and had hooked up with an aspiring young attorney. They'd lived together during most of Buck's time in the Marine Corps. His name was Ron Metzger, and life with him had evoked an interview she'd once had with that oldtime 30s movie star, Joan Blondell.

In describing her marriage to fellow actor Dick Powell, Blondell had confided: "Before having sex he always spent an hour in the bathroom soaping and cleaning every crevice. Then he gargled with Listerine for about five minutes before rushing to bed to do his duty. In five minutes he was back in the bathroom, showering and gargling *après sex*."

The same had been true with Ron. She'd never known such hygiene.

When Buck had returned to the *Examiner* after a long absence, he'd been surprised to find her working for the paper. She'd been hired by his grandfather. Buck had adopted a flirty air with her, but nothing ever came of it. He was always talking about why she never went out with him, but he'd never called and asked her out on a date.

In eighteen months, she'd called him three times asking him to different events. She never got him on the phone, but always spoke to a chilly Robert instead. At the sound of her voice, Robert sounded like the wind of an Artic night. She never really knew for sure if he gave Buck her messages or not.

A call came in for her. She reluctantly picked up the receiver, fearing it was another irate reader offended by her series on wild sex parties at the university.

The caller was anonymous. His voice was belligerent.

"Listen, bitch, and listen good. I'll tip you off to a real story."

"What might that be?" she asked with growing impatience. At least he'd called her "bitch" instead of the usual "cunt."

"What would you say to this? There's a house right here in our fair city where teenage boys are being auctioned off every night to older men. Some of the buyers are the biggest names in town. They call the boys 'Lolitos'."

"Wha..." she said into a dying phone. He'd hung up.

"Probably a crackpot," she said to herself, turning to that mountain of mail. She nervously looked into her IN basket. She wondered what new assignment Buck would give her, following her series on the university. The basket was empty.

After she'd opened her first three letters, all of them attacking her, the voice of that petulant man came back to haunt her. Unlike the usual crank call, his voice had a certain conviction to it. A teenage boy auction. The idea was so bizarre that she had to consider that it just might be true. After all, it was the 70s.

***

In his office, Buck III ignored the stern, foreboding portrait of old Buck I staring down at him and turned instead to face the smiling, beaming face of Robert. Regardless of how condemned he might be in other quarters, there was one sure thing in life: Robert was always glad to see him even though he'd just kissed him goodbye at his house only an hour before.

Everybody called Robert his "male secretary." But Robert was hardly that. He was a co-partner in life. He was not only Buck's right-hand man, but also his best friend, and had been ever since they'd first met in their freshman year at the university. Robert was the primary moral support of Buck's life. "I couldn't get through life without you, kid," Buck always told Robert.

Once the door to the suite was closed, Robert wrapped his arms around him and gave him a deep kiss. "I've missed you something terrible," Robert said.

"I was away only an hour."

"It seemed like an eternity to me," Robert said. Buck raised his arms as Robert slipped his soggy T-shirt over his head. "But anything's better than when you were away with the marines."

"You were always there waiting when I got leave. If I recall, you missed me so much I couldn't even take a crap without you hovering over me."

"You got it, big guy. I didn't want you out of my sight for a moment. I nearly died when you joined the corps. There I was, like Lili Marleen waiting outside the barracks gate."

"I'm back," Buck said. "I'm yours."

As he trailed Robert into the shower room in back of the office, he was struck by his friend's seemingly ageless quality. He and Robert were the same age, and both had been graduated from the university in '71 along with Gene Robinson and Susan Howard. Robert looked much younger than Buck, or even Susan, for that matter. He could easily pass for twenty-one. Buck could no longer do that. If anything, his years in the corps had made him more ruggedly handsome than that pretty boy look he'd had when he'd first enrolled at the university. He and Robert had looked much more alike back then. Through all his workouts and military training, Buck had put on more beef whereas Robert still could wear the same blue jeans he'd bought in his freshman year.

Many people thought Buck and Robert were brothers because of their incredible resemblance to each other. With Robert's tall, lean physique, and with his deep blue eyes and dark blond hair, he could easily have been Buck's twin. Robert's features seemingly remained locked in some time capsule whereas Buck's look was moving ever so steadily toward the ripe old age of thirty. On two occasions before joining the Marines, Buck had had Robert impersonate him at two social functions, and the masquerade had come off. He doubted if they could get away with that today.

Robert had lived in Buck's house ever since he'd been a struggling university student. After Buck had learned that his newly found friend didn't really have enough money to pay for adequate living space after his tuition bill had been settled, he'd insisted that Robert move in with him. After all, Buck owned a big house left to him by his parents.

Ever since that day, thanks to Buck's generosity, Robert hadn't gone hungry or without money. In fact, he was the only one left in that house when Buck had gone into the service.

Robert didn't just accept handouts. He'd earned his keep, becoming virtually indispensable in Buck's life from the first day he moved in. Buck wasn't great at details and, as a Virgo, Robert ran his life, handling all the little horrors that came along. Over the years, Buck had come to rely on him completely.

Robert always arrived at the office an hour earlier than Buck to have his desk ready for him and to lay out emergency communications. He was also here to help him through his morning shower.

Kneeling before Buck, Robert pulled down his jogging shorts. Taking both hands, he caressed Buck's butt and in one sudden move pulled down his jock strap with such force Buck's cock sprang out and hit Robert in the face. Availing himself of the opportunity, Robert flicked his tongue across it.

"C'mon, I'm all sweaty and smelly," Buck said in way of feeble protest.

"That's the sweetest aroma I've ever smelled. You can put your shoes under my bed any time."

"I think I already do that." He pulled Robert to his feet, gave him a quick kiss, and stepped into the shower.

He turned his face up to the showerjet, and it seemed to wash away everything that was troubling him this morning. As much as he tried to make Robert his equal, his best friend always insisted upon the servant role. "It's my life, and I can do what I want with it," Robert had once told him. Buck finally caved in and gave up, fully recognizing that Robert wanted to wait on him.

Their relationship had always been about compromise, ever since that first day he'd discovered that Robert was gay. "A straight man and a gay man can be friends, even best friends," he'd told Robert after their first month together. "Hell, dude, it's 1968."

As he put his face up under the waterjets, Buck wondered how straight he still was, after lying night after night in bed with a hot gay male who did the most tantalizingly delicious things to him without ever demanding that he reciprocate. "It's not fair to you," Buck had said. "This is a master-slave relationship. You service me. I do nothing for you. You deserve better."

"It's okay," Robert had always assured him. "I could never settle for anyone but you. You'll grow to love me as I love you."

Even though Robert had been endlessly patient with him, their love had never blossomed like Robert wanted. It still wasn't a full relationship, and Buck felt troubled by this. He knew they were moving closer and closer together as the months went by, but, even so, there was a part of Buck that wanted to experiment and have other relationships— yes, even affairs with women. He thought a lot about Susan but hadn't done anything about it. Hurting Robert wasn't exactly a turn-on for him. He hated himself for not totally sharing Robert's vision for their life together. Even though he secretly experimented on the side, he always came home to Robert.

He made a vow to the running water and to himself. He was going to begin, regardless of how awkwardly, to give more of himself to Robert. If he could give more, it would ease his guilty conscious about his sexual experimentations on the side. Or so he thought as he rinsed the last of the shampoo out of his hair.

Stepping out of the shower, he found his ever-faithful Robert waiting to rub him vigorously with a towel. He hummed a low tune as Robert dried off every inch of his body, paying particular attention to his genitals and pubic hair. Robert always kissed both cheeks of his butt to signal he was dry enough to get dressed.

Wrapping a towel around his waist, Buck headed for the dressing room where Robert had laid out a suit and a tie for the business day. The white shirt was starched very lightly, just like Buck preferred it. Robert always knew.

"What's it going to be today?" Buck asked. Robert was a nut about selecting his underwear.

He took the latest offering and held it up in the air. "How in the fuck am I going to fit all I've got into such a small pouch?"

"It'll work." Robert helped him into the underpants which seemed designed to show off genitalia more than conceal it. Reaching into the pouch, Robert artfully arranged Buck's cock.

"Stop it!" Buck said. "You're giving me a hard-on."

"Wouldn't be the first time." He stood up and looked Buck in the face with a fierce determination. "Or the last!" He gave him a quick kiss and headed back to the office.

Buck turned from him and slipped on his suit. After a final inspection in the mirror, he pronounced himself okay to enter his office and take up the day's work.

***

Buck smiled as he walked in and saw Robert at his desk. Casting one glance at his grandfather's portrait, Buck asked facetiously, "Can't we liven this place up with a de Kooning?"

Robert laughed softly, as if agreeing the place could sure use one. A frown crossed his brow. "You can't afford one. Not with the salary your granddad's got you on. Those girls who want to go out with you think you're so rich. You're not. I should know. I try to balance your checking account."

Buck smiled sardonically at the truth of that. "And you do a great job. But do you have to keep me on an allowance? Like some kid?"

"Yeah," Robert said, smiling to soften his words but meaning them. "Until you stop acting like one."

"Christ," Buck said. "I'm afraid I'll never grow up despite your attempts to drag me kicking and screaming into adulthood."

"You're doing just fine."

"Thanks a lot. You always make me feel good even when the rest of the world's against me." Buck meant what he said. But a lot of emotions and feelings between Robert and him remained unspoken. It was as if each would go just so far, then pull back abruptly at the brink of something.

In his inner sanctum. Buck glared at the tight confines and dowdy furnishings of his tower office. Even though his granddad had given him complete editorial control, the old man severely limited how much money he could draw from the corporation.

He glanced up suddenly, feeling Robert's eyes. Sometimes when Buck wasn't looking, he'd sense Robert staring at him. Good, dependable Robert knew all his secrets. Buck wished he didn't have to hire Robert as a secretary, but Robert insisted on keeping the job. Three times he'd turned down promotions to more important managerial posts on the paper.

Buck's fingers tightened on a news release. "Stick around," he told Robert, as a determined look crossed his brow. "One day I'll have eight de Koonings in this office. Paid for with money *I've* earned."

Robert faced him squarely. "Maybe more. Even a Matisse."

Buck glanced briefly at the rest of the papers Robert had marked "urgent" and left on his desk.

"I got a call from Sister Rose early this morning," Robert said. "About tonight's dinner."

"What about it? She cancelled, I hope."

"No such luck. You'd better get ready to slip through the womb again."

"Is that a reference to being born again?"

"You got it." Robert's face made it obvious what he thought of Sister Rose.

"I think she'll want to convert me tonight. Might make a headline. Like Jerry Falwell winning over Bob Guccione and having him turn *Penthouse* into a religious journal."

The buzzer from the receptionist's office alerted him that his granddad was on the phone with his ritualistic morning call. Muffling the receiver, he turned to Robert and, with a sigh, whispered, "He's just checking up on how I'm doing in potty-training."

Thirty minutes later, Buck stood alone on the balcony of his tower suite overlooking the city below. Old Buck always claimed that standing here gave him a sense of power over Okeechobee. But Buck didn't feel that way this morning. If anything, he felt impotent. Old Buck gave him power, then threatened to take it away.

He tried to forget the argument he'd had on the phone with his granddad, who'd objected to his column on capital punishment, published only yesterday. In it, he'd called the governor "Bloody Bob," placing the *Examiner* as a firm opponent of the death penalty his granddad had always staunchly advocated. Much to Buck's deep regret, it seemed that they couldn't agree on anything. Robert, when he was being extremely critical, said that most of Buck I's ideas were formed before 1914. In some sad way, that seemed true.

Later that morning, Robert told him that an anonymous caller had given the city desk "a hot tip." Some corporations were buying up those seedy hotels on South Beach, moving out—or trying to—retired elderly Jews, leaving them homeless. A few men working for those companies had boasted to about-to-be-evicted tenants. "We're gonna get rid of every Jew on the beach."

"That sounds like Hitler and the Warsaw Ghetto," Buck said.

"It also sounds far-fetched," Robert cautioned. "We get a lot of crank calls."

"I've got a hunch there's some truth to this one. Let's at least put a reporter on it. I liked Susan's series on the university. This might be her kind of thing. She's also a close friend of Rose's sister and nemesis, our darling Hazel. If anybody knows what's going on at the beach, Hazel Phillips does, especially now that she's running for mayor."

"Are you going to vote for Hazel over your old buddy, Barry?" The subject of Barry for some reason caused great apprehension in Robert.

"Of course, I am. Barry Collins and I, even when we were friends, never agreed politically on anything."

"Have you forgiven him for marrying Pamela?"

"Now you're being bitchy," Buck said. "You know I never loved Pamela."

"What do you call it then? Making love to her?"

"That was a long time ago. I hear she's drinking a lot these days."

"A complete alcoholic. Never got over the loss of you."

"I'm sure there are other reasons," Buck said.

"Bullshit! Once anybody goes to bed with Buck Brooke, he ruins them for all other sex partners."

"That's very flattering."

"In my case, it's the truth," Robert said. "If you want Roland to assign Susan, I'll convey the message." He turned and walked away.

Later, behind the glass enclosures in his office, Buck stood silently after Robert left to give his message to Roland Hunter, the city editor.

Minutes later, the shuffling, bedslipper-shod feet of the city editor headed toward the desk of Susan. Roland placed nicotine-stained fingers on her shoulder as he apparently told her about the tip Buck had received.

Tall, reserved Roland Hunter never liked Buck, and Buck wondered why he kept him in that post.

Hired by Buck I, Roland was good at his work—thorough, competent, efficient, always demanding that a reporter "dig a little deeper."

All his life he'd been plagued by "my afflictions," to hear him tell it, and he gobbled pain-killing pills for his ailments, many of which Buck considered hypochondriacal. Roland tried to control his belly-aching with what sometimes turned out to be two or three extra gin martinis at his long lunches.

Through the glass partition, Buck met Roland's eyes. The city editor turned from the sight of him without acknowledgment.

***

On the way to Sister Rose's bayfront-bordering Paradise Shores, Buck suspected that she was going to make trouble for the *Examiner*. Before he took over the paper, his granddad had devoted a lot of space to praising the Rose Phillips Charismatic Association, of which she was the founder and director. It was said to be the nation's largest anti-Communist movement. But, in spite of his granddad's policy, when young Buck took over the paper he'd told Roland, "If Sister Rose wants publicity, let her take out an ad, and pay for it!"

He didn't like the taste of her heady stew of far-right politics with old-time fundamentalism. He didn't know why she needed his paper anyway. She knew how to get her message across, as she'd become the consummate TV and radio reverend—America's most controversial and flamboyant preacher.

Sister Rose's thirty-two room bayfront mansion occupied an entire island, Paradise Shores, with a short coral runway connecting it to the mainland.

"So this is where Miss Flower Petal lives," he said to his driver. "I'm jealous already. Religion sure pays better than the newspaper business."

Once the retirement home of a Detroit car manufacturer, the 1920s winter mansion had been changed and wrenched apart to meet Rose's needs. His limousine entered a tall wrought-iron gate, with a rose petal motif intricately worked into each crossbar. The car came to a stop in the driveway, and he got out and headed for the door. Along the way he passed a heart-shaped pool, each of its two voluptuous curves extending toward the bay. Parked right in front of her entrance stood a Rolls-Royce in dusty rose.

Even though he'd heard stories, he was still awed by the opulence of her mansion and statuary-filled grounds. As he rang the doorbell, he was greeted by the chimes and recorded voice of Rose singing a chorus of "Amazing Grace." The sound beamed not only through the house, but into the courtyard. With a slight smirk, he mumbled to himself,

"This pussy's not to be believed."

A black maid led him into the parlor where he waited for Rose to appear. The room itself was a mass of white—not only the carpet, draperies, sofas and chairs, but even the heart-shaped pillows, all fringed and ruffled. In the center was an overscaled coffee table, also heart-shaped. Even the stained-glass windows were heart-shaped. White roses, her symbol, filled every white vase.

Striding into the room in a low-cut, form-fitting white gown that did little to conceal her breasts, the tall, statuesque Rose exuded euphoria. All smiles, she made a striking presence, giving off joyful radiation, the way Loretta Young used to make entrances on her long-ago TV series. Rose was one hell of a sexy woman. Without the need to appear sanctimonious in public, in her private life she could be gutsy, even in the presence of a critical young newspaper publisher.

As he took her slender, delicately soft hand, he could see a flirtatious challenge dancing in her eyes. She wore her hair long, and it was almost the exact color of Susan's, a deep auburn that evoked some autumnal scene in a Vermont forest. Around her alabaster throat hung a gold necklace, holding a heart-shaped white locket.

He knew she had to be fifteen years older than he was, and he was surprised at her youthfulness. The woman smiling before him didn't look thirty. He searched for telltale clues of a massive face-lift, finding none.

She moved through the room like a whirlwind, giving instructions to her maid, telling her butler she couldn't come to the phone. In every action, she emerged as a definite personality—strong-willed, aggressive, yet possessing a savoir faire that diffused those qualities.

When she did stop in front of him, he looked into the depths of her almond-shaped eyes, finding a turbulence that he hadn't noticed before. Beyond the self-assurance, he detected a fear, like that seen in the face of a terrorized girl. As if sensing he wanted to see behind her mask, she said, "I summoned you here tonight to give you hell. Now that I see how good looking you are, I'd rather make eyes at you."

The naïveté of that old-fashioned expression put him at ease, suggesting she had more innocence than he'd initially felt. Up close to him, she smiled again. He noted how big and strong her teeth were, like the Chiclets he used to chew as a child.

Her voice was that of an American radio announcer, showing no regional influence. "What would you like to drink?"

"A Bloody Mary." He gave his request no thought until he noted the shock on her face.

"What about a Virgin Mary? This is a Christian house."

"Very well, I like virgins." Even as he said such a crass remark, he regretted it, feeling it made him sound like an ass. He'd slip out later and sneak a drink from the bar in the back of the limousine. By then he'd need one. Virgin Mary in hand, he followed her on a trail that led across her patio into floodlit gardens.

"I didn't want to live in Okeechobee at first," she confessed, walking close to him and reaching out to take his arm. "I came here originally to visit my sister, Hazel. That was back in the days when she still spoke to me and didn't follow a line directly from the Kremlin. Do you know her?"

"Yes, quite well. Our next mayor."

Her face froze with hostility, but she softened it, smiling again. "I was just a smalltown girl, and the way I see it, this wicked place is no spot to bring up kids. I have a wonderful son, Shelley. You know, Shelley was originally a man's name. I adopted him even though I've never been married. Except, of course, as a bride of Christ. We launched our foundation in Tulsa. That is, until every acre of Oklahoma got overrun with evangelists. You know, with Oral Roberts and everybody else who could throw up a tent moving in, I felt I'd better stake out the sinners along the Gold Coast."

"We have quite a few of them here." He'd come here to challenge this woman, but her charm and grace made that difficult. She made him want to protect her from any imaginary ghouls wandering around in her garden.

"If it wasn't for my work, I'd move back to some small town," she said. "You know, where a kid could wander barefoot in the woods, build a treehouse, play with tadpoles, things like that. A place where they've never heard of child porn. I could just see Shelley rushing off fishing in the old hole, even skinny-dipping if nobody was around."

As she spoke, he looked over at a luxurious cabin cruiser, *Rose II*, docked at the evangelist's private pier. "Down here you can take the kid fishing." Noting the size of the cruiser, he added, "Deep-sea fishing."

The sarcasm struck her. "I know," she snapped. "That's not what

I'm talking about. My kid will never know the simple life, the simple values, the way I was raised. Even though I send him to a private school, I have to hire a full-time bodyguard to protect him from all the kidnappers and child molesters..." She paused awkwardly, as if forgetting something. Her reflective eyes took in her night garden, and in those eyes a sadness prevailed. She turned to him and reached out affectionately, a little desperately for his arm. "I bet you're starved."

On her back patio, ready for dinner, he'd been the polite guest long enough. After all, he was no candy-ass, but the crusading liberal publisher; Sister Rose, the enemy from the far right. "I read the file we keep on you at the *Examiner*." Adrenalin flowing, he felt fired up. He paused a moment, letting her think he possessed more information about her past than he did.

He smiled and edged back in his chair, examining her closely. The wind blew through her hair, and he was struck by the loveliness of it, how freely it flowed and how gracefully it moved when she turned her head. As she edged closer to him, a lock of it fell over her forehead. She brushed it back with carefree abandon, the way a model might do in a TV commercial advertising hair conditioner. He kept repeating one thought, that she was like no preacher he'd ever known. "Why did you invite me here?" he asked, deliberately abrupt.

She shuddered as if chilled. "You've made me a victim of the press." The words, soft and gentle, failed to conceal the bitter charge.

"I've never written anything about you."

"That's exactly what I mean," she said rising. Nervously, coming to a stop near him, she reached for his hand to plead her case. "An attack is better than silence. You're trying to freeze me and my work out of existence. Old Buck ran our ads free."

He looked away from her eyes and at the white statues of the gods and goddesses standing against her wall. "I'm not that generous."

She moved away slightly, but remained close, as if aware of the mesmerizing influence of her body. In a more conciliatory voice, she added. "You're not the only one. I can't get on a talk show. They tell me that most guests don't want to be taped sitting next to Sister Rose. Rod McKuen's allowed to come on and propagandize. Not me! It's a media conspiracy."

"Like hell!" he said, showing anger. "You're constantly on TV and radio. Always in the papers. More so than any other woman in America.

Few people, even the president, get so much media attention every time they open their mouths. You don't need our support over at the *Examiner*. You'll start the war without us."

"What does that mean?" she asked, her eyes widening.

"I don't know," he said, surprised at his words. "Sometimes I just blurt out these things, and then—real eerie-like—they come true."

Feverishly excited, she seemed in some triumphant possession of the truth. Returning to her seat, she became less tense. "Old Buck warned me I'd have trouble with you. He thinks of you as a rebel." She faced him squarely, wetting her lips with her tongue. With a calculated effect, as if searching for the right camera angle, she said, "I think you're anti-Christ. That doesn't scare me. I'm used to confronting children of the devil and winning them for Jesus."

She exasperated him. He knew she was serious, yet she left open the possibility her remark was a joke. Charm was used like a weapon.

In imitation, he leaned over the table and caressingly took her delicate hand, letting a lock of his hair fall over his eyes. That always turned women on. In a voice used for whispering words of love, he said, "I don't run stories about you because I consider you the bigot of the year!"

With a gasp, she slipped her hand from his hold and sat back in stunned silence.

Growing stronger now, the wind burst open the door to the utility room and a harsh flow of exposed electric light flooded the patio, altering the romantic setting she had so artfully cultivated. He detected the smell of gardenias in the air, a heady tropical blend of intoxicating odors. She rose quickly and went to the door, slamming it with a ferocity, taking out her aggressions on the door instead of him. The black maid arrived with dinner.

Without mentioning the charge, Rose faced him again with a brave smile. "We're having my favorite food—a juicy hamburger with lots of raw onions and an RC Cola."

Although he considered himself the gourmet of Okeechobee, he entered the spirit of the occasion. "Pass the catsup."

Over dinner, fake pleasantries returned, but when he'd finished his hamburger and had refused another one, he turned to her again. "The B'nai B'rith Anti-Defamation League has for years considered you one of its most dangerous critics. Your foundation has even lobbied secretly to prevent America from selling military equipment to Israel."

She slammed down her fork, no longer able to conceal her emotions behind her facade of grace and charm. "Just a minute, I've had enough of this. I mean, someone told me Gore Vidal in the Forties disliked the Negroid people. Now he's a flaming liberal and civil rights advocate." She slowed down for a moment to regain control. "People change, you see. I had never seen a Jew until I was seven years old. In my early days as a preacher, I made some remarks I'm not proud of. But I've grown."

Her candid admission came as a surprise. "I'm not convinced." He stared for a moment at the remains of the hamburger. Feeling leaden, he excused himself and followed the maid in the direction of the toilet. More than wanting to go, he needed to escape her overweening presence.

When he came out, he was shown to her petite salon, with its wallpaper of white roses. She had arranged herself invitingly on the white sofa, her feet curled up under her gown. A collection of foreign dolls—gifts from admirers—lined the walls of her study. All were dressed in frilly white.

"You know," she said, "defending yourself against anti-Semitism is so difficult."

With swan-like grace, her hand directed him to a comfortable winged armchair. Her face reflected a kind of martyrdom, making him feel she masochistically liked to listen to accusations from the infidel.

Surrounded by mirrors and splashy white flowers, he was encased in a powder box of her images. He fancifully, with secret pleasure, pictured himself as the invading Hun, storming the citadel of a Renaissance madonna.

She got up serenely, seeking a chocolate-covered mint to give him. Was it a peace offering?

Upstairs, he could hear recorded music playing. It sounded like a children's choir singing. "I don't think we'll ever know your final position on Jews. Lady, it looks to me like you're thirsty for some real power."

"Aren't you?"

"*Touché.* The *Examiner* isn't going to help you one step of the way. We'll be in very different camps in the months ahead." He got up. "I do apologize for the news blackout on you. Starting tomorrow, I'll assign a reporter to investigate your background. We may even do a profile series on you. From reading our file on you, I found a lot of missing gaps in your life."

"I see I haven't won you over, sinner?" Close to her again, he felt her nearness, the subtlety of her expensive perfume. "Come back and see me real soon. I don't give up easy."

In the hallway she presented him with an autographed copy of her autobiography, *Hallelujah!* "In this little book is the entire story of my life. Stay up and read it tonight. I think you'll find it inspiring."

"No little volume like this contains the entire story of anybody's life. Maybe the *Examiner* will fill in some of those gaps."

"I hope that's not a threat. I've been threatened before. Besides, we've all got closets we wouldn't like to open."

At the door she surprised him by kissing him on the cheek. No mere brush, it was a full, sensual caress. Did he detect a flicker of her tongue?

On the way to his limousine, he passed a stunningly beautiful teen-age, blond-haired boy crossing the lawn. The smell of marijuana permeated the air.

"Hi, kid," he called out, wondering if this could be Shelley. "Turning on before burger time?"

The boy appeared startled. "Fuck off!" He disappeared inside the big white door, as a chorus of "Amazing Grace" echoed across the lawn.

***

It was after midnight when Gene Robinson turned his Volkswagen at the corner and headed down the street where he lived in spite of the Cuban invasion. His yellow stucco house, with its unkempt garden, lay in the sprawling Hispanic ghetto south of the river. Hastily erected after World War II, these bungalows had been haphazardly added to over the years.

He'd grown up on this street when it was filled with low-income Protestant families—white ones. After the past ten years, he was the only Protestant still left. The Catholic "beaners" had taken over. He hated beans, and that was all they seemed to eat. Even the grocery store on the corner carried every variety.

On the way to his house, he heard the sounds of TV sets blaring through open windows. The "beaners" had their own Spanish language TV station. He couldn't understand it. The way he saw it, they lived in America now, parasitically drawing their lifeblood from this country, but stubbornly clinging to their native Spanish—demanding that signs, government documents, and classroom studies be taught in both Spanish and English. "These creeps never go to bed," he mumbled, remembering how quiet the street used to be after ten p.m.

His own modest home had been built by his now-dead parents who'd settled here in 1947. He was determined to stay on in the house they'd left him. The "beaners" wouldn't force him out, in spite of the high crime rate. The first Cuban who ever broke in to rob him would get a bullet through his head.

Some of his new Cuban neighbors had tried to make friends with him. Only the other morning a middle-aged, stringy-haired housewife from across the way had knocked at his door. When he'd opened it, she'd smiled seductively at him, introducing herself as Clara. "I can't find Maria," she lied. "I thought she might be playing over in your yard." She'd breathed in deeply, sucking the air to make her breasts stick out more prominently, thinking in her foolish way that she might lure him. "My husband works days," she'd volunteered, craning her neck to get a look inside his kitchen.

When he glared at her, not saying a word, she hadn't been intimidated. "Your curtains are always drawn. I never know when you're home, except when I see you pull into your garage. You rarely turn on your lights. Saving on energy, huh?" She'd smiled flirtatiously again, holding up her pudgy little hand to shield her eyes from the sun. "Say, do you have some coffee? I'm fresh out, and I could sure use a cup."

He'd slammed the door in her gaping face, knowing the bitch wasn't after her stinking little kid or coffee, either. That had just been an excuse to talk to him. She'd hoped to insinuate herself inside.

Driving the Volkswagen into the garage, he padlocked the door behind him. Once inside his bungalow, he surveyed his spotlessly clean, spartan kitchen before heading to the refrigerator where he poured himself a glass of milk, his favorite drink.

Then he headed down a long corridor to the rear of the bungalow to his own little stuffy bedroom, where he'd long ago boarded up all three windows. For his retreat from the world, he wanted complete privacy.

Entering the pitch-black room, he turned on the lamp. He was tired, but he still looked good, he thought, as he ran his comb through thick, wavy, black hair.

Only his large eyes had lost their once lustrous life. A deep black, they now reflected anguish, as friends and relatives had dropped away. His wife, Susan, had deserted him when he'd been disgraced. Arrested for exposing himself to that little girl. That's why he wore sunglasses now, both day and night. They were mirrored glasses. He wanted nobody looking into his eyes. His mother said his eyes were sensitive, just like the black Irish from which he was descended. "I can always tell what you're thinking just by looking into those black eyes."

On his bed, he removed his black, shiny boots, then rubbed those eyes which rested under brows full and heavy. He pressed his hand against his square-jawed face, fingering the bottom of his deeply molded lip, full and red, fearing he might be getting a fever blister. He winced at the thought, just as he did at the idea of any imperfection. He didn't want the slightest blemish spoiling his good looks. Down at police headquarters, he was known as Tyrone Power, and he liked that—at least he did until he read some unfavorable newspaper publicity and a book about his former screen idol, suggesting that Power wasn't a real man like Gene had imagined him to be. Gene still shared one thing in common with Susan. Both of them were constantly compared to movie stars. Tyrone Power and Susan Hayward, who'd once made a movie together. Dead movie stars, it was regrettable, but movie stars, nevertheless.

No wonder the Cuban woman calling herself Clara was attracted to him. Nearly everybody was. He could tell by the hungry look in their eyes.

That had been more evident than ever tonight in that smelly latrine at the far end of the park. Three of the "beaners," all *mariposas*, one even with a mouth painted lipstick red, had knelt on the piss-stained floor to swallow him whole, each with gaping mouths eagerly waiting to have their turn with him. He'd been particularly rough on the last kid, who didn't look as if he were out of high school. At his climax, he'd grabbed the faggot and shoved it all the way down his throat and held it there until the Cuban boy nearly choked. Filth like these *mariposas* deserved no better treatment. Once his climax had occurred, he'd zipped up and made it out of that park as fast as he could. He couldn't stand to look at those sex-hungry faces any more. At least they got to see and feel what a real man was like.

What they didn't know when they'd tried to lure him back to their apartment, what he didn't reveal to anyone, was that he was saving his real self for *her*. He'd never met her, yet he knew she'd want him to be pure. That's the kind of lady she was.

Like an angel.

***

Robert was waiting in the foyer of Buck's house as Buck turned the key and entered the all white marbled hallway, with a sweeping Tara-like staircase in the background. In jeans and a white T-shirt, Robert appeared warm and relaxed, and it was obvious he'd had a few drinks. Buck walked over to him and kissed him on the mouth, a little harder and firmer than he usually did.

Robert responded with equal pressure. "I've missed you something awful," he said.

"I wasn't gone that long, and Rose didn't convert me." He pulled at his necktie and took off his jacket with a certain force, tossing it over a sofa as he made his way into their larger parlor furnished exactly as his mother had left it on the day she'd died. "I need a real drink."

Robert appeared in seconds with the drink. "I heard your car coming up the driveway. I rushed to make it."

"As you rush to do everything for me day and night," Buck said. "God, I feel guilty. You do everything for me, and I give you so little." He belted down a hefty dosage of the Scotch offered.

"You give me reason to live. Isn't that enough?"

"It's a good reason. But it's not enough. I've got to give you more. I'm not sure how to go about it."

"You're all the reward I want."

"That's damn nice to hear." He downed another drink of that Scotch as if he were preparing for something and he wasn't quite sure what. "I want to turn in early tonight. And I hope you'll join me."

"Haven't I always joined you any time of the day or night you wanted to turn in? Turn on is more like it."

"Right from the first." He reached over, taking Robert by his blond hair and pulling him over for a kiss. "What pleasure it's been for me. I didn't know how good it can get until you came here. If I recall, I invited you to live out in the cottage, but from the first night you would have none of that."

"Why in the hell would I want to be in a lonely cottage out back with the dogs when the hottest man in the state of Florida was lying upstairs alone in his bedroom?"

"Why indeed?" Buck asked.

"I won you over on the first night. Your liberal philosophy dictated that a straight man and a gay man could be friends. You admitted you'd slept with your straight men friends many times. Bare-ass on camping trips, dormitories, or at school conventions. I just asked for equal treatment."

"You got it."

"It took a little push and shove. That first night you were going to get into bed with your briefs on. Such awful briefs they were. Blue. You know I insist on white."

"Have I ever worn anything but white since?" Buck asked.

"Always white—that's true. I wouldn't have you in anything else."

"You were right. I wouldn't hesitate pulling off my briefs in front of a straight man. With you, I was holding back. A little afraid of what might happen. But off came the briefs."

"And such a sight it was. And is. Unlike anything I'd ever seen. I think I was already in love at that point. Of course, I had already seen you in the shower at the unviersity."

"Stop it! You're giving me a hard-on, like you always do." He downed more of his drink. "I'll be up in a minute." He got up abruptly and adjusted his suit pants. Crossing the living room, he opened the French doors leading to the terrace overlooking the garden.

Alone in the night air, he felt he was coming unglued a bit. All sorts of contradictory feelings were racing through his blood. There was no place he wanted to be right now more than with Robert.

It wasn't a perfect picture, though. There was something missing, and he always knew what it was. He didn't love Robert with the same intensity that his friend loved him. In sex, Robert was always the giver, Buck the object of affection. Every night Robert explored every crevice of his body with his talented tongue, bringing Buck to moments of such ecstasy he didn't think he could bear another second of such exquisite torture. That's when he usually begged for more. Buck wasn't exploring Robert's body with the same intensity. The truth was, Robert, after bringing him to climax, masturbated with Buck's deflated cock in his mouth. Several times he'd come close to penetrating Robert and still held back as if that were some final frontier to cross. Ever since he was fourteen, Buck had always been willing to receive blowjobs from almost any source, and he'd had a lot of offers, particularly among his fellow marines. In his mind real fucking was something you did with women. He knew that the moment he fucked Robert he would be a card-carrying gay male, and he wasn't ready for that.

He still felt he was straight, and somehow Robert, the skilled gay seducer, had come along and diverted him from his natural inclinations. Buck wanted to test his limits more. In some ways, he felt he was living only half a life. He desperately wanted to give as much love as he received. Robert deserved more from him.

Even though Robert accepted their present arrangement, Buck couldn't continue to treat Robert like some sex slave while he, the Arab sheik, lay back and demanded to be serviced.

Starting tonight, he was going to try to bring about a shift in their relationship. He'd make love to Robert instead of having love made to him. The world's greatest seducer and most talented sexual artist would no doubt view Buck's attempts at certain forms of love amateurish. But if he knew his friend, Robert would be only too willing to accept what was offered, unskilled or not.

Even as he mounted the steps to his bedroom, he was filled with a haunting feeling. On the one hand, he genuinely believed he was doing the right thing by trying to love Robert as Robert loved him. But another gnawing thought troubled him. Was he giving more of himself to Robert to make up in some way for his upcoming betrayal of his friend?

At the door to his bedroom, he unbuttoned his white shirt and unzipped his trousers. As he turned the knob, he knew Robert would do the rest.

***

It was early morning. The first streaks of light were creeping into the bedroom. Buck turned over gently, not wanting to disturb Robert. Then he realized he was in bed alone. From the sounds, Robert was in the bathroom showering.

Stark nude, he made his way across the darkened bedroom and opened the doors leading to his balcony. Here he plopped down in a dew-moistened chair to watch the dawn split the sky. The morning sky was reason enough to live in Florida. Watching the horizon light up was like a ritual for him.

He didn't want to recall every detail of last night, and he especially didn't want to have pictures going through his mind of all the sexual plumbing involved. But he couldn't think of anything but that. The night had been different from all the hundreds of others he'd spent with Robert. It had set a new pattern for them and a new relationship between them.

It wasn't the perfect man-to-man sexual relationship, but Buck was on his way, and last night had sparked a significant change.

From the first, he'd suspected that Robert had sensed it was a different man crawling in bed with him. Robert certainly must have been aware of it when Buck had reached out and pulled him so close to him it was as if they were one. He'd kissed Robert, but the kiss was different from before. He'd kissed Robert firmly before, even wet before, but last night he'd plunged his tongue in his friend's mouth, and he'd never done that.

The moment he'd inserted his tongue into Robert's mouth, he realized what a fool he'd been all along in not giving his friend something he wanted. Robert had sucked his tongue, giving it the bath of its life.

As he'd engaged in his longest kiss ever with Robert, his friend had used both hands to explore every inch of Buck's body he could reach.

Tentatively, very tentatively, Buck had run one of his hands down Robert's back, settling on his buttocks. With his index finger, he'd ever so slowly inserted it inside Robert who'd opened up and accepted the invasion. If anything, it had made Robert suck on his tongue even harder.

Impulsively, he'd thrown Robert on his back and lay on top of him pressing down hard. With one hand, he'd run his fingers through Robert's hair, pulling at the strands. He'd nibbled at Robert's right ear before inserting his tongue in that ear for a bath. Then he'd done the same thing to his friend's other ear. This action had made Robert squirm, and for the first time ever Buck took pleasure in giving Robert joy, instead of the other way around.

Ever so gently he'd bathed Robert's chest with his tongue, almost imitating what Robert did to him night after night. When he reached the left nipple, he'd circled it with his tongue. Robert was moaning and pulling at Buck's hair at the same time, as if goading him on.

He'd seemed to know what Robert wanted. He'd bitten hard into the nipple and Robert had screamed in ecstasy. It wasn't a scream to tell Buck to stop but to go on to give him even greater pleasure. When he'd had his fill, he'd moved to the other nipple and repeated his action. Robert's chest had been heaving at this point, and Buck had traveled even lower with his lips and tongue, going where he'd never gone before.

The moment of truth had come. It had become time to take the plunge. Why had he dreaded it and resisted it for so long? Robert's hips had been rearing up from the bed signaling what he wanted Buck to do. He'd leaned over Robert and in one gulp had consumed the man. Buck had overestimated his ability in that area. He'd immediately gagged but didn't back off. Filled with determination, he'd plunged up and down on that prick which had swelled to an even greater thickness. Even as he did, he was glad it wasn't a whopper. He didn't know how Robert managed to swallow all of him. The salty-sweet taste of Robert had tasted good in Buck's mouth.

Such white-hot intensity couldn't continue, and it didn't. In a rapid, shuddering spasm, Robert had filled his mouth with a milky, musky substance. Buck had gagged and didn't feel he'd be able to swallow it. Summoning all his steely reserve, he did manage to swallow it and not only that but had stayed on until he'd drained the last drop from his friend. Only then after a few departing kisses and licks, had he fallen back on the bed totally exhausted.

Ever so gently Robert's mouth had found his, parting his lips so Robert's tongue could clean his mouth. When Robert's mouth had reached his right ear, he'd whispered softly, "Thank you, lover."

Buck had closed his eyes and breathed deeply, but had said nothing. From that point on, he'd known how the evening would end. Like it always did. From his ears to his neck, from his fingers to his arm pits, from his chest and nipples, from his thighs to his feet and toes and back along his calves, Robert had begun his nightly ritual of devouring every inch of Buck. Robert always turned Buck over and licked his back before caressing each buttock. Then the real good part came when he'd opened Buck up and plunged his tongue as deeply as he could inside him. Robert always stayed there a very long time, and last night it had been more than an hour until Buck was moaning and squirming for relief.

The journey from there to all the hidden crevices of Buck's body, including a thorough wetting down of his testicles, always ended in the same place, with Robert opening his throat to Buck. Last night Buck had been ready to blast off before Robert had even plunged down on him. When his relief finally came, it had been shattering. His entire body had seemed to explode, and long after the spasms had died, he'd held Robert down on him. His friend had shown no inclination ever to leave the spot, but Buck had held him there as if the idea of his pulling away at that moment was unthinkable. With Robert still buried there, with him still in his friend's mouth, he'd gradually fallen asleep and he guessed that Robert had too.

As if to erase last night's memory, Buck abruptly got up from the cool terrace and stretched himself in the dawn light, noticing how the sky had reddened. It almost seemed on fire.

Some impulse was stirring in him and he didn't know what it was. He headed toward the bathroom. There was no sound of a shower. As he threw open the door, he spotted Robert standing in front of the mirror shaving, a towel draped around his still wet body. He always shaved and then showered but Robert preferred to shower then shave.

He stood looking at Robert for a long time, wanting and desiring him as never before. Robert looked over to him with more love and devotion than he'd ever seen in his friend's eyes.

He walked right over to Robert and grabbed him and pulled him close, inserting his tongue in Robert's mouth. He hadn't brushed his teeth or shaved, but Robert never turned him away.

Robert clung to him, digging his fingers into Buck's back. He pushed Robert away slightly and knelt before him, ripping the towel from his nude body. Robert's sex looked tasty, tender, and ever so succulent to him. He reached out and started licking and kissing everywhere until he got what he wanted. A full, raging erection. He plunged down on Robert, and this time he didn't gag.

As he worked over his friend, Robert ran his fingers through Buck's hair, encouraging him to plunge deeper. Minutes went by, and he wasn't keeping time, but Robert's quivering body told him what to expect and very soon. He got his reward as spasm after spasm jerked Robert's body. He swallowed every drop and didn't gag, and that made him proud. When he was certain there would be no more reward for him, he stood up and faced Robert squarely eye to eye. Then he pulled him close and plunged his tongue in his mouth.

Breaking away, Buck headed for the shower with one glance back at Robert who stood by the mirror, still half shaven and looking stunned as if he weren't sure what had happened and even if he was sure, couldn't believe it.

"Listen, motherfucker," Buck said to him, "don't you ever call me a cocksucking faggot or I'll beat the shit out of you."

In the shower, he turned on the water full blast and held his face up to the jet sprays. For one brief moment, he forgot about Robert, himself, and the day that was rapidly rushing toward them.

Chapter Two

The call came in at 4:31am, and Susan turned over on her side, as if that would shut out the noise. The ringing was persistent. At first she was tempted not to answer it, but feared it might be Roland calling from the office with an assignment, as he often did at this hour. That city editor never seemed to sleep.

"Hello," she said with sleepy hesitation into the phone.

"Listen, bitch, and listen good," came a petulant voice. She immediately recognized it as her crackpot caller from yesterday. She was tempted to hang up on him but decided to hear him out.

"What have you done about that tip I gave you yesterday? About that auction of boy Lolitos."

"Nothing," she said. "I doubt if it's true."

"You doubt it? Who in the fuck are you to doubt my word? I tell the truth."

"You offer no proof. It's a wild accusation, without strong, hard evidence."

"I'll give you something hard. Real hard."

"I'm hanging up," she said.

"I've got proof."

"Yeah, right."

"Don't get smart with me," the caller said. "I've even got photographs. And some documents I stole."

"How do I know you're not bullshitting?"

"Come over to this cheap motel room I rented last night, and I'll show you my proof."

"There's no way in hell I'm coming to your motel room."

"If you're worried that this is all a trick to rape you, guess again. I don't go that route."

"Okay, I'll meet you somewhere this morning in a public place. Bring your proof with you."

"Not so fast. I'm broke. I can't even pay the bill here at this motel. I need one-thousand dollars before I let you in on this scoop."

"I don't pay for news," she said. "I never did."

"What would you say if I told you I had a photograph secretly snapped of our mayoral candidate?"

"I don't believe it. Surely you don't mean Hazel. Barry Collins?"

"The one and only. The one running as Sister Rose's hand-picked crusader to clean up Okeechobee."

"If what you say is true, that's news," she said. "But I'm still not going to pay for it."

"Listen, I'm desperate. I've got no food, no money, no place to live. The operator of the Lolito house kicked me out. I was the custodian. He didn't even give me ten dollars before showing me to the door."

"I'll tell you what I'll do. I have only five-hundred dollars in the house. If you have some genuine proof, I'll give you the money. But it's a gift to help you out. Call it a charity donation."

"Shitty little charity it is, you cunt. My information is worth much more."

"Take it or leave it," she said.

"I'll take it because I'm caught between a rock and a hard place. There's a place next door to this fleabag, Vista Linda Motel, that serves breakfast to truckers. It's called Crazy Mabel's. Out on Indian Creek Trail."

"I know the dump. I'll meet you there in thirty minutes."

"I want you to buy me breakfast, too, and we're talking a five-egg breakfast."

"It's a deal. How will I recognize you? I don't even know your name."

"I know what you look like. You're always getting your damn picture in the paper. I'll find you." He slammed down the phone.

At first she was tempted not to show up. He could be a true crackpot or else it might be some sort of trap. But through all his hostility and aggressiveness, there was a ring of truth and conviction in his charges. If he told the truth, this was major news, and she didn't want anybody else on the *Examiner*, much less the competition, getting such a big story.

Jumping out of bed, she headed for the shower, then set out on the trail. She'd quickly apply her warpaint later. Under the jet streams pouring from the shower head, she pondered over possible headlines Roland might apply to her exclusive. "Boy Lolitos" sounded catchy. It was definitely the kind of story that wire services would pick up. The potential of a news story like this was one of the reasons she became a news reporter in the first place. Ingrid always warned her not to pay for news, but in this one case maybe mother didn't know best.

***

Pulling into the oil-stained parking lot at Crazy Mabel's, Susan got out of her car and was immediately confronted with a tall, lean man who was unshaven and in his late twenties or early thirties. "I'm Terry Drummond. Did you bring the money?"

"The *cunt* brought the money. Where's your evidence?" she said, slamming the car door behind her.

"Let's eat first. I'm starved."

Early morning truckers, many of them Hispanic and eating omelets with hot sauce, filled the crowded diner. Susan managed to find a small table for them in the back. She ordered only black coffee and orange juice, but he went for a massive plate of bacon, ham, sausage, and five eggs with grits and fried potatoes.

He looked at her while waiting for his order to be cooked. "I had a job as a custodian at the boy brothel. I also had to perform stud duty for the house's owner. Get this, the owner doesn't like young boys. He likes fully grown men. In fact, his alltime fantasy male is Gene Robinson."

She winced at the mention of her former husband.

"I know you were married to him. Leroy's had a crush on him ever since they were in school together. Collects every picture he can find of him, including *that* one. He's got the negative and has had hundreds of copies made. In fact, he was the one who originally snapped that picture of Robinson. The coach later barred Leroy from the locker rooms. He worked for that campus *Tempo* magazine, the one that always used to run you on its cover as Hurricane Beauty."

"I know *Tempo* very well, but I never knew who took that picture of Gene. Anyway we're not here to discuss Gene. Who is this Leroy? Not who I think it is."

"You got the money?"

"I've got the money."

"Leroy Fitzgerald."

"I know him, if it's the same Leroy who was in the class of '71."

"One and the same," he said.

"I remember he campaigned for and eventually won recognition for a gay rights group on campus."

"That's our Leroy. Now he's a bordello owner. He gives twenty-five dollars to each of the boys every night. Sometimes the men give the boys big tips, especially when they go to private rooms together. But that's only after the show."

"What show?" she asked.

"Leroy calls it the flower-petal show. The johns come in and are seated. A spotlight goes on. The young boys parade in naked. They form a ring in the middle of the floor and lie down with their heads touching. Then the customers get up from their chairs and go down on them, moving from one to the other until each john has sampled each boy. Then Leroy auctions off each boy to the highest bidder. Sometimes when a boy is particularly desirable, the bidding can go real high. Steve almost always goes for a thousand a night."

"Are these boys underage?" she asked.

"All of them except one guy, Angelo. He's eighteen. But to look at him you'd think he was only fourteen. He looks real young."

"This is going to be a hard story to nail down, particularly for me as a woman. If I were a young boy, I could become one of Leroy's troupe and write an eye-witness account. You mentioned pictures."

"I've got lots of pictures," he said. "Leroy secretly tapes the action every night. He always claims these pictures—snapped without the john's knowledge—would not only be an insurance policy for him but something he might possibly use as blackmail."

"What a guy! Are you really sure Barry Collins is one of the patrons? He looks like such a straight shooter. In fact, he systematically denounces gays."

"I've got lots of pictures," he said, "but the one I wanted to tantalize you with was one of Miss Barry herself. She was so busy sucking boy cock she didn't know we were capturing all the action for posterity." He reached into his jacket and pulled out a glossy photograph. As he handed it to her, the waitress arrived with his breakfast.

Susan concealed the photograph until the waitress had left, then studied it carefully as Terry slurped down his breakfast.

The photograph was quite clear. It appeared to be Barry, whom she knew well. Although she realized it could be a fake, it didn't seem to be. The right-wing mayoral candidate was performing fellatio on a boy who appeared to be no more than fourteen, if that. "May I take this?"

"Yeah," he said, his mouth full, "if you've got the five-hundred dollars. But before you get any more pictures I'm going to want a lot more money. Leroy's very fickle. I knew he might kick me out when he got tired of me. So I stole as much incriminating evidence as I could get on him. I've got pictures of some of the most important people in this state. Leroy's johns are strictly from the A-list. I even got a picture of a bigtime movie star."

"What's the address of this place?"

"I'll tell you. But that's all I'm going to tell you until I get more money. It's 230 Bayshore Drive."

Susan scribbled that down on a piece of paper.

"It's owned by Leroy. He's tried for years to get a job on the *Examiner*. But old Buck would never hire him. He was just too sleazy. Maybe the new Buck will hire him—he's so fucking liberal. But Leroy's taking in so much money today he doesn't need a job. He's shot two centerfolds for *Playgirl*."

"How can I get in touch with you?" Susan asked.

"You can't. I'll call you. That's the deal. Frankly, I don't know where I'll be from night to night."

"I wish we could set up some permanent contact," she said.

"Wish again. I want that five-hundred, and I want it now. I've spilled the beans enough."

"Here it is." She handed him the money, which he grabbed from her hand so greedily that he scratched her skin.

"I'll see you around, when I run out of money." He took one final sip of his coffee, wiped the bacon grease from his lips, got up, and quickly left the restaurant.

As she watched him go, she suddenly had an idea. This was not just a story for the *Examiner*, but it was a case the police should be working on too. She wanted to do Gene a favor even though it had been years since she'd seen him. At the *Examiner* that morning, she was going to send him an anonymous tip, informing him of what Terry

Drummond had told her. This could be a big case for Gene, and it might in some small way redeem his tarnished reputation if he could break it.

***

After his morning jog, a cold shower, and a long, lingering kiss from Robert, Buck walked to his office from his dressing room.

"Not so fast, big boy," Robert said, taking his hand. "You've made me the happiest man in the world. I'm in heaven."

"I should have put you there long ago," Buck said. "I'm just a slow learner."

"It was worth waiting for."

"Expect a repeat performance tonight," Buck promised, as he opened the door and entered his office where Robert had neatly arranged his messages and mail. Through his large windows, he spotted Susan crossing through the newsroom. She spoke briefly to Roland at the city desk, then headed for her own desk in the far corner. On an impulse, he dialed her on his intercom. "Morning," he said, deliberately making his voice sound huskier than it was.

"Buck, good morning. I bet you're calling to find out how I'm doing on that South Beach thing. Today's the day to get onto it."

"Come on up to the office," he said. "Let's go over a game plan."

"I'll be right up. That is, after I pay a quick visit to the ladies' room. No former beauty queen meets Buck Brooke III without a quick check of her make-up. Besides, I got up much too early this morning. I didn't get my full beauty sleep because of a mysterious phone call I want to tell you about."

The moment he put down the phone he feared her reception in the office would be a bit chilly from Robert. He pressed a button summoning Robert to his office.

He rushed in right away. "I'd kiss you but I just washed my hair."

"It's a slow morning and you've got everything under control here," Buck said. "I want you to do something for us. I'm tired of seeing you in the same white T-shirt and jeans all the time. I want you to get more of a 70s look. Buy some new outfits. Since I suspect you'll wear them only in the privacy of our home, I don't mind if they're very revealing."

"That's what you want?" he asked, looking astonished.

"Men like to see women in lingerie, don't they?" Buck asked.

"I suppose. God only knows why."

"Why can't I enjoy looking at my boyfriend in some fun night wear?"

Robert's face brightened. "Wait till you see what I come up with." At the door, he hesitated. "You never called me your boyfriend before."

"Everybody else calls you my boyfriend. Why can't I?"

"I'm honored." He looked at Buck and smiled. "Honored, shit. I'm thrilled out of my God damn skin." He turned and left.

Within the next few minutes, after Robert had gone shopping, he went to the door and ushered Susan into his office. "I don't get many invitations here. Robert keeps you under heavy guard."

"He's a great guy. You just don't know him."

"I don't think I ever will."

He was embarrassed by this talk of Robert and wanted to change the subject. "You know Hazel better than I do. I mean, I know her and all but you know her much better."

"Hazel and I have always been good friends."

"Would you see if you could make a date for both of us to see her in her apartment on South Beach?" he asked. "By now, she must have a good idea of what's going on there."

"I'll set it up if she's free." She walked into Robert's office and dialed Hazel's number. She was back in Buck's office within minutes. "It's on. She can see us at nine o'clock tonight."

"That's fine with me. What say we meet at seven-thirty for drinks at The Rusty Pelican?"

"It's a date."

"You've always been promising me one. We'll try to keep this one strictly business."

"We'll try," she said enigmatically. A frown crossed her brow. "I've come across some really disturbing information."

From the main office, he could spot Roland staring through the large windows at Susan and himself. The city editor always became furious when Buck met privately with one of his reporters.

Susan quickly outlined to him all the data she'd learned from Terry about the boy Lolitos and the male auction.

"This is fantastic, but I don't really know how to proceed with it."
He looked at Roland again. On an impulse he was tempted to call Roland
in on their conference, but decided against it.

"There's this picture. Apparently they have a lot of incriminating
evidence on some of the johns who patronize the place."

"Let me see it," he said, reaching across and taking the photograph
which she'd concealed in a manila envelope in her purse.

He studied the photograph carefully. "If I didn't know better I'd
say that was Barry Collins. It's not a picture he can run in his campaign."

"It sure isn't. It'd be the end of him. I understand some of the
town's leading figures—judges, bank executives, a college president—
are involved in this club."

"Who's behind it?" Buck asked.

"Leroy Fitzgerald is the front man."

"The same Leroy we went to school with? The one who was always trying to take frontal pictures of the school jocks."

"The same Leroy," she said.

"This is a hot one. The boys are underage, right?" he asked.

"Sometimes only fourteen."

"Wait till Sister Rose hears about this."

"Her own hand-picked candidate..."

"We're sitting on a time-bomb," he said. "If I knew a young man
who was of the age of consent, a hustler really, but very young looking,
we might pay him to infiltrate the club and get all the dirt for us. I don't
know anybody like that. Perhaps Robert a few years ago. Maybe there's
someone out there who would do it for us."

"The whole idea disgusts me," she said.

"Does me too. The story's too hot not to touch."

"I must tell you I've gone ahead and sent anonymous word to Gene
about this sex ring," she said. "I figured we'd better get the police
involved. He needs a big case. Besides, these kids are minors, and
Leroy must be stopped."

"That's fine. If the police start to move in on the place, we can
report the news. It would remove us from the position of being criminal investigators ourselves."

"I still want the scoop," she said. "Why don't you keep the picture?" she asked. "Locked up in a safe."

"I will." He stood up. "Barry? I never would have thought it. I wonder if Pamela knows."

"I doubt it but she might. If she knows, she's a very understanding wife."

"She's very understanding," he said.

"You'd know that better than I would. Still carrying a torch?"

"Pamela and I once talked about getting married. That was a long time ago. Could I let you in on an secret?"

"Fire away."

"Pamela got drunk one night..."

"Pamela is always getting drunk one night."

"This night was different. She told me she didn't love me at all but was carrying a torch for Gene."

"Gene!" she said with astonishment. "Pamela in love with Gene? Maybe that's why she's always hated me so."

"She told me she'd married Barry on the rebound."

"Any more secrets?" she asked.

"Maybe. But I'm not telling them now."

"It's amazing," she said. "All of us went to college together. All of us were involved in some way with each other. But I wonder how well any of our classmates knew each other."

"I don't think we did at all. We're a mixed-up class of '71."

"Except now we're playing adult games," she said. "Look at the lives that this story alone will destroy—that is, if it's printed on the frontpage."

"I don't want to destroy Barry," he said.

"Barry shouldn't be sucking little boy cock," she said.

"Not while running for mayor and not while campaigning to clean up the filth and smut in Okeechobee. We've got to be careful." An urgent call came in for him and he picked up the receiver, signaling an end to his dialogue with Susan. "I'll get back to you on this."

She rose, renewing her a promise to meet him tonight. "This is a little scary," she said. "You'll have to call the shots."

"I'll do my best," he said. As she neared the door, he asked the caller to hold a little longer, and said to Susan, "Do you mind if I call Gene and meet with him?"

"It's a great idea if Gene will cooperate. He's very bitter, you know. About you. About me. With some justification, he feels we let him down."

With sadness, he looked into her eyes. "We did. At least I did. In some small way, I want to make it up to him."

"Good luck."

***

As he drove across the causeway to The Rusty Pelican, Buck sucked in the night air. He headed north to that glittering waterfront strip created solely for tourists. The ocean-bordering sandbar existed merely for pleasure.

He steered his car into the parking lot of The Rusty Pelican, which increasingly was becoming a horny, uninhibited singles bar. As he got out, he noticed two male punks distributing bumper stickers.

"Here, put this on your bumper," one of the young men told Buck, handing him a sign. "Honk every time you see someone with the same sign."

He read the neat lettering: CONVERT A JEW TO CHRIST.

He confronted the young man whose face was a mask of hostility. "Who's paying you to hand out these signs?"

"Fuck you," the man said, grabbing the sign back from Buck.

His companion shoved Buck. "In case you haven't heard, faggot, this is a free country!" With their bumper stickers in hand, both men turned and left, heading toward a pick-up truck.

Buck watched them go. He knew if someone were printing bumper stickers like this, other amusements were on the way.

Glancing at his watch, he saw that he'd arrived twenty minutes early. Inside that bar, he passed waitresses in rakish wide-brimmed hats with red scarves and pink feathers. He headed for the pulsing red lights flashing in the rear under a mirrored ceiling. Paintings of voluptuous nude women covered the walls and upper-level balconies which overlooked the dancing couples below. Foxy ladies and handsome guys, all suntanned and scantily clad, danced inside this ripe maraschino cherry.

In the rear room, where the actual food was served, he confronted the maitre d', a dime-store Liberace dressed in a jacket of shiny pink sequins.

"I'll get you a table," he lisped.

"Great!" Buck said. "Just a minute. I have to say hello to someone first."

"Okay," the manager said as if annoyed. He turned and swished away.

In the far corner of the dark bar sat Pamela Collins.

***

Pamela was already deep into a Tom Collins lineup. He stood looking at her for a long moment. He had at one time been in love with her. So had half the rest of Sigma Chi, his fraternity. Of all the women on campus, only Susan herself had been more aggressively pursued when they'd attended the university together.

Unlike Susan, Pamela hadn't aged as well, and she'd put on unflattering pounds. Her face looked ashen and puffy, but still retained enough of its beauty to evoke her former look when she'd represented Miss Florida at the Miss America Pageant at Atlantic City. Traces of that youthful beauty and natural grace remained. Her long blonde hair was still lustrous, but in the blue of her eyes he sensed a sadness.

Here she was sitting alone in a singles bar with a defiance, although her politically conservative husband was running for mayor. She'd never given a damn what people thought about her.

"Have you come back into my life again?" she asked, looking up at him. He found her as serenely cool as ever. With her slightly upturned nose and expressive wide lips, she was still sexy.

"Mind if I have a seat at the table of the woman who got away?"

"I'd be honored," she said in a honey-coated voice. "Your God damn newspaper makes me sound like a southern magnolia. Can't you at least say my blossoms are made of steel?"

"I don't think Barry would like being known as the husband of a steel magnolia. It doesn't sound right on his family values ticket." He ordered a Scotch from the waiter.

She slammed down her Tom Collins, as a simmering dissatisfaction came over her features. Barry and I just aren't compatible."

He feigned surprise, although he'd heard plenty of rumors.

The muscles in her face tightened. "I'm tired of being the one who's always smeared by every gossip. Barry's forever getting written up as Mr. Goodie Two-Shoes. I'm the threat to his career, the one with the drinking problem. And..." She paused for a long moment, her eyes staring deep into his. "You know what they say? That I've fucked half the state troopers in Florida."

Since he hadn't heard that one, he only nodded.

She moved closer to him. "Why don't you ask Barry why I'm so promiscuous? Neglected women fill up their time the best way they can."

"Any other women involved?" he asked pointedly. "I'm asking this as an old friend, not as a reporter. Our meeting is strictly off the record."

"I know you'll protect me." She asked the waiter for another Tom Collins before settling back into her chair. "Women?" she asked as if belatedly hearing his question. A smirk crossed her face.

A vision of that fellatio picture of Barry flashed through his mind. "If not women, then what?"

Intense red lights flashing in from the dance floor revealed her bloodshot eyes. "Barry spends more time with the Boy Scouts than he does with the League of Women Voters."

"You're leaving a very clear impression," he said, leaning forward, hoping she'd confide more.

She smiled petulantly. "That's all I'm saying for the moment. And nothing on the record. You can read whatever you want into whatever might come out of my pretty little mouth." A rage seemed to surge through her. She was about to say something and kept censoring herself. She was, after all, known as the Martha Mitchell of Okeechobee. "I don't want to leave a wrong impression. Although he seems to prefer to work the ball fields at junior high, he is more versatile than that."

"Meaning?"

"He's been known to throw a mercy fuck every now and then to the town's most famous woman."

"You couldn't possibly mean our dear Sister Rose?"

"You didn't hear it from me," she said.

"All day I've been met with surprises."

"I'll throw one more at you. Maybe two. Sister Rose and Calder Martin—you know her henchman, don't you?—have Barry by the balls. Maybe they're blackmailing him, I don't know. Barry's so heavily in debt he can't get out. Those vultures can command him to do their bidding. He'll make a shitty mayor, just like he's made a shitty husband. Personally, I'm not voting for him. I'm supporting Hazel."

"Now that's news."

"It would be if we were on the record, which we're not. I've always trusted you. I should never have turned down your offer of marriage."

"You loved Gene Robinson."

"I thought I did. How in hell did I know Gene was some kind of a nut? You were his best friend. Did you ever think he was so crazy?"

"Sometimes he did strange things."

"Oh, shit!" she said, looking up. Two young men had entered the bar and were eying their table. One of them looked darkly Italian, the other a sun-streaked blond surfer. "Believe it or not, those guys are my jailers."

"I don't understand."

"Calder Martin has hired them to look after me until the campaign is over," she said. "Calder thinks if they take care of me I'll stay out of trouble. Maybe he's right. But I sometimes escape."

"Do you want me to call the police?" he asked.

"Hell, no. It's part of the deal."

"What deal?"

"I've agreed to stay married to Barry until after the election. I'll divorce him later. He's getting custody of our daughters. My big payoff won't come until after he wins the election. Otherwise, they'll cut me off without a penny. I won't have any money to live on unless I play Barry's dutiful wife."

"Is this what you want?"

"With some money I can go away and make a new life for myself. I'll miss my daughters, but I don't have much choice."

He raised a toast to her as she downed the rest of her Tom Collins. She stood up on wobbly legs. "Who knows?" she said. "That new life might be with you. Haven't you heard of people starting over again? Maybe you and me?"

"I think it's too late for that."

"Robert Dante?" she asked.

"Something like that." He nodded a good night as she walked over to the bar and said something to the two young men. Casting a final look toward his table, she headed for the door with her "jailers."

He'd sit here quietly and wait for Susan.

***

Within ten minutes the image of Pamela at his table had been replaced by that of Susan who didn't look drunk, overweight, or wobbly-legged. "If I'm not terribly mistaken, that was your old girlfriend Pamela I saw in the parking lot. Being helped into the car by two very handsome young men. In other words, up to her old tricks. I don't think she saw me."

"It's not as simple as that," he said, signaling the waiter to take their order. "Barry and Calder Martin have got her on a tight leash. Those men work for Calder. Pamela, they feel, needs to be escorted around until after the election. Then it's splitsville for Barry and her."

"I'm not at all surprised, particularly after that picture we saw today. Any ideas about how to go about uncovering this?"

"Not a clue yet." he said.

After she'd ordered a burger and Buck had too, she glanced around the bar. "Where's Robert?"

He slammed down his drink. "What are you suggesting? That I can't go out the door without Robert?"

"I didn't mean to make you angry, but it seems that way to me. Okay, since the subject has come up, I might as well come out with it. Are you gay?"

Anger flashed across his face. "Hell, no!"

"I'm glad to hear that because I was thinking of asking you out tonight after we see Hazel."

Finishing off his drink, he ordered another one. "Robert is a great assistant. He helps make my life work. I don't even know how to write a check anymore. He takes care of everything."

"Everything?" She raised an eyebrow.

"Don't be provocative. It's possible, you know, for a gay man and a straight man to work together and be friends without being bedmates?"

"I know that. But from the day Robert met you in our freshman year, he's had this obsession about you."

"Considering all the people who hate me, it's nice to be loved."

"I needed to know. You do admit that you come on to me. I don't know if that's for show or if you mean it."

"Whatever I've done, I've meant. It's not Robert who's held me back. It's Gene. If I ever started dating you, and Gene found out, I think he'd go ballistic. He'd think, perhaps accurately, that we deserted him when he needed us, and then betrayed him by taking up with each other."

"I didn't think of it that way, and I didn't know you felt that way," she said. "What we thought was between Gene and me is dead and gone," she said. "And ironically, it never really existed. We were hardly man and wife. He wanted a madonna. As you might find out later one night, perhaps even tonight, I'm no madonna." She carefully ate her burger and looked at him soulfully.

Buck feared another personal question, but instead Susan, fearing she'd gone too far, adroitly asked, "Don't you think the burgers here were better when we were in college?"

He smiled and rose from his seat, taking her arm. "Everything used to be better when we were in college."

***

After Susan's sexual challenge to him at The Rusty Pelican, Buck remained quiet as he drove her to Hazel's apartment, leaving her own car in the bar's parking lot. He'd known Rose's sister for a long time. One didn't publish a newspaper in Okeechobee of any persuasion— right or left—without getting to know a lot about Hazel. She was very vocal.

Unlike Rose, the poorer sister lived on South Beach in a residential section filled mainly with elderly Jews, mostly women, of which she was a champion.

Buck parked in front of Hazel's building. In rapid strides, he followed Susan across a palm-shaded courtyard of broken tiles, with a moonlit surf curling over the litter-strewn beach in the distance.

Twice married, the recently widowed Hazel still used her maiden name of Phillips. She lived in an overcrowded, ratty apartment in a former South Beach hotel which had been converted into a condominium of retired people.

Buck's pulse raced as he made his way with Susan through the vacant-faced women sitting in rockers in the austere downstairs lobby. Taking the rickety elevator upstairs, he sensed he was getting close to the flame: Hazel Phillips, a dreaded Nemesis to her own politically conservative sister, but a champion warhorse fighting for human rights, with legions of fans.

At fifty-five, fearing youth and energy running out, she'd thrown her cowgirl hat into the mayoralty race. The hat had become her trademark, and she was often photographed in it, looking like a chubby version of Annie Oakley—her ample paunch encased in gaucho-style leather pants, held up by an embroidered belt with a prominent silver buckle. She always wore her hat rakishly over he left eye, her frazzled hair sticking out in mats.

Tonight she'd abandoned the cowgirl outfit and looked like everybody's Jewish mama, in a loose-fitting floral-patterned housecoat with wedgies. Her mouth unwiped, Hazel greeted Buck. "Did you eat? We've got plenty."

He declined but shook her hand—her grip was so hard he felt engaged in an endurance contest. The smile, the friendliest in politics, revealed yellowing teeth.

She met Susan with a kiss on both cheeks, her welcome of her warmer and friendlier than her greeting of Buck. Hazel always welcomed women with more gusto than men, as she felt men had all the advantages anyway.

She didn't bother to introduce Buck and Susan to the melange of guests, mostly campaign workers, sprawled all over the overcrowded living room floor. In the dining room, she found Buck a seat on a bench at a long wooden table. Susan had wandered off to interview some campaign workers, allowing Buck his not-so-private encounter with Hazel. Once more, he declined food from a big pot of chicken dumplings. He settled instead for a cup of bitter black coffee from a girl with long, unwashed hair.

In some way, Hazel reminded Buck of a shadowy weather-beaten version of her more delicately feminine sister. Despite their outward differences, there remained a distinct family resemblance. It was as if Rose had brought out and toned her lovelier features, whereas Hazel had brutalized hers, showing little or no concern for the way she looked.

Flashing a mischievous grin at Buck, Hazel said, "I need to move into that big mayor's house. With the crowd I've got hanging out here all the time, I'm about to suffocate."

Later, in her little study, with her desk burdened with unanswered mail, the earth mother settled comfortably on her tattered sofa, placing her stockinged but shoeless feet on her coffee table. She reached for a bowl of peanuts, firing them into her mouth like a machine gun. With a frown, she pushed the bowl aside and shouted into the next room, "Who in hell put these damn peanuts in here? You know I'm dieting."

Around Hazel, Buck felt his senses rejuvenated, his spirit cleansed, after that seductive but morbid meeting with her sister. For the first part of the interview, Hazel did all the talking, her monologue taking on extreme urgency. When she slowed down a bit, Buck realized that her face, without intense animation, appeared far older than her years—a complete contrast to the startlingly youthful face of Rose.

"If I didn't know better, I would never guess you were Rose's sister," he said. "How could two sisters be so different?"

Hazel's face took on an anxious expression. "I never wanted to be like Rose. That bitch stands up there in her pulpit, preaching hate and bigotry, using the Bible as her shield."

An aide kept repeatedly interrupting their interview, and Buck knew he wouldn't have a monopoly on Hazel's time much longer.

"Rose still thinks we can make this country free for some—and not for others," Hazel claimed.

"What made Rose oppose minorities and you champion them?"

She dropped a peanut in the ample bosom of her housecoat, then quickly retrieved it. "My husband, Bernie—you didn't know him—taught me everything I know about human rights, civil rights, whatever. I was a redneck when I married him. But as liberal as Bernie was, he would never have accepted women's liberation."

Abruptly changing the subject, Buck asked, "Don't you think Rose is easy to caricature?"

"Hell! I'm easy to caricature as some big overblown cowgirl. Take Sister Rose seriously. She's dedicated. She has said many times, 'the Lord put me on this earth to bring justice.' That means her kind of justice inflicted on people who don't agree with her." Bouncing off the sofa, she appeared robust.

A concerned look came over her face. "We've been getting reports that some of those far right creatures—types you find when you turn over a rock—have been creeping into town lately. Calder Martin, for instance."

Buck pressed her long and hard, but she could give him no details about the South Beach evictions, other than to say that she was fighting them.

"The lid's about to blow off and my people haven't gotten to the bottom of it. I wouldn't be surprised if Rose is connected with it in some way. I wouldn't be surprised at all."

He doubted that, feeling Hazel's resentment of Rose seriously discolored her judgment. After all, what possible interest could Sister Rose have in evicting some elderly Jews? Surely the evangelist pursued loftier goals.

An urgent call came in for Hazel, and she barked into the receiver before muffling her voice to whisper to Buck. "I think we're heading for big trouble here."

"What kind?" he said with growing agitation, resenting all the intrusions. A group of women came into the study to talk to Hazel.

"You're a publisher," Hazel said as a parting word. "Get a reporter, two, three—as many as it takes—to get out there and dig."

Unknown to her, Buck had already done just that.

"Find out what's going on," Hazel demanded. "What they're planning to do. In Kansas, I always knew when to head for the cyclone cellar. I could feel it in my bones."

He smiled, eager to do some snooping on his own. After all, it was too much work for Susan, and there was a sudden sense of urgency.

Going down in the elevator with Susan after leaving Hazel's apartment, he said, "She knows nothing—at least nothing she wants to share with the press. I suspect she knows a lot but just isn't ready to reveal it yet. When she's ready, we can expect a big blast. She hints that her sister's involved in some way but that seems unlikely."

"I know Hazel well. Whenever something rotten's involved, she always suspects Rose."

On this hot, humid night, he headed up the bejeweled strip of beach, wanting—at least temporarily—to forget about politics, although knowing that was impossible. He enjoyed the fresh breeze from the ocean, the glittering lights, and mostly the feel of being behind the wheel and in control of his life.

In a surprise move, Susan moved closer to him in the front seat, taking his free hand as he always drove with only one hand on the wheel, sometimes only a finger. She didn't say anything but held his hand rather tightly. Ever so gently she raised his hand to her mouth and started sucking his thumb.

"Your thumb is really nice and tastes delicious," she said. "What I did to your thumb, I could..."

He didn't let her finish her sentence, but came to an abrupt stop in the parking lot of The Rusty Pelican. He grabbed her and kissed her, inserting his tongue in her mouth. He tried to fight the image flooding his brain, but couldn't stop it. All he could think of was not Susan but Gene's penis. That penis had penetrated Susan's mouth the way his tongue was doing now.

As he kissed her longer and harder, Gene's penis became thicker and longer until it exploded in Susan's mouth. He found himself licking her lips after withdrawing his tongue. In his mind it was Gene's semen he was licking from her lips.

***

In his Volkswagen, Gene pulled into his driveway. Across the street, the stringy-haired Cuban woman, Clara, was out watering her lawn as her little girl, Maria, sat on a tiled portico sucking her thumb. Clara pretended not to notice him, yet he knew she feasted her eyes on him, devouring him, wanting him.

He gripped the steering wheel of his car as tight as he could, almost wanting to back out of the driveway and flee into the night. He wanted to leave this neighborhood behind him. Inside the house, he stripped down to his briefs and headed right for his bedroom. He didn't have any appetite tonight and wanted to sleep for twelve or fifteen hours. Before going to his chief, Biff, he wanted to get all the evidence he could about this Lolito ring. This could be the big chance to make himself a hero again, and he'd do everything in his power to break the case wide open.

Before he turned off the goose-necked lamp, he stared at his small and gloomy bedroom, with its threadbare carpeting and wallpaper of red roses that his mother had applied when he was still in high school. Now stained with age, the roses had turned a faded yellow, almost like urine streaks on the wall. He planned never to change it. The only thing he really wanted to change was the day that had ruined his life. He'd lost everything after that day, not only the most important tennis match of his career, but Susan, his hero status, and Buck.

A light had gone out of his life after that final night with Buck before the game. Buck had revealed his true nature but had run from it, even though Gene was willing to accept Buck for what he was, moving their friendship onto a different plateau. He'd been willing to make that sacrifice for Buck who had betrayed him by fleeing. Gene knew Buck wasn't fleeing from him but from himself.

After his arrest, he'd called Buck repeatedly, always getting Robert, who promised that Buck would return his calls. Buck never did, and for all Gene knew Robert never told him he'd called. Before going to bed, Gene always thought of Buck and the way their lives should have gone but hadn't. Just before that breakthrough night with Buck, there had been a bitter fight with Susan, after which he'd stormed out of the house. Susan had unknowingly driven him to find solace with Buck, who'd offered a warm refuge until he'd so abruptly abandoned him too.

Both Susan and Buck had tossed him aside. Instead of concentrating on his game the next day, he'd thought of them and their betrayals. That's why he'd lost the game. Even in defeat, the crowds had cheered him on, sensing that he was fighting for his life. It wasn't just a game. If he won the match, he could go professional after that. On many a night after that game he would remember the cheers of the crowd. Sometimes the memory of the cheering fans was what kept him alive. He wasn't to hear the cheer of the crowd ever again.

In three months of marriage to Susan, he'd grown bitter and disillusioned. He'd suspected that she was just a whore, even worse than those Cuban sluts his fraternity brothers used to smuggle into the dormitories at night.

His mother had convinced him that a woman endured sex for the sake of a man, but Susan had been completely different. She'd demanded sex for her own pleasure.

Even though she hadn't said anything on their honeymoon, he'd known she wasn't happy with his lovemaking. He'd preferred quick sex, fast relief, and she'd wanted to draw out the act. The night before the game, when he hadn't been aroused by her, she'd said, "I think I know how to bring it to life." His penis had bobbed limply only inches from her face and her fingers had fastened around it, pulling the skin back to expose the head. Then, in a flash, she'd dived for it, her lips slipping over the head, her tongue working frantically to stimulate him. He'd pushed her away and, losing control, had slapped her face. "You're disgusting," he'd shouted at her.

"It's normal for a woman to want to do that to her husband," she'd yelled back to him. "You're the one who's not normal."

Her words had stung him like no others, but it was the accusatory look on her face that had done the most damage. Getting dressed hurriedly, he'd stormed out of the house.

She followed him down the stairs, shouting after him. "What does turn you on? Why did you marry me in the first place?"

At the door he'd shoved her back. "Look at yourself," he'd said. "You're like a bitch in heat." He'd slammed the door in her face.

She'd opened the door and ran after him, as if wanting to strike back in some way. Bitterly rejected, she'd stood on the sidewalk looking hurt and humiliated, her torn housecoat half hanging on her body. In her anguish, she'd cried out loud enough for all the neighbors on the block to hear. "I thought I was getting a *real* man. You're not a man at all!"

He trembled, even now, just thinking about that confrontation. After the tennis match the next day, he hadn't gone to the showers. Still sweating profusely and dressed in white shorts, he'd driven to a slumlike neighborhood in the northern part of the city. Driving blindly, he hadn't remembered how he'd gotten there.

From a block away, he'd seen her coming up the street where his car had been parked at an intersection. She'd been like a strange girl-child, and he'd known at once she held the key to unlock some door that had been closed to him. In that inner padlocked cell—like the retreat where he now lived, boarded up from the world—lay the answer to his own manhood.

As she'd drawn closer, he'd taken in her features while at the same time, he'd felt a rising excitement in his tennis shorts. Her petulant mouth had been a deep red, her pale liquid eyes resting behind long lashes. She couldn't have been more than eight years old. Blonde ringlets had fallen casually about her head and the skin of her slim bare arms was the whitest he'd ever seen.

What had attracted him to her was a look of such openness that he'd felt it could reassure him when confronted with the challenge he was about to present to her. Her face had been like a blank piece of paper, waiting for him to make his mark on it.

How could he have known then that in the next fleeting act, his life would be changed for all time? Maybe hers, too. His blood running even hotter than in the heat of the game, he'd called her over and she'd come willingly, innocently, toward him. In vivid detail, he could still recall how eagerly she'd approached the car, as if she'd known and responded to the deep need he had for her.

At the window she'd looked down for the surprise he'd promised her. A chill of delight had come over him. Reaching in, he'd taken out his penis, and she'd watched in stunned fascination as he'd pulled the foreskin back, letting the thick, vermilion head assert itself—blossoming toward her, the blood pulsing through the rope-like veins of his shaft. Her piercing scream had made it stiffen all the more. Susan had been a liar, accusing him of not being a man. He had his evidence. His manhood was so fierce and powerful that its exposure had filled the girl with fear, and had sent her screaming up the street. The motor of his car still running, he'd stepped on the accelerator and had driven away. It could have been the end of that, if only a neighbor, spotting the running, screaming girl, hadn't taken down his license plate.

With all the willpower he had, he tried to blot out that scream that sounded as real now as it had back then. Kneeling beside his bed, he clasped his hands, his face still in shadows. He prayed that God would see him through the night.

After his prayer, he got back in his bed and slowly drifted off to sleep. He didn't know how long he'd slept or what time it was, but he was awakened by the ringing of the phone which he kept in the kitchen. Slowly he made his way through the darkened house to the phone. The only people who called any more were those at the station. It was probably some emergency duty that had come up. He didn't really want to go back to work, and only with great hesitation picked up the phone. "Yeah," he said in a gruff manner.

"Hi!" came the voice on the other end. "Hope I'm not calling too late."

The caller didn't have to identify himself. He knew at once who it was. "Old buddy." That's what he'd always called Buck. "It's been a long time. Five years to be exact."

"Right you are. Five years, seventy-nine days, thirteen hours, and eight minutes."

"At least you're better at keeping time than being a friend."

"I'm ashamed. I was fucked up in the head. I want you to forgive me."

"That I can do."

"I also want my friend back," Buck said. "We have a lot of things to talk over. The Lolito case. I know you're aware of it."

"How in the fuck do you know that?" Gene asked.

"We heard about it at the *Examiner* too."

"Is this call about the case or is it about us?" Gene sounded angry, feeling almost betrayed again, and he'd only been talking to Buck for a few seconds.

"Fuck the case," Buck said. "It's got to be about us first. You don't think I could meet with you again and talk about anything else but us?"

"That's more like it. You know the address. Haul ass."

"I'll be there in an hour." Buck put down the phone.

Gene stood alone in the darkness of the kitchen. He couldn't believe what had just happened. With Buck coming over, with him about to break a big high-profile case, his second chance at life had come again.

***

After hanging up the phone, Buck found himself trembling at the prospect of a reunion that was about to happen within the hour. He stood in Susan's apartment, surveying her living room. Susan had retreated to the bathroom where she was running bath water. By mutual agreement, he'd followed her from the parking lot of The Rusty Pelican in response to her invitation, after the meeting with Hazel, for a nightcap in her apartment. He could hardly take her to his mansion with Robert there.

Her apartment was sparsely furnished, and filled with the smell of stale beer and cigarette butts. Nothing in it suggested her delicate beauty or feminine nature. This was the apartment of two fraternity brothers living off campus.

"What do you think?" she said, coming out of the bathroom and wearing only a robe and a smile.

"A little too macho for me," he said. "Haven't you heard of curtains?"

"Back here in the bushes we're not overlooked by anybody. If I lived in the house up front, that would be different."

"Someone could easily slip back through the bushes and peer in the windows."

"I hate to disappoint you, but I don't think I'm that popular these days. Maybe I was once, but that was back in my beauty queen days."

"Still it's a little scary." He looked her up and down, suspecting she was nude under that robe. Was this a sexual invitation?

"What about a drink?" she asked.

"I'd like some Scotch if you have it."

"That I do have. Scotch and vodka—the only two poisons people drink any more. Would you get an ice tray from the refrigerator?" She motioned toward a door in the rear.

In her small, shabby kitchen, he opened the refrigerator finding only a bottle of fizzled-out Perrier and a dried-up lime. He removed an ice tray and headed back to the living room. "You don't keep much of a larder either. I'll have to send care packages."

"That's why I stay so slim. Actually I'm a career girl. Not much of a cook. If I'm eating in, I just pick up something at the deli. It's not much fun living alone. If I'd known you were coming over, I would have stocked the refrigerator just to impress you." She poured some Scotch on the rocks and handed him a chipped glass.

"Cheers," he said, clinking glasses with her. He looked deeply into her eyes, which seemed to be dancing.

She'd become suddenly playful. "I've run a tub for you. Real hot. Care to join me for a bath?"

He was amazed at her frankness. After denying he was gay, it was an invitation he couldn't refuse. He'd always been intrigued by her and now was his chance for intimacy, a chance that both of them had postponed for years in spite of opportunities. Blocking off thoughts of Robert, he followed her to the bathroom.

"You can take off your clothes and put them on the chair over there," she said, dropping her robe. Suspicion confirmed. She was completely nude under that robe. Her beauty matched or even surpassed that of Pamela in her prime. Her breasts were extremely rounded and full, although not grotesquely large. He glanced briefly at her nudity and her auburn bush. She eased herself swanlike into the tub. "Come and join me."

He unbuckled his trousers and stepped out of them before removing his white shirt and undershirt. He slipped off his socks, leaving him standing before her in only his white briefs. He reached for the elastic band.

"Don't! The moment of unveiling I like to reserve for myself." With deft hands she reached and pulled down his briefs, his big cock bouncing up toward her face where she gave it two quick kisses.

In the hot bath water, they kissed for a long time, stroking each other's bodies. His whole body tingled with excitement as she played with his fully extended erection. The water was scented with something sweet smelling. With a fluffy sponge, she bathed his chest.

A red silk ribbon held her auburn hair in position above her head. Around her white neck a few stray strands dangled. With his fingers, he made curls of them. His hand sliding across her skin, he gently traced his fingers along her neck and shoulders, cupping her breasts and toying with the nipples. His hand glided through the curve of her narrow waist and then went below to explore further.

He gently lowered himself over her and kissed her. The taste and touch of her lips excited him. His hands continued to feel every inch of her body, and he pressed toward her in complete naturalness. They didn't seem like a man and a woman discovering each other for the first time, but familiar lovers who knew secret spots to touch. His hand moved up and around to her shoulders and neck and then, gently, back down to her stomach and hips—sensual, stimulating.

She was different from other women he'd known. He found himself doing things he usually didn't—kissing her hand and holding the palm of it against his hot, uneven breath. She made him feel like something special, that he'd been hiding a part of himself to give only to her. Her soft, caressing hands moved gently, yet hungrily, over his body. Just as he cupped her breasts again, she reached below to fondle his jewels.

He pulled her to him, lifting her from the waist and seating her on his lap, impaling her. He bobbed back and forth, the way a cork rises and falls in water, the scented suds swirling around them, waves churning against soap-polished skins. He surged against her, plunging deeper and deeper, lunging faster and faster to make up for the lonely, lost time he hadn't discovered her before.

Arms locked around his neck, she kissed him with passion, holding him tighter and tighter, sucking his tongue. He could tell by the frenzied look on her face that he was filling some void deep within her.

He imagined that no man had filled her like this since Gene had gone. Gene and he were alike in only one way. Although their look was different, their genitalia equally matched each other's.

At the memory of Gene's full erection, his own urgency increased. He made her gasp for breath like Gene must have done at one time. Wrapping her long legs around his waist, she clutched him to her.

The water spilled and splattered, and no one cared. Spasm upon spasm overwhelmed him, as her own body gyrated with the force of their flow. Even at the moment of climax, he wondered if it had been like this with Gene. He wasn't seeing and experiencing the glow of her body any more but recalling his plunge into the tight confines of Gene. Images of his friend exploded in his brain, and he couldn't blot them out. He was plunging into Gene and not Susan—buried inside a woman who'd known Gene's powerful strokes.

He looked into her face fearing in some miraculous way she knew what his secret thoughts and desires were.

Her eyes tightly closed, she gave no clue that she knew a third person had intruded into their love-making. She uttered low, soft moans—strange gurgling noises, as she covered his face with wet kisses, tiny bites. Her hair had come undone and fell like a tangle of spaghetti along her neck. She looked like a little girl.

As they lay in the tub together, he gently withdrew from her. The water was turning cold, and he had a reunion to attend. He didn't dare leave her so abruptly. He still stroked her smooth skin, and his hands continued restlessly across her, as if there were new parts of her yet to be explored. But he was not going to be the explorer of this new geography. Not tonight anyway. Gene was waiting for him and even beyond there was Robert in an empty bed.

As he got out of the tub, he felt dirtier than when he'd entered it. He was confused and uncertain of himself.

"You can spend the night, natch?" she asked.

"I'd love to but I can't." He dried himself vigorously with a towel. "Old Buck is sick tonight and he's demanding that I come over. Each time he gets sick, he thinks it's the last time. He always summons me over for last-minute instructions about the future of the Examiner."

"If that's who you're going to see, I can forgive your leaving like this. You'll miss out on a lot of fun and games. Sure it's not Pamela you're secretly meeting later tonight?"

"I'm sure," he said as he hastily dressed. He suddenly felt embarrassed at being nude in front of her.

"There's one thing I'm certain of," she said.

"What's that?" he asked, slipping into his trousers and zipping up.

"There's no way in hell you can be gay."

"That's for damn sure," he said, giving her a long, lingering kiss. "Gotta go."

***

Buck hadn't been to Gene's house in five years, and he was shocked at how the neighborhood had deteriorated. The streets were once quiet and deserted in the late evening, but now were filled with bodegas and taverns playing loud music. The whole area reminded him of certain streets in Santo Domingo, and he was amazed that Gene had tenaciously held onto his home here and hadn't sold out and went to another area.

If his old friend were still the same, Buck knew Gene didn't like Hispanics. Buck had been attracted to Gene for many reasons, including some strange chemistry between them, but they'd never agreed on politics. In politics, Gene was much more on the side of Sister Rose and even old Buck himself that he was in Buck's camp.

As he pulled up in front of Gene's house, Buck at first thought he was at the wrong address. The dilapidated house with the yard unmowed looked uninhabited, with no light coming from it. He'd visited the house far too many times to be mistaken. He strode rapidly up the walkway and rang the doorbell. A long time went by and he rang again.

This time the door opened slightly as someone from behind peered out. "Old buddy, get your ass inside." It was unmistakably Gene.

Buck stepped inside the dark foyer, there to encounter Gene. He was nude except for a pair of skimpy briefs.

"It's good to see you again," Buck said, standing only inches from Gene who smelled like he'd just showered.

"It's good to see you too," Gene said. "Strike that good. I'm fucking overjoyed!"

"What are we supposed to do in a situation like this?" Buck asked. "Shake hands."

"How about a hug?" Gene asked. "Just like we used to."

Buck put his arms around Gene and pulled him close. Gene pressed his body hard against Buck as if one embrace could make up for an absence of five long years.

Neither man wanted to break away, and Buck was severely tempted to let his hands start traveling on a journey of exploration across Gene's body. That was one temptation he wasn't going to give in to.

Gene held on tighter and began to cry. Buck ran fingers through Gene's hair and pulled back to look into his face. His eyes were watering. He kissed Gene firmly on the mouth, taking his hand as he led Gene into his own living room.

"I could offer you a beer—shit like that," Gene said, "but you didn't come here for that."

"I came to see you—and to apologize. I'm ashamed." Even as they sat down on the tattered sofa, he held Gene's hand firmly. He looked into his eyes. "I want you to forgive me."

"And I want you to promise never to leave me again."

"I'll always stand by you—no matter what. That is, if you'll have me back."

"You're home." He leaned over and kissed Buck hard on the mouth.

Buck kissed him back even harder. It was a fairly large sofa but they occupied only a small part of it. "Remember when we'd known each other for years and were afraid to kiss?"

"All too well," Gene said.

"Then one night on that fishing trip I just leaned over and kissed you."

"It felt good," Gene said.

"When you didn't beat the shit out of me, I kissed you again. And again."

"I didn't want you to stop. But you did."

"I held back," Buck said. "Back then we thought it was okay for men to kiss. Not to go beyond that."

"I know. Missed out on a lot of fun by holding back."

"Today I wouldn't hold back. We both got big hard-ons every time we showered together. We'd get erections every time we wrestled."

"There were plenty of clues we had the hots for each other."

"What do you mean had?" Buck asked. Breaking his hold on Gene, he got up from the sofa.

Suddenly, Gene was behind him, standing real close, rubbing up against him. "You've been looking down at the mound in my briefs ever since you came in the door. If you want to rip them off me, feel free."

Buck moved away, going over to the far corner of the room and sitting down in an armchair. "I have taken your briefs off before."

"I remember it well," Gene said, coming over to Buck and sitting down at his feet, wrapping an arm around Buck's legs. "It was the night before the big match. I'd stormed out on Susan and called you. We met at that cheap motel near Crazy Mabel's. God, we had a lot to drink that night. I was coming unglued. The most important match of my life and I was drinking heavily. Blowing my big chance."

"I tried to get you to stop but then I had too much to drink, and one thing led to another."

"A lot of that night is fuzzy for me," Gene said. "I remember standing at the latrine. I couldn't unzip my pants."

"If I recall, and I recall very well, I volunteered to assist. A little too willingly if I remember it right."

"Your reaching in and taking me out was something that almost sobered me up."

"Friends have to help each other at the urinal—that's understood," Buck said. "But did I really have to reach in and take out your big balls too? You only wanted to piss."

"Maybe you wanted to feel them," Gene said.

"Maybe I did."

Gene looked up at Buck. "Maybe I wanted you to feel them. Maybe I could have pissed fine by myself. Maybe it was just a trick to make you reach into my pants."

"The whole night seems unreal," Buck said. "We checked into that motel. You asked me to take your clothes off, and I undressed you like an expert. Everything except the briefs. I left them on."

"But not for long," Gene said.

"Not for long. I had to take them off because I was determined to suck your cock, and I'd never sucked a cock in my life."

"Shit," Gene said, getting up abruptly. "You're giving me a fucking hard-on." He walked across the room, not certain of where to go. Only his rear faced Buck. He seemed embarrassed to turn around.

Buck got up and stood behind him. "I've got to go on. I've denied it to myself too long. I've got to actually say what I'm about to say. I swallowed every damn drop. That wasn't all. When you turned over to go to sleep, I attacked your ass. First with my tongue, then with my dick. I'd never fucked a man before that night—and, believe it or not—I haven't since. But I fucked you. Fuck, Hell! It was rape."

Gene turned around, his erection sticking out of his skimpy briefs. "I met you thrust for thrust, and when you came, I came again."

"I know. I was the guy who then spun you around and licked up every drop."

"We both fell asleep. I was drunk and I don't remember your leaving. When I woke up the next morning, you were gone. No note, nothing. Gone. That was the last time I ever saw you—until tonight."

"I know." Buck said, "God damn it, I know!"

"I've got a bedroom back there, all boarded up from the world. I owe you one for that night." He gently moved Buck toward the rear of the house.

Buck protested. "Aren't we going a little fast here?" He came to a stop near the bathroom, resisting taking any more steps. "I've got to tell you something: I've never been fucked before. I don't think I can take it."

"Your dick's as big as mine. I'd never been fucked before that night either—or ever again. If I could take it like a man back then, I guess you can do the same tonight." Gene leaned Buck against the wall, kissing him real hard and inserting his tongue which Buck eagerly sucked.

Buck reached for Gene's briefs and pulled them down. Very gently but firmly Gene pressed Buck's head lower. Buck dropped down to his knees as Gene's erect penis bobbed in front of his face. He planted tiny kisses on it before venturing lower to lick Gene's balls. He pulled Gene's foreskin back, took a deep breath, then plunged down.

***

On the drive back home, Buck could not believe the sudden change that had occurred in his life. His involvement with both Gene and Susan had come about so quickly and without plan that even now it seemed like a film spinning inside his head. That he'd made love to both of them on the same night was unreal.

Yet he knew it was painfully real. In fact, his ass ached from Gene's assault. At last he'd been fucked and by an expert. The searing pain of Gene's entry had been followed by the most exquisite pleasure he'd ever known. Gene literally had him sobbing with pleasure and begging for more. Once Gene got him to his darkened bedroom, Gene had attacked him with a ferocity in love-making unlike Buck had ever known.

Gene had almost eaten him before the penetration. There was a hunger in Gene that both attracted him and repelled him at the same time. He sensed that if flood gates were opened deep within Gene there would be no way to put a stop to them.

Buck agreed to meet Gene tomorrow and talk about the Lolito ring, and other matters. Their reunion tonight had hardly been the occasion for business.

As he pulled into his driveway, Buck was certain of only one thing. Regardless of what he'd done only hours before, his love was only for Robert.

In a robe, Robert was at the door waiting for him. He kissed Buck hard on the mouth but said nothing.

"I know it's late, and I'm sorry," Buck said. "I should have called. You must have been worried."

"Half out of my mind."

"Let's go stand on the terrace," Buck said, taking Robert's hand and leading him across the living room. "Let's breathe the night air together."

Out on the terrace he reached for Robert and pulled him close, inserting his tongue in Robert's mouth which the young man eagerly sucked.

Robert pulled away slightly. "If I didn't know better I'd swear you just had a shower."

"I always smell as sweet as the ocean breeze," Buck said, pulling him close again. "That's what you always tell me, even when I'm back from a fishing trip and haven't had a real bath in two days."

"I think that's when I like to give you a tongue bath the most."

"Stop it," he said, biting and licking Robert's ear. "You're giving me a hard-on."

"I can feel it."

"I stayed later than I thought at Hazel's."

"No, you didn't. You left early and with Susan."

"She's assigned to the story, you know."

"Just so long as she's not assigned to anything else."

"She's not," Buck said. "I don't have sex with my employees. After I dropped her off at The Rusty Pelican parking lot, I went for a long drive and an endless walk along the beach."

"I might not believe that most nights, but strangely tonight I do. You've been loving me like you've never loved me before, and I know this sudden turn of events—after all these years—has been playing on your mind."

He took Robert's hands and held each palm up to his lips, planting gentle kisses. "Thanks for understanding and being here for me. I don't know what's happening to me these days. Like that attack on you before I left to visit Hazel."

"I loved it."

"I'm all mixed up," Buck said.

"You're falling in love with me. Really in love with me. The way I've been with you for years. Now you're feeling what I have always felt. You didn't think it would happen to you."

"I certainly waited long enough."

"You sure did." He took his hand and unbuttoned Buck's shirt and reached inside to feel his chest. "I fully expect you'll do something really crazy over the next few months. I mean, really far out. But I know it's what's expected before you make a final commitment to me. You'll do some things to really piss me off. But what I also know is that in the end you'll be mine. You'll never belong to anybody else.

"I never will," Buck promised. "Why don't we go to our bed and exchange some body fluids?"

After closing the terrace doors, he followed Robert as he headed up the steps. Midway, he slapped Robert playfully on the butt. "Don't be surprised if I get a little kinky tonight. Go a bit farther than before."

"With you, there are no limits."

At the door of their bedroom, he removed Robert's robe. He was nude. "You're beautiful," Buck said, "the most beautiful man I've ever seen."

"Your exclusive property."

He bent down and kissed each of Robert's nipples. "Tonight my tongue's going to go where it has never gone before. If you can get so much pleasure out of licking every crevice of my body, the same pleasure can be mine." He picked up Robert in his arms and carried him toward their bed. He didn't have to worry about getting undressed himself. Robert was an expert at doing that for him.

**

Susan placed her receiver back on its hook and returned to her bed. She'd just called old Buck's estate and had spoken to his black butler. Buck had left some important-looking documents at her place when he'd hurried out, and she felt he might need them early in the morning. She was going to volunteer to run them over to old Buck's estate.

"I'm sorry that Mr. Brooke is ill," she'd told the butler.

"He's not ill. He walked for about a mile along the beach today. One of his longest walks. After dinner, he went to bed at eight thirty."

"You mean he's not sick and his grandson isn't coming over tonight?"

"That old man's not sick. We haven't seen that grandson around here in more than a week."

"I see. Thanks anyway. I'll take the papers into his office in the morning."

"That would be very nice of you. Even as a kid, that child always forgot something."

"Good night." She returned to her bed but couldn't go to sleep. Why had Buck lied to her? Where could Buck have gone that he didn't want her to know?

This was a troubling beginning to what had the promising ring of an exciting relationship in her life. She turned over in bed but her mind wouldn't go to rest. A thought occurred to her. He didn't go off for a reunion with Gene, or did he? He'd already told her that he was going to do that, so his intentions were hardly a secret.

Brushing it from her mind, she shut her eyes and went to sleep remembering that scene in the bathroom with Buck. That's what she'd thought life with Gene would be like but wasn't.

With Buck, she'd found a new reason to live.

Chapter Three

After the sexual marathon of last night, Buck was tired and instead of sitting at his desk, he lay on the office sofa on his back, dictating some urgent letters into a machine. He flip-flopped to his stomach and reached for another cigarette, though his present one still wasn't burned down. Sticking it in the corner of his mouth, he continued talking into the tape recorder. The telephone rang but he didn't bother to answer it. Robert had stepped out of the office briefly to deliver a contract to the legal department.

Finishing the letters, he proof-read his Sunday column which Robert had left for him. He decided it was crap. He wanted to tear it into pieces, tossing the bits of paper around the room like confetti. But he decided to run with it anyway. With everything that was happening in Okeechobee, he didn't need to be writing about why plans were stalled for a new city hall. The town was more interesting than that. A hell of a lot going on, and he was not reporting any of the action so far.

A rap at his door, and Roland—shod in his bedroom slippers—came into his office in his usual lurching gait. "You're here early, boss," he said, wandering over to open the draperies and plop himself in Buck's favorite armchair.

"Yeah," Buck said, blinking in the glaring morning light. "My column for tomorrow is shit." He rubbed his dazed and glassy eyes. "Proof it for me if you will. Throw in a few better lines if you can think of any."

"I'll do that." Roland spoke in a dull, hoarse monotone, almost a whisper. "I've been cleaning up your copy for years."

"Don't rub it in."

"You look like you've had a bad night," Roland said.

"You got that right. Hell, man, with half the beauty queens in town clamoring for my bod, what's a guy to do?"

"You're lucky. With my ailments and afflictions, I have only my memories."

Buck glanced at his disappointing column again. "I thought I'd do something about the mayoralty race. Speculating on Hazel's chances against Barry. And to tantalize the reader, the prospect of Rose coming out against her own sister to support Barry." He waited for Roland's reaction.

When none was forthcoming, Buck went to the bathroom, pulled off his shirt and started to shave. He'd showered earlier, but had completely forgotten about his beard. He left the door open so he could talk to his city editor.

"Did Rose convert you the other night?" Roland asked, an amused look in his eyes.

Buck twisted his head and glanced at Roland and then at his own face in the mirror. "Not quite." He turned to Roland, his eyes imploring, "Do you think she's a hypocrite?"

Roland took out his handkerchief and mopped his brow, as the faucet was creating a lot of steam. "In many ways she reminds me of an old-time Los Angeles faith-healer, Aimee Semple McPherson. Before your time, I know. She once stunned her congregation by roaring out on a shiny black police motorcycle—dressed completely in black leather, even thick black leather boots. A traffic cop for Christ. That beat all I've ever seen."

"Yeah," Buck said, almost kicking himself. "I remember that story. Something about a fake kidnapping when she'd run off with her lover."

"Aimee *really* lived a double life—believe you me. I was almost one of her converts."

Buck smiled and rinsed the lather from his face. "I didn't know you had a past," he said jokingly. He reached for his shirt and headed back to the office. "I'm suspicious of Rose. I just don't buy her act. She comes on real pious in public, so I've heard. I think there's a very sensual woman there."

"I'm convinced of it," Roland said. "There have been many, many stories. In my day, I've seen enough of these self-styled messiahs who blend theater with salvation. I've seen them create their fantastic temples and their big bank accounts. We used to call them the 'P.T. Barnums of religion.' Nowadays, they don't need a circus tent. They have TV. I think we've got another one on our hands. Sister Rose herself."

"Someone told me she finds the wages of sin just great if it leads to a big collection plate."

"Exactly."

Buck sat down at his desk, a strong, determined look coming onto his face. Looking up, he said to Roland, "I think we'd better start looking at her pretty closely. Grandpa thinks she's a saint, so he did nothing but puff her. But I think she's not that at all. She's very mysterious. There's a lot going on we don't know a damn thing about. Do you think she's got a lover? Lovers?"

"More than one. I'm sure just one man could never satisfy Rose Phillips." Roland settled wearily into his armchair. "Sex and religion among the big-name evangelists have mixed in this country for a long time. If you remember your mythology, many of the ancient gods and goddesses had greater sexual appetites than you and me put together."

"Speak for yourself," Buck said facetiously. "I know something about mythology, but mainly I remember psychology at the university. My professor said that many Freudians felt religious feelings were libidinous."

"If behind this preacher against sin, we find a sinner herself," Roland said, "I wouldn't be surprised. It'd be following in the footsteps of tradition. Many—maybe most—religious cult figures in America enjoyed voracious sex appetites."

Buck fell silent, his mind preoccupied. His phone rang again and he motioned to Roland not to answer it. He closed his eyes, remembering the smell of Rose and how her auburn hair had brushed across his cheek as she'd kissed him good night.

"Are you willing to expose her without mercy?" Roland asked pointedly.

Buck didn't want to be committed like that. "I don't know...maybe," he said. "I've heard a lot of reports about her. Megalomaniac. Outright psychotic. She's a strong and powerful woman, with a big following that's growing fast with this charismatic movement. Any attack the *Examiner* might run could just increase her contributions. Of course, we'll be branded as part of the 'godless Commie lunatic fringe.'"

Roland rubbed his back and seemed to suffer some intense pain. "You're used to that."

"I suspect Rose is giving a new twist to a long tradition of religious fakery and fanaticism in this country." He placed a bottle of aspirin in front of Roland and handed him a glass of water. "I think she's going to better known than Billy Graham."

"What is she after?"

"I can't figure her out yet. Money. Power. Her foundation is already one of the most heavily bank-rolled in America. The country's changing real rapidly, and Rose provides a lot of easy answers to complex riddles. In her vocabulary, good is good and evil is evil, and she doesn't want to talk about the graduations in between."

"You seem really..." Roland paused, then added, "troubled by her."

"I know," Buck said nervously, "Rose seems aggressive, ruthless. I mean, she could acquire a lot of power. She's got a lot of power now, but..."

"You mean, big power?"

"Yeah. She could be *real* big. I guess that's what scares me. She was quoted as saying, 'You can't fight the devil with just a gospel song.' I'd like to find out what she means by that."

"Sounds ominous," Roland said.

Buck raised the shade to the window overlooking the news rooms. Just as he did, he spotted Susan heading for her desk, after handing over some documents to Buck's receptionist. He realized he'd left important papers behind at Susan's apartment.

"I suspect Rose wants to lead a moral crusade—you know, clean up America," Buck said. "I've heard rumors to that effect. I think she can pull it off, too. She's already a cult figure. She's got a glib tongue. Like your friend, Aimee, she has real showmanship. She knows enough about people to play on their deep-rooted fears." He looked toward Susan again. "Rose also has that chief prerequisite. A real ego bordering on the narcissistic."

Roland got up, after making a few notations on a pad. "If she's going to launch a moral crusade, let's find out something about its leader."

Buck turned and faced Roland squarely. "I plan to do just that. Her so-called autobiography is a lot of braying brass. Lines like 'my recorded gospel songs have provided inspiration for millions of lost souls.' I want to find out what that voice of sunshine and sweetness is like when it warbles off-key."

"It's just a hunch," Roland said. "You know, an old news hound's hunch. But I wonder if Rose and the South Beach thing are part of the same story."

Just then, Robert came into the office, looking toward Buck. "God's anointed is on the phone."

Bolting to attention, Buck signaled to Roland that he'd like to take this call in private. When the city editor had gone, he picked up the receiver. "I was going to call you," he said, "and thank you for dinner the other night."

Like a cooing, billing lovebird, she said, "I called you last night. I got your unlisted home phone. No answer...I bet you were out dating some very pretty young girl. I've heard tales about you."

Buck recalled last night, but said nothing.

After a slight, awkward pause, she said, "I want to extend another invitation. I'm known, you see, for my Southern hospitality. This time, I want you to attend services at my temple. Tomorrow morning at ten." Her soft laughter was almost like a girlish giggle, "*Sinner*."

"I'm not much for church going." In blurred vision, he remembered her face telling him good night. For some reason, he hadn't dared look into her eyes as she'd kissed him good-bye. The kiss, weirdly distinct, lingered on his cheek.

"No, seriously," she said in a more businesslike tone, "this is going to be totally different from my usual gospel hour. It's going to be..." She paused, as if to hold him in suspense. "Newsworthy. I'm not telling you any more. Bye, handsome." She hung up.

Robert stood staring at Buck. "If I heard right, I assume she invited you to her temple. You're not going, are you?"

At first Buck wasn't certain. "Hell, yes, I'm going. I'm starting a series on her, and I've never seen the bitch in action. Want to come with me?"

"Do I ever want to come with you! After last night, more than ever. If you step into our little private room in back, I'll prove it."

"Come on, now. Don't think about sex all the time. You know what I mean. Will you get me out of bed Sunday morning in time?"

"I'm not too good at kicking you out of bed."

"This one time. Promise."

"I promise. But on one condition."

"Conditional love," Buck said. "What are the terms?"

"That you do to me tonight what you did to me last night."

"You got a date, hot stuff." His thoughts turned to Rose again. "Sure you don't want to go with me Sunday morning?"

"I'll get out of bed, I'll bathe you, I'll dress you, but I need the rest of Sunday morning for my beauty sleep. With all the competition I have for you, I've got to look my best."

"As you wish, but this Rose is no ordinary woman. She's carefully packaged herself and is hell-bent on cashing in while she's in her prime. I have a funny feeling she's planning some special entertainment for me Sunday morning at her temple."

***

As much as Gene tried to concentrate on his work, images of Buck flashed through his mind. He felt he was coming unglued. One part of him wanted to run in one direction, whereas another part of him told him everything was wrong and urged him to take a different path. There were times, and he didn't want anybody to know this, that he felt he was two different people. With Buck, the bad Gene had taken over, doing everything the good Gene told him not to. He'd need to seek redemption for that, yet at the same time he was eagerly awaiting his late afternoon meeting with Buck. In fact, he could hardly get his work done for thinking of Buck.

In the past few months, except for those dark furtive times when he ventured into the cesspools of the city, the good Gene had taken over. He'd tried to do what was right, but he'd never been able to prevent himself from giving in to the world's temptations.

In spite of himself, he couldn't deny the pleasures he'd experienced alone with Buck. He'd never known such exquisite joy could be possible with another human being. He'd have to be careful. His meetings with Buck had to be conducted in secret. Even though he wanted to be with him every minute of every day, that wasn't possible.

Although he'd been condemned and nearly ruined by his exposing himself to that little girl, he knew that in some pockets of the city lived people who welcomed his exhibitionism. Wherever he went there were places, ranging from latrines to bathhouses, where people wanted him to display himself before them. They were not condemning but worshipful. They wanted to see him in all his male glory, exposed and fully aroused. He was treated like a God. In some way, they made up for all the rejection. And after last night he'd won Buck over too. The way Buck had bitten his ear, licked his neck, and moaned in passion had told Gene all he needed to know: no one had penetrated Buck Brooke before. No one had reached the deep inner recesses of his body, certainly not Robert Dante. Gene had been sailing in virgin waters. He eagerly awaited a repeat performance this afternoon.

His face tightened in a fierce grip as he tossed some papers in a pile on his desk, creating a cloud of dust. As he looked around his tiny cubbyhole of an office, he dreaded the morning's police interviews, the new revelations. As a sudden chill that swept across him, he slapped his arms across his body and rubbed his hands across his broad chest.

He was deep into an investigation of the Lolito ring but had a long way to go. The address at 230 Bayshore Drive appeared to be the center of an underage boy sex ring. In an hour or so he'd learn the name of the owner of that building. That owner, from all he could gather, arranged for older men, so-called pillars of the community, to meet young boys at sex parties. The oldest boys were probably no more than sixteen. He had to find some way to penetrate that ring. He'd told none of this to his chief yet. He wanted a good, strong case before presenting his evidence. It was his big chance and he couldn't fuck it up.

The call came in from City Hall earlier than he'd expected. The owner of the house at 230 Bayshore Drive was Leroy Fitzgerald. Gene slowly put down the phone and got up and walked over to the lone window in his office. He looked out at the morning sunshine through the dirty streaks in the glass. The window hadn't been washed in years. He felt a sense of suffocation. Leroy had to be the same photographer who'd snapped the frontal nude of him in the locker room back at college. He knew that Leroy had always lusted for him, and had printed copies of that photograph of Gene to distribute among his gay brethren.

He also knew that Leroy had photographed two centerfolds in Florida for *Playgirl*. He'd begged Gene to pose for one, and Gene had almost hit him in the face. He was lucky to have this police job. All he needed now was to expose himself in a national magazine. That would be the end of his career for sure. How he wished the owner of that house had been somebody he didn't know, not someone he'd gone to the university with, not someone who had a connection with him, regardless of how remote.

He'd always spurned Leroy's advances, and could have prevented him from snapping that frontal nude. But he hadn't. When he'd spotted Leroy taking pictures back in that locker room, he'd turned his back to Leroy and had soaped himself, making himself even larger than he already was. When he'd turned around, Leroy had snapped away. Pretending not to notice, Gene had closed his eyes and turned his face up to the jet spray of water. He'd both welcomed yet shunned Leroy's attentions.

The only way Gene could define himself was through his contradictions. He reached for his jacket. Leroy or not, he had to get on this case. To do that, he was headed for the Combat Zone. At least some of the boy prostitutes who worked there had to know about Leroy's Lolito ring.

***

Heat wiggles wavered over white sand as Buck pulled off his clothes on his own private beach located on a secluded cay about three miles from the Okeechobee coastline. After getting out the *Examiner*, he'd come to his island with Robert. His parents had acquired the small cay when he was just a kid, and Buck felt he'd virtually grown up here, retreating to the island whenever he could get away.

Although he had to return to the city in the afternoon, Buck wanted to be photographed on the island for the magazine that very likely would name him "The Sexiest Man of the Year." He felt silly about the whole thing, but was determined to see it through. His own public relations department had set it up in the belief that such massive publicity would forever erase the image of the old ultra-conservative *Examiner* as led by his grandfather and would ignite a fire in the circulation department when the paper's dynamic new leadership under the third Buck Brooke was widely revealed across the nation.

Robert had insisted on coming along for the shoot. "There's no way I'm going to let you be photographed on a deserted island without me there hawkeying every shot."

Robert had been relieved when he learned that the reporter from the magazine was a well-known dyke. "We'll have no trouble from her," he said. Britt Smithey from their own paper was hired as the photographer. "That guy's so straight he'd make Richard Nixon look like a faggot," Robert had said. "So I think you're going to be okay, but I'll be here anyway seeing that you don't expose too much."

A blinding orange ball, the sun rose high in the sky over Buck's own mangrove swamp. From the beachfront house, Robert emerged, walking down the sandy path with a white terrycloth robe.

His back in the sand, Buck flexed his muscles, kicking his legs in the air as if riding a bicycle.

"So that's how Arnold Schwarzenegger does it," Robert said with a mischievous grin, as he handed Buck his robe.

"Listen," he said, rising up from the sand and squinting his eyes in the sun. "I want to look as good at fifty as I do now."

"You mean, like Rose Phillips?"

He didn't answer, closing his eyes and turning his face to the blazing sun. He wanted to look tanned.

At the beach bar, Robert splashed a Bloody Mary with another drop of Tabasco and handed it to him.

"You make the best Bloody Marys in the world, and you know I couldn't get through a Saturday morning without one. Or a Sunday morning."

"I'll make you a stiff one before you leave the house tomorrow morning to listen to that bitch preach."

Not wanting to talk about Rose, Buck opened his robe and grabbed his balls. "I may give you a stiff one right now."

"Promises, promises. We'll have to put it on hold. I'm going to have you tonight. Every bit of you. But just as soon as you finish that Bloody Mary, I'm going to give you a bath. You've got sand all over you."

Nude with Robert in the shower, Buck liked the way he was being soaped down by his friend, every part of his body washed. It was a time to relax and let Robert do the work. Robert even washed his ears for him.

On signal from Robert, Buck bent over, making himself an easy target for what Robert was going to do to him. Buck braced himself against the tiles, and Robert knelt down and firmly massaged Buck's ass before opening his cheeks. Within moments, Robert was tonguing him, making him moan in passion. Nothing in his life ever felt this good, and Robert was clearly an expert. Robert couldn't seem to get enough of this very private part of him. One Saturday afternoon, alone in their bedroom on the island, Robert had stayed glued to his target for almost two hours.

A loud knock on the bathroom door ended Buck's pleasure far too abruptly for him. "Mister Robert, Mister Robert," came the voice of Henry, Buck's tall black servant. It was an emergency call. Robert stood up and kissed Buck on the mouth before stepping out of the shower and covering himself with a terrycloth robe, as he opened the door and headed for the phone.

A little later Buck walked nude into their bedroom, toweling himself dry.

Robert was just hanging up the phone. "Oh, shit! Britt was riding in Bayfront Park on his motorcycle. He slid, fell off, and broke his arm."

"There goes my best photographer. I'm sorry. We'll call him and wish him a speedy recover. Does that mean today's shoot is off?"

"Not at all. At least from the magazine's point of view. From my point of view, I want to cancel the whole thing."

"What do you mean? They can get another photographer."

"They have. Leroy Fitzgerald."

Buck was startled. "Our little sleaze Leroy. Happy school days. Happy golden rule days."

"There's no way that I'd want Leroy photographing you. He's a centerfold photographer for *Playgirl*."

"This shoot is for a family magazine. I'm not posing nude, and they don't run nude photographs anyway."

"I guess it'll be okay if I'm around to watch Leroy's every move."

"I want some time alone with him," Buck said.

"What's that supposed to mean?"

"This is my opportunity. He's the leader of that Lolito ring I told you about. I can't let him know I know that. I need to figure out some way to entrap him into giving me information. After the shoot, I'll go for a walk along the beach with him. I may learn something."

"Okay, if that's the way it is. I'll entertain the dyke. We'll talk about pussy, I guess." At the table Henry had set up for them on the patio, Buck tasted the raw conch marinated in garlic and key lime juice.

"What's the matter?" Robert asked. "You look real troubled."

"I am, and it's about us."

"You and I are doing fine. Damn fine. The last two days have been the most terrific of my life."

"You're still working too hard to please," Buck said. "You're always doing things for me, and I feel guilty about it. I do so little for you."

"You provide everything for me. You always have."

"I want you to take more time off. At least when you come to this island with me. You're not the hired help. Henry can take care of us."

Robert looked into Buck's eyes, and he knew at once how much he'd hurt his friend.

Robert dropped his fork and stood up. "Did it ever occur to you that my whole life is based on doing things for you?" He turned and left the table, heading alone down the stretch of white sandy beach.

Shoving his plate of conch aside, Buck ran after him, easily catching up. He reached for Robert's arm. "I was a shit. Forgive me. Everything you do for me is just great. If you say I don't have to feel guilty, then..." He paused awkwardly. "It's just great."

Robert's look was open and trusting, almost like a child's. "You mean that?"

"Hell, yes." Buck put his arm firmly around Robert and directed him back toward the patio. "Hey, kid," he said. "Finish your lunch. You're going to need all your strength when I attack you tonight."

Robert reached over and firmly gripped his hand. "Don't ever tell me to stop doing what I do for you."

"I won't. I promise." Sensing some deep need within his friend, he said, "After lunch, and only if Leroy and the dyke are late, would you massage and lick my balls like you always do? I'm tense today. Nothing makes me more relaxed than that." Remembering the shower, he quickly added, "That and the other thing you do."

Leroy and the reporter were late. Buck got his massage and licking while he enjoyed a cigar, leaning back on the soft sofa to enjoy both Robert's mouth on him and the smoke. What he hadn't really told Robert was how much he liked it this way, with him in charge and Robert doing his bidding. How different it was with Gene, when the roles were reversed, when Gene was the aggressor demanding and taking pleasure from Buck's body like no one else had ever done before. He couldn't understand how both men brought out a completely different side of his personality. His only wish was that Gene and Robert could be found in one man.

When Robert had completely satisfied him, he ran his tongue along the length of Buck's penis, raised up and kissed him long and passionately on the mouth. Robert then got up. "I wish those guys would hurry up so we could get this shoot over with."

"I do too," Buck said. "You know I have to return to the city this afternoon. A little investigative reporting around Rose's charismatic foundation before tomorrow morning. Want to go with me?"

"I'd better stay here. Get things ready for our romantic Saturday night dinner."

Buck was delighted when Robert turned down the invitation. He deliberately concealed from him that he was meeting with Gene.

While Robert went to answer the latest calls that had come in, Buck returned to the white beach. Once here, he let the hushed, muted beauty of the cay fill his system. He didn't want to think—at least not now, fearing his thoughts would betray him.

On the beach, he soaked up every ray of the sun and braced himself for the coming afternoon.

When he got back to the house, Robert said, "They're here. I told them to wait in the living room. I got this pair of jeans and T-shirt for you. Buck Brooke III, young publishing executive, at rest on his private island."

"Thanks a lot." He took Robert's hand and held it up to his lips, kissing the inner palm.

Robert kissed him lightly on the lips. "I've got to go." At the door he paused. "Oh, Susan called. She wants you to call her right away."

"It's about that story I've got her on."

"I hope that's what it is," Robert said before leaving.

Buck walked over to the phone and started to dial Susan's number. He dialed only three digits before he put down the phone. Talking to Susan was a little more than he could handle right now. He headed for the living room.

***

At the Combat Zone, Gene cruised by in his unmarked police car, hoping to appear as a prospective john. He noticed two young Cuban *mariposas*, looking no more than sixteen, eying him. At the sight of him, one of the young boys licked his lips lasciviously but Gene ignored them, driving around, circling the square.

As he neared one teenage boy on the street corner, memories of exposing himself to that young girl came back racing through his mind, causing him to break out in a cold sweat.

The young boy with red hair appeared no more than fifteen. Beautifully featured and lithe, he looked like the type of boy Leroy would recruit to work his Lolito ring. Gene reached over and unlocked the door on the right side of his car. Without hesitation and with perfect ease, the teenage boy opened the door and eased into the front seat. He was sipping coke from a Dixie cup. "You look like one handsome stud," the boy said. "Hi, I'm Sandy. What's your name?"

"Ralph," Gene said, inventing a name. "Care to go for a drive with me?"

"I'd love to. But I get twenty bucks if you want to fuck my tight ass."

"There will be a twenty in it for you."

"I hope you're not a cop," Sandy said. "The other night two cops grabbed me. I thought they wanted to make it with me. Nearly all the cops I meet want sex. I dig uniforms. I've had at least a dozen cops in the past year. When I get older, I'm gonna join the force, too."

Gene didn't like the smirk on the boy's face as he turned his car and headed away from the twilight zone. The boy looked as if he knew too much, far beyond his years. Gene found himself perspiring heavily, and the young boy seemingly sensed his discomfort. He slouched down in the front seat provocatively, cupping his crotch and beginning to rub it for Gene's benefit.

"Stop that!" Gene shouted louder than he'd intended. "Sit up and behave yourself."

At first Sandy looked as if he hadn't heard right. "Isn't playing with my crotch what it's all about?"

"Later, perhaps."

"Oh, I get it. This is your first time with some boy ass. You're married, right?"

"Something like that," Gene said, steering the car down by the old water reserve. This was always a nearly deserted park except for some sex-hunters.

As they neared the park, Sandy looked disappointed. "Don't you have a place to go? I was hoping to get worked over by you in a nice comfortable bed. With a guy who looks as good as you, I wouldn't even charge to let you fuck me." He reached over and felt Gene's crotch. "I don't know if I can handle one that big."

Gene firmly removed Sandy's hand from his crotch.

"You're one uptight mother-fucker."

"Yeah," was all Gene said.

Parking near some deserted picnic tables, Gene got out of the car and signaled Sandy to follow him along the embankment with a stone wall marred with graffiti.

"You're not much of a talker," Sandy said. "What are you into?"

"I'll tell you. Instead of that twenty, how about a hundred instead?"

"A hundred dollars!" The boy looked astonished, then a frown crossed his brow. "Oh, shit. You're a sadist. You're going to torture me for that, aren't you?"

"I'm not going to touch you."

Sandy stared at him in disbelief. "I don't get it. I can't believe you're going to give me a hundred dollars just to have me jack off in front of you."

"You don't have to do anything like that. In fact, keep your fly zipped—and I mean that. What I want is information."

"What kind of information could I have that you'd be willing to pay one-hundred dollars for?"

"I'm in the closet. I've got to watch my step. But I hear there's a house in town. A place where men like me can go and meet young boys like yourself. Where it's all private and confidential."

"You want to get included in one of those little parties, right?"

"Yeah, Gene said."

"That's information I can supply. I work there every Friday night. I pick up quite a few bucks that way. One night I had seven different guys. Did I have a sore ass the next morning."

Gene reached out to touch the boy but instinct made him withdraw quickly. He looked up ahead along the path that led by a stone wall. Not another person in sight. "Kid, if you want to earn that hundred bucks, as we walk along I want you to describe one of those parties for me. Go into as much detail as you can. I like a lot of detail."

Sandy smiled. "This is gonna be the easiest hundred dollars I've ever earned. I'll give you the juicy scoop. A blow-by-blow description."

Sandy kept his promise. As they walked along, he related to Gene in vivid detail one of Leroy's parties where underage boys danced with older men to booming sounds as in a disco. The boys then stripped and formed a circle in the middle of the room under a chandelier, creating a giant flower of flesh, their adolescent limbs fanning out to evoke petals. The older men—doctors, educators, lawyers, bankers, even politicians— formed a choo-choo train, crawling around on their knees to taste each "flesh petal." Later, each of the older men bid for their favorites at an auction and took them to one of the private bedrooms upstairs.

At the end of his walk and after an hour's description from Sandy, Gene came to a stop at the clearing where the water drained into tanks. He reached for a cigarette.

"Could I have one, mister?" Sandy asked. "You don't have a joint, do you? I mean, a joint different from that mound between your legs?"

"Here, take a cigarette," Gene said, handing him one and lighting it for him. "Considering what you do for a living, giving you a cigarette seems relatively harmless."

"Did I tell you enough to earn my bread?"

"You did." Gene sucked in the smoke as images of that sex ring flooded his brain. Gene now knew the mechanics of how the place worked and even some of the club members. Leroy was definitely the master of the bordello. There was no doubt about that, and the address was indeed 230 Bayshore Drive. What troubled Gene was his awareness that for such an operation to function smoothly, it had to have protection high up. Someone big and important had to be profiting from this operation. He turned to the boy again. "How can I get included one evening?"

"That I can't help you with. Not just anybody can join. It's very secretive. Leroy has to approve of it in some way. Occasionally bigshots from out of town get invited by a member. But it's hard for a local guy to get membership—or so I've heard. It's all very hush-hush. Leroy likes to keep it quiet."

"I bet."

Sandy reached for Gene's crotch again. "There's a men's room over there," he said, pointing to a little concrete structure a few hundred yards away."

Gene removed the boy's hands from his crotch. "I'm fine."

"C'mon," Sandy said. "At least let me blow you. You're the best looking man I've ever seen. If you can get an invite to one of Leroy's parties, please go up to one of the rooms with me. I need a real man to shove it up my ass. Not those two-inch dicks I usually end up with. Did you know that a two-inch dick hurts more than a ten-incher?"

"I don't think I'm into finding that out."

"I figured you for the fucker—not the fuckee," Sandy said.

"You got that right." Gene reached into his wallet and handed the boy five twenty-dollar bills.

"That's great, mister, even if you won't plug my ass."

"I'm taking you back to the Combat Zone. How do I get in touch with you if I need to talk again?"

"I'm homeless, but you can always reach me in the zone."

Before returning him to the square, Gene stopped at a roadside diner where Sandy wolfed down three fried eggs and six pork sausages. "I've got an idea how you might get invited to one of Leroy's parties. But you've got to put out."

"Forget it. There's going to be no sex between us." Gene looked around nervously, hoping no one recognized him at this place dining with a teenage boy.

"I didn't mean sex with me. I mean sex with Leroy. Although he recruits young boys, he actually likes older studs like you."

"How's that going to get me an invitation?"

"Every morning around ten o'clock Leroy heads for the Vulcan Baths. You know where they are, don't you?"

"What do you think?" Gene asked.

"I thought so. You flash all that meat you've got—and we're talking meat for the poor here—and Leroy will be slurping away. He'll fall for you and big. He's always complaining he can't find enough guys with big meat at the baths. Wait until he gets a glimpse of you."

"Thanks for the tip."

Back at the Combat Zone, Gene turned to Sandy and thanked him. He liked the boy and felt a pang of regret at turning him loose into that square again, not knowing what weirdo he was likely to meet next.

Sandy looked briefly in Gene's eyes and seemed reluctant to get out of the car. "I'd like to make it with you, mister. With you, I'd do anything. You could fist me if you wanted to, although I don't like that. I'd even lick your asshole clean after you've taken a big crap."

"Stop it!" Gene said with an anger in his voice.

"That's not all..."

"I don't want to hear it."

Sandy grabbed Gene's hand, his eyes tearing. "Why don't you take me home with you? Let me live with you. I'd treat you really nice. I make a great chili. My scrambled eggs are the best."

"I can't."

"That's right. You're married. Probably have a kid of your own."

"I'm not married. I sometimes tell people I am. I used to be."

"I could be a wife to you. I'd be a better wife to you than your first wife, I bet."

"I'm not ready for that yet."

"Hey, I have an idea," Sandy said.

"What?"

"Tomorrow's Sunday. You don't work on Sunday, do you?"

"No, but I go to church in the morning."

"Tomorrow afternoon around two o'clock I'm going to be walking along by that reservoir. I'd sure like some company."

"I can't," Gene said.

"Hey, mister, I'm going to be there." He held Gene's hand in such a firm grip that it almost hurt.

He sensed Sandy's desperation but decided to brush it aside. "You'd better go, kid. I've got to get back to work. You helped me a lot."

"Glad to oblige." Out on the sidewalk again, Sandy held the car door open as he glanced around and surveyed the square. "This may all end soon."

"What do you mean?"

"It looks like Barry Collins is going to be mayor. He's threatened to clean up the zone."

"He's a man of his word. Even Sister Rose is backing him as a candidate."

"He's one of those two-inch dicks I've been talking about."

"I don't get it."

"He's a regular at Leroy's parties. Likes 'em real young."

Gene didn't believe Sandy. "You must have gotten him mixed up with somebody else. "Barry Collins isn't into young boys. I'm a pretty good judge of character."

"And Barry Collins is a lousy fuck. See you tomorrow at two."

"I might not be able to make it."

"You'll make it all right. Know why? Because you're not going to find anyone else in this whole fucking city who loves you and understands you the way I do. Hell, I've just met you and I want to move in with you."

"How many guys do you use that line on?" Gene asked.

"Only you, Ralph. Maybe tomorrow you'll tell me your real name. With all the other creeps, I can't wait to get away from them. I don't want you to leave me and turn me out on this God damn square to hustle a buck. Please, don't do that to me."

Perspiration had coated Gene's body, and he felt he was smothering. "I've got to go."

Sandy wiped his eyes. "You'd better be there tomorrow, you good-looking son-of-a-bitch."

"I'm Gene." With that, he reached over and shut the car door on the passenger's side. He couldn't bear to look back at Sandy. Without a glance, he drove away from the square, turning down a side street. His whole body was shaking.

Only then did the full revelation of what Sandy had confided in him settle into his mind. Barry Collins? There was no way. Any man who could satisfy a sex maniac like Pamela and get her to marry him couldn't be gay. He'd never heard stories like that about Barry. He'd dated all the most gorgeous girls at the university and now had two of the most beautiful daughters in town. He didn't think Sandy was a liar, but the boy could be wrong. Maybe it was someone who looked like Barry.

A sudden chilling thought came over Gene. Barry was Rose's handpicked candidate. If this story about the Lolito ring broke, and if Barry were implicated, he would not only be finished in politics, he might be arrested. Worse than that, at least in Gene's eyes, was that such a revelation and exposure could become a cancer growing on Rose herself.

***

Leroy was far from the sleazeball Buck had remembered. Unlike Pamela, time had been kind to him. He'd developed into a rather handsome young man with a swimmer's build. He wore his raven-black hair fashionably long and well coiffed, and his sparkling green eyes and relaxed smile made him look more like a tall model in a male fashion magazine than the master of a boy bordello.

Immaculately groomed and attired in a tasteful elephant-gray outfit, Leroy resembled the kind of a dream date a daughter might bring home to her conservative father. He made a slight concession to the style of 1977, but did not overdo anything. There was nothing flamboyant about him in spite of Buck's memory of him being rather outrageous at the university. Back then he'd been a bit of a campus rebel. But the man reaching out to shake his hand looked like he could run for mayor in a few years. If anything, Leroy appeared smoother and more publicly acceptable than Barry Collins who always had a five o'clock shadow and a slightly disheveled look, in spite of his handsome features.

Leroy shook his hand firmly. "It's been years."

"You're looking good," Buck said.

"Thanks and so are you. I can easily see why they want you for the sexiest man of the year. Remember I tried to get handsome hunk contests going at the university. But you guys gave the beauty queens all the publicity."

"You were before your time. Somehow the idea back then was that women weren't interested in seeing men with their shirts off."

"Imagine that." Leroy turned around to introduce Isabella de Nicola, a statuesque beauty who wore no makeup and had closely cropped her brown hair. "Glad to meet you," she said, shaking his hand even more firmly than Leroy had. "If you look as good on film as you do in person, you've made our job easy."

"Thanks," Buck said, smiling.

"I must say you, Leroy, and Robert are three good-looking men. But you don't do anything for me at all so I can be completely objective."

"Sorry, we don't turn you on," Buck said.

"Don't you have any beautiful women on this island?" Isabella asked, taking a Bloody Mary from Robert.

Buck turned from her to guide Leroy over to his sunken living room where the first shots were to be made. Isabella joined Robert on the sofa in the foyer to work out details.

"This is a beautiful home," Leroy said, taking a hefty sip of his Bloody Mary. "I always wanted to get invited here but I think Robert Dante got to the goodies before I did. At least I'll get to photograph them."

"Just how sexy do you want to make these photographs?" Buck asked.

"Very. I even brought a red bikini for you to wear when I go out to shoot you on the beach. Most men couldn't wear it but I hear you can fill its cup. My gay brethren who showered with you in college gave me a full report. You were the only man on campus whose endowment could match Gene's."

"Hold it here. I'm a publishing executive with a reputation to up-hold. I'm not going to be one of your centerfolds. This assignment is not for that kind of magazine."

"Will you at least try it on?" Leroy pleaded.

"Sure, I'll give it a try."

"Can I go with you to try it on?"

Buck motioned toward Robert in the next room.

"I see. I hear that girl is real jealous," Leroy said.

"He is." Buck glanced at his watch. "I've got to go back to the city this afternoon when the shoot is over. When do we begin?"

"Right now. Right in your living room. You look plenty hot in those jeans and T-shirt. Let's do some shit of the young publisher relaxing in his living room, no doubt fretting over his Sunday column."

Buck looked up at him and smiled. "No doubt."

The first hour of the shoot went reasonably well, even though Buck felt Isabella was directing a military campaign instead of a photographic layout. At one point over a camera angle, Leroy lost his cool and called her a bitch, although she seemed to pay no attention to that. Robert remained watchfully in the background.

When time came for the beach shots, Buck disappeared into his bathroom to try on the red bikini Leroy had brought to the island. As he slipped off his jeans and white briefs, he flexed his muscles before a full-length mirror. With all his exercise and jogging, he felt he was prime meat for the shots on the beach. But when he slipped into the bikini, he knew there was no way he could allow himself to be photographed in that skimpy wear. The bikini clearly showed the length of his cock and the size of his balls. He didn't think the magazine would print it anyway, even if he agreed to pose for it.

Robert opened the door and walked into the bathroom, bringing him a pair of swim trunks that would reveal nothing to the camera. "You're looking good, stud," Robert said. "Slip these on over that bikini." He handed the trunks to Buck.

"You're right. Leroy's bikini isn't swimwear; it's a posing strap," Buck said.

"One that leaves nothing to the imagination."

Buck put on the trunks, without taking off the sheer bikini.

Leroy was disappointed Buck hadn't worn the bikini, but Isabella was delighted. In the trunks, or so she claimed, Buck had just the look they wanted to convey in their magazine.

Out on the beach and after a few shots of Buck jogging along the sands and rushing to take a dip in the water, Buck signaled to Robert he wanted to be alone with Leroy as they had already agreed.

Robert kept Isabella distracted as Buck walked down the beach with Leroy to a lonely strip of sand.

"Sure you won't let me photograph the goodies?" Leroy asked.

"I'm sure," Buck said. He paused briefly, looking out toward the sea. "I'm sorry we never connected at college. I like the way you handled the shoot today. I feel we might have become friends."

"There are all kinds of friends. How do you mean?"

"I mean friend friends," Buck said.

"Don't you find me attractive?" Leroy asked.

"Very. But I've got to confess something. What really turns me on is someone really young. Someone who looks like Robert did about eight years ago.

"I see." Leroy appeared as if ready to say something but thought better of it. "Not me, man. I like my men fully grown and mature. Gene Robinson, for example. And most definitely Buck Brooke III."

"I can't help it. It's what turns me on."

"I get it. Robert's getting a little long in the tooth for you."

"Something like that." Buck steered him to a hidden cove clearly out of eyesight from Robert and Isabella.

"What would you say if I could get you an invitation to a very private party Friday night?" Leroy asked.

"What do you mean?"

"A place where a lot of important men in this town with your same proclivities can meet guys."

"You mean...like real young," Buck said.

"As young as you want."

"I would say I'd died and gone to boy heaven," Buck said, feeling he was a convincing liar.

"Say I could do that, what would you do for me?"

"For openers, I'd take off these trunks and pose in that red bikini. I'm wearing it now."

"Shit, you would?"

"Yes, I'd even fluff it a bit if you want."

"Hot damn, I'm into it. No one can see us. Take off those baggy swim shorts."

Buck took off the trunks and stood in front of Leroy's trained eye.

"Grade A stud meat."

"The agreement is, I'll let you photograph me only from the waist down. I can't have my face showing."

"Honey, when guys get a look at that meat, they won't care about your face. With the ugliest face in the world and with meat like this, you could still score and score big."

As Buck posed for Leroy's camera, he said, "You're serious about inviting me to this party?"

"Very serious. I'll call you Tuesday and tell you the details. Will you let me watch?"

"I like to keep it private."

"Too bad. That's one show I would have enjoyed. I never knew you liked them young. Like Gene himself. Exposing himself in front of that little girl. Nothing surprises me any more."

"So it's a deal?"

"It's a deal, stud. Any time you want a grown man's love, call on me."

"I'll think about it," Buck said.

"I hope you will. Thanks for letting me shoot you. Both the public photographs and for my private collection."

"Glad to help out."

"You know something, sport," Leroy said. "I think today marks the beginning of a beautiful friendship."

***

Later that afternoon, Buck returned in his boat to the mainland. He'd decided to check out a few bars in the seedy midtown to see if any were displaying that bumper sticker, CONVERT A JEW TO CHRIST. He figured that any group of Jew-haters willing to invest that much money to launch bumper-stickers throughout certain pockets of the town must have a lot more prejudice and even bigger plans.

At the third bar and into his third Budweiser, he was about to give up, but as he drove along he spotted Captain Bogey's on Front Street. This bar catered to an increasing number of rednecks flocking to Okeechobee from North Florida or South Georgia. In this bar he ordered a Coors instead of a Budweiser. Because of the ultra-conservative management of that company, it sounded more right wing. He saw no evidence of any bumper sticker displayed until he went back to the men's room to get rid of some of that Bud. Over the toilet was the sticker he'd been seeking: CONVERT A JEW TO CHRIST.

As he came out of the toilet, he noticed young men in undershirts playing pool or backgammon in the back. An occasional retiree in Bermuda shorts drifted over to the bar for packaged liquor in very small bottles. At the grease-smeared front tables, out-of-work veterans in army fatigues exchanged war stories or fish tales. A real macho WASP place, Buck thought, and just the type of establishment to display such a bumper sticker. Even the open-air pissoir in the rear confirmed the masculinity of the place.

Sensing what he was smelling, the bartender said, "Sometimes we put ice on it to cool it down a bit. Haven't seen you in here before. I guess you're new in town."

"I've been here a few weeks," Buck said.

"Drop around Saturday night. That's when the local cowboys do some mighty fine picking and singing."

"Sure," he said, looking back at the men's room. "My uncle's got a bar way out on the trail. He could sure use one of them bumper stickers you've got in the toilet."

The bartender nodded as he finished washing a glass under cold water and then slowly went over to the cash register, returning with a card on which a telephone number had been printed. "They're giving 'em out free. Will even deliver."

"Do you know who's printing them?" Buck asked.

"How in hell do I know? A lot of money guys have the dough to develop that little Jew haven over there on South Beach. The Jews there are paying cheap rent. But the place could be big. Big new construction projects. All these men you see hanging around here could get real high-paying construction jobs. But the Jews are blocking it." Someone up front called the bartender.

Slipping the card into his pocket, Buck paid for his Coors without finishing it.

Later, at the Tin Palace—a hamburger joint by day, a jazz tavern in the evening—he enjoyed a plain burger at a private booth with check-ered cafe curtains. A frequent lunchtime visitor, he went over to the gray-ing owner, Harry Foresman, and asked him if he'd join him for a beer. In the booth again, he explained he was on a story but couldn't discuss it, and asked him if he'd call the number on the card and order some bumper stickers.

He reluctantly agreed, but explained he couldn't display one. "We cater to all types here," he said. "Anybody who can pay the freight."

"Harry," he said in exasperation. "I'm not asking you to put it on the wall—only order some."

About ten minutes later, Harry returned to the table. "That line sure was busy. Maybe everybody in town's ordering one. The guy on the other end told me he'd deliver mine at four o'clock. About an hour from now."

At the appointed time, Buck was waiting outside in his car.

At four-fifteen p.m., a pea-green truck arrived and double-parked at the entrance to the Tin Palace. Package in hand, a driver hastily went inside and came out a few minutes later. When he pulled out into traffic, Buck followed in his car and, five bar stops later, he sensed the driver was ready to return to the distribution source. It was nearly six o'clock, quitting time.

On the south side of the river, in a decaying section of warehouses which originally had been used to store freight, he slowed down but kept close enough to have a clear view of the truck up ahead.

The driver parked in back of the biggest warehouse, got out, and entered through a rear door. Leaving his own car two blocks away, Buck headed toward the large red-brick building to the front entrance and there, to his surprise, found the big bold letters of The Rose Phillips Charismatic Association emblazoned like zebra stripes across the center of the facade. This was the printing headquarters of Rose's propaganda machine, where her monthly magazine, *Charismatic*, was set in type, reaching a circulation of four-million readers.

He walked into the foyer and met a receptionist who immediately asked his business. He claimed he wanted to pick up some copies of *Charismatic* to distribute to his Sunday school class tomorrow. With a slight shrug, the receptionist disappeared into the back as he turned and quietly slipped through a side door, going down a long, musty corridor to the men's room. Once here, he concealed himself in one of the enclosed toilets as he heard the printing press grind to a halt for the day.

There was much banging of doors and, from a slightly opened window, he heard motors of cars starting in the parking lot out back. No one, however, had come into the men's room.

As a long, dreary hour passed, he had been seriously tempted to smoke a cigarette, but instead waited patiently in the foul-smelling toilet until he thought the building was completely clear. Going out, he peered through a dirty window at the vast printing plant. Once in it, he could find only fresh copies of next month's edition of *Charismatic*.

Climbing the rickety wooden stairs in the rear, he reached the second floor—a large ramp with an open pit looking down into the plant below. Small rooms opened off the ramp. In the first he found neatly stacked copies of Rose's autobiography, *Hallelujah!*, ready for shipment across the nation. A large, naturalistic-looking poster of Rose stared back at him, giving him a sensation of having the evangelist in the room with him. All the books he examined had been personally autographed.

Back on the ramp, he took in the rest of the building in the fading glow of the day. Through the large skylights overhead, the sun cast a yellow-orange glow over the plant. In some way, the warehouse was like a nostalgic reminder of the twenties, when this section of town had been part of the thriving port activity before the river became too shallow for large freighters.

In other rooms opening off the ramp, he inspected enough merchandise for a blitzkrieg. All of it seemed newly manufactured and he'd never seen any of it on the streets before—everything from charismatic T-shirts with a long-stemmed rose printed on them, to rose petal buttons, to rose bumper stickers and, of course, plenty of glossy movie-star type photographs of that Doctor of Divinity herself, autographed, "Your fellow servant in Christ—love, Sister Rose."

He searched eight rooms before opening the final door. "Pay dirt!" he said out loud. Piles of anti-Semitic bumper stickers—awaiting distribution—had been neatly stacked along the walls on wooden shelves.

Holding up one of the stickers, hoping to use it as a prop for an *Examiner* photograph, he edged his way out of the storage room, heading for what he thought would be an exit toward the back. The first two doors he tried were bolted, but in the fading light the handle to the third door turned. Stepping inside, he was aware of the pitch darkness of the room, unlike the twilight visibility along the ramp. The room had no windows.

He searched for the light, finding it to be an exposed electric bulb overhead which he turned on with a dangling chain. The bulb cast a cruel patina over the room.

The powerful eyes of Sister Rose, as seen in that poster seemed to follow him here to this forbidden territory. The poster face of Rose remained like the image on a retina after exposure to a blinding flashbulb.

Here, stacked from floor to ceiling, were crates, boxes, even trash bins filled to overflowing with tabloid-type newspapers, printed on what he knew was the cheapest paper available. He grabbed the first paper, TORCHLIGHT, holding it up to the light. Quickly he scanned the contents, finding it to be an eight-page tabloid billed as "the Revolutionary newspaper of White Christianity."

On the front page was splashed a hideous caricature photograph of Hazel, caught stuffing a dill pickle in her mouth at a Jewish delicatessen on the beach. The caption read, "This grotesque horror of womanhood, a defender of child-molesters and a Jew-lover, a champion of Communist spies and the lesbian-dominated women's movement, has polluted the city commission for years with her moral stench. Now she dares run for mayor. A card-carrying Communist, she has turned her back on her own Christian heritage, ignoring the rights of white America, and has exploited the Jewish human garbage to gain political power. She has gone far enough. SHE WILL NOT RULE OKEECHOBEE."

He grabbed a sheaf of the racist papers which, along with the bumper sticker, would be his evidence. At what sounded like a noise from the plant below, he switched off the light and stood silently. Sneaking back to the ramp, he noted a night watchman making the rounds. He waited for him to go through the plant, fearing he might come upstairs. When he didn't, Buck tiptoed back down the ramp and the rickety stairs, heading for the front of the building. Once here, he found the doors locked from the outside. Down the musty corridor, he entered the men's room again, forcing open the window. He tossed the papers outside.

Sliding through, he fell five feet to the ground, bruising his knee on a rock. Picking himself up, he half ran, half limped to his car with his loot. He got in quickly and drove back to the heart of the city. He'd attend Rose's services tomorrow morning, but only after he'd filed a story for the front page. He'd still have just enough time to make the last edition.

***

The young police recruit, an attractive Cuban woman with dark brown eyes and matching shoulder-length hair, liked to tell the men in the department she was "just as ferocious, just as tough as a wildcat." As part of a training program, Gene had been anxious to wrestle with her in one-to-one combat. Along with his chief, Biff, he'd resented it when the department had been required to hire women for jobs Gene felt should be handled only by men.

Before Sofia entered the gym, Gene had decided he wasn't going to give her any breaks. He intended to be just as rough with her as he'd be in training a male police recruit. The whole setup wasn't fair in his opinion. On the mat, he was forced to stick to traditional wrestling holds, yet a woman was allowed to try any tactic she wanted, except a kick in the groin.

As the women recruits lined up to face their male opponents, the coach blew the whistle. Sofia slammed into Gene's chest, kicking his legs. Like her reputation, she struck like a wildcat, catching him off guard. Lunging for his throat, she captured his neck in a stranglehold.

Although she'd had the advantage of a surprise attack, he came back in fighting force moments later. With manic cruelty, he broke her stranglehold, savagely grabbing her neck, hurling her across his head, her body landing on the mat. Recovering quickly, Sofia rose to her feet and kicked him again, gouging his eyes.

Losing control, he grabbed her wrists and tossed her on the mat again. Against the rules, he slammed his fist into her breasts. Pinned down, the writhing woman tried to break away and, also against the rules, brought her knee up, stabbing him. He slapped her face—once, twice, harder each time—and in lightning rage socked her in the mouth, then in the nose, her head flopping from side to side like a rag doll. As blood spurted out, she screamed. He seemed blind, his features contorted in rage. Dizzy with pain, he reached for his testicles and gently rubbed them, the sharp hurt searing deep within his gut.

The coach frantically blew the whistle, as two policemen rushed to pull Gene away from the battered Cuban. Fighting to hold back her tears, Sofia was led toward the showers by two other women recruits.

Getting up, Gene felt lost, not remembering clearly what had happened. It was as if a pin had been removed from a grenade inside him. Worn out by the ordeal, he felt humiliated and vulnerable, standing in the presence of his colleagues, facing the stern, beet-red face of the coach, the veins in his neck popping out just like Gene's old man's had done.

"Better get a grip on yourself, man," the coach said in a strong-willed attempt to control his own fury. "These things happen sometimes. No man likes to get kicked down there. She won't pass my program. I'll see to that. But you've busted out of control five times in the past three months. We don't want you volunteering for training any more." He turned and looked at Gene, his face filled with despair. "I'm sorry to tell you this, but I've got to recommend you for a psychiatric evaluation next week. It's just routine. Several other guys have already been forced to go. You're not alone." The coach turned and with barely concealed anger made his way across the gym to his office.

Frustrated, swept by an overwhelming sense of defeat, Gene staggered toward the locker room. What he feared most was a psychiatric examination. He didn't want some shrink probing inside his head. His thoughts were his own, and that's the way he wanted to keep them. He knew a cadet who'd recently been evaluated. If he got in touch with him, Gene felt he'd at least have a good idea of what to expect before being examined.

Since he was going to meet Buck later on at the tennis court, he kept on his gym shorts but gathered up his street clothes and headed out back toward his car without bothering to take a shower since he was certain to be hot and sweaty after playing tennis in this heat.

Out on the street again, he breathed in the fresh air. Increasingly, violent rages had consumed him. He resented being singled out like that by the coach, lectured in front of the other policemen. He wasn't the only one in the department who'd lost control. Only the other day an officer he knew had answered a routine call and, in the course of the investigation, with no apparent motivation, had pulled out his pistol and fatally shot a fifteen-year-old black boy.

He'd seen other members of the department breaking down, too—drifting into alcoholism, wife-beating, divorce, suicide. In the face of such weakness, he had prided himself in keeping himself together, as he felt superior to the others, especially the Cubans and the blacks.

Policemen were constantly faced with sexual temptation and he'd known many who had succumbed to it. But not him. He'd held firm, steadfast, regardless of the offers received—and, as the handsomest, most virile-looking member of the force, those invitations had been frequent and persuasive.

He feared word might get out about him that he, too, was breaking down, giving in to stress—the unrelenting stress, with which all members of the department lived.

Psychiatrists had studied several of the men he worked with. Despite denials, it'd been rumored that the aim of the study was to eliminate those men and women whom the psychiatrists judged emotionally unsuited for police work.

Today had been worse than all the others. He'd hated that Leroy had been linked to that case. He wished it had been some anonymous person he could arrest without guilt. He had some strange link with Leroy although he'd always spurned the man's advances. He feared if he broke the Lolito case, his link, regardless of how tenuous, with Leroy might be revealed, even that frontal nude photograph. He'd be on display again and connected with exhibitionism. At times—even with a big case like this one—he felt he couldn't win. Everything seemed stacked against him.

"God damn it," he said out loud and in rage and, for the first time, realized he was still in the parking lot, speaking to himself. One woman police recruit looked at him strangely, before hurrying to her own car.

If he fucked up this Lolito case, he could kiss his big dream goodbye. Here was a chance to win the praise and shouts of the crowds who had once cheered him as a tennis champ. More important than that, he wanted to call Rose's attention to him. Even though he'd never met her, she'd surely hear of this. She'd understand and be proud of him. For all he knew, she'd praise him from the pulpit at her Sunday services which he faithfully attended.

He'd made so many arrests, only to have judges turn the men out to rob, loot, and kill the next day. Facing that dilemma year after year, he'd so easily understood Rose's rallying cry to clean up the town. If the police were so ineffective, then somebody—the decent people—had to step in to restore order.

He was on the street again behind the wheel of his car, driving and taking charge. He knew his meeting with Buck was a descent into evil, but Buck was like a drug to him. He couldn't resist.

Buck was going to take advantage of his weakness, and he knew he couldn't stop him from doing that, but had to give in to unnatural desires. He wanted Buck's friendship and needed it desperately even if it meant he had to submit to acts that were unspeakable.

It was just hours from Sunday morning when he'd be at her temple, hearing her clear, crystal voice. Her voice alone would cleanse him of the dirt into which he was about to plunge.

***

After inserting a sidebar in the Sunday's *Examiner* about what he'd found at Rose's charismatic center, Buck drove to the old Ada Merritt tennis courts where Gene still played every night. Gene and he had gone to junior high here together. He parked his car in the overgrown lot, remembering this place as having been better maintained. Now litter filled the grounds and all the surfaces had been marked by graffiti. He found a seat on the empty bleachers.

On the court, Gene played against a younger man who was clearly not the tennis expert that this former champion was. Behind Buck, the sound of youthful Hispanic voices mingled with the traffic noises, and in a park across the street a few people strolled with dogs. It was a friendly neighborhood setting, even if the setting wasn't as pristine as it used to be. A seedy decay hung heavily in the air.

After Gene easily won the game, he ran across the court and slapped an arm around his opponent's shoulder, just the way Buck used to watch him do. The defeated younger man seemed bitter at the loss and resentful of Gene. They were replaced on the court by two young women, and the first ball that one of them served went low, thudding into the net.

As Buck watched Gene head across the court, he appeared the same as Buck had remembered him in his days of athletic competition at the university. The same athletic build, the graceful body movement, the thick black hair.

As Gene spotted Buck, he ran to him quickly and slapped his arm around him. "You're looking good."

Buck gazed into Gene's once-sparkling eyes, and it was in those eyes he noticed the first major change in Gene. His eyes had grown dim with pain. "You're the one looking good. Still a champ after all these years."

"I just get better with age," Gene said. "Want a sample?"

"I've sampled the merchandise, and it's pure gold." He extended a mock punch to Gene in the stomach. "I wouldn't mind a repeat performance."

"You got yourself a date." Gene turned and looked at a graffiti-marked concrete building at the far corner of the courts. "The showers don't work here. I'll have to shower at home. But I'm dying of thirst. Would you join me for a beer across the street?"

"I'm game."

At a neighborhood tavern, Sloppy Louis, there were only three customers. Buck selected a table covered with a dirty red cloth and an ashtray filled with cigarette butts.

As they waited for their beer to be served, Gene tossed salted peanuts in his mouth and relaxed on a ripped red vinyl banquette. The barmaid was flirted with Gene, and he pretended to admire her legs as she walked away. "I expected you a little earlier. Got held up?"

"In this neighborhood that means held up with a gun."
Buck said. "I was delayed. I had to insert a last-minute story. A sidebar about that charismatic center of Rose Phillips."

Gene looked at him intently as the waitress came back with their beer. A blousy woman with bad stringy hair, she sized Gene up. "There's more where that came from," she said.

"I bet." Ignoring the waitress for the moment, Gene turned to Buck. "What kind of story?"

"That charismatic center is being used to distribute anti-Semitic propaganda."

"I can't believe that," Gene said.

"I was there. I saw it."

Gene sucked in the air and forced a nervous smile that barely hardly concealed his rage.

Buck wondered what possible reason Gene could have in wanting to protect Rose.

"Is it too late to kill the story?" Gene asked.

"It's running now."

"That's too God damn bad." He reached across the table and gripped Buck's wrist so hard it hurt. "You're not fair to her at all. She's really trying to clean up this cesspool of a town, and all you do is attack her."

"Maybe she isn't the evangelical angel she pretends."

Gene tightened his grip on Buck's wrist. "You can't go running bad stories about her. You've been fed lies by her enemies. Especially by that fat pig, Hazel."

Buck pulled his hand away. Gene looked half-crazed. "You and I could never talk politics and religion. Remember how we once agreed to never bring up those subjects?"

"I guess you're right." His facial muscles relaxed.

"We were friends in spite of our differences," Buck said. "It's important to remember that."

"C'mon," Gene said, pushing his beer away. "Let's get out of this dump. I've got to shower. With all the sweat I've worked up, I smell like a Havana whore in heat."

Buck left the money for the beers on the table and followed Gene out the door.

"Let's take my car to my place," Gene said. "I'll drive you back to the parking lot later. On the way home I'll tell you what I've learned so far about the Lolito ring."

Even as he got into Gene's car, Buck was tempted to tell him about his photo session that morning with Leroy and how he planned to gain admission to one of the Lolito parties. He decided against it. Gene might rule that out, and Buck was determined to go through with it, with or without Gene's consent.

Once safely inside Gene's stuffy house, there was no more talk of Rose, the *Examiner*, politics, or even the Lolito ring. Buck knew why they were here, and he could feel that Gene did too. There was tremendous tension between them, because it was still so new. Buck knew what he wanted from Gene.

No sooner was Buck inside Gene's living room, with the front door shut, than Gene grabbed him and pulled him tight against his sweaty body, inserting his tongue in Buck's mouth. Buck eagerly sucked that tongue as if it contained some life force.

Gene was the first to break the hold. "You smell fresh and clean like you always do. I'm a little ripe. Get yourself a beer while I take a shower."

As Gene headed to the bathroom in the rear of his house, Buck called out to him. "There's nothing wrong with the smell of a natural man. If I'm going to get into this man-to-man sex stuff, maybe I like a dude who doesn't smell like a bottle of deodorant."

"You mean that?" Gene raised an eyebrow as if he hadn't heard right.

"Try me."

Gene came and stood before Buck again, not doing anything at first, even though he was only six inches from his face. Buck wrapped his arms around his friend, and this time inserted his tongue in Gene's mouth where it was expertly sucked. Buck ran his hands across Gene's chest before his fingers traveled lower, unfastening the gym shorts. Buck reached inside and tightened his fingers around Gene's prick. It was rock-hard and throbbed at the touch of Buck's fingers. "You're big."

"Just like you. Are you man enough to take it?"

"I've had it before," Buck said.

"You're going to get it again." Gene led him toward the bedroom where he removed his own T-shirt and let his shorts fall to the floor. Buck knelt in front of him, pulling down Gene's jockstrap. As he did he reached to pull back Gene's foreskin before planting tiny kisses on the tip of his prick.

Gene forced Buck to his feet and slowly helped him out of his clothes until Buck was as nude as he was. Suddenly, Gene reached forward and grabbed a handful of Buck's hair, shoving his face so hard against Buck's it hurt. He began kissing and biting Buck's face, ears, and neck. "You taste good."

Gene rather forcibly lowered Buck onto his bed, and in seconds he was smearing pre-coital fluid across Buck's lips. This foreplay seemed more than Gene could handle. He slid the knob of his penis between Buck's lips. It scraped against the roof of Buck's mouth but Gene continued to push into the tight confines of Buck's throat. Buck choked but Gene did not give up until Buck could feel the dense, tight curls of his black pubic hair grinding against his nose. Gene's large balls banged against Buck's chin.

As Gene was clearly approaching orgasm, he pulled out suddenly. His mouth traced a wet trail across Buck's chest and navel before reaching the blond pubic hair. Gene pulled at the hair with his teeth, causing Buck to squirm. It was painful but also highly erotic. Without gagging, Gene lowered his mouth on Buck's prick, swallowing it slowly but unrelentingly until it was down his throat. His throat seemed to open up with a struggle and to adjust immediately to this enormous penetration. He held Buck in his throat so long Buck feared his friend would suffocate. Then he pulled back, gasping for air. He stayed on Buck until he felt him approaching a climax, and then he raised up after giving the knob a final lick.

"Not that way today," Gene said. "I'm going to fuck the juice out of you." Gene's face went lower as his tongue darted out, bathing Buck's testicles. He licked both clean and tried unsuccessfully to put one orb into his mouth. His tongue and lips traveled even lower on their journey to Buck's rosebud. When Gene parted Buck's cheeks and forced his tongue up inside Buck, Buck was squirming and moaning uncontrollably on the bed, enough so that Gene had to restrain him, holding him down. Gene delivered a final wet kiss before pulling away, raising himself up over Buck and forcing his tongue deep into Buck's mouth. He pulled back slightly to whisper into Buck's ear. "It tastes so good I want to share it with you."

He raised Buck's legs in the air, and Buck braced himself for a rough penetration. When it came, he screamed and pulled at Gene's hair as if that would force him to withdraw. It didn't, only serving to goad him on.

Gene didn't allow Buck to adjust to the thick hardness of his cock. He plunged deep inside Buck. Buck screamed again. He was in great pain. After a minute of searing agony, he began to adjust to this invasion until he welcomed it. Gene slammed more and more forcefully into him. Buck felt like his entire body had been invaded. Wave after wave of the most tantalizing pleasure shot through Buck. In one final lunge, Gene plunged into him almost as if crashing. Staccato bursts of hot juicy fluid were suddenly released like an explosion. Buck could hold back no longer. He erupted too.

His pulsation-racked body collapsed on the bed, and the next thing he remembered was the feel of Gene's tongue and lips, devouring his last orgasmic spasms, licking him clean all over. Gene's lips milked Buck's softening cock with a caressing tongue.

Buck ran his fingers through Gene's raven-black hair, caressing and loving him, fondling his ears and running his hand gently across the back of his neck. It was only when Gene was lovingly giving him his final caresses that Buck remembered he had another rendezvous. Robert was preparing a late-night dinner back on their private island, and Buck knew he must rush home to him.

"How about that shower now?" Gene asked raising up and licking his lips.

"Mind if I join you?" Buck asked.

"You're welcome. But I'm not going to turn my back to you for one moment. Guys like you can't be trusted."

***

After the violent passion with Gene, Buck was happy to return to the security of Robert and his own private island. What he needed most tonight was tender love, not throbbing passion, and he knew he could find that in Robert's arms.

As he steered his boat close to the pier, he could see Robert standing by and waiting for him. Even as he neared the dock, he was rewarded with Robert's trusting smile.

The moment he landed, Buck sensed something was wrong. Robert raced to greet him and planted several kisses on his mouth, but it was different somehow. As Buck returned the kisses, he felt tension in Robert. Had Robert found out about Gene? He parted slightly from Robert but still held him close. "What's up?"

"I have to go to Miami," Robert said. "I got a call from the hospital. My mother's dying."

"You haven't spoken to her in years."

"I know." Robert looked grim-faced as he took Buck's hand and guided him toward the living room. He said nothing but poured Buck a Scotch and came and sat with him on the sofa where they'd so recently entertained Isabella and Leroy.

"Do you want me to go with you?" Buck asked.

"I want you to go with me everywhere, but I sense there is going to be a lot of news breaking. Mother wouldn't speak to you anyway even if you showed up. I don't know if she'll even speak to me."

"Over the years she hasn't struck me as the most thankful person in the world. After all, we've paid for her to live in a condo, and we've sent her a monthly check. I don't recall ever seeing a Christmas card."

"She's a bitter old woman and mean as hell. I've been so grateful for all your help."

"I'm amazed she could accept our charity and still hate us so," Buck said. "She feels I corrupted you."

"Mother doesn't understand our kind of love," Robert said. "Come on, let's take a shower together before dinner." She'll go to her grave hating gay people and especially her gay son."

As he stood with Robert under the jet spray, Robert kissed him and whispered into his ear, "I want you to marry me."

Buck broke away. "You mean like married married"

"The real thing. I know of a minister in Miami who performs such ceremonies. I want you to marry me. In front of witnesses and a pastor."

Buck took a bar of soap and rubbed it across Robert's chest, and as Robert lifted his armpits, Buck bathed each of them lovingly before Robert returned the favor.

"Well, what do you say?" Robert asked.

"I love you, Robert, and I'll never leave you. Let me think about this marriage thing a bit?

"No matter how long it takes, I want that wedding band on my finger."

"You little devil," was all Buck said. He took Robert's finger, the same one where Robert wanted a wedding band placed, and raised that finger to his lips, then sucked it deep within his mouth.

Chapter Four

At the airport the next morning, Buck embraced Robert before he boarded the flight for Miami. Their hug went relatively unnoticed. Passengers had long grown accustomed to Hispanic men embracing at this airport. As Robert started to walk away, Buck ran after him and embraced him again.

"I can't wait until I get back to your arms," Robert whispered in his ear.

"I'll think about marriage. Just give me a little time."

Buck stood watching Robert go and almost impulsively wanted to run after him. He glanced at his watch. If he didn't leave this minute, he'd be late for morning services at Rose's temple.

Until that Sunday morning, Buck had never visited the temple of evangelism that Rose built in the northeastern sector of Okeechobee. Many charismatics, fundamentalists, and Pentecostals traveled from all over the country, as well as Canada and Europe, to worship at the multi-million-dollar shrine.

Built of reinforced concrete, the temple had raised funds by selling little bags of cement mixed with crushed seashells at fifty dollars apiece. All the temple's art work, including two stained-glass windows by Chagall, had been contributed by "fat cat" supporters, and was estimated to have a value in excess of eight million dollars.

In the flower gardens that led to the entrance, Buck rubbed his sunburned hands, then looked up at the gleaming white building, dazzling in the morning sun—a gaudy extravaganza created in the shape of a cross and crowned by an overscaled dome, which was pierced with lunette windows. He was reminded of reading of Rose's humble beginnings, a pigsty over which she'd preached early in her career.

Inside the church, painted a sky blue, he had a hard time finding an empty seat, locating a cozy perch down front near the white-robed choir. Under the dome stood a golden pulpit with thousands of luxuriously upholstered pale rose armchairs fanning off from it. All the large, roomy ramps and aisles converged at this metallic point, where it seemed that every square foot of floor space was devoted to whomever stood at its golden focal point.

He wondered how many people had read the *Examiner* before coming to church. On Sunday, the *Examiner* appeared in the morning like its rival the *News*. He had run his story on the front page, claiming that the printing headquarters of Rose's association was used as a distribution center for racist literature. It'd been impossible to reach Rose for comment last night, and he eagerly waited to confront her, as she'd invited him to come backstage to meet her after the sermon.

Planting his feet firmly on the rose-colored carpeting, he stared straight at the pulpit. He didn't have to wait long. In blazing sound, a Jesus rock band rose from the orchestra pit. It reminded him of the opening of a splashy Broadway musical. For sheer hoopla, Rose knew how to exalt the Lord in surroundings worthy of an imperial coronation.

Hidden microphones waited to capture her voice for her syndicated radio gospel programs over eighty stations, and cameras were ready to record her appearance for thirty-eight television stations, from Florida to Louisiana to Texas, all the way to Portland, Oregon.

Rose appeared—a real star's entrance—and to him, she possessed instant appeal. He had a hard time associating this image with the woman who'd passed the catsup at her patio dinner. Her arrival was greeted by a standing ovation, the congregation raising outstretched hands toward her.

Clad only in a sheer white, flowing Grecian gown, and holding a long-stemmed white rose, she had let her auburn hair cascade down the sides of her face. Shouting: "Joy! Joy! Joy!" she cut a striking figure, tall and slender, as she moved gracefully to the center of the stage to the thunderous applause of her fans.

After the demonstration had gone on for an embarrassingly long time, she extended her hands toward the dome to summon the faithful to quiet down. However, shouts of "Hallelujah!" and "Praise the Lord!" still echoed through the cavernous temple. Unlike anything he might have expected, this jubilant Christian assembly seemed gathered to have a good time, even though he noticed some of the faces around him were vacant-eyed, as if fixed on some star in their own firmament.

The sleeves of her Grecian gown billowing after her, Rose turned her full face to the audience—with her spectacular eyes and mouth, beautifully shaped nose, and a fine high forehead. She waited until the audience had quieted down, giving her a sense of control and mastery. "I can do all things through Christ," she quoted Philippians 4:13. "Like Paul, I've gone through many trials in my public and private life, but I've triumphed...and I will again!" One of her arms shot out toward the congregation, her fist tightening in an iron-willed determination. "Jesus has summoned me to carry on his battle here on earth."

Somehow Rose transferred the feel of her own metallically tense body to him, and he sensed the change in her mood and voice, depending on the point she wanted to emphasize. At one moment, she appeared belligerent, then folksy.

Suddenly Buck, along with the audience, gasped as she tripped over a cord on the platform. She seemed to have broken the heel to one of her pumps. Kicking off both shoes, she tossed them aside and walked back to the podium in her stocking feet. This act of bravado endeared her to her fans, causing spontaneous clapping. "I never had a pair of real shoes 'till I was eight years old anyway." Again, loud applause, even shouts of "Right on!" Now he suspected she'd deliberately tripped, using the shoes as a piece of stage business.

"I have called you here today to launch a moral crusade," she shouted in clear tones, her voice reverberating through the temple. With one lightning-swift glance to the dome, she tossed her head back, her hair moving rhythmically as she spoke. "If every sex pervert, bomb-thrower, abortionist baby-murderer and radical revolutionary intent on destroying this country through violent means can come out of the closet and assert his rights, then so help me, with Jesus backing me up, I can say that the *normal majority* had better get out of our attics and shout them down before they grab our country right from under our noses."

This stinging call to arms burned right through Buck's skin. He was aware of the shuffling of feet and the sounds, at first a murmur, and then a roar of "Amen, Sister!" She was getting her response—and fast.

The evangelist held up her hands as if blessing the audience, but perhaps to calm them. At first her voice had been halting. The more she launched her attack, the mellower and more vibrant it became—an odd tone for so powerful an assault. Even her face looked younger—effervescent innocence itself. Charging into her subject, she said, "I think there's a lesson to be learned from the movement of the far left. They have taken to the streets to demand their rights, while the rest of us have sat at home watching the action on TV."

She seemed to reach up in mid-air, take a bolt of fire from Jesus himself, and hurl it into the audience. "When one of us stands up—a normal American, like you or me—and says, 'Hey, just a minute. What about us? We've got rights too. The rights to raise our children in a God-fearing country.' What happens then? We're labeled racists, like I was so painfully characterized by that muckraking newspaper, the *Examiner*, this morning."

Reddening, Buck was at the same time prepared to face the assault.

"I might as well say it," she added. "In polite circles, they call us the fanatical right. But, to card-carrying Communists, we're always..." She paused, leaning closer.

He knew the word she was searching for, but didn't think she'd have the guts to use it. He misjudged her.

In a throaty sob, she shouted, "We're called Nazis!" She stopped short, as if catching her breath. Near tears, she cried out. "Lies! Lies! All lies to discredit us. Let them accuse." He felt she'd momentarily lost control and was improvising now. She recovered quickly. "I'm not advocating violence. No way. Not like the violence our enemies have inflicted on us. I'm calling for massive demonstrations of normal Americans who want to put an end to the wave of filth and perversion destroying our landscape. If the judges and the police are powerless to fight the rising tide, then we have the strength." The audience rose to its feet, extending its raised hands to show its support. Despite the contemptuous stares of those who sat near him, he remained in his seat, knowing he was so opposed to her methods and even her moral purpose that he expected any day to rise to the top of the enemy list.

"Call it revolution if you want," she shouted over the murmur of the crowd. "I call it confrontational politics. Go out...find the sinner. Stare him down—eyeball to eyeball."

He tried to imagine such bizarre encounters, and wasn't at all certain what she advocated.

Restoring calm by the magnetism of her presence, she said, "Tonight, I'm leading a march into the Combat Zone, a parade by Christian warriors that heads directly into the dirty heart of Sodom and Gomorrah itself. I want you to join me and my family in this candlelight parade. We'll not carry bombs, we'll not break windows. But we'll let the merchants of filth along the way know what we think of their wares which they peddle to corrupt our youth. Our march will be a signal to the prostitutes along the street that they'd better ship out to places like San Francisco that encourage such ilk."

Her voice changed again and, to him, it seemed even more stirring than ever. "If we succeed tonight," she said, "our cause will set an example for the rest of this great country to follow. I promise you, my friends, we'll clean up America, and we'll start right tonight in Okeechobee."

At the end of her battle cry, she broke into her theme song, "The Battle Hymn of the Republic," accompanied by a thirty-six member choral group and the Jesus rock band. Her voice soared, capturing emotions the words themselves could not express. Everybody in the audience, except Buck, seemed transposed to another plateau.

As she sang, tears streamed down her cheeks. The song itself took on a different meaning as interpreted by her. She made it sound bullish, a symbol of triumphant America embracing the moral fervor of the past century.

He shuddered at what her "terrible swift sword" would do to those who stood in her way—not only minority groups, but other Christians who differed from her Biblical interpretations. He felt he already knew which hearts of men she'd sift out before God in his judgment seat had a chance to look over the flesh.

***

In the far corner of the temple, Gene sat silently, mesmerized by Rose's rallying cry. In her virginal-appearing state, she sucked in the air, expanding her already full bosom, and sent her gracious voice rolling like an ocean wave over him. He allowed it to envelop him, bathe him, almost drown him.

His spirit, too, wanted to cry out with her the same agony of outrage. For years in the police department, he'd been forced to languish in bitter stagnation, though his idealism burned within him. In Rose's large, feverishly intense eyes that seemed to penetrate to the very core of his body, he felt her command in a hypnotic way.

After the devastation of his marriage, he had every intention—and still had—to save himself from one temptation after another. He was a thrill seeker, and couldn't help himself. It was all he could do to resist when Sandy had invited him to that men's room. He liked having sex in public places, as if he wanted to get caught. Again. Although he told himself he couldn't face more public humiliation, he did everything he could to invite it.

He always thought his sexual involvement with Buck would be confined to the dark recesses of his brain, but it had suddenly become a reality. In this temple this morning, he wanted to feel clean and pure again.

"I need each and every one of you," she called out from the pulpit.

He felt that she'd been talking to him directly, and he'd wanted to go up after the sermon to tell her that. He was willing to fight for her in her cause. It was his cause. But how could he, a lowly cop, approach an angel?

On his way home he felt feverish, knowing an excitement unlike any he'd experienced in years. Making his way down to the altar along with other milling bodies, he'd reached out to almost touch her gown. Under the brilliant light coming in from the dome, she'd looked into his trusting face, her eyes like a blast of sunlight, the radiance blinding him. In the midst of a crowd, her eyes had made contact with his, creating a great sense of intimacy and, for a moment, though surrounded by thousands, they stood alone in the temple.

Back on his own street an hour later, he was filled with a tremendously pressing need to begin the battle she'd talked of. He'd be there in the Combat Zone, marching by her side tonight.

Pulling into his garage, he found his flagging spirits revived. As if to remind him of all the evil still lurking, he spotted Maria playing in his backyard. As he yelled at her, the little Cuban girl stood glaring at him—contemptuous, defiant, as if asserting her right to use his private property.

When he moved menacingly toward her, she screamed and ran across the street to the outstretched arms of her stringy-haired mother, who grabbed her up and took her inside their house.

Back in his own kitchen, he poured himself a glass of natural apple juice. He found the air heavy and hot, yet he refused to raise a window. Still, it didn't matter. At least with the windows shut, he could keep out the noise from the Cuban neighborhood.

In his back bedroom, he pulled off his clothes and collapsed. He wanted to remember every detail of what Rose had looked like at the temple. He'd never seen her more beautiful. With no thought other than of her, he could lie in his bed peacefully, anticipating the rapidly approaching night and the candlelight parade through the Combat Zone.

That was a long time from now. The rest of the day was rapidly filling up. He looked forward to renewing his contact with Sandy at two o'clock down by the reservoir, and Buck had left a message that he wanted to meet him for a Jacuzzi bath, a cigar, and some vintage brandy at his cottage on the estate of Buck Brooke I.

Gene turned over in bed, lost in his dreams. After years of loneliness, he felt needed again. Sandy wanted to be with him, Buck was back in his life, and he knew it would be only hours—maybe even tonight—before Rose too acknowledged him and wanted to be with him.

***

An hour had gone by since a well-groomed attendant, in a maroon and gray uniform, handed a card to Buck. It was from Rose. On the back she'd written, "See me backstage. Love in Christ. Rose."

He'd waited impatiently in an anteroom decorated with large blow-ups of Sister Rose attending various rallies. He kept being told by attendants that Rose was still wishing good-bye to her followers, all of whom planned to march in tonight's parade through the Combat Zone.

Finally, the same attendant who'd initially given him the card told him that Rose had asked for him to meet her in her dressing room. She promised to be there shortly but had been overwhelmed by the massive outpouring of support for her crusade.

In the corridor leading to the dressing rooms buried underground at the temple, Buck collided with Calder Martin, the stench of whiskey and Clorets powerful on his breath. The leading hatchetman of the far right, Calder, at fifty-five years of age, stood in the shadows of American politics. The original Mr. Dirty Tricks, he was considered far too controversial a personality for even the pre-Watergate Nixon White

House to hire, though Calder had repeatedly applied for a post "behind the scenes." Nixon had turned him down three times, claiming, "We want an open administration."

Buck knew all the rumors. Reportedly, Calder's overall strategy was to form a coalition of the "new majority." Up to now, it'd been assumed that he planned to organize his caucus from a variety of right-wing hate groups. His appearance at Rose's temple caused Buck to wonder if he were trying to enlist the support of the more militant right-wing church people as well.

Calder had never made a foray into religion before, preferring to devote his considerable talents as a fund raiser to the "grass roots majority."

Known by his enemies as "liver lips," he stood only five feet, five inches tall, a pudgy person whose thick neck seemed to bulge out in all directions from his stiff white collar. With a bulbous nose, a puffy face and sunken eyes behind horn-rimmed glasses, he reminded Buck of his former biology teacher at the university. He had met Calder once before when he'd covered a Republican political convention.

"Don't tell me," Buck said sarcastically, "that America's most confirmed atheist is about to be born again."

Calder gave him a wide, insincere smile and then in a booming voice said, "Religion's bullshit and we both know it. But when you're trying to save this country from a Communist takeover, you've got to sleep with some strange political bedfelllows."

"You mean Rose Phillips?"

Calder ignored the question. "Take the *Examiner*. With your granddad, it was on our side—until you took over with your high school Marxist ideas."

"I see you read our story."

Calder leaned closer to him and, like an amoeba finding its prey, seemed to surround him. He steeled himself against the onslaught. The feel of the sterile windowless corridor was depressing enough without getting assimilated into the protoplasm of Calder Martin.

"When I was thirteen, I used to be an ice-shaver for snow cones," Calder confided. "I learned to shave pretty close in those days. Make real thin ice. And that's exactly what you're walking on, boy, if you publish another crock of shit like you did this morning."

"May I quote you?" Buck asked facetiously. "MARTIN THREAT-

ENS *EXAMINER.*" His eyes tightened and he moved menacingly toward Calder, just as the hatchetman threatened him.

"You can't quote me at all," Calder said. "I don't want my name mentioned in your rag. You got that? If you fuck with me, the old ice-shaver, you might end up with your balls cut off."

"Is that tantamount of Kate Graham getting her tit caught in the wringer?"

"Far more dangerous—and painful!" Calder threatened.

"I know you types would like to fondle my balls, but exactly how do you plan to cut them off?"

"What if I told you you're in danger of losing the *Examiner?*"

"I'd tell you you're full of shit. The *Examiner*, the last I heard, is owned by my granddad. I haven't heard he's turning it over to you."

"There's a lot a stupid liberal punk like you doesn't know. And I'm not going to be the one to enlighten you."

"I'm having lunch today with my granddad. Perhaps I'll ask him if I'm in any danger of losing the *Examiner.*"

"Go ahead and ask that old whore-hopper."

"Your challenge is accepted." Buck stood tall, towering over Calder. "Strictly on the record. Just what are you doing in our fair town?"

"I don't talk to assholes from the press!"

"Your being here doesn't have anything to do with big development planned on South Beach, does it?"

Calder looked up menacingly at him. "Listen, faggot, don't you connect me with that. I'll sue you for more money than you've got if you print one word of crap like that."

"I'm printing nothing for the moment, but know that we're definitely going to check you out. You see, we want to know why you're here. You're not in town for your health—that's for damn sure."

"I'm warning you. I have the power to shut down your slimy rag tomorrow. If you don't think I have that kind of power, just put me to the test."

"I suspect I will," Buck said.

"Get out of my way, scumbag." Calder pushed past him.

As Calder faded, Buck watched him go. He was right about one thing: Calder was definitely an amoeba, flowing down the corridor, trickling into every dark corner, every deep crevice, absorbing, filling, then oozing on.

Buck stepped up to the door of Rose's dressing room and rapped lightly, even though he suspected the evangelist was still up front, shaking hands and accepting contributions or pledges—including a lot of personal checks. A boy's voice called to him to come in.

At a backstage mirror, lined by a row of electric bulbs, sat one of the world's most beautiful boys. He was wiping makeup from his face with cream. "Fucking pimple," he said into the mirror, dabbing at his cheek with Kleenex.

Buck could not recall seeing a boy who possessed such physical perfection. It would have taken the most skilled of Renaissance painters to capture his essence. He looked androgynous as he pursed his cupid mouth. Ringlets of honey-colored curls covered his head. His blue eyes with long lashes, were luminous, and in spite of his protestations about some alleged pimple, his skin was unblemished and peach colored. His features were flawless—his nose, his ears, his forehead appearing as if carved by a sculptor.

At first Buck couldn't say anything. He stood staring, and then he was struck by an overwhelming feeling that this is what Robert must have looked like when he was fourteen. The boy wore a rose-colored suit, a red bow tie with white polka dots, and red leather cowboy boots, an outfit obviously selected by Rose. This boy appeared too hip for such garb.

His eyes darted to Buck, returned to the mirror, and then reverted to Buck again. No whore in any sleazy bar when he was in the service ever evaluated him as carefully as this angelic looking child. Buck felt that the boy possessed x-ray vision and was completely undressing him as he stood for inspection.

"You must be my new driver," he said, his eyes lingering below Buck's belt. "You're one sexy hunk. Rose always hires such old men to haul my ass around. I can't believe she'd trust me alone in a car with the likes of you."

"I'm not your driver. I'm Buck Brooke."

"Holy shit!" The boy rose to his feet. "Forgive me. Fuck! Mistaking you for a chauffeur. On closer examination, I see you're definitely the type to be hauled around with your own chauffeur. I'm Shelley

Phillips. Rose's adopted son, as she keeps reminding me."

"I saw you in the garden the night I came to Rose's house for dinner."

"I sorta remember that. If I had known what you looked like, I would have invited you to my bedroom. What an arrogant little prick I was that night."

"Forget it."

"I didn't shake your hand. Rose always insists I shake hands." He reached for Buck's hand and held it firmly in his grasp. "If you're not much into hand-shaking, you can slip your tongue down my throat."

"Mind if I take a rain check?" Buck asked.

"Honey, you can take anything of mine you want." He took Buck's hand and placed it across his left breast. "You think licking women's saggy tits is a turn-on. Wait till your mouth devours my sweet little nipples."

Buck pulled his hand away. "You know," he said, "the penalty for child molestation is severe in this state."

"I'm no God damn child," Shelley said, looking disappointed at the loss of Buck's hand. "I'm eighteen and legal if you'd like to consummate this meeting."

"Hell, I thought you were fourteen. You look fourteen going on forty."

"It's this fucking drag Rose makes we wear. I was supposed to go on today. But she dominated the whole service."

"What do you mean, go on?" Buck asked.

"I was supposed to do my bit as a child preacher."

"Of all the fields open to you, evangelism isn't what I would have picked."

He stared at Buck, then burst into laughter. "It was God's decision. God, I said. Surely you know who *she* is."

Buck smiled. "I can't see you preaching."

Shelley sat back down at the dressing table and continued to eradicate his makeup. "I should have been a fucking movie star, and I would have been if Rose had listened to me. There were roles I could have done. Children possessed by the devil, shit like that. You know, spin-offs from *The Exorcist*. One of them was really great. I would have been brilliant in the role. About a kid who had a fourteen-inch cock by the age of four. The character's name was Damon."

"Sounds like a big part."

"It was!" A cold fury came over Shelley's features, his face blanching under the golden curls. "If they actually showed the cock, I bet they could have done a close-up of your dick instead."

"I think I'm about three inches short."

"I just knew it!"

"Knew what?" Buck asked.

"That you have a big dick. I have this inner radar. Just by touching a man's hand, I can tell the size of his dick. The most I've been meeting up with lately is five and a half inches, or even less. I haven't been plowed by a real man so long I've forgotten what it feels like."

"Maybe your luck will change."

"Maybe it already has, handsome."

Strange as it seemed, Buck enjoyed Shelley's company. With smug satisfaction, he was glad Rose had adopted such a far-out son.

Shelley turned once more to the mirror. "Rose wanted me to try out for all that Disney crap. Let's face it: Great pictures don't carry G ratings. She tried to turn me into a boy Shirley Temple. But the world wasn't ready for that crap." He smiled and looked up at Buck, rubbing off the rest of his make-up. "Who in the fuck is?"

Buck couldn't help staring at the boy. Shelley looked like some seductive pubescent, a true Lolito.

Shelley smiled with a knowledge far beyond his years. He seemed to know what effect he was having on Buck. "Don't be ashamed," Shelley said. "Most men, even the straight ones." He paused. "Especially the straight ones want to plow me when they meet me. Even when I'm shaking their hands, I look into their eyes, and I know what they want. But not everyone gets to plow into the hottest, sexiest, tightest boy ass in Florida. I don't know who you've fucked before. But you've never had a rosebud like mine. It's ready to suck you in any time. You just name the night."

In spite of himself, Buck felt a hardening in his pants, a fact that Shelley noticed too. "Again, you've got to give me a rain check on that. I'm here to see your mother."

"Fuck that cunt! She's always getting the men I want. That's at first. Before it's over I win them over in the end. Get it? The end."

"I get it!"

"I don't think that bitch will be glad to see you. Not after what you wrote in the *Examiner* about her this morning. Of course, in spite of her denunciation from the pulpit, everything you wrote is true."

"I know it is."

"All this stuff is off the record, stud. Rose doesn't allow me to grant interviews, unless she's around. In fact, I'm hardly allowed out of the house—and never alone!"

"I can see why," Buck said, thinking as he did that if Shelley ever met up with a child molester, it'd be the molester who got seduced.

Shelley wheeled around and stared up at Buck. "You're about thirty, aren't you?"

"I'm getting there. Give me some more time."

"I didn't mean that in a bad way. Normally I don't go to bed with a man until he's thirty. I'm not into skinny boys. I like real men. There are so few of them left. You're a real man."

"Thanks."

"I mean that. I'll also let you in on a secret."

"About Rose? Something I can print in the *Examiner*? An exposé?"

"Cut the crap! The secret's about us. I'm psychic. I've always been psychic. I'm getting vibes about something in your past right now."

"What in fuck are you talking about?"

"It's awful." He wheeled around and put his hands over his eyes. "I don't want to see it." He burst into tears.

Buck walked over to him and placed his hand on Shelley's shoulders. "It's okay."

Shelley looked up at him with a certain trust, then wrapped his arms around Buck's waist, holding him tightly. His sobs diminished and still he held onto Buck.

When he felt Shelley was all right, Buck gently broke the hold on his waist and backed away. "Can you tell me what you saw?"

Shelley looked up at him through tear-streaked eyes. "I saw the agonized look and screams of your parents as they crashed to their deaths. It was ghastly."

Buck turned from the sight of Shelley and gasped for air in the stale dressing room. He really believed the boy. It was a scene he had imagined a thousand times in his nightmares, and he felt that Shelley had actually witnessed the event. The whole idea made him shudder.

"It's okay," Shelley said in a soothing voice. "My head is clear now. It's not something I can forget easily."

"Me, too." Buck choked back the tears. "I miss them."

Shelley came up close to Buck and stood before him. He reached for his hand and held Buck's palm to his lips, gently kissing the inner skin. "I lost both my parents too. We have that in common. It's a bond between us. I ended up with this world-class bitch for a mom. What a trip!" He sighed. "I've got to take a shower and then I'll be escorted home, the gates to Paradise Shores shut behind me. It's a fucking prison."

"Excuse me, I'll leave."

"No, stay. Rose will join us soon." Shelley reached to hold his arm and detain him. "I haven't told you my psychic vision about us, and I'm never wrong about these things. Just ask Rose."

"What about us?"

"You're going to take me as your lover. We're going to spend the rest of our lives together. But there's a lot of hell we've got to live through before that happens. A lot of bad things are going to happen."

Buck didn't say anything. At first he wanted to dismiss the boy as crazed, yet he believed he did have that vision about his parents. "Can you tell me what's going to happen?"

"I can't. We can't change it. We've got to live it."

"You sure?"

"I'm sure." Right in front of Buck, Shelley began to undress. At first Buck was tempted to turn away. But it was obvious Shelley wanted an audience. One by one, each piece of clothing was removed. When Shelley took off his undershirt, Buck almost gasped at the pure male beauty of his body. His skin was golden, his chest perfectly formed but not overly developed. His breasts were tantalizing.

Shelley stood before him in a pair of rose-colored briefs which matched the color of his cowboy outfit. Very carefully, he reached for the waistband of those briefs and slowly removed them before Buck's eager eyes. A nest of blond pubic hair trailed to a long uncut cock which seemed out of proportion to the rest of his frame. Shelley was no fourteen year old but was clearly a man with a man's genitals. Reaching for his robe, he turned around slowly. Buck knew what he was doing. He wanted Buck to admire his ass, which Buck did. It was the most alluring ass Buck had seen on anybody, even challenging Robert in that department. End of show," Shelley said. "For now. But you're going to have years and years to enjoy every bit of it." He slipped his bathrobe on and headed for the shower in back. He stuck his head out again. "If you write something about me in your paper, for Christ's sake, say I'm pretty. The last story the *Examiner* ever ran on me made me sound like a sick little faggot." He slammed the door shut.

As Buck turned around, another door from the corridor was thrown open.

There stood Rose herself.

***

"I didn't think you'd show up." Rose stood in the doorway, her soft lips parted. She quietly shut the door behind her and moved toward him, her face reflecting an infinite variety of moods from sad to exuberant.

The changing moods of her face fitted his own conflicting feelings toward her. She appeared so delightfully feminine, so vulnerable, that he felt once more that he wanted to protect her. Yet, he reminded himself, that would be like committing treason. Behind the fabulous flesh, he suspected, lay a soul blacker than the sins she ranted about from her pulpit.

"I wanted to catch your act." He'd already decided to relate to her sermon as a show business performance. "You didn't convert me. If anything, you stiffened my resistance."

She sat down in front of the dressing table just occupied by Shelley and checked her makeup. In her most tantalizing way, she caught his eye in the mirror. "It's good to know I can stiffen something in you."

Holding that glance for a long moment, he laughed, her remark having broken the tension between them.

Excusing herself, she disappeared behind a screen to remove her gown.

He could still hear the shower running in the bathroom. Frankly, he'd expected her to launch into an immediate attack on the *Examiner*'s story about her headquarters. She said nothing. "What about my story?" he asked.

Her head appeared around the screen. "My headquarters doesn't distribute racist literature. I called in reporters from the *News*. They inspected every storage room. Found nothing. Just my autobiography."

No longer respectful, he moved closer to the screen and then, in a perfectly controlled voice, said, "Babe, you're not fooling me for one moment. That creep, Calder Martin, had trucks remove the goodies in the middle of the night."

For a while he didn't hear a sound from her, and even her body stood motionless behind the thin screen. "Listen, I'm not stupid enough to have stuff like that around."

That actually made sense to him. "I know you're not. But your field marshals are."

From behind the screen, he could see her sticking out a leg, removing her sheer white hosiery. As she emerged, wearing a thin rose-colored robe that did little to conceal her slim figure, he felt it wasn't only the gorgeous legs, but the subtle and expressive way she moved her body, that made her such a turn-on.

"Why don't you write about my moral crusade? Not fantasies."

His back arched, he faced her squarely. "I'll write what I God damn please. And you're not going to like it. We're natural enemies."

She sat before him, her hair carrying a subdued jasmine scent, and the fragrance lingered in his nostrils ever so lightly.

"Is Calder taking over your operation?"

"Certainly not!" she said, smiling provocatively. "You know yourself Calder would cut off his grandma's breast if some rich Texas oilman offered him just five grand."

In exasperation, he said, "Then what? Do you want to become the duenna of the far right?"

With confident eyes and an impudent chin, she asked. "And why not? That prize is up for grabs. My appeal isn't just to rednecks any more. That old Bible Belt won't hold up a pair of pants. We're bursting at the seams, going national."

"I don't believe for one moment you're trying to offer spiritual help. And Calder's appearance here confirmed my suspicion. You want to bring church and state together. If somebody's not a born-again charismatic, how is he going to fit into your new America?"

She stood up defensively, her face tightening with her strength and determination. "I believe in the Bible. I adhere to orthodox Christian doctrine. I am personally committed to Christ. Given that belief, what makes you think I have any obligation to advance the cause of Jews, much less Communists?"

"You must not trample on the rights of others, sweetheart, in advancing your own cause."

"Jews make up only three percent of the population, yet their influence extends insidiously far beyond that. They dominate publishing, the media, you name it. They have powerful groups working night and day to protect Jewish interests. Don't you think, in all fairness, the true Americans who live by the real Bible need just as tightly knit an organization working for our rights, too?"

"The normal majority," he said sarcastically. "For one thing, I don't know who in hell's going to decide who's normal. For another, what frightens me is the tyranny of that majority." Without a good-bye, he turned and left her dressing room, slamming the door in her face. Even before he'd gone far, he knew he'd behaved in a childish, petulant way and wasn't proud of that.

If she were ugly, like Calder Martin, she'd be easy to hate. But she wasn't. She was beautiful. For him, that made her potentially dangerous.

It wasn't that she was an attractive older woman. He could have all those he wanted. From the age of fourteen, when he'd visited his mother between school terms, good-looking older women had always been after him.

It was more than that. He certainly wasn't a male Unity Mitford swooning after a Lorelei Hitler either.

Frankly, if Rose didn't have power, he would have met her and probably ignored her. It was her possession of power that intrigued him, making him in some way fantasize about taming her.

Her control of a vast and powerful right-wing propaganda machine had an effect like an aphrodisiac on him. If he could win her, have her groveling at his feet, he felt in some way he would be capturing and vanquishing that machine. It didn't make sense, but it was the way he felt.

Even as he tried to concentrate on Rose, his thoughts drifted to Shelley's nude body. It should be against the law to look like that. Other thoughts about Shelley fought for control of his mind, but in the glaring heat of a particularly ferocious noon-day sun he blotted them out.

***

In the early part of the afternoon and before lunch was served, old

Buck Brooke I was in a rare confessional mood.

Secretly, the younger Buck felt that the newspaper czar was nearing the end of his life. Up to now, the old man had never explained anything, especially one of the actions he'd taken in the past. "Never justify," he'd warned his grandson, although ever since Buck had arrived at the Brooke estate, he felt that's what the tycoon was doing.

"I'm not as clean as a hound's tooth," he told Buck III, coughing even as he talked. He could still walk, but preferred to spend most of the day in a wheelchair with a small day quilt offering him protection, even though the day outside was blistering hot. "I've done a lot of things in my life I'm ashamed of."

"All of us can say that," Buck said, hoping to dismiss his grandfather's revelations, which embarrassed him.

Old Buck seemed determined to continue. "Believe you me, the sins of mine play like a movie in my head every night. I've got a lot of guilt I can't get rid of." He looked over at his grandson through tired, gray eyes. Although born in the late 19th century, he'd always had a robust physique and a handsome profile until the 1970s. If anything, he appeared to be slowly withering away, losing more and more weight every time Buck saw him. "If I could go back and relive my life, I would, knowing what I know now. I was a man of great passion. I had a great love of life. You're not looking at a saint. My passion for life got out of control at times. I went too far. I would get caught up in something, and there was no way I could control my impulses."

"Why are you telling me all this?" Buck asked. "You've never confessed anything before."

"Listen, fucker, I'm not telling you this for my obit. I sense you're the same man I used to be. A man who can't keep his passions under control. Your father was different from us. He met your mother in the tenth grade of high school, went to the same college with her, and married her on graduation. You're more like me. I don't think you could be true to one person for more than six weeks. You've always got to find out what the pussy is like on the other side of the river." He looked long and hard into his grandson's eyes. "Or, in your case, whatever."

"I don't know what in hell you mean by that."

"We'll go into it later." He coughed again.

Young Buck got up to assist him and get him some water, but old Buck brushed him aside. "A glass of water won't help me much now.

Maybe a brandy."

"Coming up." At the bar Buck poured his grandfather a stiff brandy, his favorite, an unmarked brand he'd always imported from some remote province of France.

Old Buck sniffed the brandy and drank a heavy swig. He closed his eyes briefly and then opened them. He looked as if he wanted to say something. The brandy seemed to ease his mind. "One little vixen turned out to be too much for me. I guess she didn't like what I was making her do to me. The God damn bitch just up and bit off part of my dick. Only my doctor knows how much. I don't care to go into any more graphic details. But the stud of Okeechobee could never quite function properly again, and it ruined my life. I even considered suicide. My plumbing was permanently damaged. I continued to have sex with young girls, but I could never satisfy them the way I used to. I had to find another way, and I did. I still carried on a sex life until about four years ago. After that, sex didn't seem to matter any more."

"Did grandmother know about this? I mean, all your affairs."

"Nellie always knew, but never said anything. Once she caught me under the most suspicious of circumstances in that cottage out back. I had my pants down. I told your grandmother the maid was removing an ingrown hair from my inner thigh. She just turned and walked away. She never brought up the subject ever again, but she fired the maid the very next day."

"I always loved Nellie. She was wonderful to me."

"She was a good woman. As good as I was bad. Some of my worst excesses came much later in life. Your grandmother, bless her heart, had the good grace to die in 1940 before I'd made some of my really big mistakes."

"Care to tell me about them? I think in some way what you're doing here is not confessing but warning me somehow."

"You're right about that." He took another hefty swig of brandy. "I want to go to my grave with the dirtiest of my secrets. I can't stand having you or anybody else learn too much about me. I was a dirty old man. Let's leave it at that."

"Calder Martin threatened me this morning. Do Calder and Rose have something on you?"

"I will make no deathbed confession. In my day men went to their graves with their secrets. Today the fuckers go on talk shows."

"You're trying to tell me something, and I think I know what it is."

Buck I finished the last of his brandy and held up his empty glass to Buck III. Buck got up from his chair and went to refill it. "The bottom line is, you can't expose Rose," the old man said. "I know you're planning a series on her. It will never run in the *Examiner*, not while I'm alive."

"Like hell it won't! I'm going ahead with my investigation. That little bit of news about Rose and her anti-Semitic propaganda that you surely read this morning—that's only the beginning."

"If you expose Rose, she'll go public with what she knows about me. That's no idle threat, not with Calder Martin in town. I'll be publicly humiliated." He reached out his withered hand to grasp Buck's fingers. "I want to die in peace. You owe me that much. I've lost nearly all the papers, except two or three minor ones. I used to have twenty big ones. Now, only the *Examiner*."

"And even that is in danger," Buck said, taking hold of his grandfather's hand and squeezing it. "Are you saying it could be taken away from us?"

"Anything in life can be taken away."

"Won't you give me some more details? My life is tied up with the *Examiner*. I need to know. I'm the publisher."

"You are the publisher, but not with as much power as I gave you at first. In fact, just this morning I've empowered Roland to have a publisher's say. From now on, he can overrule you on any story or series."

"He's only the city editor," Buck protested.

"He's a city editor with the power to overrule the publisher," the old man said.

"I've never heard of such an arrangement," Buck III said, edging closer to the end of his seat. "You can't stop me from exposing Rose."

"You're right. I can only stop you from exposing her in the *Examiner*, and only for as long as I live."

"I'll sell my story to a national magazine."

"If you expose Rose, and if you expose what Calder and Rose are up to, your career at the *Examiner* is over. I'll see to that."

Buck got up and headed for the bar. He poured himself a strong Scotch. "I think my career at the *Examiner* just ended today. You've given me no choice. I'm too proud to stay on. It'll take several weeks,

in various banks. I've also got about eight hundred thousand dollars worth of jewelry that belonged to your grandmother. I also own a big hunk of land in Central Florida that I bought in 1934 for peanuts. It's worth about eight million dollars, and by the time you're fifty will probably be worth fifty million dollars. That's not all. I own half a block on South Beach, including the very apartment Hazel Phillips lives in. But I'm selling that particular asset for maybe upwards of five million."

"Who would pay that? It's not worth anywhere near that amount of money."

"The buyer's a secret."

"Is Calder Martin behind this? Rose?"

"That's for me to know and you to find out. Until you inherit everything, I'm saying nothing more. When you go over my papers when I'm dead, a lot of things will become clear to you. Even though I have a shaky hold on the *Examiner*, I am providing for you. Just in case those ambitious plans of yours don't work out."

"I knew you were loaded but I didn't know how much. I don't think even my father knew."

"He didn't know. I never told him, and I'm only telling you because I'm dying, leaving you one of the richest men in the State of Florida. But all those millions come with a price tag."

"What's the price?"

"I want you to marry Susan Howard."

"You can't tell me who to marry."

"I not only can, I am. You'll give up that faggot Dante and marry a good woman and become a real man, or I'll disinherit you. Give every penny to charity."

Buck III looked bewildered. He wanted to blast out at the old man, but sank back into his chair instead, his stomach feeling like it'd been kicked in. At that moment, the butler came into the room. "Miss Howard has just arrived."

"Wha...?" Buck III sat up in his chair. He turned to his grandfather. "You've invited her here for lunch?"

"Time is running out for me. Everything must be speeded up. My last public appearance will be at your wedding."

***

When Susan walked onto the veranda with all its potted greenery to greet Buck I and Buck III, she sensed a bitter argument had just ensued. Young Buck seemed startled to see her. Hadn't he been told that she was a guest for lunch?

Recovering quickly, he walked rapidly toward her, giving her a quick kiss on the mouth. "I've been meaning to call."

"I know," she said demurely

Buck I didn't get up from his wheelchair but appraised her from afar. "Susan, it's been a long time."

"Only four years," she said walking toward him to give him a kiss on his withered cheek.

"How time flies," he said. "But you're still one mighty fine looking heifer."

"Grandpa," Buck III said. "They don't call them heifers any more."

Buck I looked up at Susan in surprise. "What do men call women these days? You young people keep changing the terms all the time."

"As I was getting in my car, two Cuban men yelled at me, 'That's one hot *puta*.'"

"I think I'll stick to heifer." He called to his butler. "Get Susan here a drink."

"A martini," she said. "Make it with gin. I'm an old-fashioned..." She paused, looking down at Buck I, "...gal."

Over drinks, Buck I continued to down his brandy, brushing off the doctor's warnings as conveyed by his butler. "I'm going to die. I probably won't even make it to Christmas. But for all I know, this brandy will keep me alive for another year or so."

"You'll live another quarter of a century," Susan said with a kind of breezy optimism. "I hear all the Brooke men are big and strong." She looked at Buck III.

"We've all been studs to be proud of," Buck I said. "But even the biggest bull in the pasture has to give up one day."

"It will be a loss for the women of the world." She smiled faintly at Buck III. "Thank God you've left an heir to carry on the tradition."

Buck III smiled back at her, looking embarrassed.

As it appeared to Susan, this was obviously not the lunch of his dreams.

"I want to get some unpleasant business out of the way before we move on to the festivities of the day." Buck I managed to sound just as forceful as he did in his board room heyday. This exertion of his lungs brought on another coughing spasm. The butler kept giving him fresh handkerchiefs, as he always refused to use paper tissues.

"What unpleasant business?" Buck III asked, appearing distressed.

Susan noticed that when Buck I spoke, he looked only at her, ignoring his grandson. "Roland told me that young Buck here assigned you a new series: the investigation of this South Beach thing."

"That's right," she said, "and I think we're on to something big here."

"Forget it!" He looked harshly at her. "This is one story the *Examiner* is not going to break. Let the *Okeechobee News* drown in it. The *Examiner* will do no investigative reporting on the subject. If something breaks on the TV channels, we can pick it up from there. But only pronouncements from public officials, providing those pronouncements aren't coming from Hazel Phillips."

Susan felt as if all the air had left the room. She looked at Buck III for confirmation of this order. His face remained blank.

In lieu of no protest coming from her superior, Susan turned and confronted the old man himself. "I think this is a big mistake. You've been one of the great newspapermen of this century. You would never have said this twenty years ago. Why today?"

"Because, I'm an old and dying man. I know more about life than the two of you will ever know. I'm doing what's right to protect the *Examiner*."

"I don't know who you are protecting," she said harshly. "Obviously not the *Examiner*."

Buck I glared at her. He bitterly drank the rest of his brandy.

"For the moment," Buck III finally said. "I'm still the publisher of the *Examiner*. But Roland has been given authority to kill every story or series. I've had my balls cut off."

"You'll find them again," Susan said.

"I hope so." He glanced disdainfully at his grandfather. "Perhaps not as publisher of the *Examiner*."

"Now, now," Buck I said in the way of consolation. "Time will tell."

A silence fell over the patio. Something seemed to disturb the three birds of prey Buck I kept on his veranda. Susan didn't know one bird from another, but knew that they were considered dangerous if unleashed from their cage. She felt right this minute that Buck I wanted to cage Buck III.

Finally, it was Buck III who spoke. "There are just so many things that we can control from the grave."

"Tell me something I don't already know," Buck I said like a reprimand. He called for his manservant. "Why don't you people go for a walk in the garden? I need a little help getting to the table. Come back in about ten minutes when I'll be artfully arranged to preside over my last luncheon."

Neither Susan nor Buck III said anything, as he took her hand and guided her to the garden.

"What does all this mean?" she asked, once they were out of hearing distance from the house.

"It means he's dying. It means he's deeply mixed up in this Rose mess. Even this Calder Martin mess. It's my worst nightmare."

"But what are you going to do? You can't let him dictate terms like this."

He turned her around and looked deeply into her eyes. "I've just spoken with his doctor. Grandfather has days, or at most, only a few weeks, to live. I'm just going to play along. Take his orders. Put up with his shit. He'll be dead soon and I'll do what I want to do after that. Even if it means taking on Rose herself in battle."

"You mean that? You won't give in to Rose the way old Buck has?"

"Hell no. That's a promise."

"All of this is happening so fast, I don't know what to think."

"Think about this," he said, pulling her to him and kissing her long and deep. He broke away slightly, as if gasping for air. "Will you marry me?"

***

As he sat down at the luncheon table, Buck couldn't believe that Susan had accepted his proposal of marriage. Even more surprising to himself, was the fact he'd made the proposal at all. Old Buck knew him well. The temptation was too great. He decided he'd be a fool not to accept the agreement. Under the circumstances, the marriage might be a bit of a sham, as he had no intentions of leaving Robert. Once he inherited old Buck's millions, he would be free to do what he wanted, both as a husband and a publisher. He was convinced he could win Robert over to his point of view. What he didn't want to contemplate, at least not now, was Gene's reaction. That he feared most of all.

"I had my cook fix me corned beef and cabbage, my alltime favorite," Buck I was telling both of them, although he aimed most of his talk at Susan. "Always did make me fart. You've been duly warned."

Susan pretended to laugh. She was uncomfortable.

The butler served Buck I first. "Forgive this breach of etiquette," Buck I said to Susan. "My good man here knows I'm likely to die at any moment, so he always serves me first."

"It's okay," she said.

"Grandfather," Buck said, "I have to tell you something. During that brief time when we went for a walk in the garden, Susan agreed to marry me."

Buck I dropped his fork, as if his hearing aid were malfunctioning. "I wanted you to speed this thing up, but you were faster than I could imagine. I was going to goad you into asking her hand in marriage after we've chowed down on this corned beef."

"You didn't have to goad me. I've been thinking about it for a long time."

"It came as a surprise to me, too," Susan said. She smiled demurely at Buck III. "Imagine? After only one date."

Buck I stopped chewing the grainy meat for a minute. He looked proudly at his grandson. "That must have been a hell of a date."

Buck I looked around for his manservant who sensed he was needed. "Bring me that box." In moments the servant returned to the room where he handed Buck I the box he'd requested. Buck I brushed it away, motioning for him to give it to Buck III.

"What's this?" Buck III asked, opening the box.

"It's your God damn engagement ring, considering that you don't have the money—or the time—to buy this pretty gal a proper one."

Buck III opened the package slowly and stared at one of the most beautiful gems he'd ever seen. "It's a sapphire," he said to Susan.

"Sapphire, hell! Buck I said. "This is a rare blue diamond. One of the finest you will ever see. It's worth a fortune."

"How did you get it?" Susan asked.

"Back in the 20s. I was going to foreclose on a mortgage of a guy who lost everything in the stock market crash. He offered me this blue diamond. After I had it appraised, I accepted his offer. I tried to give it to my wife, but she was a simple woman. Locked it in our safe where it's been ever since."

Buck III took the ring out of the box and walked around the table. In front of Susan, he got down on his knees and looked up into her eyes. "Will you marry me?"

She smiled. "The answer, handsome, is the same as in the garden. A definite yes."

He placed the ring on her finger and kissed her lightly on the lips.

Buck I beamed with a certain pride. "Something tells me about nine months from now there's going to be a Buck Brooke IV to carry on the family name."

Susan laughed teasingly. "Does it have to be Buck Brooke IV? Can't we name him James after my own father?"

"Your father is a fine man, but I just know you'll want to name him after me. After all, some time in the next century it will be my millions he'll be living on. He'll want to remember the old man who set him up so well in life. Too bad I won't be around for the birth."

"You'll be around for the birth," Susan said.

Buck III said nothing. He wasn't even certain if his grandfather would be around for the wedding, and he doubted very seriously if there ever would be a Buck Brooke IV.

"I'm flying to Switzerland soon," Buck I said. "I'm entering this clinic in Geneva. It's my last straw. They have ways there of prolonging life, or so I've been told."

"I didn't know that." Buck III said.

"You know it now, boy."

"I hope you'll be all right," Susan said.

"I'll never be right again," he said in way of dismissal. "But I'm going to hang on to what life is left in me. We Brookes don't commit suicide. Which brings up my final wish. I fully don't expect to return to America. I have one last event I want to attend before flying out of here."

"What are you talking about?" Buck III said. "We'll take you anywhere you want to go."

"I've had your wedding speeded up. It's to take place at six o'clock in the garden here."

"But we've got to get a license," Buck III said. "A minister. Blood tests."

"Not when you're the grandson of Buck I. I've arranged everything."

"This is sudden." Susan said. "I've got to go home and get dressed. Find something to wear."

"No problem about that," Buck I said. "I still have a rare lace dress worn by my wife at our wedding. It's stunning and in perfect shape. You and she were the same size. Right now that dress is being put in the back of your car."

"This is pretty fast going here," Buck III. "I don't even have time to think."

"Think about it later," Buck I said. "I even have the marriage ring to go with that blue diamond."

"What about it, Susan?" Buck III asked. "You game?"

"Yes," she said. She turned to Buck I. "If this is what you want."

"It's what I want all right."

"I've got to warn everybody," she said. "I have a plane to catch at eight o'clock tonight. Ingrid is being honored at a large banquet in New York. Jim feels too ill to go. I've been asked to present an award around midnight. I can just make it. The following day I'm supposed to deliver a speech at this writer's conference."

"There will be plenty of time for a honeymoon later," Buck I said.

"I would go with you, honey," Buck III said. "But I've got to be in town tonight for Rose's moral crusade. That event is going to be a big news story."

"You're right," Buck I. "Your first duty is to the *Examiner*. "A wife always comes second."

"I'm glad we've gotten that priority straightened out," Susan said, getting up from the table and excusing herself. "If I'm getting married in just a few hours, I've got to go home and get ready, and also get packed for New York."

"I'll walk you to the door," Buck III said, getting up and heading around the table to her.

Susan kissed old Buck on the cheek again. "Very soon, sooner than I ever imagined, I'm going to be part of this family."

"Welcome aboard," the old man said.

Just as Buck III was escorting her out, the butler appeared. "Telephone for you. It's Robert Dante calling from Miami."

Susan looked imploringly into Buck's eyes before taking his hand and kissing him lightly on the lips. "I know the way out. See you at six." She hurried from the house.

Buck I looked glaringly at Buck III, almost defying him to take that phone call.

Without looking back, Buck III headed for the front hall and Robert's call.

***

Gene didn't mean to and even at the last minute he swore he wasn't going to show up, but at a quarter to two he found himself getting in his car and heading to the reservoir where he'd talked with Sandy.

It was shortly after two as he walked along the wall where Sandy had shared secrets about Leroy's Lolito ring. There was no one in sight. Did he really expect the boy to show up?

As he turned the corner he spotted the red-haired boy tossing rocks into the water. For one brief moment, and if life had gone differently, he felt that he could have been Sandy's father taking his son for a long walk after a family Sunday dinner. That's the way Sister Rose said was the only right and decent way to live.

Spotting him, Sandy called out, "Gene." He raced toward Gene and threw himself into his arms. "I missed you."

Gene felt awkward holding the boy in his arms, so he gently broke Sandy's hold on him. "How you doing, kid?"

"It was awful."

"What happened?" Gene asked.

"After leaving you, I was confused. I tried to go back to work but I met this old guy who wanted me to piss on him. I found everything so disgusting. In some strange way, I felt I belonged to you. I couldn't mess myself up with anybody, because from the very first I felt I had to keep myself pure for you from now on."

"You're not talking sense," Gene said, fearing this sudden intimacy. "What did you do?"

"With the money you gave me, I went and rented myself a cheap motel room. They had a little restaurant next to it. I went in there last night and ordered myself a steak. I hadn't had a steak in a long time, and I was really hungry. Then I went back to my room, lay in bed, watched TV. Mostly I dreamed about being your boy. About you taking care of me and about my loving you."

"You're talking shit. Cut it out!" Gene turned from the sight of the boy and walked rapidly along the wall as if trying to escape his presence.

Sandy raced to catch up. "I didn't mean to say anything wrong. I was just telling you what's in my heart. Is that bad?"

"I appreciate your being honest with me," Gene said, coming to a stop and looking into the boy's trusting eyes. "But this talk of love. You hardly know me."

"You're right. I'm trying like hell to get to know you. You won't let me."

"You're just a kid."

"Hell, yes, I'm just a kid. I've got no one. No parents. I'm homeless. I need someone to help me out, mister. Take care of me. The only thing I've got to offer is my body. But with you I've got something else to give."

"What are you talking about?"

He reached for Gene's hand and held it, squeezing it hard. "That something else is love. I want to love you, and you won't even give me a chance."

"It's not that..."

"It's what? Tell me. What is preventing you from loving me and taking care of me? Are you trying to bullshit me and tell me you don't need love?"

Gene turned away from the boy's intensity, walking over to a park bench.

In moments, Sandy joined him on the bench. He reached to hold Gene's hand but Gene pulled away. "I know a lot about you," Sandy said. "More than you think I know."

"What do you know?" he asked, his mouth dry. He didn't really want Sandy to answer.

"My friend Jill remembers you very well."

"I don't know anyone named that." Gene felt his anger rise.

"Jill Henson. You remember?"

The mention of that name sent shivers through Gene. That was the name of the little girl he'd exposed himself to. She'd be about Sandy's age today, maybe two or three years older. It couldn't be the same Jill. How would she know a boy prostitute like Sandy from the Combat Zone?

"I know you're Gene Robinson. You've had your picture in the papers a lot. Jill told me what happened. She understands. She's a hooker now. She told me that you caused her no harm."

She's forgiven me?"

"There is nothing to forgive."

"I wish I could go back and relive that day. It's haunted me ever since. Do you think my doing that to her made her a hooker?"

"It was her damn mama who made Jill a hooker. It was my own God damn mama who made me become a whore. When you kick a twelve-year-old out onto the street with no money and no clothes because you think he's gay, how's the kid supposed to live?"

"I know," Gene said.

"Jill knows how to take care of herself. She's tough and into karate in case some john tries to get really kinky with her. I've seen her once or twice in the Combat Zone deliver some really chopping blows."

"I don't want to talk about her any more," Gene said, getting up and continuing the walk.

Sandy jumped up and trailed him, falling in with his rapid strides. "I don't want to talk about Jill either. I want to talk about us."

"There is no us to talk about. You're just an underage kid. I shouldn't be seen with you. Probably subjecting myself to another arrest."

"Let me come home with you. Give me a place to stay. I'll work hard for you until I'm old enough to get a regular job. Then I'll pay you rent. I promise."

"I can't."

"Do you want me to go back into that Combat Zone? Trying to find some old creep who wants me to piss on him. Or, even worse, have him piss on me. Someone who's gonna torture me. Is that what you want for me? Someone who loves you."

"You don't love me."

"Try me." Sandy reached for his arm and with a surprising strength held it firmly and looked into Gene's face. Tears were streaming from Sandy's eyes. "Give me a chance, mister."

Gene felt he'd lost his mind but he put his arm around Sandy. "I'm taking you home with me." He looked into the young boy's face, which was filled with gratitude. "It's not about sex, okay? It's about caring for someone. Maybe I could take care of you, and you could take care of me."

"You'll never regret this," Sandy said.

"I can only hope so." Gene looked up as a flock of birds flew low over their heads. "You told me you make a great chili. Let's stop by a grocery store and pick up some ingredients. I love chili. I've got an appointment later in the afternoon, but when I get home I want to smell that chili pot."

"You've got yourself a deal."

He reached for Gene's hand, and this time Gene freely offered it. "And you've got yourself a boy. From this day forth, I'm your boy."

Gene swallowed hard, enjoying the first strong breeze of the day. As he took the boy's hand and walked along, he realized how incriminating this appeared. He felt he was walking into madness, but could not turn back.

***

In the cottage in back of the Buck Brooke I estate, Buck III eagerly awaited Gene's arrival. He'd already stripped in anticipation of their Jacuzzi bath, and he'd acquired some illegal Cuban cigars and a choice bottle of Armagnac from his grandfather's cellar for the occasion.

The cottage had always been his retreat from the world, even from his own parents. Buck I had given it to him and the old man had never visited him here ever since, recognizing that it was forbidden territory.

Buck III had never invited Robert here before, although Gene had visited several times during their university years. Once when they'd taken two campus beauties here for sex, they had made love to the women in the same king-sized bed. Buck had become more excited than ever, not by his woman, but by watching Gene in action. He'd caught Gene looking at him at the time, and was left with the odd sensation that they were not making love to the women, but to each other.

Buck plopped down on a chaise longue on his back veranda overlooking a ravine. His talk with Robert was fresh in his mind. Robert's mother was holding onto life but her doctors didn't give her much time. Robert said he wanted to return, but was advised to stay on for another day or so because the end appeared close at hand. Buck had promised to fly to Miami for the funeral. Robert claimed he was going out of his mind missing Buck so very much and would call him later tonight.

Buck was glad Robert wasn't in Okeechobee. What Buck couldn't tell him was that he was marrying Susan. That would have to be explained to Robert in person, and it would take all of Buck's persuasive powers to overcome Robert's objections.

Buck shuddered to think what Susan's reaction would be if she learned that her former husband was about to have a rendezvous with her future husband.

As soon as he'd entered the cottage, and before stripping down, he placed a call to Milton Green, his attorney who also represented many of his grandfather's affairs as well. Very quickly Buck told "Uncle Milty" of Buck I's demands and threats of disinheritance.

"He absolutely means what he says," Milty said. "He'll do it too. You'd be a fool not to agree to it, providing Susan will cooperate. We're told that he has maybe weeks left to live. His will contains no provisions beyond the grave. What the hell, you could get a divorce the day your grandfather dies."

"It doesn't seem right somehow," Buck said.

"A lot of things don't seem right. Everything I do every day of my life isn't right. When you're your own man, you can do whatever you want. I'm sure you'll make it up to Susan somehow. I could propose some sort of settlement for her that would be fair to all parties."

"Maybe."

"There's no fucking maybe about it," Milty said. "It's an open and shut case. Buck I might have quoted you figures about his worth, but he's completely out of touch with reality. I'm sure he's quoting valuations from the fifties. Hell, this is 1977. His estate is worth millions more than he thinks it is. If all of us live to see the New Year ten years from now when you're only thirty seven years old, can you imagine what it's going to be worth then?"

"I'm sure behaving cold-blooded."

"Don't worry about it. It's time you grew up and quit thinking with your liberal heart and soul. One of your former girl friends told me you've got a big pair of balls on you. About time you started clanking them before you turned thirty."

"I don't know."

"Cut the hesitation crap! Go through with the marriage. If it turns out to be a mess, old Uncle Milty is here for you. I've got you out of messes before, and we don't even have to go into what they were."

"No, we don't."

"Trust me on this one. Listen to me. Your grandfather bought land in central Florida during the Depression. He actually made money during the Depression when most of us here didn't have a pot to piss in. I remember as a kid I had to steal oranges and avocados from the fields to stay alive. I even stole chickens for my family so we'd have some meat on the table. When I was a little boy doing that, old Buck was acquiring land for peanuts in Florida. I though he was going to buy up the state. Even though much of that land is wilderness now, I predict that in your lifetime entire towns are going to be built on land he owns. Or, as the case may be, land that you will own. You'll be one of the richest men in this country.

"As rich as Sister Rose?"

"Maybe not that rich. But then she's got a staff of twenty-five just counting her contributions. Every time she appears on television, contributions start flowing in. A lot from Social Security checks."

"I don't want to think about that."

"Do what the old man says. If you don't, you'll spend the rest of your life regretting it."

"It really scares the shit out of me."

"If you're dumb enough not to do it for yourself, think of Robert. You guys could have a future of diamonds, champagne, and roses. What a life. A big yacht to sail the world with your own crew. If you can't do this for yourself, do it for him."

"It's all but certain it's a done deal. I've got a lot of explaining to do. Not only to Robert but to someone else."

"Who is this someone else? I thought you kept me informed of all your nocturnal adventures. After all, I'm your lawyer."

"Uncle Milty, as much as I love and trust you, I can't bring myself to tell you about this involvement."

"Shit, man, I know who it is. After all, I'm the smartest lawyer in Florida. That's why you love me. You're talking Gene here."

"You guessed it."

"Better talk yourself out of it pretty damn quick. You're dealing with a nut case. I learned privately that he's up for a very serious psychiatric examination in a day or so. I hear he's going to get thrown off the police force. There's more than one screw missing in Gene. Also, what's he going to think when he learns you're marrying his former wife?"

"That I shudder to think about."

"Drop him—and I mean that."

"I've got to sort things out in my own way."

"Take my advice," Milty said. "You pay enough for it. Marry Susan at six. Dump her later with a settlement. Get rid of Gene. Other than Shelley Phillips, Robert is the most beautiful boy in Okeechobee. Maybe in all of Florida. Even when you're an old man, Robert will be going down on that big eighty-five year old cock of yours. Robert is marriage material. A companion for life. Go with Robert. That's my advice. I'll send my bill tomorrow."

"We'll keep in touch, Uncle Milty. I need you."

"I need you, too, you handsome hunk. If I were twenty years younger, and didn't have my own darling Patrick, I'd go after you myself, even though I hear you stretch assholes out of shape."

"Just flattering rumors."

"As soon as Robert gets back from that Miami shit he's going through, I want you two over to our place. You know you like Patrick's cooking better than anybody else's."

"It's a date."

"I love you, baby. Not just as your attorney. You're like my son. I love you Gentile boys with your foreskin intact. I'm crazy about each and every one of you. You and Robert, Patrick and me will be sailing the world one day. Having a gay old time."

"Give Patrick a kiss for me," Buck said.

"Hey, I hear you're going to be named sexiest man of the year. The only thing wrong with that, you should be named sexiest man of the decade."

"Is that for sure?"

"It is indeed. I heartily concur. They were late in discovering you. I've always known how hot you are."

"That's really nice, Milty. While I've got you on the phone, I've got to ask one big favor."

"For you, anything."

"Has your tux come back from the cleaners?"

"All twenty five of them in all colors. Kept ready and waiting for any occasion."

"Fine, then get your fat ass over here at six o'clock. You're my best man." Buck hung up the phone.

Closing his eyes, he let the breeze blow across his body. He opened his eyes again, enjoying the way the sun broke through the shade trees. He heard footsteps coming up from the ravine. By the sound of those booted feet, it could only be Gene.

***

In T-shirts and jeans, Gene stood before a naked Buck on his veranda, as the sun headed down over the trees in the ravine. "Thanks for stripping," Gene said. "Saves me the trouble of having to remove all your clothing. I want you naked as a jay-bird for this romp in the Jacuzzi."

"You're looking good," Buck said. "Why are you being so modest wearing all those clothes? Got something you're ashamed for me to see?"

"Just for that, I'm going to have you screaming very soon, 'Take it out. It's hurting me. I can't handle anything so big.'"

"Promises."

Gene lowered his body over Buck on the chaise longue and inserted his tongue deep within Buck's mouth. Gene ran his tongue across Buck's eyelids before washing each ear. He raised up slightly as Buck helped him remove his T-shirt. He enjoyed Buck's hands as they traveled over his chest and arms. Gene reached below to find Buck fully aroused. "Christ, I just walk in the door and you get a hard-on."

"I wish I could arouse you as well."

"You have." Gene stood up and removed his jeans, all except his jockey shorts. Buck preferred to do that himself. When Buck slipped down the jockeys, Gene's full erection rose in Buck's face. He gasped for breath as Buck took it in his mouth and expertly with his tongue pushed the foreskin back so he could savor the taste of the head.

Gene lowered himself over Buck again, kissing and licking his lips, enjoying his own taste on Buck's mouth. "I'm hungry today," Gene said. "Real hungry. There's not one inch of your body that's going to be missed."

Buck took the plunge into the hot, bubbling waters of the Jacuzzi. Gene followed right behind and spun Buck around, kissing his mouth and biting his neck.

"You're a fucking cannibal," Buck said, breaking away. "I think there's vampire blood in you."

"You don't want me to stop, do you?" Gene asked.

"Never that."

Gene resumed biting into Buck. He pulled back slightly when he sensed Buck was experiencing acute pain. Gene was overcome with a sudden desire to taste Buck's blood. Maybe it was that talk of a vampire that did it for him. He didn't know how he was going to go about this, but was determined to taste Buck's blood before he emerged from the Jacuzzi. Drinking his saliva or even his semen weren't enough. He actually wanted to taste blood.

Instead of that, Buck reached over to the ledge and poured him an Armagnac that was followed by a Cuban cigar which Buck lit for him before lighting his own and lifting his own drink.

"I don't know what this is, and I'm no fucking food and drink connoisseur like you are, but this is the best stuff I've ever drunk. The second best drink. That stuff you make for me in your balls is pure nectar from the gods."

Buck moved closer to Gene and put his arm around him, resting his drink at the edge of the Jacuzzi. He blew cigar smoke in Gene's face, and Gene returned the favor. The aroma of Buck himself, the brandy, and the cigar was a total aphrodisiac to Gene. He found himself growing harder.

Maybe it was the lethal brandy, but one side of Gene's brain seemed to be winning out completely over the other side. He didn't want the austere life he'd contemplated. A life dedicated to a Jesus he couldn't touch, feel, or love. What he wanted—now more than ever—was a hot body next to him. That could only be Buck himself.

The way he felt now, he wanted to spend the rest of his life with Buck. No more sneaking around. He wanted to walk open and free with Buck, even hold his hand in public if it came to that. What did his stupid job matter any more at the police department? With Buck by his side, he didn't have to grovel for a dollar. If someone ever tried to make trouble for Gene again, he knew that Buck would be there to destroy the enemy for him. At first he'd been confused, thinking Sister

Rose was the answer for him. Now he knew differently. Buck was that safe refuge.

Hell, they might even adopt Sandy and give him the good life too. He just knew Buck would like Sandy, and might become a surrogate father for him.

Gene crushed out his cigar in an ashtray at the edge of the Jacuzzi. Seeing him do that, Buck did the same. Noticing a hefty swig of brandy left in his glass, Gene raised it in a toast to Buck. "Here's to us."

Buck smiled and looked deeply in his eyes. "Here's to us."

Gene turned and faced Buck in the bubbling water. Gene knew what was going to happen next and so did Buck. But both men hesitated for a few seconds before the action began, in anticipation of their mutual pleasure.

He pulled Buck to him and stuck his tongue in his mouth to savor the rest of the brandy. He licked Buck's lips and found himself biting harder and harder, and Buck involuntarily tried to back away but he held him closer, chewing on his lower lip. When the first blood came, he sucked it into his mouth and exerted such a powerful suction that he tasted more and more blood. Instead of Buck pulling away, he moved in closer to Gene. It was as if he knew what Gene wanted and was determined to let him drink from him, in spite of the pain. Finally, he pulled away and gently tongued Buck's neck and ears. He whispered in his ear. "I got carried away. I'm sorry."

"It's okay."

"I've never wanted to taste anybody as much as I've wanted to taste you," Gene said, lifting Buck from the water and spreading him along the edge of the Jacuzzi, face down. He kissed each cheek of his ass, biting gently, before opening Buck up to fully explore his secret spot. As much as he savored the taste and smell, it was not enough. Slowly he lowered Buck into the water, pressing Buck's back up against his body. It wasn't gentleness that prevailed when he abruptly entered Buck. There was no gradual easing in but a violent thrust.

Buck screamed out in pain but Gene held him closer and tighter. The more Buck struggled to free himself from this impalement, the greater the pleasure for Gene. The squirming brought greater thrills racing through Gene's body. Buck fought back but Gene held him onto the penetration.

The struggle between two evenly matched men seemed to go on

forever. Eventually Buck stopped squirming and trying to free himself. He moved his body up against Gene which Gene accepted as total surrender. Even as Gene began he knew it was going to be the fuck of a lifetime, one he would remember always. He'd found his mate.

He bit Buck's neck and reached around and fondled Buck's cock, before weighing his heavy balls. Gene's hand returned to Buck and it was then he felt his friend's orgasm. Buck couldn't restrain himself. Even as Gene was feeling Buck's body going through the throes of orgasm, he continued unrelentingly. For all he knew hours could have gone by as he found himself thrusting even harder. Only when he felt Buck going through his second orgasm did Gene release himself inside Buck.

Long after both bodies had stopped spewing, they clung to each other until Gene gradually pulled out. Even then, Buck's muscles clenched around him.

In the shower they were tender with each other, soaping and rubbing each other's bodies. Gene tenderly and ever so gently kissed Buck's bruised lips. "I'm sorry," he whispered in Buck's ear under the running water. "But it tasted good."

"You're kinky," Buck said, breaking away and stepping out of the shower. As he was drying himself off, he threw a towel to Gene. The phone rang. Buck answered it. "Okay," he said, "send it on down." He turned to get dressed. "You'd better find your jeans too. Someone's coming down from the house."

Without questioning it, Gene went out to the veranda and picked up his discarded jeans and T-shirt and put them on. He stared into the distance, noticing how much lower the sun had gone down since he'd first raced up the ravine. Stepping into his boots, he wondered if Sandy were indeed at home making tonight's chili. He was going to invite Buck over to join them. As soon as some apparent delivery was made from the main house, he'd ask Buck one very important question, the most important question he would ever ask anyone in his entire life.

He was going to ask Buck to live with him as husband and husband. They wouldn't have to go to any church to have any ceremony performed. A total commitment from Buck was all that was needed.

He watched as Buck headed for the front door to answer the buzzer. As Buck walked across that room, Gene realized he loved him as he had no other person on earth. Yet at the same time he was filled with this awful feeling that something horrible was about to happen. It should be the happiest moment of his life yet there was something ominous in the air.

Buck opened the door. It was old Buck's manservant, carrying a dark suit or perhaps a tux for Buck. As Buck shut the door, Gene walked into the living room.

A look on Buck's face told him that something was dreadfully wrong.

"There's something going on here," Gene said.

"It's all happened so fast," Buck said apologetically. "I'm going to tell you something and you're not going to like it. You've got to promise to hear me out."

"What is it?" Gene asked, a growing apprehension crossing his mind. He was breaking out in a cold sweat.

"I'm going to marry Susan at six o'clock."

Gene wasn't sure he'd really heard the words right. All he knew was he found himself running down the ravine. Vaguely he remembered Buck calling after him. He was on his motorcycle and long gone before Buck could ever catch up.

As he drove into the oncoming evening, he heard Buck's voice more clearly calling to him. It was as if Buck were right behind him. But when Gene looked back from his speeding cycle, there was no one.

***

As Buck rushed Susan to the airport, she turned to look at the man she'd just married. As long as she'd known him, he was a stranger to her. His lower lip was bandaged. He told her that in his nervousness about their imminent wedding, he'd cut himself with a razor.

When he'd arrived at the ceremony, she was left with the distinct feeling that he'd been in some sort of violent argument.

"Why did you marry me?" she asked.

"I'm madly in love with you," he said, turning to smile at her.

"The real reason. I'm a tough hard-nosed reporter, remember?"

"Because my granddad threatened to disinherit me if I didn't."

"Not very flattering," she said,

"He may have only days to live," he said, his eyes still firmly on the road in front of him. "You and I will have the rest of our lives to sort this out. It was an old man's dying wish."   " W h e r e does that leave us?"

"I don't know. Fly north, do your thing, and come back here. We'll work on it."

"Does Robert know?"

"I haven't told him yet."

"You're planning to soon, I hope, before he reads it in the paper."

"We're not announcing it to the press yet," he said. "At least not now. Everyone's sworn to secrecy at the moment."

"How do you think Robert is going to take this?" she asked.

"He'll go ballistic over this man-and-wife shit."

"Shit? Is that what you think of our marriage?"

"Come on, get off my case. I can't even sort out my own reactions to the marriage—much less anybody else's."

"On the plane north, I'll think about what I've gotten myself into," she said. When I get back, we'll see where this marriage is going to go."

"Let's be rather blunt," he said. "It's a marriage of convenience. If it's to become something more, time will tell."

"Where do you want me to live when I get back? At your home?"

"No, Robert lives there and has for many years. It's his home. For the time being, why don't you continue to live in your apartment?"

"Thanks," she said sarcastically.

"I didn't mean forever. I have three beautiful condos on the upper beach. My parents gave them to me. You can take your pick. Move into the one you like best."

"That's a generous offer. After all, I have married up in the world."

"You'll have a new car waiting when you get back. Charge cards. Whatever you want."

"That's very generous. You make me sound like the mistress of a very rich man."

"Forgive me."

"There's nothing to forgive. I'm going into this marriage with my eyes wide open. I'm no longer some idealistic school girl like I was when I married Gene Robinson."

"It's only fair that you get something out of this marriage," he said. "You're doing me a God damn big favor."

"I know you're a man of your word. It looks to me like I'll get a lot out of this marriage. The only thing I won't get is a husband. But what the hell."

"One can't have everything," he said. He didn't say anything else, and neither did she, until they arrived at the loading ramp.

His kiss good-bye was perfunctory, but after all, he had a cut lip.

***

The moment he came in through his back door, entering his once dark kitchen, Gene could tell a transformation had occurred. The place was brightly lit, and the open windows let in the dying sun. The smell of chili bubbling on the stove permeated the air. The floor had been scrubbed, the surfaces brightly polished. The place looked like it did when his mother was still alive. Sandy was nowhere to be seen.

Gene searched for him, going first up front to the living room before checking the dining room and even the bathroom. Thinking Sandy might have fallen asleep, he checked the guest bedroom. No one. There was only one room left: his bedroom. He walked back to his bedroom to find Sandy making up his bed with fresh sheets.

"Don't you ever clean up this joint?" Sandy asked, rushing to give him a hug. The boy wore only a pair of cut-off denims, and Gene hugged him briefly, fearing the intimate contact of skin.

"I wasn't gone that long," Gene said. "How did you get so much done so soon? I thought all you teenage kids like to live in a pig sty."

"Not me, handsome. I like things sparkling clean, and this house looks like it'll take me weeks to get it in shape. I'm a good gardener too. That yard really needs work."

"Thanks for everything. I needed someone here when I came home tonight." He turned and headed for the kitchen for a beer.

"I hope things didn't go wrong at your appointment," Sandy said.

"It didn't go the way I planned."

Sandy washed off the beer can and opened it for him. "I'm here if you want to talk about it."

"I can't right now."

Sandy went over to stir the chili pot. "The phone has been ringing off the wall. Buck Brooke has been calling. He sounded really desperate. I know the name. He's the publisher of the *Examiner*. I feel some major story is breaking."

"If he calls again, tell him I'm not home," Gene said. "I'm starved, man. I like my chili fiery hot."

Sandy rubbed his fingers across Gene's cheek. "I bet you do."

"I'd like to stay here with you tonight but I can't. I'm on duty. That march through the Combat Zone. There could be violence."

"I'm coming with you," Sandy said.

"You're staying here."

"Promise me, you'll take care. You're all I've got in the world."

Gene smelled the bowl of chili set before him before reaching for some crackers. "I'll take care of you, kid."

"I trust you," Sandy said, reaching for his hand.

Gene tasted the chili. "That's the best I've ever had. Do you know how to cook anything else?"

"I can make a great western omelette. I can fry a mean steak, and I know how to stuff a chicken and roast it. I noticed a cookbook on that shelf."

"It belonged to my mother. *The Joy of Cooking*."

"I bet if I read it, I'll learn to cook a lot more dishes."

Gene smiled at him before devouring the chili. "I bet you can." His gargantuan hunger surprised him. He didn't think he'd be hungry at a time like this, but he was ravenous.

Sandy sat across from him, enjoying a coke with his chili. "Thanks for giving me a place to stay. I don't remember when I've been so happy. I'll have our bed waiting tonight."

"You'd better fix up the guest room. I'm not wanting sex from you. But I do need to have you here. Every man who's brought you home with him wanted sex. I just need your company."

"If you want me to sleep up in the guest room, I'll be there. If you want some company, just pick me up in your arms and carry me to your bedroom."

Gene put down his fork. "All I need now is a hug."

Sandy got up from the table and walked across to Gene. He grabbed the boy and held him as tightly as he'd ever held anybody before. Then he burst into uncontrollable sobbing, and he was a man who never cried.

***

Ever since three o'clock that afternoon, protest marchers, answering Rose's call to arms, had been assembling at the entrance to the Combat Zone. Through Roland, Buck had assigned every reporter the *Examiner* could spare, and he planned to write an eyewitness account himself, hoping it would perk up his column.

He put through a final hasty call to Gene. A young man—or perhaps a boy—answered the phone. He was unaware that Gene lived with someone. The boy told him that Gene was on duty tonight.

After putting down the phone, he dialed Robert from their home before heading for the zone. "How's your mom?"

"Hanging on. She's in a coma."

"I wish I could be there with you tonight, but I'm covering Rose's march."

"I'm going to watch it on TV," Robert said. "In the safety of the hospital." Fear came into his voice. "You'll be real careful, won't you?"

"I can look after myself."

"You can't even take a bath without me," Robert said.

"Just don't become part of the violence—and don't play hero."

"I love my baby," Buck said."

"I miss my man."

"Gotta go." Buck put down the phone before Robert could say any more. He just couldn't bring himself to tell him about his marriage to Susan.

***

As night fell over the city, Rose's parade had begun. Buck, trapped in a parking lot of buses and cars, missed her first appearance. He noted a lot of pickup trucks driven in from the central part of the state.

At the completely disorganized tail of the candlelit march, he finally set foot on The Strip. By then, Rose was at least ten blocks ahead, moving toward People's Park at the end.

As he made his way through the crowd holding candles, he tried to stay on the sidewalk so he could observe the action better. He kept getting pushed and shoved to the center of the street, lost in a milling sea. Drawing a few Yoga breaths, he tried to calm himself and estimate the number of marchers.

They seemed to be in the thousands, and he refused to believe that the march had been spontaneously called only that morning at the temple. He'd learned that the demonstration, at least in the vanguard, had been carefully staged. All afternoon, buses had fanned out to the suburbs, not only hauling in protesters, but recruiting them as well. The *Examiner* had discovered that all the cultist churches in the city and neighboring suburbs had been notified, with appeals to the various congregations to turn out en masse.

In a shirt and jeans, he found himself swimming in a sea of brightly colored polyester leisure suits. He wondered if all this synthetic fabric were inflammable, because many people were pushed dangerously close to burning candles.

The police had long ago cordoned off the entire Combat Zone so that marchers could parade down the center of the street, the fiery glow of their candles competing against the glaring marquees of the porno movie houses, advertising such X-rated pictures as Jack Wrangler in "Heavy Equipment" at the Adonis and a "luscious new Italian star" at the Pussycat Cinema.

To him, some of the protest demonstrators—spiritual descendants of Cotton Mather—seemed rigid-faced and frightened to be in such hostile, unfamiliar terrain. Many held Bibles and waved American flags. One woman, whose face reflected her firm belief in God and patriotism, carried a placard on which she'd mounted a stern, foreboding photograph of John Foster Dulles, as if she'd been forced to search in America's attic for a man she could trust.

From the lobbies of the seedy, "hot bed" hotels lining The Strip, television sets blared with fresh reports of the marching taking place right outside their doors. Not since the anti-war protests of the Sixties had Okeechobee witnessed such a massive street demonstration.

Most of the "johns" who frequented the zone at night had disappeared from the street, probably going home to their wives. He suspected that some of those sex-hunters had joined their wives in the protest march in a neat piece of hypocrisy.

It was one of the hottest nights he had suffered through in the city, a bubbling ninety-six degrees Fahrenheit—just the type of weather to make tempers flare. He needed a drink in the worst way. At a singles bar on The Strip, he fended off at least two women who wanted to relieve him of his solitude.

At first his drinking had been cautious but, the longer he sat at the bar, the more he drank. Here he was in a bar spending his honeymoon night when he should be out covering the march like one of his reporters, or even flying north with his bride.

Getting up from the bar, he paid the bill and headed back into the street.

***

To Rose, the march lived up to her expectations and, at the beginning of her crusade, she knew she'd struck a responsive chord in the public's mind.

The crowds were almost hypnotic to her. With such mass support of her stand, she believed she could light bonfires across America. Everything depended on Okeechobee. She'd selected it as her test city, knowing she had to win here, and win big, before storming the continent.

That afternoon she'd suffered almost a seizure, as a kind of madness whirled around her. For two hours her staff feared she might have to cancel her appearance. But without her presence, she realized, the entire plan she'd worked on for so many years would fail.

Toward sunset, she'd regained control of herself and that horrible shaking feeling that had come over her had left her. She'd felt serene and her mirror had confirmed she'd never looked better. She was ready to face the cameras, and she knew that before midnight in California, her image would be beamed into millions of American homes.

When she faced the biggest glare of the TV news cameras, she'd deliberately moved away from some of the older and more overweight followers and toward the direction of a tall, young, and handsome man who kept getting closer to her, looking up at her like a love-sick puppy. He bore an amazing resemblance to Tyrone Power.

With him at her side, she hoped to hit the front pages across the nation tomorrow. She wanted her crusade to appear to be a spontaneous demonstration of the young and vigorous. At no point did she want to connect herself with caricatured members of her own generation. That's why she'd tutored Shelley so carefully for his appearance tonight.

She held her hand to her chest, as if embracing herself. The delusion and panic gone now, she knew she was on the verge of fulfilling some of the wildest dreams that had grown out of her dark moments.

***

Caught unaware, a few ultra-left groups had tried to mount a hasty counterprotest. They appeared weak and vastly outnumbered. Some lesbian mothers wheeled empty baby carriages, and a few shirtless bartenders from the topless singles bar paraded, along with a scattering of black militants. One young minister carried a placard asking, "IF JESUS HAD HIS PETER, WHY CAN'T I?"

Buck was astonished to find a group of male high school students in Ku Klux Klan hoods. Accepting one of their tabloids, he learned at a glance that it was the same newspaper he'd discovered stored at Rose's printing headquarters. He stepped up to one of the hooded boys. "Who prints this shit?" The boy yanked the paper from Buck's hand and ran in the other direction.

Buck was distracted by a wide-eyed, almost crazed-looking girl who ran right into the sea of marchers, flaunting a large blowup of Anne Frank at them, with a provocative question hand-lettered on it. HAVE YOU FORGOTTEN HITLER? Her boyfriend, dressed as an American Indian, carried another placard with the bold claim, DISCIPLES OF HATE ARE NOT CHRISTIAN.

Not only were the two trying to block the marchers, they seemed to tantalize them, as if goading them to strike back. Buck immediately feared for the couple's safety. A burly man knocked the young woman down, and her boyfriend slugged her attacker in the jaw. This seemed to anger the marchers even more. A few people kicked the young man as he lay screaming on the sidewalk, his nose bleeding, his placard crushed under marching feet. A group of counter-protesters, sensing the brutality of the marchers, rushed into the melee, even though policemen tried to cordon them off. The police flailed the air with their night sticks, sparing no victim.

Buck watched in horror as a TV camera recorded a scene. Suddenly, the acrid smell of tear gas permeated the street, as hundreds fled with running eyes, raw throats. Covering his mouth with a handkerchief, he stumbled back into an alleyway, hoping for a breath of air to cleanse his lungs.

In plain clothes, Gene had been assigned to the parade to spot potential trouble. To do that, he'd joined with the other protest marchers, pretending to be one of them. He felt he was. At one point he had come intimately close to Rose.

Before he left police headquarters, Biff, his chief, had made it clear to him what was *real* trouble and what was merely "just honest dissent from God-fearing people." Biff didn't need to tell him not to interfere with Rose's supporters.

Up front with Rose, Gene experienced no disorder, no clashes of opposing forces, no violence.

The presence of the evangelist herself seemed to mesmerize the crowd—not only her followers, but the spectators who'd lined both sides of the street, perhaps to jeer and hurl insults. Even they appeared subdued, their gawking faces aware they were witnesses to a spiritual phenomenon.

When Rose passed in front of a massage parlor, Jupiter's Retreat, she stopped and mounted the steps. All the patrons had fled. Only the maintenance crew flocked to the entrance to see what was happening.

At first she didn't speak, standing there regally, waiting for the marchers to quiet down. Someone gave her a hand microphone. Her violet eyes glanced neither left nor right. She stared straight ahead, as if fixed on some star unseen by the rest of her followers. In her radiant face, with its wet sensuality, Gene detected an irresistible combination of the angel and the devil, and in that moment he knew Rose had struggled with the same demons he had. It was obvious to him that she'd already conquered hers.

In her soft, well-modulated voice that seemed to grow in power and tempo as she talked, she told her audience, "God drew a ring of fire and invited me to step into it." As she spoke, and Gene moved closer to the steps, her voice took on a curious erotic quality to him.

"In tomorrow's newspapers," she said, "I'll be attacked, abused and libeled, as I always am. My own life will be threatened by forces working to undermine and ultimately topple the government of this great country. One way to weaken us is to encourage degeneracy, destroy the nuclear family."

As she looked up at Jupiter's Retreat, the windows overhead appeared as dark as the lust they hid within. The evangelist's face became pallid with bitterness, the more she stared at the fortress-like windows. The candlelight caused her silver earrings to shimmer and, more than that, it made her face suddenly luminous as she turned from the windows and into the soft glow again. Shadows streaked her cheeks, making her infinitely desirable to Gene, a feeling he'd had for no other woman, not even Susan. Yet at the same time, she seemed to pull him into a sphere of terrible temptation, as one might be drawn to death.

"They call this a pleasure palace," she said. "We call it a cesspool of human depravity. Join our crusade in wiping it out!" Loud cheers went up from the protesters. She raised her hands to acknowledge the support and to quiet the marchers.

"We feel sorry for the poor, mentally disturbed individuals on this street who have lost their way. Not knowing life's real blessings, its true joy, they have turned instead to the artificial and the tawdry, the sinful and evil. For that, we pity them. What we can't do is to allow them to pull us along with them in their leap to suicide." Again, more shouts of approval, none louder than from Gene himself.

When she resumed her leadership of the vanguard of the march, she'd picked up a lightness of step, almost a waltz. Gaily triumphant, she headed for People's Park, where she knew a police squad car waited to take her away before any trouble began.

No longer fearing his flesh would betray him, Gene joined her in a kind of liberation. Never before had he felt so confident of conquering the demons within himself, and also those who lurked outside, waiting not only to destroy him, but to harm Rose. Even though Rose might not know it, he'd be out there, protecting and defending her, following her wherever she appeared in public. After all, she'd warned tonight that there were those waiting to take her life. Before that happened, those forces would have to kill him first—and he didn't destruct easily.

***

Buck fought his way to the bandstand in the center of the park where, to his disappointment, he learned Rose wasn't going to appear. Policemen in gas masks holding shotguns stood ominously by as children ran through beds, trampling over the flowers that someone had worked so hard to plant. Seeing the well-armored policemen, one girl near him said, "Somebody could get killed."

On the bandstand, a group of Tennessee "Possum Hunters" were soothing the crowd with sound of—

"Gimme that ol' time religion,
Gimme that ol' time religion,
Gimme that ol' time religion,
It's good enough for me..."

One fiddle player in pink sequins seemed straight from the stage of the Grand Ole Opry. A dumpy, over-the-hill blonde deep-throated the microphone.

Uncle Skeeter Hay, the chief "Possum Hunter," stepped up in front of the microphone in his ten-gallon hat and pot belly that bulged over his buttercup yellow, double-knit trousers. His chartreuse jacket had a covered wagon imprinted on its back. He announced, "We've got some spontaneous words from a little preacher, a child of God."

Buck braced himself, knowing, but still not wanting to believe, that that could only mean Shelley himself.

And it was. Shelley at first seemed nervous, terrified of his audience, and Buck feared he could never make it as the Billy Graham of the pubescents.

"I will not be recruited into sin by one of my teachers," Shelley promised his audience. "No law in the land is going to force me to look upon moral lepers as role models."

Buck winced at this blatant slander and gross vulgarization, as he realized what kind of tone Rose's moral crusade was ready to sound.

As Shelley moved deeper into his speech, Buck felt that the boy was warming to his task, showing greater ease and stage presence in front of the audience. The boy switched gears, becoming more emotional, his voice filled with a mounting hysteria as he beseeched his audience to, "Join me and my Christian family in a nation-wide campaign against the offensive on God and his moral laws. Though the deviates in all walks of life will try to sabotage our moral crusade, with God's help we'll fight them every step of the way."

The air seemed heavy and hot to Buck. He found himself arching his body, as if poised for a fight.

"The moral lepers of this world are going to hell where they'll burn for eternity," Shelley predicted. "The anti-Christs. The job before us tonight is to save the children—young boys like me—from such a road of sin. Keep us out of the jailhouse of the damned!"

Buck was fascinated at Shelley's blue eyes as they were cast upward to the spots lighting the stage, making him appear almost cherubic, although Buck, with wry amusement, felt that Shelley was probably the most blatant moral leper in the park.

"Even though I'm very young," Shelley said, "my mother has taught me what it means to be lost to Jesus. Because I believe in my mother's holy war against the worshipers of the devil, I'm going to set aside my school lessons, all my personal dreams, in fact, to devote my little self to the cause of saving our children from the clutches of the godless moral lepers. I'm giving up everything to help my mother, Sister Rose."

The mention of her name brought an almost overwhelming roar of approval from the crowd, followed by a few catcalls at the far end of the park.

As Buck turned and made a hasty retreat through the crowds, he heard Shelley's final words. "We need your help, your contributions."

Still trapped in the middle of the spectators, Buck believed that both Shelley and Rose would get that help, and certainly those contributions which he imagined would pour in from all over the country once this story hit the wire services and the late night news.

***

Back on The Strip, the crowd had scattered. Many of the protest marchers had been in the Combat Zone since mid-afternoon, responding to Rose's rallying cry. Tired and hungry, they headed now for the security of home, having stood up, they felt, for decency.

Maneuvering through a throng of spectators, Buck came to a stop near a small contingent of mounted policemen on sleek horses whose hooves made fiery sparks when they hit the pavement.

The band's rendition of "When the Saints Come Marching In" was interrupted by an explosion that sounded as if someone had tossed a small bomb into the crowd. Buck jumped back before realizing it was only the popping sound of a giant balloon. Others, not knowing that, ran screaming in fear. Not wanting to be swept into the mass of milling bodies, he darted into the entrance of a building and just stood there, taking in the scene for a long minute before he realized he'd come to a stop at the doorstep to Jupiter's Retreat.

At the sound of another explosion, a large chestnut horse whimpered in fright, then jolted into the air, his forelegs poised menacingly over a group of running people. The patrolman mounting him pulled the reins, but was thrown onto the street. His helmet jarred loose to roll down the sidewalk. Two other patrolmen rushed to their fallen comrade's aid. As they did, the horse broke away, galloping toward the crowd which was pouring out of the park.

An old man slipped and fell down on the street. The runaway horse—his head tossing frantically from side to side—galloped over the victim, an iron-shod hoof pounding the old man's head into the pavement.

To the squawk of bullhorns and the rasp of police radios, the old man, only ten feet from Buck, lay dying. Cops crouched over his body and a helicopter circled overhead. Even now, the man looked rigid-faced, his yellowing teeth clenched in a bitter determination that fell like a pallor over his death mask.

Buck swallowed hard, knowing this was the first of what could be many casualties in Rose's moral re-armament.

The riderless horse raced toward the terrified crowd. A small child broke free from his mother's hand and ran toward the horse. Misdirected and confused, the child—a little boy—stumbled and fell. Caught in the frantic, darting horse's path, the boy was crushed under the hoofs of the powerful animal.

One man whipped a gun out of his pocket holster and shot the horse in the head. It whimpered in fright and, with its last gasp, tried to hurdle a fence bordering People's Park. The animal impaled itself on one of the sharp spikes and hung suspended there, blood running from its eyes. With one weak whine, the horse collapsed in death.

Running up the street, Buck recognized Gene as the man who'd fired the shot.

Two other patrolmen came up to Gene to talk to him, and in seconds he was gone, racing away with the men to confront some other emergency.

A great animal lover, Buck was sorry that Gene had to shoot that horse, even though he recognized the need for it.

His head low, Buck turned and headed back to People's Park.

***

Fear, rage, humiliation—all these emotions combined to make Buck come to. He found himself slumped over in the alleyway, where the Nazis had attacked him. An aching lump reminded him of the descent of the bronze eagle on his skull. The teenage girl had disappeared.

He licked his lips, his throat feeling sore and parched. Vividly he recalled the agonizing pain that had shot through his body. His side hurt, as if someone had kicked him in the gut.

Every muscle in his body winced in sharp agony as he forced himself to stand up, his head spinning. Dizzy and nauseous, he stumbled toward The Strip.

Once there, he noticed that a heavy rain had fallen, just what was needed to thin the crowd and cool the excessive heat. The steamy street was nearly deserted, except for a few patrolmen and late-night stragglers. Broken glass and debris littered the sidewalks.

The cold light of night was reflected by the puddles of the wet car roofs of the patrol cars. He headed back to People's Park, where the gingerbread bandstand had been washed clean by the pelting rain.

At the opposite end, the bonfire had turned into a pile of flaky ashes, with only a few dying embers remaining from the most defiant of books.

A policemen in a rain jacket shouted for him to move on and, as he started to, he noticed some books, not quite burned, near the edge of the bonfire. He scooped four of them up and, in the night light, looked for their titles.

Though charred around the edges, the jackets were clearly visible. He'd assumed that sleazy porno books had fueled the bonfire. These were hard-cover editions. The first title page revealed to him the book was the property of the Okeechobee Public Library. It was an English translation of Proust's Remembrance of Things Past. Quickly he looked at one of the other books, Whitman's Leaves of Grass. The third, Oscar Wilde's The Picture of Dorian Gray. The final one was a more recent edition, Tennessee Williams' Moise and the World of Reason.

He scooped up the books, planning to take them back to his office to be photographed for tomorrow's edition. Evidence in hand, he still found it hard to believe that someone in self-appointed judgment had actually removed these titles from a public library shelf for book-burning. The hate literature circulating had been bad enough.

Trudging along in the light rain, he felt his shirt and jeans were sopping wet. The moisture ran down his shins into his boots, leaving a cold, trickling sensation.

With a determination to get a good grip on himself, he walked with a fast step along the Combat Zone.

***

From the darkest alley she'd emerged, standing before Gene in the light cast from the street lamppost. The girl was oddly familiar to him, but different from some vague memory in his head. Her face was badly bruised, still showing traces of blood, and her blonde hair looked as if she'd just showered, or else had been caught in the rain.

She looked up and down the street before returning her attention to him. The crowd was gone, the violence over. She appraised Gene suggestively. "Hi," she said. "As soon as I fix my lipstick, we can get on with the business of the night."

"You okay?" he asked.

"I'm fine. Johns, even Nazi johns—especially those—have roughed me up before."

"Aren't you a little young to be working the Combat Zone?"

"Sugar, men like 'em young. I'm old enough. Name's Jill."

That name always made him shudder. It was the same name of the little girl he'd exposed himself to.

"I need to make some money something awful tonight," she said. "But when a john looks as hot as you, I'm almost tempted to throw a free one."

"I'm not here for that."

"Don't kid me. They're all here for that."

"Not me. I think you'd better get checked at a hospital. I'll drive you there."

"Yeah, right. Once in that car with you, it's no telling where you'd haul my ass."

"I'm not going to harm you." He stumbled over some debris left by the march. Bracing himself, he stood up, his face fully lit by the streetlamp.

"I know you. You're Gene Robinson."

"How could you know me?"

"You're famous. You and me—how shall I put it?—were once linked romantically."

"What in hell are you talking about?"

"I'm that girl—grown up now—that you showed your hard-on to. What a grand sight it was. Been looking ever since for its mate."

He stepped back, feeling he was lost in darkness. This couldn't be happening.

"Don't worry about it," she said.

"I'm sorry," he stammered awkwardly. "I've been sorry about that every day of my life."

"Don't carry around such a guilt trip. All is forgiven. In fact, I wouldn't mind a repeat performance," she said. "And this time you can do more than just show it to me."

"I'm not going to touch you. Let me help. I'll take you to the hospital."

"I'm not going."

"Wait a minute," he said. "I have a young friend who knows you. His name is Sandy."

"I know Sandy. He's practically my best friend."

"He's living at my place now."

"Lucky boy," she said. "It's just my luck that you'd turn out gay. All the good-looking ones go that route."

"It's not what you think."

"Sugar, it's always what I think."

"If you won't let me take you to the hospital, come home with me and hang out with Sandy. At least you can get a bath, and Sandy will put something on your bruises. He also makes a mean bowl of chili."

"I know," she said. "We've often shared motel rooms together. You know, the type with kitchenettes."

"Then you'll come?" he asked.

"If it's with you, Gene, just say the word."

He glanced apprehensively around him, as he helped Jill into his car. He had a feeling he could be arrested at any minute. Once in the car, Jill was silent. He knew he was reliving that day he'd exposed himself to her, and he suspected she was recalling it too.

He pulled into his driveway, hoping none of the neighbors was observing him.

"I think I'm a little more bruised than I thought at first," she said. "It's beginning to hurt a lot."

"We'll fix you up," he promised. At the back door and before he had a chance to turn the key, Sandy threw open the door.

"You're safe," Sandy said. "I called everywhere. Even down at the station."

"I'm okay," he said. "A couple of bruises—that's all." He ushered Jill inside. "This is the one who's beat up."

"Jill," Sandy said. "What happened to you?"

"A pack of Nazis roughed me up, but I'm gonna be okay. Handsome here rescued me."

"I did nothing like that," Gene said. "I think some other guy tried to help you, but he got hit over the head."

"Come on in," Sandy said. "My new home. Come with me to the bathroom. I'll tend to those bruises."

Gene sat at the kitchen table having a beer and listening to the sounds coming from the bathroom.

Sandy was the first to come back into the kitchen. "She's more beat up than you. I've put a couple of bandages on her. Now I'm going to heat up that chili."

"Thanks for helping out. I offered to take her to the hospital but she wouldn't go. Since she knew you, I thought of bringing her here. I hope this won't get me into trouble."

"Jill won't make trouble for you."

"That's good to know."

In minutes Jill was back in the room. "I may look a little roughed up, but I can take on both of you guys in a three-way."

"That won't be needed," Sandy said, pulling up a chair for her. "Have some of my chili instead."

"That's hotter than a three-way," she said, sitting down and reaching for the crackers.

"You okay?" Gene asked. "I hope you can stay the night."

"Sure I can. As many nights as you want." She dug into her chili bowl with a spoon.

"You can take the guest room up front," Sandy said. "I get the back room with Gene." He eyed Gene provocatively. "I have to warn you in advance."

"What's that?" Gene asked, sipping his beer.

"I don't sleep with my underwear on."

"I'll get you some pajamas." Gene pretended to ignore him, turning to Jill. "You got a home?"

"Any hotel will do. Whatever john's got the room rent."

"You can stay the night. Tomorrow, I'll start trying to find a home for you."

She looked about the kitchen. "Good chili," she said to Sandy before turning to Gene. "This place will be just fine. It definitely needs a woman's touch."

"You got any parents?" Gene asked.

"None that know me," she said.

After dinner, Gene helped Sandy wash the dishes, and he checked the front bedroom to see that it was right for Jill. As Gene was telling her goodnight, she reached to kiss him in gratitude. He backed away, her lips only brushing his cheek. "Thanks for the bed, I'm grateful."

"We'll take care of you." He turned to Sandy. "Let's hit the hay, sport. I've got an early call."

In the bedroom he felt embarrassed taking off his clothes in front of Sandy. He could see the boy eying him appreciatively. He stripped but retained his briefs. He slipped quickly under the covers.

In the glow cast by the lamp, Sandy stood in front of him and removed all his clothes. His body was young and thin as if he'd missed many meals.

Gene turned over, his back to Sandy. "Get in. We both could use some sleep."

Sandy crawled in and reached to hug Gene. Gene pushed him away gently. "No stuff like that. I mean that."

"You can at least kiss me good night."

Gene reached over and planted a light kiss on Sandy's cheek. The boy clasped Gene's face and kissed him hard on the mouth. "I can kiss a lot more places than that."

"Enough men have used you."

"All except one—and he's the only one I want."

Gene turned over, lying flat on his belly. He didn't trust Sandy's roving hands. "Good night."

Chapter Five

The next morning found Buck again on the beach of his private cay. He'd had a troubled sleep and only minutes ago had called Robert in Miami to see how his mother was. It didn't look good. Mrs. Dante's doctor had warned Robert that he didn't think she would last another day.

"Are you coming back before the funeral, or will you stay in Miami until it's all over?" Buck had asked.

"I don't know yet. I'll let you know."

"I'll fly down for the funeral," Buck said.

"I don't think I can face it without you."

"I'll be there," Buck promised. "I'm also popping the big question."

"Hot damn!" Robert said.

"Make the arrangements down in Miami," Buck said. "We'll get married when I fly down."

"Hot double damn."

"Go buy our wedding rings," Buck said. "Make sure they match."

He put down the phone only to take a call from Roland at the city desk.

Buck had left the office early today because he'd resented Roland's taking charge. The staff seemed to have sensed there had been a shift of power. Key issues and major assignments were funneled toward Roland, not to Buck's office.

On the phone, Roland told him that he'd had to tone down his column about Rose's march through the Combat Zone. "You were pretty rough on her," the city editor said. "We can't offend much of our readership. A lot of good people marched in that parade. It wasn't exactly a Nazi rally."

"I'll tell you what," Buck said. "You've got plenty of stories about last night's march, right?"

"Tremendous coverage."

"Then kill my piece," Buck said before slamming down the phone.

Impulsively he had dialed Gene's house only to hear the same voice, that of a young boy. He'd left urgent messages for Gene to call him after the boy had told him that Gene was already at work. When he'd dialed Gene's office at police headquarters, he'd suspected that Gene was there but was refusing to take his call.

After that phone call he put on those bikini briefs Leroy had given him but decided to slip his trunks on over them—not that he was expecting company but somehow it seemed more discreet.

Before going to the beach, he'd put through a call to Susan only to find she was not in her hotel room in New York.

Alone on the beach, he removed his trunks, enjoying the feel of the tight briefs hugging his genitals. As the tide reached its flow, he lay back, gazing at the sky, letting the warm water wash over his feet.

"Mr. Brooke, you have visitors," Henry said. "I don't know who."

Slipping on the jeans his servant held out for him, a puzzled Buck strode bare-chested and barefoot down to his pier where another yacht had anchored beside his own.

There, all glistening shell pink in the morning sun, stood the luxury cruiser, *Rose II*. Running up the gangplank, he called out, "What's going on here?"

From the cabin below, Rose emerged in a flowing white robe, her auburn hair wrapped in a turban, her violet eyes concealed behind large sunglasses. "Is that any way to talk to a lady?"

He stood staring at her, his emotions churning. Two of her crew sat at the far edge of the deck. "What do you think Jesus would say of your coming unannounced to Buck Brooke's erotic paradise?" he asked.

"From what I know of Jesus, he would definitely approve." She removed her sunglasses, her eyes dancing. "It'd be a race between me and him to see who got you first." In the sun, her face was exuberant, as he'd remembered it—excitingly flamboyant, daringly provocative, deliberately flirtatious. "Then you, Jesus, and me could have a *menage à trois*?" She kissed the tips of her fingers, releasing the caress to the wind.

As she moved across the deck of her yacht, he had the same feeling he'd had about her at the temple—total confusion. It was a relief to know that a woman who seemed to take Christ so seriously could also be flip about him. He couldn't connect the public Rose with the private woman, for, in a schizophrenic way, those two Roses spoke a different language.

The quiet, reserved Henry had set up a breakfast table right on the wooden pier, with its peppermint-striped awning. On the linen-draped table stood a freshly brewed pot of coffee and a platter holding slices of papaya.

"I might as well invite you to breakfast," Buck said.

"Thanks." She reached for his arm. "Shelley's still asleep."

He frowned. "How great for me you brought him along. I heard his speech last night."

Active distress came over her face. "If I knew how Shelley would turn out, I would never have adopted him. But enough about him. Did you read my book?"

Feeling the curve of her back under his hand, he guided her into a director's chair. "I'm not too much into fantasies."

She leaned over to him and shaded her eyes with her free hand. "Cruel, but I still love you." With graciousness, she focused on Henry, showering him with her charm. Henry didn't seem too concerned with her as he poured coffee.

A light breeze blew in, enough to chill Buck. The coffee felt good and warm going down.

Whatever she was doing—drinking coffee or adjusting her turban—she never took her eyes off him. "You have a magnificent physique. Your face, too. So strong. And I love the way that forelock dangles over your brow. Like a fallen cockscomb. In some way, you're a child-man."

"I'm fully grown," he said. "Wanna climb the mountain?"

"What a fabulous invitation," she said. For a while she sat there in silence, gazing at him, a slight tremble on her lips. "After the horror of that march, I needed a place to retreat to. More than that, I realized that I needed to be with you."

A quick shiver of apprehension went down his back. "I don't know why. You've got the racists, the anti-Semites, the crypto-Nazis, and the patriotic simpletons marching for you. What do you need me for?"

She reached out tentatively for him, never actually touching. "Don't talk like that. You know I can't help but attract some far-out types. I just try to do what I think is right."

She seemed to cling to his hand, and her face turned pale in the orange glow of the sun as she stared at a slight mist that hadn't burnt off the horizon yet. She pressed her head against his nude shoulder, and he noticed her rapid breathing. Her soft hair rubbed against his unshaven face and it, too, felt as fresh as the morning.

With a will of its own, his broad palm cupped the back of her neck. His free hand traced her delicate bones, beginning at the curve of her brow and descending along her cheekbones to her chin. His hand traveled to her thin waist, and he crushed his mouth over hers and tasted her lips—soft, moist, yielding.

***

Although Buck had been pissed when Shelley, awakened from sleep in his cabin on the yacht, had walked up, catching him kissing Rose, he'd forgiven the boy later in the day when he'd taken him for a stroll along the beach. It was hard to be miffed at Shelley for long. He was so incredibly beautiful you almost had to forgive him. If anything, he was the type of boy you wanted to grab and shower with kisses. Today he appeared more luminous than ever.

Rose had gone to the house to make some very private telephone calls, which gave Buck time alone with Shelley before Henry prepared lunch later in the day for Buck's two uninvited guests.

As Shelley played in the water, Buck had a chance to observe him closely. He looked fourteen, not his true age. The boy, bathed in a golden glow, belonged nowhere and to nobody. Yet at the same time he seemed to be crying out for someone to come and possess him.

At the breakfast table, Shelley had been filled with self-mocking humor, his commentary on Rose's moral crusade and his own role in it so crackling, his mother had asked him to leave the table. Delicate and fair-skinned, Shelley had a thin face that seemed masked, like one of those ghostly countenances one glimpses briefly behind a curtained window.

At first Buck had been tempted to teach him to swim, but he'd resisted that impulse. At People's Park, Shelley had preached about what he couldn't accept in a role model. It seemed ironic to Buck how much the boy did need someone to look up to. Rose herself was the worst choice, forcing Shelley into the hardsell evangelical movement.

Buck was lying on a blanket on the white sands with Shelley when he was overcome with an impulse. He got up and peeled off his jeans standing only in the see-through red bikini Leroy had purchased for him. Shelley was treated only to his rear view as Buck rushed toward the water, hoping that the boy would follow. He didn't. Shelley still lay on the blanket staring in the distance at him.

When Buck emerged from the water, he didn't look down but felt that in this wet bikini he might as well be nude. It left nothing to the imagination, hugging every line and contour of his genitals.

Back at the blanket he stood with his hands on his hips, his long legs widespread. Shelley did not look into his face but seemed mesmerized by the attraction below his navel. It was all Buck could do to admit to himself that he liked displaying himself in front of the boy.

The day was hot and getting hotter, and the heat made Buck's mind bubble. The sun seared the beach, turning the white sand whiter, creating a glare.

"You've got quite a pair of balls on you," Shelley said when Buck caught him looking.

"I need them," he said, sitting down on the sand.

"I knew you had a big dick—suspicion now confirmed—when I first met you," Shelley said. "I didn't know you had big balls too. Even on that rare occasion when you can meet up with a man with a big dick, the balls are often small. Lucky you. You've got both pieces of equipment. Or lucky the person who gets to drain those balls every night."

"How you talk for a sweet little evangelist being rescued from all the moral lepers in the world."

"Don't bring up that religious shit when I'm talking about the big dick of Buck Brooke III. My eye is like a tape measure. You've got five and half inches soft. Maybe even six. I bet a dick like that expands to twice its flaccid size when hard. With my sweet ruby red lips sucking it like a lollipop, I bet I could run a flag up its pole."

Shelley's talk was giving Buck a hard-on.

"You know you want it," the boy said, running his tongue around his lips. "Why don't we just take this blanket behind the bushes and give you some relief right now? A big juicy blow-job. I'll let you fuck me later. Before I let you dismount, you're going to come twice inside me. Not only that, when you pull out and are lying panting, I'm going down on you for a final taste."

Shelley reached out and took his hand and pulled it toward his mouth. One by one he began to suck Buck's fingers in the most lascivious way. "I've got to have that big dick in me. I can't stand it any more. You can make this real easy for me or else I'll have to revert to other means."

"Other means?" Buck asked.

"Even if you don't pull off that bikini, I'll get it off you one way or another."

Shelley's sucking of Buck's fingers fully aroused Buck until the red bikini could hardly contain him. Jerking his fingers from Shelley's devouring mouth, he flipped over on his stomach, his hard cock rubbing into the hot beach blanket, as he became embarrassed by his own arousal. Looking intently at Shelley, he asked sharply, "Do you hate Rose?"

"I don't want to say hate," Shelley said, a smirk on his face. "It's just that I have dreams at night. You know, torches all around me lighting bonfires. White-robed choirs singing *Hallelujah*. Then Rose, with these great big white wings, swooping down. In the dream she's got a face like a falcon. She grabs me and swings me in mid-air. Then tosses me into hell's fire. Some dream, huh?"

"Powerful stuff!"

"Listen," Shelley said in a soft, confidential voice. "I know it's smart-ass for a kid like me to tell a super-honcho like you anything, but I'm stuck with the bitch. You aren't. Rose will snip off those big balls of yours the first chance she gets. She's already got a trophy room of testicles. Don't you be the latest catch."

He got up quickly, wondering as he did if Rose possessed such ruthlessness, or if Shelley was exaggerating in his usual overstatement. "Thanks for the tip. I intend to hang onto my jewels." He quickly slipped into his jeans.

There was little motion on the beach, not even a slight breeze. The waves seemed lethargic. The blinding sun had momentarily robbed Buck of energy. Sand flies droned in the air, circling him, then landed on his neck. He slapped them away.

As he strolled the beach, he noticed Shelley following along behind. Whipping the towel from around his neck, he snapped it at Shelley, tanning his buttocks.

"I love it!" Shelley shouted playfully. "More, more."

At the crest of a hill, Rose, still clad in her sheer white robe, stood regally, gazing down at them.

As Buck headed across the sand dunes toward her, he found his pace quickening.

With all the emotional complications in his life, did he need these two new and strange bedfellows?

***

After a lunch of conch salad prepared by Henry, Rose was summoned to the phone on her yacht. In minutes she returned to join Buck at table with Shelley. A look of great distress was on her face.

"Something wrong?" Buck asked.

She hesitated. "There have been some complications. I have to meet with Calder Martin this afternoon."

"Oh, shit!" was Shelley's only comment.

"Enjoyed your visit," Buck said.

There was a hint of desperation in her voice. "I didn't come all the way over here just for lunch. It's urgent that I talk to you. I'll return at six, if I'm invited back?"

"Come back for dinner," Buck said.

"I'm loving it here," Shelley said. "Can't I stay on until you get back?"

Rose looked first at Shelley, then imploringly at Buck. "That depends on your host."

"Sure, kid, you're welcome to hang out." He reached for the salad bowl. "Have some more conch. It'll make a man out of you."

At the pier Buck told Rose good-bye, then returned to table with Shelley.

"As soon as we get this luncheon out of the way, I'm ready for action," Shelley said. "Prepare for the fuck of a lifetime. I don't know how many holes you've plugged, but with me you're going to face your ultimate turn-on."

"Not with you." Buck said.

Shelley reached across the table taking Buck's hand as he'd started to lift a cup of coffee. "As Rose's friend, Nixon, might say: let me make something perfectly clear. I've never wanted any man as much as I want you."

"Forget it," Buck said, removing his hand from Shelley's grasp.

"That's where you're wrong. Shelley gets what Shelley wants, and, big boy, Shelley wants you."

Shelley tasted a Bloody Mary that Henry had prepared for him and frowned at its flavor. "I think I'm the only one in the world who knows how to make a real Bloody Mary. Someday I'll tell you my secret, because I heard it's one of your favorite drinks. Do you also like margaritas?"

"I love margaritas. I could drink them all day and night."

"I've also make the world's greatest margarita."

"I've had some pretty good ones," Buck said.

"You haven't tasted mine." Shelley's eyes traveled Buck's body suggestively.

"So I haven't."

"Let me go into Henry's kitchen and return shortly with pomegranate margarita. I saw some of that tasty fruit in there."

"A pomegranate margarita. I'm game."

"Why don't you go out and rest in that Florida room? I'll join you there."

"It's a date," Buck said.

Shelley stood up but looked back at him. "More so than you can ever imagine."

***

Gene put down the phone. It was nearly three o'clock, and he knew he was due at the office for a psychiatric evaluation in just thirty minutes. He'd learned what he wanted from a cadet acquaintance of his who'd only last week gone through the same evaluation.

"That guy spent more time evaluating what's in my pants instead of what's in my head," the cadet, Phil Graham, had told him. "He couldn't take his eyes off the outline of my meat. What a cocksucker! I had him so flustered he couldn't hold his pen steady."

"Did he put the make on you!" Gene had asked. "You could report him."

"He wasn't that much of a fool. But I'm sure if I'd whipped it out for the faggot, he would have gone down on me right in his office. After all, he locks his doors."

"Thanks, pal," Gene had said before hanging up the phone. An idea had quickly occurred to him. Instead of appearing in a suit, he had another plan. Back in his bedroom, he pulled off his clothes and headed for his closet. He was glad Jill and Sandy were out shopping.

In the back of his closet he took out a pair of faded jeans he hadn't worn since he was in college. Stepping out of his briefs, he slipped into the jeans, having a hard time buttoning them. Even though his waist was still trim and his stomach hard, the jeans were clearly a size or two too small. Over the years the jeans had been laundered so many times they were now a very pale blue. These jeans outlined the full length and thickness of his cock and formed a perfect basket to capture his low-hanging balls. He was so exposed in them that he felt almost nude.

At the psychiatrist's office, Gene waited for what seemed like an hour before he was finally ushered in. A bald, short man with a tendency to put on weight looked up as he came in. Seeing Gene, his dead eyes seemed to come alive.

"I'm Dr. Valibus," he said, reaching for Gene's hand and perhaps holding it for too long.

"I'm Gene Robinson."

"Sit down," Dr. Valibus said, motioning to a chair to the side of his desk.

Gene eased his frame into the chair letting the army shirt slip open. The chair seemed to make his jeans ride higher up his waist, revealing more of his genitals.

Dr. Valibus gave him a long, steady appraisal. It seemed hard for him to ask questions. "You work out a lot?"

"Yeah."

Dr. Valibus stammered, checking out Gene's basket. "I've been going over your file. An interesting record."

"You mean, that I was once accused of exposing myself? I've got a lot to exhibit."

"I can see that," the doctor said.

"I don't mind flashing every now and then. That little girl was one thing, but the rest of the world seems mighty interested in what's hanging."

"What do you mean?"

"I noticed when I go into a men's room, guys often follow me in. Even if there are ten urinals there, two guys always stand on each side of me waiting for me to expose myself."

"Do you?" the doctor asked.

"I've got to take a leak, don't I?"

"Does it ever get hard?"

"Sometimes I shake it and stand there at the urinal for a few extra moments. Often I drop my hands or light a cigarette while standing there. That gives them extra viewing time."

"Do they reach for it?" the doctor asked.

"Nothing wrong with touching."

Beads of perspiration were forming on Dr. Valibus's forehead. "This is not the usual procedure. Most of my exams are here at the desk. In some unusual cases I also conduct a physical exam." He motioned to an adjoining room. "Why don't you go into the other room and remove your clothes? Even your briefs."

"I'm not wearing any today," Gene said.

"Fine." The doctor put through a call to his front desk before following Gene into the examining room.

In the examining room and in front of Dr. Valibus, Gene removed his army shirt and slipped his T-shirt over his head. Sitting down, he removed his black boots and socks, then stood up and unbuttoned his jeans, sliding them down slowly until his penis burst free of its tight confinement. Dr. Valibus's obvious excitement was causing Gene to harden. Totally nude, he placed his hands on his hips and stood with his legs widespread.

Dr. Roland moved closer to him and reached for his low-hanging testicles. He gently encased one of them in his sweaty small hand. "Cough," he said.

Gene didn't even attempt to cough, and Dr. Valibus didn't seem to notice. The doctor began to play with Gene's testicles, as Gene's cock expanded to its full size. The psychiatrist seemed fascinated by the length and thickness of it. He pulled the skin back and began to plant tiny kisses on the head of Gene's cock, nibbling on the sides. He turned his head from side to side, giving the cock a circular, caressing movement. Then he took the cock into his mouth, pushing down on it, taking as much as he could swallow. And he could swallow a lot. He was extremely skilled. The head of Gene's cock pressed against the doctor's throat which miraculously opened for him. Gene enjoyed the tight confines and kept his cock in as long as he dared before withdrawing so

Dr. Valibus could breathe. A slurping, gurgling noise filled the room.

Gene seized both sides of the doctor's head, raising himself on tiptoe. "Eat me!" he commanded, increasing the speed of his pumping. "Your tonsils are going to get a bath."

Dr. Valibus cupped a free hand under Gene's balls, squeezing and tickling them, pulling at them as he prepared his throat for another deep penetration. Gene continued to pump furiously. "Damn it," he said. "Oh, damn it." Almost without warning, he filled the doctor's mouth to overflowing. Although he found the doctor personally detestable, he'd been one of the most skilled cocksuckers Gene had ever discovered.

Even when he was spent, the doctor's mouth remained glued to Gene's cock, milking the urethral canal empty of its last sweet drops. Long after Gene had gone limp, the doctor continued to tongue and kiss him. Finally, Gene slowly pulled himself from the man's eagerly devouring mouth.

"What a blow-job," Gene said, rising to his feet, although the doctor remained on the floor, staring up at him. "Where did you learn all those tricks?"

"I have been a psychiatrist for the men in blue for twenty years," he said, slowly getting up. "You learn a lot in twenty years."

Gene quickly slipped on his clothes.

"You were the best ever. I imagined your come was blue like a police uniform. That it was sprinkled with sapphires and diamonds."

"In that case, you've got a lot of jewelry in that fat belly of yours."

Dr. Valibus didn't seem in the least offended at this insult.

"Going to give me a good evaluation?" Gene asked, buttoning up his jeans.

"I definitely am going to report what a healthy specimen you are, both mentally and physically."

"Thanks, doc."

As Gene was heading for the outer office, Dr. Valibus called him back.

"There's a catch, though," the doctor said.

"What's that?" Gene asked.

"You've got to report to me every week at this same time."

***

Buck felt he'd been on a long journey somewhere but was slowly returning to earth. It was something like the feeling he'd experienced when he'd been knocked over the head by those Nazis. But this time, although his mind had been sent on a long drift, he felt intense pleasure—not pain.

As he gradually began to come to, his body still didn't seem connected with his brain. In some way, he felt he'd just smoked six powerful marijuana cigarettes and was a bit giggly from the experience. His head was swimming in a most delightful way.

His cock was fully hard and was being serviced by an expert. This sex dream was too real and vivid. He didn't want it to end and hoped it would go on forever.

He was dreaming about Robert. Only his friend could satisfy him so expertly. He was certain that Robert had returned from Miami and was going down on him, causing his entire body to experience the most incredible sensations. This was Robert's welcome home present to him. Only Robert, not Gene, could swallow all of him this way.

Keeping his eyes fully closed, Buck pumped harder, raising his hips from the bed, wanting to receive more and more of this suctioning mouth and throat. He reached down and placed his broad hand on his seducer's neck, the other hand on the back of his head. Almost unconsciously he wanted to force his seducer down on him for the final blast-off.

When his release came, it was violent and overpowering, almost like none he'd ever experienced before. It seemed to go on forever, and his seducer showed no signs of letting up. There was no need to use force here. If anything, he felt he'd have to use force to withdraw from the mouth which seemed to want to hold him in bondage until it was certain it'd drained him to the last drop.

Buck fell back on his bed, panting. He seemed to still be in the throes of orgasm. His recovery was slow. Gradually he opened his eyes, finding himself in his bedroom. He could tell by the light coming in that the afternoon had faded.

All he remembered was tasting that pomegranate margarita. Shelley had fulfilled his promise: it was the best Buck had ever tasted. The only sensation that disturbed him was a slight almond taste. He'd taken another long sip, savoring the taste. That was all he'd remembered.

The drink must have gone to his head. He'd felt an overpowering need to sleep.

He opened his eyes, looking up his bedroom ceiling. The last he remembered was when he'd been in his Florida room, drinking Shelley's margarita. The devouring mouth was still on him, gently licking his cock and planting tantalizing little kisses on it.

Raising up on his elbows, he looked down at his seducer. It wasn't Robert. "Shelley!" he said harshly. "What in hell are you doing?"

The boy raised his head and looked up at Buck with a kind of wonder and awe. "Hi," he said.

"What in the fuck do you mean, Hi? What have you done?"

"I've just had the most thrilling experience of my life. I've found the cock of my dreams." He ran his fingers along the length of it.

Buck pulled away but made no effort to cover his nudity. There seemed little need to prevent exposure now. "Do you plan to spend the rest of your life drugging me and seducing me?"

"The next time I won't have to drug you. You'll be begging for it."

Buck eased himself from Shelley and headed for his closet and a fresh pair of jeans.

"That's some bubble-butt ass you've got," Shelley called after him. "I should know. I've been an hour licking it and tasting the sweetest rosebud God ever gave to a white man."

"You got to that too?" Buck said, slipping into a pair of jeans, although remaining shirtless. "Is there any part of me you're not intimately familiar with?"

"My tongue has been over every inch of your body so many times I know it better than my own."

"It'll never happen again."

"It'll happen thousands of times. This is only the beginning of a lifelong affair."

"You may be the world's most beautiful boy—there's little doubt about that—but beautiful boy might be a little touched in the head."

"Not at all," a fully dressed Shelley said, getting up from the bed and licking off the last flavor of Buck on his lips. "I'm not going to brush my teeth for the rest of the night."

"Don't you ever do that again, and I mean it."

A light rap at the door and Buck was in front of it, opening it to discover Henry.

"Mrs. Phillips has returned from the mainland," Henry said. "She's asking you and Mr. Shelley to come down to the dock for a drink on her yacht."

"We'll be right there," Buck said, looking for a shirt.

"Great," Shelley said with a smile. "I'll whip up some pomegranate margaritas."

***

At New York's Waldorf-Astoria, Susan eyed her mother with great approval. Ingrid always wore Chanel dresses, some of them twenty years old. Her hair had turned a lovely salt-and-pepper, which softened her features as she moved deeper into her fifties.

"Thanks for agreeing to go shopping with me," Susan said. "Somehow clothes always look better on me when I buy them in New York."

"You'll be able to buy any outfit you want now," Ingrid said. "Mrs. Buck Brooke III."

"I didn't marry Buck for his money."

"He married you to hold onto his money," Ingrid claimed.

"Are you sure?"

"I'm not called the smartest woman columnist in America for nothing. Robert Dante has his claws in your man and will never let go. Buck is moving you out of your tacky apartment and into a luxurious condo—not his home."

"I could hardly live under the same roof with Robert."

"Where will your husband spend his nights? With Robert or with you?"

Susan frowned. "I'm prepared to share him if necessary."

"Is Robert?"

"I don't think so." She frowned again. "Buck hasn't even told Robert about the marriage."

Ingrid leaned back, reaching for her coffee. "I've always suspected that there was also something between Gene and Buck."

"You're far too suspicious."

"I have an unfailing instinct about these matters. I'm not a homophobe even when one of those guys marries my only child. I just don't want unhappiness for you."

"I managed to find plenty of that before I married Buck."

"I don't want you to set yourself up for heartbreak again," Ingrid said.

"I entered into this marriage with my eyes wide open."

"It was a smart career move," Ingrid said. "You certainly married up in the world. Your husband is going to be one of the richest men in Florida."

"He's also a great lay."

"In that case, we can assume he's bisexual." Ingrid smiled again. "The marriage might work. If Buck is cynically using you, use him back."

"I wish it could be a full marriage. If it's not, I'm prepared to live with that too."

"You can always have someone on the side. Buck would be very understanding. If he's fucking Robert and maybe Gene too, why wouldn't he?"

"I'll probably have to make an appointment with Robert just to see him," Susan said.

"You don't love him, do you?"

"I think of him as a great date—not a husband. When his grandfather dies, he can always divorce me. By then, he will have gotten his inheritance."

"I don't think he's going to divorce you at all."

"What do you mean?" Susan asked.

"If he's really gay and wants lovers on the side, I think he's going to need a cover like you. He's going to want that understanding wife for public consumption, pictures in the news. You're perfect. You'll be the most charming and romantic couple in Florida. The *Examiner*'s circulation will climb."

Susan stood up from the table and reached for her mother's hand. "When I land back in Okeechobee, I'll have a new wardrobe, a new look, even a new husband. Guess where I'm sending the bills?"

***

At sunset, Buck's cay turned golden until shadows fell across the hill. Out on the patio, Rose's cheeks glowed with color.

He eyed her, hoping to turn on the sexual current that had flowed between them when he'd kissed her at breakfast that morning.

He poured her a dry sherry. As he offered her the glass, he detected a tremor in her hand. She reached out and gently caressed his fingers.

The twilight air was clear and he felt proud of himself for getting Shelley to take a nap. Finally!

At first Rose had wanted to talk business, but he clearly wasn't interested. As if compelled, she persisted in discussing what an important force religion was in TV programming and station ownership.

Slim and elegant in her clinging white gown, she braced her shoulders as a triumphant glee came across her face. "Since launching my moral crusade, I've picked up ten new stations. "I'm going national with a *60 Minutes* type of program that will begin where the religious broadcasts leave off."

He closed his eyes, letting the fresh breeze bathe him. What terrifying, special dark vision did she plan to broadcast to America?

As if asking herself that same question, she said, "In my own 60 Minutes, I'll see to it that the grievances of the silent sufferers will be heard and the unjust exposed without mercy."

"I get it," he said with weary resignation. "The overburdened taxpayer against the welfare cheat; the God-fearing Christian against the deviate, godless Commie, the puritan WASP against the child-molesting Jew pornographer. That program should run forever."

Her eyes still filled with the vision of her goals, she seemed not to notice the sarcasm in his voice, and went on spinning her dream.

"That Arab-Israeli war ten years ago regrettably has resulted in a wave of Arab stereotypes. The Jews have objected violently to their own stereotypes, but the Arabs have never found a voice in America to champion their rights. If an Arab speaks, no one listens."

"You'd like to become the spokesperson for Arab America?" The prospect left him dumbfounded.

"There has been no effective society to stand up and defend the rights of Arab-Americans. Such a society could counter the demonizing stereotypes. It could lobby in Washington for policies favorable to the embattled homelands of the Middle East that live in fear of aerial bombardment by Israel."

"I'm sure if you set up such an organization, contributions would pour in by the billions from Arab states. As spokesperson, you'd be richer than you already are. You might even be given vast oil wells to call your own."

"Be as sarcastic as you want, but what you just said is true. My organization will dwarf that National Association of Arab-Americans set up in 1972."

"Why? Because of your love of Arabs? Why would a little Christian Oakie like you love Arabs and want to advance their cause in any way?"

"There's nothing wrong with financial gain," she said defensively. "The last time I checked this was still a capitalist country, although Hazel and such ilk would like us to take our orders directly from the Kremlin. Is it illegal for me to take a public relations job in this country?"

"Do you want to do this?" he asked.

"Coming from a Christian leader like me would give the Arab movement a validity it's never had. There are at least three million Arab-Americans in this country. Probably a lot more than that. Most of them are Lebanese. But there are many other Americans here who came from Iraq, Syria, Palestine, Egypt, wherever. They need a leader."

"You?"

"Who else? I could serve as a bridge between them and the Christian world. Calder Martin has enormous political contacts. He could make the voice of Arab America heard in Washington."

"A daunting prospect," he said. He could take this talk no more. He got up and headed for the liquor cabinet and a vodka.

Later, as Henry served dinner, she wondered why Shelley was still asleep. "I usually can't get him to go to bed."

He didn't want to tell her he'd placed a sleeping capsule in the boy's soda.

Out on the patio after dinner, Buck manipulated the buttons that controlled the lights in the house. In a second, everything went dark. Only the sound of fountain could be heard, and then a frantic gasp from inside the living room where she was caught unaware.

He rushed to her side, finding her trembling. He reached to turn on a lamp and she stopped him. "I'm terrified of the dark," she said, "unless someone holds me."

"There are no demons here," he said calmly, pressing his body close to hers.

Her long fingers reached inside his shirt, feeling his chest as if it were a flawless piece of sculpture. He quickly yanked off his T-shirt.

Creating a slow-moving choreography of their own, he danced with her around the center of the room, no longer listening to the rhythm of the background music, but to their inner melody. Their bodies moved together, tighter and tighter, and she gracefully let him slip off her gown. She was completely nude.

Her skin felt terrific to him. She seemed as strong and energetic as he was. Reaching, exploring, he put his hand on her thigh, and the quiver of her body was a compelling clue she wanted him to go farther. He groaned as she rubbed against him, and though her features were indistinct, he knew she had a funny little smile of accomplishment on her face.

The lines of her body were lovely, sensual and ripe, the breasts large with prominent nipples. With both hands, she tugged at his jeans.

He eased her onto the sofa, mesmerized at how her shapely arms and legs glistened in the soft, natural light. His chest pressed harder against her breasts. As she lay her head back on the cushions, he gently kissed her neck and, reaching to pull him closer, she laughed softly, her tongue flickering in his ear.

Under his deft fingers, he felt her heart beating fast and in this moment of love-making, he was still aware that this was a famous evangelist, a self-professed moralist, but also a passionate woman whose skin was just as smooth and fragrant as any he'd known. He slid his tongue over her mouth and then put it deep inside her, as if trying to reach the voice that had preached to millions over the radio and TV about sin, adultery, and fornication.

His penis thickened in anticipation as her fingers slid over him. He writhed in pleasure as she continued to stroke and tease. As her hand reached lower, he uttered a low moan, only to find her slipping beneath him, licking and biting his chest like a lioness lusting after warm meat. Her mouth encircled his shaft and, once inside her, he finally reached the throat from which sprang the voice that brought reassurance of heavenly rewards to the devout. That throat existed only for his pleasure, and he'd silenced that voice except for a deep gurgle. Pounding with excitement, no longer wanting to delay, he lubricated her throat.

Later when they were in his bedroom, he took her, her writhing hips creating a frenzy of joy within him. She seemed to swallow him whole, and the more deeply he penetrated, the greater her rocking thrill.

The irresistible force of orgasm gathered within him. She hard-gripped him, and he never wanted to break free. Arching his back, he tried to gain more momentum. She held him down with a masterful light touch, as if she were taking control, directing his movements, telling him as if by some inner radar where to move and how to bring her even more excitement. Soon, actual movement wasn't needed, and he collapsed on top of her. She grabbed him tightly, her climax surging through her.

At this point he was overcome with a sense of dread, as if he'd desecrated a national monument.

Getting up from the bed, she strolled through the open doors that led to the pool and dived in.

Nude, he ran after her, plunging in with her. The sudden coldness of the water startled him. He caught up with her and pulled her close, kissing her face and inserting his tongue in her mouth

Her left hand traveled and fondled his jewels. He was soon fully erect in the water and wanting more relief. He decided to take her right in the pool. Her back was against the tiles of the pool, and she could not see the lone figure who'd emerged out of the shadows.

It was Shelley. The sleeping powder had obviously worn off. He was wearing only a pair of briefs.

The pool lights were on as Shelley remained in a dark corner of the unlit patio. Rose's eyes were closed as she moaned and gripped Buck tighter.

Buck knew Shelley was watching their every move. Strangely, instead of deflating his hard-on, Shelley's presence seemed to thicken and lengthen his penis as he plunged deeper into Rose, who was now digging into his back with her fingers and nibbling at his ear.

Shelley pulled down his briefs and began to masturbate. As if he were having sex with Buck—not his mother—he beat himself furiously. Even though Buck couldn't clearly see, he knew that his orgasm and that of Shelley's were perfectly timed.

***

When Gene drove into his driveway the windows of his home were open and the place looked bright, cheery, and inviting. The house had been boarded up for so long, it was always dusty and mildewed. Not today. Jill and Sandy had aired out the place. As he came into the kitchen, he saw that everything was freshly cleaned and polished. Someone had taken down the curtains at the kitchen sink and washed them. Not only that but a stew was cooking on the stove.

Coming from the bedroom with a stack of old newspapers, Sandy broke into a smile when he spotted Gene standing over the stove inspecting what was in the pot. "My man," Sandy said, putting down the papers and rushing toward Gene. Almost before he knew what was happening, Sandy kissed him on the mouth.

"Cut that shit!" Gene said but not in a harsh way

"Since when can't a boy kiss his old man?"

So as not to reject the boy totally, Gene ran his hand across Sandy's smooth face, "What's going on here?"

"You may be the best looking man who's ever walked the planet, and the sexiest, but you are the world's worst housekeeper."

Gene smiled and squeezed Sandy's arm. This time it was he who reached over and kissed the boy on the cheek. "Thanks a lot."

Sandy took his hand and led him up the corridor. "The living room actually looks like someone might live here."

"Where's Jill?"

"You won't believe this, but she's out back planting some flower seeds she bought with her ill-gotten gains. She said she's always wanted to have a garden."

At that moment, Jill, dirty from the garden, came into the living room. "Welcome home, big man. We've missed you." She walked over and with perfect naturalness kissed Gene on the cheek. "Do you like our little transformation?"

"I love it," Gene said. "Thanks."

She sat down across from Gene. "In a few weeks we're going to have some flowers growing in our secret garden."

Sandy reached for Gene's hand and held it like a caress. "Jill wants to ask you something."

"Fire away," Gene said.

"I knew your invitation for me to stay here wasn't forever, but could I stay on a few more days? I don't have any place to go and I love it here with you and Sandy."

Gene tightened his grip on Sandy's hand. "You can stay here as long as you want. That goes for both of you."

No one said anything for a long moment. Jill got up and kissed

Gene again on the cheek. "That's damn good news to a girl who has never had much good news in her life."

When she was off in her bedroom showering, Gene turned to Sandy. "Having Jill here and letting me help her and take care of her in some way helps me get over the guilt of what I did to her."

"It's all gone and forgotten." Sandy took Gene's hand and raised it to his lips, planting a long, lingering kiss on his inner palm. "I love you, daddy."

With some awkwardness, Gene pulled his hand away.

Sandy got up from the sofa and looked down at him. "You liked my chili last night but you're going to love my beef stew."

"Thanks for cooking it."

"And thank you for leaving some money on the kitchen table so we could buy some groceries." Sandy said.

Later, in their bedroom, Gene noticed that it was never so brightly cleaned and polished. The pillow cases looked fresh. Inside their bathroom, all the mold had been washed away.

In front of an open dresser drawer, Sandy said, "What do you think?"

Gene looked inside. All his briefs had been neatly washed and stacked up in three piles.

"You sure wear sexy briefs. Before I put them back in the drawer, I kissed inside each pouch knowing what goodies it will contain."

"That wasn't necessary," Gene said.

"It will have to do until I can get the real thing down my throat."

Gene reached out and touched the boy's arms. "You don't need some grown man using you for sex. Haven't you had enough of that?"

"I've had enough of that. I could never get enough of you."

"C'mon, you're too young. I can't give in to my temptations."

"It's gonna happen," Sandy said.

Gene reached over and kissed Sandy's cheek again. "Right now we're going to go into that kitchen and have an old-fashioned family dinner."

***

After a good dinner, and after Sandy and Jill retired to the living room to watch some television programs, Gene excused himself and headed for the back bedroom.

Relieved that Sandy didn't follow him to the bedroom, he stripped off his clothes and headed for the shower. His mind was preoccupied with Buck and Susan. Were they together right this very moment making love? He turned his face up to the spray, and, even though the water was a bit too hot, he let it wash over his eyes, lips, nose, and throat, as if that act alone would blot out the memory of Buck.

His face still under the jet spray, he was aware of a movement in the shower. He jerked his face away from the water to discover that a nude Sandy had entered the shower with him. The boy was fondling Gene's genitals. Gently but forcefully Gene removed Sandy's hand, although as he did he could feel himself hardening.

He turned his back to Sandy to avoid contact with him but the boy sank to his knees and began planting tiny kisses on Gene's buttocks. Within moments the kisses became licks. In one lunge, the boy's tongue was slurping at Gene's most private part. He moved to force the boy's head to break the contact but Sandy clung to him tenaciously as if he were not going to be denied this pleasure.

With one hand he slipped his fingers from Gene's buttocks to his genitals where with expertise and skill he massaged Gene to a full hard-on. The boy seemed to be lovingly measuring the length and thickness of Gene's penis as he continued with his tongue to explore as deeply into Gene as he could. Gene was gasping for breath, the blood pounding inside his head.

Sandy abruptly stopped his assault on Gene's buttocks and moved his head between Gene's legs. His lips slid tightly along Gene's throbbing cock, encasing a good part of it, a feat that amazed Gene. One part of his brain told him to push Sandy's mouth from him. Instead of pushing Sandy's head away, he held the boy even more firmly to his body. In minutes rapid-fire swellings in his spasm-wracked prick told him the inevitable was happening. Erupting with a loud, gasping cry, he shot hot bursts into the boy's eager mouth, coating far back into his throat. Sandy devoured the offering and held on until he'd milked every last sweetness from Gene.

After this explosion, Gene felt awkward in the boy's presence. He let Sandy make the next move. The boy took the soap from Gene and began to lather and clean Gene's body. Even when Gene had stepped from the shower, Sandy was still at his side, wiping him dry with a thick towel.

Neither had said a word to each other. In bed with Sandy, Gene turned over on his stomach. Sandy seized on this opportunity, running his fingers along Gene's back and planting tiny kisses there.

"You're so tense," Sandy said. "I'm going to massage and relax you."

Gene closed his eyes and said nothing even when Sandy's caressing fingers were replaced by Sandy's tongue. He wetted each of Gene's legs and sucked and washed each of Gene's toes in his mouth before returning to Gene's buttocks.

Gene drifted toward the sleep he so desperately needed. He was only vaguely aware of Sandy masturbating as he tongued Gene's rosebud, but he felt he was incapable of calling a halt to this.

Long after he'd drifted into sleep, Gene woke up suddenly. When he came to, he felt drenched in his own sweat. Sandy was sleeping peacefully at his side. Gene had been dreaming.

In the dream he'd been in some warm, sensual place with Rose. He was just a boy in the dream, and Rose was his mother. At first she'd held his hand and guided him through the vastness of a tunnel and, as long as she'd been with him, he'd felt secure. Then she'd run away from him, and his legs had been too short to keep up with her long, graceful strides. The wind blew through her long auburn hair and though he reached to clutch it, it was beyond his grasp.

As darkness closed in, he stumbled, falling several times.

Yet he kept picking himself up and running faster. The air that had been as protective as the womb suddenly grew harsher. From out of nowhere a strong wind blew in, so cold it made the liquid in his eyes turn to ice.

He called out to her and she answered, her voice a faint, distant echo, urging him to run faster. Then no sound at all.

He was trapped in the cave, buffeted by the wind, encased in darkness.

Blindly he ran on, banging into rocky walls. Up ahead her face appeared, illuminated by purplish spotlights on the wall of the tunnel. As he rushed to catch up with her, the image faded, only to reappear shortly at some more distant point.

She taunted him and he begged her to stop. "I love you!" he shouted. She didn't seem to hear him and her melodic voice changed, becoming cruel in tone, harsh like the cry of a great wild animal in the forest.

He fell down a ravine and when he pulled himself up from the jagged rocks, he became aware he was touching the tip of a white diaphanous gown.

Slowly he hugged the woman's body close to his. Then he discovered that the body wasn't Rose at all, but a hissing snake disguised as a woman. Shrieking in horror, he stepped back, the ground giving way under him. Falling into space, he woke up with a start.

He got up and stumbled to the bathroom, slapping cold water on his face. When he came back, the sheets on his bed seemed on fire. Even though he needed sleep, he dared not return to bed. In sleep, the demons came out and took possession.

At 3am, as Sandy slept, Gene dressed silently and left the house. At a marina he got out and stood briefly under a streetlamp before heading for the pier. Streaks of early dawn appeared in the sky, and the screech of unseen birds could be heard.

Back in his car, he swung onto the causeway as the sun broke through, casting bright reflections on the green-blue bay. He reached for his mirrored sunglasses

The radio announced another record-breaking heat wave, with the temperature expected to climb to ninety-eight degrees. He knew he could stand the heat.

Chapter Six

A sliver of light cut through the drawn shade of Buck's bedroom. It fell over the curved, naked thigh of Rose. Not the world's most youthful thigh, it was still creamy, well-preserved and smooth enough to elicit lust in him, making him want to touch and feel her as he had last night. His passion was made all the sweeter the more the sun progressed and sparkled on her body. Relaxed now, innocent in veil of sleep, she had driven him into a whirlpool of excitement last night until somewhere in the half-dreamy hours of morning he'd fallen asleep, her arm resting casually across the expanse of his broad shoulders.

Her face was covered with an eyeless scarlet-colored satin domino to protect her from the morning glare. He was more exposed, vulnerable to the piercing light that crept through.

Outside his window he heard the shrieks of birds and the sound of the wings of sea gulls descending on their prey. Immediately, he was overcome with a sense of cannibalism. He wanted a cigarette but was hesitant to light one.

The island was bathed in silence, yet within his head he heard the toll of church bells, a choir singing "The Alleluia Chorus." He'd been to bed with an angel, except, in truth, she wasn't *that* any more than he was.

Filled with bitterness and hatred, she could also deliver wild, passionate love. After their thirsts were satisfied last night, they'd seemed to huddle together like two lost children, and it wasn't sentimental. She held him with a kind of dignity he imagined two brave people might summon when they were about to face a firing squad.

She was lonely and afraid, and she'd clung to him with a tenacity he'd found in no other woman. He brought her a joy, comfort and fulfillment he suspected she'd known in few men. What troubled him was his reluctance to continue to provide it. He'd never entered into any relationship that had all the earmarks of a catastrophe right from the beginning.

He kept his eyes tightly closed, enjoying the languid heat of the room. They'd agreed to turn off the air conditioner and to leave the doors to the patio and pool open all night.

He was fully awake, no longer dreaming. Uncomfortably aware of the invasion of some foreign presence, he opened his eyes and looked down near his feet where Shelley slept peacefully, clinging to his leg. He'd thought Rose's feet had become intertwined with his.

Gently removing his leg from Shelley's embrace, he also eased out from under Rose's arm and slipped out of the room, dressing quickly in the bathroom.

In the kitchen, he told Henry he wouldn't be joining Rose and Shelley for breakfast.

On his yacht, he spoke to one of his crew, telling him he wanted to return to Okeechobee at once. As the yacht pulled out, he paced the deck in his bare feet, watching the cruiser, *Rose II* fade.

He sat down to compose a note to her, telling her he couldn't see her any more. His words were too empty for the message, so he tore up the paper and tossed it to the wind.

Last night her offer had been stunning and had taken him by surprise. Although she'd made it clear there was a "cancer" growing on the *Examiner*, and she might not be able to save the newspaper for him, she promised far greater rewards if he'd join her in her crusade. She'd promised him a position with a massive salary as her media director-- television stations, newspapers, whatever. It could all be his if he came aboard her staff and worked for "Jesus instead of for the Devil."

A gnawing restless energy, an itch to get back to the office, filled him. Even if he had to give in to Roland's expanded command, he wanted to make himself a presence there.

He stood looking at the restless ocean in silence. The sudden rise of a wave somehow reminded him that two major items loomed on his agenda: Susan returned from New York today and he was going to pick her up at the airport. He also had a date to fly to Miami to join Robert. Another marriage loomed for him, even if the second one were only the mock. He went below to get dressed.

***

Off-tune, Shelley's singing must have awakened her. Before she figured out what he was doing in Buck's bathroom, Rose turned over in bed after adjusting her satin domino.

The memory of last night stirred her flesh. Buck had loved her with a fervor she hadn't known in a man in years. He'd worshipped every part of her body separately and at his touch, she'd felt like a work of art. Cheeks, thighs, hair, feet—each part of her had been fondled and adored.

His love-making had left her half-drugged and as she lay here quiet and languid, she desired him again.

Once, while he was still asleep, she'd removed her domino just to stare at his body, sprawled next to hers. In the rosy, pre-dawn light, everything had looked beautiful—especially him. His hand had lain gently across her stomach. Completely relaxed, the hand an hour before had been a feverish tool of lust, probing every inch of her nudity. She'd gently fondled his hand, circling his fingers until he'd started to stir. His handsome face had nestled almost innocently against the curve of her breast where her nipple had looked slightly puffy and bruised from his all-night attack. Her whole body had tingled as she'd traced the light feathering of blond hair on his chest, across his washboard stomach until she'd stopped to fondle the source of so much pleasure.

Still remembering that scene, she reached out and searched for his body in bed, coming up empty-handed. Sitting up, she jerked off her domino and stared in fright, as a sense of loss came over her.

A towel draped around his shoulders, Shelley paraded nude into her bedroom, a beaming smile on his radiant face. She resented his youth and beauty. It made her feel old somehow. Would Buck one day desire Shelley more than he wanted her? Why hadn't she adopted someone ugly or even deformed? Why had she adopted the world's most beautiful boy?

Ever since puberty, he'd been her sexual competitor. The first time she'd caught him with a lover, the All-America football player, Don Bossdum, had come as a shock and had led to a screaming fight over who was to have the six-foot-two-inch blond hunk. Even now, she recalled Shelley's words, *"He's practically signed an affidavit that he prefers my tight rosebud to your overripe charms."* She'd cringed at those words and feared her son might be right. Don had, in fact, ended up spending more evenings with Shelley than with her.

"Buck's gone," Shelley said. "Maybe we wore him out yesterday."

"We?" she asked, sitting up in bed. "Don't tell me you tried to move in on him."

"My lips are sealed."

"Get out!" she shouted. "You're disgusting."

Tossing the towel at her, he stood completely nude in front of her, then headed for Buck's pool and an early morning swim.

Rising reluctantly from her bed of lust, she headed for the same bathroom from which Shelley had emerged.

In front of the full-length bathroom mirror, she examined herself critically, hoping Buck would not apply so keen an eye. Even if he did, he'd find a slender, youthful-appearing body, in spite of her years. Perhaps not as young nor as firm as his own, but one possessing immense physical appeal all the same.

Through an open window a sudden ray of light stabbed the room, one of such brilliant intensity it momentarily blinded her. When her eyes adjusted to the light, her body appeared more vulnerable, indecently nude. Instead of a perfect curvature of figure, she detected telltale clues as to future and ominous sags of flesh. She retreated into the shower to avoid seeing her own body.

As she showered, her troubled mind realized she'd have to leave the cay at once to place her one important phone call of the day. Buck's line might be tapped, and this ritual international call demanded total secrecy.

As she dried herself, she found herself trembling at having to face her problems back on the mainland. All the violence, horror, and bloodshed. It seemed impossible to her that she'd surrendered so much of her own life to others. How wonderful if instead she could have spent the day in Buck's arms, making love again. She'd sold out long ago, and now her bosses were insistently demanding the return of that loan in ways she'd never imagined.

Buck remained her one grand hope. If only he'd accept her deal to become her media director. She knew that Calder wanted the job and felt he had the post in his pocket. There was a great struggle for supremacy with Calder within her own organization. She couldn't fight him alone. But with Buck firmly allied with her, she could slay Calder.

She might not be able to save the *Examiner* from a hostile takeover by Calder, but there would be other newspapers to conquer, new television and radio stations. The salary would be fantastic. As proof of her generosity, she was this very moment having a treasured gift sent to Buck's office. This gift would remind him that there was plenty more where that came from, if only he'd cooperate with her and write glowing praise of her image instead of his attacks.

Coming back into the bedroom, she wrapped a robe around herself and headed for the patio where Shelley was completing several laps in the pool. When he pulled himself from the water, he looked like an Adonis.

She realized she had to be very clever about her son. Instead of viewing Shelley as a competitor for Buck's sexual favors, maybe she should look upon him as part of the package. Buck would not only get her, but Shelley too. Surely the two of them would be more than adequate to satisfy Buck's sexual needs and keep him in permanent residence at Paradise Shores.

She knew Buck was involved with his secretary, Robert Dante. Calder had presented her with all the evidence, including secretly taped messages between them. But she also knew that Buck liked women and had made many conquests. It would serve her purpose if Buck developed an interest in Shelley. She feared the boy's philandering would eventually lead to a sexual scandal that would threaten her own image and her charismatic foundation. At least with Buck fucking him, he might stay home at night and out of trouble. Judging from last night's performance, Buck was certainly man enough to satisfy both of them.

She might even invite both of them into her bed at the same time. She'd always been curious about why men turned to each other for sex and rejected women. Maybe she could learn this lesson up close.

When Shelley came up to her and stood tantalizingly looking down at her from her position on a chaise longue, she tossed him a towel. "It's quite generous in size, darling," she said. "But Buck's got you beat by several inches."

"You should know after he lubricated your tonsils last night," he said. "Not to mention what else."

"You sound jealous. You want him just for yourself." She sat up as Henry appeared on the patio with morning coffee and juice. "This time I might let you share some of the goodies, but not possess him totally. I think I'm falling in love with him."

"He really must have been good for you. You don't love anybody."

"I've never been in love, and I'm not sure I am now. But I'm thinking about it. Don Bossdum had the physical endowments of Buck, but he didn't have the brain power. I think we both got tired of a man who sat around in his jockey shorts all day watching sports programs."

"Don had his charms. It was he who left us, remember?"

"I don't exactly recall. There have been so many. Buck is special. He could become part of my dream."

"You mean your nightmare."

"Drink your coffee, faggot," she said harshly. "We've got to get back to the mainland. I've got God's work to do!"

***

Robert had mysteriously disappeared. Back in Okeechobee, Buck had placed several calls to his friend but could not locate him. A call to the hospital revealed that Robert's mother had died only hours before. Buck was amazed that Robert hadn't called right away.

In the park that morning he needed his morning jog more than ever before facing whatever it was back at the office. For all he knew he would return to the news tower and find Roland occupying his main office instead of sitting at his usual place at the city desk.

A faint breeze was stirring but even so the day was muggy. He felt his clothes soaked in perspiration only five minutes into his jog. A red headband was catching his sweat that otherwise would pour down into his eyes, clouding his vision.

Only vaguely he became aware of a white limousine moving slowly along the street, following his trail as he jogged. Fearing trouble, he decided to veer inward through the park instead of running along its border. As he cut deeper into the park, the limousine stopped abruptly. The back door was thrown open, and a portly man with some difficulty emerged.

"Brooke! Wait up!" The voice was that of Calder Martin.

Seeing it was Calder, Buck ran toward the limousine. Nearing Calder, Buck stopped abruptly. One didn't want to get too close to pit vipers. "The last time we accidentally met," Buck said, "you told me you didn't talk to assholes from the *Examiner*."

"Get in!" Calder commanded.

At first the thought of a kidnapping flashed through Buck's mind. Even Calder wouldn't dare that. Buck decided to get in. Surely Calder had news.

In the air-conditioned back seat of Calder's limousine, the hatchet man of the far right offered him a whisky.

"No thanks," Buck said.

"Too early in the morning for you, sissy boy? Real men can drink at any hour."

"Help yourself, macho man."

Calder poured himself a generous drink from the limousine bar, then settled back against the plush upholstery. "Rose, so I've heard, has been making you all sorts of tempting offers. You can forget them."

"Why so?"

"I'm the only media director that cunt will ever need."

"But what if she wants me for the job?" Buck asked.

"Listen, and listen good, you little faggot. Rose and I are jockeying for position within our organization. She thinks she can run things. She's wrong. She's got no power to offer you anything. I'm the only one who can make offers."

"I'm not convinced of that."

"Rose is not convinced of it either."

Without responding, Buck called to the driver. "Take me to the *Examiner* news tower." He looked over at Calder. "Don't worry. I'll pay him the regular taxi fare."

"Cut the bullshit! This is a serious talk. I don't think you realize how easy it is for me to ruin somebody. I think you need a demonstration."

"What in hell are you foaming at the mouth about, liver lips?"

"Don't you ever call me that name. I can't stand to be called that."

"Get used to it."

"Fuck you! Okay, I'll prove something to you. I know how—what can I say?—fond you are of Gene Robinson. Let me demonstrate to you how easily I can destroy him. When you see how I do that, you'll get just a tiny preview of what I'm going to do to you."

"You leave Gene out of this," Buck said, perhaps a little too defensively. A look into Calder's steely eyes revealed a determination that frightened Buck. "What do you want?"

"You must never see Rose again. Stop any plans you have to expose her in the *Examiner*. In other words, back off!"

"She's too hot a news item for a publisher to ignore. And on a personal side, far too alluring."

As the limousine neared the news tower, Calder looked over at Buck intensely. "You've got to be taught some lessons. A little too cocky for me. This old ice shaver has warned you about my ability to cut off balls."

"You fucker! Don't you do anything to Gene. Your fight's not with him. It's with me. If you want to threaten somebody, make it me. Let him alone."

"Too late now. Get the hell out of my car. Somebody might see us together and think I'm a queer like you."

"Go to hell, you slimebag bastard."

"Let's lunch," Calder called mockingly after him, as the limousine pulled away from the curb.

***

Buck's stay on the island had stretched out far too long. He didn't like anyone thinking he was doing a bad job as publisher, deserting his post as Okeechobee became a hot news beat. He hoped Roland didn't know he'd just slept with one of the prime news figures herself.

When he came into his office, a temporary secretary had been hired in Robert's absence. "Any messages for me?" Buck asked, anxious to hear from Robert.

"Nothing," she said rather curtly.

In the rear quarters, Buck showered and dressed hurriedly and headed for his desk. A memo from Roland was waiting. "I know you've had Susan Howard on special assignment. Please abandon any long-range investigative reporting you may be doing about Sister Rose. In the future, I will direct any such coverage."

The secretary knocked on his door and entered. "You've got a surprise." She ushered in two security guards from Rose's temple, carrying a carefully boxed frame. Buck identified the men quickly from the emblems on their uniforms.

"What's this?" he demanded to know.

As if Buck had surrendered his soul, the secretary announced. "Would you believe a de Kooning?

A frown crossed Buck's face. The only person he'd ever confided in that he desired a de Kooning was Robert. Robert hardly had conveyed that request to Rose. That meant his line had been tapped. "Why don't you tear off the casing?" Buck asked.

One of the security guards removed the casing. The secretary picked up a tag attached to the painting. "It's called *East Hampton II, 1977*. Painted only this year. A review attached says it's in shocking magentas, blushing Neapolitan yellows."

Buck took in the painting and found it thrilling. It was one of the best de Koonings he'd ever seen.

Minutes later, the secretary buzzed him. "Ms. Phillips is on the phone."

"Tell her I have to meet someone at the airport, and I'm gone."

In the foyer he paused and turned to the secretary. "Are you certain Robert Dante didn't call?"

"Yes," she said rather matter-of-factly. "But someone did call while you were in the bathroom."

"Who?"

"Leroy Fitzgerald."

***

The Vulcan Baths at the Twenty-Third Street Beach had been built at the turn of the century, but now were deep in decay. The four-story building was painted a pea-green, and many of its outsized windows had been broken and never repaired.

Gene walked up the steps to the second floor and registered at the desk. After checking his watch and wallet, he was given a locker in a dormitory room with plain iron cots covered with sheets. Opening off these were a few private cubicles with a single cot in each. The attendant told him the steam baths, massage room, and swimming pool were in the basement.

After signing in, he wondered if he'd been wise in giving his real name. He stripped, placing his jeans and T-shirt in the locker assigned to him. He put on a robe of white sheeting similar to a hospital nightgown. It reached mid-thigh. On the way to the steam room, he noticed that the private cubicles were divided by wooden partitions reaching up about nine feet, but not touching the tall ceiling. He spotted holes drilled or crudely cut in the walls, perhaps by voyeurs.

At the entrance to the steam room, he left his robe on a numbered hook outside and entered nude, his sudden appearance attracting much attention from the sex shoppers.

He hoped he'd be able to spot Leroy in the dim light. Sandy had told him the leader of the Lolito ring hung out here at this time of day.

Brushing caressing hands from his body, Gene perched on a shelf, lined with Cuban tiles. The other bathers paraded around just to look at him. After fifteen minutes, he could hardly breathe and decided to go outside. Maybe Sandy had been wrong.

At the point he'd given up hope, he spotted Leroy joining the shopping circuit. At least he thought it was Leroy. He couldn't be sure. On closer inspection, he definitely recognized his old schoolmate.

Leroy cruised him, not making eye contact. Leroy was the only man in the room who hadn't been rejected by Gene. One elderly man warned him to stay away from Gene, though Leroy didn't take the man's advice. He sat down beside Gene and groped him. "Let's go upstairs," Gene whispered in his ear. "I don't want to put on a show."

Almost feverishly with excitement, Leroy gladly acquiesced. As Leroy turned to leave with the prize catch, he faced hostile stares from the other men.

In the shower stall outside, Gene kept his back turned to Leroy as he rinsed off his sweat. "Got a room?" he asked.

"Yeah," Leroy said, as he dried himself and reached for his robe. "Twenty-one."

"I'll meet you there," Gene promised, turning his face up to the water jet.

"Don't forget," Leroy called over his shoulder, bouncing toward the stairs. "I'll be waiting."

After Gene finished showering, he dried himself off and reached for his robe. So far, his plan was working.

After a quick rap on cubicle twenty-one, he was ushered inside by Leroy. "The bastard," Gene thought to himself. "He still hasn't looked at my face." Not that Leroy could see anybody's face very well in the near blackness of the room. Without saying a word, Leroy removed Gene's robe and dropped to his knees.

"You've got a big one," Leroy said, fondling him. "And the balls to match."

At that point Gene informed him he was under arrest. "You son of a bitch. You still don't even know who I am. The next time, look at his face when you proposition a guy." He grabbed the string of an exposed bulb overhead and turned it on.

There, to his horror, Leroy saw who it was. "Oh, my God," he said, his eyes wide with terror. "Please, let me off."

"You creep. Do you want to leave peacefully, or do I have to hand-cuff you?"

"No," Leroy said, trembling. "Don't make a fuss," he sighed in a resigned weariness. "I'll go."

Gene left the cubicle and went to his locker on the same floor. He rapped on Leroy's door again and when he opened it, he was dressed too, in jeans and a T-shirt just like Gene. He'd put on his sunglasses this time, and so had Gene. Leroy's face was reflected in Gene's mirrored lens. "I thought you guys had stopped all this entrapment shit."

"Biff's decided to crack down all over again," Gene said. It was a lie. He grabbed Leroy's arm. "You should have kept your brownnose clean, cocksucker!"

Gene had no intention of arresting Leroy, at least not at this point. He wanted to scare him into giving him information so he'd be better prepared for his meeting with his chief, Biff, later that day.

At the squad car, he shoved Leroy in and got in himself, taking the wheel.

His neck stiffening, Gene felt an uneasiness that had settled first in the pit of his stomach. "Do you want to go to police headquarters?" Gene asked. "Or do you want to take me to that Lolito house where we can talk first? I'm giving you a choice. You can also call your lawyer."

"Let's go to my condo instead," Leroy said with surprising confidence. "Unless you're afraid to be alone with me. Afraid of what it might lead to."

"Shut up, faggot!"

"I think before hauling me into the police station, you'd better learn some things and see some things I've got to show you. I'm saying this for your own good."

As Gene took his eyes off the road to observe Leroy closely, he felt he had touched only the tip of an iceberg. Today it felt more like a red hot poker. This was no simple boy prostitution ring, he feared, but something bigger.

"Your taking me in could cause more harm for you than for me," Leroy threatened.

"Cut the shit, man!" Even as he harshly rebuked Leroy, Gene feared the photographer might be telling the truth.

Leroy stared vacantly out the window, waiting for Gene to decide. "You're in big trouble," he warned Leroy.

For some reason, Leroy seemed to have the upper hand. "Take me to my apartment. It's at 400 West View Street."

Without saying another word, Gene drove in that direction, wondering as he did how many times Leroy had seduced Sandy. The idea of Leroy's hands and mouth crawling all over Sandy disgusted him.

"This whole thing is messier and bigger than you think," Leroy said finally, as the squad car neared his apartment. "I'm their victim too. They make me do what I do. I'm not taking this rap alone—not by a lone shot."

Going up on the elevator, Gene said nothing. When Leroy stood in front of the door to his apartment and inserted the key, Gene entered quickly, glancing down the hallway as he did.

Once inside, Leroy said, "You can relax now. I'll get you a drink. You can take off anything you want. I've seen it all. Years ago I even photographed it. What an impressive sight!"

"We didn't come here for a seduction," Gene said.

"Too bad. You're missing out on the thrill of a lifetime. I'm an expert sword swallower."

"I'll take a raincheck," Gene said.

"I can't believe you're here in my apartment. Do you know how many nights I've dreamed about this? I've known many men, but you're my all-time fantasy. If you don't believe me, take a look at my bathroom."

"What are you talking about?"

"Go on, take a look. It's just down the hallway."

Out of curiosity and feeling no longer in charge, Gene walked down the corridor and flipped on the light switch in the luxurious bathroom. To his amazement, the walls were covered with reproductions of that frontal nude photograph Leroy had snapped of him in the shower room at the university. He wondered how many men Leroy had invited here to view the show.

As if anticipating his question, Leroy stood behind him. "All my gay friends have seen it. They all have a crush on you. You don't need to exhibit it to that little girl. You can exhibit it to my friends any day. We'll even pay you and I mean a lot."

Gene turned around and grabbed Leroy, shoving him up against the wall. "You little shit. I should beat the hell out of you right now."

"That's okay with me providing it ends with a brutal rape. I love that! From you, it would be divine."

"You don't really run this show, do you?" Gene snarled. "Who's the big enchilada behind it?"

"I'll make a deal with you. If you fuck me with that big cock of yours, I'll nibble on your ear while you're doing it. As you blast off in me, I'll whisper the name in your ear. Is it a deal?"

Gene stood in the bright sunlight of the apartment, with its views of a nearby park. There was a sudden stillness in the room. He moved closer to Leroy's picture windows. All he was thinking was about that long ago day when Leroy had photographed him. He'd known what Leroy was doing. It was hard to admit it but he was thrilled to be photographed totally exposed that way. He'd wanted to be desired by the worshipping eyes and lens of Leroy. In site of himself, he felt his penis lengthening.

***

In a black Chanel suit, Susan felt she'd never looked better than when she'd entered a terminal at the Miami International Airport. Before disembarking, she'd gone to the airplane bathroom to apply the final touches to her makeup. Getting her hair styled in New York had helped too.

As she raced toward a waiting Buck, she felt secure in her marriage, although knowing that was only a fleeting impression. As he ran to hug and kiss her, he evoked an image of his university days when she used to spot him jogging on campus in a pair of shorts that revealed an endowment greater than that of the university.

After kissing her on the lips a second time, he lifted her off her feet and whirled her in the air. He seemed delighted to see her, but perhaps he was putting on a show for the other passengers milling about.

"I send you off to New York a country girl and you come back a fashion star."

"Wait till you get the bill," she said.

"I'll survive."

"Glad to be back," she said. "We haven't even gone on a honeymoon."

A frown crossed his brow.

She wondered if it were an indication there would be no honeymoon.

"Come on," he said. "I'm driving you to your condo. I hired someone to get it ready for you."

She noted that he said "ready for you"—not ready for us.

In his car on the way to the beach, she kept the talk light with tales of her experiences in the north. She confessed she'd like to go there at least once a month, preferably with him.

He didn't immediately accept such an invitation. "I'm such a Florida boy. I always feel out of place in New York. Anywhere for that matter. Except Okeechobee."

"Don't tell me you're as provincial as all that."

"I'm a simple man with simple tastes. All I want is a mansion, my own newspaper, a private island, a luxurious yacht, and the most beautiful woman in Florida."

"You've got those, except perhaps the most beautiful woman in Florida. Some of my worst enemies say I'm only the second most beautiful." She smiled to indicate she was teasing.

He laughed and didn't say anything for a long while, as if thinking about something he didn't want to tell her. She wanted to ask him about Robert. Had he been told of their marriage?

"It's been very rough at the *Examiner*. Roland's clanking his balls. I gave you all the details on the phone. Old Buck went ahead and told him to take you off the South Beach thing. I don't think Roland even knows about the Lolito story."

"The son of a bitch." Her heart seemed to sink.

"I don't know what's going on," he said. "but there's been a mysterious transfer of most of the company's voting stock. Who will own it or run it, especially after old Buck is gone, I don't know."

"I always thought you owned twelve percent."

"That was left to me by my parents. But that's hardly a big enough percentage to control the paper."

"Buck is going to will you his share, won't he? Especially now that we're married?"

"I assume he will. He owns twenty-five percent. That would give me thirty-seven percent—still not enough to control the paper."

"You'd at least be the biggest shareholder. The other stocks are diversified. No one has complete control."

"What if someone acquired the majority stock?" he asked.

She reached for his hand on the wheel and delicately ran caressing fingers across it. "I don't want you to be in harm's way."

"Deep down I feel I am," he said.

As Buck's car neared the condo, so much more luxurious than the one Hazel occupied, she realized that she didn't know this man riding with her. She had married a stranger.

***

With his back on the living room carpet, Leroy eagerly received Gene's pounding thrusts. Leroy sighed deeply each time Gene plunged into him. Instead of thinking about the present penetration, Gene's mind had drifted to only minutes before when he had strained Leroy's jaws wide and exerted pressure against the lining of his throat. Leroy's devouring mouth had welcomed the pain.

A burning desire kept Gene at fever pitch. He wanted those final two inches in Leroy. With all his strength, he lunged into Leroy. Leroy screamed in pain but his hands reached to clutch and claw at Gene's back. Gene knew that Leroy's insides were turned into a boiling pit.

A feeling of triumph came over Gene as he neared his climax. He liked having Leroy under his control. Gene pressed his body brutally against Leroy's. He would pull out until the lip of his cock head was showing, then he would drive into Leroy with greater force than he'd ever used on anybody.

Leroy was not only yelling loudly but crying as well. Gene's pulsating, hammering cock spewed forth within Leroy which triggered his own spectacular climax, bathing Gene's chest. Collapsing on top of Leroy, he lay here for several minutes. Leroy was still moaning softly and running his hands caressingly over Gene's body.

Leroy put his lips against Gene's left ear. "Calder Martin."

Gene pulled out abruptly and headed for the shower. Glancing only briefly at the nudes of himself lining the bathroom walls, Gene welcomed the cleansing effect of the hot water spray jets from the shower. He wanted to wash off all traces of Leroy.

Gene thought not of the Lolito investigation but of Rose. Little did she know that two key figures in her moral crusade, Calder Martin and Barry Collins, were part of the filth she rallied against. If only he could get to her and warn her.

If Calder were behind this, Gene had to be extra careful. Calder Martin didn't operate a sex ring for his own gratification. If Calder were behind the ring, blackmail would be the motive. Who was he blackmailing? Barry Collins, for openers.

As Gene held his face up to the water jet, he feared this case was too much for him. The very men he investigated had the power to move in on him at any moment.

After drying himself and wrapping a towel around his body, he came back into the living room. In his bathrobe, Leroy was putting down the phone.

Gene stopped and looked intently at Leroy who only smiled.

"That was the most thrilling seduction of my whole life," Leroy said. "It was worth the wait all these years."

Gene heard not the sexual flattery but was left with the distinct suspicion that Leroy had just hung up the phone on Calder Martin.

***

"It's severe and masculine—that's why I like it," Susan said, surveying her new home, a nine-room condo overlooking the ocean. Her own possessions, she noted, had been moved here, and they appeared shabby in contrast to the luxurious furnishings. The decorator obviously liked shades of black and brown.

"It's certainly not pink and girlish," Buck said.

The sunlight streamed into the apartment, making his blond hair blonder. She had never seen him look this handsome before, and found it hard to believe that she was married to him.

"I'm glad you moved my stuff over. That took a bit of phallic thrust."

"I thought if we took all your stuff and mixed it in with the new stuff, you'd feel more at home," he said.

"Something old, something new. And you...are you what is borrowed?"

"I'm a free agent," he said.

She walked toward the kitchen to pour herself a drink. "Want one?"

"It's a bit early, isn't it?"

"Perhaps, but I thought I needed a bit of fortification before I pursued this conversation. Have you told Robert Dante about our marriage?"

"No." His voice turned a bit hostile. "Robert's in Miami. His mother died. I don't even know where he is right now."

"Don't you usually know where Robert is every minute of every day?" she asked.

"Yes!" he virtually shouted, turning his back to her and walking toward the picture windows overlooking the ocean. "Every minute of every hour of every day of every week of every month of every year." He turned and glared at her. "Is that what you wanted to hear?"

"I want to understand how things are. I'm to live here. Robert is to live in your home. I'm not to go there, is that right?"

"You've got it."

"It's a new marriage. My second, your first. I want to understand the ground rules."

"Well, those are the rules. You live here. Robert lives there."

"I can accept that. Are you in love with Robert?"

"I don't know about the 'in love' part. But I've loved him from the very first moment I ever saw him. He and I share a bond that's unbreakable."

"You'll be spending your nights with Robert?"

"Robert has rights too," he said.

"You mean rights to you?"

"Any time—day or night—that he calls for me, I'm there for him."

Drink in hand, she stood only a few feet from him, facing his back. "I'm not opposed to anything you told me. I went into my marriage with Gene like a blind fool. I'm not going into a marriage with you with the same innocence."

"Thanks," he said, turning around to face her and staring deeply into her eyes. "Can we be friends? Sometimes lovers?"

"Yes," she said. "We can be fantastic friends and occasional lovers."

"I'm prepared to make it work," he said.

She downed the rest of her drink. The phone rang, and she went over to pick up the receiver.

It was old Buck's butler. "You and Mr. Buck have got to come over right away. He's demanding to see both of you immediately. He's flying in a few hours to a clinic in Switzerland. Maybe for good."

"We'll be right there." She put down the phone. "Old Buck wants to see us right away. And why not? That's what this marriage was all about anyway, wasn't it? A show for a dying man about to leave you a vast fortune."

"Sounds a bit harsh," he said.

"Let's go!" she said, looking for her purse

***

Leroy, drink in hand, trailed Gene to the terrace. "Calder Martin's known for some time that you've been investigating the Lolito ring. There's nothing in this town that escapes him."

Gene shot a quick glance at Leroy, then stared vacantly at the sea. "Does Biff already know of this sex ring?"

Leroy smiled enigmatically. "What do you think?"

Gene could feel his own heart pounding. The investigation for which he'd anticipated receiving the praise of the department had begun to crumble. "Do you think Biff and Calder know the *Examiner* is onto it too?"

"They know all about it. They even know that a guy named Terry Drummond met with Susan Howard. I'm sure you remember her well."

"Cut the shit, man! You know I was married to her."

"Of course, I do." He walked over to Gene and reached for his arm, as Gene pulled away. "C'mon," Leroy said. "I'm giving you some hot advice: drop this thing. Pretend it doesn't exist. These men can destroy you. And if you don't believe me, read an item on page two of this morning's *Examiner*. It's right over there on the sofa."

Gene scanned the page quickly. All the news was international except one local item. A vagrant, Terry Drummond, had been found dead this morning along Indian Creek Trail near the Vista Linda Motel. Apparently while wandering drunk along the side of the highway, he'd been struck down by a hit-and-run driver. "Who is this Drummond?" Gene demanded to know.

"He used to be my lover," Leroy said. "We had a fight. I replaced him. A big mistake on my part. Unknown to me, he'd accumulated hardcore evidence about the boy ring. He even sold some of it to the *Examiner*. Susan now owns some incriminating photographs of Barry Collins."

All this was too much for Gene. Still close by his side, Leroy took the *Examiner* from Gene's hands. "The brothel has already served its purpose. Even before you began to investigate it, Calder had gotten all the blackmail evidence he needs. He's really got some of the top men in this town by the short hairs."

"Like Barry Collins?"

"When Barry beats that dyke Hazel for mayor," Leroy predicted, "Calder will own his ass."

Gene felt trapped. "I'd better drop this Lolito thing. Like right now."

"If you know what's good for you. You don't have to be some stupid policeman. Not with what you've got. I could market you. That's like as in meat market. Within a year you could be rich. Hell, you could make a fortune in porn. I've got connections. My friends in this town will pay—and pay plenty—for exhibitions...or whatever. You can always come and live here with me in luxury. Why not opt for the good life with plenty of money? No one at that crooked police department gives a damn about you or your moral crusade." Leroy raised his eyebrows provocatively.

"Thanks for the offer. I'll consider it. But aren't you worried for your own safety? You do know a hell of a lot."

"I've protected myself. I'm not some dumb turd like Terry."

Gene was overcome with a strong suspicion that Leroy would be dead within weeks.

Leroy went into a small library off his living room, as Gene trailed him. In the room Leroy opened a safe and handed a small book—bound in black leather—to Gene.

Slowly Gene read the names in that book. It was a list of Leroy's most preferred customers, stating their preferences in young boys and detailing the sex scenes they were into. In stunned disbelief, Gene sounded each name on his lips, substituting the position of the man in the community—the vice president of the Okeechobee First National Bank, the dean of men at Okeechobee High School, a Catholic priest from the neighboring town of Cypress, the president of the Okeechobee Memorial Hospital.

Then his eyes focused on one name. It stood out from all the rest. "Barry Collins," he said out loud. Trembling, Gene continued to turn the pages. A local Boy Scout executive. A circuit judge, William F. Gamble. "My God, the chief's best friend." He closed the book quickly.

Leroy placed the book back in his safe. "That's not all. I have pictures too." He reached into his safe and removed a manila envelope. "This is just one envelope. There are many others. Of course, Calder has the first ones I developed. After all, it was his idea to open the brothel—just to blackmail. But this one fox had copies made. I'm not going to end up like Terry Drummond." He presented the envelope to Gene. "If anything happens to me, I have the negatives locked in a bank vault. They're going to go to the *Okeechobee News*, the only honest paper in town."

As Leroy went to pour a drink, Gene opened the envelope. There were pornographic pictures of the men whose names he'd seen in the black book—glossy eight-by-tens of the so-called pillars of the community, photographed secretly in various sexual positions with teenage boys.

He swallowed hard when he came to the picture of Barry. The face of the mayoral candidate was clearly obvious. In one picture he was sodomizing a teenage boy. Another photograph showed his fully nude body, as two young boys, really children, made love to him. Secretly he slipped three of the most revealing pictures of Collins under his shirt.

He returned the manila envelope to the safe as Leroy came back into the room. "I don't think I'll have that drink after all. I have a meeting with Biff later in the day, and I don't want to show up drunk."

"Suit yourself."

"One thing you said really bothered me. You said Calder might be taking over the *Examiner*. I happen to know that Buck Brooke—the young one—hates Calder."

"Don't be naïve," Leroy said, heading for the safe and removing another manila envelope. "Buck's one of them. He's all part of the sorry mess." He reached into the envelope and pulled out a picture of Buck snapped on his private island.

Gene took the picture from him. Buck was wearing a bikini so transparent he might as well be nude.

"I shot that of him recently. He agreed to pose because he wanted a favor from me. I'm fixing him up with my most delectable boy. Buck is a child molester too. Just like Barry Collins."

Gene thrust the photograph into Leroy's hand. "I'm out of here. It's been fun," he said to Leroy, heading quickly for the door.

"You come back any time," Leroy said, racing after him. "Any time of the day or night. You can make big money."

"Thanks for the invite." Gene felt his blood bubbling.

At the door, Leroy said, "You know what I think? I think you made up that story about arresting me. I probably caught you at the Vulcan, and you had to say something. Frankly, dear, you weren't very convincing. I just played along."

"Let's keep that one of our little secrets."

Out on the street again, the rich stench of frying grease and onions from a Cuban hamburger reminded him that he hadn't eaten all day. He couldn't take time for that now. Another hunger gnawed at him.

***

Later in the day the police chief read the *Okeechobee News* and, at the same time, seemed impatient with his interview with Gene.

Gene glared at Biff. It was all he could do to conceal his hatred and contempt from his chief. No more than five feet, Biff was thinly built, a shade hunchbacked, and he'd taken a little gray hair and spread it across his nearly bald head. His desk had been placed on a platform, giving him a decided advantage over persons he interviewed who were forced to look up to him.

Biff slammed down his paper and turned intense eyes on Gene. "I'm telling all my men that the aim of this police department is to do whatever we can to see that Barry Collins becomes mayor. He's a great friend of this department. I know that you've known Barry for a long time. I heard rumors you've come up with something on him. Spill the beans."

Gene hesitated for a long moment. "There's nothing, I guess. Clean as a hound's tooth, as I'm sure you know."

"I know plenty, and I'd say that was a truthful evaluation. Clean as a hound's tooth."

Gene suspected "they" had bought Biff, too. Was Calder Martin in charge of the police department?

"All men have a weakness o r two. Even me who likes to drink too many sometimes." Biff went over to his liquor cabinet and removed a bottle of Chivas Regal, offering Gene a drink which was refused. From a bucket filled with ice, he extracted two cubes and poured himself a generous one. "Deciding which law breakers to pursue and which to leave alone is tough for me. But that's why they made me head of the department. You can't lock up the whole fucking town. There's probably a million people in Okeechobee right this minute breaking some God damn law. Selective enforcement—that's what the law is all about. Every day an honest citizen breaks some law, maybe a law he doesn't even know he's breaking. There are so many damn laws on the books, we can't enforce them all."

Gene knew at this point a protest to Biff would fall on deaf ears. He didn't have his heart in the Lolito case any more.

Biff slowly sipped his drink and eyed Gene cautiously. "Harming Barry would allow that cunt, Hazel Phillips, to get at our soft underbelly. Could you imagine what the police force would be like with Hazel as mayor?"

"Would you be proud to serve under Barry?" Gene asked.

The chief moved menacingly toward him, the way Gene had seen him do with criminal suspects. "Barry Collins might have pumped it to a little boy with that boy's consent, with that boy getting paid and with that boy being nothing but a cheap hooker who loves to get plowed anyway." He came to a stop only inches before Gene and was forced to look up to him. "Gene Robinson, on the other hand, exposed himself to a little girl and, as you damn well know, destroyed that poor child's life."

As Biff returned to his desk, Gene had a sinking feeling. Dreading what was coming next, he feared he'd throw up.

"Do you know what the guys call you around the department?" Biff asked sarcastically.

Gene cringed, not answering.

"The flasher! Yeah, you heard me. The flasher!"

The word cut into Gene and he headed for the door.

Determined to go on, Biff called after him. "Just the other day, one of my men washed off a little ditty someone had written about you in the men's room. I had him make a copy before erasing it." The chief reached into his desk and pulled out a piece of paper which he held up for Gene to inspect. Gene made no attempt to retrieve the paper. "I'll read it," Biff said threateningly.

A lover of tennis, 'tis said, named Gene
Could piss on his friends with a golden stream
And though we hear that his penis is thick
We regret to say that something is sick
Whenever, well seasoned, it came into sight,
A little blonde girl would quickly take flight
A pity, you say, that matrons do lack
So often for dick in the depths of the sack
When sickies like Gene, a tad adolescent
Jerk off in the face of females pubescent.

Gene closed his eyes, then opened them to the blazing light streaming in through the large picture window. He stood very still and, though the office was air conditioned, he felt intense heat.

"You don't look well," Biff said. "Frankly, I've been hearing reports that you're coming unglued. Acting real irrational. I thought you might be fucked up in the head. But then I've just received this psychiatric evaluation of you. The psychiatrist we hire to observe you men thinks you're in great mental and physical condition. Still, I have my doubts. Those shrinks don't know everything. I want you to take the day off. Hell! Take the whole week off. It will do you good."

At the door, Gene looked back. "Thanks." He felt defeated. "When I come back on the job, you tell me what you want me to work on."

The look on Biff's face revealed his pride in knowing he'd won this round. "You're lucky I hired you in the first place. You should have been thrown in jail as a child-molesting flasher. Now get out of here."

Gene closed the door behind him, trying to blot out Biff's words. Biff had humiliated him to the point where he felt he could not tolerate it. He went to the phone and dialed the psychiatrist's office, and was granted an appointment right away. Even before going home, he needed to be with that psychiatrist. That shrink made him feel big and important, and he'd even written a report that Gene was in good mental and physical condition. Biff had stripped Gene of his dignity and manhood. He knew the psychiatrist could restore his faith in himself.

The psychiatrist would worship him and make him feel like a man again, the way Leroy had done only this morning.

***

At Buck I's estate, his luggage was neatly stacked in the hallway waiting for a limousine, and the old man himself was sitting in a wheelchair in his living room, wearing a heavy wool coat in spite of the stifling heat of the day.

Buck III, his arm linked possessively with Susan's, went over and kissed his grandfather on the forehead. The coldness of the man frightened him. One look into those steely blue eyes told Buck what he always knew and suspected: his grandfather was none too happy turning over his riches and his world to Buck III.

As he pulled back from the dying man and Susan kissed his forehead, Buck III suspected another reason. His grandfather truly hoped there would be a Buck IV to carry on his name.

After he'd been dutifully kissed, Buck I glowered at his grandson. "It took you long enough to get here. A dying man doesn't like to be kept waiting."

"The plane doesn't leave for three hours," Buck III said. "We've got plenty of time to get you there."

"I like to get to the airport real early and watch the people," Buck I said. "You young people today wait until the last minute for everything." He looked toward Susan with more kindness than he showed his grandson. "You even wait too long to get married. Right now you should be holding up Buck IV for me to kiss, and I fear he's not even in the oven yet."

"We're getting there," Buck III assured him. "In time."

Ruefully, Buck I said, "Time..." He paused. "That's something I don't have in great supply."

"You're going to be fine," Susan said, although her voice didn't sound that reassuring. "If you've got anything that can be cured, the doctors of Switzerland can cure it for you."

"I've got something that can't be cured," Buck I said. "Old age."

"You'll live a lot longer," Buck III said, placing firm fingers on his arm. In a display of affection that was real, Buck III lifted his grandfather's withered hand and pressed it against his cheek before kissing the palm.

The old man withdrew his hand. "We Florida swamp studs don't go in for hand-kissing." He called for his butler to bring him a final brandy. He offered one to both Buck III and Susan. Clearly this was their final drink together.

"A toast to your marriage and a toast to the future Buck IV." The old man lifted the glass to his parched lips and downed the brandy in one gulp. That set off a coughing spasm.

"Are you okay?" Buck III asked.

His grandfather looked at him harshly. "No, God damn it!" he said. "I'm not going to be okay ever again."

"We still have hope for you," Susan said reassuringly. "Buck and I want you to live to see little Buck IV grow up. I bet he'll take after you."

Buck I looked up at her and smiled. She was obviously catering to the dying man.

From a slight distance away, Buck III realized she was better at these goodbye scenes than he was. She was playing her role. A vast fortune was at stake. He'd definitely owe her one for this.

"As soon as I arrange some things here in Okeechobee," Buck III said, "I'll fly to Switzerland to join you."

Buck I looked up at him with the first kindness he'd shown him all day. "That would be nice, providing those arrangements you're making here in Okeechobee aren't my funeral."

"Who knows?" Buck III said. "As tough as you are, you might outlive us all."

"That I doubt," Buck I said, coughing again but the sound came out more like a clearing of his throat this time. "There are one or two final requests I have before heading out."

The butler came into the room to announce the limousine had arrived.

"Tell him to wait." He motioned for Buck III to come closer to him. As Buck III neared his chair, Buck I reached out and yanked at his grandson's tie, choking him and pulling his face almost against Buck I's nose. When he spoke, spittle peppered young Buck's face. "I want you to promise me something."

Buck III pulled back slightly but instinct told him not to take his hand and wipe the spittle from his face. "What do you want me to do?"

"I don't want Robert Dante to set foot in this house. Have I made that perfectly clear?"

"He'll not come here," Buck said.

"Another thing. I want you to will this house to Buck IV when you're finished with it. I want him to get married and settle down here, and the little fucker had better leave all the portraits of me hanging on the walls. I want him to remember that it was his old grandpa—not you—who fixed him up so grandly in life."

"He'll treasure your memory," Susan said. "His only regret will be that you weren't around to see him grow up. But who knows? We'll pray that you will always be with us."

"That's nice," he said. He looked over at Buck III. As if to warn his grandson that he'd hardly become a sentimental old fool, he reached for Buck III's arm and again pulled him close. "Hear this one thing, and hear it good. In case you think you can pull a fast one, and divorce Susan the moment I die, I've had a provision written in my will. It was signed at ten o'clock this morning."

Buck III looked startled. "What is it?"

"The provision reads that if you and Susan divorce, everything I've left you will go to my favorite charity which is dedicated to pre-serving the wildlife of Florida."

Buck III felt overheated and he knew sweat was about to drip from his brow, but he dared not make the gesture of wiping it away. He walked over to Susan and kissed her lightly on the lips. "We have no intention of ever getting a divorce."

Susan smiled back and then leaned forward and kissed Buck I on the forehead again. "We'll be together when we're old and gray."

"Or until death do you part," Buck I said. "That's the way it was with my Nellie. I was at her bedside the night she died." He looked at Buck III with a disapproval in his eye. "A man and a woman. That was God's intention."

"You'll be proud of your grandson," Susan said, "and definitely of your great-grandson."

"Can't we go with you to the airport?" Buck III said.

"Hell, no! We can handle that ourselves. Now I want both of you to leave. The garden is beautiful this time of the year. Go walk in it. I don't want you seeing the way they lift me into the limousine. I want you to remember me here in this living room."

"We'll go," Susan said, reaching to kiss him again.

"No more kisses, no more hugs. I hate farewells. Just go." He signaled the butler to come for him.

"Until we meet in Switzerland." Buck III said, taking Susan's hand and heading for the garden. He stood with her in the garden enjoying the flowers, the trees, and the bright day. "You're beautiful," he told her. "I've never seen you more beautiful." He pulled her to him and kissed her passionately on the lips. "If only we could lead the dream life envisioned for us by the old man."

"If only we could," she said, breaking away to inspect a bush around which a butterfly hovered.

A breeze drifted up from below where the cottage stood. Although the day was peaceful and the scene looked harmless, Buck felt someone was spying on them. He couldn't be sure. He excused himself, claiming he had to retrieve something from the cottage. He walked rapidly to the back where he spotted a recently smoked cigarette ground out in the dirt. There were tire marks too. They looked like the marks of a motorcycle. He reached down and picked up the cigarette butt. As he did, he heard the sound of a motorcycle in the distance.

He walked back toward the garden and Susan. This tranquil scene was no longer peaceful to him. The day and the garden had grown sinister.

Chapter Seven

The session with the psychiatrist had gone well. Gene could still feel the excitement of the sucking mouth taking pleasure from his body. He had been worshipped, his manhood had been praised, and he'd literally reduced the doctor who was to evaluate him into a quivering ball of lust. When he'd left the office, the doctor had begged him to stay. "I'm in love with you," he told Gene. "I've had a hundred police officers—maybe a lot more. Married, unmarried, whatever. No one is the man you are."

When he got home, he came in through the kitchen door, wondering where Sandy and Jill were. He thought they might be up front in the living room. As he walked up the hallway, he heard noises coming from Jill's bedroom. He knew the sound well. They were making love. Not just love, but mad, passionate love.

So as not to disturb them, he tiptoed back down the hallway and into the kitchen.

The house felt strangely confining. Almost overnight, it'd become a love nest. Feeling excluded, he retreated to his garden.

The sun had made its full rise in the clear sky and was beginning a slow descent. Its rays reflected across Gene's shaded backyard, turning the plants a green-gold. He entered a gate and went behind his garage where he'd built a sundeck. It was completely fenced in and could only be entered through this private gate. Nervously he ran fingers through his hair as a shadow fell across his forehead.

Removing his T-shirt, he sucked in the fresh air, enjoying how it inflated his broad chest. He slipped off his jeans and jockey shorts. He could still smell the aroma of sex that lingered after the psychiatrist had devoured him. Sitting down on a canvas chair, he shut his eyes, enjoying the velvet flashes of red, orange, and yellow that came through the trees overhead. Drops of sweat lubricated his skin. Opening his eyes, he admired the form of his taut body, tanned to a deep bronze except for the vee which his brief bikini usually protected. Tracing his flesh with his hands, he lay back again, shutting his eyes once more.

Under feathery clouds gathering on the horizon, he eventually dropped off to sleep. He didn't know for how long. A burning sensation on his skin caused him to wake up. Maybe it was a mosquito bite. At first he didn't open his eyes, but lay there calmly as he began a slow, stroking movement of his cock. As he massaged it, it started to swell. Buck may have rejected him, and it appeared that Sandy had found other interests. But Leroy thought he was a god. After only two sessions, the psychiatrist had fallen in love with him.

Eerily, he became aware of a presence. Slowly, he opened his eyes. No longer blue, the sky was streaked with pink. He cast his head up and, as he did, he saw her standing there, her wide eyes filled with a child's wonder.

Maybe it was a bad dream. Perhaps he was reliving that awful experience of long ago when he'd exposed himself to that little girl, the same little girl who was grown up now and making a woman's love to Sandy in the front room.

Maybe it was a blurry dream, a flashback from his past. But he wasn't in his car. The little girl didn't look the same. Not blonde and fair as before.

She was one of the "invaders." The little Cuban girl, Maria. Her stringy hair was as black as her eyes—heartless, vaporless. Her grubby fingers were held like a shield at her unwashed face. "You're dirt," she accused. "It looks like a snake."

The muscles in his stomach tightened as he sought to get control over his rage. Before, with the other girl, he'd seen the blush of tender bloom. Today, he confronted vulgarity—a coarse, crude little monster who cringed at the sight of him.

Jumping to his feet as if in a state of madness, he lunged toward the trespassing girl, ordering her out of his retreat. She backed off, letting out a scream that pierced the air.

Without his clothes, he hurried to his back yard where he wanted to retreat into the privacy of his home.

Hearing her daughter's scream, Maria's mother, Clara, came onto the grounds. She shouted something in Spanish at him he didn't understand. At the sight of his nude body, she crossed herself and protectively grabbed her sobbing daughter, who'd rushed into her arms. Once safely cuddled there, Clara shielded her daughter from the sight of Gene.

From the adjoining backyard, two Cuban women crossed into his driveway to see what the disturbance was. Enraged at the spectacle, they stared defiantly at him. He stood menacingly at the head of his steps leading into his home.

Here he was, caught without his clothes. He didn't even have his mirrored sunglasses to protect his eyes from the probing stares.

"*Policia!*" one of the Cuban women shouted.

"Call the emergency number," Clara yelled. Picking up her daughter, she carried her in a run toward the street. The other women followed behind.

Gene darted into his kitchen, slamming the door behind him, locking it, and pulling down the shades. A note was on the kitchen table. It was from Sandy and Jill. They'd gone shopping for fresh vegetables. The flounder they planned for dinner had been left out to defrost. Without a protective wrapper, blue-green flies buzzed around it, descending. He imagined them laying filthy eggs to contaminate their meal.

He rushed into his bedroom, as if approaching an abyss. The hallway itself was actually like a serpentine stream, seeming to move.

Outside came angry shouts, then enraged men shouting in Spanish at his front door. Was it Maria's father backed up by a posse of other men?

He'd locked the back door tightly as if that would keep out the world. He'd done nothing wrong. But who would believe that?

Angry voices continued to be heard from the street outside, resounding inside his tortured head. In the far distance, he imagined he heard the sound of happy children playing.

***

Haunted by the fear that Gene had been secretly spying on Susan and him at Buck I's estate, Buck III jogged in the park, inhaling the fresh breezes from the sea. He'd agreed to meet with Susan on his private island in the early evening, and needed this time alone.

He'd made several efforts to reach Robert, who seemed to have vanished. In his frequent calls to Miami, he'd learned that Robert had made no arrangements for the funeral of his mother.

As he ran close to the northern tier of the park bordering the boulevard, he spotted a stretch limousine in a bright shade of rose. A memory of a similar encounter with Calder Martin crossed his mind. That luxury car could only belong to one person in Okeechobee. As if to confirm his suspicion, a chauffeur in elephant gray attire opened the driver's door and got out to assist the passenger in the rear.

Rose emerged onto the sidewalk. She was clad in a form-fitting white dress with a rose-colored belt which was matched by a scarf in the same color at her neck. White high heels effectively called attention to her shapely legs. Her auburn hair seemed set afire in the afternoon sun and, as she walked toward him, she appeared like a young girl. In spite of her years, Rose's body looked just as young as Susan's.

Slowly his jog came to a dead stop, as he stood and let Rose approach him. Her skin was porcelain, her face vibrant. Her flame-red lipstick gave her the look of a 40s movie star, almost like Betty Grable.

Without saying a word, Rose stood in front of him and kissed him deeply, a kiss that evoked possession as much as passion.

"I won't dare ask," he told her, "how you knew I wanted a de Kooning. I loved it. Too bad I can't accept it."

"Don't be a fool, darling. I paid nothing for it. It was a gift from one of my followers. She left it to my temple in her will. I can't stand de Kooning. But I must admit I kept the Matisse she left for myself. Shelley, that precious dear, took the two Picassos and hung them in his bedroom. I don't like Picasso either."

"I feel it's presented like a reward for a great roll in the hay—which it was."

"Indeed it was. I think we both owe each other something for that. It was the greatest I've ever had, and I'm not exactly the Virgin Mary. As for the de Kooning, I know how to make you keep it."

"What do you mean?"

"If you return it to Paradise Shores, I'll slash it to ribbons."

He looked deeply into her eyes. "I believe you would."

She returned his look with a certain defiance. "You know I would!"

"Then it's settled. The de Kooning is mine."

"Let's get in the back seat of that limousine and head for Paradise Shores."

"I can't," he said, breaking away. "I've got another appointment."

"Bullshit!" she said. "I have two important dinner guests tonight.

Ronald and Nancy. They're flying up from Miami but I'd turn them down if you asked me to."

"I didn't know they were coming to town. We should cover it for the *Examiner*."

"It's a secret visit. This broken down actor wants to be president of the United States. Can you imagine? He's privately seeking the support of my foundation. Of course, he'd like millions of voters delivered to him, not to mention how much cash."

"Are you going to sign up?" he asked.

"In the weeks ahead, Ronnie and Nancy will deny ever having met me."

"Why's that?"

"That's for me to know and you to find out." She smiled enigmatically. "Reagan's okay. I once went to bed with him."

"How was it?"

"Just so-so. He likes to shower before the act, then rush to shower at the end. Squeaky clean sex. Not down and dirty like we had last night. Reagan doesn't have your stupendous equipment."

"That's enlightening, I guess."

"Nancy is the problem. I just don't like her. She and I have competed for the same guys before. You know, she was known as the fellatio queen of Hollywood. But I think I'm better at that than bitch Nancy."

"You're very good. I haven't sampled Nancy yet."

"I'm sure she'd go for it. I have an idea. Why don't you join us at dinner tonight? While I'm entertaining Ronnie, I can arrange for you and Nancy to go for a walk in the garden. I'm sure you two can duck into my guest bungalow. She can try out her fabled technique on you, then the next morning you announce the victor. Nancy or me."

"That sounds tempting, but I can't."

"Very well," she said. "You turned down my invitation to lunch. Surely you can't deny me afternoon tea when I tell you I have some top-secret news to report to you about the *Examiner*."

"You're going to tell me the secret?"

"You'll love the tea, but not the news I have to tell you."

"With that build-up, how can I say no?"

"Let's crawl into the back seat of that limo. I like a man who's all hot and sweaty."

"I need a shower."

"Paradise Shores has the most luxurious showers in town. Shelley told me if you'll agree to come over, he'll help bathe you."

"I know how to wash my own ass." A memory of Robert in his shower crossed his brain as he headed for the rear of the limo to disappear into the afternoon with Rose.

As the chauffeur sped off, Rose said, "You can either fuck me now, while you smell like a randy jock, or after you take a shower if you want to make Ronnie your role model.

***

It was *déjà vu*. Arrested on the same charge as before. Gene felt trapped in the back seat of a squad car. His head spinning, he sat grim-faced, a cold sweat bathing his body. When the two officers had arrived at his house, he had let them in. He'd expected them and was dressed and ready to go. Routinely, they'd frisked him. That he'd understood. But he did feel he deserved better treatment than having handcuffs placed on him.

What had been worse was walking the gauntlet of leering-eyed Cubans who'd lined up along the street to witness his arrest. Even now, on the way to the police station, the hysterical babble of their voices resounded in his ears. One contemptuous woman had spat in his face. He had never been as humiliated and defeated. After all these years of holding out against them, the "invaders" had caught up with him.

He'd learned from the officers what the charges were. He'd been accused of enticing the little girl into his garden where he exposed himself and had started to masturbate in front of her. All of it one big lie.

He knew the papers, especially the TV night news, would pick up the story and sensationalize it. The press would rehash those old charges, even though they'd been officially dropped. Shivering in the heat of the late afternoon, he feared his latest arrest would destroy him. Clara had planned all this. She'd wanted to go to bed with him and when he'd rejected her, she'd plotted against him.

He feared that Rose might hear about this. Maybe she'd even attack him from the pulpit, citing his case as that of a supposed defender of the law who secretly preyed on innocent young girls. Rose might use him as an example of moral degeneracy. Somehow he had to find a way to get to her and tell her his side of it.

As he was ushered into police headquarters, two reporters and a photographer recognized him. A blinding flash, and the photographer snapped his picture. A chill came over him as he imagined what that picture would look like on the front page.

After he'd been booked, he was shown to a cell. He was to be held here until bail was raised. Though offered a chance, he'd refused to call a lawyer. All he could remember was a big steel door closing and the key turning. Then an overwhelming loneliness.

He drifted off for a while and when he woke up, his heartbeat had come under control again. Before, it had been beating so fiercely he could hear it. He got up and walked around in his cell.

He promised himself not to think about Maria or the Cubans who'd taken over his neighborhood. He'd think only of *her.*

To him, Rose was blindingly beautiful. And she was good, a woman fighting the very evil forces that threatened to ruin him. How he longed to reach out and touch her gown, feel her waist-length auburn hair, caress skin white as marble. It was her face he remembered the most from those Sunday mornings, the face of a saint who could protect him from the all-encompassing slime.

***

The porcelain tea set once used by the Queen of England, and even the tea itself, were the finest Buck had ever known. Rose poured the tea with such precision that she'd be more than qualified to entertain Elizabeth Windsor and her consort, Philip, instead of Nancy and Ronald, who were, presumably, less demanding in their tea ritual. Rose had even promised that Shelley would be arriving in less than fifteen minutes, although she assured Buck her son was no tea drinker. "Personally, I think he drinks brandy."

Buck looked at her with a certain puzzlement. She'd held out the prospect of Shelley's arrival as a kind of enticement. "Before my darling boy arrives, I must tell you what I know about what's happening at the *Examiner.*"

"The publisher is the last to know."

She sighed and slowly sipped her tea. It wasn't as if she were tantalizing him by withholding information. It was more as if she was figuring out the best way to break the news to him. "Before he flew to Switzerland for those tests, old Buck sold his twenty-five percent interest in the *Examiner*."

Buck slammed down his tea cup. "What the fuck! Without even telling me."

"There's more. The parties who purchased it already own a lot of *Examiner* stock. In other words and in spite of your holding twelve percent of the stock, these parties or party are now in control of the newspaper. You're out the door, and I don't say that with any glee."

"Do you think they'll allow me to go back into the tower and retrieve the bar of soap I use to take a shower? Not only that but my de Kooning."

"I'm sure they will."

He bit his lip. "I've been fucked."

She reached out her hand to comfort him. "Please don't blame me. I'm just a puppet in this whole God damn mess. In a lot deeper than I ever expected to be."

In spite of what he perceived as her immense power, she seemed vulnerable somehow. A spokesperson, nothing more. But a spokesperson for what?

"I don't suppose you're going to tell me who is the new power behind the *Examiner*."

"Personally, I don't own one bit of the stock."

"Who does?"

"I'm to set up the meeting between you and the new owner. I can't give you the details yet. I've told you too much already. The meeting is to take place at a retreat in Palm Springs."

"If I'm out, there's no point in my going."

"There's a major reason." She appeared to be a Lorelei leading him into some nightmarish trap.

"What?" he asked.

"You're to be presented with a check for eighteen million dollars!"

"Did I hear that right?"

"Eighteen million dollars," she said. Old Buck is turning over his entire share of the sale of the *Examiner* directly to you."

"His one-fourth interest in the newspaper isn't worth eighteen million dollars," he said.

"Darling, property is worth whatever somebody is willing to pay for it." When news of a takeover is announced, your own twelve per-cent in the newspaper will go through the ceiling. Maybe another three million over its present worth. Maybe a lot more."

"That's fantastic."

"Since you'll have no more power at the *Examiner*, you might want to sell all your stock while the iron's hot. I predict another cool twelve to thirteen million if you're interested."

"My head is spinning," he said.

"And well it should. Your grandfather was paying you only forty-five thousand a year. With your newly acquired wealth, you can lead the good life." She smiled provocatively at him. "Maybe spend more time keeping me entertained than writing those dreary editorials at-tacking me."

"I'm out of a job."

"That means, I can present my offer to you again. I want you to become my media director. I can sign you to a three-year contract at a salary of three million a year." She smiled that same provocative smile again. "There will be many fringe benefits."

"You are the devil, throwing temptation at me. Frankly, my last dream in life is to become your media director. Then you make me an offer I can hardly refuse, especially since I'm now within the ranks of the unemployed."

"It took some manipulation to get you that salary. After all, I'm not entirely controlling this operation." Her arm reached out and she ran her fingers across his hand. "You'll be asked to sing for your supper now and then."

He sat uneasily on the edge of his chair. "This is all too much."

"You'll need to think things over. Come to my dinner tonight. You'll see Ronald and Nancy grovel."

"Forgive me, won't you? I've got to call my lawyer."

"Why don't you place the call from my library?" she said, getting up. "I've got to get changed for dinner anyway."

"Thanks for the tea," he said.

"What about those millions?" she asked.

"Those too."

She moved toward him and kissed him firmly on the mouth. "You smell good," she said, backing away and running her lips across her mouth. "Pure jock sweat."

"I'm glad it turns you on." Excusing himself, he headed toward her library.

The door to the library was being held open for him by the butler. Buck went in, shutting the door behind him. He had to call Uncle Milty.

***

"It's all true," Milty said when Buck finally reached his attorney. "I've been trying to contact you all afternoon."

"The price tag," Buck said. "It's incredible."

"It made no sense to me either. That's what someone is willing to pay."

"Rose Phillips tells me there is hot interest in buying out my share, too," Buck said. "She's talking another twelve to thirteen million for my stock alone."

"Take the fucker's offer," Milty urged. "What would you want with twelve percent of a paper you don't control? One that might be run by a religious fanatic. Why not become the publisher of the *Okeechobee News*? Buy the *News* and compete with the *Examiner*."

"That's not a bad idea. I might buy it for Susan. Make her the publisher." "There's more. Rose wants me to become her media director. Three million a year. A contract guaranteed for three years."

"Hot damn! Another nine million."

"You're not urging me to do it, are you?" Buck asked.

"Nine million sounds very enticing, Milty said.

"Let me meet with Rose's lawyers. Believe me, I'll protect your cute ass at every turn."

"You handle all this for me," Buck said. "You're all I have right now. I don't even have Robert with me. I want you to hire a private detective—detectives, whatever—and trace him."

"I have been holding back on you. I know where Robert is. He's flying back here in a few hours. He knows about your marriage to Susan."

"Who told him?" Buck said.

"You know how close Patrick is to Robert. I mean, Patrick, other than yourself, is not only my lover, but he loves Robert almost as much as he loves me."

"Patrick knows everything."

"And he told everything," Milty said. "Those two girls have secrets from the two of us. I warned Patrick not to tell him, but he went ahead. Although he didn't show it at your wedding, Patrick was opposed to your hooking up with Susan. He thinks you should not have caved in to old Buck's demands. I, on the other hand, think you did just right. Patrick and Robert don't realize that we men have to pay the bills."

"I wanted to tell Robert myself."

"I'll say this for Patrick: He did explain to Robert why you were forced into the marriage. The threat of disinheritance. And Patrick really emphasized to Robert that it won't be a real marriage."

"Did Robert understand?" Buck asaked.

"Not at all. He threatened to kill himself. Maybe it was because he'd become unglued over the death of his mother. You know gay men and their mothers."

"When can I see him?" Buck said.

"As soon as I know something, I'll get back to you. I won't tell Patrick that we've talked. Robert is going to stay here with Patrick and me. He said he'll never set foot in your house again."

"He used to call it 'our' house."

"He feels you've betrayed him. He also said you promised to marry him, not Susan."

"I will marry him. Tell him that. The thing with Susan is business, nothing more."

"If you'll go through with the plan to marry Robert—right after his mother's funeral—I think that will bring him around. He's strung out right now."

"Set up a wedding," Buck ordered. "It has no legal standing, but it might mean something to Robert."

"I'll arrange for a minister to marry you in Miami. Both Patrick and I will fly down. I'll be your best man, and Patrick will be Robert's maid of honor."

"Get Robert to come back." Buck said, and put down the phone.

As he did, he became aware of a presence in the library. As he turned around, he confronted Shelley.

"It's pointless to try to get Robert back," Shelley said. "You're mine now—not Robert's."

***

"I know it's your own home, but don't you think you should at least knock?" Buck asked.

"Not when two people know each other as we do," Shelley said, moving toward him. Before Buck knew what was happening, Shelley kissed him firmly on the lips with a brush of his sweet tongue.

Buck backed away, moving toward the window, where views opened onto Rose's well-manicured gardens. It was the panorama of Shelley that clouded his vision, not the cascades of multi-colored roses in Rose's fabled rose gardens, rumored to be the rarest and most spectacular roses in the world.

Fresh from a match, Shelley was wearing a rose-colored tennis outfit, his golden legs never more shapely. Everything about the boy—his lips, his face, his eyes, his long eyelashes, his blond hair, his swimmer's build—was perfection itself. Buck suspected that never had a more rotten core been camouflaged into such an Adonis-like appearance.

Shelley plopped down in a chair, letting one leg droop over the arm.   Buck glanced briefly at how tight his tennis shorts were. With Shelley's leg raised, Buck could see upward toward Shelley's crotch. Now's the time for you to clean up." Shelley said, "How else are you going to support me in my old age?"

"What about the strings attached," Buck said.

Shelley looked up at Buck with his luminous blue eyes. "The fringe benefits are not to be believed."

"Do you come with the deal?"

Shelley slid deeper into the chair accenting the tightness even more of his tennis shorts. He said nothing, only smiled.

Instead of looking at those roses, Buck kept his eyes glued to what was even more enticing to him: Shelley's state-of-the-art boy ass.

Shelley with his hawkeye knew where Buck was looking. "A penny for your thoughts."

"I'm dreaming about plowing my dick up that tight rosebud of yours," Buck said. He slammed his fist into his hand. "Is that what you wanted to hear?"

"I wanted to hear the words coming from those lips of yours,"

Shelley said.   He jumped up from the chair and stood behind Buck, reaching out and putting his arms around him. The boy rubbed Buck's chest and traced his fingers over Buck's rock-hard stomach. Buck whirled around, grabbed Shelley in his arms and pressed him close, sticking his tongue down the boy's throat. When Buck broke free, he traced his tongue along the boy's neck and nibbled his ears before inserting his tongue in each lobe. "God damn it, I want to eat you alive, then fuck you all night."

"I'm yours," Shelley said, gasping for breath. He'd seemed to melt under Buck's touch and caresses.

Buck broke away. He couldn't control himself any more. As Shelley could see, Buck's penis was practically trying to burst out of his shorts. "I belong to Robert."

Shelley stood defiantly. "I have this vision thing. Robert is going on his way. I don't know how or why. He won't be in your life much longer. You and I are going to spend the rest of our lives together."

The library, in spite of its air conditioning, had grown oppressively hot. Buck couldn't stand to be here for another second. He walked to the door, ignoring Shelley's pleas for him to come back.

Out on the street, he hailed a taxi and ordered the driver to take him home.

Rose and Shelley wanted him, and maybe Robert did too. Even Gene might still want him. He knew Susan did.

What Buck wanted was to be alone in his empty house. There was much to sort out.

In the privacy of his garden, Buck—clad only in a robe—sucked in the twilight air deeply. Ever since Uncle Milty had called him about Gene's arrest, he'd been tempted to phone Susan. He'd wanted to tell her the news himself. Susan was en route to his private island where he'd agreed to meet with her later. He knew this latest arrest would arouse too many painful memories for her.

Near some of his more exotic flowers, he came to an abrupt stop, his face one of grief. He still loved Gene, and the news of this latest arrest struck a blow to him.

Something about Gene's arrest didn't strike Buck right. As he understood it, Gene was nude, but nude in the privacy of his own deck in an enclosed area shut off from public view. If someone could be arrested for that, then half of Florida would be in jail. What was that little girl doing in Gene's private space? Gene's chief, Biff, had suspended him from the force. It was more than a suspension. Biff told TV news that he'd never "let this child molester work another day on the police force."

Buck wanted to do what he could. On the phone to Milty, he said, "I can't let Gene down this time."

"He won't even talk to you."

"What's his fucking bail?" Buck asked.

"Ten thousand dollars," Milty said. "He can't raise it."

"Post it for him," Buck said.

"I'm out the fucking door, with the bond money?" Milty said.

"Gene's been framed," Buck said. "I was with Calder Martin. He threatened to ruin Gene. He wanted to show me how quickly he could ruin a man."

"Fucking Calder. Right-wing mad dog from hell."

"Get Gene out of jail," Buck said.

"And I'll resolve that Rose offer."

Just as he put down the phone, he heard the sound of car wheels pulling into his driveway. Had Robert returned?

***

Still clad in his robe, Buck opened the front door to confront a stunningly beautiful Rose in a diaphanous white gown and her even more stunningly beautiful son, Shelley, clad in a white dinner jacket. Shelley's only dress code defiance was in wearing a purple polka dot bow tie. In his driveway Buck noted the rose-colored Rolls-Royce limousine with an older driver attired in elephant gray.

"Don't you believe in phoning?" he asked them, standing at the door barring their entrance. His feelings were mixed. This was one gorgeous pair.

"I tried calling," Rose said, sliding past him and entering his foyer. "Your line was always busy." She turned and smiled knowingly at him. "No doubt talking to one of your other girl friends."

"Who are you, anyway?" Shelley asked, also brushing past. "The love 'em and leave 'em kissing bandit?"

Rose stood serenely in his foyer, eying the decor and looking into the large living room beyond. "We'll have to redecorate. I'll pay for it, of course."

"You always pay," Shelley said, heading for the living room. He looked around vacantly, as if having no reason to be here. "Where's your bedroom? I always like to see where a man sleeps. You always learn so much about a man that way."

"I'm sure Buck is not going to show you to his bedroom, at least not now," Rose said.

"Or ever!" Buck said, brushing past them and clutching his robe even tighter around him. In the presence of their formal wear, he felt nude.

Her face was startlingly white in contrast to her burning dark eyes. She possessed the profile of a huntress, and he suspected he was the big game she eagerly sought. "I've spoken to Nancy. She and Ronnie would be delighted if you could join us for dinner. They know who you are and would welcome the *Examiner's* support. Of course, they think your politics are the same as old Buck's."

"If she truly were known as the fellatio queen of Hollywood, I might be in luck." Buck said. "I'm real horny tonight."

"Why didn't you tell us sooner?" Shelley said, moving closer to him and reaching to caress his cheek. "You needn't look farther than mommie dearest and me."

A slight laugh escaped from Rose's throat. "Don't worry about messing up our outfits. Both Shelley and I swallow."

He was startled for a moment, not thinking he heard right. He invited both of them out to his pool area, leading the way.

Once there, Buck poured himself a splash of Scotch. "May I offer you something to drink?"

"You can," Shelley said. "Your own cocktail, white and creamy."

"Oh, Shelley," she said. "You're so graphic."

Shelley took the glass from Buck and ran his pink tongue around its rim before handing it back. Buck put the glass to his lips and downed a hefty swig.

"Let's go upstairs," Shelley said, running his delicate fingers tantalizingly around Buck's left ear lobe. "I'll help you get into your tux for dinner." Shelley slid the robe from Buck's body. He stood completely nude.

Rose turned to take in the view. "I do believe I am staring at the world's greatest male specimen."

Buck dived into the water and swam several lengths of the pool, as both Rose and Shelley watched him.

After his swim, he climbed up the pool ladder where Rose waited with a large white beach towel she'd retrieved from a nearby rack. Water streamed down his neck as he emerged from the pool, making no effort to cover himself. Shelley came up from behind, seemingly out of nowhere. He began to towel the water off Buck's back. Rose moved forward and rubbed the droplets off his chest. He felt the blood beating in his temples. Both Rose and her son had a delicate, sensual touch, as if massaging him.

Their towels and the caresses of their experienced fingers were having its effect. He felt himself rising and hardening. Shelley was toweling his ass and Rose's fingers moved lower to massage his balls. She knelt before him to wipe his legs of the water from the pool. As she looked up, she saw him fully extended in all his glory. Shelley fondled and weighed Buck's balls, dangling them in front of Rose. The boy's hands traveled the full length of Buck's penis, uncapping it for Rose.

She plunged down with consummate skill. Buck almost wanted to cry out in ecstasy as he felt Shelley's tongue entering him from the rear, delicately kissing and probing his innermost part. With one hand, he sought Rose's head, pressing her face into his body and with his other free hand he reached around for Shelley's neck and pressed his face even closer into his ass. Buck didn't want this moment to end. After ten minutes, his body signaled him that such exquisite torture couldn't last forever. His climax when it finally arrived seemed to go on forever. These skilled seducers knew how to extend it until the last possible gasp.

Even after Rose had had her fill, and had retreated to his downstairs bathroom, Shelley moved around in front of him, there to lick and to polish his shaft entirely clean and to drain any last drops.

***

Buck retrieved his robe and headed for the bar, where he joined Rose who looked so fresh and alluring it was impossible to imagine only moments before she'd been down on her knees with his cock buried deep in her throat. She poured herself a sherry from a decanter, as she eyed him. "You're one hell of a man," she said, kissing him on the lips. "I've had them all—the good, the bad, the ugly. You're the best thing that's come along."

"Thank you," he said rather formally. "Not only for the compliment, but for the action. I don't think if I traveled through all the bordellos of the ancient Orient would I come across talent such as you and Shelley. Did you teach him all he knows?"

She laughed a bit nervously. "I taught him nothing. But somebody obviously did. No doubt, one or several of my many boyfriends."

Shelley came to join them at the bar and reached for a brandy. Buck observed that these two generally took what they wanted.

"Put the fucking liquor down," Rose said harshly to him. "I don't want you showing up drunk to meet Ronnie and Nancy. And get in the God damn bathroom and wash your face. You've still got come on your cheek."

Shelley turned to Buck and smiled as he softened his voice. "Today the leading female cocksucker of the East Coast, my mommie dearest, will sup with the leading cocksucker of the West Coast, Ms. Nancy Davis. At least we know why Reagan married her."

"Get to that bathroom and make yourself even more beautiful than you are," she said to him. "Brush your teeth so that when Nancy kisses you she won't smell her favorite liquid, semen."

Shelley kissed Buck on the lips. Buck returned the kiss. What the hell! If the world's most beautiful boy kisses you on the mouth, you kiss him back.

Breaking away, Shelley said, "Mama, I want you to buy me this for Christmas." He headed for the ground floor bathroom.

"What would be your big objection to your becoming my media director?" she asked. She'd suddenly become all business.

"I'm the wrong guy for your organization," he said. "I'm not sure I believe in a God. If I do, it's not any God you believe in."

She laughed and took his hand and pressed it against her lips. "My darling man, do you think I believe in God? I don't! Do you think Shelley believes in God? Don't be ridiculous. We're not Christians. Do you think Calder Martin believes in God? We use these stupid Christians for their money—nothing else."

"I wasn't certain. You're so convincing up there in that pulpit."

"That's because I'm an actress," she said. "Believe me, I'd rather curl up with a hunk with an eleven-inch dick than the Bible. It's money, baby. Power. We can climb the highest ladder together. Do you think I want to be climbing that ladder with Calder Martin? Calder should be kept down in the sewers with the rats and the shit doing his dirty work. You, I'd like to present to the media."

"I'm tempted," he said. "In some way I think you might help me become bigger than old Buck. I'm ambitious. You're playing on that flaw in my character."

"It's not a flaw, baby." She rose abruptly and stood before him, almost whirling around in a little dance of glee. "The love of money and power is being smart." She paused. "I'm in love with you."

A long silence followed. "There can be no big romance between us. I don't love you. Fascination. Sexual attraction. Nothing more."

"I want to marry you. Look at the press we'd get!"

"We'd get press all right," he said. "I'd be indicted for bigamy."

"You are married?"

"Quite recently. Susan Howard."

"That silly little girl reporter," she said.

"She's my wife. That's why I can't join you for dinner tonight. I've promised to meet her on my private island. It's our honeymoon night."

Staggeringly wounded, she ran toward the foyer and, in moments, he heard her throw open the front door, her high heels hitting the gravel of his driveway. "I'm out of here."

He returned to the garden where the twilight glowed with a rare radiance, breaking through the gray overcast that had hung over the garden most of the evening.

Seemingly emerging from nowhere, a presence appeared in the garden. Startled, he turned around to confront Shelley. No longer in his formal wear, the boy was completely nude. The soft lighting in the garden accentuated his beauty.

Shelley's fingers were on his body removing his robe. It fell to the brick patio. Buck was nude like the boy himself.

"Welcome to the Garden of Delights," Shelley said softly, his voice a caress.

***

Consumed with rage, Gene drove home, feeling like a bottled scorpion eating his own tail. It had come as a complete surprise—a shock, really—when Buck had posted bail for him through his attorney.

When Buck's offer to post bail had come into the police station, Gene had rejected it. As he'd reconsidered, the help had grown more appealing. Why shouldn't he receive aid and comfort from Buck? He could afford it. Gene couldn't.

Exposing himself to Jill had been real. But with Maria, he had been set up for a fall. He planned to take revenge on Clara and her daughter.

Before he turned the corner of his block, he heard the clang of a fire alarm, its glaring sound followed by police sirens. The street had been cordoned off. He slammed on his brakes, abandoning his car double-parked in the street, and raced in the direction of his home.

Bumping into chattering Cubans, almost tripping, he reached his home. It was too late. Flames leaped from his windows as firemen turned on their hoses full blast. The house had long ago been built of wooden timbers, which provided easy fuel for the leaping flames. It was all he owned in the world. Every one of his possessions, even his prized tennis trophies, were being consumed by flames. The water from the hoses seemed to have little effect. To him, the water almost appeared to be gasoline fueling the flames.

"My God!" he cried out, realizing that Jill and Sandy might be trapped in that house. He shouted their names wildly into the night, but his voice was drowned out. He rushed toward his house to rescue Jill and Sandy.

Two policemen, recognizing him, restrained him, even though he kicked and fought violently, trying to break through. "They're in there," he shouted at one of the policemen. "You're letting them burn to death."

"It's okay," one of the officers shouted back. "That boy, Sandy, is in the hospital. The girl is with him."

"Is he okay?"

"He's badly burned," the officer said. "He tried to rush in to save you, thinking you were there. He's at Okeechobee Memorial. The girl's with him."

Gene gasped for air at the news, but his lungs filled with smoke instead. His eyes smarting, he watched helplessly, as curls of smoke, fed by his possessions, floated into the night sky. The flames rose fan-like toward the beams of the wood-framed house, igniting the roof.

Women and children screamed as policemen forced them back behind hastily erected barriers. The flames beat up through the rafters, making him shut his eyes, remembering his childhood toys stored there.

As he opened his eyes, he spotted Clara and Maria on the far side of the street, looking not at the flames engulfing his home but glaring at him triumphantly.

The stink of smoke choked him as he pressed as close to the blaze as the policemen would allow. He'd been born in that very house. His mother didn't believe in hospitals. Black drifts of smoke flowed down the street that was no longer his. As flames mixed with the sky, bands of red turned to orange, creating an eerie silhouette against the darkness.

Before a screen of flames, a policeman he knew spoke to him. "I'm sorry, Gene. It's arson. We found empty gasoline cans out back."

He didn't need to be told that. He could just picture the beaners—angry, outraged Cuban fathers plotting over their cheap wine-drinking to set fire to his home and chase out the one lone WASP who had remained in their neighborhood. He shut his eyes real tight, remembering how the neighborhood used to be when he was a kid. Things were so peaceful then.

For a while he stood still, watching the flames, mesmerized by them, the way he always was by Rose at her temple. When he could no longer stand the strain, he broke through the crowd and cut across a neighbor's driveway until he was safely screened by a thick row of hibiscus bushes at the edge of his own backyard. He could hear his heavy heartbeat as he stood here, watching the firemen extinguish what was now a wreck. His stomach felt like a tangled knot, as he cried, thanking God that no one was here to witness him break down like this.

He also thanked God that Sandy and Jill had not died in that fire-trap.

As he stood, trembling in shock, hours seemed to pass within a relatively short period of time. He'd lost all track of time. With the flames dead, and after inspecting the damage, the Cubans wandered off. Eventually the policemen and fire trucks departed too. Within the hour, the blaring sounds of Spanish from a hundred TV sets filled the night air.

Gene remained in the bushes, staring vacantly at the charred beams of his home. He would never re-enter what was left of his home. That was foreign territory to him now, belonging to the invaders. They had won.

There was nothing left for him to do now, other than go to the hospital and pick up what remained of his life. He was deeply touched that Sandy had tried to rescue him.

The moon blazed against one remaining side of his white-painted house, and the effect was like snow-light.

Feverish with memories, he crept toward the ruins of his house, stumbling over his rocking horse that had been stored in the attic but somehow had come to rest forlornly on the ground, its rockers broken.

He stood on the back steps looking at the still-smoking ruins in the moonlight. His house was dead.

Part of him wasn't dead at all. The bottled scorpion wasn't going to bite its tail any more. It was going to crawl out of the bottle and sting the city.

***

In the corridor of the Okeechobee Memorial Hospital, painted a pea-green, Gene dodged a stretcher carrying a young black male who'd been knifed in the stomach.

It was then that Gene spotted her. She was sitting anxiously on a bench. The moment he called to her, Jill jumped up and rushed to his side. She gave him a hug, as she burst into tears, crushing herself into his chest.

"How is he?" he asked.

"He's in a lot of pain," she said, sobbing. "His left arm and shoulder are badly burned. They're doing what they can."

Tears welled in Gene's eyes. "I wish I'd been there."

"He thought you were asleep in the back bedroom," Jill said. He broke through the police line and tried to rescue you."

"I'll make it up to him somehow," Gene said.

"You gave Sandy and me your home," Jill said. "We were so grateful."

"I'll still provide a home somehow." He brought his hands together in desperation, cracking his knuckles. "There's a way out of this. I've got two-thousand dollars in the bank. That will hold us over for a little while."

"What are we going to do?" she asked.

"I know a place that rents studio efficiencies. We can hole in there for a while. We don't even have clothes."

"I could go back to work. Make some money."

"Forget it! The main thing is to nurse Sandy back to health. To think he did that for me."

"I heard what happened to you. That God damn Cuban bitch. You did nothing wrong."

He took her hand and looked deeply into her eyes. "I can't believe you're standing by me. After what I did to you. That's when I deserved to be arrested. Not this time."

A young woman intern appeared in the corridor. "Sandy wants to see both of you. But would you go in one at a time?"

"You go first," Jill said.

In the dimly lit room Sandy shared the cramped quarters with another patient who was almost entirely bandaged. Sandy's eyes were wide open, his brow feverish. He sat up in bed but winced in pain. "Gene," he said. "Tell me you're okay."

"I'm okay, kid. It's you I'm worried about."

"It hurts like hell. But I'll heal. At least all of us are alive."

"You shouldn't have gone in after me," Gene said.

"Yeah, right, just stand outside and watch you burn to death. I had to go in. The fucking firemen wouldn't do it."

"I'll always be grateful." Gene leaned over and kissed Sandy on his brow.

With his good hand, the boy reached out to Gene. "I love you, big guy. I'd do anything for you."

"You've become the best friend I've ever had," Gene said.

Sandy squeezed his hand. "That other thing that happened to you today—I'm so sorry."

"I was set up by someone," Gene said.

"I'm with you all the way." He tried to sit up again but Gene eased him back against the pillow. "What are we going to do now?"

"I'll think of something," Gene said.

"When I'm well, I'll make money for us. It will keep food on the table. Wherever that table is going to be."

"Thanks, kid, we'll manage.

An attendant came into the room, signaling Gene that it was time to leave.

"Will you come to see me in the morning?" Sandy asked.

"First thing."

"I'm also sorry you lost your job," Sandy said. Will it be rough finding another one?"

"Easier than you think," Gene said.

"Don't get into trouble," Sandy cautioned.

He kissed Sandy's forehead, then took his hand and pressed it against his cheek. "You'll pull through this."

"*We'll* pull through this," Sandy corrected him.

"That's the spirit." Not wanting to witness the boy's pain for another second, Gene turned and headed for the door. "I'll send Jill in now."

In the corridor, he hugged Jill. "He can see you now."

Spotting a bank of phones, Gene saw a free one. In the booth next to him, a large, fat black woman was shouting into the receiver. "He's dead! They killed him. Stabbed him right in the gut. All for some stupid little container of coke."

Closing the booth behind him, although he couldn't block out her sobs, Gene reached into his wallet, searching for a slip of paper. He dialed the unlisted phone number of Leroy Fitzgerald.

***

There was still a little trace of light in the early evening sky as Buck, clad only in a white T-shirt and a pair of white shorts, stood at the gangplank of his yacht as it anchored on his own private island.

Susan was here to greet him. "That's one pair of legs you have. Not to mention everything else."

"I'd call that sexual harassment." The banter was similar to some vaguely remembered exchange they'd once had at the Examiner office. He eyed her lovely body. She, too, was clad in a pair of shorts. "You've got legs too." He smiled. "Even better than Pamela's."

She knew he was joking, but looked at him with a pretended offense. "Your old girl friend's lost her looks. I'm getting better looking every day."

He knew that was true. If anything she looked more incredibly beautiful than she had during their days at the university. Her body, slim and exquisitely formed, was like a piece of sculpture.

As he gave her a deep kiss on the pier, he vividly remembered that in a moment of passion he'd grabbed Shelley and confessed his love for him. Kissing Susan, he still felt the taste of Shelley on his lips. He looked into her eyes. "Welcome to my island."

"Its reputation has preceded it." Her voice was deliberately flirtatious as she walked to the outdoor patio where Henry had arranged supper.

Over dinner, he spoke with great pain over the loss of the *Examiner*. "We're both out of a job, but not for long. I'm considering buying the *Okeechobee News*. Let them take the *Examiner*. We'll be back in fighting form."

"That would be great," she said.

"If I can secretly buy the *News*, and I know they're in deep shit financially, I'll make you the publisher."

"You're kidding."

"You're more than qualified. I think you'd be a great publisher."

"What would you do?"

"Another well-paying job, perhaps."

Henry appeared, telling Buck that he had three urgent phone calls. Excusing himself, he went into his private library. Even though Susan was his wife, he didn't want her to be privy to any of them.

Not once during dinner had she mentioned Gene's arrest. That could only mean she hadn't turned on a radio or TV since coming to the island. The news was being widely broadcast. He'd have to tell her after he took his calls.

The first call was from Uncle Milty. "Patrick went to the airport to meet Robert. He wasn't on the flight. I've called everywhere."

"Keep trying, baby." Putting down the phone, he picked up the other line. It was Leroy Fitzgerald. "It's on for tomorrow night at eight o'clock. Be on time. Slip in through the back entrance."

"I'm game," Buck said. "Hot and horny."

"I've got the most delectable piece of boy ass in the whole fucking eastern seaboard lined up for you," Leroy said.

"Sounds enticing."

"By the way, the pictures of you came out just great," Leroy said. "You photograph magnificently."

"Thanks for the compliment." He put down the receiver and switched to another line. The third caller was Shelley. "She's taking it badly."

"What do you mean?"

"Rose," he said. "Your marriage to Susan. She's drinking heavily and making all sorts of threats. You'd better come over to calm her down."

"I can't," Buck said. "I'm on my honeymoon night."

"That puny red-haired pussy, Susan Howard? The only honeymoon you'll ever have is the one you take with me. Did you forget what you told me?"

"I'd rather forget," he said.

"You're not going to forget it. You told me you loved me. You told me I gave you the most exquisite pleasure you've ever known in your whole life. Was that a lie?"

"No, God damn it!" he said. "I've got to go now. I have an urgent call coming in."

"Talk to you later," Shelley said. "From this moment on, you and I are a thing."

"Okay, we're a thing."

"I love you, fucker." Shelley finally hung up.

A new call came in from a doctor with a French accent. "The test. "I know you've been calling the clinic here a lot. But we've had no information—that is, nothing specific until today. Your grandfather is eaten up with cancer. It is far more advanced than we ever thought. He must have been in great pain at all times but trying to conceal it. There is no hope. He has only days to live."

"I'll catch the next plane," Buck said.

"He absolutely refuses to see you or anybody. It is useless to fly over. We must respect his wishes. He has, after all, given us a huge donation for our research work. We're very grateful to him, and we're going to make his final days as comfortable as possible."

"I must see him!" Buck said.

"There is no way. If you come over, we'll bar the doors to you. I am so very sorry. This is his explicit instruction."

"What is your name if I need to call you back?"

"Dr. Euler."

"Can I keep calling you? Will you let me know his condition?"

"You are his grandson and heir apparent. That is the least I can do, but you cannot see him."

"I really want to."

"It's impossible." Dr. Euler hung up.

Coming back onto the patio, Buck looked over toward Susan who'd finished her dinner without him.

"I've got some bad news," he said.

***

Before going to Leroy's condo, Gene had installed Jill into a little efficiency in a seedy-looking neighborhood by the East River. For the moment, it was the best he could do.

At Leroy's apartment building, he took the elevator to the top floor.

Clad only in a short silk bathrobe, Leroy opened the door and beamed at the sight of him. "What a surprise!"

Without saying a word, Gene barged into the apartment as if he owned it. "Yeah, I'm back."

At the bar, Leroy eyed him with a shrewd appraisal. "My, oh my, but you've been in the news lately. That story about you and that little girl sounds fishy. More like entrapment."

"It was!" Gene said. "I was set up."

Handing Gene the drink, Leroy sat with him on the sofa. "My aim is to bring joy into your life. Not trouble." He placed his hand on Gene's knee. "Losing your job on the force. Having those Cuban bastards burn down your house. It seems you need some comfort, and you've come to the right place. After I give you a long, leisurely bath, I'll massage you." He ran his tongue around the rim of his glass. "Not with my hands."

"Sounds tempting!" Gene said, barely able to conceal his rage at having put himself in Leroy's power. "I fear I need more than that. I need money."

"I always knew you'd turn to hustling," Leroy said. "I have plenty of money. It depends on how far you're willing to go. There's five-hundred for the usual."

"What do you mean?"

"If you're strictly rough trade."

"If I'm not?" Gene said.

"We could easily turn this into a thousand-dollar night."

"What do I have to do?" Gene asked.

"I want you to kiss me. Really kiss me, then go down on me too."

"I'll think about it," Gene said. "But I'm going to need more than a thousand."

"That's higher than I've ever gone. In your case, I'll make it one thousand five hundred."

"I was thinking somewhere in the neighborhood of ten thousand. I need money."

"Wow!" Leroy said. "You are setting a high price."

"I don't mean just for our night together. You mentioned friends of yours that really dig me. I bet they're rich fags like you. Right?"

"I see what you mean." Leroy got up and went to the bar and poured himself another drink. "My feverish brain is already going into over-drive. I think I could arrange quite a party. They paid plenty for those pictures of you. I bet they'd pay a lot for the real thing. At least two-thousand dollars each for a long, all-day session."

"What do I have to do?" Gene asked apprehensively.

"Everything," he said. "You'll also have to agree to let us film it."

"A big order. But I don't know how I can make money so fast anywhere else."

"You can't," Leroy said, coming back over to the sofa. "You'll agree to everything. I just know it." He reached down and took Gene's hand, leading him toward the bathroom.

As Gene went down the corridor, he started removing his clothing piece by piece. At the door of the bathroom, he reached down to un-buckle his belt, having already discarded his T-shirt and dress shirt.

"No," Leroy said, sitting on the closed lid of the toilet and motion-ing Gene to him. "That little pleasure I reserve for myself." His hands reached into the air to claim Gene's large metal buckle.

***

Three o'clock in the morning found Buck alone on his patio where he'd romped with Rose and Shelley. They seemed far removed from his life.

Still no word from Robert. Buck had placed a call to Uncle Milty at one that morning. No news.

Earlier in the evening, Susan had drifted off to his bedroom. He knew it was expected of him that he join her there. Somehow he'd lagged behind, finally drifting off to sleep after watching the two o'clock news with its sad, tragic report about Gene. It seemed he'd slept only an hour before waking up with a start.

He felt his island had been invaded. At first he feared Gene was stalking them again.

It was here on this forlorn patio that Susan found him.

Not saying a word, she reached for his arm and, linked that way, led him down the stone path to the beach.

Clad only in his jockey shorts, he strolled along the white sands with her. Despite what was going on beneath its surface, the ocean appeared at rest. On the far horizon, the distant night lights of Okeechobee could be seen.

"It's so beautiful here," she said in a voice so soft it was like a whisper.

"Mmmm," was all he could manage.

He didn't want to talk. Neither did she. At his little cabana on the beach, he went inside and brought back a big white beach towel, arranging it for her on the sand.

She lay down on it, looking up at his nearly nude body, as he stood against the background of a sky where the first hint of dawn streaked through. Below him, she had a dreamlike quality to her, the kind of women he used to think he wanted. These days he didn't know what he wanted.

There was no compelling urgency to his love-making. He instinctively wanted to prolong it and he knew she did too.

When he'd finished plunging and darting, hungering and lusting for her body—when his surging blood was still, he lay in her arms, not wanting to move or break the mood. For an hour or so, they had lain here as the morning sun slowly returned from the other side of the world. He'd watched sandpipers run up the beach as gulls circled overhead.

After drifting off, he'd awakened suddenly to find her still here, his need back again, stronger than ever. She seemed happy to have him wake up in her arms. Putting his arms tightly around her, he buried his softly sucking lips in her neck, as she caressed his right ear with her long fingers.

There was a little moan he discovered that came from a deep recess in her throat. In his loving her, he gave and gave of himself until he could hear that little moan. When that sound became a loud gasp for breath, he knew he'd gone over the top with her.

The sun had burned away the dark shadows on the beach. Everything was streaked with red, orange and yellow; in the distance he could see the tall, slim black figure of Henry, slowly making his way down the path from the house with freshly brewed coffee.

***

After breakfast, Buck took Susan back to his bedroom to sleep. He left the doors open leading to the pool, and he drifted off in an apparent feeling of warmth and openness.

To Susan, the house was opulent, yet casual, so unlike her former barren apartment. The lush life of the island invaded every room. Cradled in his arm, she brushed aside any disturbing thought, drifting into a deep sleep—her last vision that of the mid-morning sun reflecting its rays off the pool.

She didn't know how long she slept. Maybe two hours. She woke up, sensing a foreign presence in the house. But there was no one she could see except Buck asleep beside her.

The heat of the day and the intensity of light coming from the pool told her it was around noon.

Her eyes traveled his large bed which was big enough to sleep four comfortably. The oversize pillows—so many of them—added a touch of decadence. In sleep, his body was strong, well developed and mature, yet, caught in its naturalness, it had a touch of innocence. His blond hair fell over his forehead and his mouth, which hours before had brought her such pleasure, was half-open. She listened to the sound of his heavy breathing.

Knowing it was time for them to get up, she reached over and stroked him, feeling the muscles of his chest beneath the smooth skin. She played with the light brush of golden hair on his chest as she slowly slipped the sheet from his body, revealing his penis, which lay curled over one thigh.

He twitched slightly as her mouth gently captured one of his brown-red nipples. Her tongue began a graceful journey down through the hair of his chest to his stomach where her mouth opened to engulf his navel before continuing on its way to the golden tangle at his groin. He was waking up, as her fingertips lightly combed the bush of his pubis.

She went for his jewels, taking each one in her mouth separately, pressuring them between her palate and her tongue. Her tongue climbed to the bulbous, swollen head of his penis, where it did a little dance on the tip before plunging down on him. She let the organ ease into the arch of her throat. That type of love-making, to which Gene had objected so violently, pleased Buck immeasurably. Soon he couldn't take any more, and he bubbled over. The first of several spurts splashed against her tonsils. She could feel his heat and intensity. When she'd drained him completely, his head fell back in the pillow.

As she raised her head, she was overcome with a strange feeling. She had the distinct impression that someone had invaded the bedroom during the heat of their love-making, and that Buck had seen who it was. Was it Henry?

In the shower, she bathed hurriedly, drying herself before slipping into a white robe and heading for the living room. Before reaching it, she eyed Henry suspiciously. Seemingly oblivious to everything, he poured her a cup of black coffee. Buck must have gotten up, too, because she heard the shower running in his bathroom.

To her surprise, when she did go into the living room, Buck was sitting on the sofa, his back turned to her. How could he have showered and dressed so quickly? She still heard the sound of his shower.

She slipped up behind him, covering his eyes with her hands and gently blowing a kiss into his ear.

The head jerked back and confronted her. It wasn't Buck at all.

It was Robert.

Chapter Eight

He glared at her. Long, lean and muscular, he radiated power, his beard like golden flecks against his tanned skin. He looked as if he hadn't shaved or showered in two days. She found herself strangely drawn to him. His resemblance to Buck was amazing. She always thought he looked like a twin brother. He had the same thick blond hair, the deep blue eyes.

A dreadful reality came over her. Robert had walked in on Buck and her unannounced. Henry was just too skilled as a servant to have allowed that, if he had known.

She'd always known Robert loved Buck. Until today she hadn't realized the extent of that love. She feared it went beyond mere love, and into a deep kind of obsession.

Robert was the first to break the long silence between them. "Let's go for a walk down by the pier. It's a lovely day."

Without saying anything, she left the room with him and headed out to the pier. She could still hear Buck in the shower.

Out in the bright light of day, she turned to Robert. He'd put on a pair of extremely dark sunglasses. He wore a beige linen suit, not removing the jacket even though the day was scorching.

"I was very sorry to hear of your mother passing away," she said. "Buck told me. He's been trying to get in touch with you."

"My mother claimed I would perish in hell's fire because of the way I lead my life."

"I am so very sorry she was intolerant," she said.

He moved closer to her as she came to a standstill. "I'm just as intolerant as my mother. I cannot tolerate your marriage to Buck. He belongs to me."

"Surely Buck has some say in this matter," she said. "It's his life."

"It's our lives. Mine and his. There is no room for you."

"You can't set such terms."

"Buck was forced to marry you. You married Buck just to see what you could get."

"I'm not a hooker."

"Yeah, right," he said, heading in the direction of a second boat anchored near Buck's yacht. The skipper of the craft called down to them. "Let's go aboard," Robert said.

She didn't trust him but went aboard anyway, wanting to hear what he had to say.

He held the door open for her, and she entered a small stateroom. Pictures on the wall revealed that this was not Buck's boat but a yacht belonging to old Buck I.

"Have a seat," he said. "Make yourself comfortable for some uncomfortable news."

She nervously sat down, and felt she'd been foolish for coming aboard. Was he going to kidnap her? Robert reached inside his linen suit and removed a revolver, as she recoiled in fear.

"I'm not going to kill you," he said, "At least not yet. But this gun should let you know how determined I am. There will be no more rolls in the hay with Buck. If you attempt to be his wife in anything but name, I'll kill you."

"You'd be the first suspect. The insanely jealous boyfriend."

"I know I couldn't get away with murder. So after killing you, I'd put a bullet in my own head."

She stood up, wanting to flee from the stateroom but not daring. "You mean what you say, every God damn word of it."

"You've got that right, bitch." He moved menacingly toward her. Only one foot from her face, he removed his dark sunglasses. "I'll kill you. Then I'll kill myself."

She didn't need any more convincing. "What do you want me to do?"

"I'm getting off this boat. You stay on. You'll be taken back to your condo."

"What will Buck say?"

"I'll handle Buck just fine. He's going to fly to Miami where we'll not only attend a memorial service for my mother, but he'll marry me. My marriage to Buck will be a real marriage—not the sham yours is."

"I don't want to die," she said.

"You've got a lot to live for," he said. "You don't want to fuck it up."

"Good luck on your upcoming marriage," she said. "I'm getting the hell out of here."

"The smartest move you've ever made. We'll keep our conversation private."

He put back on his sunglasses. As he left the boat, she heard the motors starting.

She turned from the sight of him, sensing his madness.

After she'd sailed away, she went back on deck. In the distance she could still see him clad in his linen suit, standing on the pier watching her disappear.

She sucked in the fresh breezes of the sea. Out here everything was clean and pure. She suddenly burst into tears but they didn't last long.

Back at her condo, she called her father to invite herself over. Sometimes a girl needed to visit her dad, and this was one of those times.

***

In the bathroom, Buck finished showering. He was uncertain about how to handle Robert. It seemed like an incredibly inconvenient time for him to have walked in.

When he pulled aside the shower curtain, he fully expected Robert to be here waiting for him with a thick towel to dry him off. He wasn't. After drying himself off, he covered his nudity with the wet towel and headed into his living room. He looked into his bedroom where he found Henry changing the sheets.

"Where's Susan?" Buck asked.

"Miss Susan returned to the mainland."

"What? My yacht is still here."

"Miss Susan took old man Buck's yacht. Mister Robert came over on that boat with a crew."

"I see." Buck was confused.

"He went for a walk on the beach."

"Thanks." Forgetting to dress and with the towel draped around him, he ran down the beach, increasing his pace until he spotted Robert in the distance. He caught up with him. "Please come here and give me a kiss and don't take your tongue out of my mouth until at least an hour's gone by."

Tears in his eyes, Robert turned to face Buck.

"How could you?"

"You know I had to marry her. If I didn't, Old Buck would cut me off without a penny."

"You shouldn't have brought her here. This is our island."

"I'll never do it again."

Robert moved closer to him. "That's one promise you're going to keep."

"I should have kept the marriage with Susan in name only. I was wrong. Forgive me."

"You belong to me."

Buck put a broad, firm hand on Robert's shoulder. "You drove me crazy when I couldn't get in touch with you."

Buck was tempted to grab his lover and force himself upon Robert. But he decided to let Robert come back to him at his own pace.

Robert took Buck's hand in his, and walked along the beach.

Buck walked beside him, his hand enclosing Robert's in a tight grip."

Robert stopped and looked deeply into Buck's eyes, then pressed his mouth hard against his. Holding Robert in a tight embrace, Buck plunged his tongue into Robert's mouth, exploring its crevices. Just as fast as Robert could produce saliva, Buck swallowed it.

Robert ripped the towel from Buck, exposing his nudity. Possessively, he fondled Buck's balls.

When Buck broke away from Robert's lips, he descended on his friend's ears, lovingly kissing and biting each lobe. He cupped the cheeks of Robert's buttocks, fondling the mounds with a devotion he'd never displayed before. With his free hand, he began to unbutton Robert's shirt.

"Are you still going to marry me?" Robert asked, tracing his fingers along Buck's fully aroused cock.

"I can't wait." Buck said.

Robert ran his tongue over Buck's closed eyelids. "Let's go to our little secret place."

Buck put his arm around Robert and guided him along the flower-lined path leading to a little gazebo where they often used to go for drinks. A huge ocean wave crashed across the beach. "Welcome home."

At the gazebo, a nude Buck removed Robert's shirt. His hands were trembling as he reached for the buckle on Robert's trousers. On his knees, he hesitated for only a moment before unbuckling the belt and unzipping the pants. He pulled them down, burying his face in Robert's white jockey shorts. Then, with his teeth, he pulled them down to Robert's knees.

Robert was fully aroused, and he became even more so when Buck planted tender wet kisses on the tip of his penis. He gently lowered Robert onto the sofa in the gazebo, as his tongue caressed Robert's balls and began its long wet trail to what was his real target for the day. Robert raised his legs in the air and rested them on Buck's shoulders. Buck reached down and parted the cheeks of Robert's ass.

***

On the Florida patio that belonged to her father, Jim, Susan enjoyed her first drink of the day. She'd told Jim everything.

"Take his threat seriously," Jim cautioned. "Stay out of it. Maintain the marriage, but at a safe distance. You're lucky this happened right at the very beginning. Before you fell in love with Buck."

At the canopied outdoor bar, she paused. "I'm not in love with him. I don't think I even know him."

"What do you mean?"

"His relationship with Gene, for one thing. I don't know what's going on between them. That's one fucked up former husband of mine."

"I know," Jim said wearily. "Arrested again on the same charge. This time it seems different, as if he were set up."

"I feel that way too," she said. "Will you represent Gene?"

"I knew you'd ask me, and I've thought it over. I'll take his case."

"I knew I could count on you." She bent down and kissed him on the forehead.

He eyed her sternly. "Your second marriage is not a tragedy. You care for Buck. And there is, I'm sure, a strong sexual attraction. Hell, if I were thirty years younger, I'd go for the hunk myself."

"Since when did you turn gay?"

"I had a couple of affairs with guys in my university days. One of them I really cared about, and then along came Ingrid. She wouldn't want me telling you this."

"I'm not shocked at all," she said. He got up to answer the phone.

When he came back, she wanted to change the subject. "You may not know this, but Uncle Milty may be spending a lot of time acquiring the *News* for Buck."

"That makes sense. Buck's lost the *Examiner*. He's going to have millions to burn. Right now the *News* needs a bail-out. Buck might be their salvation."

"Or I could be their salvation," she said. "Buck says if he can get the *News*, he'll make me the publisher."

"I'm a bit awed," he said.

"If you want to be cynical, you could say he's buying me off," she said. "Giving me a paper instead of a husband to put to bed."

"If you learn the rules, and play by them, you might have a great marriage. And your career will soar."

"Where's the love to come from? Or don't you think I need it?"

"All of us need love. Buck is not going to object to your having an affair or two on the side."

"Where? All the men in Okeechobee seem to be sleeping with each other."

"There is one who I would virtually guarantee is straight," he said.

"A straight man in Okeechobee? I don't believe it."

"Don Bossdum's back in town. He called for your phone number. He tried to reach you at the *Examiner*."

"Don Bossdum. Who could forget him? Other than Gene and Buck, he was the most pursued man at the university. Football captain. Big and blond."

"Why don't you call him? After the university, he said he got married to a Cuban girl in Miami. It didn't last long. There was some minor scandal, I don't know what."

"He didn't expose himself to a little girl?"

"Nothing like that. I think his wife caught him cheating."

She inhaled the fresh air as some distant memory came back to her. "I recall some rumor about Don getting involved for a while with Rose Phillips."

"That I doubt. What would a handsome football hunk like Don Bossdum, with every girl in the state of Florida throwing herself at him, want with a vintage tomato like Sister Rose?"

"She could be his grandmother. I'll give the stud a ring."

As she moved to gather her things, Jim got up and walked toward her. "Why don't you stay here and cook dinner?"

"There are very few men I cook dinner for. But as soon as I get settled in, I'll invite you and Ingrid over to my new condo. A fringe benefit of being Mrs. Buck Brooke III."

"We miss you," he said, kissing her lightly on the lips.

"I'll visit more often." She paused as if she'd forgotten something. "Did you write down Don's number?"

"I'll get it for you." He wandered into the hallway and returned with a piece of paper. "Enjoy."

After kissing Jim goodbye, she walked out to her car, heading for the causeway and the beach. She'd spend the night alone. But on second thought, why not spend the night with Don Bossdum?

***

Nude and exhausted, Gene lay in Leroy's bed alone. Leroy had to go to a photographer who developed film for him.

Gene had just placed a call to Jill, who was doing fine in their bleak efficiency, and another to Sandy. Sandy's pain had eased, and there was hope he'd be out of the hospital in a day or two. When Gene got some sleep, he was going to move them into a better apartment right in Leroy's building. Leroy was going to make the rental terms very favorable, providing Gene would continue to "cooperate."

Gene assured him he'd keep putting out as he had today with Leroy's rich friends, only he planned to get a real job too. He knew no one would hire him except one man. That man wouldn't want to give him a job, but Gene planned to insinuate himself into that one's life whether welcome or not.

He'd had to leave his new address with the police since he was out on bail, with a trial pending. Through that link, Jim Howard had called Jill and left a message. He claimed he wanted to represent Gene and would do so for free. Gene at first wanted to turn it down until he realized he'd accepted that bail money from Buck. Why not accept free legal representation, too?

To defend himself would costs thousands, and the ten thousand dollars he'd recently earned he wanted to use to rebuild his life and to help Jill and Sandy so they wouldn't be forced to go back on the streets.

He'd never gotten along with his former father-in-law, but right now he didn't see that that mattered. Other than Buck's so-called "Uncle Milty," Jim Howard was the best attorney in Okeechobee.

Before falling into a deep sleep, Gene relived the events of the past few hours. All his life he'd been contemptuous of whores. Now he'd become a performing whore himself.

Lying in this bed with its rumpled sheets, he could still feel the devouring mouths taking pleasure from his body. With a cameraman recording everything, five men—all friends of Leroy's—had descended with sucking mouths and lapping tongues to taste his body. The men were physically disgusting to him, often overweight and in one case at least seventy years old. He'd given them what they wanted: his flesh. It was as if they'd wanted to suck the blood from him.

Even when he rose from the bed and had momentarily escaped the camera, the seventy-year-old man had followed him into the bathroom lined with nude photographs of Gene. At first Gene had assumed that the man had wanted to watch him urinate but it soon became clear that the pathetic looking creature was begging Gene to use his open, gaping mouth instead of the toilet stool. Closing his eyes, Gene had inserted his cock into the man's mouth. The old man had eagerly swallowed every drop, continuing to suck and drain even when Gene had fully relieved himself.

"That's the sweetest cocktail I've ever tasted in my life, even sweeter than that of my sixteen-year-old grandson." The man had slowly risen from the floor. Standing before Gene, he'd fondled Gene's balls as he'd licked his lips, savoring the final taste. "I'm going to arrange through Leroy some very private sessions with you. I've got a place up in Jupiter where I go for fun and games. You won't believe what I've got planned for you."

"I can believe it," Gene had said, turning away in disgust.

Gene had returned to the bed and the camera. Here more eager, hungry mouths had waited for him. The men had sucked him with great excitement. Their prodigious talents in fellatio brought him to the brink. As the first scalding spurt of jism exploded, a mouth had withdrawn itself suddenly so that all of them could witness his explosion, especially the camera. After he'd delivered his last blast, mouths had fallen on him again to taste the hot sweetness of his sperm.

As he'd lain gasping for breath on the bed, the men had turned him over, prying open his ass cheeks for their own amusement and to record his most private spot for the benefit of the camera. Even though they'd drained him in front, those same mouths descended on him again, licking, tasting, probing with their tongues. The seventy-year-old man had firmly clamped his mouth on Gene's anus, then inserted his tongue so deeply that Gene felt that he was getting fucked. After five minutes, two of the other younger men had pulled him away. Frustrated and cursing them, the old man then descended to Gene's toes where he proceeded to devour each of them on each foot with a tenacity Gene had never known. The other men had taken breaks and gotten a drink, but through the five-hour ordeal the old man's mouth never left Gene's body, descending at one point to bathe each of Gene's armpits with his tongue.

The climax of the long ordeal had arrived when the men had lined up on the bed, each demanding to be penetrated by Gene. He'd serviced all of them, never losing his erection. As kneading, stroking hands had worked his body, he'd entered each of them, fucking wildly and brutally, not caring whether he hurt them or not. He'd been inflamed and his cock seemed to follow a life of its own, making each cry out at the enormity of his penis. He was no longer their hired whore. He was their master and they were forced to service him. As he'd plunged for a final time, the fifth man screamed when Gene had penetrated him, begging Gene to take it out. "It's killing me," the man had yelled. His obvious pain seemed to excite the other men who held him down. It was this man that Gene decided was going to get another scalding load from him. His cock had seemed to double in girth and length as it pounded into the screaming man. Gene himself screamed at his final orgasm. All he'd remembered after that was more devouring mouths descending on him to lick him clean. As he'd sat up, he noticed that the old man had finally quit sucking on parts of Gene's body and was eagerly exploring the ass of the man he'd raped, trying to suck out Gene's deposit there.

The victim of the rape had been sobbing but his tears had subsided as he looked over at Gene and ran his fingers through Gene's hair. "That was the first time I've ever been fucked. I want many more private sessions with you. I want you to do that again and again—except I want you to wear your police boots, a police cap, and a short sleeved blue police shirt with the emblem of the department sewn on. Nothing else."

"That can be arranged," Gene said huskily. "But it'll cost plenty."

"With me, money is no object," the man said. "There is just one catch. You'll have to do it in front of my wife. She loves to watch."

Gene closed his eyes. He felt he'd earned his money and it was time for them to go, as he wanted sleep. Gradually after giving him final licks and tongue lashings, all the men had gone except the seventy-year-old man whose tongue remained glued to Gene's ass.

Long after the others had left Leroy's condo, the man wouldn't leave him alone. It had taken all of Leroy's strength to pull him away from Gene and to usher him from the apartment. The old man vowed to watch the film of Gene's seduction every night for the rest of his life. "Who would have ever thought that an old geezer like me would get to eat Gene Robinson."

***

Sleep wouldn't come as Rose tossed in her luxurious satin-padded bed, reaching out and clutching a fluffy pillow, imagining it was Buck. But no sofa pillow could be the stand-in for the rock-hard body of her man. Even though she'd run out the door at the news of his marriage, and had reacted hysterically at first, she felt calmer now. The announcement of his marriage was but a temporary setback for her. Like Scarlett O'Hara, one of her role models, she would begin plotting even before morning on ways to get him back.

What could some silly little beauty queen like Susan Howard who covered university news offer him that she couldn't? In her mind, it was tantamount to the horror as depicted in *Sunset Boulevard* of Joe Gillis deserting Norma Desmond for that weak little piece of liver as portrayed by the forgettable Nancy Olsen. Joe Gillis did walk out on Norma Desmond, but what did it get him? A bullet in the back and a dead swim in a pool. If Hollywood ever remade that movie, Rose felt she'd be perfect for the part of Norma Desmond.

She felt relieved that Buck hadn't flatly rejected her offer to become her media director, although Calder Martin felt he had squatter's rights on the post.

That job was but one of many temptations she planned to place in front of Buck. She was in love with him and was still not aware of how it had happened. She'd known many men, even one as well endowed and good looking as Buck. Don Bossdum. But from the moment Buck had penetrated her, she was in love with him. It was the feel of him, the way a lock of his blond hair had fallen and kept grazing her forehead as he worked to bring her the deep satisfaction she demanded in a man.

Many men like Barry Collins had moved over her body and had penetrated her, even bringing her to climax. They'd never reached a spot deep within her body that made her want to belong to them forever. Buck did that for her. Her climax with him was the most spectacular she'd ever known. It literally made her scream, and no man had ever done that for her, except perhaps Don Bossdum.

Right this moment she wanted sleep more than anything else. She reached for a scarlet satin domino and put it over her eyes. She felt a noose was about to tighten around her neck. She'd accepted a check for twenty-million dollars, which she'd deposited in a bank in Vienna, and very soon she was going to have to start to sing in public to earn that much money. There was a promise of more money to come, but she had to convince certain interests that she could deliver on her first act.

The truth was, she wasn't the powerful personality she conveyed in front of TV cameras. She was a weak and frightened creature who needed a good, strong man behind her who would protect her even from herself. In Buck, she felt she'd found a man strong enough to guard her against harm.

She smiled confidently. As a means of drawing Buck back into her fort, she'd already unleashed one of the greatest lures in her arsenal: Shelley. The boy already seemed to be working overtime to make Buck fall in love with him. Although she pretended to hold her son in disdain, she—along with virtually everybody else—was awestruck by his beauty. He'd already seduced several of her former lovers, some of whom had presumably never had sex with a boy before. If all her charisma, wealth, and power weren't enticement enough for Buck, surely Shelley was. From what she'd observed, Buck was already falling under the boy's spell.

As a film of sleep began to drift over her body, she turned over and tried to shut out the world. Already a plan was formulating in her brain to have Buck racing over to Paradise Shores. It was a bit risky—maybe lethal—but she was willing to take the chance. It was better for her to think about that than the disastrous dinner she'd had with Ronald and

Nancy Reagan.

***

In the comfort of their island bedroom, Buck lay nude on the bed, enjoying the soft lights of the patio. Also nude, Robert had inserted himself between Buck's legs where he was worshipping Buck's balls with this tongue and lips. It was as if he were rewarding them for having given him such exquisite pleasure.

There was no doubt that Buck's life had changed that afternoon. A new doorway of pleasure with Robert had opened for him. In spite of all the opportunities, he had never penetrated Robert before. In some murky part of his brain, he'd always felt it was the last frontier with Robert. As long as he was being serviced or even doing some servicing himself, he somehow believed that didn't make him gay. Fucking a man made him gay, and that's why his experience with Gene had blown his mind. He'd crossed the frontier, first with Gene and now with Robert, and was damn happy he'd done so. It had been a thrilling experience for both Robert and him.

At first he'd had a hard time achieving entry, as Robert had winced at the pain and had even cried out, "It's killing me." Buck attempted to withdraw, but Robert had grabbed him, digging his nails into his back and demanding he continue his assault. Inch by inch, Buck had penetrated his friend who was goading him on in spite of his anguish.

In three, maybe it was five, minutes Robert had seemed to open to him. Instead of pain, the most exquisite ecstasy had come over his face, as he'd opened his mouth and stuck out his tongue for Buck to suck. As Buck had fucked him, Robert's body had come alive as never before. In spite of the initial awkwardness, he had discovered that Robert was a true bottom. Buck had nibbled Robert's ear and licked his neck, sometimes descending to devour that very neck even though he knew it would cause a hickey or maybe more than one. He couldn't help himself. At one point he even found himself biting Robert's neck really hard.

After one very deep plunge, Robert had screamed. At first Buck thought it was the pain. Robert was experiencing a shattering orgasm. Without completely removing himself from the young man's body, Buck had lowered his lips and mouth over Robert to reward himself with the liquid offering of his friend. Robert's semen had never tasted sweeter. Mounting him again, Buck had continued his deep penetration of Robert. Amazingly, before Buck achieved his own shattering climax, Robert had reached orgasm one more time. He'd seemed thrilled beyond his wildest expectations to have Buck inside him, and to judge by the way he'd held onto Buck he never wanted him to leave his body.

When Buck's own climax finally did erupt, and he'd held it back for as long as he could, he'd collapsed onto Robert and didn't want to pull out. Buck had found himself crying at the sheer joy of what he'd just experienced. Robert had licked Buck's tears away. When Buck had opened his eyes, he was greeted with Robert's smiling face.

The memory of such pleasure still raced through his body as he reached down and ran his fingers through Robert's beautiful silky blond hair. He knew that Robert was so hopelessly in love with him at this point, that Robert would never leave him again. Buck eased gently into the soft comfort of the bed, enjoying the feel of Robert's beautiful pink tongue as it paid homage to his balls. Buck was proud of their shape and size and had been since he was fourteen years old. He was delighted that Robert recognized their power and potency. Even so powerful an attraction as Buck's balls was not enough to keep Robert buried between Buck's legs forever. Robert's tongue began to travel, and Buck knew where it was heading. Buck groaned in anticipation

Robert's tongue found its target and there it would stay until an hour had passed. One sensation after another shot through Buck's body as he surrendered himself completely to Robert's expert lappings. Deep into the hour, Buck was lying moaning on the bed, clutching and grabbing Robert's head and forcing him into even closer contact with the target.

***

She must not have slept more than four hours before she sat up in bed, ripping off her domino. Her troubled mind wouldn't allow her to sleep any more, and she didn't want to become addicted to medication. She was tempted to press the buzzer and order black coffee but decided she needed these moments alone. Until now she'd tried to blot from memory her troubling dinner with Ronnie and Nancy.

If Buck had accepted her invitation, the evening would have gone better. As it went, there could have been no more incompatible grouping of dinner partners than Ronald Reagan, Nancy Davis, Shelley, and herself. Before the first twenty minutes had gone by, Rose knew she wasn't going to be asked to join the rich and powerful inner circle that was trying to propel this broken down actor into the White House.

Even though always stylishly dressed for the 70s, the Reagans still carried with them a 50s aura—barbecues in the backyard, potluck picnics, and outings at the ranch. That was hardly the evening she had planned for them.

Paradise Shores had never looked more beautiful. She'd filled it with flowers and had personally overseen the soft lighting. She'd wanted to appear stunningly glamorous before the Reagans and had dressed in a low-cut red evening gown that glittered and gave off a gentle rustling sound when she moved. The dress had cost twelve thousand dollars and had been shipped down from New York where it had required extra fittings. She wanted it to be perfect, knowing that Nancy was increasingly becoming a fashion plate.

Before the Reagan limousine arrived, she'd checked all the final arrangements and had even hired an extra staff of ten to service the dinner. Wherever she looked bowls of open roses in all colors had floated, and the candlelight had cast an enchanting glow.

She'd been determined that the dinner would be perfect, beginning with the caviar and smoked salmon. She'd even booked a world class pianist to play softly in the music room, although he'd been warned not to come out and introduce himself as he was a flaming liberal who'd detested Reagan's role as governor of California.

Shelley had remained in his bedroom getting dressed, and she'd feared he wouldn't wear the dark blue suit and white shirt she'd selected for him. Even before she had a final chance to go up and check on Shelley's wardrobe, the Reagan limousine was in the driveway.

She'd wondered which one of their fat cat supporters was paying for it, as she'd been informed that the Reagans had been virtually paupers all their lives. They certainly didn't make much money appearing in all those bad films. She'd once seen Nancy Davis on the late show, flipping off the channel after ten minutes. She'd only seen one movie starring Reagan himself. Something about *John Loves Mary*. She didn't like to waste her time on such dribble.

Nancy's dress was also red but it hadn't been half as stunning as hers. It fell just below her knee, whereas Rose's gown was floor length. Although a permanent smile had been fixed on her face as if sculpted there, Nancy had appeared to examine her critically. It was obvious from the beginning that Nancy had not approved of her, and certainly didn't like the low cut of her gown. It apparently was too revealing for Nancy. But Rose had caught Ronnie taking a peek at the goodies. Perhaps a remembrance of things past.

She'd planned to have drinks at the pier down by her yacht. It had been carefully planned, and it was also the best place to see the sun set. But Queen Nancy had intervened. "He's been on his feet all day. Get him off his feet."

Changing plans abruptly, Rose had ushered them into her sunken Florida room filled with roses. "What kind of First Lady will you make?" Rose had said after drinks were served. No sooner had the words escaped than she realized how abrupt they sounded.

As if the cameras were still turning, Nancy had said, "I'll be no Mrs. Roosevelt—that's for sure. That woman had her own agenda. I will devote myself totally to Ronnie's causes."

"What Nancy meant," Ronnie had interjected, "is, of course, that we have the greatest respect for Mrs. Roosevelt, Democrat or not."

"My mother was a southern Democrat," Nancy had interjected.

"And I too was once a Democrat," Ronnie had said. "You see, we all make mistakes and can learn from them." He sipped his drink and leaned forward. "To my knowledge, you don't have a party affiliation."

She had gotten up from the sofa to stand before the fireplace. She'd felt that her artfully arranged position there had shown off her figure to its best advantage. Unlike these former actors, she at least had a figure to show off.

"I only do a solo," she'd said.

"What do you mean?" Nancy had asked with a slightly raised eyebrow.

"I run my own show. So far, my charismatic movement hasn't backed political candidates. All that is about to change."

"We're hoping that our ideas and causes, which I'm sure you've read about, might intrigue you enough to support us," Ronnie had said, smiling with a courtly charm.

She'd studied him for a minute, checking the roots of his hair, detecting no gray. "I think in a few days when my true agenda becomes clearer to the American public, that you will not welcome my support."

"That's astonishing," Ronnie had said. "What's going to happen in a few days?"

"That is a secret," she'd said. "But I'm going public with my agenda. No doubt it will be different from your own."

"We assume that you're following an agenda much like that of Pat Robertson and Jerry Falwell," Nancy had said.

"Nothing like that," Rose had said.

"But Christian..." Ronnie had stammered, not realizing what she was alluding to. He'd seemed acutely uncomfortable, and the evening had only begun.

"Of course, I will always be a spokesperson for the Christian movement in this country," she'd said. "But I will also be representing other misunderstood interests in this country. I will become a lobbyist for another group as well. I fear this new group is too much of a hot potato for you to handle, and because of various affiliations of mine you may want to seek support elsewhere."

"I don't understand," Ronnie had said.

"You will," Rose had countered.

He'd cleared his throat which had seemed to bring on a coughing spasm. Nancy had tried to comfort him, but her steely, disapproving eyes had glared at Rose even though her smile remained permanently fixed on her face.

From that point on, Rose had known that the dinner would be a disaster. Being the consummate professionals they were, she'd known somehow they would manage to get through the evening, even though its whole purpose had vanished at the beginning with her enigmatic statements. She couldn't tell the Reagans exactly what she was planning to do, but she'd also warned them to back off and not come knocking at her temple door again. In the next few days, they'd probably deny this dinner had ever happened.

Ever the diplomat, Nancy had rushed in with something to divert the conversation. "I noticed your rose-colored limousine out in the driveway. It's very impressive. I ride around a lot in limousines these days. But my fondest times are not in these limousines, but in a red Pontiac station wagon I used to drive in the 50s."

Ronnie had sat back, as if relaxing for the first time this evening. "We used to have the best barbecues. No politics then. More show biz friends. Bill Holden came over a lot. George Burns and Gracie Allen. And long before I became governor of California, Jack Benny used to call me governor."

At this point Shelley had entered the room. He hadn't worn anything flamboyant, but had put on that dark suit, a conservative tie, and white shirt she'd laid out for him.

Far from being the menace she'd feared, he'd actually been quite delightful, charming, articulate, and completely gracious. Knowing how dangerous politics were, he'd used his extensive knowledge as a movie buff to entertain and delight them with secrets of Hollywood that even they hadn't known.

Over dinner Shelley had turned to Nancy and said, "Did you know that Olivia de Haviland maintains that Jimmy Stewart was the best lay in Hollywood."

Nancy had appeared slightly shocked but had seemed mildly titillated by this bit of information, whether true or not. Ronnie had seemed embarrassed.

After the main course had been served, Shelley had put down his wine glass. "Did my mother tell you that I have the gift of prophecy?"

"No, she didn't," Nancy had said, obviously intrigued. "In fact she didn't tell us much about you at all."

"It's true," Rose had said. "He can predict the future. He's never wrong."

"Then that brings up a big question," Ronnie had said.

"Yes," Nancy had echoed, taking a cue from her husband. "We have to ask."

"You're the next occupant of the White House," Shelley had said matter-of-factly and with such conviction that at least for one moment everybody at the table had seemingly believed him.

"That's wonderful," Nancy had said.

"There's only one problem," Shelley had warned. "I hesitate to bring it up."

"I can handle it if Ronnie can," Nancy had said, reaching over and taking the hand of her husband.

"I think Shelley has predicted enough for one evening," Rose said.

Ronnie had interceded. "I want to know. If I'm going to be president of the United States, I'll have to learn how to handle a lot of bad news."

"I see this assassination problem," Shelley had said.

The table had fallen strangely silent. After that, no topic of conversation could enliven the evening again. There were long periods of silences.

Rose had understood when the Reagans had excused themselves, not taking dessert.

"I can always tell when Ronnie is getting a cold, and he's getting one right now. I must take him back to our hotel," Nancy had said.

In the foyer Rose had stood under candlelight, bidding them goodbye. Both Ronnie and Nancy had told her what a lovely evening they'd had. Nancy even claimed how delightful it was to have met her.

"Shelley's remarkable," Nancy had said as a parting remark. The boy had disappeared. "He's certainly the world's most beautiful boy. But..." She'd hesitated. "As a prophet, I'm not so sure."

"Let's hope he's wrong," Ronnie had said.

The final good-byes and kisses were staged theatrically, and the Reagans had departed in their limousine, never to grace the grounds of Paradise Shores again.

***

At the *Examiner*'s office, only the early shift had reported for work. As Buck walked into his office, he noticed Robert's empty desk and a feeling of great regret came over him. He was going to remove only his most personal files. The rest of his papers and possessions would be gathered that afternoon by a bonded moving agency. Buck sighed as he looked at the gift from Sister Rose of the de Kooning. That he was going to take with him.

At his typewriter, he banged out copy about his resignation from the *Examiner*. Resignation sounded better than being booted. He enigmatically promised his readers to "return" soon, without spelling out exactly what that meant.

Roland came into his office, staring straight at him like a spent runner.

"Bad night, again?" Buck asked. "What's it now?"

"My back kept me up all night."

He was so used to Roland's afflictions he didn't inquire further. "Well, what do you think?" he asked, handing the copy to Roland. "My resignation. I suggest you run it on the front page with a box."

"Your wish is my command." Roland quickly read the copy. "I'll run it after correcting a couple of typos."

"Hope your back gets better," Buck called out to Roland.

The city editor did not look back or tell him good-bye. As Buck retrieved his de Kooning, he heard the persistent ringing of his desk phone. "Hello," he said hesitantly into the phone.

"At last I got you. It's Leroy. I've been calling all over town. "It's on for tonight. You know the address. Eight o'clock sharp."

Buck reviewed a few more details with Leroy before agreeing to the ever-so-secret rendezvous. Through the windows of his office, he noticed Roland looking in suspiciously.

Buck was a publisher no more, and he had no more professional interest in the Lolito investigation. The private party Leroy was staging appealed to the voyeur in him.

***

A manila envelope tucked tightly under his arm, Gene strode into the orchid-colored room of a small convention hall. Defiantly, he marched forward to take a seat in the front row. A woman attendant informed him that the red chairs, sprinkled with silvery dust, were reserved. He refused to budge. With a slightly embarrassed anguish, the attendant gave in.

In a wrinkled suit and a white shirt that should have been retired the day before, Gene seemed out of place in this hall of well-groomed fat cats. Unlike them, he'd had his clothes set afire and hadn't bothered to replace his wardrobe. He was engulfed in a gleaming "Star Spangled Banner" atmosphere, as most of Barry's supporters wore stripes of red, white, and blue.

On stage, an all-white Dixieland band played to warm up the crowd of some two-hundred supporters. About a dozen "Collins Boys & Girls," juniors from the local high school, moved through the audience, handing out leaflets extolling their candidate's qualifications. The girls wore red dresses with straw hats enclosed in blue-ribbon bands. The boys wore the same hats but white pants and red, white, and blue shirts. The fresh faces and eager eyes of the students, combined with their toothpaste smiles, suggested the youthfulness and vigor of their candidate, although they were not of voting age themselves.

Gene wondered how many of these fresh-faced boys Barry had seduced. Gene's hope was that at the exact moment Barry announced his candidacy, his eyes would meet Gene's.

To the sound of music, Barry bounded onto the stage, running up the platform to kiss the eagerly awaiting lady Republican chairman on the cheek. The lights came on for the TV cameras.

In Gene's opinion, Barry was everything in appearance Hazel wasn't: young, good looking, trim and lean—a mild-mannered man who chose his words carefully. He'd been called the John Lindsay of Okeechobee, but only in physical appearance.

The applause intensified, as balloons were released. The clapping grew louder, as did the Dixieland band. The only person missing in this cozy scene was Pamela.

A polished performer in front of TV cameras, Barry explained that Pamela was ill, but would soon join him on the campaign trail. "We're going to clean up the filth in this town," he promised his supporters, echoing Rose's familiar words at the launch of her moral crusade.

Gene looked with increased loathing at Barry, sick to his heart at how the candidate parroted Rose's challenging battle cry. Gene had seen enough. He got up from his chair and left. He decided not to ruin this moment for Barry. There would be plenty of time for that later.

Outside the convention hall, Gene—pushed and shoved by the girls waving "Barry for Mayor" signs—waited for the candidate. He noticed Barry's long, sleek, midnight-blue limousine, with its luxurious, gunmetal-gray upholstery

After announcing his candidacy and leaving the hall to loud cheers, Barry's face looked ashen. In spite of this massive outpouring of support, he seemed to want to escape from the crowd.

Barry looked warily ahead as he moved toward his waiting limousine. He plunged into the midst of his women admirers, shaking hands, flashing his smile, and nearly losing his necktie to a determined, long-nailed souvenir hunter. Swimming through a sea of wedges and rhinestone sunglasses, he was the darling of the Republican matrons.

After waving to the crowd and giving a victory sign, he crawled into his limousine. Clutching the damaging photographs, Gene reached for the badge he hadn't yet returned to Biff's department. He showed it briefly to Barry's chauffeur, then trailed the candidate into the rear of the vehicle. "Police," he muttered to Barry, turning his back to the candidate as if checking out some disturbance.

As the vehicle pulled out, Barry paid little notice to Gene. "You guys should do a better job of keeping those animals off my back," Barry protested. "Twice I had my balls pinched."

"Those broads too old for you?" Gene asked, moving closer and looking Barry intently in the eye.

Barry turned to confront him. "You." He looked astonished. "Gene Robinson."

His eyes were concealed behind dark glasses, Gene smiled. "It's been a long time."

"Get out of this car!" Barry demanded.

"I'm along for the ride."

Barry leaned forward to summon the driver to stop the limousine.

Gene held out a restraining hand. "I have pictures for you. Snapped by Leroy Fitzgerald. You make one move to kick me out, and these pictures will end up with the news services."

"Pictures?" Barry's eyes looked helpless.

"Want to see them?" Gene asked.

"Put them away," Barry said angrily. "What do you want?"

"I want to go somewhere and talk," Gene said.

After Barry told the driver where to take them, he settled back in his seat in stiff silence. Miles from the beachfront hotels, the limousine sped past scrubby palmettos and decaying stucco buildings.

At a roadside tavern, far removed from the city limits of Okeechobee, a jukebox blared and the cowgirl waitresses served barbecued spareribs to interstate truckers, hustling the orders across the sawdust-littered wooden floors. Barry ordered a double Scotch.

Barry settled back with a resigned weariness. "I know about those pictures. Biff already showed them to me. I didn't know you had copies. What's your price?"

"I'm not a blackmailer. I want a job. To be your private security guard."

"Listen, fucker, as a moral crusader, I can't have some child molester working as my security guard."

"I'll be a private security guard at your home. Never leave the grounds."

"I don't need someone like that," Barry said.

"You will as the campaign heats up. My salary will be two-thousand a week."

"You don't come cheap," Barry said.

"I don't think you have a choice."

Barry took a long drink. "I don't think I do. My advisers have set out a long agenda for me, ending up in the White House by the year 2000. I guess I have to begin compromising."

"You started compromising a long time ago," Gene said.

"Someone will pay you the God damn two-thousand dollars. Not me. But you'll get paid."

"That's good to hear."

"I heard your house was set on fire," Barry said. "I guess this means you'll be moving in with Pamela and me. She was always attracted to you." Barry raised his glass in a mock toast. "From one child molester to another. Different scene, different style, but we're brothers."

At first Gene wanted to punch him until he saw a desperation in Barry's eyes.

Sensing that none of the other patrons were looking, Barry reached over and fondled Gene's hand. "You know you look as good as you did at the university. God, were you hot then. You still are. You haven't aged at all. I think I'm going to like the idea of you moving in with me. You can share my bedroom. Pamela and I don't sleep together any more. My girls occupy the other bedrooms."

"My body isn't part of the two-thousand package," Gene said.

"Don't be unreasonable. Leroy showed me those pictures he took of you in the shower. That's some piece of meat."

"I thought fourteen-year-olds were your specialty," Gene said.

"For fun and games. But a man needs to get penetrated now and then. For that, I need a real man like you."

"I'm not going to be your boy," Gene said.

"We'll see." Barry rose from the booth and plopped money down on the table, heading for the swinging doors leading to the parking lot. Gene followed.

Later in the limousine heading back to town, Gene turned to Barry. "Do you ever get to see Sister Rose?"

"Are you kidding?" Barry said. "Pamela's got one of my balls, that bitch Rose the other. If I had a third ball, I bet you'd be squeezing it."

Gene kept his eyes on the road ahead, not saying a word. Barry's reference to Pamela and him he understood. But what could he possibly mean about Sister Rose?"

**

At the boy bordello, filled with young men known as Lolitos, Buck felt out of place. The role of male madam seemed one that Leroy was destined to play. Buck had already warned Leroy that he didn't want to be seen in the public areas of the house whose ground floors were draped in black velvet with music playing like he'd heard at night in Tangier, Morocco. There was something of an *Arabian Nights* aura about the place. Everything suggested forbidden fruit.

"We entertain important guests here," Leroy spoke softly to Buck. "We have private rooms upstairs for them. For others, being out there enjoying the fun in the arena is what it's all about."

"Arena?" Buck asked.

"You'll see what that means in about ten minutes or so when the fun begins," Leroy said. "I'll arrange a lookout post for you."

Buck had even forgotten the lie he'd told Robert that allowed him to come here in the first place. Uncle Milty and Patrick were having a dinner tonight for Robert and him. It was to be a celebration of their reconciliation.

In a small, cramped room in back of the arena, Leroy ushered him into a comfortable seat. "This is where you can sit back and enjoy the fireworks. Can I get you a drink?"

"I'm fine," Buck said.

"You won't believe the famous men who have sat in that chair before you." Leroy reached and pulled back the curtains to reveal a two-way mirror. Leroy and he could see everything inside the dimly lit arena but the audience saw only their own reflections in the mirror. "Actually the mirror was designed so that when the boy was showing frontal the men in the audience could see his backside. When he showed them his backside, they could see frontal in the mirror."

After Leroy had gone, Buck carefully studied the mirror. He could make out the heads of men in the audience, waiting expectantly for something to happen. A spotlight was turned on the stage.

A young blond boy dressed in a sailor's uniform far too tight for him came out, his cap resting at a cocky tilt on his head. He was a beauty evocative of Robert as a teenage boy. He stood on a revolving medallion much like a lazy susan.

The medallion began to spin slowly, allowing the boy to be viewed at all angles. When it had revolved around so that Buck was staring at the boy's frontal part, he saw that his sailor pants were so tight that his genitals were clearly outlined. He appeared overly endowed. Taking his eyes from the boy's crotch, Buck looked up into his beautiful face with his long blond hair, heavy eyelashes, and penetratingly blue eyes. The boy winked at him.

Buck realized that the boy knew what the rest of the audience presumably didn't: that someone on the other side of the mirror was there watching him.

The boy took his left hand and placed it on his crotch as he pivoted around on the revolving metal. He was working himself to a full erection. When he'd made a full rotation and had faced the audience frontal again, there was raucous applause.

As the medallion started its spin again, the boy tossed his sailor's cap into the audience where a hand reached up to ensnare it. He slowly removed his top, revealing a well-defined chest with golden hairs centered between two brown nipples.

Even though he couldn't see their faces, Buck knew that this talented young man was working the audience to a feverish pitch. He was nude except for his tight sailor pants. Very slowly he began to unbutton them as the audience shouted for a total revelation. Provocatively he continued to unbutton his pants and when he did that he slowly let them slide down, revealing first his blond pubic hair. As he came into Buck's vision again, Buck saw the beginning of what appeared to be a thick and hard penis.

By the time the boy had pivoted around completely, he dropped his pants and revealed his fully erect penis to the audience, which brought loud clapping and cheering. When the medallion had turned so that only his side view as visible, Buck could see the full extent of the boy's penis. The penis not only stood out straight, long, and capped, but was reinforced by an exceptionally large ballsac. When the boy came full frontal at the window mirror, he smiled, as if a private smile to Buck, then uncapped his penis to reveal a large red knob. This unveiling of the head of his penis was met with more loud applause.

The boy's sailor pants were down at his knees as he masturbated himself in front of his newly acquired fans.

The *faux* sailor had done his job. Buck was fully aroused, and he suspected that the rest of the audience was too. After this show, the house lights went black and the boy slipped behind the curtain.

When the spotlight was turned on again, it revealed an empty medallion. In a program that would ultimately stretch out for two hours, that medallion was occupied 11 more times. Buck was certain that Leroy had selected all the outfits for the stripteases: a construction worker, a cowboy, a pilot, a police officer, a U.S. marine, a football captain, a lifeguard, a Roman gladiator, a boxer, Elvis, and a Canadian mountie.

Each one performed virtually the same routine, although none aroused Buck as much as the first "sailor," no doubt because of his resemblance to a much younger Robert.

Leroy's voice came over the loud speaker, announcing, "It's not the finale but the beginning."

Each boy, beginning with the sailor, emerged barefoot and fully nude on the stage with a full erection. As each boy stepped from the stage, he lay down on his back on a gigantic fluffy white mattress in the center of the arena. Each performer continued to masturbate himself to maintain a full erection.

When the final performer emerged, the boxer, he too joined the other eleven on the mattress. Their heads came together at the center, their bodies extending outward like a giant flower petal of flesh.

Disco music suddenly came on. The first member of the audience came out of the dim glow and lowered himself onto the first boy, the sailor. The rather portly middle-aged man plunged his mouth down on the sailor's penis, swallowing it. Other members of this small audience emerged from their seats and lowered their mouths onto each boy.

After two minutes, the music stopped, as Leroy's voice came on the speaker again. "Time to move on, little doggie," he said. The music started to blare up again.

At that signal, each man changed partners, in some cases reluctantly leaving the boy they were enjoying as they moved around in the circle fellating the next boy in line. This would continue until each of the twelve men in the audience had sampled the wares of each boy.

When the full circle had been completed, the music stopped. Leroy's voice came over the speaker again. "This time we go over the top." The music, more raucous than ever, came on again.

Buck noticed that the portly middle-aged man had gone full cycle, returning to the source of his first enjoyment, the young blond sailor.

It didn't take long. The boys had already been worked to a feverish pitch, and each of them, beginning with the blond sailor, began shooting off. The sailor reached for the portly man's head, forcing him down even more onto his penis. The man stayed on him until the eruption had long ceased. With an apparent reluctance each man lifted his satisfied mouth off each performer and retreated into the dim recesses of the arena.

Over the speaker, Leroy said,"Gentlemen, the party's not over. It's time to select a boy of your choice. There are no limits to what you can do, including penetration. But nothing sadistic. If you hurt one of our boys in any way, the party's over for you. House rules. Otherwise enjoy!"

Buck remained alone in the cramped room as the lights in the arena dimmed. He found his whole body soaked in sweat from having watched the performers. He was sexually aroused.

After a soft tap, Leroy came in. "I wanted to give you a warning in case you were jacking off."

"Some show!" Buck said.

"There's more to come. I've got a surprise for you."

***

In a foyer off one of the upstairs bedrooms, Leroy ushered Buck into even more cramped quarters than downstairs. "Wait until you see this one."

"You're a real pal," Buck said.

"After posing for those pictures, I owe you a favor," Leroy said. "The boy in this show knows you're watching but the john doesn't. And you already know both the boy and the john."

"I can't wait," Buck said.

"I can't be here for the action, since I'm arranging things all over the house. Either *Call Me Madam*, or call me Ethel Merman. Enjoy, enjoy," he whispered. "Curtains up!" He headed out the door.

For some reason Buck was shaking as he pulled back the black velvet curtain to reveal another two-way mirror. A young boy dressed in white had entered the room and was slowly and very tantalizingly removing his clothes. First went the shirt revealing a perfectly formed hairless chest. The look was all too familiar. Buck raised his eyes and looked directly into the face of Shelley.

The boy stared defiantly at the mirror. A slight smile crossed his beautiful face as he unbuckled his white pants and lowered them. He was wearing no underwear. In moments he'd exposed his genitals to Buck.

In the cramped little room, Buck was sweating profusely. His mouth was dry, and he kept clenching and unclenching his fist.

Fully nude, Shelley lay down on the bed, raising one leg provocatively.

Fresh from the campaign trail, Barry Collins came into the room. On seeing Shelley, he said something that Buck couldn't hear. Shelley ran his fingers up and down his flawless body, and rolled over, presenting his buttocks to Barry.

Barry quickly removed his coat, shirt, and tie, before slipping off his underwear top. He unbuckled his pants and dropped them to the floor, easing out of them as he slipped off his loafers. Reaching inside the band, he lowered his jockey shorts and stepped out of them. Never taking his eyes off Shelley, Barry was already fully aroused.

On the bed, he reached for Shelley. Barry bit into the back of Shelley's neck as one hand traced patterns on Shelley's chest before settling on one of the boy's brown nipples which he pinched something fierce. Shelley winced with pain but made no protest.

Barry was running his fingers over Shelley's smooth ass, fondling each buttock with gentleness before inserting a finger between the crack. Buck looked into Shelley's face as the finger was inserted in him, and the boy stared right back at him in the mirror.

Barry forced Shelley to rise up on his knees, his buttocks sticking up in the air, his face buried in a fluffy pillow.

Beginning slowly, Barry slapped Shelley's ass. At first they were gentle slaps but the intensity increased until they became sharp and stinging. Shelley's buttocks were turning red. The boy writhed and arched his back as the blows rained down. The whipping hand finally stopped and Barry leaned down and licked each buttock gently.

He took Shelley in his arms, turning the boy's face to his as he pressed his body against Shelley. When Shelley's face met his, Barry kissed the lips of the boy, running his tongue around the upper lip before biting down on the lower lip. Before Shelley could protest, Barry had inserted his tongue inside Shelley's mouth.

Very gently Barry started to kiss and lick Shelley's trembling body. He had clearly aroused passion in the boy who now seemed prepared to accept whatever Barry wanted to do with him. Barry raised his body up over Shelley's after a tongue attack on the boy's stomach. Their eyes locked.

Barry leaned down and kissed the boy long and hard. Breaking from Shelley's mouth, Barry spit in his hand and jerked the boy's legs apart. He inserted two fingers in Shelley's butt as he pinched one of the boy's nipples. Barry rubbed his sweaty, hairy chest against Shelley's hairless one. Shelley wrapped his legs around Barry, who supported the boy's thighs on his shoulders. Shelley was about to get fucked.

Buck had had enough. He opened the door to his cramped little room and headed to Shelley's room. He'd noticed that Barry hadn't locked the door when he came in

At the very moment that Barry was pressing his dickhead between Shelley's buttocks, Buck threw open the door and came into the room, slamming it behind him.

Barry looked up. "What the fuck? Buck? What in hell are you doing here? Can't you see that this is private?"

"Listen, Collins, if you don't want the shit beat out of you, get off that boy, get your clothes on as fast as you've ever dressed in your life, and get the fuck out of this house."

"Hi, Buck," Shelley said as Barry rose from the bed. "God, you're handsome when you're mad."

Without saying another word, Barry rushed to retrieve his clothes, slipping into his trousers and forgetting his jockey shorts. With his trousers still unzipped, he made for the door, retrieving his shoes, jacket and shirt.

Before opening the door, he stood to confront Buck. "I know why you're here. You want the boy for yourself."

"Get the fuck out of my sight, stinkball," Buck demanded.

over him. "You're too big a guy to skip meals." She finished the last of her wine and reached for his hand, which he willingly offered.

"Don't think I'm looking at you as my next meal ticket," he said. "That call from you sure came at the right time. I mean, I hate taking money from a woman." He paused. "Unless she can afford it."

"I'm not exactly down and out," she said. "You'll see that later if you come back to my condo."

He smiled and laughed nervously. "I thought you'd never ask."

"There is something I should tell you," she said. "I'm a married woman."

"Didn't you get a divorce from Gene?" he asked.

"A long time ago," she said. "I recently remarried."

"And you're out dating me?"

"I married Buck Brooke."

"You mean the younger version and not the old crone." He arched his eyebrows. "That's a surprise. I always thought that Buck was gay. He even came on to me one afternoon in the locker."

She looked at him suspiciously, wondering if he were lying. "I thought Robert Dante had his hooks so deep into Buck that he'd never release him for a woman," Don said.

"The marriage was to save an inheritance." She feared she'd been indiscreet to have confided even this much to Don. As Don attacked his lobster, she said, "Since I'm confessing, I want us to even the score, and I want to ask you a question. You've heard rumors about Buck. I've also heard rumors about you."

He stopped eating for a moment and searched her face. "What kind of rumors?"

"About you and Sister Rose."

His face registered no emotion. "I'm not a born again Christian if that's what you mean. I've never even seen Sister Rose, much less had an affair with her."

"Forgive me for asking. It's none of my business."

"With beauty queens like you running around, what do I need with an old bag like Rose?" Avoiding her eyes, he attacked that lobster with a certain fury.

She believed his story about not eating all day. What she didn't believe was his denial about Sister Rose.

"Speaking of beauty queens," he said, "unless I'm seeing things I just saw Pamela Collins go into the women's room. My old flame. I sure don't want to run into her tonight."

"She's been known to hang out here. Which reminds me. I need to powder my nose. If I run into Pamela. I won't tell her I'm with you." Brushing his hand softly, she headed for the women's room where she encountered Pamela in front of the mirror. The former Miss Florida was checking her appearance. Her makeup smeared, she was definitely drunk.

"Susan Howard as I live and breathe. You're looking good."

"So are you. If they were giving away a prize for beauty, you'd win it. Not just Miss Florida. You were also voted rodeo queen when the cowboys hit town."

She smiled back at Susan. "There was more to it than that. I did some of the boys a certain favor."

"I see," Susan said. She turned from the woman to go into a nearby booth.

Pamela reached to restrain her. "I need to talk to somebody with good connections, but private."

"Sure, I'll talk to you." Susan reached for her purse and jotted down her new number on a pad of paper.

"I'll call you," Pamela said. She had a sense of desperation about her, as she leaned toward Susan and gave her a light kiss on the cheek before leaving the bathroom.

Two women came in. "Aren't you Susan Howard?" the older of the two asked, studying her carefully. "And wasn't that Pamela Collins? We're voting for Barry for mayor."

"No," Susan said before retreating into a booth. "We're just imposters."

***

In the back seat of his limousine with its darkened windows, Buck reached out for Shelley and pulled him close. He kissed the boy's lips feverishly. "Don't you ever let me catch you with another man." He knew the chauffeur could see him kissing Shelley but didn't care at this point.

"I belong to you," Shelley whispered as he nibbled at Buck's ear.

"I love you, boy. The first time I saw you in the dressing room at the temple, I wanted to grab you and rape you."

"Why didn't you?" Shelley asked.

"Great self-control."

"You can lose some of that God damn self-control." Shelley's skilled fingers had settled comfortably between Buck's legs. He was handling, fondling, and massaging the basket of goodies here as if he owned it.

"There can be more later—a lot more—but for the moment I've got to fill my gut with the sweetest tasting nectar on earth," Shelley said.

As Shelley unzipped him and removed his already fully aroused cock, Buck settled comfortably into the well-padded upholstery and ran his fingers through Shelley's beautiful blond hair as he was serviced expertly. Soft groans were escaping from Buck's throat.

Shelley had removed Buck's balls. When he wasn't deep-throating Buck, Shelley licked and devoured each one. He wanted more from Shelley, but this expert tonguing would have to do for the moment. He ran his hands across Shelley's back, heading for his buttocks which he squeezed and caressed. He slipped his hand inside Shelley's trousers, his finger moving gently down the crack until it found its target. Once there, Buck with ease inserted his finger as deep as it would go inside Shelley.

The boy moaned in pleasure, devouring Buck with even greater energy. After Buck had been thoroughly kissed, nibbled, licked, and sucked, Shelley raised himself over Buck, then plunged down on his cock, letting it slowly invade his throat.

Buck didn't know how the boy managed this, but it was a most delectable sexual thrill. He reached for Shelley's throat with his free hand, as if he could feel himself buried there. In moments Shelley backed up and gasped for air. When his lungs were filled, he returned again and again to let Buck penetrate his throat.

Buck couldn't take much more of this without exploding. When his eruption fired, it shot directly into Shelley's gasping throat. Shelley backed off slightly, wanting to savor the final blast in his mouth. When Buck was long spent, Shelley continued to lick him clean. He crawled up and reached for Buck's mouth. As Buck kissed Shelley, he tongued his mouth, tasting himself. He put his hand to Shelley's throat again, massaging it. "That was some sensation."

"I plan to devote my life to giving you the most exquisite pleasure," Shelley said.

"I'll have it no other way." Suddenly, a reality came over Buck. Uncle Milty and Patrick were throwing a dinner for Robert and him. Buck was hours late and hadn't called. He instructed the driver to take Shelley to Paradise Shores. "I've got to go to my lawyer's house, and I'm late. I'm dropping you off."

"I demand that you take Rose's job offer," Shelley said. "The fringe benefits alone."

"You are no fringe benefit," Buck said. "You're the pot of gold waiting at the end of the rainbow." He reached between Shelley's legs, fondling his cock and finding it fully erect. "I want to empty those luscious golden balls of yours."

Without saying a word, Shelley unzipped and freed himself, moving over Buck's body as he lay back in the seat. He plunged his cock into Buck's devouring mouth as Buck eagerly sucked and tasted the boy. It was the most delicious taste and aroma. Shelley was able to hold back for at least 10 minutes and never once did Buck release him but continued to tongue, lick and suck until he had the boy moaning. Without warning, Shelley blasted into his mouth. Buck didn't want to swallow it right away. When Shelley kept pushing into his mouth demanding that Buck swallow his offering, Buck did, savoring every luscious drop.

As the limousine sped to Paradise Shores, Buck believed he had ensnared Florida's most luscious golden boy. As he licked Shelley's lips and kissed them, Buck reached once again to cup Shelley's buttocks and to rub his finger up and down the crack.

"The next time we meet, I'm going to spend an hour or two with my tongue buried here. After that, I'm going to bury something else in you."

"That's a promise I'm holding you to, big man." Shelley licked Buck's left ear and ran his tongue along Buck's sweaty throat.

"I'm sorry I did what I did tonight," Shelley said. "But I smoked you out of the closet. I planned the whole thing with Barry to make you jealous."

"I don't want to think about it again."

At the gateway to Paradise Shores, Shelley adjusted his clothing before getting out. He gave Buck one long, lingering kiss. He reached for a pad resting on the limousine bar and wrote down a telephone number. "As soon as you have a free moment at your attorney's, slip away and call me. I have to know how I can reach you at all times. Until we start living openly together, we're going to keep this relationship in the closet. But I need to feel I can call you at any hour of the day or night."

"You can't identify yourself," Buck said.

"I've got that all worked out. I'm a man of many voices. I'm going to be Arlie Ray Minton, your associate secretary, one authorized to call you day and night." He kissed Buck once more and got out of the car, pressing a secret code to enter the gates at Paradise Shores.

Buck instructed the driver to take him to his attorney's home. It was Robert who moved into his thoughts. He loved Robert as deeply and passionately as he loved Shelley. He loved them both and wanted them both. As of this moment, he couldn't bear the idea of losing either of them. Tomorrow he would try to figure out what to do. He closed his eyes, thinking of loving and kissing Robert. As soon as Robert's image invaded his mind, it gave way to Shelley's radiance and beauty.

As he peered out the window of the limousine, he saw that he'd been delivered to the dimly lit home of Uncle Milty. With trepidation, he entered the gates and walked with dread to face what incriminations might be waiting for him on the other side of the door.

***

In a tank top and too-tight shorts, Patrick opened the door to welcome Buck. Uncle Milty's former toy boy—picked up on a beach in Fort Lauderdale in 1969—had stayed around ever since. No longer quite as young and beautiful as he once was, Patrick still had a masculine beauty and charm. His hair was blond, aided in part by bleach and in part by the sun. He kissed Buck on the mouth...hard.

"Sorry I'm late," Buck said.

"We went ahead and had dinner without you. I'll whip something up for you. Milty can always throw steak on the grill."

Seeing Robert emerge, Buck rushed toward him and kissed him and held him close. "I've missed you, baby, but I couldn't help it."

Robert backed away slightly. "Chivas Regal, is it?"

Before getting out of the limousine, Buck had rinsed his mouth thoroughly with Scotch and spat the wash on the sidewalk.

"What kept you?" Robert asked.

"Let's get Uncle Milty to hustle up a steak for a hungry man," Buck said, avoiding the question.

Out on the patio Uncle Milty with a cooking fork waved Buck over to a grill where a steak sizzled. "Come over here, handsome hunk, and give your Uncle Milty a big sloppy wet one."

"Got held up—really sorry." He kissed Uncle Milty on the mouth as he always did. His attorney demanded that. Attired in a white apron sprinkled with red hearts, Uncle Milty wore baggy shorts and, like Patrick, a tank top. Unlike the other three specimens of male flesh on the patio, each finely tuned to perfection, Uncle Milty let his pot belly grow an inch or two every year. He was a bit bow-legged, his eyes bulged, and he had craters in his face left over from what he always called "the world's worst case of acne as a teenager." Patrick obviously adored him, even though Buck used to view Patrick as a mere street hustler.

Buck was also grateful that Robert liked Patrick. He wanted Robert to have some friends and not focus exclusively on him all the time.

"Patrick's going to give away the bride tomorrow—and ain't that just great?" Uncle Milty asked, looking over at Robert.

"Come on, Milty," Buck said as a way of reprimand. "You know I don't like to hear Robert referred to as a woman."

"One of you has got to be the bride," Uncle Milty protested. "Buck looks too much like a Roman gladiator to be a bride. The captain of a football team, maybe."

"I prefer to call it a marriage of husband and husband," Buck said, taking Robert's hand and kissing the inner palm.

Patrick came up behind Buck, offering him his favorite Scotch and soda. "I give you guys at least forty years—maybe even fifty. I'll throw your golden wedding anniversary."

"Fifty would be stretching it for me," Uncle Milty said. "I'm not as young as you beautiful boys. And these God damn varicose veins."

As Buck ate his steak, Uncle Milty related the details of his meeting with Sister Rose's money boys. "There is money here from God. At first I thought this media director thing was some press secretary shit which wouldn't have been right for you. But it's big and getting bigger."

"Exactly what would Buck have to do for this kind of money?"

Robert demanded to know. "Milty told me all about it, and I'm against it."

"A little bit of everything," Milty said. "They want to take over newspapers. Buy radio and television stations. Even go into entertainment. Finance films. They're even considering buying up several TV sitcoms from long ago."

"You mean I'd end up negotiating the rights for *I Love Lucy*?" Buck asked.

"Something like that," Uncle Milty said with all seriousness. "I'd quit everything and devote myself full time to my favorite client."

Buck held a fork with a morsel of steak at his mouth. "You're not telling me everything."

"I more or less accepted for you," Milty said.

"You did?" Robert's words stabbed the air. "I'm not happy about Buck working for this Christian psychotic."

"I'm not either," Uncle Milty said. "I can't stand the holy cow. But wait until you hear the terms."

"You mean three-million big ones a year?" Buck asked.

"A little more than that," Milty said. "I'm a greedy bastard when I'm not being your loving Uncle Milty. When all those deals are being made, I'm going to see that Buck Brooke III's name comes in for a lot of stock. As far as I'm concerned, the three million is only the down payment. I'm going to take the fuckers for all I can get."

"It scares me," Robert said.

"Don't you want a rich husband?" Uncle Milty asked. "One who could buy you a mink or sable every week."

"Fuck mink or sable," Robert said, reaching possessively for Buck's hand. "We live in Okeechobee where it's hot most of the time."

"A few fur coats are always good to have," Milty said. "After all, Buck's going to own a HUGE condo in New York when the old man passes on."

"Any news on that front?" Buck asked apprehensively.

"I'm in secret touch with his doctors," Uncle Milty said. "Three times a day I speak to them. They're not hopeful, monkey gland transplant or not. They think it's a matter of just a few more months. Weeks maybe."

"I'll fly to his side at any moment," Buck promised.

"He keeps saying he doesn't want you there," Uncle Milty said.

"That could change. What I think is, he doesn't want you to see how weak and pathetic he's become."

Buck shuddered at the images flashing through his mind. "Poor man. I know he's a bastard in many ways, but I still love him."

"Your grandpappy has lived his life and it's over now," said Uncle Milty. "Yours is just beginning, especially with this deal I'm lining up for you." He signaled Patrick to bring him a piece of paper. "Here's a number for you to call. An office in Los Angeles. Rose's boys want to set up a meeting with you sooner than later. They're flying the contracts to Miami. After they're signed, they want to turn over the millions to you personally. I demanded to go but they want to talk privately with you. Of course, all future deals have to be run by me."

"What do you think they want?" Buck asked.

"Just to check you out in the flesh. After all they're paying triple for everything. The *Examiner* isn't worth what they're giving you."

"If they want me to be media director, why not let me handle the *Examiner* too?" Buck asked.

"That's a mystery to me too," Milty said. "It seems the *Examiner* was promised to someone else."

"I'd better get used to mysteries if I'm getting involved with these goons," Buck said. "I'll make the call from your library." Alone in the library, he dialed Shelley's number.

The boy sounded sleepy. "I was just dreaming about you."

"Wake up and write down these numbers," Buck said. "I'm here at my attorney's home. Here's his private number. Here's my private home number." He gave both numbers to Shelley. "I'll be home around two o'clock this morning. That media director thing's getting hot."

"They're going to make you offers you can't refuse," Shelley said.

"Who is they?" Buck asked.

"That's for you to find out."

"I've got to go, hot stuff," Buck said. He looked over his shoulder, finding that he was still alone. "I love you, boy."

"I love you too, and miss you something awful," Shelley said.

Buck put down the phone and dialed the California number. A heavily accented male voice came on the phone.

"We were expecting your call," the mysterious voice said. "Actually, there's been a change of plans. Our supervisor would like to meet with you. The venue will be at an estate in Palm Springs, not our offices here in Los Angeles. You're to make arrangements through her. Thank you for calling, Mr. Brooke." Without saying another word, the man hung up.

Buck walked back into the patio and went over to kiss Robert.

"What did they say?" Uncle Milty asked.

"A meeting is going to be set up in Palm Springs. Arranged through Rose."

"You're going to walk out of that meeting with a lot of money," Uncle Milty said. "I think I'd better start raising my fees."

"Another thing I learned," Buck said, knowing he was going to lie. "For the loot they're paying me, I've got to be at their beck and call 24 hours a day. They've got to know a number they can reach me at all times. They've even hired a guy, Arlie Ray Minton, to keep track of me." He turned to Robert. "So if Arlie Ray calls, whoever that creep is, I'm all ears."

"Okay," Robert said, looking disappointed. "I don't like them having such control over you."

"They're entitled," Uncle Milty said. "I mean, we're talking millions."

Patrick came onto the patio carrying an elaborate flambéd dessert. "This is a pre-marriage celebration," he said.

"I didn't come clean with those guys in California," Buck said.

"How so?" Uncle Milty asked.

"I didn't tell them I'm rushing off to get married in the morning." Buck paused and looked over at Robert and smiled. "To a man."

***

In bed, his body entwined with that of Robert, Buck heard the phone's urgent ring. The sound was coming from a sitting area off his bedroom but it seemed miles away in his foggy brain.

Robert separated himself from Buck and went to answer the phone. Within a minute, he returned. "It's that Arlie Ray Minton guy you mentioned. Sounds like a creep. You haven't even signed the contract and they're calling you at three o'clock in the morning." The nude Robert crawled back in bed.

Bolting up, Buck walked naked across the bedroom floor to answer the phone. "What is it?" Buck asked.

At the sound of his voice, Shelley said, "It's Rose. You've got to come over here at once. She cut her throat but she's okay."

"I'll be right over." He put down the receiver and returned to the bedroom. "I've got to go to Paradise Shores. The shit's hit the fan. Rose tried to kill herself."

Robert sat up in bed. "She's crazier than I thought."

Hurriedly dressing, he kissed Robert good-bye, promising to check in with him later. On the way to Paradise Shores, he drove as fast as he dared. The trip was agonizing, and at one point he feared a motorcycle patrolman might stop him for speeding.

At Paradise Shores, he got out of his car as a distraught Shelley, clad only in a pair of rose-colored jockey shorts, rushed out to meet him. "Thank God you're here." He threw himself into Buck's arms, hugging him tightly and kissing him on the mouth.

"Where is she?" Buck asked.

"The doctor's with her now." The boy appeared on the verge of tears. "A little while ago she called for you."

Entering the grand marble foyer, Buck turned to Shelley. "Just what happened?"

Taking his hand and guiding him into the living room, Shelley tried to piece together the story. Earlier, Rose had pleaded with him to have the chauffeur drive over to her doctor's house to obtain more Seconals. The doctor had refused. "He told me not to let her take any more pills," Shelley said. "She was already on Dexedrine."

Not really knowing what to say, Buck walked to the patio off the living room.

"Sometimes she has these wild mood swings," Shelley said, coming up behind Buck and putting his arms around him. "Tonight she was at her most self-destructive. She kept saying over and over, 'Buck wants a younger woman. I'm too old for him.'"

Buck turned around to confront Shelley. "I don't want an older woman. I think I'll swear off women forever. I want her younger son."

Shelley reached up and kissed Buck's lips tenderly. "I'm afraid."

"I'll take care of you." He slipped off his light rain jacket and insisted Shelley put it on.

He followed Shelley into the living room again. "How could I know I'd upset Rose that much after a roll in the hay?" he asked. "Don't tell me that a woman who has known as many men as Rose and who has the iron will to stand up against massive organized attack will freak out over a little rejection from me."

"Little rejection!" Shelley said with a sneer. "You told her you were married—that's all."

"I didn't know how serious Rose was about me."

"Her mind's all fucked up. With Jesus on her side, she's like a tigress—you know that. Sometimes when she leaves the stage, she'll regress. I mean, I once caught her cooing to a rag doll. About two o'clock I heard this crash coming from her bedroom. I rushed there but her door was locked. I ran around to the terrace and got in through a glass panel. The door to her bathroom was locked. I called out to her. Finally, I got our driver to bash the door in. We found her sprawled on the floor. She'd cut her throat. There was blood everywhere. She'd used a razor. The doctor is patching her up now."

"The wound? Was it bad?"

"Just a flesh wound. She may be disfigured. She'll spend the rest of her life wearing very expensive scarves."

"I'll even pretend I love her just so I can stay next to you," Buck said.

A nurse came into the living room. "Mr. Brooke, the doctor said you can go up to her bedroom. She cut herself rather badly, but the wound isn't deep."

"I'll be right up," Buck said.

As he slowly entered Rose's softly lit bedroom, shutting the door behind him, he saw her lying on pillows in her white satin bed, her throat bandaged. Her hair was combed and her face made up with bright red lipstick, yet her skin looked ghostly pale, perhaps from the loss of blood. Slowly, sensing he was in her bedroom, she opened her eyes.

"You're beautiful," he said. "Why ruin that beauty?"

At the sound of his voice, her eyes seemed to dance alive. "I didn't mean to do it. To take one's own life is wrong. It was like another side of me took over and did it."

"I understand." He sat down beside her on the cushiony bed, reaching for her delicate hand. "You're going to be okay."

"The news of your marriage—it was more than I could take," she said weakly.

"It's just a marriage of convenience," he said. "Old Buck threatened to disinherit me unless I married Susan Howard."

"I guess I never really understood," she said.

"I'd be a fool to let my inheritance slip through my fingers," he said.

She reached over and rubbed his face, running her fingers through his hair. "You're the most handsome man I've ever known. It's as if that other beauty, Shelley, were actually our real son. That he got his beauty from the both of us."

"That's a wonderful thought," he said.

"Since it's a marriage of convenience, we'll see that the bitch is paid off." She reached out and unbuttoned his shirt. "I don't want anyone enjoying these muscles but me." She paused as a thought seemed to occur to her. "And, of course, Shelley, whenever you want a little change of pace. With Shelley, we're keeping it all in the family."

"I suppose," he said, concealing his astonishment. He realized that the doctor must have given her a heavy sedative. She tried to say something, but it was only a faint mutter. Soon she'd drifted off.

He got up and pulled back the draperies so he could see the bay through her sliding glass panels. The water below shone like a metal sheet, reflecting the moon.

After he felt assured that she was sound asleep, he slipped into her study and made a call to Robert telling him that this emergency at Paradise Shores would keep him away all night.

Buck yawned as he returned to a Queen Anne armchair beside Rose's bed. No sooner was he comfortably settled in the chair than he fell immediately asleep. He didn't know how long he slept. When he woke up, he could see it was morning. His watch told him it was seven o'clock, and he still had three hours before joining Uncle Milty, Patrick, and Robert on that flight to Miami to get married. Rubbing sleep from his eyes, he headed toward the bathroom, unzipping his fly.

He met Rose coming out of the bath. Seeing he was unzipped, she reached inside, fondling his cock with its morning hard-on and cuddling his balls. "That's just to reassure myself that it's as big as I remember."

"That's all me, babe, but I've got to seek relief somewhere else for the moment." He walked over and pissed loudly into her rose-colored bowl. He stood at an angle because he knew she wanted to see his cock dangling from his trousers.

As he stared back at her, he took in her luminous glow. It was hard to imagine that only hours before she'd tried to slit her throat. She wore a rosy dressing gown and had beautifully arranged her hair. Even the rose-colored scarf concealing the bandages on her neck looked chic.

She was walking toward him. On her thickly carpeted floor, she kneeled in front of him. She reached for his cock and shook the last drops of urine from it. Then she pulled back the foreskin and slurped it voraciously into her mouth. His penis thickened and hardened at once. The throat that she'd tried to cut was back in full action servicing him. She was a true expert at sucking a man's penis, and could take his full penetration without gagging. She weighed his balls in her delicate hands, fingering and testing their size and fullness as if he were a prize bull. He let her do all the work, not wanting to plunge into her and face fuck her because of her bandaged throat. So skilled was her tongue and lips that he felt his climax building faster than it usually did. When the eruption did explode, she swallowed his offering eagerly and kept his penis in her mouth for the longest time, not wanting to relinquish her prize.

Pulling himself away from her, he stripped off his clothes and headed for the shower to wash off Rose and the night before.

When he was finished and opened the shower doors, Shelley, clad in a silk robe, was waiting with a thick rose-colored towel. The boy kissed Buck good morning. Buck drew back when he spotted Rose entering the bathroom carrying a morning cup of coffee for him. Shelley made no attempt to move away from Buck's body but licked and kissed each nipple before taking the towel and drying Buck's chest. Kneeling before Buck, he skinned back Buck's penis and dried its thick head before planting soft little kissings and tongue lashings on it.

Rose in the meanwhile took another towel and dried his back, kneeling to wipe the water from his legs before softly drying his ass. She planted little kisses on his buttocks, her tongue occasionally darting inside the crevice to sample and taste.

Breaking from his assailants, Buck went over to a rose-colored sink and reached for a red rosy toothbrush. The toothpaste was white, however. He brushed his teeth and thanked Rose for the coffee. Shelley remained in the room. Seeing a man's white terrycloth robe hanging nearby, Buck reached for the robe and attempted to put it on.

"You won't need that," Shelley said. "Rose and I know what you look like."

"What the hell then?" Buck said, striding naked into the bedroom. Rose was in her alcove talking to someone on the phone. She sounded upset, her voice taking on a hysterical edge.

Buck spread his nude frame on a rose-colored chaise longue and enjoyed his first cup of coffee. Shelley settled between his legs to lick his balls.

Rose appeared in the room looking rather solemn. At no point did she even seem to take notice of what Shelley was doing. If it didn't upset Rose, it didn't bother Buck. Besides it felt real good.

"My great aunt died this morning," Rose announced, but didn't appear shaken by the news.

If Shelley had a reaction, it was concealed by his slurping.

"She was the matriarch of the Phillips family," Rose said. "A real frontier woman. She always said I took after her. The funeral's in Durant. That's in Oklahoma where I come from. Since I'm a little unsteady on my feet, I was hoping you'd go there with me."

"I'd like to," Buck said, taking his fingers and fondling Shelley's blond hair. "But I've got to fly to Miami this morning. I'm due in court. If I don't show up, a judgment will go against me."

"Oh, I see," she said. "A libel judgment no doubt."

"Something like that. I'm flying down at ten but I'll be back to-morrow morning. I'm going with my attorney."

"That will still fit into my plans. Shelley and I aren't flying out until tomorrow morning for the funeral. I'm also due in Abilene for a big press conference. Are you ever going to be surprised."

"You're always full of surprises," Buck said.

Shelley continued with his licking and kissing, as if he'd never come up for air.

"After Abilene we fly to Oklahoma," Rose said. "There's more. After that I want you to go with us to Palm Springs. There you're going to meet the boss. He'll be your boss too if you sign on as media direc-tor, and I know you will. You'll also get the check owed to your old grandpa. All those millions. You'll also get another check if your damn attorney will ever agree on the exact price being asked for your share of *Examiner* stock. In other words, you'll fly to Palm Springs a fired $45,000-a-year publisher, and you'll return to Okeechobee with mil-lions."

At the mention of millions, Shelley removed his lips from Buck's balls. "We've got ourselves one rich stud," he said to Rose.

"We've got our own millions," Rose said defensively.

With one hand, Buck finished his coffee and with the other hand he reached for Shelley's neck, returning him to his balls. Shelley expertly went to work again, servicing Buck and bringing him such exquisite pleasure that Buck occasionally moaned in joy.

"I'll certainly be misunderstood after that press conference tomorrow in Abilene," Rose said. "But in Durant I'm understood. This will be your chance to see how the real grass roots America responds to me."

"I can't wait," Buck said. "I especially can't wait to fly to Palm Springs. I've already taken to riding around in limousines and leading the good life. That's a private charter I'm taking to Miami. I need to get a check cashed before all those bills start coming in."

Shelley raised his head and stared lovingly into Buck's eyes. "Don't you ever worry about bills any more. You've got bills to pay? Send them over to us." He looked over at Rose with a certain contempt. "We've got more money than God."

Without Buck seeming to realize it, Shelley's kissing and licking of his balls had produced his second roaring hard-on of the morning.

Rose walked over as if aware for the first time of the sexual foreplay going on between Shelley and Buck. She ran her long tapered fingers up Buck's shaft, causing him to moan again at her touch. She reached and gently uncapped his penis, running her fingertips over its engorged head. She was incredibly gentle with Buck, but when she reached for Shelley's hair, she yanked him up roughly and virtually forced him to go down on the long, thick penis. In spite of her pulling his hair, Shelley was only too willing to take the plunge.

When Buck had deeply penetrated Shelley's throat, Rose got up and headed toward the door, moving with a swanlike grace. When she turned around to face them again, Buck noted a harshness to her features. She yelled to her son, "Enjoy yourself, cocksucker, but I've already beat you to his first load of the day." Turning on her heels, she slammed the door behind her.

Chapter Nine

In their privately chartered plane, a sleepy Buck buckled up as the craft took off the runway in Okeechobee heading for the airport in Miami. Robert was beside him, smiling and looking a little sleepy too.

In a seat across from them, Uncle Milty and Patrick sat looking out the window as the plane went airborne. They were holding hands.

Uncle Milty and Robert had arranged for the matching wedding bands, but Buck had always planned to give Robert an engagement ring. He'd never gotten around to it. As he'd climbed into his waiting limousine at Paradise Shores, Shelley had raced toward the car to give him a present. "Go on, open it," Shelley had demanded eagerly. When Buck opened Shelley's gift, he'd discovered one of the most beautiful rings he'd ever seen. It was a circle of blue diamonds and rubies. "It was created for some Arab sheik," Shelley said. "Do you like it?"

"It's spectacular, but I can't accept it. It must be worth a king's ransom."

"More than that. I want you to have it." He'd taken the ring and slipped it on Buck's finger.

Before he'd gotten to the airport, Buck had slipped the ring off his finger and concealed it within his pocket. On the plane, he reached inside his pants and retrieved the ring. Taking Robert's hand, he put each finger to his mouth and sucked on each one tenderly. He took the ring and slipped it on Robert's finger. He pulled Robert close to him and kissed him real hard.

Breaking away, Robert looked down at the ring. "That's the greatest ring I've ever seen in my life." He kissed Buck lightly on the lips. "Thank you." He showed the ring to Uncle Milty and Patrick.

"I'm sure I'll be sent the bill since I'm handling all your affairs," Uncle Milty said to Buck. "Some bill." He turned to Robert. "You are worth it."

"This calls for champagne," Robert said, getting up and heading for the rear of the plane.

"I'll help you," Uncle Milty volunteered.

When they got up, Patrick rose from his seat to join Buck on the other side. He reached for Buck's hand, kissing the inner palm. "That's the most drop dead ring I've ever seen. Uncle Milty will have to tell me what you paid for it."

"There will be no bill," Buck said. "It's a family heirloom."

Patrick smiled. "It must be nice to have rich parents. I grew up in a trailer in Arkansas. We had nothing. My parents still don't. Uncle Milty sends them a two-hundred dollar check every week."

"We helped out Robert's mother but she never thanked us," Buck said.

"I dread the funeral," Patrick said. "I'd much rather attend the wedding instead."

"So would I," Buck said.

"A funeral and a wedding, all on the same day." Patrick reached for Buck's hand again, kissing the palm before suddenly licking it.

Buck withdrew his hand. "I'm already spoken for."

"Sigh," was all Patrick said. "When I saw you reach over and grab Robert to kiss him, I had to conceal my hard-on."

At that point Robert and Uncle Milty came back to the front of the plane, Robert carrying the tray with the poured champagne and Uncle Milty following with an extra bottle.

"I'd like to make a toast," Uncle Milty said. "Back in Okeechobee, there may be a *faux* Mr. and Mrs. Brooke III. Here's to the real Mr. and Mrs. Buck Brooke III."

***

After a restless night, Gene, behind the wheel of his car, felt more in charge today. He was going to the hospital to pick up Sandy who would be released. Although in some pain, the terrible ordeal was over for Sandy.

Thanks to Leroy, Gene had a beautifully furnished condo waiting for Jill and Sandy. Gene wasn't proud of what he'd done to earn that condo.

Within fifteen minutes of the hospital, Gene reviewed the events of the past evening as if it were a film being played in his head. He'd moved into the Collins household. On the first night, he hadn't met Barry's daughters. They'd left hours earlier for Tampa to visit with their grandmother. Gene had found himself alone in the house with Pamela and Barry.

In Barry's bedroom, Gene had spotted a pair of swimming trunks and had stripped and put them on, crossing the carpeted floor of a terrace which overlooked a ball-shaped, Olympic-size swimming pool. Barry had retreated to his library where Gene had heard him shouting to someone on the phone.

Pamela hadn't been sick, as Barry had told his supporters at the rally that afternoon. When the chauffeur had delivered Gene and Barry to the Collins home, they'd found Pamela, her blouse unbuttoned, sprawled on a beige-colored sofa in their sunken living room. Barry had gently slapped her to arouse her from a drunken stupor.

At first she hadn't recognized Gene but, after a while, her memory had seemed to return. Looking with contempt at Barry, she'd said, "At least now we'll have a real man around the house."

In the borrowed trunks from Barry, Gene had walked to the edge of the pool and had dived in with a loud splash. In spite of the hot temperatures, the water was cold. Going under, he'd emerged at the deep end, pulling himself out by an aluminum ladder, his body covered with water crystals, his skin glistening in the lights around the pool.

As he'd glanced over his shoulder, he'd spotted Pamela standing at the edge of the pool staring at him as if transfixed. In her white bikini, she looked somewhat as she had when she'd entered beauty contests in their university days. Picking up a towel from a nearby stand, she'd headed toward him. He'd stood completely still as she'd dried his back, her hands caressing him. Her laugh had been mischievous, low and husky. "I should think an exhibitionist like you would wear something more revealing when going into the water. Or else nothing at all."

A chill had gone through his body as her fingers had traced patterns on his chest, encircling a nipple and pinching it. "Cool it!" he'd said, breaking from her. "Barry might come out here and see us."

"Honey, it won't matter none if Barry does see us."

With a force he'd found surprising, she'd kneeled in front of him, pulling down the trunks, completely exposing Gene. She'd pushed him back on an air mattress and had fallen upon him, devouring his cock with a loud suction noise. In spite of himself, he'd found himself hardening and thickening in her experienced mouth. Maybe those rumors about her were true after all, he'd pondered. She was said to have given head to half the state troopers in Florida.

With her free hand, she'd unfastened the top to her bikini, exposing her still ample breasts. He'd closed his eyes and had lain back on the mattress. To his surprise, he'd found himself taking pleasure in her sucking and licking of him. He'd been tense all day, and her lovemaking was bringing him the relief he'd needed. Gradually rising up and pumping himself into her mouth, he'd begun to fuck her face. She'd been an equal match for him, meeting his every forward lurch with her devouring mouth.

In moments his penis had been left wet and bobbing in the night air. Barry had suddenly come onto the patio wearing only a terrycloth robe. He'd jerked Pamela by her hair and pulled her off Gene. In moments he'd replaced her suctioning mouth with his own equally skilled one.

"You fucking cocksucker," Pamela had shouted at her husband. "That load belonged to me."

Without removing his mouth from Gene's penis, Barry had not even looked up as Pamela had raced from the patio in tears.

Even before Barry had claimed his penis, Gene had been near a climax. As he'd felt himself in the throes of orgasm, Gene had reached down and captured Barry's head and forced him to go all the way down on his penis which produced a shattering orgasm. Gene hadn't cared whether he'd choked Barry or not.

Later when Gene had entered Barry's bedroom, the candidate was completely nude on the bed, fucking himself with a dildo. Upon seeing Gene, he'd said, "Get your ass over here. I need to get fucked with the real thing."

That was all Gene cared to remember of last night.

After parking his car in an open air lot at the hospital, he raced down the corridor to see Sandy.

***

In a slumlike section of North Miami, Uncle Milty directed the chauffeur to a cement-block structure with a hand-painted sign out front, "Jews for Jesus."

"What's this?" Buck asked, taking Robert's hand and feeling a surge of insecurity. "You converting to Christianity, Uncle Milty?"

"It's not always easy getting a pastor to perform these ceremonies," Uncle Milty said. "This guy, Doug Potter, will perform any ceremony for anybody. If you wanted to marry your dog, that's okay by Doug. He's not Jewish but he specializes in converting them. They give him gifts for their conversion."

"What fun," Robert said. "Is he legitimate?"

"As legitimate as any of your Christian ministers—and that's not saying a lot," Uncle Milty said.

Standing in the litter-strewn unpaved lot of the ministry, Buck almost wished he'd withheld permission for such a ceremony to take place.

Robert came up behind him. "I know you're uncomfortable here. But it's important to me."

"I thought your mother's funeral was to come before the wedding," Buck said.

"Her church is tied up this morning with a wedding. We won't be able to have the funeral until three o'clock."

The door to the temple was open and Buck led the men inside. The place was empty and two phones were ringing. Papers were scattered everywhere, including unopened mail. In the rear was a small chapel with a makeshift altar and some folding chairs. What saved the ambience were a dozen wreaths of the most gorgeous flowers, some of them exotic.

"I ordered those," Patrick said, catching Buck's eye.

"Thanks," was all Buck could manage to say.

At this point Doug Potter, the minister, stuck his head out of a side door. "Welcome guys. I'm not dressed yet. Hey, you're Buck Brooke. I recognized your picture. You know that magazine has just been published. They call you the sexiest guy alive. Get your ass back here."

Buck cringed and excused himself, heading for the minister's room.

It turned out to be a bedroom with an unmade bed. Reaching to shake his hand, Doug was clad only in a pair of jockey shorts far too tight to cover the ample load. Although older, he evoked a young Marlon Brando as he appeared in *A Streetcar Named Desire*.

"Forgive the look of the place," Doug said. "Only an hour ago I was fucking two cunts—one blonde, the other brunette. I always like two at a time. It takes two pussies to handle me anyway."

"You're a minister—not a celibate Catholic priest," Buck said.

"Damn right I am," Doug said, reaching for a white shirt. "I believe if God didn't want us to have sex, he wouldn't have invented it. I'm not one of those right-wing shitheads." He buttoned his shirt and reached for his pants. "I'm not against gay people. In fact, I conduct special services for them. I figure if they contribute to my temple, what the hell. I've never been able to tell a gay dollar from a straight dollar."

"I agree with you," Buck said.

"Indirectly gay men helped launch me in my temple," Doug said.

"How so?" Buck asked.

"I saved my bucks. For years I was one of the highest paid male hustlers in Miami. Earned the big ones. In fact, James Herlihy, the writer, used me as a role model for Joe Buck in *Midnight Cowboy*. Herlihy could really suck cock. I don't care how many women try it, it takes a man to really know how to suck cock."

"So far," Buck said, "I'm agreeing with you on every point. You've converted me already."

"Fine," Doug said, zipping up his pants and searching under the bed for his shoes. "I expect a big contribution for this wedding ceremony. I'm not charging to perform the service. I'm counting on your generosity, and I mean yours and not Uncle Milty's. He's a Jew, and they start out stingy. When I convert them to Christianity, I find they can be very generous. Two old Jewish ladies who became Christians even willed me their homes when they died. That's the kind of contribution I like."

"Thanks for agreeing to perform the ceremony," Buck said. "It's important to my friend, Robert."

"I'll make it easy for you," Doug promised.

Buck glanced nervously at his watch. "Don't you think it's about time we got moving?"

"Let's go for it," Doug said. He paused as he straightened his tie. "Do you mind if you write your check to me before I perform the ceremony?"

"By all means," Buck said.

Doug smiled and kissed Buck on the mouth.

Buck was taken aback but didn't do anything stupid like wipe traces of the wet kiss from his lips.

Doug winked at him. "I could be converted."

After that, the wedding and even the funeral itself was anticlimactic.

***

Still bandaged from his burns, Sandy was in awe at the condo. He went from room to room inspecting everything. "This is great. I've lived in dumps all my life. Until now."

Gene felt proud like a father.

Sandy ran his hands over the upholstery and felt the thick gold draperies. "It looks like a movie set." A sudden frown crossed his brow. "How did you afford all this?"

Gene went over to the bar to pour himself an orange juice. "I got a job. Special duty. It pays well."

The phone rang. Thinking it might be Jill, Gene picked up the receiver. "Hello," he said cautiously.

The voice of Leroy came over the wire. "I hope your young friends like the condo."

"They're real grateful to you," Gene said.

"They shouldn't thank me but you," Leroy said. "You earned it. "I've got to see you right away. Get on the elevator and come up here."

"Sounds urgent. I'll be right up."

"Hurry," Leroy urged.

After putting down the receiver, Gene turned to Sandy, kissing him lightly on the lips. "I've got to go upstairs to see Leroy."

"No trouble, I hope."

"I'll let you know," Gene said.

As Gene turned to leave, Sandy held his arm. "There are only two bedrooms here—not three."

"Sorry, but Leroy wouldn't give us a three-bedroom."

"That's the way I want it," Sandy said.

"You and Jill can have the front room," Gene said, "and I'll take the one in the rear."

"Correction," Sandy said. "Jill in the front room, me and you in the back bedroom."

***

It must have been one o'clock in the afternoon when Susan woke up. Don and she hadn't really gone to sleep until six in the morning. She ranked the evening as the most memorable of her life. With memories of the night, she reached over in her bed, seeking to run her fingers across Don's broad chest. Her hand came up empty.

She heard the shower running. At first she was tempted to join him, but decided she wanted to linger in bed.

Don had made her forget Buck in one night. She'd never known sex like that Don could deliver. There was no part of her body he hadn't explored with his tongue. More than once he'd made her scream with joy and pull his hair. When his deep penetration had come, it was evocative of Buck's, although he'd ridden her with a fury she'd never felt from Buck. At their first climax when she'd thought he'd withdraw from her, she'd been wrong. Still partially erect, he'd lingered inside her until a second steam had formed in his engine. He'd plowed her again, more forcefully than before.

The second time had taken much longer and in many ways it was more enthralling because the great urgency for climax was no longer there.

Opening her eyes, she felt awake for the first time today. The noise from the shower had long stopped, and Don seemed to be in the kitchen making a phone call

Since Don was all fresh and clean, her vanity dictated that she greet him the same way. She'd sneak into their shower and her powder room and look gorgeous when confronting him. Right now she feared she looked like a woman who'd taken on twelve studs in combat.

As she passed by the door, she detected anger in Don's voice. She didn't mean to eavesdrop but couldn't help herself.

"God damn you, Shelley," Don said into the phone. "You can't drop me like this just because you've captured Buck Brooke. What's he got that I don't have?"

At the sound of those words, she stopped short. That was Shelley Phillips that Don was talking to on the phone. No one else had a name like Shelley. Not only had Don been involved with Sister Rose but with Shelley too. Maybe she hadn't heard right. Shelley was also involved with Buck.

"I've been with you too long to settle for a lousy fifty-thousand dollars," Don said. "It's not enough. It was always you and me, babe, long after Rose and I broke up. Rose didn't know you kept slipping down to Miami to see me. That you've never stopped seeing me until my wife found out. I need one-hundred thousand dollars. I could make it real rough on you, cocksucker, ruin you."

There was a long pause. It was clear Shelley had plenty of reaction to that.

"One-hundred thousand dollars and in cash," Don demanded.

She put her hand at her throat. She'd landed herself the most expensive hustler in the state of Florida.

"It's not just the money," Don said to Shelley. "Sex with you is better than any sex I've ever had in my life. When you get over this God damn thing with Buck, I want you back."

She didn't really want to hear Don pleading with Shelley for the boy to come back to him. Under the shower she tried to blot out the words she'd heard. If she'd been twenty-three, she would have burst into the kitchen, grabbed the phone from Don and denounced Shelley. She would have slammed down the receiver and demanded that Don leave her condo.

She turned on the shower extra hot. To her surprise, there was no pain to burn away. Who in hell was she to judge Don? Wasn't she a paid courtesan herself? The only difference between them was that she didn't have to fuck on command. Because of the terms of her marriage, she couldn't find a regular guy anyway. What was left for her? A married man? A trick on the side? For all appearances, she had to appear Buck's dutiful and loyal wife.

Don was a great lover, and she needed that. She admired Shelley's taste: Don Bossdum and now Buck Brooke. That little preacher rat knew how to pick them.

Stepping from the shower, she reached for a thick towel. She was going to call Uncle Milty as soon as he returned from Miami to inform him of her new living arrangements and tell him to send Don a check every week for seven-hundred and fifty dollars. She'd supply the rest of the money for him, including a new wardrobe and a sports car. Don didn't need a job: he already had a job and that was being with her. Let Buck have his Robert. Let Buck even have his Shelley.

Applying the finishing touches to her face, she liked the reflection staring back at her in the mirror. Instead of diminishing her, Don's lovemaking seemed to have given her a new vitality and glow.

She paused only briefly at the bedroom door. The only sound coming from the kitchen was the television. Don was watching some sports broadcast.

She came into the kitchen.

He looked up at her. "Hi, sugar," he said.

"Good morning," she said in a soft, modulated voice. "Did anyone ever tell you you're the world's greatest lover?"

***

In a pair of shorts and a T-shirt, Leroy looked younger than Gene had ever seen him. As soon as Gene had entered the apartment, Leroy kissed him on the mouth and took his hand, directing him to the terrace.

Leroy plopped down on a chaise longue, putting his feet up on a coffee table. "I'm ashamed that I put you through that shit with my friends. Only this morning I was trying to buy back the films. I don't want anybody having that film of you."

"Maybe it's too late for that now," Gene said. "Why do you want the film back?"

"I'm in love with you," Leroy said. "From this day on, you're my own property."

Gene looked astonished. "Don't I have something to say about that?"

"I didn't mean to sound like I own you," Leroy said.

"I'm here for you—the body that is," Gene said."Not the heart."

"Do you think I'm just some silly little faggot? I know you don't love me. You can learn to love me in time."

"We'll see," Gene said.

Leroy reached for Gene's hand and pulled him down on the sofa to sit beside him. "I'm going to see you through this shit you've gotten yourself into with that little Cuban girl. Once that's behind us, I'm going to beg you to come to California with me. I've accumulated one and a half million dollars—don't ask me how. That's more than enough for us to live on. I'm also the world's best photographer. I can make big bucks out there. We'll live in grand style." He reached over and kissed Gene on the lips. "Say you'll come with me."

As Leroy embraced him, Gene returned the hug. He didn't even resist when Leroy started kissing his neck and unbuttoning his shirt.

"I'll think about it, dude."

He sighed as Leroy began to tongue his nipples, working himself up to a feeding frenzy over Gene's perfectly sculpted body. Pretending to moan and enjoy Leroy's tongue lashings, Gene smiled to himself. He had no intentions of following him to California or anywhere else.

Gene closed his eyes and imagined it was Buck down there making love to him.

***

At The Rusty Pelican, the pub was nearly deserted. It was early at a place that didn't become active until after ten o'clock. Susan sat in a deserted corner, studying the anxiety in Pamela's tremulous face. Only minutes before, Pamela had told her that Gene had become Barry's night bodyguard.

"I would think Barry would be sensitive about being seen with Gene—I mean with his latest case still pending and everything," Susan said.

"Barry's not seen in public with Gene," Pamela said.

Even though no longer married to Gene, Susan couldn't help but feel a bit of jealousy over Gene. She didn't want to think about Pamela and Gene together.

"I might still have the hots for Gene, but Barry has senior rank in our marriage," Pamela said. "I fear Gene is lost to me once again."

Susan tried to conceal the look of astonishment on her face. "I can't believe that. Barry likes them younger, I thought."

"My husband is very versatile," Pamela said. "He has many tastes."

Susan didn't want to know more. She'd hardly recovered from learning about Don and Buck with Shelley. But Gene and Barry?

"Just this afternoon, Gene flew with Barry in a private jet to Miami," Pamela said. "They're staying at this villa in Key Biscayne. Calder Martin has arranged for Barry to meet the big boys in our party. Barry is being groomed for hot shit. He'll do anything to get ahead. Make any deal."

"If he makes it big, you're along for the ride," Susan said.

Pamela looked at Susan for a long moment, then belted down her drink, her face tightening. "I think Calder Martin doesn't want me around for the long haul. He likes Barry because he can control him.

Calder feels I am a liability." She leaned over toward Susan, her voice a whisper. "I think Calder Martin wants to get rid of me."

"Buy you off, you mean?" Susan said.

"I don't think Calder wants Barry to get a divorce," Pamela said.

"Do you plan to stay married to him?"

"Calder doesn't believe in divorce, and Sister Rose preaches against it," Pamela said. "It might be better for all parties if I had an accident."

Susan sighed and, like Pamela, took a stronger sip of her drink. Was this Pamela's paranoia speaking, or was her companion truly on to something? "I can't believe they'd dare go that far."

Pamela cracked her knuckles in desperation. "Perhaps after I've had this accident, then people, including you, will believe me."

"Even assuming I did believe you, what can I do about it?" Susan asked.

"Not a God damn thing right now," Pamela said. "If I do have that accident, would you and Ingrid investigate it? She's got the column and everything."

"By all means," Susan said. "Hell wouldn't stop us."

"Even though I'd be dead, I wouldn't want the bastards to get away with it." Pamela glanced at her watch. "I've got to go." With a trembling hand, she reached for Susan's arm. "Please, carry out your promise."

"I will," Susan said.

On wobbly legs, Pamela stood up and looked down at Susan. "Twenty years from now, they want Barry in the White House. That's what this secret meeting in Key Biscayne is all about."

"You'd be First Lady."

"I'll never live to be First Lady," Pamela said. "Barry will be known as the widowed president. His hostesses will not be me but my two darling daughters."

"I don't think this nightmare is going to happen," Susan said.

"Nightmares often come true," Pamela said, heading for the door.

During their university days, Susan had thought of Pamela as her major competition. In the changing world of 1977, Shelley Phillips had become competition for the men in her life.

***

In a pair of shorts, Barry stood at the pool bar in their Key Biscayne villa. "Okay," he said into the phone. "Eight o'clock it is." He hung up and poured himself a stiff drink, calling over to Gene. "Want anything?"

In a white bikini, Gene lay by the pool, sunning himself. "I'm fine." He was surprised that Calder Martin had agreed to let him accompany Barry to Miami. He'd been instructed to keep Barry out of trouble. The way Gene figured it, he was to be Barry's distraction and amusement. Actually, he didn't want to be here at all.

Barry came over and plopped down on the chaise longue in front of Gene. "Man, do you ever fill out that bikini. My greatest disappointment in life was that I wasn't born with a big dick like yours. God made up for it, though. I'm one good-looking mother fucker. I've often wondered if God could have made me less handsome but with a bigger dick."

"There's not a hell of a lot you can do about that now," Gene said.

"I think I first got mixed up with young boys because I figured they were inexperienced and wouldn't judge me too harshly. Barry said. "They wouldn't know whether I was a good fuck or not. Men or women, who have had a lot of experience, might find me lacking something."

"Pamela married you, and she'd had a lot of guys chasing her," Gene said.

"Pamela didn't married me for sex. Sister Rose went for me in a big way."

Gene raised himself up. "You telling me you had sex with Sister Rose?" He felt his heart pounding.

"I not only fucked Rose, I fucked Shelley too," Barry said.

"Her son?"

Barry ran his fingers up and down Gene's bikini, going lower to fondle and caress Gene's buttocks. "Fucking Shelley was a lot more fun than fucking Rose. She's a bit ripe for me."

Gene tried to control himself. Barry was just a braggart. He'd never had sex with Sister Rose, much less Shelley.

"I could really go for that Shelley," Barry said. "That's one real hot number. I've lost even him."

Barry's lies were beginning to infuriate Gene.

"Shelley belongs to Buck now. Why would Shelley want to get plowed by me when he could have Buck Brooke's legendary inches?"

Gene rose abruptly from the chaise longue, brushing aside Barry's feeling hands. He headed for the bar.

"What's the matter?" Barry called after him. "You can't stand for a man to play with your ass or something?"

"I just need a drink—that's all." At the bar Gene found himself trembling. He almost dropped a whisky bottle. "I'm not myself lately."

"I see," Barry said, getting up and heading to the bar to join Gene. At the bar he poured himself another strong drink. "What I don't understand is why Buck is in Key Biscayne right now marrying Robert Dante. If he's in love with Shelley, why is he marrying Dante?"

"Slow down," Gene said. "Buck is on Key Biscayne?"

"Yeah, in a house about a mile from here. The real fancy one owned by that faggot movie producer, a friend of Buck's lawyer. That's the one that Bebe originally wanted for love trysts with his friend Tricky Dickie. But he decided not to buy it."

"You're saying Bebe and Nixon were an item?" Gene asked.

Barry laughed nervously. "No one would believe that. At any rate, Bebe and Tricky aren't in the house. Robert Dante, the bride, is there with her newly acquired husband, Buck Brooke III. That Jew, Uncle Milty, is also there with them on their honeymoon. The bastard lawyer brought along his own hustler boy friend. It must be some cozy household."

"I'm sure," was all Gene could manage to say. "I know the place."

"After my little political caucus is over, should we walk down the beach and visit them? Toast them on their honeymoon?"

"I don't attend honeymoons when men marry men," Gene said.

Barry stripped off his clothes and stood naked in front of Gene. "I'm going for a swim."

Barry raced toward the pool and jumped in with a big splash. Raising his head above the water, Barry called out to Gene. "Calder's not a total shit. He's done you a big favor."

Gene was heading for the bedroom upstairs, but stopped when he heard that.

"Calder's got all those charges against you dropped," Barry said.

"You mean that?"

"Calder can get anything done in Okeechobee. He's got Biff by the balls. The little girl and her mother are going to announce to the press that you did nothing wrong. That the girl wandered into your private space. That you didn't entice her there."

In the dying sun, Gene felt dizzy. He'd heard too much.

From the pool Barry called to him again. "You're on your own tonight—at least until the meeting is over. These blow-shits coming over tonight are going to talk about grooming this girl here to become president of the United States one day."

"You'll make a great president," Gene called to him. "I'm out of here." Hurrying to the bedroom to dress, he knew where he was going for the night.

**

The sudden approach of footsteps on the grass had caused Gene to dart across the yard of Buck's borrowed Key Biscayne villa, taking cover in the shrubbery. From that vantage point, he not only had a clear view of the "honeymoon house," but he had a coral rock wall against his back for security. He sensed that the intruder had been a servant.

It was a beautiful night, a clear one, and a full moon was out, giving the vegetation in the garden an eerie lunar sheen. He felt protected enough to breathe more easily now. He could afford to wait and watch.

From where he stood in the moonlight, he had a clear view of the patio garden yet was completely concealed.

Buck was seated at a candlelit garden table with Robert by his side. They faced Milty, his attorney, and also a young companion.

"I couldn't believe it," Buck was telling his friends. "Rose gave me her private plane. Of course, she's getting a new one tomorrow."

"The first of many fringe benefits," Milty said.

Gene sucked air deep into his lungs. Had Buck gone to work for Sister Rose?

"You've not done badly," Robert said. "You may have lost the *Examiner*, but there are other rewards."

"While you and Robert retreat to your honeymoon bed," Milty said, "I'll study those contracts Rose had flown down."

"Uncle Milty loves multi-millionaires," Patrick chimed in.

In the bushes, Gene felt hurt and excluded. This little dinner party dramatized to him that he was not part of Buck's family. Gene felt he didn't belong in this league of powerful men—Buck and Milty—with their pretty little boyfriends.

"A final toast," Milty said, "to the newlyweds." He raised his glass to toast Buck and Robert.

After a drink, Buck turned and gave Robert a long, lingering kiss in front of everybody. Gene averted his eyes, remembering Buck's lips on his.

Buck got up from the table and took Robert's hand, kissing both Milty and his boyfriend good night.

Gene didn't want to see any more. When the party broke up, he seized the moment to escape. Passing by the window of the master bedroom, he heard no sound. He shuddered in the night breeze from the ocean, and wandered across to a little pier overlooking the house. The meeting might go on at Barry's villa for hours yet, so he decided to take up a position overlooking Buck's villa.

The beach was deserted on this lovely night. His tears turned to soft moans escaping from his throat. He'd never felt so much alone as he did tonight.

***

A digital clock beside his honeymoon bed told Buck it was three o'clock in the morning. A totally satisfied Robert, who had been wrapped in his arms all night, was asleep beside him. Buck hoped to slip free of the marriage bed and go for a walk on the beach to clear his head.

He felt he'd done his job well. Robert had told him repeatedly it was the best sex he'd ever had. Buck hadn't held back.

He loved Robert, and loved him dearly, but he did not *love* Robert.

The challenge facing him was to keep giving himself to Robert but to find the time to be with Shelley. Shelley was what Buck wanted and desired. The only reason he'd accepted the job as media director with Rose was to be near Shelley. It was the perfect excuse.

What made it easier was Rose's complete acceptance of the relationship. Shelley was her bait, used as a means of keeping Buck, one way or another—in her own life.

Slipping nude from the bed, Buck reached for some clothing, finding only a pair of jockey briefs.

Wearing the briefs, he slowly opened a side door leading into the garden. In the moonlight, he headed for the beach enjoying the sand under his bare feet.

He sucked in the night air and raised his arms for a stretch. He might stay on the beach until streaks of dawn split the sky.

"I'm the sexiest man alive!" Buck whispered to the wind, parroting the headline in the magazine.

"That you are, good buddy."

From out of nowhere, the voice was from the past. Startled, he turned around to stare into the moonlit face of Gene.

***

"What in hell are you doing here?" Buck asked.

"So many questions so early in the morning," Gene said. "I'm working as a bodyguard for Barry. He told me where you were staying. Thought I'd drop by."

"I'm sorry you had to spend the night out here," Buck said.

"Good news," Gene said. "You're going to get your bail money back. The case against me has been dropped."

"The whole thing seemed a set-up," Buck said. He hesitated for a moment. "About the marriage, I can explain."

"The marriage to Susan or to Robert Dante?" Gene asked.

"The marriage to Susan. I can't explain the marriage to Robert. It wasn't my idea to marry Susan. My grandfather threatened to disinherit me. It's not a real marriage."

"I believe you. What about Robert?"

"I'm loyal to Robert, who's always been there for me. This is a mock marriage, and I went into it with great misgivings."

"I know you're in love with me," Gene said.

"Don't go on," Buck cautioned.

"Let me finish," Gene said. "Don't you know how hard this is for me? After many years, I'm finally opening up to the one man I've always loved. It's you. From the first day I met you at the university, I wanted you. I just couldn't bring myself to admit that I wanted another man. My marriage to Susan gave me the excuse to deny that I loved you."

Buck seemed to want to say something, and Gene knew it must be as difficult for Buck to declare his love as it was for Gene to confess his passion.

"Let's view this morning as a celebration," Gene said. "You've won me." After this revelation Gene thought that Buck would rush into his arms, and inaugurate a sex act right on the sands. Buck wasn't responding.

"Gene..." Buck's voice trailed off. "You don't have to go on."

"I'll need some time to set some matters straight, and I know you will too," Gene said. "We can get out of Okeechobee. Go anywhere. Start a new life together. We've both waited long enough."

"Hey, let's slow down. This is..."

Gene didn't want Buck to finish what he was saying. There would be time for talk later. Gene rose up and reached for Buck, crushing his body into his. His lips descended on Buck's, a kiss filled with commitment. Gene's magic was still strong. In moments he had Buck responding. That was all the proof that Gene needed that the attraction was still there. Gene broke away. "Will you be in Okeechobee ten days from now?"

"I expect to be," Buck said.

"At six o'clock Saturday night—that's ten days from now—I'm going to be playing tennis on those old courts. I want you to meet me there. You and I are going to start living our lives for the first time ever."

"Gene..." There was that hesitancy in Buck's voice again.

"It will be morning soon," Gene said. "You go back into that household and do what you've got to do, and I'll go back to Barry's. When you and I get together again, we'll have cleaned up the mess in our lives."

The moon shone brighter than ever, capturing Buck's face as if lit by a spotlight. Buck was crying. Gene kissed him tenderly on the lips and embraced him for one final time. "Until we meet on those tennis courts, know that I love you."

Without saying another word, Gene headed down the lonely stretch of deserted beach. One thing troubled him: he'd gotten no commitment from Buck. That was okay. Gene knew Buck had heard and accepted what he'd told him.

Gene sucked in the cool morning air. For the first time, his whole rotten life was turning around. The shadowy part of his brain was sinking even deeper into its murky recesses. A brighter side of him was emerging, and he dared to believe he'd found happiness after all.

Chapter Ten

It was like an airborne yacht. The moment Buck stepped aboard the customized Boeing 707 jetliner, his eyes drank in the splendor. He'd agreed to go with Rose and Shelley to Abilene, Kansas.

Upon entering the plane, Rose clutched his hand warmly, claiming she had to place an urgent call from the communications center up front. Buck looked in vain for Shelley.

In the lounge, a white-robed attendant fastened Buck into a bronze and ebony throne, resting on carved lion's paws, right before the plane was cleared for take-off. Once airborne, he had time to take in the sumptuousness of the decor, which vaguely suggested the tomb of King Tutankhamen. Across from him stood a cedarwood chest carved with hieroglyphs. Golden sun disks formed window shades.

For a carrier of one of America's leading evangelists, the plane was incongruously filled with pagan symbols, with many kinds of animals—such as a lioness, representing ancient gods as decorative themes. The cow Hathor formed the endpiece of a couch, with its lyre-shaped horns holding a sun disk.

Separating the lounge from the dining area was a varnished black jackal with silver claws. When the caution lights went off, he unfastened his seat belt and headed for the rear of the cabin. The attendant directed him to a suite he was to share with Rose. He hesitated. "I have some business to discuss with Shelley. Would you show me to his suite instead?"

"Of course," the attendant said, rather coldly. He led Buck down the corridor and knocked on another door.

Within seconds, Shelley, clad only in a rose-colored robe, opened the door. "Come on in, Mr. Brooke," he said, "I've been expecting you." When Buck came in, Shelley quickly locked the door, opened his robe, and pressed his nude body against Buck. "An hour away from you is hell."

Buck kissed and licked his face, as his hands wandered over Shelley's smooth body, settling on his buttocks which he squeezed and fondled.

Shelley planted lightning kisses on Buck's lips and eyelids. At a rap on the door, Buck sighed. Shelley retreated to the bathroom and Buck opened the door.

The same attendant was there, looking rather stern. "Ms. Phillips is ready to receive you now."

"I'll be there soon," Buck said, shutting and locking the door. He trailed Shelley into the bathroom where the boy stood in front of a large closet, surprising on a plane, selecting his wardrobe for the day. "The God mother is demanding an audience," Shelley said. "She'll probably want to get fucked." He kissed Buck. "You've got millions waiting for you in the desert."

The attendant showed Buck into Rose's suite. She was nowhere to be seen. Unlike the Egyptian motif up front, the suite had been customized with Rose in mind. The symbol of the rose was everywhere, even in the design of the canopy over the queen-size bed. Sculpted roses cut through the deep-pile, opera-red carpeting.

The attendant left to be replaced by a young Japanese girl in a kimono. "Her Highness will be detained briefly," she said. "In the meantime she wants you to try out her luxurious new bath."

"I'm sure I could use one," he said, not unduly surprised that she'd referred to Rose by a royal title.

"Please," the young woman said, pointing in the direction of the bathroom before leaving.

In the private bathroom, with its sunken tub in pink marble, he pulled off all his clothes. This might be his only chance to take an airborne bubble bath. He smelled the contents of an alabaster vase, inlaid with floral garlands. Picking it up, he poured some of the rose cologne into the water. He might as well go rose all the way.

Reclining in the marble tub, he raised the shade of a large-scaled window. As the sun blinded him, he tried to give a command performance to any spaceship that might be passing by. In the background someone has piped in classical music. He splashed water over his chest and stomach, then oiled his firm flesh. With his eyes dreamily half-closed, he took in the spectacle of the brilliant sky. He became aware of an intoxicating smell, foreign to the cologne and bath oils. Rose's body. Surreptiously she'd entered the bathroom. He looked up at her. Clad in a see-through, rose-colored robe, she stood staring down lovingly at him.

"Some pad!" he said.

"I'm glad you like it," she said, seating herself at her vanity and taking a quick check of her makeup. She adjusted the scarf around her bandaged throat.

"May I ask how you acquired this flying carpet?"

She smiled enigmatically. "It's not really mine. On lease."

"From whom?" He sat up in the tub. "Saudi Arabia?"

She eyed him in a tantalizing way. "If I didn't have this slight problem with my throat, I'd join you." She knelt beside the tub, taking his wet hand and placing it on her breast. Holding him there, she looked out the window. "I love it up here. Sometimes I never want to land."

Gently he squeezed her breast. "Do you think heaven is like this?"

"If so, I can't wait to get there," she said.

The feel of her breast had a decided effect on his crotch. He released her and stood up in the tub with a hard-on. She reached over and handed him a rose-colored towel. After he'd toweled himself dry, he slipped into the robe she held out for him. He joined her in her bedroom where, to his surprise, an Arab wearing a fringed turban and an elaborately knotted sash had opened a bottle of champagne. When the attendant had left, he turned to her, thinking he'd become a whore. He poured champagne into tulip-shaped glasses decorated with a red rose motif.

She took the glass from him, lovingly caressing his fingers.

"You're not only closer to Jesus up here, but you can get high too," he said.

She headed for the swan bed, her chiffon gown sweeping in a wave behind her. She slowly removed her gown and in a low, sensual voice called out to him.

The bath had given him renewed vigor and the sight of her body aroused passion in him. He felt no love for her at all, although his cock was sending him a different message. He was intrigued with the idea of an airborne fuck.

She reached for him, tasting his lips. She fondled beneath him, teasing his most sensitive spots. Careful to avoid touching her throat, his hand moved across her full breasts, along her narrow waist and flat stomach and, finally, grazing the auburn patch itself. His stroking seemed to make her purr.

Lost in his own private world, he entered her gently at first. Her muscles seemed to clamp around him, and the grip sent thrills up his spine.

Shelley had slipped into the suite and had parted his buttocks, before attacking his most private part. The sensations were driving Buck crazy with lust. He shoved himself even harder into Rose. Her face told him she had prematurely entered heaven, as she dug her nails into his back and nibbled on his ear.

For Buck, it was as if his sensations had shifted from penetrating Rose to enjoying Shelley's tongue lashings. He spread his legs even wider giving the boy more access to his target.

Time drifted by. Sometimes they'd stop and drink some more champagne. Once he noted a freshly chilled bottle, and wondered how the Arab attendant had managed to enter the room without attracting his notice.

Sometimes he'd switch positions, penetrating Shelley, his favorite sensation. When that happened, Rose would take up her duty at Shelley's station. She was equally skilled at assaulting his rosebud. His balls, too, had never received such loving care. These two really adored balls, obviously viewing them as God's special gift.

Once they fell asleep. He didn't know for how long. Rose was the first to wake up. Her mouth was licking and kissing his belly before plunging down. Amazingly she could swallow every inch of him. When he was fully erect again, she positioned herself under him for one final assault. This one she wanted from the rear. She surrendered herself to him on her knees. As he entered her, Shelley woke up and slid across her back, inserting his cock into Buck's suctioning mouth.

As the plane landed on Kansas soil, its bumpy movement provided the right rhythm for a pile-driving action he needed for one final climax.

Rose had returned to Abilene in a style her long dead parents never could have conjured up.

***

As they'd agreed, Buck remained aboard the jet after its landing in

Abilene. No reporters were allowed on board, as Rose didn't want the press to see the luxurious appointments inside.

Before leaving the plane, she'd told him she wanted to appear on camera having "beauty and fire." The state legislature had just adopted a resolution citing Rose's efforts "to restore decency to America." She was to be fêted at Rose Phillips Day, declared in Abilene for its favorite home-grown daughter.

The moment had arrived—a time of confrontation, dreaded but inevitable. Waiting behind barricades thrown up at the airport, her supporters had been trusting, believing.

The elderly had been there, and she'd expected them—those harsh, lined faces who'd survived a depression and a war. What was far more gratifying to her had been the eager faces of the young people turning out to greet her, including many married couples in their twenties who thrust their children at her, wanting her to touch their offspring.

Striding through the crowds assembled on either side of the aisle stretching through the airport, she made her way to a podium set up for her in the parking lot. She smiled at the hushed crowd whose edges were dotted with the press corps, which ranged from New York to Los Angeles.

Her opening remarks at the press conference were predictable and necessary. She knew she had to praise Abilene, even though she loathed it. She amused the crowd by telling them her daddy, Flip Phillips, had gotten her a job on the Cracklin' Jim Gospel Hour when she was just a teenager.

She talked about her ideals for the Christian state of Kansas, and led the crowd in an emotional public prayer. Finally, she raised her throaty voice to the far reaches of the asphalt-covered parking lot and said, in a tone cracking with emotion, "And to all of you well-wishers in my campaign to bring a moral revolution to our playgrounds, to our schools, and to the very institutions that have made America great, I say, God bless you."

She gracefully bowed her head in silent prayer.

She paused in front of the microphones, signaling that she was ready to accept questions.

"Are you going to export your revolution into every state?" The question came from a woman reporter who obviously dressed and talked with Barbara Walters as a role model. The sound of her voice carried a stinging criticism.

A flashbulb shot off close to Rose, making her jump. "I'm not afraid to call it a revolution," she said, regaining control of herself. "A moral revolution. We're going to export it, not only to every state, but around the world."

Cameras banged against bodies in the background and one electrician yelled, "Push me, you son of a bitch and I'll..." His voice carried across the crowd.

"Is everyone going to hell who doesn't subscribe to your moral views?" one CBS reporter asked.

"Yes, as a matter of fact." She smiled at the CBS reporter. "You didn't expect me to admit that, did you?"

"What about Jews?" came a probing question from the back.

"I believe as I believe," Rose said calmly. "Jews who don't accept Jesus Christ as their personal Savior are going to hell. We consider such Jews lost souls. Before you scream anti-Semitism, let me tell you that I'm opening up charismatic centers around the nation. There, we will help the Jew who's willing to accept Christ. Far from persecuting or condemning the Jew, we are prepared to save him!"

A murmur arose from the audience. A wild-eyed woman near the rear of the crowd made her way down front, pushing and shoving through several editors and technicians. A public relations man signaled to Rose to ignore her waving, outstretched hand. Rose stood firm. "Yes."

"What about Zionists?" the woman asked. Heads turned in her direction. "Hate sheets, believed to be financed by your association, have attacked Zionists."

Rose's hand went to her bandaged throat, concealed by a scarf. "I hope I'm not violating some gentleman's agreement in answering." A lone, nervous chuckle behind her greeted that pronouncement, then silence.

She remembered to keep her voice reasonable in tone, as she prepared to make inflammatory remarks. "Zionists can no longer have a honeymoon with the American public, and there are hopeful signs that this cozy arrangement is over. Israel itself must stand up and be judged by American public opinion, the way we judge all nations, including Russia and Cuba."

Her expression turned grim as she gripped the lectern with both hands. "Few senators are willing to speak out against Israel because they know that the big, powerful Jewish lobby is prepared to destroy their political careers. The intimidation of our lawmakers, and the threats by the Jewish lobby, must be stopped."

She detected a triumphant smile on her woman questioner's face. It was as if she'd personally trapped her on the record. "Because they've suffered, Jews feel they have to be singled out for preferential treatment for eternity," Rose said. "What about the blacks? They've suffered, too. Anti-Semitism belongs to the past. Jewish power in this country destroyed it long ago. In the case of Israel, the oppressed has now become the oppressor, invading and destroying the homeland of others." A deafening silence fell. "I find an equation between Zionism and Nazism." The mayor and other dignitaries were clearly shocked.

Live television cameras seemed to block every aisle. A few hands went up. Gaining confidence, she paused to take a sip of water. Additional television lights were turned on, "Have the Jews so quickly forgotten their own suffering? Is Israel now trying to make others suffer as much as her people did? Israel today uses Hitler's old weapons— arrest, torture, murder, and bombing of civilian populations, the forced separation of families."

She imagined how she'd look on TV news that night. "In our country Jewish Defense League members engage in terroristic practices, while our leaders remain silent, afraid to speak out against them. I dare say, if the JDL were black, we'd have the FBI rounding them up in the middle of the night."

Great excitement seemed to build in the press section. She heard noises, movement again. Still, she went on, "I am not against Jews. I'm against many of the policies of Israel and, as an American, cherish my right to state my views publicly. As for the Jews themselves, great numbers have already joined our charismatic movement. In time, I expect to have thousands more worshipping with us, renouncing their own religion."

Suddenly, there was a crash. The hushed crowd radiated tension. A reporter pushed aside two TV cameramen, knocking over their equipment. Grabbing a hand camera from a woman photographer, he broke from a security guard and dashed toward the front. Only feet from Rose's face, he hurled the camera.

A sound, not quite like a woman's scream, escaped from her damaged throat. She ducked but it was too late. The impact was instant, brutal. It blinded her. She felt a gash in her cheek and instinctively her fingers went there, only to withdraw at the feel of blood. "Oh, God," she said out loud, praying silently she hadn't been disfigured. Distorted, her vision came back, and the massive spotlights became so many burning suns. Dazed, she stumbled and fainted.

***

From Rose's own communications center aboard the plane, Buck reached the injured evangelist in her hospital bedroom. Over the phone, she assured him she was all right. "Just a bit shaken, a very minor cut on my cheek. It wouldn't be discreet to have you come to the hospital. I'm spending the night here. We'll fly out tomorrow. Shelley will be back on the plane by six o'clock. You guys can have supper aboard the plane. I've ordered the best steaks in Kansas to be sent aboard. The bedrooms on the plane are far more comfortable than anything you'll find in Abilene. They still sleep on straw in Abilene."

"Glad you're okay," he said. "That was some press conference, some homecoming."

"What did you think of it?" she asked.

"Very entertaining," he said without too much emotion in his voice. "At least I've learned more about your agenda. Whoever chose you to become a spokesperson for Arab interests in this country couldn't have made a better choice."

"I'll take that as a compliment."

"You're very skilled," he said. "America's leading evangelist. You won't have to worry one bit about losing any of your supporters. I don't think your Born Again Christians like Jews anyway. If anything, you might have increased your support."

She sighed. "I don't dislike Jews. As for Zionists or Israel, I couldn't care less. I couldn't give a fuck about any Arab country either. Give me a script and I'll read it. If Israel had approached me, I would have agreed to become a spokesperson for their interests."

Surveying the luxury of the plane, he said, "I don't think Israel could afford you."

"I have expensive tastes," she said. "Even in boyfriends."

"I'm not someone whose favors you can buy," he said.

"Bullshit! You can be bought just as much as I can. We all play the same sinful games. The only difference between people is how we choose to deceive the world." She abruptly hung up.

***

The next morning Buck was anxiously awaiting Rose aboard her jet. After a marathon sex session last night, Shelley was getting ready, knowing he'd have to face the cameras once they arrived in Dallas. Even though Buck felt relatively secure in the safety of the plane, he sensed a nasty mood at the airport. Attendants who'd left the plane had reported to him that about six-hundred dissenters had gathered at the airport to protest against Sister Rose.

Shelley joined him at breakfast, giving him several quick kisses on the mouth. "You're fantastic."

"So are you, cute stuff," Buck said. "You should see the boxes of telegrams brought aboard," Shelley said.

"I hope they've been checked for bombs," Buck said apprehensively. "Rose is inviting big trouble."

"She's getting well paid for it," Shelley said.

Buck finished the last of a mimosa and signaled the attendant for another one. "One should always be paid well for sticking one's fingers into a hornet's nest. The sting is something awful. They fight back."

"I know that and I dread what's coming," Shelley said.

"This media director thing," Buck said. "Now that I know more about Rose's agenda, I've got to pull out."

Fifteen minutes later, Rose, followed by two aides in rose-colored uniforms, came aboard. She rushed back to greet Buck and Shelley, kissing them both on the lips. She eagerly accepted a mimosa offered. In a trim white business suit, except for a rose-colored scarf, she appeared radiant. A small bandage was on her right cheek where she'd been hit by a camera.

"Thank you for those steaks last night," was all that Buck could manage to say.

She settled into the banquette, holding up a tulip-shaped glass. "You thought Abilene was fireworks. Wait until Dallas. There's more to come to this show."

"I understand we're going to see Hazel in Durant," Buck said.

"I've heard the fat cow is showing up," Rose said. "To embarrass me."

"What are our plans, mommie dearest?" Shelley asked.

She glared at him. "Shelley and I will get off the plane first in Dallas. We'll meet the press and go in a separate limousine to Durant." She turned to Buck. "I don't want you to face the press at this point. My staff has arranged for a private limousine to drive you to Durant. You'll spend the night at a private mansion there."

The Japanese attendant came into their space and told Rose that an urgent message was waiting for her at the communications center. She slammed down her glass, gave Buck a departing kiss, and headed up front. "The general has got to return to her command post."

***

Once the private jet landed in Dallas, Buck kissed rose and Shelley good-bye, planning to remain aboard for one hour until the press had left the airport in pursuit of Rose.

When the time came, he was glad to be back on the ground. Told by one of Rose's staff members there that would be a thirty-minute delay for the limousine, he retreated to a bar in the airport. It was here he chose to relax and take in Rose's press conference in Dallas.

In front of TV cameras, she waved cartoons which had appeared in U.S. magazines. "Talk about prejudice!" she said in a strident voice. "Look at these racial slurs." She presented samples of cartoons to members of the press. "Oil-rich sheiks are drawn with swarthy physiognomies. Fat, double-chinned men, with lusty eyes and billowy robes, carry daggers with eyebrow curves. This is the type of propaganda that recalls how *Der Sturmer* used to depict Jews."

He winced and ordered another drink.

"Right when we need the friendship of the Arabs more than ever," she said, "the American public is being brainwashed! Would the Jew stand idly by as *Time* depicted him with lubricity and Shylockery? No way!"

To his astonishment, he noticed supporters carrying ROSE FOR PRESIDENT signs, parading up and down the airport corridors. Surely, occupying the White House wasn't Rose's ultimate aim?

"I seriously question the loyalty of the American Jew who takes money out of this country to finance military adventures whereby Israel invades the homelands of others," Rose told TVland.

At a tap on his shoulder, he whirled around, taking his eyes off the television screen and focusing on what looked like a shadowy version of Rose. It took him a moment in the bright glare to realize it was Hazel.

"You're headed for the funeral?" he asked, hoping she didn't know he'd flown in with Rose.

"Sure thing," she said with a weary sigh. "I'm the black sheep of the family, but Martha was my great aunt, too."

"Are you surprised to run into me in Dallas?" Buck asked.

"I was too polite to ask," Hazel said.

"I've lost the *Examiner*," he said. "My grandfather arranged the deal before flying off to a clinic in Switzerland."

"The *Examiner* was my one big hope in the mayor's race," she said. "Rose is behind this."

"The deal is being closed in California." He said. "I'm supposed to pick up a check for the Brooke share of stock. Once I pick up the money, I've ordered Uncle Milty to make a serious bid to take over the *News*. I'm just switching from one paper to another."

"Hot damn!" she said. "We'll have some newspaper support in Okeechobee after all. I'll be the best mayor Okeechobee ever had, and you'll be the town's hottest publisher."

One of Rose's staff appeared before him and told him that his limousine was ready. He was asked to move fast, as a large crowd of hostile demonstrators had formed north of the airport. So far, the Dallas police had held them back behind barricades.

He crushed out his cigarette and looked into Hazel's slightly bleary eyes. "Do you know the way to Durant?" he asked.

"Hell, yes, I do!"

"Come along." He turned to the attendant. "I won't be needing that limousine after all."

Although the attendant protested vehemently, Buck took Hazel by the arm and guided her out of the airport bar.

He sat with Hazel in the lounge of the rental agency, waiting for their car to be brought up. On a television set in the lounge, he caught a glimpse of Rose's hasty departure from the airport. She and Shelley were seated in the back seat of a Zaftig Stutz Blackhawk IV. A TV news reporter informed viewers that this custom-designed limousine was a type particularly popular with the sheiks of Saudi Arabia.

**

Traveling on the open road with Hazel was a remarkably different experience from flying across the country on Rose's magic carpet. Instead of champagne, Hazel had brought along a six-pack of Budweiser.

Ten miles outside Dallas, the air-conditioning system broke down. "Where can we rent another car?" he asked.

She urged him to go on. "I can stand the heat."

The beer quickly turned hot, but they continued to drink it. He pulled off his jacket and now even his trousers seemed to cling to his body. The temperature had slipped into the nineties.

Perspiring heavily, she finally said, "I'm not trying to put the make on you, but why don't you take your pants off? If you can stand the sight of me in a bra, I'm sure I can live with you in jockey shorts."

"Good idea." He braked the car along the side of the road and slipped out of his trousers. He ducked behind the car to take a fast leak. When he got back inside, he had to help her out of her sweat-soaked pink blouse that looked two sizes too small for her.

Along the way they passed some phony cowboys working for a construction gang and, in the distance, scattered clapboard houses, turned a rosy pink from the dust.

She remembered a truck stop ahead. "It's called Dirty Edna's, and the cook there serves rattlesnake meat. You've got to sample it at least once in your life."

At the truck stop, he parked near a washing hose. He slipped into his pants and went with her inside, throwing open the screen door with a Dr. Pepper sign just as she finished hooking the top fastening on her still wet blouse.

Over a formica bar hung a picture of Lyndon Johnson, a melancholy smile on his face. They found a booth as a waitress with a dirty dishcloth came over and wiped the chipped table for them. Hazel ordered rattlesnake meat, fried potatoes, and lots of cold beer for them.

After tasting snake, he compared the flavor to chicken. "Why not snake?" he asked. "I've eaten everything from chocolate-coated ants to caterpillars."

She didn't like hers. "We can't go back, can we? Everything used to taste better."

"I feel I've been wandering around the Garden of Eden with the Phillips sisters. Rose, as Eve, offered me the shiny red apple. You serve the fucking snake itself!"

She chuckled, downing more beer. "That's a good one. At least it breaks the ice between us. I know about Rose and you."

"I think that aide at the airport made it pretty obvious," he said, cutting off another bite-size piece of snake.

"Oh, I knew before Dallas. It's the talk of Okeechobee." A look of apprehension came across her face. "I don't know how Susan fits into this picture. I also heard rumors of a marriage."

"I'm one mixed-up crazy dude."

Back on the road again, the shadows of afternoon lengthened. As seen through his alcoholic gaze, the road was like a faint blur of white sand. He headed for Oklahoma's Red River Valley.

***

In her borrowed mansion in Durant, Rose was throwing a black tie event for family, friends, and "admirers." Not being informed of this, Buck arrived in a white T-shirt and blue jeans. There was no live band— only Anita Bryant records blasting over a loudspeaker. In the main foyer, Buck felt lost in a sea of polyester. The curling irons had been busy, and entire vats of mousse had been used. A few wet slippery palms shaking hands made his own hands feel clammy. Every person he met glanced at his inappropriate dress but made no comment other than, "Welcome to the party."

Even though it was getting late, little girls with cascades of chiffon and ribbons apparently had been allowed to stay up late. To Buck, this hardly looked like a wake—more a wedding reception but then he'd never been to Oklahoma before.

One liver-spotted hand reached for him, taking him by the arm. A gaunt woman in her 80s wearing a red wig stood before him. "I'm Rose's Aunt Bice, and I bet I'm the only one at the party who knows who you are. Love your outfit."

"I wasn't told," he said defensively.

"Fancy dress is only for the middle class," she said, leading him into the garden. "Multi-millionaires can show up at a ball in their ten-day old fishing clothes, smelling like rotten shark, and they'll be perfectly welcome. Here in Oklahoma we love people with money, and we don't give a damn what they wear. Just so long as they leave some of that money behind before they depart."

"Aunt Bice, you are a woman after my heart."

She giggled and rubbed up against him. "If only I was seventy years younger. One night with me back then and you'd be the straightest man in America."

He looked at her and arched a brow. "What makes you think I'm not?"

"Shelley tells me everything," she said smiling, rubbing her hand gently across Buck's cheek. "I'm the only confidante he has in the world. What men do—especially those five husbands I was married to—never surprises me."

"He's told you everything?"

"I'm so happy for him. It's time he settled down with one man. That that man happens to be the sexiest man alive—yes, I read magazines—and also a multi-millionaire isn't bad. Did I also mention the handsomest man I've ever feasted my eyes on, and I've seen some living dolls in my day."

"This is a bit amazing," he said, looking away from her into the party which he could see in full bloom through the open windows. A sudden wind blew through the garden

"He also confided in me that there are many horses that wouldn't come off well when compared to you," she said. "That lucky boy."

He glanced at her in complete bewilderment. "He told you that?"

"One of my husbands had seven and a half inches. He won the prize. One of the bastards I married didn't even measure up to four and a half."

"I'm so sorry they disappointed you," he said.

"Don't cry for me," she said, brushing her hand across his cheek again. "I found plenty of cowboys on the side."

He glanced apprehensively around the garden, looking for Rose.

"Rose is tied up tonight," Aunt Bice said. "She told me to take care of you and that she'd see you in the morning. I've arranged for you to share a suite with Shelley at the back of the house on the fourth floor. It's very private." No one will disturb you there and you can pound it to that boy all night."

"Aunt Bice, you amaze me. In the state of Oklahoma, land of Anita Bryant."

"Oh, darling, we're not all Oakies here," she said. "Anita doesn't speak for all of us. Someone must have spiked that pussy's orange juice. Hell, I love gay men more than the boring straight assholes I encounter here. I'm known as the fag hag of Durant."

He kissed both sides of her cheeks. "Thanks for setting me up to-night."

Thunderous applause came from the main parlor. Apparently, Rose was going to sing. As her not bad voice drifted out, he listened briefly to her words, "From this valley they say you are leaving..."

"She knows how to pick her material," he said to Aunt Bice.

In the garden Shelley rushed into his arms and kissed him on the lips in front of Aunt Bice who only giggled and turned away.

"Step back and let me have a look," Buck said, "I've never seen you dressed up before."

Like a model, Shelley stepped back in the garden. The bottom but-ton of his dinner jacket had lazily plopped open. Everything about him seemed perfection itself. High-waisted, his black trousers only accented his long, slender legs and promising crotch.

"Before the funeral in the morning, I want you boys to come over for one of my famous Durant country breakfasts," Aunt Bice said.

Before fluttering away into the night, Aunt Bice turned to Buck and took his hand. "Shelley is gonna be pissed at me for blabbing, but I have to tell you something."

"Don't you dare," Shelley cautioned her.

"Hell with that," Aunt Bice said. "He'll find out sooner than later. Shelley lied to you about his age."

"You mean, he's not eighteen?" Buck said.

"He's sixteen going on forty."

Buck felt a deep thud hit his heart. "Jail bait!"

"I'm sorry I lied but I thought you wouldn't go to bed with me if you thought I was sixteen," Shelley said.

"Good night, Aunt Bice," Buck said. "Shelley and I will talk about this privately. See you at breakfast."

"Good night, my darling boys." She waved her mauve gloves in the night air, disappearing behind a gardenia bush. "Young love, young love."

Buck turned to Shelley. He looked playful and mischievous, not remorseful at all. "You're not going to spank me, are you? For lying."

"That's exactly what I'm going to do. I'm going to spank you— real hard—then I'm going to fuck that sixteen-year-old ass of yours like it's never been fucked before."

Shelley melted into his body. "I love you."

"It's too late for me to stop now. Even if you were twelve, I've fallen for you. I don't plan to sit around and wait for you to become legal."

Shelley gave him several light feathery kisses on the lips. "Look at the bright side."

"What bright side?" Buck asked.

"Men reach their sexual peak at nineteen. That means you've got three more years to enjoy me before I peak. Then when I turn nineteen, you're going to get it, big boy."

***

After the burial of Aunt Martha, Rose sent word to Buck to meet her in the pastor's private office in a wing attached to the clapboard-framed white church.

On his way to it, he ran into Hazel, her dress soaked, her makeup running. "I cried when I saw Aunt Martha lowered into her grave. All I could remember was the time she made Rose and me strip bareass and switched our fannies red."

He kissed her perspiring, flabby cheek and headed in rapid strides to the preacher's office. He looked over his shoulder. "See you in Okeechobee."

Alone in the office with him, Rose had recovered from her collapse at the gravesite, a photographic remembrance now on its way to the developing lab where it, in turn, would be transmitted over the wire services.

"I saw you out the window," she said, using for the first time her harshest voice on him. "Kissing Hazel. Such a cozy scene."

He nodded as he unbuttoned his collar, loosened his tie, and took off his jacket. "If I kiss one sister, I guess it's only fitting and proper to kiss the other." He walked over to her, leaned down and kissed her on the cheek, as he had Hazel. She took his face in her hands holding it firmly as she planted a long, wet, lingering kiss on his lips, with short tongue lashings against his teeth.

"I apologize for neglecting you so much." She smiled sardonically. "I'm sure Shelley kept you amused."

"Aunt Bice told me he was only sixteen years old," Buck said.

"He might be fifteen."

"Fifteen for God's sake. Fifteen fucking years old."

"We're not sure of his age," she said. "He was an abandoned child. We could only guess at his age."

"That scares me," he said. "There are laws."

"No harm will come of it," she said. "Calder is our problem. He and I are involved in a big power struggle. I'm trying to break free of him. He's trying to become my super boss. He's also a threat to Shelley."

"I'm sorry to hear that, because I don't want to be involved in any of Calder's shit," he said.

"Tonight in Palm Springs I'm going to introduce you to a very important man," she said. "He controls everything. I want you to do everything you can to destroy Calder in this man's eyes. Would you promise me that?"

"Of course, I will. Calder has made himself my enemy number one." He balled his fists. "If he so much as lays a hand on Shelley, I'll kill him."

"The trouble with killing Calder is he might kill you first."

Chapter Eleven

Susan wasn't in love, but she was having a marvelous time. Don Bossdum had liberated her sexually as no man ever had. After last night she was convinced that when he went to bed with a woman, he did not merely seduce her, he devoured her. Hustler or not, Don was the man to put his shoes under her bed any night.

In the pool at the condo, she loved swimming as many laps as she could. She wanted to keep in tiptop shape for her loving man. Maybe money had to be exchanged, but she didn't care. It wasn't her money any way. How could Sister Rose and Shelley have kicked him out? Of course, if given the choice, you'd go for Buck. He was beautiful, richly endowed, and had all the money in Florida, or soon would. Don was a mere hustler but worth every penny.

She loved being in charge of a relationship for the first time in her life. With other men, especially Gene and Buck, she had been at their beck and call. With Don it was different. She made the plans for the evening, she decided when she wanted to go home, she picked the restaurant—after all, she was paying for the meal—and, yes, she even decided when it was time to mount her.

With Don, his vaginal penetration was the culmination of a long series of sexual foreplays that included the most divine tongue probes a woman could ever expect to receive from a man. This was an experienced man, no little schoolboy out on his first date. Don loved women so much that it was hard for her to imagine his being with a man, even though she'd heard that talk with Shelley.

Gasping at her final lap, she pulled herself from the pool and reached for a towel. It was eleven o'clock, and she had a luncheon meeting at the home of Uncle Milty, who was going to work out the financial terms of her marriage to Buck. Milty had assured her that he didn't think Buck would object to her arrangement with Don at all. "When he married you, he didn't expect you to go to a nunnery. You are one lucky girl. Gene. Buck. Now Don Bossdum. Don't you ever got to bed with a man with a small dick?"

"God damn right I have," she'd said. With the three exceptions you named, all the men I've gone to bed with had small dicks."

Placing a towel around her wet head, she looked up at the condo tower where Don was still sleeping. As if breaking through a cloud, the sun seemed to shine even brighter to her, momentarily blinding her. A thought crossed her mind. Was she but a high-class whore who was so well paid she could afford her own hustler?

***

Only toying with a pink grapefruit, Leroy smiled demurely at Gene as they sat on his terrace having breakfast. For Gene it had been a long night, and he wanted to get back to his own condo to be with Jill and Sandy before he drove over to the Collins house later in the day. If Barry were going to be away for the day, he might even invite the kids for a swim in the would-be mayor's pool.

"Things are going very good for us," Leroy said as if holding back vital news. "When we fly out of this hell hole for California, we're going to have so much money with us the plane will have a hard time getting airborne."

"What fantasy is this?"

"I'm not bullshitting," Leroy said. "This gal has come up with a way to make the big bucks I've always lusted for. Big dicks and big bucks, my two favorite things. I've got two little pricks, Calder Martin and Barry Collins, by the balls, and I'm squeezing hard."

"Better watch it," Gene cautioned, "or you'll get your own balls cut off, especially if you fuck with Calder Martin."

"I can ruin their carefully laid plans tomorrow," Leroy said, a menacing edge creeping into his voice. "I've got evidence that could destroy Barry Collins. He'll get nowhere—certainly not the White House one day—if I come forth. I have pictures of Shelley Phillips and Barry that would put an end to the would-be mayor's career tomorrow. Not to mention what it would do for Sister Rose's charismatic movement."

Gene slammed down his coffee. The heat of the morning was getting to him. He swallowed hard, knowing he had to figure out a way to reach Sister Rose and inform her of this threat.

"I'm demanding five-million dollars from Calder's boys, or else

I'll go public with what I know. They'll have to give in."

Tightening his robe around him, Gene rose from the terrace. He'd heard enough. Leroy trailed him into the bathroom where Gene removed his robe and stepped under the shower. He showered quickly and reached for a towel, resisting Leroy's attempts to dry him. He wrapped the towel around his waist, heading for the bedroom to get dressed.

In the bedroom, Gene said, "Let me warn you about something. You fuck with Calder and you'll have an accident."

"I've already protected myself," Leroy said. "If something happens to me, the evidence goes public."

Shaking uncontrollably, Gene grabbed Leroy's arm, digging his nails in. "Don't you dare harm Sister Rose."

"You're hurting me," Leroy said petulantly, pulling away. "What in the fuck do you care about Sister Rose?"

"I believe in her."

The sound of Leroy's bitter laughter followed him as Gene headed for the door. "Don't tell me you're one of those Born-Again Christians?"

***

A distraught Barry sat beside the edge of his pool. He seemed on the verge of tears. "Calder Martin's pulled the plug," Barry said. "They're going to see me through this mayor's race because believe it or not I'm ahead in the polls. Even with Rose's dubious support. Anybody could beat that cow Hazel. But after this race Calder is going to recommend to the big boys that I be dumped. Just like that. They'll find a new guy. Bright faced. Young. Eager to please. Married to a faithful wife he met in college when he was eighteen. Never fucked around. Two adorable daughters. Just like mine." Barry got up from the pool area and headed toward his office, ignoring Gene.

Gene watched him go, vowing to assert himself one day so that he could not be so easily dismissed.

From a distant corner of the house, he heard Barry yelling into the phone. At one point he shouted the name "Calder."

The telephone by the pool rang. At first Gene was tempted to answer it but had been warned by Barry not to pick up the phone in his household. The phone wouldn't stop ringing. It must have rung twenty times. He decided to answer it. He picked up the receiver. "It's Pamela," came an angry voice on the other end.

"Where are you?" Gene asked.

"Where I am at the moment is none of your damn business. Wouldn't Barry and Calder Martin just love to know where I am? They'd come after me—that's for sure. Is Barry there?"

"He's on the phone right now with Calder."

"How cozy. I don't even want to speak to Barry again. I've decided to strike at them before they get me. I've talked to my lawyer. My demands are going to be delivered today by messenger. He should be arriving there any minute. Make sure you go to the door. If the demands in my letter aren't met, tell Miss Barry and that creep Calder I'm going to go public. A press conference. If they don't meet my demands, tell both assholes they're history."

Before he could say another word, she slammed down the phone.

Gene pulled off all his clothes and jumped into the refreshing waters of the pool. A plan was emerging. Even before he'd finished the first lap, he decided not to tell Barry about that phone call. He just needed to figure out a way to receive that package from the messenger without letting Barry know what was happening. Before he had fully thought out how he could do this, Barry came back onto the patio.

"Calder has really fucked me now."

Gene swam to the edge of the pool and raised himself up several feet from the water. "What now?"

"Leroy Fitzgerald—you remember that creep we went to college with?—that fucker is blackmailing me. He's got pictures of Shelley Phillips and me going at it. That asshole Leroy is demanding five-million dollars."

"Are the pictures real?" Gene asked.

"They're real all right. Before I lost my support with Calder's boys, I thought they might put up the money. There's no deal now. Calder wants me to go to Sister Rose. She's got money to burn. Since her own son is involved, and exposure would seriously damage her following, Calder believes she will be forced to cough up the dough."

Gene rose up from the pool, noting the admiring glances Barry was devoting to his genitalia. Even with all his present troubles, Barry couldn't resist a good view. Slowly, Gene dried himself in front of

Barry. "I hope you don't mind," Gene said, "But I'm expecting a messenger soon with a package for me."

"Fuck!" Barry said, not taking his eyes off Gene's penis which was beginning to rise. "I don't want your packages sent to my address."

"It's from Jim Howard. Papers about my case which has been dropped."

"Okay, if you've already had them sent here," Barry said The doorbell rang, and there was no one in the house to answer it but Gene or Barry. Gene pulled Barry to him and kissed him hard on the lips. Almost by instinct, Barry's hands traveled to Gene's lengthening prick.

"You're all hot and sweaty," Gene said, breaking away. "Go to the shower and I'll meet you in there. Sometimes it's fun to do it in the shower." Gene reached for a robe and headed for the front door, as Barry went toward the bathroom.

At the door Gene accepted the package but didn't have any money to tip the young man. He forged Barry's name to the slip and shut the door quickly. He noted the package was from a local law firm with five names, all Jewish.

Without bothering to open it, he took the package and headed for the rock garden behind the pool. Lifting the largest rock he could find, he slipped the package underneath, lowering the rock over its contents.

Tossing his robe on the tiles of the pool patio, he walked toward the shower where Barry was waiting.

***

As Gene pulled into the parking lot, he noticed TV cameras outside the entrance to his condo. Jerking his car in reverse, he headed out of the lot. There was no way he wanted to be photographed going into that building. He'd have to slip undetected into his condo to learn what news inside was worthy of getting on TV news.

Slipping through the back entrance, Gene managed to enter Leroy's apartment without being detected. "What in hell's all this fuss about?" Gene asked an obviously frightened Leroy, who had just gotten off the phone with someone.

"The shit's hit the fan," Leroy said, still in his robe. "Calder's playing hard ball."

"Why are those fucking TV cameramen outside the building?" Gene demanded to know.

"Someone has tipped off the press that you're living here with Jill, the same girl you exposed yourself to years ago. I guess the tonight news in Okeechobee thought that was a human interest story."

"Where's Jill and Sandy?" Gene asked.

"I called the apartment. Jill is holed up there. She's afraid to go out the door. The cameramen are right outside the apartment. Sandy is away somewhere."

"Let me try to get her on the phone," Gene said.

"She's not taking calls," Leroy said. "I've tried three times. I knew when I demanded money from Calder, he'd play dirty tricks like this."

"How is Jill tied in with this?" Gene asked.

"Calder knows we're having an affair," Leroy said. "Striking back at you is just a warning to me. Calder Martin was not the only one behind your arrest. Guess who his lieutenant is? That son of a bitch, Biff, was also behind it."

"God damn him!"

"I don't know how much you know about your former boss. I know plenty. He claims he's the biggest cocksman in Okeechobee. Actually he's impotent. I used to slip him into the Lolito house. He'd sneak into one of the rooms where he could spy on the action. He never joined in. He even disguises himself a bit and frequents the Vulcan Baths. Never for any action. Always to watch."

"That asshole hypocrite. And he ridiculed me as the flasher."

"Somehow Buck Brooke is in on this, too." Leroy said.

"I don't believe that," Gene said.

"Think again." Leroy walked over to his wall cabinet and pulled out a photograph, handing it to Gene.

Gene studied the photograph of Buck in his jogging outfit getting into a limousine.

"I'm sure you recognize that limousine," Leroy said. "It's seen enough around Okeechobee. He's getting in the car with Calder Martin."

"Fuck! Buck riding in a limo with that bastard."

"Okay, try this on for size," Leroy said. "Buck has hired your dear Clara and Maria. They're living at his private house, and you can check that out for yourself."

Gene felt himself trembling.

"The question is, why would Buck want to drive you out of town?" Leroy said. "What do you know about Buck that would make him want to do you in? Do you know something you could blackmail him with?"

"Maybe." Gene walked over to the sofa and sat down. "I want to see the six o'clock news. When it gets dark, I'll slip out. I've got things to do."

Leroy poured himself another drink. "So far I've heard no word from Calder and Barry about coughing up the big bucks."

There was an ominous look on Gene's face. "Maybe we've already heard from them."

***

Even as she sat in Gene's condo talking to Jill, Susan couldn't believe her good fortune in getting the interview. As the news that Gene was living with Jill came on television, Susan hadn't believed the slant given by reporters. She was also determined to become a working woman again, even if she'd been fired from the *Examiner*. She wanted an interview with Jill, and she was confident that the *Okeechobee News* would publish it. The way she figured it, appearing at the *News* and offering them an exclusive interview might be a good and proper introduction to a newspaper she wanted to direct in the near future.

As she noticed the polite, rather sensitive young woman preparing tea for them, Susan knew that the only reason Jill had agreed to see her was because she'd once been married to Gene.

Up to now reports had given a sexual overtone to the story, suggesting that Gene had exposed himself to the little girl and had later tracked her down and forced her into becoming his sex slave.

"What they are saying is wrong," Jill said. "Gene is the kindest, gentlest man I've ever known. I'm not his lover. What the TV people don't know is that I live here with my boyfriend, Sandy. Gene is like a daddy to us."

"I didn't know about this Sandy."

"Gene is giving Sandy and me a home we never had."

I'm glad Gene is helping you," Susan said.

Jill burst into tears. "Somebody is trying to ruin Gene. Making our lives together ugly."

"I think I can write a story that puts this whole thing in a different light."

"I hope you can. I've read other stories about Gene and me. They were all wrong. It's true: he did expose himself to me. I will always remember the look in his eyes. It was like he was saying, 'Look, I'm a man. Here's proof.' I know this doesn't make much sense, but I've always felt that something happened that day that made him feel he'd lost his manhood. He took a crude approach. It wasn't to harm me. He was reaching out to me for something. I was too young to respond back then."

"I feel I might have driven Gene to that act. I never heard his plea for help."

Jill reached for Susan's hand. "Maybe it doesn't matter what the public thinks. Just what we think."

Susan turned her head at the sound of a key in the lock

From the dark shadows of the hallway, someone appeared.

It was Gene.

***

In Palm Springs, it was already late in the evening when Buck arrived at the address given him by a member of Rose's staff. Although his invitation was valid from the moment his plane landed, he preferred to delay his arrival at the mansion for several hours so that he could collect his thoughts. Turning down the chauffeur-driven limousine, he had rented a car and driven out into the desert, hoping a long monotonous drive through a drab landscape would clear his head. It hadn't. He'd arrived at the mansion completely uncertain about the direction of his life.

Upon leaving the plane in Palm Springs, Rose had ordered Shelley to come with her. Buck was not told where they were going, although both of them promised to meet him later at the mansion.

At the gateway to the mansion, a security guard telephoned the main house to receive permission for Buck's vehicle to be allowed up the winding, palm-lined driveway that led to a pair of golden doors. He wasn't certain but he suspected the doors weren't painted but were actually inlaid with the precious metal itself. In low relief on the golden doors was a replica of prehistoric cave painting, portraying a realistic bull attacked by men with bows and arrows.

As he braked his car, the golden doors were thrown open by two servants in turbans, each clad in a flowing white disdasha. Their long, lean bodies approached his car. As one of them opened the door, Buck observed their narrow faces and light skins, causing him to believe they were Berbers.

Ushered into a dimly lit hallway where the smell of incense was powerful, he was informed that Sister Rose would join him shortly. He didn't know where Shelley was.

As he stood near painted columns under a vaulted ceiling, he gave his order for a Scotch. Looking about, he noticed that the split-level room was filled with copies of Roman statuary, including a head of Zeus and a nude Venus.

He was shown to a large patio with an Italian fountain topped by a statue of the Three Graces standing on a pedestal over a cascade of water. Branching off from the patio was a series of rooms. He strolled into one, finding it to be a private walled garden. Its terracotta walls were painted mauve, with a wide pink border around the base. The garden had been planted with large plastic bushes, holding an abundance of amazingly realistic flowers he was forced to fondle before deciding they were fakes. An illusion of ever-bearing flowery shrubbery was created, the magic garden of some child's fantasy. The roof tiles were painted a pink and orange in a checkerboard style, evoking pop art.

He left the garden, following an entry hallway to another room. Here the floor and four walls were covered with a scarlet-colored carpet, and a white silk canopy studded with gold fleurs-de-lis hung from the ceiling. The nude statues were painted, as in classical days, with meticulous realism, including careful shading of the skin tones of the genitalia. The fountain showered pink water. Around it were placed white patent leather pillow mattresses.

He walked alongside a small pond in which gardenias floated and brilliantly colored carp swam by. At the far end of the wall stood a black marble fireplace, over which hung a portrait of a man who appeared to be in his early forties.

He moved closer for an inspection. The subject of the portrait was obviously an Arab, though one attired in western dress. His face appeared vaguely familiar. An article in *Esquire* flashed through his mind. The Arab was strikingly handsome, his eyes intense and purple in their luminosity, so large and powerful they dominated his finely chiseled face.

He turned abruptly at the approach of a male servant. "Who's the painting of?"

The servant didn't understand. "Who is it?" Buck asked him again before he realized that the servant found it inconceivable that he didn't know the name of, presumably, the host. "I'm a friend of Sister Rose's. I've never had the pleasure of meeting the gentleman in the painting."

"That's Mr. Pharaon," the servant answered politely in a clipped British accent.

"Pharaon who?"

"Mr. Ahmad Pharaon." The servant gave him his drink, bowed, and walked off.

The name was not unknown to Buck, even though he couldn't immediately identify it. It sounded like so many other names buzzing in his head.

Ahmad Pharaon, Ahmad Pharaon, Ahmad Pharaon, he kept repeating to himself. Settling back on a sofa that he was certain was upholstered in the skin of some endangered species, he recalled who Ahmad Pharaon was. After all, his own newspaper—read that former newspaper—had once carried a story on Pharaon.

Robert and Buck three years ago had flown for a quickie two-day vacation to Paradise Island. While wandering around, they had spotted what the locals called "The House of Mystery" before they'd reached the Cloister at the Ocean Club. Their guide had told them that this was the most luxurious and opulent private mansion in all The Bahamas. The mansion was supposed to be owned by a mysterious sheik who'd created a bit of *Arabian Nights* fantasy on Paradise Island. Ever since it was first built, the mansion had been the subject of much local speculation. The estate was surrounded by a wall, with a total of sixteen towering lampposts lighting the night. A statue of Neptune along with four security guards protected the only gate leading into the grounds.

At the Ocean Club, a banker friend of his grandfather's had encountered Buck in the bar. The banker had told Buck that he'd heard that the house belonged to Ahmad Pharaon, who was widely known in the Arab world and probably had a long file in FBI and CIA headquarters here in America.

The reason the *Examiner* had run a piece on him, however, was that he was rumored to have purchased a sixty-two room mansion twenty-five miles from Okeechobee, a palatial dwelling far larger than Rose's Paradise Shores. The mansion had originally been built by a tobacco heiress who had died mysteriously. Her estate had put the house on the market, and it was sold almost immediately, the name of the buyer a mystery.

Pharaon was the oil-rich relative of Libya's former ambassador to the United Nations. He was known for living in extraordinary luxury around the world and was famous for his riotous extravagances. Publicly he was the head of an Arab multinational conglomerate that was founded on traffic in guns, but now backed everything from California banks to films. Privately, he was rumored to be a fund-raiser for international terrorists, with powerful connections in Iran and Algeria as well as his native Libya.

There remained little doubt in Buck's mind. Pharaon was the major source of Rose's seemingly unlimited capital.

The sound of angry voices coming from a salon across the patio momentarily distracted him.

***

"God damn you, Rose, let me alone!"

Whirling around, she screamed, "Shut up, you little faggot! I've had about all of you I can take." Words came from her injured throat as if her voicebox were constricted. She closed her eyes and everything mercifully went blank.

At times she really believed she hated Shelley so much she could kill him. Each day she regretted a little more her having adopted him. She found him threatening, fearing that at any time a quirk in his nature could sabotage her plans.

He stood before a fireplace, facing her defiantly. Even though it was his own actions, and those of Barry Collins, he somehow seemed to blame her for his misfortune. The meeting with the power brokers had gone badly. Shelley was out. He'd been ordered to go into seclusion. He was to make no more public appearances. It was deemed best that he go away for a long time, some place where he wouldn't get into trouble. She'd been ordered to pay off the blackmailer with her own funds.

She breathed in deeply. "You are being sent away—and that's that," she said as calmly as she could. "Calder Martin has arranged it. That asshole Martin won the round today. You've thoroughly disgraced me. I've indulged you. But the stupidity of your going to that boy whorehouse was far too much. Even if you're a total idiot and didn't know better, Barry should have known better. Any man with that lack of judgment shouldn't be groomed to become president of the United States. And he won't. You're not only out yourself, but Barry is finished too. They'll stick with him until this God damn mayor's race is over. They sure don't want Hazel in power. After that, they're dumping him."

"I won't go away. That's kidnapping. I'll go to the police. I'll tell everything."

"If Calder heard what you just said, he might put you to sleep," Rose said.

"Too many people would ask too many questions," he said.

"You'd be surprised what Calder can get away with," she said.

"You didn't stand up for me one time today," he said. "You let the jackals tear at my flesh."

"I can't defend you. Your stupidity is without defense. I'm buying off your blackmailer. Isn't that enough? When I get back to Okeechobee, after my little trip to the Middle East for that damn propaganda film, I'm meeting with Barry to let him know I'm bailing him out."

"You can afford it," he said.

"That's not the point. The point is, I don't intend to be placed in another position where I have to give in to a blackmailer. The arrangement we had with Bossdum was perfect."

"Really? That's what you think. I haven't told you this but Bossdum is demanding one-hundred thousand dollars."

"That's chicken feed," she said. "For God's sake, give it to him. That's a hell of a lot cheaper pay-off than Leroy Fitzgerald is demanding. I'll give Buck the money in cash. Let him meet with Bossdum for the pay-off. I'm sure they know each other. They went to college together."

"Whatever you say, as long as you're paying," Shelley said.

"I'm going to be bigger than ever," Rose said. "Make incredible money at great peril to myself. I could get killed by some crazed assassin. Do you think for one minute that I would give up the biggest chance I've ever had in my life because you're cruising around trying to get a big dick shoved up your overstretched ass."

"Things are different. I've settled down. I've got Buck. He's all I've ever wanted. We can keep him. Shower him with money and presents. There's enough meat there to satisfy both of us."

"You don't to get it," Rose said. "Buck has arrived too late to save you. You are history. They're still with me. I've been discreet. You've been nothing but a whore."

"You are a whore too," he said.

"I might be a whore," she said, "but no one ever photographed me getting fucked."

"I didn't believe Leroy would blackmail me," Shelley said.

"Anybody in the fucking world can blackmail you."

"I'm only fourteen years old," he said. "How am I supposed to know how you dirty adults play your rotten games?"

"You've learned more today than you've ever learned about adult games," she said.

"I hate everything you're doing with this Arab connection. You'd come out against motherhood if someone paid you enough. You're the slut of religion."

Irritated and enraged beyond control, she crossed the floor to him and, almost before he knew what had happened, she slapped him so hard the noise resounded through the room.

He rushed to the mantle of the fireplace, his fingers tightening around a piece of Egyptian statuary. He seemed ready to lunge blindly at her, attacking her with the figure. She moved back, sensing danger.

After a suspenseful moment, he dropped the statue, sending it crashing to the hearth. It had been stolen from a museum in Cairo and was a rare work of art handed down from antiquity. She searched his face for some sign of remorse. There was none. He didn't even look down to see how the pieces shattered on the floor.

The way the boy stared at her made her uncomfortably aware and self-conscious of her looks. By the very intensity of his glare, he made her feel old, ugly, and misshapen, hardly the kind of mood she wanted to be in when she dined with Buck.

"Okay, *Sister*," he said, mocking the word. "I owe you one for that slap."

She felt near tears, as she stood white-lipped and tense, waiting to see what he was going to do next. Like a doe facing the bullet of the hunter, she remained frozen with glazed eyes, wanting to flee.

"You really believe that Pharaon is turned on by you?" Shelley asked.

She didn't answer.

"He told me you were too old for him," he said. "Too flabby. He fucked you, he claimed, for political reasons."

The sudden shock of those words made her tremble.

He pointed at her with a swift hand movement, as if dismissing her. She knew he was about to confirm her worst suspicion.

"He finds my sweet little ass—so rosy pink, so tight—just delectable." He spoke with obvious glee. "You know Arabs, baby. They like them young, it doesn't matter which sex."

She burst into tears. He'd succeeded in making her feel ugly and frightened. Shoulders shaking, she turned from the sight of him.

After an agonizing moment, she faced him again. His smug look faded when he confronted the harshness in the lines of her face. He'd had his little moment of triumph and, as a street-smart boy, he knew it was her turn now.

She moved toward him, as in a blood-rite initiation. "You useless piece of shit!" she said, the ferocity of her own voice disturbing even her. A sharp, icy wind seemed to whip her, crackling and swirling underfoot as she came closer.

Her face and demeanor had gone through a terrifying metamorphosis in the last minute. Alarm swept over his petulant face. Right before him, staring deeply into his eyes, she said, "I'll fix you, you little bastard."

He turned from the sight of her and ran in the direction of his bedroom.

After he was gone, she checked her appearance in a Moroccan mirror, trying to soften the harsh features. To do that, she had to erase from her mind completely what had just taken place.

From somewhere deep within, a clear radiance emerged, making her eyes look translucent, shimmering like emeralds. Smiling at her ability to summon this hidden resource, she held up her finely carved lips to inspect. Her mouth had seduced Buck in his own bedroom on his private cay and had brought him inordinate pleasure.

It could still do that again. Shelley was a liar. She was at the peak of her beauty and desirability. She knew, of course, that Pharaon was involved with her son. Shelley was only a toy for him. When he wanted mature love, he turned to her. It was the same with Buck. Shelley was a mere convenience to Buck, a means of getting his rocks off with a cute trick. For adult pleasures, she was available to him. His love-making was genuine, she could tell.

Before meeting with Buck, she checked her appearance one final time. In spite of Shelley's blast, the woman staring back at her in the mirror was camera ready. The lighting in the room was flattering. More than that, she knew she'd never looked lovelier. Beauty, power, money. What man could resist her? She breathed in deeply, knowing that these moments alone with herself had restored her confidence. At last she was ready to face the challenges that still lay ahead in the evening. She'd deal with Shelley later.

***

The artificial palm tree appeared sinister-looking as the wind blew through its fake fronds. Buck sat in the garden under this golden tree with scarlet and purple fruit. Nesting in its fronds were lifelike replicas of fantastic birds of paradise. Somehow the setting seemed appropriate for what was about to happen.

The hysterical conversation he'd just heard had been predictable, confirming the image of Shelley as that of a boy sophisticated beyond his years. Rose and Shelley struck him as two persons possessed— moving unrelentingly toward their self-destruction. Or had each selected the other to deliver the *coup de grace*?

Interrupting his thoughts, she emerged from behind an Oriental drapery. It was a theatrical entrance against a dramatic scenic backdrop. Even though she'd been cruelly attacked by her son, she appeared like a woman who'd just emerged from the bed of a lover.

Later she had the grace to serve dinner without bringing up unpleasant business. The *cous-cous* was perfectly prepared, the best he'd ever tasted, though he had no appetite. He rested his hands on an elegant teakwood table, watching her face lit by electric candelabra. He smelled the fresh roses and Spanish lilies and admired the Swedish crystal and silver service that she informed him had once belonged to the Hapsburgs. He did manage in the meantime to drink a bottle of Dom Perignon. She only sipped at hers, knowing she had to keep a clear head. On the other hand, he needed a tranquilizer.

By the time the Arab coffee was served, he could no longer stand the suspense. He looked over at her and asked pointedly, "Are you buying up oil wells in Libya with your Christian donations?"

"No." Her fingers delicately traced a pattern along her tulip-shaped glass. "I have more interesting acquisitions in mind."

"Such as?" he asked.

She got up and walked over to his chair. "If you make the *right* decision, my people will buy back the chain of papers your grandfather lost." In amazement, he looked up at her. Her offer, so blatant and bold, made without hesitation and preliminaries. He met her stare, finding it fierce. "If you go with me, I'll make you the biggest newspaper publisher in America."

He slowly got up, his head reeling. A disturbing feeling of his own ambition flashed. He tried to retain his cool detachment, but on a much deeper level he was far from peaceful. In this make-believe world, he moved unsteadily.

What amazed him more than anything was that she had reached inside him and discovered his deepest, darkest ambition. God damn it, he did want to become the biggest newspaper publisher in America. Night after night, he used to dream of controlling not just the *Examiner*, but all the papers in the chain old Buck had tossed away.

The voice from behind him was imperious, the presence commanding. "Buck." The next mention of his name was turned into the most sensual of caresses. "*Buck.*"

It was an intoxicating aroma she gave off, and the smell didn't come from her expensive perfume either. It was from raw power. She wanted that, he knew, far more than the money. In that wish, his desire matched hers. She was willing to pay a higher price than he was, and both of them had totally different ideas as to what to do with that power. Her offer was tempting, the most tempting ever.

He felt like the young Trojan, Paris, in the old legend. Hera offered earthly power; Athena, wisdom, and Aphrodite, love. At the moment the thrill of power made him lean toward Hera's promise. For one brief flash, he told himself that perhaps for a small investment of himself ventured, the rewards would far outweigh the compromises.

He was still in that undecided state when he turned to face her again. For a moment she looked like Isadora Duncan among the columns of the Acropolis. But something was lacking in that image. She didn't possess Isadora's child-heart.

He confronted a cold statue, a woman of daring, a flamboyant actress who, faced with fading beauty, seemed intent on following savage whims.

Without losing eye contact, he slowly took out a cigarette and lit it. Only a foot from her face, he aggressively blew out the smoke. She stared at the cigarette, her face comprehending the arrogance of his lighting it as he did. It was his way of telling her that he wanted to be an equal partner, not some rent boy summoned to her boudoir at her convenience. She stared back at him as if each were on a battlefield. This was no longer about sex, and certainly not about love. It was about power and money. He sucked the cigarette smoke deeper into his lungs. "You have thoroughly corrupted me."

"Darling, I realized how corrupt you were the first moment I met you. It was, in fact, my bond with you."

"That's fine. What about Pharaon?"

"Sometime tonight he'll be here. I've got to monopolize his time for the first few hours. When we wake up in the morning, he'll want to meet with you. He's got some gold bars—a lot of them—to pass on to you. You may be losing the *Examiner* but you sure as hell are getting paid back for your loss."

"I know that," he said.

"All the more for you to enjoy," she said.

"Where do you want me to go?"

"Don't go up to Shelley's room tonight," she said. "He and I have some very important arrangements to work out. I've arranged for you to spend the night at Frank Sinatra's villa. Everything is there."

"Great!" he said.

She smiled at him before turning and walking from the courtyard, heading for an adjoining parlor. "Let's have a brandy and a long, lingering kiss before you disappear into the night."

He followed her trail, noting the beauty of her body and how gracefully it moved across the courtyard. He wondered about Shelley.

Thoughts of Robert, Susan, and Gene flashed through his mind, but only briefly. None of them belonged here in this exotic setting, and the more he lingered here, the more he wondered if he too were out of his depth.

***

Susan looked at Gene for a long moment. The years had gone by but they had been kind to him. If anything, he appeared handsomer and more virile than he was the night she'd married him. That lost little boy quality that had attracted her to him was gone. It'd been replaced by a more strong-jawed man.

His very stance challenged her. "You had to slip your way in here to interview Jill, didn't you? Was that really necessary?"

"It's cool, Gene," Jill said, walking over to comfort him and kiss him on the cheek.

"Jill's right," Susan said. "I'm here as a friend. I'm hoping to get your side across."

He turned from the sight of her. "Isn't that what all news reporters tell their victims?"

Jill kissed Gene on the cheek again and excused herself. "You two guys had better be alone. I'll be in my bedroom if you need me."

Susan watched her go, regretting it. She was apprehensive about being alone with Gene.

Gene drank some tea, then slammed the cup into the saucer. "A lot of people are out to get me."

"Who?" Susan asked.

"Your new husband for one."

"Buck...?" Her voice grew hesitant. "I can't believe that."

"What if I told you that Maria and Clara are living in Buck's house right now?"

"Surely not," she said.

"I've checked it out. Robert Dante hired them."

"Maybe Robert felt sorry for them," she said. "Buck would never do anything to harm you."

"How well do you know the man you married?" Gene asked.

Her throat tightened. "There's a whole side of him I don't know."

"You don't even know who he's in love with," he said. "It's not you."

"You mean Robert?" she asked.

"Somebody else," he said.

She swallowed hard, not wanting Gene to go on.

"Buck's in love with me. Always has been."

She sank back into the sofa.

"I made a woman out of him," he said. "He can't live with that. The sexiest man alive is nothing but a woman." There was a long awkward silence. "Your new husband can't stand up to a real man. He picks faggy little boys so he can play the big man. He can't deal with his true nature."

"Please don't judge Buck until you know more about the truth," she said.

"I'll find out that truth in my own way. In the meantime, I think you'd better leave. My condo's a little small."

She reached for her tea because her throat had grown dry. The tea had turned cold.

"I knew what I was getting into the day I married him."

"The son of a bitch loves me—not you," he said. "He's too much of a coward to admit that. He was planning to run away with me. But now I know he just tricked me into thinking that. Instead of letting me go peacefully, he thinks he has to strike back at me."

Jill burst from her bedroom. "A call came in from the police. Sandy's been arrested!"

***

Seated on a divan in the desert night, Rose wore a melancholy face in the glow of candlelight. In a sudden move, she flung herself onto the silk sofa, hugging a satin pillow, whose motif looked like it could have belonged to Cleopatra. "It was a cold, cruel act—your making love to me, getting me to feel again. Until you came along, my heart had died. Now I feel weak and vulnerable."

"That's hardly what happened," Buck said defensively. "If I walked out that door today, I feel I would not be missed. That I would be immediately replaced."

She still wanted to speak of love, even though he felt that she didn't believe her own words. "At this moment, I'm facing the greatest challenge of my career. I need all my energy channeled." She leaned forward and reached for his hand.

He took it and caressed it, holding it to his lips for a gentle kiss.

"Without you in my life, I'd be helpless to stand up against the onslaught."

"The moment you popped out of the womb you were no longer helpless," he said. To soften his words, he added, "That's because I believe you're a strong and powerful woman who can stand up to anything. Certainly Calder Martin."

The windows in the room were closed, and the heat of the desert afternoon had settled. Although cool outside, the night air seemed not to have entered this room. No one had turned on the air conditioner. He got up and faced an empty fireplace, his back to her. He turned again to look at her.

She defiantly stood up too, and somehow in the movement of her body, in her command of it, she admitted the truth of what he'd just said.

"You were born with great male beauty. I was born with great beauty too. Both of us have used our beauty as a weapon to charm the world. When it's gone, when the sun comes out and reveals the devastation of the years, one must reinvent oneself. Find another weapon to use."

"That is hardly your problem," he said. "I doubt if you've ever looked greater than you do now."

"That may be true." She staggered toward the bar to get herself another brandy. It was only then he realized she was drunk and getting more morbid by the minute. "In your case the loss of beauty won't matter," she said. "Women, or whatever, will still be attracted to you, regardless of how burnt out and old you become. For every man, there's somebody out there salivating. For a woman...for me, it's different. We have a shorter time to dance on the stage."

"I'm not the only man you're capable of attracting," he said. "There will be many others."

"You don't understand," she said, moving closer to him with her drink. "How much longer can I hold out?"

Until she'd raised that question, he'd never considered it. She did appear to be a woman working on a very tight time schedule.

"Right now I can create an illusionary fire of beauty," she said. She paused, her overstated self-assessment giving way to doubt. "Even at my age. But what of the next few years?"

It was a rhetorical question, he felt.

"With you, I had begun to feel love when I thought all such feeling in me had died," she said. "When you said there will be other men, was that but a signal that you'll leave me?"

"I'm just suggesting that other men will throw themselves at your feet." He smiled flirtatiously. "I'll have a lot of competition."

"I can just imagine what other men I'll meet. Boys at beach cabanas. Boys in hotel lobbies. In bars where one is not known. Through discreet introductions at parties. Maybe at gatherings of my church. At fifty I'll probably be using a call service."

Suddenly, she lunged toward him, pressing her body against him as tightly as she could, as if trying to arouse some passion that had been lost. "Oh, Buck, if all those young men emerge in my future, all their faces will become one great blur. They'll all mesh into...you!"

He grabbed her and kissed her. He was too close to collecting his millions for him to fail her now. She was moaning, clutching him, but it was only mechanical love-making for him.

A male Arab servant entered the room. She broke away quickly.

"Mr. Pharaon called," he announced. "He's arrived at the airport and will be here soon."

On unsteady legs, she headed for the bar again to refill her glass. She motioned for the servant to open the glass doors leading to the garishly lit patio with its bizarre nude statuary. He followed her, noting that the lights of the patio, combined with the flickering candles of the salon, made grotesque patterns on her face. Momentarily, she looked demented until he realized it was her fear of meeting Pharaon.

"I must go to Sinatra's," he said. "Too bad. You and I might have had one hot evening."

She didn't seem to hear him, appearing lost in her own drunken world. Running one hand across her cheek, she seemed to want to assure herself of her own smooth beauty. She raised her hand to her mouth as if to muffle a sound coming from her damaged throat.

"I'll tell you what age is," she said in a forlorn voice, not quite her own. "Age is climbing a tree. At first its branches are firm and covered with greenery. The higher you climb from the roots, the weaker the branches become. Eventually the leaves decay, turn colors and fall off. Still you must climb higher and higher. The branches grow brittle and break off under your weight. Soon you see the top of the tree and you know it's the end. You're compelled to reach for it. You know you can't stay where you are forever. The clothes you used to drape yourself in have grown ragged by the time you reach the top. They barely conceal your skeletal nudity. At the top, you're assaulted by the coldest, bitterest wind that ever blew across the glacial desert."

He swallowed hard. She wasn't lamenting the loss of her beauty. Echoing Shelley's fears, she was sensing her own upcoming doom.

He approached her to tell her good night. She seemed on the verge of igniting before his eyes. Her eyes glistened with tears. She held up her right hand, her fingers arched, but it had no function to perform.

"Life has placed me in a position of trust," she said. "Millions of my devoted turn to me for guidance. For whatever reason, I inspire them." She winced and passed a nervous hand across her forehead. "I'm not going to help those souls. I will only bring out the worst in them."

He kissed her on the cheek and said good night, but she didn't seem to hear him or note his passing. She was completely enraptured by her own alcohol-induced world. He could only imagine what would come out of her meeting with Pharaon.

In the foyer of the mansion, the servant handed him neatly typed directions for reaching Sinatra's house. He looked longingly up the stairwell, wishing he could go and find Shelley's bedroom. As if sensing his impulse, the servant stood in front of the stairwell.

As an attendant brought his car around, Buck looked back once more at the gates of the mansion, wondering what secrets this house held.

Chapter Twelve

Buck left the Pharaon estate, heading for Sinatra's mansion. He didn't know what awaited him there, and at this point he didn't much care. Celebrities never impressed him, and because of his newspaper work he'd met his share of them. If he'd been star-struck, he wouldn't have turned down that invitation to meet Ronald Reagan and Nancy Davis. After all, the man might become president of the United States, although he seriously doubted that.

Without bothering to read the directions, he found himself driving aimlessly, wanting to get away from Palm Springs and escape to the desert on a road to nowhere. He welcomed the incredible blackness of the night that only the desert could provide.

Suddenly, from the back seat, he heard a movement and then a head popped up. It was Shelley. Buck jammed his foot on the brakes. "What the hell!"

"Keep on going," Shelley said in a commanding tone. "The farther I get from that stinking rose garden, the better."

Buck slumped over the wheel in astonishment, then turned to look back at Shelley. "Christ, man, I'd better take you right back to big mama. The next thing I know she'll have me up on a kidnapping charge."

Shelley crawled over the seat and anchored into a front position with Buck, reaching for one of his cigarettes in a package on the dashboard. "Give me a break, love. Let me go away for the night with you."

Buck steered the car into the desert.

The hard white eyes of an onrushing car—the lone sight visible for miles around—roared passed them, then was swallowed up by the desert. The only sound was of his rented car rolling across the empty mesa to the mountains in the distance.

Shelley turned, smiled at him, then stuck his unfinished cigarette between Buck's lips, lighting another for himself. "We might as well kill this night together, honey."

Buck rubbed sweat from his eyes. "Okay, what are you planning to do?"

"They think they can just dismiss me because of a little transgression here and there—nothing serious. A boy's attempt to have some harmless fun. They've got another thought coming."

"My advice is to pay Leroy off and get rid of the fucker," Buck said. "I love you, and I want to protect you."

"That's cute. But I've got to have my revenge on both Rose and Calder. They want to send me into exile as a moral leper. They are the moral lepers—and that's the exact message I plan to bring to the world. Rose is not going to be a threat to anybody when I finish with her. I've had it with that bitch. And when I tell what I know about Calder Martin, he might end up in jail."

Buck was tempted to stop the car and shake some sense into Shelley's blond head. "You do that and you're dead."

"It will be a disaster for them," Shelley said. "Not for me. I've got a few million held in trust for me until I turn twenty-one."

"If you fuck with Rose and Calder, much less Pharaon, you'll never get to be twenty-one."

"They should be afraid of me."

In the dim light, Buck studied Shelley's face as best he could, finding it contemptuous, defiant.

"By standing up and denouncing them, the press will call me a hero," Shelley said. "Standing on my own golden little feet and denouncing bigotry and hatred. Shit, they'll give me the fucking Nobel Peace Prize."

The speedometer registered seventy-five, eighty, eighty-five, ninety. The road ahead was blurred. He knew his driving was dangerous, yet somehow he needed the speed.

Buck had no intention of returning to the resort and finding Sinatra's house. He'd been tempted to steer Shelley to some desert motel, there to spend a troubled night with him. He suspected that would end in an argument, with him devoting the night to a vain attempt to get Shelley to keep quiet for his own safety.

As if sensing the same thing, Shelley reached for Buck's arm. "You'd better take me back to the lion's den, handsome. If I'm going to pull off my little stunt, I don't want to arouse suspicion."

Buck slammed on the brakes, turned the car around in the middle of the road and headed back to the center of Palm Springs. "Would you make a promise to me?" Buck asked.

"Don't ask me to change my mind," Shelley said.

"Can we talk about it tomorrow? Privately. Just the two of us."

"It's a deal," Shelley said. "We're a team."

"If you're going to go through with this, then I'm pulling out after I meet with Pharaon," Buck said. "I'll pick up my money for the sale of the *Examiner*, then I'm out of there. Instead of becoming some media director, I'll need to spend the rest of my days covering your ass."

The boy didn't say anything for a long moment, as if mulling something over. "Let me out several blocks from Pharaon's place. I know how to slip back in undetected."

As Shelley started to get out of the car, Buck reached for him, pulling him close and kissing him long and hard. For the first time ever, Shelley appeared unresponsive, as if something else was distracting him. "Kid, take care," Buck said.

"I know what chance I'm taking," Shelley said. "I'm going to give the old finger to Rose." Buck heard only the slamming of the car door and, in moments, Shelley's white shirt and trousers were no longer visible.

Buck sat for a long while behind the wheel   "The kid has balls after all," he muttered to himself. Sighing deeply, he stepped on the gas and headed for the loneliness of a desert motel room.

***

In Biff's police station, Jim Howard had come through for Susan again. Sandy was out on bail. He'd been arrested and charged with prostitution.

When they came out of the police station, Susan was waiting for them where they'd parked above the elevated highway. She'd lit a cigarette and was watching the moon shining on the water. In spite of all the trouble swirling around her head, the moonlit Florida landscape at night was reason enough to live here.

Until an hour ago, she'd never heard of the boy approaching her, but had found herself begging for Jim's intervention. As Sandy came up to her and she could make out his features, she was struck by how handsome the boy appeared, not the type she'd immediately associate with street hustling. He had almost the classic choir boy look about him.

"I know who you are," he said, "You were married to Gene."

"I plead guilty," she said, extending her hand. "I'm Susan." She looked at Jim, thanking him with her eyes for his rescue.

"I'm Sandy." He shook her hand firmly. "I'm sorry we had to meet like this. I've seen your picture in the paper many times. You're very beautiful."

"Thank you."

"Let's get in the car," Jim said, obviously angered by something that had happened in the police station.

The boy got into the back seat as Susan joined Jim up front. "I was going into the drug store to buy some things, and suddenly this squad car pulled up and forced me inside," Sandy said. "They took me to the police station where I was interrogated by the police chief. They said I was hustling."

Jim sighed and turned to Susan. "I think the boy is telling the truth. The only trouble is, he's been arrested for solicitation twice before. It's on his record."

"I was guilty then," Sandy said. "I'm not guilty now."

"How did you meet Gene?" Susan asked.

"He picked me up one day on the square."

"For sex?" she asked provocatively.

"That's what I thought at first," Sandy said. "He didn't want that. God knows I would have been willing."

"What did he want?" she asked.

"Information about this Lolito ring," Sandy said. "Do you know about that?"

"Not as much as I should."

I think he also felt sorry for me—and for Jill too. He came to like us and provide a place for us."

"I was curious," Jim interjected. "Why are you bandaged?" Did someone beat you up? It might help my case."

"I was burned when Gene's house was set afire," Sandy said. "The firemen wouldn't go in to save Gene. I thought he was trapped in his back bedroom. I broke away from the firemen and rushed in to save Gene myself. Thank God he wasn't there that night."

Later in the evening at their home, Ingrid and Jim talked to Sandy over sandwiches and colas in their patio, Susan went into the hallway and dialed Gene. When she'd fully informed him of everything she knew, he sighed, "I feel a rope is tightening around my throat."

"I think someone's got it in for you, and I still refuse to believe it's Buck," she said.

"I think someone's setting me up for something," Gene said. "I have this instinct."

She started to ring off, but there was something in his voice that made her stay on the line. "Gene...is there anything I can do?"

"You've helped us out plenty tonight," he said.

"There's something else, isn't there?"

He hesitated. "If something were to happen to me, would you help out Sandy and Jill?" Even before she could respond, he put down the phone.

***

Gene let himself in through the secret garden gate leading into Barry's compound. He crossed by the rock where he'd hidden Pamela's document, wondering when she'd make another attempt to get in touch with Barry's attorneys.

Barry was talking on the phone, his soft, cajoling voice heard through an open window.

"I'm lonely tonight, and I want to see you," Barry said. There was a long pause. "I know you love him, but does he love you? Robert, you and I have always been real tight. Let me come over."

Could this be Robert Dante on the phone? Surely Barry wasn't an old friend of Robert's.

Barry's voice grew harsher. "No one will know I'm seeing you. Buck's gone."

Gene swallowed hard. It was Robert Dante.

"That's more like it," Barry said into the phone. "I'll be right over." He put down the phone.

Gene didn't want Barry to know he'd entered the compound, and he concealed himself behind the bushes.

Barry emerged from his office and walked over to the pool. He reached into his pocket and pulled out a cigarette. He lit it and smoked only a few draws before tossing it into the pool. He headed for the garage.

Gene would wait ten minutes, then follow him. Invited or not, Gene was heading to Buck's house.

An hour later in the dark shadows of Buck's garden, Gene concealed himself behind a hedge, as he watched Clara bring drinks to Barry and Robert, sitting in a gazebo at the far end of the lawn. Maria sat on the steps of Buck's pillared back veranda, eating what looked like a popsicle.

The presence of Clara and Maria at Buck's home was clear evidence of his friend's betrayal. His plans to run away with Buck seemed but a dream. Gene felt he'd been had. Buck must have secretly mocked him when Gene had revealed his love.

When Clara came back to the veranda after having taken the drinks to Robert and Barry, she went inside through the large wooden doors, heading to the kitchen. Maria got up off the porch and trailed her mother inside.

Silently moving along the cover of the hedges, Gene positioned himself about five feet from the gazebo where Robert and Barry sat drinking.

"You know I told you never to come here again," Robert was saying.

"All during the time he was in the service, you didn't object to my being upstairs with you. Buck wasn't fucking you. You had to get it from somebody. You're a natural bottom."

"It's different now," Robert said. "It's not like it was before when I had to turn to you."

"I thought you loved me," Barry said.

"That was back then," Robert said. "This is now. We've made a commitment to each other. I'm not going to be the one who breaks those vows."

"What if Buck breaks the vows?" Barry said.

"I don't believe he'd do that. Not now anyway."

"He's betraying you right this minute," Barry said.

"With whom?" Robert asked, a growing alarm in his voice.

"Shelley Phillips."

"I can't believe that." There was such uncertainty in Robert's voice.

"I'm not making this up," Barry said. "Buck's fallen in love with Shelley. Before Buck came along, the boy belonged to me, or as much as that little whore can belong to anybody."

"I can't believe this," Robert said in a choked voice. "I was having this thing with Shelley at Leroy's bordello," Barry said. "Buck rushed into the room like a maniac and kicked me out and took Shelley away."

"That explains a lot," Robert said. "Sometimes when Buck comes to me, I've had the feeling that he's just risen from a hotbed with somebody else."

"I want you to leave Buck and come back with me," Barry said. "As my political assistant and lover. No more chasing boys for me. I've got to settle down with one good man I can trust."

"I don't know," Robert said.

Gene couldn't clearly see but apparently Barry had taken Robert in his arms and was kissing him.

"If you come with me," Barry said, "it will be just like the old times. We had good times back then, and we'll have good times in the future. But very discreet times. As my assistant, it's the perfect cover."

Robert seemed to be standing up and walking away. "I'll think about it."

"Will you promise to call me every day?" Barry asked.

"I promise," Robert said.

Barry walked over to Robert who broke away. "Not now," Robert said.

"Okay, kid, here's looking at you," Barry said. "My offer is genuine. It'll be a disaster for you if you stay with Buck."

"We'll see," Robert said in a forlorn voice. "I want to be alone tonight."

"I understand," Barry said. "Just a kiss. A good night kiss." Barry must have held Robert for a long time.

In the safety of the bushes, Gene liked hearing other people's dark secrets. It gave him power over them.

***

The sobering cold of the night air sent an added chill through Shelley's body as he used a secret key to open a tiny gate at the far end of Pharaon's estate. As he moved across the garden, he rehearsed his upcoming press conference.

At the patio doors leading into the living room, he stopped, breathing deeply all the fresh air he could. Soon he'd be asleep from sheer exhaustion. He had to look his best for tomorrow.

Later in his bedroom, he stripped and crawled into bed, watching reflections the moonlight made in Pharaon's garden.

Soon he drifted off, and he didn't know how long he slept. Maybe it was a dream. He woke up at the feel of something heavy on his chest. Opening his bleary eyes, he met the foreboding stare of a Berber as a light in his room went on. One of Pharaon's bodyguards stood over him. Shelley tried to get up, but the firm, broad hand of the Berber pinned him down.

"Look what we've got here, Rose," came the familiar, chilling voice of Calder Martin.

Rose remained motionless and silent beside Calder.

In his hand, Calder dangled a tape recorder, flipping it on. The sound of Buck's familiar voice could be heard.

To Shelley's horror, he realized that Buck's rented car had been bugged.

As Buck's voice still sounded on the tape recorder, Shelley, in a sudden move, slipped from the Berber's hold and darted starkly naked toward the patio door leading to his terrace. Momentarily taken aback, the Berber rushed after Shelley, grabbing the boy's arm, twisting it behind his back, totally restraining him. Shelley cried out in pain.

Just then, on a signal from Calder, a second Berber came into the room. He headed toward Shelley with a needle. The first Berber still held him with one hand and with the other repeatedly slapped him, very hard and very fast, making him dazed, ready to receive the needle.

Nearly blinded from the slapping, Shelley was half conscious, too weak to resist the needle that was shot in his arm.

Rose stood over him. At least he thought it was Rose. His eyes took in only the white of the gown and, of all the things he could be thinking about right now, he remembered that Rose always liked to wear white. "You're not going to meet the press," he heard her say. "But to our place in St. Moritz. I think the time has come for you to be born again!"

At these words, a tortured scream escaped from his throat. He knew what that meant. Rose had taken everything from him but the freedom of his mind. He kicked the Berber holding the needle and spat in the face of the bodyguard restraining him.

Calder towered over him. In one swift kick, Calder plowed his foot into Shelley's groin. The pain was unbearable. It lasted only a second before Shelley descended into blackness.

"Listen, you little fag!" he heard Calder say. The voice sounded as if it were bouncing off the walls of a tunnel. "You've caused enough trouble."

Although he had at first resisted it, Shelley now invited the point of the needle as it penetrated the surface of his skin. His blood seemed on fire before he drifted into oblivion.

***

It was three o'clock in the morning, as Gene sat alone in a roadside tavern. The bar was so dimly lit he felt the power had gone out. A man and two women occupied a table up front. They were having some sort of argument about who owned a mobile home in the Cactus Grove Trailer Camp. Gene couldn't have cared less. He had other things on his mind.

Even now he couldn't believe what had happened in the past two hours. It had not been planned. If you'd told him at midnight where he'd be at 3am, he would not have believed it. It must have been a dream. He'd raped Robert.

After Barry had left the garden, Gene had emerged from behind the bushes to attack Robert. Gene had already removed all of his clothing so his garments wouldn't get in the way. Panic had come over Robert. As he'd started to scream, Gene's fingers tightened around the young man's throat. "You scream and you're dead," Gene had said. "I can kill a man in an instant. It's your choice."

"I'll do anything you say," Robert said.

"That's more like it," Gene had told him, as he ripped off Robert's shirt and tore open his fly. His shorts had fallen on the ground. Gene had pulled down Robert's jockey underwear. Roughly he'd thrown Robert onto the garden sofa covered with weather-proof cushions.

In the light of the night garden, he had clearly seen Robert's face, although his own face had remained in shadow. The young man had trembled, but had offered no resistance.

Gene had taken his hand and held it over Robert's mouth even though he'd made no attempt to scream. Gene had known what would eventually happen. Considering the sheer size of Gene's cock, Robert would not have been able to keep from screaming.

With his hand muffling Robert's mouth, Gene had guided himself to his target. First he'd slapped Robert's ass, first one cheek, then the other. Robert's legs had been up in the air, resting on Gene's broad shoulders. But he hadn't opened for Gene. With a sudden move, Gene had grabbed Robert's balls, squeezing them as hard as he could. The target had suddenly opened. With a sudden plunge, he'd completely penetrated Robert. Robert had cried out in pain. Gene had removed his hand from Robert's mouth and had descended upon Robert, biting and sucking his lips and blowing his hot breath inside Robert's mouth. Robert had grabbed him and tried to push him away but Gene had shoved and pushed even harder.

As intense pain wracked Robert's body, Gene's teeth had descended on Robert's ears and neck. He was biting Robert and biting hard. Robert had continued to resist him, pushing and shoving him away. But Gene had him completely pinned down.

No longer able to hold back, Robert's tears had flowed. Ignoring them, Gene had continued to pump Robert furiously. Gene's weight had crushed against Robert who had moaned softly.

Very soon Gene had heard a different moan coming from Robert. He'd no longer pushed Gene away but his fingers had traced caressing patterns across Gene's back. Gene had felt the wiry muscles of Robert's legs stiffen as his stomach had tightened. With a high whimper, Robert had shot a stream of pungent semen across Gene's chest and had grabbed the back of Gene's head, forcing his mouth onto Gene's. Gene's tongue had shot into Robert's mouth. There it had been eagerly sucked, the most powerful sucking it had ever received. Robert no longer pushed him away, but had wrapped his arms around Gene as if demanding a deeper penetration.

Suddenly Gene had let out a muffled cry as he'd emptied himself into Robert. Gene had collapsed onto Robert. He had lain very still, gasping for breath before rolling off his victim. Within moments, Robert had moved his position and had virtually fallen on Gene's stomach, where his tongue had cleaned off his own semen. He had licked inside Gene's navel before descending to his testicles where he'd licked and sucked, giving them a bath. His head had moved upward to clean and lick Gene's penis. He'd been tender and gentle, almost arousing Gene to another bout of passion.

When he'd completely cleaned Gene, Robert's lips had moved up his chest, gently kissing his nipples. At Gene's neck, Robert had licked the sweat from him before pressing his mouth onto Gene's.

"Stay with me," Robert had pleaded. "No man has ever taken me like that before."

As Gene had tried to slip into his jeans, Robert had fallen before him, licking his thighs and fondling his testicles. "There's so much more I can do for you," Robert had said.

Gene had pushed him away and gotten dressed. Robert had walked toward him, hoping for one final embrace. Gene had moved quickly from the garden and had disappeared, driving endlessly until he found this all-night bar.

On an impulse he stood up in the bar, paid his tab, and got into his car. He knew exactly where he was going.

In less than thirty minutes he was on the veranda of Buck's mansion ringing the doorbell, wondering if he'd awaken Clara and Maria. If he encountered them, he didn't know what he was going to do.

It was Robert—clad in a robe—who opened the door. Seeing it was Gene, he reached out and took his arm, guiding him inside, as he shut the door. Gene pulled Robert into an embrace, inserting his tongue in Robert's mouth. Robert opened his robe and pressed his nude body against Gene's clothed one. With one hand, Gene massaged Robert's velvety smooth back. With the other he caressed the cheeks of Robert's ass. Robert moaned in Gene's arms, giving of himself up completely.

Robert moved from Gene's lips, planting little flickering kisses and licks on Gene's neck before bathing his ear. Into that ear, he whispered, "Take me upstairs and do anything to me you've ever wanted to do. No limits."

***

Back at the Pharaon mansion, Buck was ushered into the large central patio. He'd asked an Arab servant where Mrs. Phillips and her son were. "They're not available," the man had said.

Buck waited forty minutes, and he was growing impatient. Finally, the same servant arrived with a pot of coffee for him and a selection of juices. "If there's anything else, press this buzzer over there." He motioned to the bar. "We have everything. Caviar. Anything you want."

"I want to speak to Mr. Pharaon," Buck said firmly.

"He sends his apologies and will be here shortly."

As Buck paced the patio, he began to feel the exotic vegetation was cannibalistic and might swoop down to devour him. There was a movement in the far corner of the patio, and then a man emerged. It was Pharaon. Buck recognized him immediately from his portrait. Most portraits flatter. Pharaon's portrait was but a shadow version of himself.

In real life, Pharaon was an exotic beauty from some *Arabian Nights* fantasy. Dressed entirely in white, he was as slender as anyone could wish. He was wearing what was most definitely the world's most expensive and most exquisitely tailored silk suit, with a violet shirt and a mauve tie. He wore the suit with the careless confidence of a man born to wear the world's most expensive clothing. From the tips of his manicured nails to his perfectly groomed hair, from his discreet but paralyzingly priced jewelry to his violet-colored eyes, he exuded sex appeal. Even though he must be over forty, his olive skin had the bloom of youth. His thin cheeks appeared as if made up, but Buck knew that was his natural tone. Even his pinkish red lips looked painted with discretion but they were real. He did not owe his beauty to art or discipline. The facility of his carriage and the grace of his gestures immediately attracted Buck to him, as Pharaon reached to shake his hand.

He surprised Buck by taking his hand and placing its inner palm against his lips. He gently kissed Buck's hand, then pressed the palm even closer to his lips. His tongue darted out to lick Buck's palm. Before releasing Buck's hand, he swallowed two of Buck's fingers.

"God, you taste good," Pharaon said. "If we were not civilized the way we are today, I would kidnap you and make you the favorite in my harem."

"What an introduction!" Buck said. "I assume this is not your greeting for everybody."

"It's my greeting for you," Pharaon said. "I've never met anyone quite like you. You are the world's most beautiful man. No, I'd better take that back. I am the world's most beautiful man. You are the world's sexiest man."

"How can I hate you and view you as a dreaded terrorist and international murderer if you come on like that? Buck asked.

"I heard you were a Marine," Pharaon said. "I always liked big, handsome U.S. Marines with blue eyes and blond hair, except when they invade my country."

"I thought you liked little boys like Shelley."

"As playthings. Sex with Shelley would be like a tiny diversion. Not my true agenda. Back home I go for the little boys. It's part of my legend. My real desire is for a U.S. Marine like you. At home I am always the top. When I go abroad, I become my true self: a bottom."

Buck sat down opposite Pharaon. "Have you seen Rose and Shelley this morning?"

"I saw them last night. Rose and Calder left this morning to fly to the Middle East. Rose left you a note. Calder said you could go fuck yourself. Shelley had to fly to Europe. He too left you a note. I guess that leaves you and me alone together. Except for thirty-eight very discreet servants."

"You know why I'm here," Buck said.

"Indeed I do." He pressed a buzzer. An unfamiliar servant emerged with a leather case. In front of Pharaon, he reached in and removed two checks. Pharaon glanced at them only briefly before signaling the servant to hand them to Buck. After doing that, the servant quietly left.

Buck studied first one check, then the other.

"One is for your stock interest in the *Examiner*," Pharaon said. "The other for your grandfather's. Are they satisfactory?"

"I don't want to sound like a country boy, but this is the most money I've ever seen in my entire life." Buck said.

"Of course, if you prefer I could take the checks back and deposit gold bars in some bank account in Geneva."

"The checks will do fine," Buck said. "In this country we have something known as the IRS."

"A deplorable institution," Pharaon said.

"Thank you," Buck said. "Losing the *Examiner* was painful. These checks have helped ease it."

"Are you also going to become my media director?" Pharaon asked. "Rose highly recommends you."

"That we need to talk about."

"I have planned to spend the rest of the day talking about nothing else—except, perhaps, your raw magnetism and male beauty."

"You know how to make a man feel good," Buck said.

"The media director's job will give you incredible power, not to mention the money."

"Before we go on, I must tell you I have no stomach for advancing Arab causes in this country, attacking Jews, or exploiting Born Again Christians."

"Neither do I," Pharaon said. "As the afternoon progresses, you will see that I have another agenda. I wouldn't be so stupid as to involve you in shit like that. I need a person to represent me in this country. With television stations. Radio stations. Especially in Hollywood. I plan to bankroll American films. I would never insult your intelligence or abilities by using you for this propaganda garbage. I have Rose for that crap. For my dirty deeds, I have Calder Martin. He's a scumbag. I know Rose told you to undermine Calder with me. Hold your breath. I know more about Calder than you ever will. Regrettably, he also knows too much about me. I can't get rid of him. The propaganda thing with Rose will not be part of your job description. I want us to move into the media elite in this country. I'm an Arab and I can't do it. But you're a blond American hunk. You can go where I'm not accepted, and I want to use you to advance my interests. Believe me, in this case, I'm interested in making money—not making war or propaganda."

"Strangely, I believe you," Buck said.

"Let's spend the day talking about it. Tell me all the reasons you're wrong for the job, and I'll tell you all the reasons you're right for it."

"The day is yours," Buck said.

"The day is ours." Pharaon got up and walked over and sat down with Buck. "I want you to go for a swim with me in my private pool. It will not be necessary to put on a swimming suit. I understand from Rose you have nothing to be ashamed of. We'll talk and we'll talk. We'll make love and we'll talk some more. You can use me the way a man uses a woman. Think of me as your love slave." He bent over and pressed his lips hard against Buck's. Buck returned the kiss, his mind blurring.

"Your taste is of the Gods," Pharaon said. "I want to taste every inch of your body. But I don't offer you just my body. I offer you the world or at least that part of the world I can give you. Those checks over there are just the beginning."

"That's a mighty impressive beginning."

"There is so much more to come." He took Buck's hand. "Let's go for that swim so I can see your nude body in action. I have the best trained masseurs in the world." He reached for Buck's hand again, putting it to his mouth and licking it. "But only you can give me the ultimate massage."

***

Buck awoke in the most luxurious bedroom he'd ever known. As his eyes slowly took in the wonder of the place, he imagined it was what Cleopatra's bedroom might have looked like. It seemed appropriate for the queen of the Nile—no one else. He wasn't quite sure where he was until he remembered he was in Palm Springs. He was in Ahmad's bedroom. He'd spent the most sensual day of his young life. Regardless of what experiences awaited him in the future, he felt nothing could compare to the day just gone by.

He ran his fingers across the satin sheets feeling for Ahmad but no one was in bed with him. He picked up rose petals, however. Someone—no doubt Ahmad—had covered his bed with rose petals. Picking up a handful of petals, he dropped them one by one across his face. It was then he became aware of a large ring on his finger. It was studded with precious gems, and it looked as if it'd cost the annual budget of the United States. He suspected that ring was no doubt once owned by Alexander the Great or some such towering historical figure.

In the place where the body of Ahmad had so recently rested, he picked up a piece of gold paper with mauve-colored ink. He read the words slowly: "All my life I've searched for the one perfect man, knowing that such a divine creature must exist somewhere on the face of the earth. Today I have found him. You are descended from the Gods. I have tasted every part of your body. I have known the most passionate kisses from you and the deepest penetration. You have transported me to a heaven I thought I'd never experience on the face of this earth. I'm a little black and blue, and your teeth marks are on me. You've branded me and made me yours. Your passion for me was so great you had to bite my flesh, even drawing blood, to relieve the exquisite torture I was putting you through. YOU ARE MY HUSBAND. From this day forth, everything I have is yours. A silly contract between us is meaningless now. I possess one of the fabled fortunes of all time. It is yours to share with me. In spite of all my pretense, I am not a man after all. Today you made me a woman. When I am alone with you in the future, I will dress and act like the woman I have discovered in myself. I have left your bed only to prepare myself for you when you awake. When you have rested, please come to the boudoir upstairs. I will be there ready and waiting for you. When you come to me, we will speak of our glorious future. It is all right to continue with your boy-toy in the harem. Shelley is but a mere plaything to amuse yourself with while I am away, as I must often be. But I am the chief wife. When I am around, you will have need of no others. Your semen fills my body. I want you to think of my body as a willing receptacle of your nectar in the future. It will always be there for you willing to give you pleasure that you've never known before with anyone else—man or woman. I have fallen in love with the world's most spectacular man. Your darling wife, Ahmad."

Buck rolled over in bed. "Oh, fuck," he said out loud. And he thought he'd had a complicated life before. What was the point in returning to Okeechobee now? It looked like school days down there. This afternoon he'd entered the adult world, and what fun it was.

He would soon rise from this bed and head for his bath. Immersed deep in that bath, he would remember in precious detail each thing Ahmad had so recently done to his body. He'd never known such pleasure or experienced such orgasms.

There was a gentle knock on the door. Thinking it was Ahmad, he called out, "Come on in."

A male Arab servant appeared with two notes which he handed to Buck on a gold platter. "Thank you." Without saying a word, the servant turned and left.

He picked up the first note and opened it. It was from Rose. "I will be out of phone contact for one week. Don't ask me where I am. God, have I gotten myself in a mess with this shit. As soon as I finish this project, I'll fly back to Okeechobee and your loving arms. I am so sorry I wasn't here to say good-bye to you, but I am sure Ahmad will entertain you royally. Love, Rose."

He picked up the second note. It was from Shelley. "Buck, it was just great. Just great!!! While it lasted. But all good things come to an end. The end has come for us. Remember, I'm just a kid, and kids change their minds from day to day. One day they want to grow up to be a cowboy. The next day a fireman. One day I want to be the lover of

Buck Brooke III. The next day I have another agenda and some other man. I'm sure you'll understand. To tell you the truth, you have begun to bore me. I bet we don't even have the same taste in music. Please, don't try to contact me. It's over between us. I'm sure you'll find someone your own age. Why not go back to Robert? He seems ever faithful. Don't forget to drop off that money to Don Bossdum. Rose had it gift wrapped—a cashier's check. He deserves it. Gotta go now. Love and kisses, Shelley."

Buck crushed the note in his hand.

***

Dust covered the American-built jeeps until their colors were completely obscured. Mounted on a swivel-head tripod at the rear of each jeep, machine guns faced the vastness of the desert, waiting for some unknown enemy to appear on the horizon.

Under the scorching sun, Rose stood as the finishing touches were applied by an Arab girl who wore a tight blouse and skirt. Instead of concentrating on Rose, she smiled invitingly at one of the cameramen. Rose sighed to herself in lament at how modesty had seemed to disappear from Arab women these days. Taking the brush from the girl's hand, she said, "God damn it, I'll do it myself."

Throughout the long hot hours, the relentless director had kept her and the crew working until her narration was "just perfect." She hadn't seen the film yet and, frankly, was grateful that her appearance in it had been limited to some introductory remarks. When she told the director of how she suffered in the heat, he reminded her of what she'd been paid. She shut up.

Surrounded by men in white robes and *keffiyeh*, she feared that in this inferno her makeup would run and distort her appearance on camera. To solve this problem, the director ordered two air-cooling machines to be blown on her for the next take. In her white Grecian gown, she imagined what she would look like on screen, her dress gently rippling in the winds. The air-cooling machines solved a lot of problems, including hot tempers.

The cooling breezes reminded her of last night when she'd slipped nude into the sparkling waters of the Red Sea. As she'd slowly cooled her overheated body, she'd seemed to wash away memories of Buck,

Palm Springs, even Shelley. Of all the thoughts troubling her mind, the one she wanted to obliterate was the memory of Shelley. How could things have gone so wrong?

Later in the evening, as she'd prepared herself to face the desert heat of the morning, she'd been all too aware that she didn't write the script any more. At dawn, she'd left the camp in a jeep. That bastard Calder had remained near the water, sitting under a Quonset hut on the beach in the company of two young girls.

Before the cameras again, she stood in front of a bleak-looking boulder, symbolizing the barren land. The glare from the mid-afternoon sun was so intense it created prismatic colors that reflected against her face. She hoped such brilliant light would remove any imperfections a cruel camera lens might pick up.

She sighed as she looked out at a "valley of the moon" landscape, in a setting of pink sands and distant black mountains.

A young man, Abdul, who'd been assigned to her as a bodyguard, had been unusually attentive all day. She'd welcomed the comfort of his presence. "After the shooting," he said, "you must come and see my town. It's a rose-colored city—just like your name." Abdul's dark, lusty eyes bored into her, thrilling her with their savagery. "My city is half as old as time."

"I feel as old as your city," she said, wanting to be contradicted.

"You're not old—you're young. A very beautiful lady."

She smiled at him, wondering if she should invite him inside her tent tonight. Shelley had been very wrong about her. She could still attract young men, without having to pay.

Sucking in the dry air, she rehearsed her dialogue—words familiar to her. "The Arab point of view is seldom heard in America. Evangelicals, in particular, avoid the subject. But the strong Zionist bloc in the United States should not affect Christian movements. We must keep our minds free to form our own opinion in a rapidly changing world."

The screeching whine of a helicopter passing directly over her head interrupted the filming, forcing the director to call "Cut!" It turned out to be Calder.

"Fuck you, Calder!" she yelled at him. "We almost had a perfect take."

In fifteen minutes, filming resumed. Only her words in the desert were heard: "Menachem Begin was once voted one of the most admired men in America. Yet this is the butcher who committed a stormtrooper-like atrocity on April 8, 1948, when he led bloodthirsty, revenging soldiers upon the small Arab village of Deier Yassin, near Jerusalem. On that infamous day, Begin and his hoodlums massacred 250 men, women and children. Menachem Begin, the perfect candidate for the Nobel Peace Prize!"

Calder smiled at her as if he were reviewing an honor guard marching for his inspection. These were his words anyway. This piece of information he had written surprised her. To her, Begin didn't look like a stormtrooper—more like a shopkeeper or the owner of a delicatessen.

"European Jews illegally confiscated and occupied Arab homes, even villages, where families had lived for centuries," she went on in a brave hope this was the final take. "There were no repatriations, no compensations for Arab losses. Fearing another Begin-led massacre, entire villages fled. The American Indian knows such atrocities well. The Jews who fled Hitler's Europe did so only to inflict the brutality they'd known there onto an innocent people. A terrible irony of history!"

Calder's presence was no longer visible. All she saw was a blur of white and orange, as she continued speaking in front of camera. "As a Christian woman, I am here in this Palestinian-held territory hoping to do my part to make right a grievous wrong. I want to bring righteousness, justice and mercy to this land of suffering, homeless people."

A shiver traveled the length of her body as she realized the repercussions she'd have to face back home for making such a propaganda film. In her cold fury, she silently cursed Calder for talking her into such a scheme. The bear's claw was at her throat—not his. Suddenly, her voice choked in that familiar strangulation.

The director seemed pleased and didn't stop the camera. It appeared as genuine concern for the people of Palestine.

She gasped for breath. Her throat was parched. "For too long, Christians have avoided getting involved in this conflict. Yet it is a conflict close to our hearts. It is our Holy Land. Ground that Christ walked upon. Just as I have sympathy for the Jews after the terrible Nazi Holocaust, so I have sympathy for the Palestinians upon whom the Jews have inflicted such suffering."

"Cut!" the director yelled. "That's it for today."

"That's it—for good!" she said. "Let me out of this hell-hole." As she stumbled toward her tent, she felt the strong arm of Abdul around her waist. In the desert heat, he sweated heavily. Far from offending, the smell attracted her. It was the smell of youth, of vigor, of freshness. She stayed close to him until they'd escaped into the darkness of her tent.

She shuddered as she turned to him. His skin was smooth and soft to her touch. His eyes held out such promise it filled her with a delirious kind of joy. "Don't ever leave me," came her desperate whisper in his ear.

***

In a favorite Palm Springs haunt of Sinatra's Rat Pack, Buck noted the eyes of interest cast at his table. He and Ahmad did make a stunning couple—he, the handsome blond hunk looking like a recruiting poster for the U.S. Marines, and Ahmad, his date, appearing as a beautifully gowned young lady of elegance and refinement, perhaps some oil-rich princess from a Middle East kingdom.

Ahmad possessed great beauty as a male, but as a woman was a stunning delight, with some of the flair and grace of Audrey Hepburn at her finest moments. He played the role so well that Buck felt even the sharpest eye couldn't detect that Ahmad was a man. Every trace of his manhood had been artfully concealed.

His makeup and hair were perfect—nothing overdone but with just the right amount of allure to be sexy and beautiful at the same time. Ahmad's perfect features, including a sensual mouth, were highlighted with the discreet use of makeup including pale mauve-colored lips.

As Buck studied that mouth intensely, he knew all to well what pleasure it could provide for a man. In the presence of Ahmad the woman, he felt he'd become straight again. When he was with Ahmad, his balls felt bigger than they were.

"You're staring," Ahmad said, smiling gently to soften the accusation. "But, of course, that's what it's all about. How can I complain that you haven't taken your eyes off me all night?"

Buck reached for Ahmad's hand, taking it caressingly and holding it to his lips for a soothing kiss. "Even now I can't believe what's happened."

"You mean my transformation into a woman?"

"That too. What I'm really thinking about is what you did to me all afternoon. I'm not exactly a virgin but I've never had sex like that in my life."

"I learned it in school," Ahmad said.

"You're joking."

"I actually did go to a school for sex. It's in Egypt. I decided early when I was a teenager that if I wanted to attract men, I'd have to learn to please them. At this school you learn techniques passed down by the ancients."

"You learned your lessons well," Buck said. "I can't wait for a repeat performance."

"There will be many more nights to come. After all, you are the husband I've waited for all my life."

"Aren't we going a bit fast here? I never proposed."

"You're not turning it down, are you?" Ahmad asked.

Buck smiled and took a sip from his drink. "The ring I'm wearing answers that."

"You're not marrying me for my money?" Ahmad asked.

"I guess you're not poor," Buck said.

"I don't even know how much money I have—an endless supply. As my husband, you'll not want for anything."

"What are you telling me?" Buck said.

"For openers, I'm going to give you a codeword and access to a numbered bank account. With the codeword, you can tap into all the money you want, should you—for example—decide to buy the Empire State Building, perhaps a less prominent building, an ocean-going yacht, whatever you want to buy. If I have overlooked something and didn't buy it for you already, then you're free to purchase it yourself."

"Awesome," Buck said.

"There will be so much more. What's the point in my acquiring all this money, if I can't enjoy spending some of it? Take our new Florida home. It's the largest and most splendid mansion in America. The one you wrote about in your paper."

"It is yours?" Buck asked.

"No, darling, it's ours. Whenever I can fly into Okeechobee, it will be ours. I've already left instructions that the place is yours to do with as you like whether I'm there or not."

"I've always wanted to see that mansion," Buck said.

"The estate is called Desire," Ahmad said. "I designed it myself as a love nest for my husband, long before I knew I'd find you."

"As soon as I get back to Florida, I'll go there," Buck said. "Will you accompany me through the gates?"

"I wish I could. I've got to leave early in the morning. I'll be out of touch for a few days but we'll schedule a rendezvous somewhere. Marriages like ours are the way relationships will be in the future. One will actually have to schedule an appointment to be with one's husband. In the meantime, I've assigned twelve bodyguards to you."

"Am I that precious?" Buck asked.

"To me, you are divine," Ahmad said.

"It'll be like I'm the president of the United States guarded by the Secret Service," Buck said.

"Who knows? You might be president one day. It's unlikely that Barry Collins will ever make it to the White House. We need to groom someone else. Barry and Shelley weren't discreet."

The mention of Shelley brought back the reality of that note. Buck reached into his breast pocket and retrieved Shelley's note, giving it to Ahmad to read.

Ahmad studied it carefully. "It could be genuine."

"Do you think I could see the boy?" Buck asked.

"I don't know where Shelley is," Ahmad said. "I never interfere in battles between Calder and Rose."

"I want to see him."

"I'll force them to arrange it if nothing else," Ahmad said. "It will take a few days. I'll be incommunicado for a while. As soon as I've re-emerged into the world, I will look into this matter."

"Are you jealous of Shelley and me?"

"A young boy should never interfere in the mature relationship of a man and woman like you and me."

"You are the most intriguing person I've ever met in my life," Buck said.

"You'll never meet another Ahmad. Life doesn't bestow blessings twice like this. So you'd better enjoy me while I'm here."

Buck slid closer to Ahmad. "You know what I want and want now."

"We're in a restaurant," Ahmad said demurely. "You men. So demanding."

The waiter appeared to take their food order. "I'm not too hungry," Buck said.

"Eat a steak," Ahmad ordered. "You'll need all your energy before we take our separate planes in the morning." He turned to the waiter. "I'll have a light green salad—hold the dressing—and my husband will have a T-bone, rare, with a baked potato and some broccoli."

"That sounds just great," Buck said after the waiter had left. "How did you know that's one of my favorite meals?"

"It was in your file. We've been keeping one on you for years." Ahmad raised his glass. "Let's toast our marriage."

"To our marriage," Buck said, raising his glass. He just knew he'd wake up tomorrow in some bleak California motel room and all this would be a dream.

***

Although Gene was shaking all over, he wasn't cold in the night's wind. Like white foam, a huge wave rose above his boat, a double-ended yawl with a black hull. His blood froze, and for a moment he was filled with fear. The wave seemed to seize the boat, making it rise. It crashed and shuddered to a halt until it lurched free. Hands locked to the wheel, he slumped over. God had saved him from being hurled into the watery grave.

Earlier that day he'd driven to Fort Lauderdale, where he kept his boat in a rundown marina. It had been his only luxury in life, and he'd lovingly cared for the vessel. Now the vessel had become more important to him than ever, a vital part of his plan.

His breathing grew more relaxed. The boat was still under him, still plowing over the water.

His eyes stung from the burning salt as the water slapped his face. A splintering flash of lightning cut across the sky, followed by an explosion of thunder. He should have listened to radio reports before impulsively taking the boat out. Or he should have returned to port earlier. Getting caught in a storm was the last stupid mistake he'd make.

Rose would soon return to Paradise Shores and when she did he'd drive with Barry to meet her. Barry hadn't wanted to take him along, but he'd demanded it. He tried to blot out the visions of expectation that drifted through his mind. She might not like him. He must not hope too much.

Though alone, he was comforted by the feeling that Rose was already at his side. The boat continued its wild gyrations and he took grim pleasure in this, knowing he had to protect not only himself, but her. As the sea fell on him unrelentingly, he took little notice of it. Not even the turbulent waters could alter him from his course.

It would be so easy to give in, abandoning the endless humiliation, allowing the sea to claim him. Perhaps that would come later. Not now when there was so much to do.

His sodden coat provided some protection from the wind. He wasn't cold because she was beside him, giving off warmth.

Another wave hit his boat, causing the bowsprit to rise menacingly in the white-capped sea. It pointed at the heavens and, in one flash, he imagined his ascending there. Then it fell with a crash, plowing back into the rain-lashed waters. Like a dipper, the boat scooped up gallons of the churning sea. Flood waters hurtled along the deck. He hadn't closed the hatch cover, another mistake.

His eyes still stung from the salt and his whole body ached from the strain of staring into the black frenzy. The shore line approached. He'd have to hold out a little longer. His nerves knotted tighter at the prospect of reaching the marina.

Bringing the boat back was a kind of triumph for him, letting him know that his nerves were steady enough to do the job ahead.

The lurching of the boat had made him sick at his stomach. As he got closer to shore, he noted how the full-throated roar of the wind had become just a faint cry. The boat rose and fell the way it had earlier in the evening, like an out-of-control elevator, madly going up and down.

Safely ashore, he took a taxi to a cheap apartment he'd rented in Fort Lauderdale under an assumed name. Inside the dank rooms, the smell was musty. He didn't bother to turn on the lights. Stripping, he toweled himself dry. The only sound in his bedroom was the hum of a ceiling fan and an occasional snore from the old man who lived next door. Sounds traveled easily through the thin walls. He'd slip in and out of the apartment. After the trauma with that little Cuban girl and her mother, he vowed never to let his new neighbors see him.

Under the bed he kept a rifle and an M-16 which he checked carefully. The M-16 had been shipped back from Vietnam, piece by piece, by a soldier Gene had known. He'd bought it from him. For some reason not clear to him, he'd had the vision to remove the weapons and store them in a locker at the Greyhound bus station. He'd visited the weapons frequently, not only to see that the locker fee was paid up, but to check on them. It seemed a miracle to him that he'd had the foresight to remove the weapons because they would have been destroyed in the fire that swept across his home. It was as if God had intended for him to keep these weapons.

He lay in silence, waiting, too excited to rest. He fell asleep with exhaustion but woke to the voice of the old man next door. It was morning. The man chased two gray alley cats from the garbage can.

He knew Sandy and Jill might be worried about him. No doubt they'd think he had spent the entire night at the home of Barry Collins. They were never to know of this secret place.

Returning to his womb-like room had safely cradled Gene. He felt sealed like a royal mummy for the long voyage ahead.

***

Arriving at the airport, Buck was informed that Ahmad had flown a private jet to Palm Springs to pick Buck up and take him to Okeechobee. Buck felt foolish boarding the plane with a flank of security guards. It was as if overnight he'd become a potentate. Before mounting the stairs to the plane, he looked once more at the ring Ahmad had given him. In some way, that ring symbolized that he'd become Ahmad's property.

The chief security guard, a handsome, blond-haired Norwegian, Lars Hensen, welcomed Buck aboard. "Your companion is in the main suite. He's asking for you."

"My God, he's come back to me. You mean the one with the blond curls?"

"That's the one," Lars said.

"Then the note was a cruel joke," Buck said.

"I don't know about any note, sir."

Ignoring him, Buck fast-stepped his way to the back of the plane. He entered the darkened suite, shutting the door behind him and locking it. In the dim light, he saw Shelley's blond curly head lying on a pillow.

"You didn't leave me after all," Buck said. "I knew your note was a lie. I love you, Shelley."

The figure rose from the bed and turned on the bedside lamp. Slowly he removed his blond curly wig. Robert's own blond hair emerged from under the wig.

Buck stared into Robert's face, not believing he'd been aboard the plane. So much for Ahmad's security check. Turning his back at the sight of Robert, he went over to the bar to pour himself a drink.

"What did you just say? I love you...*Shelley*?" Robert said, mocking his words. "You've betrayed me."

Still not looking at him, Buck belted down a strong dose of alcohol. "So you know."

"All my life I've been faithful to you," Robert said. "I've never looked at another man. Look how you rewarded that trust."

As he took in Robert's features, Buck couldn't understand how he'd ever loved him, much less married him. All feelings of love had vanished. He wasn't staring into the sophisticated face of Ahmad who'd understand sexual indiscretions with the wisdom of the ages. If anything, Robert appeared to have become a shrill of a nagging wife.

"Don't you have anything to say to me?" Robert asked.

"I didn't mean to fall in love with Shelley," Buck said. "A lot of good it did me. He's left me."

"That's the first good news I've heard all day." He sat up in bed, revealing his golden chest which had brought such pleasure to Buck in the past. He gazed at Buck's hand. "I see you've acquired another ring, not just our wedding band. You've even got your own personal security guard. Lars thinks I'm still your boy."

"All right, I've cheated on you, and I've fallen for another guy. What do you want from me? I'll give you anything within reason."

"I want your complete commitment to me," Robert said.

"That's more than I can deliver." Buck downed the rest of his drink. "I'll give you money. The only thing I can't promise is myself."

"You just said the little brat left you."

"I married you too soon," Buck said. "Hell, I only came out of the closet yesterday. Before I started sucking cock, I thought I was straight. Straight maybe with a gay streak. I'm not ready to settle down to a domestic life in Okeechobee."

"Are you sure you're not a hustler?" Robert said. "You've suddenly got a private plane, security guards. Who pays for all this?"

Buck suddenly realized that he absolutely didn't want to be with Robert for the rest of the flight home. He wanted to retreat to the other suite, there to dream about carrying out Ahmad's plans for their Hollywood debut. "You'll find a man worthy of you. I'm a two-timing bastard, not worthy of you."

"It's not too late." Robert slowly removed the sheet from his nude body. "You can come over here and reclaim me."

Buck closed his eyes, not wanting to take in the sight of Robert's body. "I don't feel well. I've got to go to my own cabin."

"This is your cabin," Robert protested.

"I'll go somewhere else," Buck said. He turned and walked quickly to the door. He shut it behind him, emerging into the relative freedom of the communal area of the plane. At the plane's bar, he confronted Lars. "I've had a fight with my companion," he told Lars. "I don't want to see him for the rest of the flight. I'll be in the other suite."

Buck headed for his cabin, knowing that in the last five minutes just played out with Robert, he'd changed his entire life.

Chapter Thirteen

It was not the homecoming Buck envisioned. A driver was waiting at the airport in a limousine. Sitting near the window, Robert remained sullen on the way home. Once in the house, he headed for his own private suite which he'd never used before.

After Robert had gone upstairs, the new Cuban maid, Clara, came into the parlor and asked Buck if he wanted anything.

He declined, resenting her presence in his household. He was angry at Robert for hiring her in the first place. It seemed like a deliberate betrayal of Gene. As she turned to leave, he called back to her. "Stay out of the pool area. I want to go for a nude swim."

"I've seen you American men nude before," Clara said.

"I'm sure you have," Buck said, "but I didn't want to have you calling the police to have me arrested for indecent exposure."

Clara only glared at him before stalking toward the kitchen. Regardless of what Robert said, Buck was going to fire her the moment he got back from Switzerland. Pouring himself a drink, he dialed Susan.

She picked up the phone right away. "My errant husband returns. How did it go?"

"I brought back all the gold in California. Winter's coming. How many furs do you want?"

"I've already found something to keep me warm," she said.

"Uncle Milty told me. Don Bossdum. Not bad. All America. What a catch. All the girls were after him in college."

"You mean the ones not stalking you and Gene?"

"Yeah, those." He hesitated a moment. "I'm calling about our wedding pictures. The announcements to the press. Stuff like that. I'm flying to Switzerland soon to see the old man. Could we get this done tomorrow morning around noon?"

"I'll arrange everything," she said. "Could you come to the condo around ten thirty in the morning? I should be back from the beauty parlor then. I want to look gorgeous when I'm photographed announcing my marriage to Florida's handsomest and richest man—not to mention the sexiest stud alive."

"I'm sure that honor should go to football-playing Don."

"He isn't as handsome as you."

"Flattery will get you everywhere," Buck said.

"I doubt that," she said with just a ring of sarcasm in her voice.

"See you in the morning, love." He hung up and headed for his balcony overlooking his gardens and fountains. As wonderful as they looked to him, he was daydreaming about what the gardens and fountains at Ahmad's Desire looked like. Just as soon as he could slip away, he planned to have his chauffeur drive him to his new home.

As he made his way across the veranda, he spotted five of Lars's men on the grounds of the property next door.

Lars appeared out of nowhere. "I'm sorry, I haven't secured your property yet. All of us are installed in the mansion next door."

"How in the hell did you arrange that?" Buck asked.

"Ahmad knows how to get things done from afar," Lars said.

"That house is even bigger than this one," Buck said. "I've always envied it."

"It's yours," Lars said.

"What do you mean?" Buck asked.

"Before he left America, Ahmad acquired it for you. After all, my security force needs a place in which to operate. We need bedrooms, stuff like that."

"What happened to the Markums?" Buck said. "They've devoted their lives to restoring and furnishing that place with antiques and paintings. That super rich bitch Pat Markum is a collector from hell. She always put us to shame."

"They left with only their clothing," Lars said. "Everything is still intact, furnishings, paintings, everything. It's yours now. Ahmad made them an offer they couldn't refuse providing they'd evacuate the house within six hours. We're still packing up their things." Lars looked at Buck enigmatically, a smile breaking across his handsome Nordic face. "Please come over tonight or as soon as you can and take a grand tour."

"It's a deal," Buck said. "But the property I really want to see is Desire."

"The limo is waiting to take you there any time you say. I'll go with you. I know the place well. All its secrets."

At sundown Buck raced across the lawn to the Markum estate, as evening shadows fell. His mother had a long ago feud with Mrs. Markum—they'd once been friends—and he'd never set foot on the neighboring estate since he was thirteen. Feeling like an intruder, he appeared on the veranda of the Gothic-style manor. At any minute he expected Mrs. Markum to appear and chase him off her property.

As he approached the door, it was thrown open by Lars himself. "Welcome, lord of the manor."

"Thanks," was all he could manage to say. Standing in the foyer, he was overcome by the grandeur of the mansion. Since he'd last seen it, Mrs. Markum had looted more of the showcases of Europe. It was a house filled with *objets d'art* from all over the world.

"I have an inventory from the appraiser," Lars said.

"Later," Buck said. "I just want to take everything in."

"Many of her paintings are minor, although worthy of display in a minor museum," Lars said. "However, she sold us eight world-class masterpieces. Munch. El Greco."

"I want to wander about on my own," Buck said, "then look at every item individually. I think I've died and gone to heaven."

"You have," Lars said. "Ahmad is incredibly generous. Wait until you see Desire."

Long after he'd finished his own tour and then a closer inspection with Lars explaining what each item was, Buck settled into a sofa on the veranda in the rear overlooking the garden. When he used to come here with his mother, he was more interested in the tennis courts and swimming pool, both bigger than his own. "I'm impressed," Buck told Lars, who poured him a Scotch. "I can't believe this is all mine. A bit conservative and traditional, but fabulous."

"That little table in the tiny foyer off the hallway is worth $175,000 alone," Lars said. "Where did she get all the money?"

"Before he retired, her husband was in steel, but she had her own money. She was an heiress. Her father once owned huge real estate in North Miami Beach which he sold off. They could afford anything they wanted, and they were world class shoppers."

Lars looked around him. "Obviously."

"When will I see Ahmad again?" Buck asked.

"He will just suddenly appear out of nowhere without warning.

I'm almost certain you will see him within six days. He's never gone more than a week or so at a time. He spends all his time in airplanes—his own."

"I can't wait to see him again?" Buck said, smiling. "I owe him so much."

"While you're waiting for Ahmad, if I can be of any assistance, I'm here for you." Lars leaned over and kissed Buck gently on the lips.

"Later," Buck promised. It was an empty promise but not that empty.

***

Crossing through the gardens with Lars, heading back to the Brooke house, Buck stopped near the gazebo. Lars too came to a halt, watching as Robert walked across the back veranda and headed for the driveway that led to the end of the property near a back street, Carroll Place. At first Buck thought he was going to the garage. It seemed unlikely Robert was going for a walk.

After he'd passed them, Lars whispered to Buck. "We know all about where he's going if you're interested."

"I want to know," Buck said.

"I don't want you to think we're interfering in your private life," Lars said. "But we're checking everything that remotely involves you in case of a threat to your security. Your phone is tapped. Robert is meeting Gene Robinson. A little ironic I would say. Your wife's first husband."

"Surely you're wrong." Buck felt his own heart beating.

"They agreed on the rendezvous late this afternoon," Lars said. "He's walking three blocks from your house. Robinson is waiting in a car for him on a side street."

"But Robert hates Gene—always has," Buck said.

"We could tell from the conversation, this hot and torrid affair has been going on for a few days at least," Lars said. "Do you want to hear the tapes?"

"No way," Buck said. "I can't believe this." He headed toward his house. "I want to pick up some things and then I'm headed for Desire."

Three hours later Lars had delivered him to the gates of Desire. In many ways, it was like the mansion in Palm Springs, with the same fountains and painted nude statuary, only a much more gargantuan version. It was not really a home but some giant museum, although there were pockets of comfort everywhere. It looked like no one had ever lived here or could ever live here. Wherever the eye peered, there was splendor, art and antiques from all over the world. The gigantic pool, the largest he'd ever seen, was surrounded by Carrara marble replicas of antiquity's most famous statuary. Alabaster globe lamps created the illusion of moonlight. Marble colonnades stretched down to the sea.

In the center of the garden was a large domed movie theater. In one part of the garden a Chinese Teahouse had been erected with a tiny railroad constructed to ferry footmen bearing tea from the main house. The gardens captured his heart. He felt he could live in them forever. They were dotted with gingerbread gazebos and fountains lit at night to color the water displays. The bronze statuary competed with the marble nudes, and there was an amazing variety of shrubs and trees, and seemingly endless sunken courtyards.

The kitchen looked like it could serve one thousand guests with no problem. The wine cellar seemed to stretch across the state. Each bedroom was decorated differently but all in luxurious taste, with the finest of silks.

In the center of one gigantic enclosed courtyard was a 23-karat gold coronation coach seemingly having no purpose in being here and no place to ride. One part of the mansion was modeled after the Petit Trianon at Versailles. It contained the most ornate gilt-encrusted ballroom Buck had ever seen.

The main dining room was dominated by a Sienna marble fireplace outlined in opalescent Tiffany brick tiles. The bronze chairs at the fifty-foot-long table looked too heavy to be lifted. The paneling was mahogany. But, Lars assured him, the ceiling was pure gold.

Back in the main foyer Buck was struck by the multicolored marbles used throughout, the arched double loggia, and the mosaic ceilings. The music room, Lars said, had been constructed in Austria and shipped here for reassembly. The billiard room was in gray-green marble, yellow alabaster, and mahogany.

"Even in the Gilded Age, robber barons didn't live this well," Buck said. "I've had enough for one night, and it's getting late. I think I could live here a year and always discover something new."

"Ahmad always claims the place is smaller than it is," Lars said. "I think he says there are sixty-two rooms, something like that. Don't hold me to it. Actually, I counted them one day. There are one-hundred and ten rooms."

"It's a fantasy house," Buck said. "Do I have a bedroom here?"

"The choice is yours," Lars said.

Buck's first night at Desire had begun. He knew it would not be the last.

***

Robert had the world's gentlest hands, as they caressed Gene's body as Gene pounded into him. Slowly and lovingly Robert's fingers traced the contours of Gene's back goading him on. One had traveled even lower, cupping the heavy globes hanging between Gene's legs. Robert gently squeezed them, spurring Gene to more intense action. Robert was chewing on Gene's left nipple, pulling with his teeth at the little tufts of hair there. Ending that action, Robert licked Gene's chest. Kissing his chin, Robert moved his lips to Gene's left ear. "You're all man," he said between gasps. "I've never known a man like you before. You're the best."

Robert might as well have finished his statement. "Better than Buck." That's obviously what he meant, and Gene knew that. These were words he wanted to hear.

Even though Gene was only in the middle of his attack on Robert, he suddenly buckled his body as Gene's balls bounced against his ass. He bellowed and blew a thick shot of jizz up over Gene's torso and onto the motel bed where they bounced.

Gene pumped him harder, knowing he was reaching all the right targets. Robert was completely under Gene's spell. "Don't stop," Robert whispered in his ear. "I've never felt anything this good."

"Jesus," Gene cried out. His body shook as he poured what seemed like liquid fire into Robert. He wrapped his arms around Robert and pulled him close to his chest, covering the top of his head with passionate kisses. He cradled Robert against his heaving chest before collapsing on him. "I could stay inside you for the rest of the night," he whispered into Robert's ear.

Robert's mouth blindly sought Gene's. Their tongues dueled, and Gene felt a pleasurable jolt he'd never known before. Robert had awakened a side of Gene he never knew existed. Robert brought an intensity to love-making he'd never captured with Buck. Gene thought Buck was his peak experience. That was no longer true.

A half hour later, Gene took delight in soaping Robert's smooth skin, as Robert lathered Gene's own muscular body.

Over an early morning breakfast in the motel coffee shop, Gene leaned over and asked Robert, "Why did Buck hire Clara and Maria after what they'd done to me?"

Robert's face looked startled for a minute as if caught unaware, then a grim look appeared. "He did it to humiliate you. I don't know why but Buck wants you destroyed. If he finds out I've fallen for you, then it will be really bad."

"I think you're right. He's turned on me." He reached for Robert's hand which was willingly extended. "There's not much future for me in this town. I've got to get out."

"I'll help you but I need a few weeks," Robert said. "Buck has betrayed me too, and I want revenge. It's payback time. At first I was going to hang on to him making every day of his life miserable. After falling in love with you, I have another plan. I'm going to take him for every cent I can get out of the bastard."

"God, I hate his ass," Gene said.

"Will you go away with me?" Robert asked, squeezing Gene's hand all the harder.

"You don't have to ask," Gene said. "I'm your man."

"I knew from the moment I smelled you in the garden," Robert said, "you were there to rape me. It was as if I'd spent an entire life waiting for the right man."

Gene liked hearing that. Buck might have all the money and power in the world, but Gene knew he was the better man. Robert was the best source to judge. It was ironic. Buck had married his former wife, and now he was going to run away with Buck's "wife."

All Gene's life he had wanted to take something away from Buck and now his chance was at hand. Gene rose from the table, motioning for Robert to follow him. Robert belonged to him. He'd taken him from Buck.

The day was his.

***

On the elevator to Susan's condo, Buck carried a cashier's check for one-hundred thousand dollars to pay off Don Bossdum, compliments of Shelley and Rose. At some point he'd slip the money to Don when Susan was distracted elsewhere. Considering the five-million dollars Leroy was demanding, Don's request seemed modest. At the door to Susan's condo, Buck rang the bell.

In moments the door was hesitantly opened but only a crack. "That you, Buck?" Don asked, peering out. "Come on in."

Inside the apartment, Don smiled as he greeted Buck. "Forgive me, I just got out of the shower and haven't had a chance to put on my bikini briefs."

"Great to see you again, Don," Buck said with all the enthusiasm he could muster. "I just didn't expect to see so much of you."

"What you see is what you get," Don said, walking over to the serving bar to pour Buck some coffee.

"I once invited you for a beer," Buck said. "You turned me down but I guess I can accept a drink from you even if it's only coffee."

"I can explain that," Don said apologetically, handing Buck his coffee black. He just seemed to know Buck didn't take cream or sugar. "I was fucked up in the head back then. I know a lot more about myself now. Why don't you extend the invite for a beer tonight? See what I'd say now."

Ignoring him and looking around the condo, Buck asked, "Where's Susan?"

"She's still at the beauty parlor. She called just a little while ago. She'll be here any minute now."

Don sat across from Buck, raising one bare leg and putting it on the sofa, giving Buck an even clearer view of the ample load suspended between his legs.

"Before Susan gets here, I have to tell you that Rose gave me the one-hundred thousand dollars you wanted. It's a cashier's check. Made out to you for the right amount. It looks like you and I have changed partners. You've got my wife now, and I've switched to Shelley. At least until recently. He's written me a Dear John letter."

"Shelley—that whore—was always good at French leave," Don said, getting up and taking the check from Buck. As he studied it, his equipment dangled only inches from Buck's face. He returned to his seat but made no attempt to get dressed. "I'm sorry you found out about this. Please don't let Susan know."

"She'll not hear it from me," Buck said.

"Thanks. I'll owe you one. You name the time and place."

"Thanks, but no thanks," Buck said. "I've got a full agenda."

At the sound of a key in the door, Don bolted for the bathroom to get dressed.

When Susan came into the apartment, Buck got up to welcome her, kissing her on the mouth.

"Welcome back from California," she said. "We've kept the home fires burning."

"You look really nice," he said, admiring her tasteful hair-do. "But it's gilding on the lily. You're a natural beauty. You don't need fancy hair-dos."

"You're too kind." She danced around in front of him playfully. "Is this the right outfit?"

"It's something Jackie might have worn for an appearance with JFK."

"I guess that's a compliment." She looked around the apartment. "Where's Don?"

"He's getting dressed to come with us." He noted a look of suspicion in her face. "I just got here."

"I see."

When Don came out fully dressed in a blue suit, he rushed to Susan, kissed her on the mouth, then picked her up off the floor and whirled her around. "You look terrific."

"She always looks terrific," Buck said, as Don put her down. "I want to introduce you as the dude who was my best man at the wedding. You know, former U.S. marine marrying beauty queen. All America football hero as best man. It's best to give people images they can deal with."

***

Without explaining to Uncle Milty what his plan was, Buck asked to be driven to Sun City, a failed real-estate development opening onto the water forty miles from Okeechobee. Lars got in the front seat, and Uncle Milty crawled into the back with Buck so they could talk privately.

"You made one handsome groom," Uncle Milty said. "I saw the wedding pictures."

"By that, I guess you mean my first conventional wedding," Buck said. "To Susan, not my marriage to Robert."

"Robert has called me," Milty said. "He's not the Robert I have known. Someone different. Demanding, aggressive, he wants a cool five million. Or else..." Uncle Milty paused. "Or else he's threatening a palimony suit."

"The fuck!" Buck said. "I never thought Robert would do this to me."

"I think I can maneuver him down," Milty said. "When he turns, I turn on him."

"I know where he got the idea of five million," Buck said. "That's the exact figure Leroy is demanding in blackmail from Calder and Barry." Buck sighed, sinking back into the luxurious upholstery of his new Blackhawk. "He's been loyal up until now. He deserves something. I don't know how to come up with a dollar amount. If anything, I'm relieved. Robert was smothering me to death. He's just solved that problem for me."

"Five-million dollars is a lot of money," Milty said.

"I don't want him to have it all at once. We'll sign contracts. Pay him so much a year. A trust fund. It's his new lover I don't trust. I think it's because of his new lover that Robert is making these demands. Suddenly he needs money."

"What in hell are you talking about?" Milty said. "New lover?"

"Gene Robinson."

"The most unlikely coupling on the globe," Milty said.

When the driver reached Sun City, Uncle Milty and Buck went for a walk on a nearby hill overlooking the development. It looked ghostly. The developers had gone belly up, and the project had been abandoned before it was half finished. Gaping condos without windows greeted them at every turn.

"Don't tell me you want to take over this project?" Uncle Milty asked.

"You've got it," Buck said. "For openers I'll move in all those poor souls losing their homes on the beach. You know, in Hazel's neighborhood."

"You can't afford it although you could pick up Sun City for a song," Milty said. "You'd have to have the money to develop it and see it through."

"I think I can afford it," Buck said.

"Not with what you got from the sale of the *Examiner*, especially if you acquire the *News*."

"Rose chases out the Jews," Buck said. "I find homes for them. Isn't that a butt-grabber?"

Buck walked over to the edge of the hill and looked at the abandoned project. He closed his eyes and looked again. In the glaringly bright light of the Florida sun, a city had miraculously emerged before his eyes.

"I guess you didn't hear me," Milty said. "You can't afford it."

With twinkling eyes, Buck turned and faced him squarely. "Believe me, I can afford it. You're my lawyer. We've got to talk. It's about time you learned what your favorite boy has been up to."

***

Word reached Buck at Desire that Rose had slipped back into town unannounced. Buck ordered Lars to arrange a private meeting.

Lars got back to him at once. Rose had agreed to the meeting but it was not to be at Paradise Shores. Their meeting was to be aboard her yacht. Buck was to take his own smaller yacht out to see and meet her offshore. His yacht was to pull up alongside her own, at which time he was to come aboard.

As Buck headed for the shower to get ready for his meeting at sea with Rose, Lars handed him a note from Robert.

"Dear Buck,

With Uncle Milty's permission, I am going to temporarily stay on your island. You note I said your island and not our island as I used to. Your offer of your home in town was very generous but I must decline. I plan to leave Okeechobee and all its memories of you. I feel you have betrayed me on a very serious level, and I don't find it in my heart to forgive you. I'm sure Uncle Milty has told you of my financial de-

mands. I am taking you at your word—that you are going to be very generous. I have devoted a considerable amount of my life to you, and I expect to be fully compensated. If you were still making forty-five thousand dollars a year, I would not make such demands on you. But you now have millions, and I fully expect more millions are in your future. Although my demands may be excessive, or appear that way, they are but a small amount taken from your bag of gold. I hope you will not resist giving in to my requests. I feel I have earned the money I'm asking. Please do not contact me on the island or come here to see me. I will use old Buck's yacht to get to the island. I hope you don't mind. Uncle Milty said it was okay. You have even destroyed my friendship with Patrick. Now that I am threatening to expose you in a palimony law suit, he doesn't want to have anything else to do with me. His obvious loyalty is to you because of your connection with Uncle Milty. Patrick knows which side of his bread is buttered. I've wasted no time giving my heart to another person in the wake of your betrayal. I am truly in love with this person. I used to think I was in love with you. But I didn't know what true love was. I know that now. I view my involvement with you as a sick schoolgirl crush. Please give me my money as soon as possible so I can leave Florida and you behind me.

Robert."

At the pier, the door to his limousine was opened by his driver. Beside Buck's own rather small yacht was a sailing ship of impressive size.

Lars took Buck's hand and guided him not to his own yacht but to the ship nearby. "Ahmad has a present for you."

Buck looked at the ship in astonishment. "You mean this is mine?"

"Ahmad has just had it completely redone," Lars said.

Buck stood looking in awe at the sleek ship.

"It's called *Mandalay*," Lars said. "Before that it was called *Mein Kampf*. It used to be one of the most famous and luxurious ships in the world. When it was built by the arms baron, Alfred Krupp, it was the only armor-plated sailing vessel in the world. Its armaments influenced the outcome of the Franco-Prussian War of 1870. Hitler once came aboard to award the Iron Cross to one of its U-boat commanders. The United States seized it as war booty in 1945, and it was eventually sold to George Vanderbilt as a private yacht. It became the fastest two-masted sailing vessel off the California coast. It once managed an almost frightening 22 knots under full sail. Come aboard."

Feeling like a schoolboy with his first car, Buck came aboard. Lars introduced Buck to the captain and the rest of the crew.

After greeting them, Buck went to look over the railing, as the captain started the vessel, heading for a rendezvous with Sister Rose. "I've got to see Ahmad," Buck said privately to Lars. "He just steps into my life, gives me the world, and then disappears."

"Don't worry. Ahmad will be back with you soon. But I have to tell you, he's afraid you don't really love him. He hopes to shower you with extravagant gifts so you'll never lose interest in him, especially now that he's getting a bit older."

"He doesn't have to do all this." Buck surveyed the ship and all its splendor. "But I'm glad he does. First, letting me turn Desire into my home. Now *Mandalay*."

Ahmad has other yachts, but he wanted you to have this one in your own name. It's so very special—even historic. He knows you're a real sailor, and he thought you'd appreciate it."

"Appreciate it! I love it! You tell Ahmad to get his ass back to me real soon if he really wants it fucked. Before meeting up with Sister Rose, let's go on a tour. I'm dying to see everything."

Later, when *Mandalay* had anchored next to Rose's ocean-going yacht, Buck with Lars and two security guards crossed a hastily assembled drawbridge connecting the two vessels. He really wanted their rendezvous to take place aboard his new toy, *Mandalay*, but Rose had wanted to see him aboard her own yacht.

"She's in her suite," the captain of her yacht said. "She wants you to come there."

Buck headed below. An attendant in a rose jacket showed him to the door to Rose's cabin. The attendant knocked lightly, opened the door, and invited Buck in.

With a slight trepidation, Buck entered the sumptuous suite, all decorated in various shades of rose. Emerging from her bathroom, Rose rushed to him and threw her arms around him. He held her tightly, kissing her long and hard.

"I've missed you," she said. "I don't think I could go another day without being in your arms."

He broke away from her and looked around her cabin. "I think I need a drink."

She quickly called the attendant and ordered drinks sent down. "You may wonder why all the secrecy," she said. "Meeting at sea."

"I was wondering," he said, turning around to face her, as she kissed him several times on the lips. "Ahmad ordered it. He doesn't want you seen at Paradise Shores and doesn't want you to appear with me at all during the next few weeks. A lot of shit is about to happen, and he doesn't want you connected with it. I know all about what he wants you to accomplish for him in Hollywood. He wants you to arrive there looking clean as a hound's tooth and not involved in any of the political crap I have contracted for." She stood back, looking at him with a steely eyed appraisal. "You're not going to become my media director after all. That meeting with Ahmad must have gone very successfully. Instead of becoming my media director, you're going to be his media director."

"He told you that?" Buck said.

"That and other things." At a discreet knock on the door, Rose went and opened it, ushering the attendant in with the drinks.

After he had left, Buck took a hefty swig of his drink before turning to Rose again. "What's happened to Shelley? I don't think he wrote that note to me." She sighed and sat down on a luxurious sofa covered in rose-colored Thai silk. "I've already spoken to Ahmad about this. Whether Calder and I think it wise or not, Ahmad demands that you be allowed to see Shelley."

"Have Calder's goons beaten him up?" Buck asked. He noticed tears welling in her eyes.

"It's all very complicated," she said. "Shelley had to be detained. We used to be able to handle domestic disputes like this without Ahmad. Now you've involved him."

"God damn it, we're talking about your son. My lover. I have to hear it from Shelley's own mouth that he doesn't want to see me again."

"The Shelley you're going to meet isn't the Shelley you knew," she said.

"Calder has done something to him?" Buck asked.

"Calder had to intervene. As much as I hated sending Shelley away, I knew it was in my own best interests."

"Where is Shelley?" Buck asked.

"In my chalet outside St. Moritz."

"How convenient," he said. "I'm flying to Switzerland to see old Buck. He's dying. I'll be in the same country."

"I'll arrange it through Lars for you to see him if you insist."

"Set it up," Buck demanded.

"Consider it done," she said, disguising a certain hostility in her voice.

Another knock on the door, and Lars entered. "You've got an urgent message," he said to Buck, ignoring Rose. "Your grandfather's had a heart attack in Geneva. His doctors want you to come at once."

"I've got to go," Buck said, putting down his drink and turning to Rose."

"He's in a coma," Lars said. "They think he may never come out of it."

"I'll join you in a minute," Buck said. Lars turned and left.

When she looked up at Buck, she appeared lost, needing his company and dreading his leaving. "I was so hoping you could be with me tonight."

"I can't stay. The old man is very important to me."

"He's dying. I'm alive. We're alive."

He looked imploringly into her eyes. "I can't stay."

She got up from the sofa and called the attendant to bring her another drink.

"I'll call you frequently," he said. "I've heard rumors about some march. A controversial dedication. Hazel's spreading a lot of shit, and it sounds like big trouble for you."

"It will be," she said, as if hopelessly assigned to the task. "So sorry you won't be here. Even if you were, Ahmad wouldn't let you appear by my side. He fears the contamination. Did you think this would ever happen to me? That I would sell out to the point where merely appearing by my side could contaminate another person?"

"I can only imagine the dreadful games you're playing."

"You're playing the same dreadful games," she said. "You're getting—or at least will get—far greater rewards than me, but you're not out there on the front line taking the heat like I am. I'll be the victim of hatemongers—even a potential assassin. You'll go to Hollywood and start spending Ahmad's millions and will be the toast of the town. It doesn't seem fair somehow."

"Maybe it's not and you've got a point. But then I wouldn't sign on for your particular duties."

"Surely your darling Uncle Milty has cashed Ahmad's checks for the sale of the *Examiner*," she said. "Isn't that all the money you'll ever need? But, like me, you're seeking even more money and power as Ahmad's boy. If you want money, you've hooked up with the right sugar daddy. Ahmad has millions he hasn't even counted yet. I know how he got much of that money but somehow I don't think I'll get around to telling you."

"My time is up," he said, glancing nervously at his watch.

"Let's have our embrace here away from prying eyes," she said.

He took her in his arms, kissing her long and hard, wishing it could be any number of other people he was kissing. She clung to him, clawing into his back. He'd never seen her this desperate before. He broke away.

"Oh, God," she called out. "I may never see you again."

The words were delivered to his back, as he turned and was walking out the door.

Aboard the *Mandalay*, he stood on deck, surveying the calm sea. As he looked back at her yacht, he saw her standing on her own deck, her white gown billowing in the wind. She looked like a ghostly figure, not real somehow.

Was this the last time he'd ever see her? He shuddered in the wind before going below.

Chapter Fourteen

Once again in the comfort of Paradise Shores, Rose settled back in her favorite armchair covered in a silk upholstery of red roses. Looking across at a nervous Barry, she could never imagine why she'd ever been attracted to him. Of course, he was extraordinary handsome and had a great body, except for his penis. It was just too small, hardly enough to satisfy a woman who had known Don Bossdum and Buck Brooke III.

If he didn't have to take off his clothes and perform, he might be the kind of guy you could look at. He was pretty enough to be a fashion model. It seemed that women he met on the campaign trail were awed by his male beauty. In fact, she'd rank him as the handsomest male she'd ever seen go into politics. John Kennedy wasn't handsome. Barry Collins was handsome. With the passing months, he'd drifted away from her bed, and she was hardly anxious to invite him back. On their last encounter, if she recalled, he was unable to get an erection. Barry had been more successful getting an erection for Shelley than for her.

At first she'd never known of Barry's interest in young boys. She once said that Barry Collins was probably the only certifiably straight man in Okeechobee. How wrong she'd been on that call.

Although he'd not been her most ardent lover, he'd always been persistent and convincing, at least back in the days when he courted her support. She realized belatedly that he'd been no more than a hustler, perhaps regarding making love to her as a distasteful duty. He obviously liked his bodies much younger. As he rambled on about the mayoral campaign, she didn't listen. She knew and he knew what the real purpose of this meeting was. It was about those photographs and her coming up with five million to pay off the blackmailer, Leroy Fitzgerald. She studied his face instead. There had been almost no changes—perhaps a small line she'd never known before. He was incredibly photogenic. If any man could win an election on looks alone, it was Barry Collins, particularly when his opponent was ugly, fat Hazel.

Sitting here studying him closely, she realized she'd definitely picked the wrong man to run for mayor against her sister. This man was weak and indecisive and his wife, Pamela, was definitely a bomb waiting to explode. Yet she knew she was locked into Barry and had to ride out the campaign with him.

She decided to interrupt him. "Cut the shit! I don't care about what TV ads you plan to run. I'm only interested in one thing. The five-million dollars needed to pay off this cocksucking blackmailer. I love how you and Calder have just determined that I am to come up with all the money."

"I just don't have it. You know I'm not a rich man."

"I know what you've got." She looked at his crotch. "Or don't have."

"Okay, so I'm not Buck Brooke III with his endowment...and millions."

"Nor will you ever be. I don't know why Shelley ever took up with you. He usually likes studs."

"He thought I was very handsome. Please stop this. It's humiliating to have to come here and beg you for money."

"You call five-million dollars money. That's not money. That's a fortune!"

"I will be ruined if Leroy goes public with those pictures," Barry said. "But the backlash on you will be tremendous. The whole world will know that your darling Shelley isn't the innocent cherub you've made him out to be. When you arrive majestically in your pulpit, they'll boo you off the stage. They don't give a fuck about your licking Arab ass. Your Born Again Christians hate Jews too. That won't harm you at all. The only thing that drives those fuckers ballistic is homosexuality."

"You don't have to tell me what the damage will be," she said.

"I made a mistake and I'm sorry."

"She rang a glass bell resting on an end table, summoning a woman servant to bring her a strong drink. She didn't bother to offer Barry one. When the servant had gone, she turned to Barry, her face in deep distress. "I may have to buy myself out of this trap you've set for me."

"Say yes. It's for both our sakes."

"If I do it, it will be to save my own beautiful skin. I couldn't care less if Calder threw you to the sharks tomorrow." When her drink arrived, Rose took a hefty swallow. "How's Pamela?"

A pained look came over his face. She was all too aware of the rumors that Pamela had deserted the campaign and disappeared. He tried to change the subject. "You don't like Pamela, do you? Do you think it better if I get a divorce and marry some woman the public would find more acceptable?"

"Calder will have to decide that," she answered. "I was misled by Pamela. She's right pretty, a little overweight. Her clothes are too frilly. Like an aging woman trying to recapture her university days. That we could deal with. We could always hire a stylist for the bitch. It's her tongue that bothers me. The only thing that would stop it is to cut it out!"

He got up and walked the floor, circling her chair in a nervous way. "Look, this whole fucking thing is about to blow up in my face. Instead of becoming mayor, I could be ruined."

She stood up and confronted him. "Where is Pamela? I don't buy this bullshit about her being sick."

"She's visiting some relatives out of state," he said.

"If you're going into politics, you've got to lie better than that," she said.

"Okay, God damn it, I don't know where the bitch is. She ran off."

"I think what you're trying to tell me is that any day you'll be getting Pamela's demands for millions," she said.

"That won't happen, I can assure you."

"Listen, faggot, and listen good. You bring Pamela here. I want to grill the cunt, put her in the hot seat. I'm not going to pay off Fitzgerald, then be confronted with demands for more millions from Pamela. This is a bottomless sea. How many more do you have who'll appear out of the woodwork demanding more millions?"

"I don't know where she is."

"Fuck that! Before I put up five-million dollars, I want to see your wife."

"I'll try to find her." He turned on her with anger. "I'm not taking part in any dedication on the beach, and I'm not marching in any of your parades. I'd like to put some distance between us right now. Your coming out against the Jews like that sure caught me off guard. My campaign headquarters has been bombarded with hostile calls. A lot of people want me to denounce your support. Attacking the Jews! Have you lost your mind?"

"You don't have to attend anything as far as I'm concerned. I can't let my enemies think they're driven me underground. It's not only my enemies I'm worried about, it's my so-called friends. We've just learned the Nazis and the KKK are going to march in my support. Right into the heart of the Jewish ghetto."

"Call the God damn thing off," he said.

"No! Calder and I knew from the beginning a campaign like ours would attract the lunatics."

"I think shit will blow in your face," he said.

"Get out," she ordered.

He lingered behind. "I've got a request. I've hired this bodyguard. He's out on the patio now, and he's dying to meet you. The guy worships you. He used to be a policeman until he got arrested for exposing himself to a little girl. He's Gene Robinson."

"I've heard of that case," she said."

"There's a screw loose somewhere. But he wants to be your bodyguard for the parade and the dedication in case somebody tries to harm you. Frankly, if you're going through with this shit, you'd better have him there."

A smirk came across her face. "Maybe you're right. I could always give Mr. Robinson an autographed white Bible." She walked over to the window and parted the drapery slightly. From where she stood, she could clearly see Gene. "My God, he's a beauty."

"And hung like a horse."

"Does he like women or have you cocksuckers got him fully booked?" she asked.

"He's straight. He was once married to Susan Howard, your darling Buck's wife."

"How intriguing," she said. She looked back to the patio and at Gene. The policeman's very presence was magnetically male. He didn't just walk the patio, he stalked it. She thought he had tremendous animal magnetism. "Why don't you go home without him? I'll go and introduce myself to your young stallion."

***

Emerging from the darkness of the house into the colored lights of the patio, Rose's face was alive—so alive it seemed on fire. For one flashing moment, Gene feared such intensity would shatter both of them. He'd seen her at the temple and had marched real close to her in the parade. The image in front of him was not the woman he'd viewed then, but the vision he'd conjured up in his dreams. Drowned in her beauty, he reached to take the hand she extended. Her handshake was more like a caress.

"Mr. Robinson, welcome to Paradise Shores."

He was so filled with admiration he hesitated an awkward moment. "It's the most beautiful place in the world." He'd wanted to say she was the most beautiful woman in the world. He'd touched her hand, yet she still seemed untouchable. She was not a vision to be sullied by man.

She walked ahead, leading him toward a gazebo. Down a flower-lined path, she retreated into a dark pocket of the garden. Here she stood for a moment, waiting for him to catch up. She glanced at the foliage on the other side of the gazebo and reached for his hand. His large hand enclosed her delicate one. He hoped his palm wasn't sweaty.

"Lately, I've been afraid to walk in my own garden," she said. "There have been so many phone threats on my life."

"You need a bodyguard," he said, his pace matching hers.

She came to a stop just long enough to look deeply into his eyes. "I know."

In the gazebo, she offered him a cola which he took with trembling hands. She leaned forward, her eyes lighting up with discovery. "I think I've seen you somewhere before."

He shuddered at the revelation she was about to make, fearing she'd viewed his face on the television screen at the time of his arrest.

"You marched with me in my parade," she said. "Right alongside me."

He breathed easier. "I didn't think you'd remember."

She leaned back and smiled. "I think both of us looked terrific, don't you?"

He took in her sly smile, her disarming dimple, her auburn hair piled high and carelessly on her head. "You certainly did, Miss Phillips."

"Rose." It seemed like a command. "We don't have to be formal.

Not if you're going to protect me tomorrow from the loonies."

"Barry has already asked..."

"I accepted your offer." She spoke tenderly as they sat sipping their drinks. She wasn't at all the forceful woman who stood in the pulpit, preaching to her congregation. She was warm, loving, giving—a person you could open up to.

After their first hour together, he'd begun to relax in her presence. She was infinitely desirable, but beyond the reach of man. Her earrings shimmered in the night light of the patio, and he found himself drawn closer to her. Her eyes, her mouth, her hair—everything about her fascinated him.

Her voice had become a whisper as she invited him back to the house. "It's getting damp," she said. He took off his jacket and gave it to her, and she smiled her appreciation of the gesture. Her hand fondled his as he draped the jacket across her shoulders, covering her thin gown.

On their walk back from the garden, she slipped her fingers into his and, at that signal, he locked hands with her, perhaps a little more tightly than he'd meant. He didn't want to hurt her.

In the living room, she confided, "Most men I've known have resented my strength. They believe a woman should be delicate, tender, you know—not strong. What do you think?"

"You are strong, yet a woman, too, a gentle person. You make your points without having to shout. Unlike..." he stopped himself.

"My sister, Hazel, you meant to say," she said.

"I'm sorry."

"Don't be. We have no love for each other."

Over dinner, he didn't bother to ask where Barry had gone. Although a lamp lit their table, he didn't need its light. The glow coming from her was enough. The more she talked, the huskier her voice became, her eyes feverish as they turned a cloudy violet.

She got up from the table and reached again for his hand. "I'd better get my beauty sleep if I'm going to face those TV cameras tomorrow." She led him toward the living room. "Why don't you spend the night in my guest room? I'd feel a lot safer with you in the house. It's okay with Barry."

"I don't have to report to Barry," he said defensively.

"I'm glad to hear that."

As she stood before the door to her guest room wishing him a good night, he seemed enveloped in her warmth. He didn't want her to leave, but didn't know how to ask her to stay. Suddenly, she kissed his lips and, before the tingling sensation of it had traveled his body, she was gone.

Later, as he tossed and turned in bed, he still couldn't believe he'd actually met her, that she'd kissed him and made him feel like the center of her world. She'd asked him to protect her, just as she had in his imagination. Was tonight just one of his many dreams about her, having no reality at all? In the morning when he woke up, would she be gone, like a fantasy of night?

***

In his Blackhawk limousine en route to the airport, Buck asked Lars to turn on the radio. To his astonishment, he learned that Rose's dedication ceremony was already under way. It had been announced for ten o'clock that morning, but had started at eight-thirty. Buck suspected that this was done deliberately by Calder. Perhaps Rose hoped to get through the dedication before ugly crowds formed to protest against her, or some of her lunatic supporters showed up. The last thing she wanted was to have newsreel cameras capture her making a speech with swastikas in the background. As in her candlelight parade, she also wanted to retreat to safety before any violence broke out.

Over the radio came the sound of Rose's melodious voice. "Not only will I dedicate the greatest religious center, spiritual retreat and hospital in the entire southland, but I plan to establish one of America's greatest universities. Like a phoenix rising from the ashes of urban blight, we will have an open university where free thought is allowed. Not a university where Zionist die-hards control the curriculum."

Buck greeted that news with amazement. There was more. He signaled Lars to turn up the volume.

"In one building we will have a research institute called the Middle East Center," came Rose's voice. "The door to thought and information has been closed long enough in America. In our Arab studies center, we will open that door, shedding light on the people who figure so importantly in our destiny today. Nobody questions Hebrew studies at the big American universities. Why is it then that a study of the history and culture of the Arab nations is called propaganda?"

He sighed. Rose always managed to surprise him.

"We must explore both sides of the conflict in the Middle East," Rose claimed. "The charismatics in my own foundation are not afraid of the truth. Why should other Americans be?"

As her voice went off the radio and her all-woman chorus began to sing, "Onward, Christian Soldiers," he signaled Lars to turn off the radio. He'd heard enough.

Later, after a thorough inspection of the plane, Lars came to Buck. "The plane is secure," he said. "We're heading for Geneva." He paused. "A message came in from Rose. She's asking you to reconsider and not go to St. Moritz."

"Hell with her!" Buck said. "I'm on my way now."

As his jet became airborne, he was glad to be leaving Okeechobee behind. He thanked the gods he didn't accept some media director's job with Rose. Hollywood on the arm of Ahmad was more his scene.

He was relieved to be high in the clouds and off the earth for a few hours. Lars was removing his shoes and socks. All of a sudden he missed Ahmad. Where in the hell was Ahmad? Ahmad was the man who made all things possible.

An assistant to the pilot came into the rear, handing Buck a communication from Uncle Milty. Ahmad had granted the financing for Sun City. The project was on. "There's more," Uncle Milty wrote. "The *News* is yours. I've been unable to reach Susan this morning to tell her she's the publisher. I didn't have to spend a cent of your *Examiner* millions. Ahmad's firm has provided financing for the whole thing."

Buck leaned back into the soft upholstery of the plane. "There must be a downside to all this," he said to no one in particular.

Tomorrow would be time enough to encounter the downside. Right now he felt like king of the world.

***

Susan had learned that militant right-wing groups planned to march down Washington Boulevard into what was often called the Jewish ghetto, to an old bandstand which hadn't been used in twenty-five years. She wanted to see it all.

On the fringe of the area, she passed through a mob of milling, beer-swigging young white men, many of whom wore T-shirts, proclaiming BE A MAN, JOIN THE KLAN. Some of them had stock-piled bricks, coke bottles and firecrackers, and other brandished base-ball bats.

The wail of sirens announced the arrival of dozens of policemen in the area, including Biff himself. Susan made her way through the surging crowds. She turned and headed rapidly to the bandstand.

The sidewalk had filled up with onlookers, mainly elderly Jewish women who'd come out of their seedy retirement hotels and decaying apartment houses. They appeared bewildered and confused. Several of the women appealed to stonily silent policemen to call off the parade.

"People could get hurt," one woman told Susan.

"Including you," she said firmly. "Now get back to your room." She led the woman over to the doorway of her apartment house, and for some reason she obeyed and went inside.

Hurrying as fast as she could, Susan cut through the largely partisan audience assembled around the bandstand. Once there, she realized she was too late.

Rose had already finished the dedication ceremony and the white-robed chorus had disbanded. Under heavy guard, Rose was hustled from the bandstand to a waiting limousine.

Susan spotted a man at Rose's side who looked amazingly like Gene. She got only a glimpse of him before he disappeared inside the limousine with Rose.

Susan felt she was mistaken. What would Rose Phillips be doing with Gene Robinson?

***

A sizable crowd had already formed about the limousine, in spite of police efforts to hold it back. Some were from Rose's own temple, and Gene knew they were harmless. It was the protesters from the decaying apartment houses he feared. During the dedication, the mob had already grown restless and had started to push and shove.

As he guided her to her limousine, he could feel Rose holding his hand tighter and tighter until it became almost a death-grip. Although she appeared serene on the surface, that grip told him how frightened she really way. It made him feel all the more protective of her.

"Just head straight for the car," he cautioned her. "No matter what happens."

Once he'd gotten her through the sharply divided crowd into the safety of the car, he could still hear angry voices filtering through the limousine's heavy glass windows. Rose was immediately on the phone in the limousine, calling Calder to summon more police protection. "God damn you, you promised me this wouldn't happen."

The voice was unfamiliar to Gene and he was surprised to hear her curse, to take the Lord's name in vain like that.

The shouts of the huge crowd had grown angry. He feared serious trouble. Those strange women from the apartment houses who were about to be dispossessed shouted at members of the temple and raised mocking, threatening fists to Rose in the back seat of the limousine. They'd been caught off guard when Rose had launched her dedication ceremonies an hour and a half before they were scheduled, but word had traveled fast through the ghetto.

The crowd had completely surrounded the limousine until the driver couldn't move the vehicle. People continued their shouts as they pushed and shoved. Most of them appeared to be protesters, but some were clearly celebrity chasers—as they waved pens, pencils, and autograph books, hoping Rose would lower the window and reward them with her signature.

She seemed terrified as she edged closer on the elephant-gray seat to Gene.

The police threatened the crowd with nightsticks, but that didn't seem to work. Some women pounded on the limousine with their fists, spitting on its windows. Other younger people climbed on top of it, peering upside down into all the windows.

"Make them get out of the way," she shouted to policemen who couldn't hear her. "I feel like a caged animal in some fucking zoo."

For a moment Gene was paralyzed, then he was goaded into action. "I can handle it!" He squeezed her hand once more to give her assurance. Like an athlete, he bolted from the car, slamming and locking the door behind him. He knocked one woman down as he opened the door to the driver's seat, shoving the chauffeur aside.

Behind the large wheel, he started to move the limousine, using its large bumper as a people-prodder. Faced with a slow-moving car, the crowd parted, as police joined the effort to clear a path. It worked. Through his rear-view mirror, he could see Rose's tense face as she perched nervously on the edge of the seat, her hand at her throat as if gasping for breath.

As the sedan turned east on Washington Boulevard, he swallowed hard. An angry mob had formed there in front of TV cameras. With her cowgirl hat, Hazel stood out in the crowd. She'd been summoned to the bandstand so early she'd grabbed her hat, but hadn't changed out of her morning robe.

"She's planned it this way!" Rose shouted through the screen. "Look at those cameras. Don't run over her. That bitch wants to be a martyr."

Backed by a phalanx of protesting tenants, Hazel stretched out her arms like a giant bird, defying the sedan to run over her.

Gene braked the car as his mind whirled. A dark impulse came over him, but he struggled with it. One part of his brain wanted to step on the accelerator and plunge the limousine into the blockage of women.

Siren wailing, a squad car carrying Biff pulled up near the intersection. The chief got out and grabbed a loudspeaker, shouting for the rapidly swelling crowds to stand back. On Biff's orders, two policemen tried to restrain Hazel. Her own booming voice competed with the amplified shouts of the chief.

Hazel broke free of the policemen and ran to storm the limousine. Another policeman grabbed her and they tangled, a mass of arms and legs, until the overweight woman lost her balance, falling back into the bay of the fountain that stood in the center of the square. The event was recorded by TV cameras.

Two of her campaign workers pulled the screaming warhorse out of the water. To Gene, a wet Hazel was an even more formidable presence, as she stood hatless before Biff, threatening him with hell and damnation.

Meanwhile, a mob had moved in on the limousine from the rear, surging against the car, threatening hands balled into fists reaching out to pound the car. Rose opened the window in the limousine's divider, clutching Gene's hand. The sedan shook violently. He sensed at once what was happening. About twenty protesters tried to overturn the heavy limousine.

Protected by glass, Gene felt the mood of the crowd. A smell of blood was in the air.

He had to make snap decisions and he prayed he'd do the right thing. He appeared completely blocked by abandoned cars and demonstrators. Impulsively he opened the door again, slamming its heavy metal against two protesters, knocking them back. A woman tried to slap him but he bashed her face, shoving her down on the cobblestone square.

He signaled Rose to open the door. At first thinking he wanted back in, she raised the lock, only to have him yank her off her delicate perch on the edge of the seat. Realizing what he was doing, she clung to a leather strap, holding on tenaciously, refusing to be pulled into a deadly sea. He broke her grip. "No, no!" she screamed at him. "Let me go!"

He pulled her anyway. Up close and out on the square, she clawed at his face with a fury, a sharp red nail digging into his forehead.

Ripping his jacket off, he covered her head and completely blinding her vision, carried her in the direction of Biff's waiting squad car. Past the fountain where Hazel had fallen, he looked back just in time to see the limousine overturned, making a crunching thud on the sidewalk. The chauffeur was still trapped in the front seat.

Elderly bystanders from the apartment houses were shoved aside as two young men broke through a barrier of blue-helmeted policemen. Both carried containers of gasoline. One long-haired boy fell down on the cobblestones, dropping his can. A policeman delivered chopping strokes to his head. In a stupor, the boy crawled toward the fountain, protecting his skull with his bare hands.

Gene winced as the other kid tossed gasoline on the limousine. By the time two policemen reached the boy with their flailing nightsticks, he'd covered the overturned hood. The boy was grabbed, screaming and crying as the cops leaped on him.

Churning feet crushed his toes, as Gene tried to escape with Rose. The attack on the limousine had momentarily diverted the attention of the demonstrators, who seemed carried away more with the symbol than the actual target herself. Pushing hard, he crossed the tidal wave of humanity, protecting Rose as best he could. He feared cracked ribs. Globs of spit spattered his face.

Finally, he was able to shove Rose into the back seat of Biff's squad car. He gasped for breath, feeling free of the entangling mess. Just as he looked back, the limousine went up in flames, the chauffeur trying to struggle out through the window. Flames leaped to his uniform, turning him into a human torch. Gene had seen enough.

Rose screamed hysterically, sensing what was happening, although his jacket still covered her head.

Just then, he became aware of a sharp pain that pierced his leg right above the ankle. It throbbed but his concern was for her. "You okay?"

"Get me out of here!" she screamed.

In the background, Biff and his men struggled to keep the crowd from the flaming limousine.

The driver of the squad car turned on the flashing dome light and siren. The people in front of them instinctively moved out of their way. A pathway was cleared. Onlookers screamed and trampled each other as they fled in all directions before the onrushing car. The wail of firetrucks rushing to the scene could be heard in the distance.

He crushed his eyes shut, hoping the stabbing pain in his leg would go away.

Crouched down on the seat beside him, Rose pressed tighter and tighter to him. Her lips near his ear, she whispered, "Don't ever leave me...please."

***

It all started with the sound of bricks pelting the stained-glass windows of a synagogue at the opposite end of the square. The parade down Washington Boulevard was already under way.

In the vanguard marched about two hundred blue-collar workers, all of whom were said to be jobless. They'd been protesting to the city for months about their plight, but to no avail. The retiring mayor had promised them construction jobs on Rose's new charismatic center.

Following them were about thirty white-robed members of the local chapter of the Ku Klux Klan, some of whom carried large placards proclaiming JEWS BEWARE.

Goose-stepping behind them paraded about forty marchers of the American Nazi Party, dressed in khaki uniforms and supporting swastika insignias. At the sight of these arrogant marchers, a roar of loud boos rose from the sidewalk.

Coming from the opposite side of the mall was a group of about two hundred Jewish women and men, led by Hazel.

"Stand back," a policeman cautioned Susan.

"Like hell!" she said, jerking his arm away. "I'm getting a picture of this." She reached for her camera.

Biff had ordered about thirty policemen to cordon off the Jewish marchers so as to allow the coven of Nazis to pass through and into the bandshell.

And then it happened—a full-fledged riot. Susan was caught in the middle. Bottles filled with ammonia were hurled from upper windows of the decaying apartment houses. She ducked for cover.

People ran and screamed, tearing through the trees of the park, as hugh tear-gas canisters seemed to crash around them, filling the air with an acrid smell. A phalanx of police advanced, swatting at crumpled figures. Large street-cleaning trucks swept toward the crowd, spraying more tear gas.

New police reinforcement came out of the park, armed with plastic riot shields to ward off a rain of brick and bottle missiles. Metal-studded clubs flayed the air. Fist fights broke out. The cries of *Sieg Heil* pierced the dying morning.

The crowd of young men Susan had seen earlier in the park advanced against the elderly Jews on the sidewalk, tossing the bricks, coke bottles and firecrackers they'd stockpiled in the arsenal. They broke through the police lines formed to protect the spectators.

One policeman, hit in the head by a flying brick, fell to the ground as another mounted policeman accidentally ran over his squirming body.

Her eyes smarting from tear gas, Susan jumped back as another squad of police charged up to the scene. Loudspeakers urged the mob to clear the streets.

Hustled and shoved, she tried to breathe through her mouth. She made her way through the surging crowd and climbed the steps of an old apartment building, stopping on the second-floor landing where a door stood open. The tiny efficiency was abandoned. She entered the ill-kept rooms that smelled of mildew, heading for a tiny open-air terrace to get a better view of the riot.

Ambulance sirens screamed and she shuddered at the wailing moan. She felt she was choking to death. Closing her eyes in agony, she became aware of a throbbing pain in her left shoulder, not having noticed it before. She must have been hit, and didn't even know it. Mucus smeared her face. She ripped open her blouse to inspect the wound. With a handkerchief, she tried to stop the blood, apparently caused by a piece of flying glass.

Down below mobs roamed the streets. Plate-glass windows were smashed. Bricks were thrown into hotel rooms. Trash cans were turned over and set on fire. Fire engines fought for space with the ambulances. Missiles were hurled through the air.

In the distance, above the roar of the clashing crowd, large white crosses were set on fire in the bandshell—the smoke rising, billowing, curling ominously against the noonday sun.

She'd stayed long enough, and now had to get back to the condo. She needed a doctor.

Leaving the building, she ran in the direction of her car. Blood soaked through her blouse. She came to a stop about a block from the riot, which had shifted to the far side of the park. Sirens still wailed, loudspeakers boomed, but there was a new sound—that of gunfire. Her eyes smarted from tear gas.

From one of the smashed store windows at the far end of Washington Boulevard, five young men dressed as U.S. marines piled out onto the street, armed with stolen clothing.

She tried to take a picture of the looters, but they fled too quickly in the other direction.

She finally managed to reach the car fifteen blocks away. Across the causeway she drove as fast as she could, the fresh sea air momentarily reviving her.

At one point, blackness swirled around her, and she careened dangerously into the other lane, narrowly missing an oncoming car. She came to again and was clear-headed. To the left she could see the news tower of the *Examiner* rising in the distance. In the old days she'd be on her way there to file a story, whether bloody or not.

For one brief moment, she thought of rushing into the *News* building, announcing to the staff that she was the publisher, and sitting down and banging out a story for the next edition. That seemed like something done only in the movies. She had to make it back to the condo. There she'd demand that Don get a doctor for her.

Back in the safety of her condo, she'd have time to collapse, giving in to the awful memories.

***

Her tensions had come visibly to the surface. Gene had noticed the wild, jerky rhythms of her speech. He'd comforted her. He was a much stronger personality than she'd thought at first. Originally Rose had seen him as a lovesick fan. After his rescuing her in the demonstration, she'd come to look upon him as much more of a man she could depend upon.

He would soon learn that her passion matched her beauty. At first he'd been reluctant, but she'd gotten him to remove his trousers. She had dismissed the maid, preferring to help him soak his foot herself. Her hands had moved gently, yet hungrily, along his perfect leg. She'd massaged the muscled calf until he'd winced in pain. She'd eased his foot into hot, salted water, and with a soapy sponge she'd washed some blood off his kneecap where he suffered a cut.

Finding a terrycloth robe for him, she'd kissed him lightly on the forehead and invited him to sleep until tonight when she'd asked him to accompany her to her temple for the showing of a special film.

In the early evening she was so eager to be with him again she wanted to tiptoe to her guest room and wake him up. The night air was warm, and she'd refused to take all calls or to listen to any more disaster reports about the rioting on South Beach. She'd been interested in only one news item. Hazel had been badly bruised, but at least she hadn't been seriously injured. Rose feared Hazel would gain much mileage from today's event, especially when newsreel footage of her was flashed across the nation's TV screens. "God damn it," Rose said out loud. "The bitch always manages to make herself the victim!"

Through a picture window, she noticed the water around her yacht appeared turbulent. Waves from the bay came crashing into shore. Bathed in an eerie white light, *Rose II*, her cruiser, looked like the vessel to sail to an adventurous escape. Right this minute, instead of attending film ceremonies, she wanted to go on that craft and run away with Gene somewhere.

Just then, a sliding panel of glass opened, and Gene came out onto the patio. In the background, classical music played.

The sight of him, the mere presence of the man, thrilled her. Unlike Calder, who sent her into traps, Gene was her real protector.

He grew more handsome every time she gazed upon him. The terrycloth robe was open at the neck, revealing his smooth, full chest. She closed her eyes for a moment, experiencing the joy of having clutched his well-muscled arms. Images of the V-outline of his jockey shorts and the promising curve flashed through her mind. A solid, large mound.

She got up slowly and made her way toward him, extending her arms for an embrace. "If it weren't for you, my obit would have been broadcast on tonight's news."

He seemed genuinely embarrassed, both wanting the intimacy of her presence, yet afraid of her at the same time. "I wanted to help."

"You did," she said, enjoying the odor of him. He'd sweated heavily in the protest march and still hadn't showered. His breath smelled of sleep, and she found its staleness intoxicating. She wanted to kiss his full lips, settling instead for his cheek and a murmured thanks of appreciation for his rescue. "Can you walk?"

"Yeah, a light limp—nothing serious."

"Are you able to go with me tonight?" she asked. "If you aren't, I'm calling the whole thing off. I can't face any more mobs unless you're with me."

He leaned closer to her and, in a voice that was a whisper, promised, "I wouldn't let you go out of this house alone."

***

Hundreds of pickets had formed in front of Rose's temple. With her injured shoulder, Susan was able to pass between the police barricades and into the main lobby where a press ticket awaited her. Through the glass doors of the temple's lobby, she stood in horror watching the cops fighting back, kicking and punching some members of the Jewish Defense League. Some protesters carried placards denouncing Rose. Members of her temple tried to rip these placards to pieces. At first Susan feared the surging demonstrators would break through the glass doors of the lobby. Police efforts to hold them back were successful. The glass doors withstood the stones hurled at them by youths.

She'd been assigned a luxuriously upholstered seat near the front of the temple, and was almost the last to arrive. Every chair was full. There was a hushed stillness—no shuffling of feet, no rustling of paper.

She estimated that at least two-hundred members of the press—many sent down from New York—were in the audience. She looked for Barry Collins, but didn't see him. He had wisely chosen not to attend.

The lights dimmed. Any minute Susan expected a spot to be turned on Sister Rose as she made her welcoming address. Instead, fake stars went on overhead, bathing the temple in a rosy glow. A wide screen was lowered.

When it was fully in position, the sound of Sister Rose's melodious voice was beamed over the speakers. "I have just come from Palestine," the voice claimed. "The dust of that glory road of Jesus is still on my weary feet. I have gone there hoping to find peace as I walked in the footsteps of the Lord." She paused for a long moment before going on. Her voice seemed more strained when she spoke again. "What I found instead was unbelievable suffering and injustice. I'll let tonight's film speak for itself. I just ask that you view what you're about to see with an open mind."

Before a large boulder in some mysterious desert, Sister Rose's face flashed on the screen in full color. The desert light seemed to illuminate her bone structure, giving her a finely chiseled look. Her deep-seat eyes, her soft and sensual lips, and her free-flowing auburn hair brought an aura of enchantment to her. Susan realized at once what a fascinating screen personality Sister Rose could have been if she hadn't become an evangelist instead.

Ten minutes into the film, Susan knew the audience was witnessing a powerful, convincing documentary. It was a brilliant plea for the Palestinian inhabitants and their struggles for their ancient homeland. The film had obviously been made at great cost and with the most skilled of technicians.

Just as she watched donkeys and oxen pull plows to cultivate terraced hillsides, it came. From the back of the temple, a shattering blast. A burst of flame shot through the air, cascading into the temple's auditorium.

Stunned seconds passed before she sensed what had happened. The audience, too, remained quiet for those deadening seconds. Then an eruption of sounds and movement. Screams resounded through the auditorium as panic swept through the spectators. A wild, mad dash had begun for all available exits.

Joining in this stampede, Susan tried to protect her injured shoulder as best she could.

People cried out. Families were divided. Angry shouts filled the air.

Once she'd escaped to the parking lot, she found the traffic hopeless. Sirens sounded all around her as emergency equipment came in from every direction.

Ambulances converged in front of the temple to haul off the injured. Fire-fighting equipment raced to the scene, along with additional police vehicles.

In the parking lot, cars were hopelessly stalled as motorists, fearing another blast, had rushed from the temple. Traffic jammed together, nosing and wedging each other into an impossible tangle. Finally, most drivers realized they couldn't pull out of the temple's grounds. They began to abandon their cars, fleeing on foot.

Reporters, photographers, demonstrators, temple members, maintenance men—all staggered from the parking lot. Some had head wounds. Blood ran down the faces of others.

Susan ran ahead until she reached the top of an artificially created hill on which Sister Rose had mounted a white cross, looking out over her temple gardens, its extensions like protective arms guarding her flock.

Susan felt safe from the driven, scattering people. After being pounded and clubbed by the hysterical mob, she could breathe more easily and was grateful she hadn't been injured again or blown away. The fire at the front of the temple appeared to have been brought under control. She wouldn't know how many people were injured until she heard the news broadcast later over television.

Away from the pushing and prodding of the mob, she experienced a calm. Sirens and shouts of the crowd rose up to the hill.

She heard them only distantly.

***

Gene had not understood what was happening all night. To his surprise, Rose had not wanted to go into the main auditorium of the temple, and had directed him instead to the dressing rooms in the cement cellars below. There he'd met Calder Martin in wraparound sunglasses and a green paisley tie. Although Gene was introduced to Rose's campaign manager, Calder had ignored his extended hand, turning to answer an urgently ringing phone.

The atmosphere was charged with tension. Rose seemed as nervous as she had been during the riot on South Beach. In front of her dressing room mirror, she wiped her brow with a tissue, as her makeup ran. "God, it's hot in here."

"Is the air conditioning broken?" Gene asked.

"We had to turn it off," she said. "Its noise interfered with the sound of the film." She smiled in a cute, upturned lip fashion. "I'm used to the heat."

At first he was reluctant to call attention to it, finally remarking casually, "Your lipstick's smeared."

"Oh, that," she said, glancing back in the mirror. "I'll repair it on the elevator."

As they stood in front of the elevator bank, she had grown fidgety, her movements and speech jerky. She sucked in the hot, stale air of the underground vaults and kept swallowing as if she had a lump in her throat.

Then he heard it. A loud blast. "A bomb!" he shouted, instinctively darting for cover. He grabbed her, pressing his body against hers, bracing for another blast.

For some odd reason, she no longer appeared frightened.

"We've got to get out of here!" he yelled in panic, his eyes darting for the nearest emergency exit.

"It'll be okay," she said reassuringly.

"What in hell do you mean?" he asked. "Another bomb might be set off!"

As the elevator doors opened, she paused in the bright neon lighting from the hall, looking back at him. She reached out for his hand, indicating he was to join her. "I'm sure the police can handle it. Come on, I'm holding that press conference."

In one of the bustling studios of the temple, where she filmed special broadcasts without an audience, two fleeing electricians collided with them. "Over here," she urged Gene, passing a crew throwing color cables over the balcony before rushing out.

A control room engineer reported to her that the blast had gone off in the front and some people had been injured. Right now, no one knew just how many.

"That's a distance of about half a mile from here," she said, showing no concern for the injured. "Show the press in."

"You're calling it off, surely!" the engineer said.

"Like hell!" Her face was adamant.

"The press is running like hell," the engineer warned.

"They'll come back," she said calmly. "Let's get started." She turned to Gene, embracing him affectionately and pressing extra hard against him, not caring if she messed up her hair, makeup or gown. "You'll stay with me, won't you?"

"Right beside you." He was perplexed and could only hope she knew what she was doing.

A press agent whispered something to her as he took a position near Gene in front of a door. The smell of salted peanuts and peppermint Life Savers on the agent's breath nauseated Gene. He was anxious to get upstairs to see what damage had been done. But Rose wanted him at her side.

Suddenly, the door burst open and she rushed into the second studio as if she'd fled from the bombing.

An announcer stood in front of a TV camera, reporting the first news of the blast. Seeing her, he called out, "Sister Rose." Turning back to the camera, he said in a nervous voice, "Ladies and gentlemen, Rose Phillips is in the studio." The announcer extended a hand-held microphone in front of her. "Can you tell us what happened?" Seeing how distraught she looked, he said, "You okay?"

"I'll be fine," she said. In front of the camera, a magic came over her face. Fatigue and nervousness had been replaced with an appealing, charming personality backed up by a beguiling voice. Other members of the press filed into the studio room.

"The reports are now coming in about the injured," she said on camera. "At the sound of the first blast, I ran from the main auditorium down a long corridor to the underground cellars. To tell the truth, I thought it was an assassination attempt. I receive daily threats."

Gene noticed that more and more members of the press were coming into the studio.

Wavering at first, Rose's voice picked up volume. "I had refused to bow to Zionist pressure and went ahead tonight with plans to show this important film. I made a grave mistake."

"Do you blame the Jewish Defense League?" a reporter shouted.

She ignored him. "I should have know that desperate Zionists would prevent the truth about the Palestinian people and the Palestinian Liberation Organization from being heard. The film, *To Die in Palestine*, presents the heroic and determined struggle of a valiant people."

Reporters shouted more questions to her as she continued to speak calmly into the cameras. "The Palestinians have had to fight every step of the way in their age-long struggle to free themselves from foreign domination." Her speech seemed to have been already prepared.

"I call upon Christian America to support these people in their struggle. Don't let bomb-tossing Zionist hoodlums destroy freedom in America. Join me in my struggle to bring out the truth about the Palestinians."

Just then, the press agent stepped forward and whispered something into her ear. "Oh, God," she cried out. "No, no, no!"

"What is it?" the announcer inquired, thrusting the microphone at her strained face. "At least ten members of my temple have been killed in the bombing." She buried her face in her hands and broke into hysterical sobbing. The press agent led her away from the announcer, as the camera followed. Stumbling, she was directed back to the second concealed studio.

As he rushed to her side to help her, Gene was overcome with a haunting suspicion. She had known that a bomb was set to explode.

***

Her bedroom was definitely feminine, in shades of pink and white. In the center stood a heart-shaped overscaled bed with a white ruffled and skirted cover. Gene sat on a gilded Louis XV chaise longue of pink satin with white lace pillows, and Rose perched at her Italianate dressing table in painted gilt with a three-way mirror. At the push of a button, the lights could be either harshly realistic or else flattering. In front of him, she switched to the flattering version as she splashed herself with some rose water, her favorite scent. She'd quickly restored her disheveled look and appeared superbly groomed.

"My favorite musical was *Oklahoma*," she told him. "I liked what Aunt Eller tells Laurey. 'You gotta be hearty, and you gotta be tough. You can't deserve the sweet and tender things in life less'n you're tough.' Aunt Eller's words are the code I live by. And from what I know of you, you're the same way."

He hesitated before asking. "Rose, what about the bomb?"

She didn't want to hear the rest of the question. Her features appeared contorted before she relaxed again, giving him a plastic smile. "I want the laws of God and the cultural values of man to be vindicated!"

"I do, too." Even though agreeing, he felt a sickening thud in his stomach. "You said you wanted to accomplish things peacefully. Without violence. Have you changed?"

She stared harshly at her own face in the mirror before gazing up at his reflection. "I know I said that. I was wrong. All those years in the police department must have taught you you can't accomplish some things peacefully." Quickly she got up, walking over and reaching for his hand. "Let me show you our bathroom." Her voice was jubilant, like that of a little girl sharing a longed-for Christmas gift.

As he trailed her, he was stunned at the use of the word "our."

In her dimly lit bathroom, she pointed with pride at her sunken tub, all in gold and edged by pink roses. During the day it was lit by a skylight. On glass racks rested dozens of bottles of unusual, exotic perfumes. "I think a lady should smell pretty, don't you?"

"No," he answered sharply. "Just fresh and clean. I like unscented deodorant." He left the bath, heading back to her bedroom. Such an intimate setting embarrassed him. He shouldn't have accepted when she'd invited him into her bedroom. Nervously, he glanced around the room, studying one wall of photographs revealing her in triumphant moments of her career.

When she came in, her face indicated no concern at his leaving the bath so abruptly. She directed him to her moonlit terrace overlooking her garden, where the smell of night-blooming jasmine filled the air. Being with her in such a place had been his most cherished moment in all his dreams. Now that it actually was happening, he was deeply disturbed to be alone with her.

After enjoying the night air, she took his hand, leading him back into her bedroom. Here the lighting—muted and indirect—reminded him of a Hollywood set, strictly Art Deco.

Over the bed, softly lit by pink spots, hung an idealized portrait of her in a long, flowing Grecian gown. In one arm she cradled a dozen white roses—her trademark. Her face turned heavenward, and the artist had captured a look of rapturous joy. She found the most advantageous spot on her chaise longue. Reaching out, she signaled him to join her.

Reluctantly he did. Her auburn hair was loose and flowing, her white gown opened to reveal the large cleavage of her breasts. In spite of the horror she'd gone through, she appeared calm, not affected by the injuries and death which had been caused—at least indirectly—in her name.

In spite of that, he had to admit she'd never looked more desirable. He sought her eyes, and for a moment was mesmerized by her. Those eyes—so large and inviting—clearly extended an invitation. He fought to blot out the image, picturing his golden tanned body, completely nude, contrasting with her skin, so white and pale it was as creamy as milk glass. Excited by the closeness of her, he was erect, so powerfully he could not conceal it.

Her eyes focusing on his fly, she said, "My, oh my, what do we have here?"

He sweated heavily. Instead of a grown man, he felt like a boy again, the way he'd been when an older woman had tried to seduce him when he was only fourteen years old.

In a low, soft voice she said, "Ever since that first night I saw you on the patio, I've wanted to know what it looks like. Those two little girls you exposed yourself to know more about you than I do. That doesn't seem fair."

He jerked back, not wanting to believe he'd heard her right. Gently she pulled down his zipper and his penis reared up with a heated desire. She stroked and placated it as it grew more swollen and stretched. She reached deeper into his pants, tickling him, the globes so sensitive, her fingers caused him to wriggle in pleasure. If only she hadn't said what she'd said. If only...

She moved her lips to his mouth and kissed him gently at first. The longer she kissed, the more ferocious her lips and tongue became. "My God, baby," she whispered, breaking away from his mouth to explore his ear with her tongue. One hand still held him, stroking him. "It's so fucking big! Bigger than Buck Brooke's—and that's saying a lot!"

"What...what do you mean by that? You and Buck?"

"That's right, darling," she said, amused. "He is also my lover. Talk about changing partners."

He was astonished. Drawing away from her, he got up from the chaise, trying to stuff himself back into his pants, pulling his rapidly deflating erection down his leg.

"Just a minute," she said, her voice turning angry. "We've got some unfinished business."

"No!" he shouted at her. He sucked in the air as a serene mask came over him. Regardless of what happened—what she said and did—he wouldn't lose control, the way he'd done when he'd wrestled that police woman. Avoiding her eyes, he said, "That'll have to wait till we're married."

"Till when?" she asked.

She made it difficult for him. "You know."

"No, I don't know!" The calmer he tried to be, the louder her own voice grew.

"When we're married, it'll be different," he said.

"Married?" she cried out, her mocking, derisive laughter exploding inside his head. "I'd use you for a stud, but not for marriage. That's a joke. So that's why you're holding out? You'd like to marry me, wouldn't you? Live like a king on money I've earned the hard way. No way, *flasher!*"

Hearing that word from her was the most humiliating moment of his life. When he looked at her, he didn't like what he saw. She was no goddess, no unattainable angel. There was nothing sacred about her, and in her own bitter frustration she no longer appeared desirable to him. With her legs vulgarly spread apart, her face distorted by her own unrequited passion, she was just another bitch in heat. More revolting to him than Susan had been.

"Get out of my house!" she shouted at him.

"I'm leaving," he said, zipping up and tucking in his white shirt. He could hardly breathe in this room and the smell of her rose water made him feel ill. He looked at her once more, though he'd promised himself he wouldn't. "You'll see me again."

"I doubt that!" She headed for the bathroom, slamming the door.

In the foyer he picked up a set of keys the maid had left on a silver tray. Quickly he slipped them into the pocket of his jacket.

He'd be back.

***

Geneva was a city of international conventions, and Buck never liked to go here. It was a duty call. With Lars and a security force, he checked into the Hotel des Bergues because he liked the location at a point where the lake becomes a river. From his bedroom window he could see Rousseau Island in the middle of the water, its towering poplars pushing toward the sky. Quickly he dialed the clinic and, after a short talk with old Buck's doctor, agreed to go there in an hour. There had been no improvement in his grandfather's condition.

For Buck, going to a hospital was like the shot of a surgical needle. In the early afternoon sun, the little Swiss doctor who stood before him smelling of some strange chemical didn't offer much comfort, either.

"When your grandfather checked in, he told me, 'Do what you can for me. I want to hold on as long as possible.' He's in a coma."

"He'll never come out, right?" Buck asked.

"I fear so. If you wanted to have any last words with him, it's too late."

When Buck was shown into the sick room, the doctor and attending nurse left, leaving him alone with the old man. Buck III had a headache and felt shaky inside. A lump filled his throat. His grandfather might technically live for months in a coma, but Buck knew he was already dead.

He felt scared. He wanted to shake the old man awake. There were so many questions he wanted to ask.

A wave of sadness washed over him. He leaned over the old man. His eyes were closed and his mouth formed a large O as he sucked in the chilled air.

As he stood looking, Buck felt the end of their struggles. No more fights, no more reprimands.

Buck stood up, taking one last look at the old man's face. "Dad," he said softly. "I won't be coming to see you any more." He slowly traced the shape of old Buck's almost skeletal head and withered cheek. His grandfather's frail hands were clasped in a tight grip, his fingernails blue. Some tiny little noise escaped from his throat.

Buck turned away, not able to face him any more. He whispered, "Peace at last."

He left the cold and quiet stillness of the room. Outside, he found himself walking faster toward Lars.

***

After a short flight into St. Moritz, Lars had Buck's luggage transferred into a rented limousine for immediate delivery to the wedding-cake style Palace Hotel. Its V-shaped gimmicks and spires—all architectural frosting—suggested a holiday mood Buck didn't feel. In the lobby, Cartier of Paris had staged a multi-million dollar display of rubies, sapphires, diamonds, and emeralds. Passing through the salons, with burnished paneling and beams, Buck overhead women in long, supple silks claiming that diamonds were declassé.

After checking into the hotel's most lavish suite with Lars, Buck retired to the marine bar overlooking a glass swimming pool built among rocks and a waterfall. With Lars he sipped champagne as a chaser to his first beer. In an hour at an agreed upon time a tall, red-haired, stocky driver came to tell them they were to trail him in their limousine to Rose's estate on the outskirts of the spa.

He'd never seen St. Moritz except in February. Without heavy snows, the resort had a dullness to it he'd never imagined—not at all chic. On his last trip, the temperature was well below zero, and he'd arrived with a French model with glossy hair and perfect teeth. They'd worn technicolored ski outfits with Abominable Snowman boots in yellow and red plastic. That was long ago, a part of his life to which he no longer felt a link. Everything had changed. Today instead of a French model he was pursuing a fourteen-year-old boy.

It was already dark when the sedan reached a large stone wall where a grill gateway was automatically opened, allowing them to enter a graveled circular driveway leading to a large stone mansion. The house appeared cold and foreboding. He couldn't imagine Shelley living here. It was too fortress-like for such a flamboyant boy.

Inside, the place reminded him of a monastery. A woman in a stiff white uniform showed him into a large living room lit by antler chandeliers. Lars waited outside the room in a grand foyer. Though the day was warm, a fire burned brightly. Offered some *Kirschwasser*, Buck refused it.

Nervously he waited for Shelley. In about fifteen minutes, the boy was shown into the living room by the woman attendant. She walked out immediately, leaving Shelley alone with him.

Buck wanted to rush over and take Shelley in his arms, but he feared they were being spied upon. He looked deeply into the boy's eyes. They were cold and distant, obviously not an invitation to an embrace. Buck studied him closely. He wore a simple uniform, like a military cadet. His face was drawn and disconsolate, and he looked gaunt, dangerously thin. His once-lustrous blonde hair seemed just a shade darker. He didn't look himself at all.

At first he didn't seem to recognize Buck. After an awkward silence, he asked hesitantly, "Buck?"

"Yeah, it's me, kid."

Shelley turned from the sight of him and walked to large picture windows opening onto dark mountains. "It's a beautiful night. The skies are so clear this time of year you can see every star in heaven. It's great."

"Sure." He walked over to join Shelley looking out the window. He hadn't remembered him as being so young, at least not this vulnerable looking. The boy's back was held rigidly, and he seemed ill at ease, like a young actor caught in a stage drama unable to recall his lines. Buck asked if they could sit down. Shelley said he wanted to remain standing.

"You okay?" Buck asked, definitely feeling observing eyes from somewhere intruding on what he hoped would be a private moment. "No one's hurt you or anything?"

The boy's gaze swept around the living room. When his eyes looked into Buck's, he smiled shyly. It seemed to be an appeal for sympathy and understanding. No longer cocky and arrogant, Shelley's manner was gentle, his voice soft-spoken. "I'm fine. No one's hurt me. I hurt myself the way I was. I've changed deep down."

"In so little time?" Buck asked with great suspicion. "I find that hard to believe. How have you changed?"

"I found Jesus." His face remained calm. "All my life I've been looking for someone to love me. I've found him."

"Until a few days ago I thought I was that someone to love you. I also thought you loved me. If you didn't, you gave a very convincing act."

"Please," Shelley said, walking away from him. "I'm a fourteen-year-old boy. You're a grown man. You should let me grow up away from you. You should leave me alone. Let me find myself in my own way. You shouldn't have done some of the things you did to me. It was taking advantage."

Buck felt his heart beating faster. He couldn't believe this was

Shelley speaking. He walked over closer to the boy. In a tiny whisper, he asked, "Is it Calder? Want me to rescue you from this zoo?"

Shelley backed away, his face indicating genuine fear, as if Buck were about to harm him. Buck reached for his arm, but Shelley jerked it away. "It's not Calder," he said in a voice loud and clear enough to bounce off the walls like an echo. "I want to stay here. I want to devote my life to serving Jesus. I want you to go and let me alone. I don't want to play your dirty games."

Moving toward Shelley and at close range, Buck was overcome by an eerie feeling, as he stared deeply into the boy's eyes. This was not Shelley. The boy's clear eyes were almost completely glazed. He just didn't seem to be anything, not even a person. Looking into Shelley's face revealed nothing. It was a pale zombie staring back at him.

"They got to you," Buck said. "Calder's done a job on you. I want my old Shelley back."

"That Shelley left you in the Palm Springs desert." The boy's voice was firm as he averted looking into Buck's eyes. "He's gone forever." Some life came to his face, but it was only momentary. Buck felt Shelley was reading from a script handed to him. He appeared in a trance, like old Buck lying in the clinic bed in Geneva.

Shelley stood rigidly in front of Buck, as if defying him. "You tried to lure me into your perversions. I was stronger than you. I'm a fourteen-year-old. Aren't you ashamed of yourself?"

"If I recall, and I do recall, I think you enjoyed it as much as I did and begged for seconds."

"That's disgusting." He stepped back from Buck and looked at him with a hostility he'd never seen in the boy's face before. "You're a pervert! A child molester!"

After those accusations, the attendant appeared in the living room, and Shelley rushed to her arms. "The interview is over, Mr. Brooke," she said. "Won't you please leave?"

"Okay, God damn it, I will." He grabbed Shelley from the attendant's arm, forcing the boy to look into his face. "You're in a jail. They've got your mind. I can help."

Shelley's face seemed to crumble before Buck. He screamed out in agony, returning to the attendant's arms to bury his face in her breasts. She stroked his hair. "Please" he said to the attendant, "make this filthy man leave me alone."

Buck felt the strong pressure of a hand on his shoulder. It was Lars. "The car is waiting."

Buck stood for a long moment, watching Shelley disappear down a corridor with the attendant. As he felt Lars's firm hand on his shoulder again, he turned and headed in rapid strides to the front door.

Back in the comfort of the limousine, tears welled in his eyes.

"A message has come into the Palace Hotel from Ahmad," Lars said. "He wants you to fly to Cairo at once."

***

In his car, Gene drove out of the city heading for the sleazy marina a few miles from town. He couldn't afford to keep his boat moored in the expensive marinas in Okeechobee. In an hour he would be on Buck's own private island with Robert in his arms. The air conditioning in his car gave off foul-smelling fumes. Earlier he'd passed a slow-moving vehicle, its lights a hazy yellow in the black Florida night. Otherwise he had the road to himself.

Something struck his windshield and at first he feared it was a bullet. Someone had targeted him for assassination. It was only a gigantic insect or small bird. He couldn't tell. Whatever it was left most of its guts splattered across his windshield. Fumbling for a wiper, he turned on the blades. That only made it worse, the guck blinding his vision.

Just then, he crashed. Slamming on the brakes, he swerved off the road, going into a swampy embankment. The motor died as his wheels spun in the water. Something seemed torn loose in his shoulder when he hit the wheel. He pulled himself up, opening the door and getting out. He had veered off the road after ramming a broken down refrigerator. What idiot would leave a refrigerator in the middle of the road on the darkest night? It looked like it'd fallen off a dump truck.

He looked at his car. Even if he could get it started again, he could never haul it from its hole. There was no phone nearby to call for help. His breath came in such ragged gasps, it sounded like sobs. He felt utterly frustrated and defeated.

He locked the dead car and headed down the highway walking to the marina. It couldn't be more than an hour's walk. He headed in rapid strides toward the water, as a sharp pain shot through his shoulder.

Once he accidentally kicked a piece of coral. The sound of it hitting the pavement made him duck for cover. Picking himself up again, he moved more cautiously down the road. "Christ, I'm paranoid tonight." A bird from the swamp swept by with a rush of sound. After that, the only music was the croaking of frogs which sounded ominous.

Later, on Buck's island, Robert's gentle massaging of his nude shoulder made him feel better. Robert had magical hands. When Robert had finished, Gene placed his right hand behind Robert's neck and pulled him close for a long and deep kiss.

"I'm so sorry," Robert said, going to get one of Buck's cigars for Gene. "I'll call a tow truck first thing in the morning and get it hauled away and repaired. Better yet, in a few days, I think I'll be able to buy you a new car. I think Buck's coming up with the money."

"He can afford it," Gene said, getting up and walking nude to the pool. Henry had retired for the night, and Robert had asked Gene to take off all his clothes while he was here. Robert had modestly retained a pair of white shorts to wear himself.

Gene liked showing off his body before an appreciative audience like Robert. Robert kept feasting his eyes on one part of Gene's anatomy, and Gene liked that. After that disastrous encounter with Sister Rose, Robert made him feel good again.

Out by Buck's pool, Gene smoked Buck's cigar, enjoying the luxury of this island retreat. Robert had gone into the kitchen to prepare him a light supper.

Gene felt that both he and Robert deserved to be richly rewarded for the suffering Buck had caused them.

With Robert he'd found the love and passion he'd sought with Buck. Robert was upfront about his need for sex with Gene. Robert loved every inch of Gene's body, licking it, kissing it, massaging it. Gene had privately cringed when Leroy had done that to him. But he loved it when Robert worshipped his body. Robert's adulation of him was always followed by the same act: a deep penetration of Robert that left him crying out in ecstasy. Gene was thrilled with his sexual power over Robert. What he most loved to hear was how much better he was than Buck at love-making.

Robert came in with the tray of food which Gene quickly devoured, as he was enormously hungry. As he ate, Robert nested at his feet, massaging his legs. "I think you're the most beautiful man I've ever known. Your body is a work of art. It's the body all men want to have and few end up with." He reached for Gene's penis. "And your cock— it's fabulous. It's so much bigger than mine that I'm ashamed."

"This is not a competition, and you're not exactly small."

Robert crawled up Gene's body, fondling and caressing his chest and biting his nipples before coming to his mouth where he tried to find out what Gene's tonsils tasted like. It was then that Gene took two fingers and began a probe of his target for the night. Robert shivered and slammed forward into Gene. It was all too clear what Robert wanted.

Not wanting to lose body contact with him, he picked Robert up and carried him to Buck's bedroom. Robert's eyes focused onto the thick cock standing tall and fierce as Gene prepared it to enter his newly found love. Robert's tongue nervously flicked out across his lower lip in anticipation of the assault. As Gene moved onto him, Robert lifted his legs, granting Gene complete access. Gene locked his elbows behind Robert's knees and leaned low over his face. He wanted to stare deeply into Robert's face, so he could witness every flinch or grimace Robert experienced. If Robert screamed, that would be music to his ears.

***

"Do you want a woman, sir?" A slender, dark-skinned boy came out from behind a potted palm in full view of the setting sun across the Nile. Buck looked not at the boy but at one of Lars's security forces who kept his hand on the gun in his breast pocket. The fading rays turned the boy's white shirt scarlet, as he fixed purple-black eyes on Buck. More suspicious than ever these days, Buck returned the stare.

Before the question, he'd watched the sun begin its descent across the Nile where a felucca—an ancient craft loaded with water skins— floated beside a barge transporting raw cotton. It was the same falling sun Iknaton had watched.

In the hot, slow breeze, Buck continued to stare at the youth as if he didn't hear the question. The boy had turned to face the sunset which made his eyes an albino-red, like the Nile itself. He faced Buck again. "I said, sir, do you want a woman?"

"I've got my own," he answered before getting up from his peacock chair, heading back to his hotel suite. Lars was already in the suite making arrangements. The boy looked disappointed. Two security guards trailed Buck through the lobby.

In just fifteen minutes, he was due to meet with his former classmate, Ismail Pasha, who'd been named after a 19th-century khedive of Egypt. Buck was amazed that Ismail was aware that he'd be in Cairo. Ismail had called him for the meeting. Buck found himself in a strange new world where everybody knew how to get in touch with everybody else.

Ismail was late and that was predictable. When he'd gone to the university with Buck, he even showed up late for the graduation ceremonies. Finally, he did arrive, just half an hour after he was expected. Embracing his longtime friend, Buck called for room service to bring them some mint tea, then he led Ismail to the terrace of his suite. The sun had set. From across the water came a long haunting cry.

"I love this hotel," Buck said to Ismail. "I expect Sydney Greenstreet to appear at any minute, what with all the overhead fans, peacock chairs, and potted palms."

"You're just a colonial," Ismail teased him, "nostalgic for an Egypt that no longer exists."

Over tea, the talk was filled with reminiscence, although Buck was impatient for some news of the arrival of Ahmad. At one point, Ismail showed him a picture of a pretty, plump girl he'd married. Buck did his best to offer compliments.

After tea, they smoked a ceremonial cigarette, as Ismail observed him closely. He obviously knew Buck hadn't come here to talk about old times. "Today your hometown made the front page of our little paper in Cairo."

"I know that. The bombing."

"Exactly. Naturally the paper blamed Zionist radicals. Dr. Phillips has been invited to Cairo to show her film here. We are most interested."

A brief anger flared in Buck. "Okay," he said, anxious to change the subject.

The story also said that our old classmate, Barry Collins, may defeat Rose's sister and become mayor," Ismail said. "If you see Barry, remember me to him. I recall some good times with him, but even more so I remember the beautiful blonde lady he married. Pamela, I think she was called. She was my special prize."

"All of us knew Pamela sometime during those four years—so you weren't alone in that line-up," Buck said.

Rolling his eyes, Ismail appeared suddenly business-like. "If Calder Martin and Dr. Phillips gain control of Okeechobee, they'll take their anti-Jewish campaign nationwide. A propaganda blitz, as you call it. They'll blame the Jews for everything. Inflation. World recession. Unemployment. They'll reveal that conspiratorial Jewish lobbies pull the string of U.S. foreign policy."

"What fun," Buck said sarcastically, heading back into his suite. It was dark, so he turned on an exposed bulb overhead. In spite of the heat of the day, the room had a chill to it.

They talked more, but something was gone between them. No longer the young men they used to be, they had different points of view and the past years had formed a deep chasm between them.

"I must say I've not been completely honest with you," Ismail said. "I have not given you—how do you say in America?—complete disclosure."

"What do you have to disclose?" Buck asked.

Ismail studied him with a certain wry amusement. "You must have found it surprising that I knew how to contact you. After all, your visit to Cairo was rather sudden."

"I was very curious but was too polite to ask," Buck said.

"I'm a very respected journalist in the Arab world," Ismail said. "But I hardly make my living working as a journalist. I arrived at your hotel in a chauffeured car, and I own a sumptuous villa on the outskirts of town."

"I get it," Buck said. "You're on someone's payroll."

"Not just someone," Ismail said. "Ahmad Pharaon's payroll."

"I see. What you're telling me is that you know all about my connection with Ahmad."

"I do and I want to congratulate you," Ismail said. "You could have made no finer choice. Long before you, I used to be Ahmad's boy but I fear he tired of me. At some point Ahmad decided he didn't really like sex with Arab boys. He now prefers blonds. In parting, he was incredibly generous. He'll probably be spectacularly generous with you."

"He already has been and he hardly knows me," Buck said.

"Ahmad has provided well for me. He purchased the villa for me, the chauffeur, everything. He pays me such a ridiculously high salary that I am embarrassed when I go to cash his checks."

"He's a loving, tender man—not at all like his reputation—and I have passionate interest in him. Of course, his money and power are part of the turn-on. But what would Ahmad be without money and power? That's who he is."

"I miss those tender moments I enjoyed with him," Ismail said. "You are one lucky man."

"Do you know if I will get to see him soon?" Buck asked. "I came all this way."

"My friend," Ismail said, "all you have to do is turn around and he'll be there."

"Yeah, right." In spite of saying that, Buck whirled around.

In back of him stood Ahmad who had silently entered the suite.

Chapter Fifteen

His mind in disarray, Gene planned to pick up some possessions at Barry's and head over to Leroy's condo. He was not only going to quit the job he'd forced Barry to agree to, but he was planning to tell Leroy that he wasn't going to California with him and wouldn't be visiting his apartment again. Robert had assured him that they had enough money to keep Jill and Sandy installed in their present condo.

At the Collins house, he found only Barry. Once again his daughters were gone. Barry lay on a sofa in the living room. He was unshaven and wearing only a pair of jockey shorts. Even though it was still morning, he'd been drinking. Barry seemed to hang here, as if suspended in space, not knowing what to do, although several campaign appointments had been made for him. He didn't look like any front-runner in the mayoral race. Gene thought how weak Barry appeared compared to the fighting spirit Hazel had shown in the South Beach riot.

Gene wanted to hate—Rose, Barry, the whole filthy mess, certainly Buck—all part of the Okeechobee dirt that covered his body with slime. He had a special venom reserved for Biff, Calder, Clara, and her daughter, all conspirators against him. When presented with that forlorn look on Barry's face, with its wide and handsome cheekbones, Gene felt a tug of sympathy for him.

The moment he saw Gene, Barry got up off the sofa and came toward him. "Thank God you're back."

This welcome aroused suspicion in Gene. "I've got good news for you. I'm out of here."

Barry's eyes blazed. The stench of liquor was strong on his breath. "You don't have to go." The voice was inviting.

Gene headed upstairs for Barry's bedroom where he tossed some clothes in a suitcase.

Barry appeared at the door, holding a glass of liquor in one hand.

"Could I ask you something?"

"I don't have time for an interview." Gene stuffed his white shirt over his jeans and two pairs of slacks, then fastened the buckle of his suitcase.

"What happened when I left you with Rose?" Barry asked.

"None of your fucking business."

"She seemed real taken with you. Now that I'm no longer her lover—God, what a distasteful job—I'm reduced to pimping." His face turned angry. He walked over to the window, tossing his drink, glass and all, into the patio below. The sound of breaking glass echoed back, the noise like ice cubes tumbling into a bucket. Barry headed back to the living room.

Gene glanced at his luggage and looked briefly around the room, fearing he had forgotten something. The phone rang. He hesitated before picking up the receiver. "Hello," he said.

"Who's this?" came the gruff voice of a man on the other end.

At first Gene had been reluctant to give his name. "Gene Robinson."

"Barry's bodyguard," the voice said. "I'm glad I got you. Calder knows where Pamela is. She's checked into the Pier House in Key West. Tell Barry the problem is going to be handled." The man slammed down the receiver.

In the living room, Barry had poured himself another glass.

"You've always hated me," Gene said, "except when you're horny."

Barry poured a drink for Gene before walking over in a bold stride. Gene accepted the liquor. He needed something strong and, even though it burned his throat going down, he welcomed the stinging sensation. His guts were already on fire.

"You're right," Barry said. "I let all our college friends know how filthy I thought you were. How abnormal! What you did to wreck the life of that little girl."

Gene was tempted to bash Barry in the mouth.

"I didn't really feel such hatred against you," Barry said. "I felt that by attacking you, I'd thrown the wolves off my own dirty scent. You exposed yourself to that little girl. I did much worse with little boys." No more than two feet away, he looked deeply into Gene's eyes. "You know, I hated you when you blackmailed your way in here. I hated you for having power over me, just as I hate Rose and Calder for having even more power, just as I hate Pamela for all her threats.

I've never been able to lead my own life, do what I want to do. Everybody is trying to control me. With you, it's been different." You really turn me on. I want you to stay."

"What about Robert Dante?" Gene asked.

"Robert's okay," Barry said nonchalantly. "In fact, I've asked him to come back to work for me."

"What about Buck?"

"In case you don't know this, Buck has found other interests. He's dumping Robert. I wouldn't mind having Robert for myself. Robert is the kind of guy who's convenient to have around. For real sex, I need to turn to a guy like you."

Gene sighed. He couldn't deal with Barry any more.

"This is a bad time for you to leave," Barry said. "Why don't you stick around? Even if Robert Dante comes to live here, we can work out some sleeping arrangements. A threesome, perhaps."

"No thanks," Gene said, picking up his suitcase and heading for the door.

"Stay," Barry called after him.

Gene slammed the door, heading toward his rented car and Leroy's condo.

He'd called Jill and Sandy earlier but they were out. He wanted to see them, but he'd promised all his nights to Robert.

***

In the quietness of the luxurious suite, Buck cradled Ahmad in his arms, planting tender kisses on his neck. "Don't leave me, guy. I can't stand it," Buck said, whispering in his ear before inserting his tongue which caused Ahmad to squirm beneath him.

"I wasn't gone for that long," Ahmad said, running his fingers through Buck's blond hair and fondling his neck before moving lower to feel the muscles of his strong back.

"It was like an eternity," Buck whispered to him. "You come into my life, you make me fall in love with you, and then you disappear."

"I have secret business I need to take care of from time to time," Ahmad said. "But I will never be away from you for more than a few days at a time."

"That's a promise I'm going to hold you to." Buck leaned forward inserting his mouth over Ahmad's. Ahmad kissed him passionately, his hands traveling lower to fondle Buck's genitals. "Don't tell me," he said, measuring Buck's penis with is delicate fingers, "That I was able to take every inch of that prime U.S. Marine dick."

"You did it and I must say it was the most satisfying fuck of my life, even better than the first one."

"And, poor me, I won't be able to walk for a month."

"You loved every minute of it and after dinner you're going to get it again," Buck said.

"I can't wait." Ahmad rose unsteadily from the bed. "Let's dress for dinner. I've arranged a private dining room for us at the hotel so we won't be disturbed." He put on a robe and looked down at the nude Buck who'd deliberately removed the sheets so Ahmad could feast on his body. "I want you to do me a favor. In the closet over there you'll find the uniform you wore in the U.S. Marines. I had Lars steal it from the back of your closet in Okeechobee. I want you to wear it to dinner tonight."

"If that is what turns you on, it's great by me," Buck said.

"I, on the other hand, will wear something different. It'll take me a while to get dressed. I've had the outfit flown in from Paris."

"I'll use the other bathroom and be dressed and ready for you," Buck said.

Before heading for his own dressing room, Ahmad bent over and inserted his tongue under Buck's foreskin. "Why do Arabs and Jews remove one of the most delectable parts of a man? I could spend hours making love to that part of you."

Buck fondled his head as Ahmad brought even more tingling pleasure to him. "Knowing how much you like it, I'll insist you pay homage to it every day."

Long after he'd showered and dressed in his military outfit, which still fitted perfectly, Buck wandered through the suite waiting for Ahmad to appear. He poured himself a drink and walked to the terrace to enjoy views over the city at night. He always liked hearing the sounds of cities in the Arab world. There was a forlorn, haunting quality to these sounds, evoking mystery and all the enchantment of *The Arabian Nights*.

He wasn't just playing the hustler with Ahmad. He genuinely loved the man. Who wouldn't love somebody who gave you the greatest sex you'd ever known and bestowed millions of dollars upon request or else just as a spontaneous gift? The sex, the money, the power were all there. Buck was eager to leave Okeechobee behind him and move on to California, except he could never leave Desire for long. He wanted to spend as much time at the mansion as he could. No matter where he'd ever live, he knew that nothing would ever compete with the splendor of Desire.

At a sudden movement, he whirled around. Ahmad had transformed himself into a grand lady in a white low-cut gown. Buck looked stunned. Ahmad might be incredibly handsome as a man but as a woman he was one of the world's most stunning beauties. Perfectly made up and elegant of stature and bearing, Buck looked upon Ahmad in astonishment. Buck felt an instant erection growing in his marine trousers. He loved Ahmad as a man but was sexually excited by him as a stunning woman as well. Perhaps he hadn't completely abandoned his love of women.

"I want to rush to you and crush you in my arms," Buck said. "You're beautiful. But I fear I will mar perfection."

"You're very kind. But the perfection stands in front of me. My ultimate sexual fantasy. A U.S. Marine. Six feet two. Blond, blue-eyed, with a muscled body honed to perfection. A true golden boy of the American plain. Not to mention a horse cock with balls to match. You are a gay man's fantasy."

"I want to be your fantasy. Always. I also want the pleasure of escorting you to dinner."

Ahmad planted a gentle kiss on Buck's lips, not wanting to spoil his makeup. He locked his arms with Buck's as they headed for the door.

Over dinner Buck poured out his total rapture at being allowed to live at Desire. "It's a dream place," Buck said. "I'm happiest when I'm there. I want to be there with you."

"It is the next place where we'll meet," Ahmad promised.

Buck held up his hand to make a point and became aware of the ring Ahmad had given him the first time they'd made love. "I can't thank you enough for this ring." He started to say he loved the ring but wasn't that much into jewelry when he noticed Ahmad signaling one of the waiters. The waiter arrived with a red satin box. Ahmad presented it to Buck. "Go ahead and open it."

Buck smiled at him and opened the lid of the box. Twelve of the world's most stunning rings greeted him. His eyes were dazzled by the stones.

"They were among the rarest and most beautiful stones in the world," Ahmad said. "A king's ransom. I hope you treasure them always."

Buck stammered. "I don't know what to say. Each and every one, more beautiful than the other one. Ahmad, this is too much. You're spoiling me."

"These rings are cold stones." He raised a glass of champagne to toast Buck. "I'd throw them all away for just one taste of that foreskin of yours. I'd give away a sumptuous villa for the aroma of your beautiful butt before I plunge my very skilled tongue into its depths."

"Stop it, you're turning me on, and I need to eat dinner. I'm hungry."

"That type of hunger we can deal with immediately," Ahmad said. "There will be other types of hunger to satisfy later. I've hired the three finest chefs in Egypt to prepare us a special meal tonight."

"I'd enjoy a burger and fries if I were with you," Buck said.

"Aren't you just saying that to flatter an old man who's fallen hopelessly in love for the first time in his entire life?"

"I just made love to you," Buck said.

"I don't think the most skilled hustler in all the world could fake love-making like that. Perhaps I'm kidding myself but I think you are in love with me. Not as much as I'm in love with you. Nobody could be that much in love with you. But we are in love."

"I never expected it to happen," Buck said. "With you, it's different. I can't wait until we are in California together. But I bet your place there is not as grand as Desire."

"That's true," Ahmad said. "It's not Desire. But I still think you'll be amazed. There's nothing like it in California."

"I'm sorry you have to be away so much."

"I am too. But I must continue to make millions for us. How I make those millions need not concern you."

"I don't even want to know," Buck said. "I'm amazed at what you've done for me. Let's list a few things. The Markum estate for openers. But that was just the hors d'oeuvres. Sun City. *The Okeechobee News.*"

"The Markum property is just a trifle," Ahmad said. "I've known about Sun City. It's a great investment idea. I've wanted to move in on it for some time. When the call came through from your lawyer, it just goaded me into action. I predict that in our life times an entire city will grow up there. It'll be spectacular. I'll make you the mayor."

"I believe in the project too. And the *News*."

"You lost the *Examiner*."

"I was amply rewarded," Buck said.

"The *News* one day will become one of the most important papers in Florida," Ahmad said. "The *Examiner* will be reduced to a mere house organ for Rose. Believe me, you got the better deal."

"Thanks to you."

After the most sumptuous dinner of his entire life was served, Buck decided to bring up the subject of Shelley. At first he didn't dare but Ahmad made him feel so secure and comfortable that he forged ahead. "I've met with Shelley in Rose's villa outside St. Moritz," Buck said.

"Oh, yes, I've been there once or twice but only in February."

"I think Shelley is being held there as a prisoner," Buck said. "He's been brainwashed. I want to get him out of there. Do you know a way?"

"My darling, man, please believe me when I tell you I have the power to abduct the president of the United States. Normally, I don't interfere in the domestic problems between Calder and Rose. If you want him rescued, you are indeed looking at the right woman."

"You'd do that for me?" Buck asked.

"Of course, I would. But you must not mention a word of this to Rose and Calder. I even have a suggestion where to take him after he's kidnapped."

"I hadn't thought about that," Buck said.

"Take him to Desire. I'll have him flown to Desire and slipped into the country. No one will know where he is except you, me, and Lars. I'm sure Lars didn't tell you but I have a completely closed off apartment at Desire. Locked away from the rest of the world. I never know if I'll ever have to detain someone. No one can escape from it. I'll put Shelley there. If he's been brainwashed, he can become unbrainwashed. I don't know if that's good English."

"It doesn't matter," Buck said.

"I must warn you. It won't be easy cleansing his mind again. Brainwashed victims don't immediately revert to their old selves, and, even if they do, they're different somehow. I know of such things."

"Do you think it would work?" Buck asked.

"Oh, please. I don't think you know the kind of woman you're dealing with. Let me show you what power really means in this world." He signaled the waiter to bring Lars in. When Lars came to the door, Ahmad quickly whispered something in his ear. Lars then disappeared. Returning to his seat, Ahmad glanced at his diamond watch. "By this time tomorrow night, Shelley will be at Desire."

"You're amazing."

Ahmad leaned over and kissed him lightly on the lips. "I'm more amazing than you'll ever know. Each day of your life with me will be filled with surprises. Now let's finish our dinner and return to our suite."

At three o'clock that morning, Buck stood nude on the balcony. Ahmad was asleep. Buck went back into the living room when he heard a light tap on the door to their suite. Opening the door, he confronted Lars who had a grim look.

"Your grandfather passed into Valhalla an hour ago. He died in his sleep."

Without saying a word, Buck stumbled toward the balcony. There he burst into uncontrollable sobbing. Lars comforted him, before going to wake up Ahmad.

As Buck stood looking at the city where night was dying and morning was on its way, he felt the presence of Ahmad behind him. Ahmad put his arms around Buck and held him closely. "I've made arrangements for you to fly to Geneva in the morning. You can claim the body and bring it back to Florida on your own private plane for a proper burial."

"Thanks, Ahmad. I don't know what to say."

"He was your refuge for years even if you refused to admit that. He is gone now. You have a new protector. I will keep you from harm."

Buck leaned back, pressing himself into Ahmad. "I need you now more than ever."

***

When Gene came into Leroy's condo, nothing appeared in disarray. There was, nonetheless, an ominous foreboding. The doors leading to the terrace were open so he walked outside in the hot air, feeling he might find Leroy here. The birds that nested in the gardens below were unbelievably noisy.

The time had come to say good-bye to Leroy. Gene had been Leroy's paid sex toy. With Robert, it would be different.

As he went back into the living room, his stomach felt hallow. Always an instinctive person, he feared he was in some sort of deadly trap. Coming in from the blinding sun, he had to readjust his eyes to the light. Dark shadows filled the room, and he wondered why Leroy had pulled the draperies so early in the day.

Gene headed for the bedroom. If Leroy were asleep, he'd just have to wake him up. Gene could stay in that apartment no longer.

Silence greeted him when he went into the bedroom. Leroy liked to pull black draperies real tight when he slept. He couldn't stand any light in his bedroom.

He pulled back the draperies. There on the bed lay a dead Leroy. A wire like a telephone cord was wrapped around his neck. In death, his eyes were open, staring at Gene. Those eyes were gaping wide, pop-eyed, and accusatory. He was nude. There was some horrible flesh-like raw guts trapped in his mouth. It was a bloody mess.

Slowly Gene's eyes traveled the length of Leroy's body. Leroy had been castrated, his genitals stuffed into his mouth. A bloodstain the size of Brazil had formed on the white sheets on which he lay.

Gene looked back once more into Leroy's face. He could only imagine the whimpers beseeching mercy that must have come from that mouth before the garbled protests were snuffed out by his own body parts.

Gene felt dizzy. In all his years on the police force he'd never encountered such a sight. He'd only read about such mutilations. His lasting memory of Leroy was his right hand gripping a pillow. It was a death grip. The pain must have been unbearable. Gene looked down at the body on the bed again. Leroy seemed to be staring directly at Gene, as if blaming him for his brutal murder.

The word blame stuck in Gene's brain. He was going to be blamed for this murder. His fingerprints were everywhere. Massive evidence. Biff would no doubt make this a gay lovers' quarrel. Gene knew it was but a matter of time before he was arrested for murder. The cops were probably on their way here now.

He walked rapidly toward Leroy's safe. It was open and empty, the incriminating evidence gone. He headed for the front door, opening it with caution.

He thought of Pamela. Was she the next victim? He had to get to her before they did. Maybe by saving her, he could also save himself. Slipping out the back entrance, he headed for his rented car. He didn't want to take a chance at the airport in Okeechobee. Biff's officers might have staked out that airport. He would be immediately recognized. He'd drive to a neighboring town and book the first immediate flight to Key West.

Time was running out.

***

The plane ride had been smooth from Okeechobee to Miami, and the transfer easy from there to the Key West airport. Once on land, he boarded a taxi to take him to Duval Street.

In this end-of-the-line city, the taxi drove through streets crowded with revelers. Key West was filled with bars, character, and a certain mystery just as he'd found it in the days when he'd visited it with Susan. He saw two men, both drunk, leaving a bar arm in arm. In the bright lights of a street lamp, they stopped to kiss long and passionately.

Spotting a flower shop, he asked the taxi driver to let him out there. In the shop he admired some brilliantly orange Birds of Paradise and purchased a large bouquet.

"I really shouldn't tell you this," the sales clerk, a young woman in her twenties, said, "but these are from South Africa." The saleswoman seemed worried about the political correctness of purchasing flowers from South Africa. He couldn't care less.

After purchasing the flowers, he crossed the street to the Pier House where Pamela was registered. He had to get her room number, and he suspected she was staying here under an alias.

At the reception desk, he was greeted by a tall, thin man with bleached hair and an earring. He smiled and seemed to take an undue interest in Gene. "We're completely full," the young man said, "but I have an extra room at my apartment. It's on William Street nearby." He looked Gene over appreciatively. "It'd be free."

"Thanks," Gene said. "I might take you up on that. But first I've got to deliver these flowers to Pamela Collins' room. Could you give me her room number?"

"Why don't you leave them with me, and I'll have a member of the staff take them up?"

"This is a little embarrassing," Gene said, leaning over the desk. He rubbed the crotch of his tight and very revealing jeans. "You see, it was more than flowers Ms. Collilns called for. I run this ad."

"Oh," the clerk said, brushing back his bleached blond hair. "Do you do only women? What about men?"

"Men are my favorite." He leaned over the desk. "It's big. We're talking real big. Why don't I go to the men's room?" Why don't you excuse yourself and join me there?" He winked at the clerk. "After I finish my duties with Ms. Collins, I'll meet you after work."

"You've got yourself a deal, big boy."

In the men's room, Gene waited for the clerk at the urinal. He was masturbating himself to a full hard-on. In minutes, the clerk had taken the urinal next to him to observe the show. Seeing that the room was empty, he reached over and played with Gene's penis, reaching inside to free his balls. "That's the biggest I've ever seen. I've got to taste it. He leaned over and took the penis in his mouth and was trying to go all the way down on it. At that point, he heard the door open. He jerked up and stood rigidly at the urinal. "I get off at ten," he whispered to Gene. "I'll meet you outside the front door."

"You've got yourself a date," Gene said. Back at the front desk, Gene described Pamela in detail to the clerk.

"There's a woman in room 201 who meets that description completely," the clerk said. "I checked her in. She said her name was Barbara Bennett."

"Thanks," Gene said, gathering up the flowers. "She's married and doesn't want her husband to know what she's up to."

He hurried through the gardens to the back stairs. Upstairs he walked rapidly down the corridor, hearing the sounds of a drunken party and singing.

He didn't dare knock at her door. If she knew who it was, she might scream for help, alerting the party-goers next door. Instead he had to figure out a way to force her to listen to him.

Gene could detect no light coming from her room. Knocking lightly, he muttered, "Housekeeping." Still no answer. He tried the door, finding it unlocked. If she wasn't there, he'd wait for her return, subduing her if he had to—anything to make her listen.

Opening the door, he quietly entered the room, feeling like a rapist. Right away he knew something was wrong. Someone had pulled back the draperies and moonlight streamed in. The room overlooked the water where the Atlantic meets the Gulf of Mexico. Seeing that the bed was empty and unmade, he stole across the room and pulled the draperies shut. The room was in pitch blackness.

He switched on a lamp. With an instinct sharpened by all his years on the police force, he was overcome by an eerie feeling deep in his gut. Swirling around, he spotted her.

She lay on the floor beside the large double bed, her legs tucked up toward her stomach. It was like a fetal pose. She wore bikini panties. They were still wet, indicating her death had been recent. In her struggle for life, her right breast had slipped out of a cup of a flowered bra. A white nylon rope had been looped twice around her neck. Her dead eyes seemed to stare at him. Her hands were bunched up near her throat as if she'd clutched the cord cutting off her air supply. He checked her body for pulse, finding her wrist had the coldness of death.

Shaken, he moved fast to turn off the light. He had to get out of here at once. It already might be too late. He waited at the door. From across the hall came the sound of partying. Cracking the door slightly, he checked the corridor, finding it deserted. As he slipped out, the door from across the hall opened and two men, one supporting the other, staggered out, "This party's dull. Let's go to Tony's."

Gene could tell the eyes of the more sober man sensed something wrong. He shut the door behind him, not wanting to appear panic-stricken. As he did, a burly man came up behind the two guys. "What's going on here? That's a woman's room. A sexy blonde. Not your room. You're a fucking thief!"

Gene turned and fled down the corridor as the burly man shouted after him. It was all too convenient. How had that burly man known he was a thief? He jumped the railing and cut through the garden before the police could be summoned.

Cutting off Duval and heading down a side street, he found a taxi and asked to be driven to Stock Island, a seedy backwater adjoining Key West. Here in the garden of a broken down trailer, he had to figure a way out of all this. A road block might be set up.

He ripped off his jacket and shirt, wearing only a T-shirt. Mussing his hair, he wished it were longer. With a pocket knife he cut off the legs to his pants, making shorts of them.

Later, on the highway, he hitched a ride in a large van with a fat, bearded young driver who introduced himself as "Whale Man." Gene took a seat near his stringy-haired girlfriend. They were headed for Pompano Beach. He told them he was going to Fort Lauderdale.

Up the Keys the van rolled, passing seemingly endless bridges. To him, it was like riding with a bunch of god damn freaks, but he knew their language well, pretending to be one of them. He didn't admit it, but suggested he'd run into a problem in Key West peddling drugs. The girlfriend, Allison, offered him a smelly sleeping bag in the rear of the van, and he retreated there to avoid conversation. He only pretended to sleep.

They reached Miami just as the Beatles began to pump out "Here Comes the Sun" on the tape deck. After breakfast in a greasy spoon, Whale Man headed up the coast to Fort Lauderdale. Gene was let out five blocks from his secret apartment. He had to go there and change clothes and pick up his weapons before heading back to Okeechobee in his old car which had belonged to his mother. It was parked in the garage at the apartment house, and now he could thank God he'd kept it in good running order.

By the time he reached the apartment, the first light of day streaked the sky.

He pulled off his clothes and headed for the shower, until the whining of two gray cats in the garden below caught his attention. The cats, who annoyed his neighbors by raiding the garbage, looked up sorrowfully at him. It seemed to him that their hungry, accusatory look resembled the expression trapped in Pamela's dead eyes. He couldn't stand that look. In the kitchen he opened a can of sardines, wrapped them in a thin sheet of newspaper and tossed the soggy mess to the cats.

That would be his last act of kindness. Already his mind spun with plans for the day.

***

At Desire, Lars led Buck down a long corridor to a distant wing of the property. He inserted a security code, and a steel door opened for him. Lars turned and looked at Buck with trepidation. "Do you want me to go inside with you?"

"I'll be fine," Buck said.

"He didn't want to leave Switzerland. Fought like hell. There are no blunt instruments in the suite. The room is monitored. If you're in danger at any time, my men are coming in."

Buck walked down the hallway and into the open-doored suite. At first he couldn't see Shelley in the darkened room until he detected a movement in a chair. Shelley sat in a silk-upholstered armchair gazing upon what appeared to be an outdoor scene with vegetation. The vegetation was real but the effect of the outdoors was fake. They were underground.

"Shelley," Buck said.

The boy rose to face Buck. He was clad only in the briefest of bikini underwear. He looked thinner than Buck had ever seen him before. "Who do you think it is? John Wayne?"

Buck stood looking at him for a long moment. This was not the Shelley he'd known. How could he be so different and have changed so much in such a short time?

"Why did you kidnap me?" Shelley asked.

"I'm going to try to undo whatever has been done to you," Buck said.

"Let me go. I promise if you free me, I won't bring kidnapping charges."

"I don't even know if you're in control of your own mind," Buck said.

"I'm fine. I want to go back to where I was. I was safe there. I'm afraid here."

He walked closer to Shelley who backed away, an alarming fear growing in his eyes. "Don't come any closer. I'll scream."

"Go ahead and scream. What good will that do you?"

A look of hopeless despair settled over Shelley's face. Buck walked over and sat down in the chair, looking at the vegetation in the fake daylight. "I'm not going to keep you here forever. Just long enough to get your own free will back."

"I know my mind," Shelley said.

He came tantalizingly close to Buck, who took in the luminous beauty of his body before meeting his eyes. "I want to go back to Switzerland."

"It looked to me like you were in a prison there. Here in Florida or
in California you could have the glamorous life you've always wanted.
I could get it for you. You said you wanted to be a movie star. I'll have
the power to get that for you."

Shelley looked bewildered. Tears welled in his eyes, as a pathetic
look came over his face. "I just don't know."

Buck faced the boy. This time he didn't back away. "I don't want
to hurt you." He reached out and rubbed Shelley's smooth cheek with
his hand.

The boy was trembling.

"Why are you so afraid of me?" Buck asked.

"I know why you brought me here," Shelley said.

"I'm not going to rape you," Buck said. "I wouldn't want you in
this frame of mind. I will never force myself on you."

"You're not going to rape me?" Shelley asked.

"I'm not going to hurt you ever. But I am going to bring two or
three men here to talk to you. I need their professional assurances that
you're okay. There may be quite a few sessions. These men are trained
to work with brainwashed victims. I hope you'll cooperate."

"You don't have to bring those men here." He moved slightly closer
to Buck. "Do you really mean it? You'd take me to Hollywood and
everything."

"Of course," Buck said. "In the meantime, I'll take care of you."
He paused and looked deeply into Shelley's eyes. "And I'll ask nothing in return." Buck turned and walked toward the door.

Shelley called back to him. "Don't go."

Buck came back and took Shelley in his arms and hugged him
affectionately but not too tightly. He kissed him but only on the neck.

The boy was shaking all over. "I don't know what to do." He started
to cry. Buck attempted to break away but Shelley held on to him.

Buck took his hands and ran his fingers over Shelley's body. This
seemed to put the boy at ease.

"Please pick me up and carry me over to that bed," Shelley whispered in his ear.

Buck easily picked Shelley up in his arms and carried him to the
bed where he gently lowered him onto the mauve sheets. Buck started
to raise his body up but Shelley reached out for him, pulling him down

on top of his lithe frame.

"Would you kiss me?" Shelley asked.

Gently Buck pressed his lips against Shelley's and kissed him tenderly, then withdrew.

Shelley looked disappointed. "I thought you were going to rape me."

"It's not going to happen—not today."

"Will you come back and sleep with me tonight?" Shelley asked.

He looked into Shelley's deep blue eyes. "When the world's prettiest boy makes a request like that, what can I say but yes?"

***

After leaving Shelley locked away, Buck called Susan and Don, letting them know he was back in Okeechobee. He invited them to Desire. Instead of arriving in a limousine, Don volunteered to drive Susan over in his new sports car, which Buck had bought for him.

In the library, locked away from the rest of the house, Buck seated himself before a giant TV screen. Lars propped Buck's feet up on an ottoman and gently removed his shoes and socks.

Buck knew what the lead broadcast was: the death of Leroy Fitzgerald. Gene was the prime suspect, and a manhunt was on for him. Even with such overwhelming evidence, Buck still couldn't bring himself to believe that Gene had killed Leroy. Buck suspected—and he couldn't even begin to prove this—that Calder had ordered Leroy killed.

Buck wondered if Gene would make contact with Robert. Impulsively he dialed Robert on the island. Henry picked up the phone. "Is Robert there?" Buck asked.

"He sure is, and driving me crazy. He's pacing up and down all the time, asking if Mr. Robinson has called. There ain't been no calls from Mr. Robinson."

In a minute, Robert was on the phone. "What is it?" he asked sharply without a greeting.

"I just wanted you to know that Uncle Milty has made great progress in drawing up our documents. We're prepared to meet all your requests."

"Do you mean that?" Robert asked.

"I not only mean it, but in case something should ever go wrong with you in the future, I will always be there for you."

"My future will be just fine when I get the money you owe me," Robert said. "Could we keep this phone call short? I'm expecting an urgent call."

Buck wanted to ask about Gene but didn't. "You've got to come into town to sign the documents. I've booked you the presidential suite at the Rooney Plaza. Uncle Milty will call you and arrange a meeting."

"What would Uncle Milty be if not the little Jew doing the bidding for the rich man."

"Please don't say that," Buck said.

"I liked Patrick. I never liked Uncle Milty. He always had a crush on you. Always giving you wet kisses. I didn't even want you to kiss me after Uncle Milty had liplocked you. I thought he was disgusting. Now Patrick has betrayed me too. He won't even take my calls."

"They are my friends," Buck said.

"Everybody, including slutty little Susan, is after your money," Robert said, sighing. "I'll go to the Roney Plaza. But right now I have to stay by the phone."

When Buck put down the phone, a great sadness swept over him.

***

Concealed in the Collins' backyard, Gene waited patiently until his former chief, Biff, had left after grilling Barry—no doubt about Leroy's death. He suspected that the chief also knew about Pamela's death as well.

He'd left his mother's old and battered car parked eight blocks from the Collins' home and had walked to Barry's house. Pamela's murder, he knew, would bring on a massive manhunt, making Leroy's death dim in comparison. After all, Leroy was only a fag; Pamela was the wife of a candidate.

He'd listened to the radio. The news concerned Leroy's murder and the death of Old Buck I, with no mention of Pamela's death.

When all the police officers, including Biff, had left Barry's house, Gene knew that Barry had not accused him in any way. If he had, Biff would have ordered police protection for the candidate in case Gene came back.

He crossed the lawn to get nearer to the back door, concealing himself behind a hibiscus bush. He still had Barry's keys. He pressed a lever on his red-faced watch and the ruby plastic lit up 12:01, a minute past his deadline. He smiled at the slight delay, knowing he'd given Barry one more minute of his life. Although he carried a pistol in his holster, he gripped a nylon cord in one hand. He wanted Barry to die as Pamela had, struggling and clutching the cord as he whimpered in muffled gasps for precious air.

He inserted his key and entered the house. Passing quietly through the kitchen, he slipped into the living room, concealing himself behind a library shelf. From across the room he could see most of Barry's body, curled like a fetus, as if he'd passed out on the sofa, his still full drink resting on the floor behind him.

Gene had worn mirrored sunglasses. As Barry choked to death, he wanted him to see, not his eyes, but his own eyes and, in witnessing the fright and panic there, to know and experience what Pamela had felt.

All day he had been haunted by billboard pictures of Barry, staring at him as he drove through the streets of Okeechobee. There Barry was projecting a false image to fool a naïve public. Not only was Barry's picture on billboards, it would soon be on the television news and on the front pages of newspapers, depicting him as a grief-stricken husband, winning more undeserved sympathy for him. Pamela's murder would hold nationwide interest.

Barry got up from the sofa. "Gene," he said in a hesitant voice. "I know you're here. Come out of hiding."

Nothing could have surprised Gene more than that invitation. He deftly removed his pistol from his holster, wiping the sweat from his brow. Pointing the pistol directly at Barry, Gene stepped out of the shadows.

"I knew you were coming," Barry said, "I didn't tell Biff. I don't believe Biff even knows of Pamela's death. The maid hasn't even gone into her room. Like you, I learned about Pamela's death the hard way."

"How did you find out?" Gene asked.

"I was tipped off by someone on Calder's staff." With pleading eyes, he moved closer to Gene. "Believe me, I didn't know."

"You guys set me up like a fucking patsy!" Gene yelled in a hoarse voice, his face reflecting bitter anger.

"Calder set you up. Calder and your dear, beloved Rose. Pamela could have ruined me, but I wouldn't have killed her." His hands thrust into his dressing robe pockets, he fixed his eyes on Gene.

He had Barry at his complete mercy, but he was in a fog. He almost believed him.

"I could have had the police stay and guard me if I'd fingered you. I didn't. I think I wanted you to come back here and kill me."

"You're crazy, man," Gene said.

Barry turned his head away as if looking for something. "See that statement I'm working on for the papers?" He pointed to a letter resting on his secretary. "I'm resigning from the mayor's race."

"Are you denouncing Calder to the press?"

"He'd have me killed if I did that," Barry said. "Calder and Rose only have power over me if I want power myself."

Barry reached for a box on the stand, but Gene slapped his outstretched hand, knocking over cigarettes, scattering them all over the carpet. "You are going to die!"

"I know it," Barry said. He bent down and reached for one of the cigarettes. Gene let him light it. "In the meantime, I'm going to have a smoke."

Gene pointed the pistol at Barry. The trigger clicked. He didn't fire it. Barry was pushed back into a chair. It was high time he killed him.

"I'm like you," Barry said. "I'm one of their victims, too. Like Pamela. As bad as she was, she didn't deserve that."

The weapon felt limp and clumsy in Gene's hand. He'd forgotten about the cord.

"That one moment, that little girl," Barry said. "One silly mistake, and you've paid all your life. I think Buck Brooke had you framed the second time around. What's her name, Maria? Her mother works for Brooke now. Come on, man. Don't be stupid."

Gene knew he couldn't kill Barry.

"I'm no good," Barry said. "I don't pretend to be, at least not with you. I'm not as rotten as Rose. No one's as rotten as Calder. I never killed anyone. What originally got me into this slime was making love to bodies, not killing them."

Gene looked at his wrist watch. He was wasting time. "Are you calling the police the moment I leave?"

Barry sighed in relief. That question confirmed that he wasn't going to be killed. "No, because I think I know what you're going to do. For once, I've outguessed Calder. You're the only person who will get me out of this sick business. Because of you, I might one day be free of them."

"You want me to do the job for you?" Gene asked.

"You're their new game. I just hope you get them before they get you."

"Biff wants me dead, doesn't he?" Gene asked.

"He'll never arrest you. He's not going to bring you in. His men are going to shoot to kill. You know too much."

"If Biff is working so closely with Calder, why doesn't the chief know Pamela is dead?"

"With Biff, Calder operates only on a need-to-know level. Biff will learn about Pamela's death soon enough. Surely in an hour or so."

"Where is he now?" Gene asked.

"He's gone to the Vulcan Baths for his little afternoon luncheon break."

"How can he go there without being recognized?"

"When he takes off that wig and that red mustache, he blends in completely with all the other old sex hunters at the baths," Barry said.

A vivacious buzz played in Gene's head like a medley of voices, each calling him in different directions. The bullets in his pistol seemed like capsules, and in those capsules a heady elixir danced. He turned and headed toward the kitchen, through the open door and into the backyard.

While he was free, there was much to be done.

***

Susan came into the foyer of Desire looking so fresh-faced that Buck felt embarrassed at her seeing him in his rumpled clothes, unshaven, with ruffled hair and red eyes from lack of sleep.

In contrast, Susan appeared like a wildflower in full bloom, with her long auburn hair, her prominent breasts, her ivory skin. She wore a well-tailored suit with a porcelain rose necklace on a satin cord around her neck.

Taking in her exciting presence, Buck said, "You look great. All except the rose necklace. My least favorite flower."

In a dramatic gesture, she unfastened the rose necklace and tossed it on the sofa.

"You don't have to go that far," he cautioned her.

"I don't like Sister Rose either." She kissed him firmly on the lips. As he pulled away, he spotted Don, in blue jeans and a T-shirt, coming into the foyer. Don came over to him, holding him in a tight embrace. When he backed away, he said, "Welcome home, boss man. I've missed you."

Buck put his arm around Don's waist, tightening his grip and liking the rock hard stomach he felt.

Ignoring them, Susan was taking in the splendor of the mansion. "This is fabulous. Incredible."

"You certainly have come up in the world," Don said, looking around. "I can't wait for the guided tour."

"Lars is going to take you on a tour," Buck said. "He'll even show you your private suite. I want you to feel free to live here."

"I'm spellbound," Susan said. "Thanks for the invitation. I'll take you up on it. How about you, Don?"

I was born to live in such a place, and now I'm here," Don said. Lars appeared to take them on a tour.

Two hours later, Buck stood looking out the gigantic picture windows of Ahmad's living room, opening onto the pool down below. At the far end of the pool, he could see Don removing all his clothes for a nude swim.

"A magnificent specimen," Susan said, coming up behind Buck and putting her arms around his waist. "He's good at his work. Let's keep him around."

He turned to her and smiled, kissing her lightly on the lips. "Let's do that."

"Actually Don has heart, feelings, sensitivity," she said. "Somewhat."

"We're the best thing that ever happened to him—and he knows that," Buck said.

Lars appeared in the living room. "You have an urgent call from your attorney."

"Do you want me to leave the room?" Susan asked.

"No, stay," Buck said, picking up the phone. "Uncle Milty, my darling man! I'm here with Susan."

"You'd better be watching TV," Milty said. "In about three minutes there's going to be an hour's retrospective devoted to the old man.

They even have newsreel pictures of you when you were a kid. It's on Channel 13."

"Turn on Channel 13," he called out to Susan.

"Gene seems to have gone insane," Uncle Milty said. "Killing Leroy and all."

"If he did kill Leroy," Buck said.

"If not Gene, then who?"

"Calder Martin."

"You can't prove that." Milty coughed slightly. "I just had to tell you of some alarming discoveries being made. My staff and I are going over old Buck's assets. He may have been forced out of top management by stockholders of all those papers he used to own. But in every case he was incredibly rewarded in a settlement. He took millions and poured the money into land most realtors viewed as worthless. What was viewed as worthless land in the Fifties isn't necessarily looked upon that way today."

"Exactly what are you getting at?" Buck asked.

"You may be America's greatest land baron. In the past hour we have read only some of the holdings. It appears, to cite only one example, you may own Eastern Oregon."

"I've never been to Oregon," Buck said.

"Perhaps a visit is long overdue," Milty said.

"On the way there, we might stop off in Northeastern Maine. Also Indiana."

"Indiana?" Buck said in astonishment. "No one's ever heard of Indiana."

"Old Buck Brooke has heard of Indiana, and Indiana has heard of him. Not to mention Oklahoma."

"Now that's a state I've visited, although under unusual circumstances," Buck said.

"Have you ever been to Northwestern Texas or Western Kansas?" Milty asked.

"No one in his right mind would go there," Buck said.

"Let's make one final stopover. Montana. You are now the cattle queen of Montana."

"Wasn't that an old movie with Barbara Stanwyck and Ronald Reagan?"

"Who knows? You're taking over the role now."

"I've never been to Montana either. But I've been skiing in Wyoming."

"I don't think you own anything in Wyoming. But you do own a condo in Sun Valley, Idaho. Did you know that?"

"I didn't know any of this. He paid me forty-five thousand a year."

"Hurry and watch that TV show," Milty said. "Another thing. I'm afraid of Gene. If you didn't have all those security guards, I'd hire plenty of them to protect you and Susan. For all I know, your lives could be in danger."

"What about Robert?" Buck asked.

"You know what I think?" Milty said. "Gene is in love with Robert. It's all tied up with you in some sick way. Let's give Robert his five million. Not in installments. The whole thing."

"Why?"

"Because with all that money they could flee the country. Give them your plane. Offer to fly Robert anywhere. Don't say anything but set it up so that Gene can be slipped aboard that plane. Perhaps as one of the members of the staff. I could arrange that. When I meet with Robert, I'll make it perfectly clear without making it perfectly clear. They'll probably head south. South America, some place. I'll hint at all that. Let's have that meeting with Robert like now."

"You may be right," Buck said. "We could be in some sort of danger." Susan had seated herself in front of the television, but that remark caught her interest. She looked at him with grave concern. He nodded at her, hoping to assure her that everything was all right.

"I also need to know your funeral plans at once," Milty said. "The press is pounding on the door. Or do you want me to handle it?"

Buck looked over at Susan. "I'm going to ask Susan."

"No better choice unless you could get Jacqueline Kennedy herself. Gotta run. I love you. The show's about to begin."

Buck went over to the sofa and sat down beside Susan, reaching for her hand. On the screen flashed the title of the show: AMERICA'S LAST CITIZEN KANE.

***

Twelve minutes into watching the biography of old Buck, the program was interrupted for a news bulletin. Pamela had been found murdered at the Pier House in Key West. Broadcast first as a rumor on radio, the report had been officially confirmed by the police. Gene Robinson had been spotted leaving her motel room. The manhunt for him had been intensified. Reporters were clamoring for Biff to hold a press conference but his office claimed the chief was involved in a high-level investigation and wasn't available.

Locked in seclusion with his two daughters, Barry too was unable to face the press. A spokesperson said that Barry's first obligation now was "to console and offer comfort to his grief-stricken daughters."

As a commercial went on, Buck turned to Susan. "That's the news. What's the truth?"

A despondent look came over her. "I think he's innocent."

"So do I," Buck said. "While we wait for more news, we've got to go ahead with the funeral."

"I'll handle everything," Susan said. She came over to him and put her arm around him to comfort him.

"It was the worst of lives and the best of lives," Buck said, looking at the TV set. "Old Buck did a lot of good in the world, and a lot of other things best forgotten. He wanted to be cremated and to have his ashes thrown from his yacht into the sea."

"That's very dramatic—just like him," Susan said.

Mention of the yacht brought back a memory of Robert on the island. Right now Robert had control of his grandather's yacht. Buck planned to reclaim it when Robert came back to town. But before he did, Buck wanted one final meeting with Robert. He excused himself and headed for a library off the main living room. "I've got to make an urgent call."

Locked into the privacy of the library, he dialed Robert, hoping that he hadn't left the island. Henry picked up the phone. After greeting Henry, he asked, "Has Robert left?"

"He's still here," Henry said.

"Put him on."

In a minute Robert came on the line. "I was just getting ready to leave. I was writing a note thanking you for use of your island."

"I'd like to be thanked in person," Buck said.

"What does that mean?"

"It means I'm coming to the island," Buck said. "You used to think I was a pretty hot guy before you developed other interests. I thought for old time's sake, we should say good-bye face to face. Man to man."

"I don't see what good it will do," Robert said. "But if you really want to see me, I'll wait here for you."

"I'm leaving now," Buck said.

***

The police chief, Biff, had not really been part of the day's choreography. But Gene changed his mind after Barry told him that he'd find him at the Vulcan Baths. Since the law wasn't going to punish Biff, Gene would have to.

On the portable radio, as he drove in his mother's old car, he heard the news that the manhunt for him had intensified. He was wanted for questioning in connection with Pamela's murder. A maid had discovered her body at the Pier House. A radio station, beating the TV news, had broadcast the sketchy and still unconfirmed reported. Gene had been identified by that burly man who'd seen him leaving her room.

With all the police business whirling around his head, Biff must be a sex addict requiring his daily fix at the Vulcan Baths.

After checking into the baths, Gene went directly to an anonymous cubicle where he stripped down, putting on a flimsy robe. He headed for the shower room with slanted boards, dishes of soap, stacks of graying towels, and a smell of disinfectant.

He ignored the stares of middle-aged men with paunchy midriffs and brushed away a wandering hand or two. After half an hour, he'd almost given up hope that Biff would ever come down to the steam room. Time was valuable—the most valuable it had ever been to him—and he feared he was wasting it.

Back upstairs, he wandered the floors for another half hour with the sex hunters. Wet tongues flicked out at him, and the sound of convulsing bodies assailed his eardrums.

As eyes riveted on him, he was king of the mountain, the superstud center stage. He let the eyes feast on his thick, muscular legs. He let them dream of the delights his body would give them.

The smell of marijuana and amyl nitrate filled the air. One old, fat man, leaning up against a peeling wall, reached out to grope him. He slammed his fist into the guy's guts. That ended that. No more hands reached out for him. No one followed him any more. He wanted it that way from now on.

Finally, Biff emerged from one of the cubicles, heading for the shower and sauna room. At first Gene didn't recognize him. Without his red wig and mustache, he looked completely different, and almost twenty years older. He blended in perfectly with the other middle-age sex hunters at the baths.

As Biff left the floor, Gene trailed him. In the whirlpool area, no one was in sight. At the far side of the pool, two men lay in each other's arms, fondling each other's genitals.

Gene checked the toilets. Empty. Biff could be in only one place. He'd gone into the sauna room.

Gene stripped off his gown and removed a nylon cord he'd carried in a towel. Slowly he opened the creaking door and entered the sauna. Only one body was there. It had to be Biff. The sight of his former chief's heavily perspiring nude body with its shriveled sex disgusted Gene. He thanked god they were alone. Anyone could walk in at any moment.

He moved toward Biff. As Gene's massive frame came into view, he could almost see Biff's eyes light up, as if his heart were pounding furiously. Biff's eyes were transfixed by Gene's genitals.

Before Biff could look up in his face, Gene walked to where the Chief was sitting on a tiled wall seat. Gene's cock was only two inches from Biff's mouth. At this point Gene knew Biff wouldn't look up.

Biff's stubby fingers reached out to fondle and weigh Gene's balls. With his other hand, Biff pulled back the skin from Gene's penis and plunged down on his cock. He was an expert, taking the whole mass of flesh down his throat. Gene hardened at once. He was overcome with sexual excitement.

As Biff slurped and devoured him, his hands traveled up to Gene's nipples. For the first time Biff looked up into Gene's face. It was a look of such astonishment Gene would remember it always, even if always had become a short time.

Biff withdrew suddenly from Gene's cock. Before either of them could say anything or make the next move, a look was exchanged between them. It was the look of the victim meeting his executioner.

That look ended quickly, as life preserving forces welled in Biff. "What the hell...YOU!" His accusation stabbed the steamy air. It was an accusation no jury would hear.

In one lightning move, Gene slipped the cord around Biff's bloated neck. Like a wild animal, Biff crawled about three feet toward a broken tile ledge. Gene tightened the grip on the cord, pulling him back. Biff kicked and moaned but didn't have enough air in him to let out a real scream. His left hand jerked wildly as if looking for a target, finding it in Gene's muscular leg, where his fingernails dug in, drawing blood. Still holding him by the cord, Gene jerked it tighter and tighter before smashing Biff's unprotected head against the tiles. Biff's claws gradually withdrew from their blood-sucking hold on Gene's leg.

Up close he could smell the foulness of Biff's liquor-soaked breath. The chief's eyes bulged, a desperate plea for help.

As Gene held his former chief in his grip, Gene knew that Biff was already dead. Seconds before, a gurgling sound had escaped from Biff's throat, the last rattle before oblivion. Gene released his grip on the cord, letting it fall on the damp tiles. Biff's body collapsed on the tiles in a crumpled heap, his gaping mouth forming a large O.

Gene hurried from the steam room. Now fully erect, the two men were still engaged at the other end of the pool. Upstairs, Gene took a handkerchief and tied it around his bloody leg. He quickly slipped on his clothes. He hadn't checked any valuables. Instead of returning to the front desk, he slipped out the back entrance.

No sign of life anywhere. He raced across the parking lot and headed for his next appointment. His upcoming victims didn't know their time had come.

On the way to the next fatal encounter, he stopped at a deserted beach. He got out of the car and decided to go for a walk. He needed a few minutes between appointments. If anyone spotted him running, Gene could easily be taken for a jogger. The air smelled clean, fresh, and, though the ocean wind had a slight chill to it, he was on fire.

About half a mile up the beach, he stopped—panting, breathless, collapsing on the sands, hoping to summon energy for what lay ahead. His thoughts were on Robert. He had to reach Robert but feared he couldn't call the island, knowing the phone was tapped. Maybe he'd take his boat there to make contact with Robert.

Pulling himself up, he brushed off sand and decided to jog back to his waiting car. He looked up at the bright sun. The day was moving rapidly along.

***

The mid-afternoon was at its hottest but Gene knew that the sun would soon begin its descent. He made his way across the garden to Buck's villa. The lawn seemed to have grown used to his footsteps. No sound came from inside the house. A yellow lamp glowed by the rear door, leading to the kitchen. It was a night light but Clara, the maid, hadn't bothered to turn it off all day.

Deftly he removed the globe and unscrewed the bulb. He didn't have to do that, but felt compelled to. As he extinguished the light, it seemed like all breath and life had left him, too. His body trembled as he removed a knife he'd bought. With it, he cut through the screen door, unfastening the latch. Slipping onto the porch, he took out a glass cutter from his leather bag and slashed into a window pane of a door opening onto the kitchen.

Inside the house was still. He could only imagine what life was like when Robert and Buck inhabited the house. The kitchen was like one of those houses where he used to work as a boy, taking odd jobs where he could find them, often mowing people's lawns and carrying out their garbage. Those kitchens are all the same. Butcher block counter tops, gleaming stainless steel double sinks, copper utensils hanging from a cork board.

He just knew Clara and Maria were still in the house, but there was no sign of them. He crept upstairs to the master bedroom where he'd made love to Robert. The door to the bedroom stood wide open. The draperies were pulled. In the shadowy afternoon light, the bed was perfectly made, not a wrinkle. No one slept here any more.

As he turned his head, he heard a sound coming from an adjoining bedroom which opened onto a rear garden. He concealed himself behind a door and waited.

Another sound. Someone was getting up. Whoever it was flipped on a radio. It was one of those Spanish stations which broadcast programs to the invaders who refused to learn the language of their new country

In the hallway, the sound of approaching footsteps alerted him. As she passed him, she didn't look in Buck's room. He saw only the side of her face and the back of her head. He knew who it was. The Cuban woman's eyes had followed him for months as he'd come and gone from his house which no longer existed because of her. Seeing the back of her head, he remembered his house going up in flames. She'd been responsible for that. Clara and Maria. How he hated the sound of those two names.

In a chenille robe, Clara slowly descended the winding staircase in her loose-fitting bedroom slippers. Rubbing sleep from her eyes following her afternoon siesta, she took one step at a time. When he heard her shuffling feet on the tile floor downstairs, he, too, trailed her down the carpeted steps, one stair at a time. One of his hands iron-gripped a stiletto.

She went into the kitchen, turning on a light since the blinds were drawn. At first he feared she might see the glass cut but she was too sloppily indifferent to notice a detail like that.

She headed for the utility room right off the kitchen, a liquor bottle in her hand. She turned on the light and poured herself a drink. She left the door open. From where he stood, he could see her clearly, as her back was to him.

She rubbed her back, as if she had a sharp pain, then removed her chenille robe, hanging it on a hook. On the adjoining hook she reached for her maid's uniform. Bending over to remove her bedroom slippers, she thrust her chubby ass virtually into his face.

He moved forward, shutting the door to the utility room and locking it. He was alone in the small room with her.

Completely nude, she whirled around to face this invasion. Her hand reached to cover her breasts. Her face flashed an immediate recognition. Other than Biff facing his execution, Gene had never seen such terror as that reflected in the woman's eyes.

Before she could scream, he'd muffled her mouth with the big palm of his hand, holding the tip of the stiletto at her throat. From a mirrored wall, an image of the two of them—locked in a grotesque embrace—swept before his eyes. They just stood there for a few brief seconds, locked in this dance of death, swaying back and forth. Her dark eyes were wide and luminous.

"If you scream I'll kill you," he threatened her. He slowly removed his hand from her mouth. She was too choked to utter a sound. Tears ran down her face. He seized one of her large breasts, his fingernails digging in. At her first outcry, he jabbed the tip of the stiletto into her neck, drawing blood. Her startled cry became only a low, soft moan. "Señor, señor, señor."

"Did Brooke pay you to frame me?"

The woman looked as if she'd suddenly been reprieved. "Sí, sí, sí." Her terrified eyes sought his. "He forced me. He made me lie. *Kill him!*"

He brought his knee up sharply into the softness of her belly, as he kept the stiletto at her throat.

Her fear finally overcame her. She fell on the floor, writhing.

He towered over her, holding the stiletto. Her ugly sex was widespread, as clearly visible as a gaping wound. His face tightened. "You wanted me, didn't you? You get your wish."

He fell on her, stabbing at her sex repeatedly—he didn't know the number of times. Her squeals were like those of a pig at castration. Blood spurted from the wounds as her bellowing cry for help filled the room. As her screams died, her throat made only gurgling noises.

After the stiletto rape, he slashed again up toward her chest. The stiletto entered so fast it hit a bone, sliding from his grasp. He clutched it again, as if fondling it, then his grip tightened once more as he slashed her neck where she'd sucked in the air that gave breath to lies against him.

He'd been oblivious to the sound. Now he heard it clearly, as it grew louder and louder, like a drum beating inside his head. Someone pounded on the door. "Mama, mama, mama!"

Getting up, covered with blood, he stood before the door for a long moment before turning the lock. He needed this respite to summon his courage. "God," he said. "God." He knew what he had to do and, even this late in his choreography, he resented the part he'd been assigned.

Maria opened the door, rushing into the room. With a life all its own, the stiletto plunged right into her heart. She didn't have a chance to scream. The sight of him holding the weapon and her own blood-soaked mother on the floor had captured her in a paralytic trance. He left the stiletto in her heart. He would have no more need for the weapon.

Maria stood there for a lost moment before falling over. When she had joined her mother in the blood bath on the tiles, he held both of his hands up to his face. Empty, but bloody.

He bolted from the room, slamming the door behind him, wanting to be free of the memory. He ran up the stairs and into the master bedroom. Here he peeled the clothes from his body, clambering toward the shower. He turned on the water at full blast, fiery hot, letting its jet spray cleanse him thoroughly. It was an act of purification. By the time he'd showered and had come back into the bedroom, he had calmed down considerably. A kind of peace had come over him. Opening the door to Buck's closet, he removed a pair of slacks and a sports shirt. He slipped into them, finding that they were the same size. Bundling up his bloody clothes, he took them with him, planning to get rid of them later.

Downstairs again, he hurried past the utility room, not looking inside. In the kitchen, he poured himself a cup of coffee, imagining Buck doing that before he left for work. By the coffee pot he noticed a pad. On it someone had scribbled the name, Señor Dante, and a telephone number.

Impulsively he dialed the number, letting it ring seven times. It was four o'clock in the afternoon. Finally, it was answered. He recognized Robert's voice.

"Hello," Robert said into the phone. He seemed ready to hang up. Gene was afraid to speak to him, fearing the line was tapped. "Gene, is that you?" Robert asked hesitantly. When there was no answer, Robert hung up.

Gene slammed down the phone. The call had confirmed that Robert was still on the island. Gene would take his boat and go to Robert's side.

Outside the lawn was still wet as if a light rain had fallen for only a minute or so. Birds nested in the trees and the sound of their chirping filled the air. It was a perfect day.

Carrying his blood-soaked clothes, he headed five blocks down the street to his mother's old car. Beside his car an old and half-dead mongrel had come to rest. Brittle-boned and mangy, it won his sympathy immediately. He was almost tempted to go back in the house and get the dog something to eat. He was reminded of the cats and the sardines he'd offered them. He had no time for any more kindness to animals.

In his car again, he headed for the distant marina. With Robert, he would make plans for his escape after he'd accomplished one final mission in Okeechobee.

In the late afternoon breeze, he liked the way he'd fitted into Buck's clothes. If life had been different, if he had gotten the breaks Buck had, he could fit very well into an easy life.

He'd felt he'd really belonged in Buck's house, yet knew such a dream was only to be dreamed. Perhaps in some far and distant land, Robert and he would also have a fine house. It would be a beautiful place where the weather was always warm and sunny. Maybe they'd acquire some pets. Pets would be nice. Too many animals were homeless in the world. Perhaps Robert, when he came into his millions, would hire Sandy and Jill to run the house and grounds for them

He no longer thought he was going to die. Right now he felt that he'd live forever in Robert's arms. He could enjoy the good life just like Buck. After all, Robert had assured him he was a better man than Buck.

***

On the sofa, in the living room of Buck's private island, Gene spotted Robert sitting, watching a news broadcast about Gene himself. Gene was wanted by the police for questioning in the murders of both Leroy and Pamela. Gene slipped up from behind, reaching out and muffling Robert's mouth. "It's me, baby," Gene whispered in his ear. Satisfied that Robert knew who it was, he removed his hand.

"Gene!" Robert practically cried out his name. "I've been half out of my mind with worry."

Gene reached to hold him in a tight embrace, before giving him a long, deep kiss. "I'm back with you."

"The police..." Robert seemed hesitant, unsure.

Gene felt that Robert needed to be reassured. "We've got to talk. I don't want the black guy to know I'm here."

"I know what to do." Robert gave him a quick kiss. In minutes he returned. "It's handled."

"He's still here," Gene protested.

"He lives in a cottage at the far end of the island. He won't disturb us. Let's go into the kitchen. I bet you're starved unless you grabbed some fast food on the run."

"I didn't. I felt the fewer people who saw me, the better off I was."

In the kitchen Robert quickly prepared Gene a plate of roast beef

Henry had recently cooked. Gene devoured the food eagerly. Until Robert suggested it, he didn't know he was starving. He consumed a large can of V-8 juice. Only then did he settle back in the chair.

"I know you didn't kill anybody," Robert said.

Robert's conviction was a little too weak for Gene but it was a proclamation of his innocence he wanted to hear.

"I've killed nobody," Gene said. He sensed distrust in Robert's face. "You don't have to ask: I know your next question. What in hell am I doing wearing Buck's clothes?"

"I was wondering."

"I went to his house and slipped inside the door. I was looking for you. I figured you would either be here or still on the island."

"Did Clara see you?" Robert asked.

"The bitch was gone. No doubt on a shopping trip with all the money Buck is paying her to blackmail me. I went upstairs and showered and shaved. I borrowed some of Buck's clothes."

"I'm glad you did." He leaned over and kissed Gene. "I'm also glad you came looking for me."

"When I learned you weren't at Buck's house, I came here in my boat. I've been driving around in my mother's old car. It hasn't been seen on the streets in Okeechobee in years. I kept the license up to date."

Robert glanced at his watch. "You can't stay here. We don't have much time."

"Are you expecting someone?" Gene asked.

"You might as well know. Buck is on his way here now."

"Buck?" Gene was startled. "Why is he coming here? I thought it was all over between the two of you."

"He wants to meet with me to work out the final details of our financial agreement. After that, I'm taking old Buck's yacht and going to that meeting with Milton, the lawyer guy."

"How can we hook up?" Gene asked.

"I want you to meet me at the presidential suite at the Roney Plaza. It's on the grounds of the property. You don't have to go through the lobby or anything. I've already checked. The suite has three doors. You're to come to the door numbered 1001. It will be open. I'll be waiting there."

"What happens then?" Buck asked.

"We'll flee the country together," Robert said. "I'm trying to figure out the safest way."

"You're saving my ass." Gene pulled him over and kissed him long and hard. "I've got to go."

The television set in the far corner of the living room had been left on. A news bulletin caught their attention. The police chief, Biff, had been found strangled to death in the parking lot behind the building housing Gene's condo.

Gene looked at the news report in shock. "I had nothing to do with it," he shouted. What he couldn't bring himself to tell Robert was that he had strangled Biff inside the Vulcan Baths. The owners of the baths had obviously arranged for the chief's body to be removed. Calder Martin no doubt had other men working for him in the police department.

Robert turned from the TV set to Gene. "Now that the chief is dead, the police will be looking for you like a mad dog."

"We've got to move fast."

Robert kissed Gene and hugged him a final time. Gene glanced apprehensively at his watch. He had so little time to accomplish his final mission.

"Damn!" Robert said. "That's Buck's yacht pulling into the pier. Where's your boat?"

"I anchored it down by the beach," Gene said.

"Hurry," Robert said. When he broke away, there were tears in his eyes. "Be safe. Be safe."

Gene looked long and hard at Robert before fleeing across the terrace by the pool and heading down the beach. He found himself shaking, as if coming unglued. Killing Clara, Maria, and Biff had been easy compared to the challenge that awaited him now. Before boarding a plane to freedom, the guilty had to be punished.

***

Even as he stood before Robert, Buck didn't know why he'd done it. Before disembarking from his yacht, Buck had taken off his clothes and slipped on a white bikini stored on ship that Robert had bought for him four years ago. Virtually sheer, it was so revealing that Robert had never let him appear in it before anybody else. Before facing the crew,

Buck had slipped on his robe. Once on his island and before going in to see Robert, he had taken off the robe. He might as well have been nude.

In the living room Robert looked at Buck in amazement, paying particular attention to the bikini. "I haven't seen you wear that in years." "Does it bring back a memory?" Buck asked provocatively. "If I remember correctly, and I do, you never let me wear this little string for long. You were always taking it off me to expose the goodies."

"I recall that too." There was a look of longing in Robert's eyes and a tenderness to his voice that Buck hadn't heard since he'd come back from California.

Buck returned Robert's look. Each man seemed to wait for the other to make a move. "What's holding you back?" Buck finally asked.

A desperate cry escaped from Robert's throat as he moved swiftly toward Buck to immerse himself in the strong, outstretched arms of his friend.

Robert planted the most incredible kiss on Buck's lips. Buck's tongue probed Robert's mouth, as his broad hands explored every inch of his body he could conveniently reach. Robert's own hands were rediscovering the skin he knew so well. With his eyes closed, he knew every curve and line, especially the tender spots. Robert's hands glided, pressed, and stroked until the white bikini could no longer contain Buck. Robert slipped it off him.

Robert's tongue began methodically tracing patterns across Buck's flesh, as if preparing him for some ritual. Robert squeezed, kissed, licked, and sucked the flesh with a dedicated sense of devotion.

The little moans coming from Robert told Buck what he wanted to know: Robert was back again. If Buck stood beside Gene, and Robert were given a choice, Buck knew in his heart that Robert would rush to his arms, deserting Gene for his greater love. Robert had had his fling. Buck had had his fling—more than one. Now it was time for each man to come home.

Buck picked Robert up in his arms, carrying him from the living room to their bedroom. Buck removed Robert's T-shirt and shorts. Robert appeared in a half-dreamy trance. After completely stripping him, Buck threw him on the bed. He was deliberately rough with Robert. The moment had come to cross the final frontier with Robert.

Buck did not care to remember when he'd first realized what Robert wanted. Perhaps the knowledge had come on one of those mornings he got up early to watch the sun rise in Florida, always his favorite time of the day. Even when Buck had grown more experimental and kinky with Robert, it still hadn't been enough. Buck had held back, not letting himself give in to what was demanded of him from Robert. It wasn't in Buck's nature. Or he didn't think it was in his nature until this moment on their deserted island.

He lowered himself over Robert's body, looking deeply into his friend's eyes. The men had known each other too long and too intimately for words. There was an unspoken language between them. Robert's eyes seemed to defy him, goading him on, almost daring him to take the next move.

With one hand, Buck grabbed a fistful of Robert's blond hair, yanking at the roots with his tightest grip and pulling hard. With the other hand he slapped Robert across the face. As he got into it, the slaps grew harder and harder. Robert cried out in pain and seemed to struggle to get away but Buck held him down tighter, slapping him more violently. He didn't even stop when Robert's nose started to bleed. The young man's erection pressing hard and firm against Buck's belly was all the confirmation Buck needed. He stopped slapping him, tightened his grip on the hair, and spat once, twice into Robert's face. Robert moaned in ecstasy.

He flipped Robert's body over until he lay spread across Buck's stomach. He explored Robert's ass with his fingers, encircling the rosebud but not penetrating it with his finger. Robert seemed in a state of perpetual joy, as Buck fondled him roughly. Buck's first smack was quick, sharp, and stinging. He saw Robert's ass redden before his onslaught. Buck's hand came down hard and slow. Robert screamed out in pain. Buck felt the young man's erection seemingly grow even harder and thicker. Buck used more force on Robert's ass, the slaps growing more vicious on the tender skin. He knew Robert's flesh was on fire.

Robert responded by arching his back and raising his ass to meet each blow. His flesh was beaten tender and the feel of it was achingly hot. His buttocks had turned a deep scarlet.

Without preparation, Buck inserted his finger deep inside Robert. Robert cried out. Buck grabbed Robert's hair, forcing his face up and slapping him hard.

Robert was reeling high from the beating. Buck inserted another finger, then another. Moaning at this invasion, Robert was breathing harder and harder. As Robert's explosion came, Buck felt it erupting all over his stomach.

In the throes of Robert's orgasm, Buck hauled the boy up to his face and forced open his lips, as his tongue began to explore the depths of Robert's suddenly dry mouth. Buck's fingers still probed and explored Robert's ass. He pierced as deeply as he could.

Buck turned Robert over as he quickly withdrew his fingers. He positioned his cock, then pushed hard and entered Robert as violently as he could. There was a popping sensation and a scream from Robert that brought Buck's strong, firm hand down, slapping his face repeatedly.

"You dirty little two-timing, bitch," Buck said. "This boy-pussy belongs to me. You got that?"

"I love you," Robert called out. He was crying now from the slapping. "It was never this good."

That made Buck pound all the harder. Robert seemed to open up to him as never before, drawing him deeper and deeper. The pleasure was too incredible for Buck. He had to distract him in some way. He descended on Robert's neck and began biting him furiously. Every time he bit down, really sinking his teeth into Robert, Robert cried out with joy, goading Buck on. With his thrusts, he seemed to push Robert's body deeper and deeper into the bed. He felt Robert's muscles gripping and holding him like a vise. Breathing hard, Buck knew he couldn't last much longer. Robert's second eruption came before his. As Robert was experiencing the final throes of another orgasm, Buck exploded inside him. Spent, he fell across Robert, deliberately grinding his body hard against him.

Robert burst into tears. "I've waited so long for that," he whispered into Buck's ears, as he gently fondled the muscles of Buck's sweaty back.

Bathed in perspiration and cum, Buck pressed his body even harder against Robert's. "You'll never leave me again."

Robert's warm, familiar arms tightened around Buck.

After time had passed, Buck pulled himself off Robert's body and carried him to the shower where he bathed Robert before his friend bathed him.

Dressed and at the pier, he stood before Robert. "I'm taking old

Buck's yacht back to town and leaving mine. He wanted his ashes spread at sea from his own yacht. We've got to have this for the funeral."

"I won't be needing your yacht," Robert said. "Thanks anyway. I'm staying here until you come for me."

"I'll be back later tonight," Buck said. "I've got some things to take care of." He paused a long time looking deeply into Robert's eyes.

"You can keep your fucking five-million dollars," Robert said. "I don't want the man's money. I want the man himself."

"I've always known that. My flings are over." He pulled Robert even closer to him. Unlike the violence of the late afternoon, Buck's kiss was passionate but tender. "Have the bed warm for me later tonight," he told Robert before a final kiss. Heading up the gangplank, he turned again for a final good-bye.

As he stood on the deck of old Buck's yacht, watching Robert fade into the distance, Buck dreaded facing Ahmad. He had to do it. He'd never been comfortable with the idea of belonging to just one man, but that's what he wanted now. He didn't need Ahmad or his power and money, and he certainly didn't need to force himself on a young boy like Shelley.

He looked back at his island growing smaller and smaller. It wasn't just his island. It belonged to Robert too.

***

"You didn't have to have her killed!" It was Rose's voice.

From his concealed position in the hallway, Gene could easily overhear her. Undetected, he'd slipped into Paradise Shores, using the keys he'd stolen from her after she'd kicked him out.

In her white living room, she was having an angry confrontation with Calder.

"I had no choice," Calder said with biting anger. "Pamela was about to fuck up everything. There's one thing you just can't accept. When you make a grand commitment, you've got to see it through, no matter what happens. When the heat's on, you're chicken shit!"

"The next time you get ready to go off on another one of those grand commitments, you clear it with me first, liver lips." Her words lacerated the air. It was a voice Gene had heard before in the back seat of the limousine at the South Beach riot. "If there's a chance my neck is on the guillotine, ever, you let me know that. It's my neck, but it's going to be your neck if you fuck up like this again. And so soon after the Shelley thing. I'll never forgive you for that, you bastard."

"Okay, with Shelley, things got out of control. And now that boy's been kidnapped by Buck Brooke. God only knows if that boy starts talking. If Buck finds out the truth, it could be the end of both of us. Ahmad would toss us to the sharks. He'd side with Brooke. He's acting like a lovesick schoolgirl. I've never seen him like this."

"I wish I could throw you out of my house," Rose said.

"I've been ordered here. You don't think I'd be here if I didn't have to, do you? I can't stand the sight of you. But we may be called upon to issue a statement to the press. I don't trust what you'd say."

"You don't trust me. You're the fuck-up—not me."

"I run this show, and don't you forget that. Deep down, you're still a backwoods preacher waving her tambourine and shaking a collection box at a Sunday night bunch of smelly niggers."

"Go to hell!" Rose shouted.

"Besides, you won't be implicated in Pamela's murder. Your lover boy—the flasher—will take the blame if he's not killed first."

"That's what Biff thought," she said. "Now he's dead."

"I at least had him die in the line of duty," Calder said. "The press didn't find out the cocksucker died at the Vulcan Baths."

"You murder people and have Gene take the rap," Rose said. "Even for the death of Leroy Fitzgerald."

"That was one trouble-maker who thought he had me by the balls," Calder said. "The faggot wanted a mouthful of cock. He got it on his death bed. His mouth stuffed with his own tiny dick."

"You're a disgusting piece of shit," she said. "I have enough on you to send you to the electric chair."

"Forget it," Calder said. "I'll die a rich old man on some Caribbean island in a big mansion."

"The way you've been carrying on, you and I will never live to collect Social Security. For all I know, that boy is talking to Buck Brooke right now. Telling him everything."

"It was you who allowed Brooke to get in to see him in St. Moritz. I had things under control."

"Ahmad ordered it!" she shouted.

"That fucking lovesick puppy. He's going to screw everything up."

"It seems you're doing a perfect job of that all by yourself," Rose said.

"So far, my plan has been brilliant. I get rid of Pamela and Fitzgerald, and the flasher takes the rap."

"What if Gene is captured and brought in?" she asked. "What if he has a spirited defense?"

"Gene isn't going to be brought in alive," Calder said. "The police will hunt him down. The story's already written. He was armed. He fired at the police. They had to shoot him."

"You bastard!" she said. "You really taught me the lower depths."

"Your first big lie of the day. Your record is as black as mine. I know plenty about you. All except one thing. I don't know the answer to it."

"What in the hell is that?" she asked.

"Do you believe in God?" Calder said.

She paused a moment before answering. "I stopped believing in God a long time ago." She turned and headed for her bedroom.

"Where in hell do you think you're going?" Calder asked.

"To get some sleep. I haven't slept in days. I don't give a fuck what you're planning to do tonight. I want no part of it—or you."

"After I take a bath and have another drink or two, I'll work on that press release. Your grief-stricken response to Pamela's death. I've already helped Barry prepare his statement for the press."

"Oh, goodie, goodie." She left the room.

His heart pounding loudly, Gene was relieved that the conversation was over. He'd heard enough. At this point, it didn't matter. It was like Calder had said. The plan was ready to swing into action.

From where he stood, Gene could see into the living room. Drinks were stacked on the table. The room reeked of alcohol and tobacco.

Unshaven, Calder sat on the sofa, his flabby flesh hanging loosely from his structure. The way his skin fell from his frame, it looked as if it were several sizes too large for his bones. Finally, he got up and stumbled toward the guest bedroom, the same one Gene had occupied. A drunk Calder would make his job easier.

***

Gene waited in the hallway before following Calder inside. From his leather bag, Gene removed a blackjack. The bedroom, the same bed he'd lain in, was empty.

From the bathroom came the sound of water running in the shower. He gripped the blackjack, as he made his way across the carpeted floor and into the bathroom where Calder had conveniently left the door wide open.

Once his feet touched the tiles, he paused only briefly, before pulling back the shower curtain. In an astonished moment of recognition, Calder opened his mouth as if to yell. The scream never escaped his throat. The blackjack smashing against his skull caused him to crumple over, falling under the running water.

Quickly, Gene turned off the shower. Returning to the bedroom, he picked up his leather bag and carried it into the bath. From it, he removed a gag and two nylon cords. First he gagged Calder tightly, then tied his hands over his belly with one of the cords. With the other cord, he securely tied his feet.

Placing Calder's head under the faucet, he turned on the cold water. In a few minutes Calder came to, his eyes widening at the sight of Gene, they way they had when he'd pulled back the shower curtain. Calder struggled to raise himself, only to have Gene knock him back against the porcelain.

From his bag, he removed a straight blade razor. With a slash, he cut deep into Calder's right wrist. The man winced in pain, although he feared he hadn't cut deep enough. This time he cut more deliberately, slowly and accurately. Calder's eyes told him he'd hit his target this time. Blood streamed like a fountain.

Clutching his razor tighter, he slowly cut the vein on the left wrist. Blood spurted out, forming pools in the bathtub as it ran down Calder's flabby belly into the patch of hair above his shriveled sex. Every time he struggled up, Gene pushed him down. Deep low moans—easily drowned out by the running water—escaped from Calder's throat.

In a haze, Calder grew weaker. Gene moved his arms about, drawing more blood. The fight was out of Calder. He no longer struggled to get up. "You'd love it, wouldn't you, if I'd gone to the electric chair?"

Calder moaned. His eyes watered heavily, mucus poured from his nose, and blood flowed in thick streams from his wrists. Desperately he tried to draw breath through his gagged mouth. Overcome with nausea, he retched and vomited. The vomit soaked through the gag, most of it returning to his throat. His nose clogged, his mouth gagged, Calder was suffocating.

Gene's own eyes were blurred over at this point, his body rigid and cramped from bending over Calder. He wanted Calder alive and awake to see his final action. Untying the gag, he ripped it off. Calder coughed, choking and vomiting. Gene held his head under the running water.

Grabbing a fist full of Calder's hair, he held him inches from his own face. He looked deep into Calder's squinting eyes which opened and shut, shaking off the water.

Calder's eyes fully opened in time to see the blade of the razor before it slashed across his throat.

***

The day was softer somehow. Removing Calder from it had made the world a brighter place. Still, that voice inside him demanded more. Gene slowly moved down the carpeted hall leading to Rose's bedroom. Once that room had been the vision center of his dreams. All that had changed.

He was in love with her, still. When he'd been alone with her in her bedroom and she'd moved close to him, he could recall the tendrils of wild hair on her white neck. Everything had been perfect, except the timing—her wanting to rush things. Then a voice had come out of her soul and her wide mouth—made for soft caress—had turned instead to mocking laughter. It was a devouring mouth. The tongue in it had lashed like a whip, the voice whirling like a sand-laden simoom wind.

He could not listen to her voice, only the other voice inside him which urged him forward. He was possessed, the voice inside him confusing, not always clear in its message. A cold fire burned in his bowels.

Before her door, he gave himself a moment of silence. The servants were in the rear wing. Calder was dead. The only hearts beating in the house belonged to Rose and him. Now, at her door with his leather bag, he wasn't sure of his purpose.

With Rose, he had never been certain. She'd always aroused conflicting feelings in him—maternal, sensual, mystical. How he wished he could go back to that bright Sunday morning in her temple.

It had taken him until now to realize it, but he'd been happy then.

When you had your dreams and the wonder and beauty of life were still before you, you could look up at the shining mountain capped by a blue sky. It was only when you climbed that mountain and saw the vast emptiness beyond, that innocence ended. At the top of the mountain he'd expected glory and splendor and had found instead evil.

To kill a person, even a black devil like Calder, was a sin—and he could be punished for that. Soon he'd be far away from the cesspool, out of the reach of those who would kill him.

Rose still had evil in her heart—vanity, cruelty. She'd have to live to atone for those sins before she'd be allowed to join him one day in heaven.

In heaven, where both of them were cleansed of their earthly deeds, she'd be his beautiful angel again. He'd kiss her hand and worship her and bring her pretty flowers to put in her hair. Once freed of the desires of flesh, their love would be pure.

He clutched his leather bag, having arrived at the perfect solution on the boat back from Buck's cay. Rose had used her beauty to entice and seduce men, to lure innocent, unsuspecting persons down a trail to disaster. Her weapon, that beautiful face, had to be taken from her so that she could discover her soul.

A panic seized him. The voice had grown angry. Lost in maudlin thoughts, he was delaying, not fulfilling the mission the voice had commanded him to.

Opening the door, he stood in the silence of her bedroom. The draperies were drawn. From the meager light that filtered in through a crack, he could see her lying in her large bed, a satin domino keeping the world in blackness. He shut the door softly, moving rapidly toward her.

***

Perhaps it was the onrushing air, the noise of racing feet. Whatever it was, she knew she wasn't alone. Jerking up in bed, she ripped of the domino just as a weight was thrown against her legs. A man's heavy body fell on top of her. The room was in darkness, but she knew who it was.

She tried to scream but his strong fingers cut off her breath completely. Overwhelmed with one thought, she was paralyzed with fear, knowing she was going to die. Gene had selected her as his next victim.

In the struggle for her own life, thoughts of Pamela flashed through her mind. Had it been this way with Pamela, too? In panic, her mind refused to accept what was happening. "My God," she managed to say as he released his grip on her throat. "No, no, no!" It was useless to scream. Who could hear her? Calder? He was probably dead.

He threw her face down, turning it into the pillow, muffling her sobs. He yanked her arms behind her back. Handcuffed, she kicked and fought, biting into his wrist with her sharp teeth. She drew blood but he didn't let up until the cuffs were securely fastened on her.

"My God," she repeated. How stupid of her not to realize she'd be targeted as his next victim. Calder should have hired bodyguards to surround Paradise Shores.

He tied her kicking feet with a nylon cord, then flipped her over to face him. "Gene, please...anything. Anything you want."

Grabbing one of her strong silk scarves, he gagged her. Then he lifted himself off the bed, turning on a lamp.

Nausea rose in her, flooding her throat with hot bile. If only he hadn't gagged her, she felt the persuasive power of her voice would have reached him, stopped him from whatever he was about to do to her.

His broad trembling hand reached out to touch her face. As she softly moaned, he lovingly circled her eyes, brows, nose—his fingers slipping beneath the gag to touch her tender lips. He was like a sculptor feeling the contours of her face.

As he removed his fingers, she tried to cry out. Sobbing, she had only blurred vision. In fear and pain, she braced herself to face the terror of her own death.

From a leather bag, he removed a glass vial with a cork stopper, putting it on her night table. She bit the gag and twisted her handcuffed hands, desperately trying to free herself.

He let her struggle until she tried to slip from her bed. Grabbing her, he forced her back into the middle of the bed, his strong hand jamming her face against a satin pillow, suffocating her, stifling her moans.

It was only then that she'd finally realized what he was going to do to her. She preferred death.

***

Gene looked down on her now. Sweating and panting, she was still a beautiful sight. After he was gone, no other man would know that beauty. She would never dare show her face to anybody ever again, particularly a young man. Forever she'd wear the dark veil of mourning for him.

Her eyes were wide as that terrified horse he'd been forced to shoot during her protest march through the Combat Zone.

On the table beside her bed, he reached for the glass vial of sulfuric acid. Before coming to Paradise Shores, he'd broken into a university laboratory and stolen it.

He removed an eyedropper, sucking in the sulfuric acid. Drop by drop, this would be a slow, agonizing process. He only prayed that Jesus would reveal to Rose the absolute necessity of what he was going to do. She'd know it for what it was: an act of purification. Not to harm her, but to cleanse her soul so that she could one day join him in heaven.

For what minor pain she'd suffer on this earth, it seemed worth it to him, considering the ultimate reward—a place in heaven beside him.

As he held the eyedropper of acid over her face, he had never known such terror reflected in the eyes of another human being.

The first drop of stinging acid hit her face, sizzling and eating into her skin, disfiguring it for all time.

She was a trapped animal awaiting slaughter.

***

Back on the mainland, Susan waited with Don in the back seat of a limousine. She could clearly see Buck, accompanied by Lars, on the deck of the old man's yacht, which he'd retrieved from his private island.

As Buck came down the gangplank, she was there to greet him with a kiss. Buck seemed extremely agitated. In the back seat of the car, Buck asked to be taken to his old house. "My grandfather personally selected the music played at the funeral of my parents. I have everything in a safe place at the house. I think we should play the same music he wanted."

"That's a great idea," Susan said. "Frankly, I didn't have a clue what to do."

Don reached for Buck's hand. "Glad to have you back," he said. "We missed you."

Buck squeezed his hand and settled back. Leaning into the upholstery, he closed his eyes.

As the chauffeur pulled the limousine into the driveway of Buck's darkened home, Susan stiffened, feeling the coldness of her own hands.

"You guys can wait in the car if you wish," Buck told them. "I won't be long."

"No!" she said in a sharp voice that surprised her. "We want to go with you."

It was important for her to be with him now. She could trust him to pick up the music and probably change his clothes by himself, couldn't she? It was something else. A dread anxiety swept over her, a lingering doubt and a deeply rooted fear that had something to do with Gene. In the deepest corner of her heart, she feared that Gene might strike back at them in some way.

Something about the garden was ominous, and she didn't know what it was. The moon was shining, the flowers were still growing, and every statue or chair seemed in place. Still, it seemed too perfect, too intense, and deadly quiet.

Lars and two of his security guards were checking the grounds. She saw one of the men disappear inside a garage.

Buck climbed the steps of his back veranda. He paused at the door. "The screen's been cut!"

"Don't go inside." She called out to Lars for help.

Bounding up the steps, Lars yelled at his men. He tried the door, finding it unlocked but shut. He came into the kitchen, ordering his men to check the front rooms. "I'll go upstairs."

"I think we were robbed," Buck said. "It wouldn't be the first time."

"I'm frightened," she said.

He hugged her for comfort. "Clara and Maria probably went to visit relatives. The stuff I'm looking for is in my study."

"Go with him," Susan said to Don.

When they had gone, she felt the coldness of her hands again.

"Anybody home?" Buck called into the empty living room.

The phone in the corridor rang, a persistent ring, and no one answered it. On the way to the phone, she looked down. A pool of blood had seeped out of the utility room, running under the door. In shuddering horror, she looked at it, too frozen to call for help. She knew—somehow she knew—what was beyond that door and, for that reason, her hand rested a hesitant moment on the knob before she turned it.

The sight that greeted her caused a sudden spasm of choking. Maria lay on the floor. Susan looked at her first, avoiding the vision of her mother. Dressed in jeans and a little pink blouse, Maria seemed to have fallen asleep. Only the back of her head was visible as she faced the tiles.

Clara lay sprawled in a massive pool of blood. Her blood was everywhere—covering her body, the tiles, the washing machine nearby. Splotches of it had been splattered on a mirrored wall, as if there had been a violent struggle. Her body was nude. Her throat had been slit and the gaping wound had festered into an ugly sore. She resembled a carcass of beef, badly butchered and thrown to the side in a slaughterhouse.

Gasping for breath, Susan felt the blood drain from her face. As if obeying a command, some unwritten rule, she tried to touch Maria's body, to feel for pulse, some sign of life. Yet her hand only hovered there. She couldn't bring herself to rest it on the girl.

She backed away until she stood in the hallway. There she realized she'd tugged at her blouse until she'd ripped the buttons from the front. She'd done that instead of screaming.

She began to sob uncontrollably, sounds forming in her throat. As she looked into Clara's eyes—so wide, so open—she screamed. Her scream grew louder and louder. She turned and faced the wall, beating her hands against it, as if that would drive the horrible vision from her memory.

She was only vaguely aware of Buck's presence. At her scream, he'd rushed in, moving up behind her, holding her in his arms.

Seemingly within seconds, Lars had staked out the area. Gun pointed, he entered the utility room.

Don looked as if he were going to vomit. "Did Gene do this?" No one responded to his question.

Lars ordered one of his men to call the police.

Buck turned and escorted her toward the back veranda. "Let's wait outside."

"No," Lars shouted at him. "I want all of you to go into the library. It's the most secure room on the property. Someone might still be in the garden with a gun. It's not safe out there."

Susan needed to be told what to do. No more could she think for herself. She stumbled blindly toward the library with Buck and Don.

She sat crying softly in a chair placed in a bay window. Looking out over the grounds, she suspected that at any minute Gene would appear to kill them. Everything told her that her former husband had become the madman of the night.

***

In Gene's boat again, the winds remained light. The sky was darkening but there were streaks of light. All around him the blue-green sea had turned into a deep black cesspool. After leaving Paradise Shores, Gene experienced a great release of inner tension. "Why go on killing?" he asked himself. "Let it all go." He was tempted to take his boat as far into the sea as he could, there to let himself run out of fuel and drift into a slow death, a total yielding to Jesus.

He wouldn't do that. Not when a new life with Robert awaited him. But he didn't deserve that life until he completed the final mission Jesus had sent him on. It was a terrible mission, but he had to see it through, regardless of the consequences.

In thirty minutes, he reached Buck's private cay where moon rays cut into the water over the reef. With permanent smiles, conchs heaved forward as he moored his boat. Earlier in the day he'd seen sulphur yellow sponges and corals, between which rainbow parrot fish glided. Such beauty didn't greet him now. The shore looked like a watery grave.

Wading through the water, he reached the white sands. He'd landed at the west side of the cay, at the farthest point from Buck's house. Armed with his rifle, he very slowly, very carefully plowed his booted feet through mangrove swamp, brushing back palmetto bushes. At a piercing call, he froze with fear. It was only the cry of a cicada. He passed a nest of red-blue orchids, a miniature pond of crystal-clear water on which lily pads floated and a banana tree that bore fruit only wild things ate.

In fifteen minutes the house had come into view. Concealed in shrubbery, he was close enough he didn't need to sight his target through his six-power scope. In shadows, he stood no more than fifty yards from the sundeck.

As he suspected, Buck had remained on the island. His yacht was anchored at the pier. Old Buck's yacht was gone. It was clear to him: Robert had taken the yacht and gone back to town to collect the money that would buy them their freedom

Henry appeared on the patio, setting up a supper tray. He went away to reappear with a tall drink. Gene smiled to himself. This was one elegant supper Buck would never finish.

Gene stood at his post, waiting, trying not to think. He wasn't even sure at this point why he was supposed to kill Buck. The voices told him to. Up to now, he'd killed merely the jackals. Buck was the lion awaiting slaughter.

***

About three minutes went by before Gene's target came out from the bedroom onto the deck where he saw the tray waiting for him. His body was muscled to perfection, a real man's physique, like his own. Gene's hand tightened on the trigger. He didn't want to fire right away, letting his victim stretch his arms and extend his handsome face up to the bright moonlight. Gene couldn't make out the face, but he'd know Buck's blond hair anywhere.

A flicker of excitement swept over Gene's body, the feeling of spying on another man in unabashed secrecy, knowing he held the power of life and death over him.

No longer mesmerized, in complete control, he fired once, twice, hitting his victim both times in the chest. The man collapsed in death, like a youth sacrificed to the gods in some ancient pagan rite.

Gene stood there for a long moment in the same spot where he'd fired the shots. He could afford to take such a chance. The weapon made him confident. Crouched, unmoving, he continued to stand there, his mind racing. It'd been so easy. He dropped the rifle. No more need for it.

He spotted Henry rushing to the patio, stooping over the slain body. "Oh, my God!" he heard Henry cry into the night air for no one to hear but Gene himself. "Jesus, Lord Almighty!"

Turning, Gene forced himself to walk—not run—back to his boat. His booted feet splashed through the mangrove swamp, and he found himself feeling carefree and light, as if the final burden Jesus had assigned him had been removed. His only duty now was to get to the Roney Plaza Hotel where Robert would take him in his arms.

Elated by his success in carrying out his mission, he was overcome by an uncontrollable joy. He wanted to shout and praise the Lord. He felt delirious. The jackals were now dead. He'd slain the lion and left the lioness so badly disfigured she'd never show her face in public again but under heavy veil.

In the name of Jesus, he'd brought death where it was called for. His enemies would burn forever in the fires of hell. No doubt those fires were consuming their bodies right now. They were doomed to live in hell where the fires would burn them for all eternity. They would pray for death but it wouldn't come, only the pain of eternal burning.

Before getting on his boat, he stopped and picked a wild orchid as he'd done before. It would live for such a short time in his pocket, and that made it all the more precious. If he didn't succeed in escaping with Robert, his fate would be that of the flower. For that reason he wanted it near to his heart. He put it in his shirt pocket as he headed toward his boat.

***

As Buck was being questioned in his library by the police, two officers stood before Susan taking her report about the discovery of the bodies. The phone near her rang and she picked it up, excusing herself from the police, who chose to remain at her side while she took the call. For one impossible moment, she felt it might be Gene himself calling.

"That you, Mrs. Buck?" came a voice courtly and polite like a black servant in antebellum days.

"It's Susan, Henry."

"I've got to speak to Mr. Buck right away."

"Oh, God, what's happened?"

"It's Mister Robert. Someone's shot him. He's dead."

"Robert..."

Coming into the foyer where she was speaking on the phone, Buck heard her mention Robert's name. He faced her as she held the phone tentatively, not knowing what to do with it, wanting to protect him from the message at the other end.

"What...WHAT?" Buck said.

His impatient face demanded answers and she tried to deliver, but her throat was too choked for her to speak at first. "Robert," she blurted out. He knew. She'd never seen such anguish on a human face.

"Robert," he said, in a soft and gentle voice. After the initial shock on his face, he appeared calm, pathetically accepting the news. Then his whole face collapsed. "He's dead, isn't he?"

She didn't need to answer.

***

On the grounds of the Roney Plaza, where security was so lax it almost didn't exist, Gene tried the door of the suite. It was locked. Robert promised it would be open, and he'd be waiting there for him. How could he have forgotten? Gene feared he'd been trapped in legal difficulties with Buck's lawyer and hadn't been able to get over here yet. Gene decided to conceal himself on the grounds and wait for Robert's arrival.

Nearly an hour had gone by and still no Robert. It was getting late, and the suite remained in total darkness. He was anxious to hear the news. He knew Henry had called the police. He anticipated that the news of Buck's shooting would soon be on television news, with all its lurid speculation.

Gene feared he'd made a terrible mistake. Uncle Milty may have learned of Buck's murder and was withholding Robert's money. Maybe Robert himself was being held for questioning in connection with Buck's murder. His dread was that he'd placed Robert in jeopardy. He shouldn't have killed Buck, and even now couldn't figure out why he did. There was no joy in killing Buck. He wanted him back and alive.

Desperate for some news, he slipped around to the back of the suite which opened onto a vine-covered stone wall. There was no one in sight. At the French doors leading into the courtyard of the suite, he cracked a glass pane and turned the door knob inside.

Inside the darkened suite, he walked slowly across the living room, spotting a TV set. He quickly turned on the set to watch the local news roundup. A picture of Robert's handsome face stared back at him. Only then did he realize what was being reported. He didn't need to hear the bulletin. He already knew what the announcer would say.

He'd killed Robert instead of Buck!

Robert's connection with Buck was being flashed across the screen. Robert was being identified as Buck's longtime secretary. Pictures of Buck's recent marriage to Susan dominated the wide screen. A lump formed in Gene's throat, choking him. He didn't want to see any pictures or hear any more. As he moved to switch off the set, something the announcer said held him spellbound. Shortly before his shooting, Dante—or so it appeared—had been brutally raped.

In stunned disbelief, Gene tried to absorb the bulletin. It made no sense. How could Robert have been brutally raped? Gene knew he was meeting with Buck. But Gene found it unbelievable that Buck had raped Robert.

The world was spinning out of control. After turning off the television set, Gene collapsed on the floor. All the tears he'd ever shed before were nothing until now. This was the real cry of his life. It started deep within his guts and traveled upward through his throat where the sound nearly choked him.

He wanted Robert back. A grandfather clock ticked away in the center of the room. Sobbing, he wanted to go over to that clock and turn back the hands of time. If only he could start the day over again. If only this day hadn't begun in the first place.

Robert was his chance for freedom. His one last hope to have a life, and he'd destroyed that.

He had to summon a steely reserve, pick himself up, walk out of this suite, and do what he must before fleeing Okeechobee.

The voice that had told him what to do, the same voice that had deserted him for the past two hours, now returned. It was speaking to him again, directing him. He felt so relieved. He didn't have to think of killing Robert. The voice told him to erase that memory. He had other tasks to perform and he'd need to give his full attention to the deadly game that lay before him.

***

In the darkened living room of his parents' house, where he'd lived so long with Robert, Buck sat quietly with Susan and Don. He stared vacantly into space, trying to forget the sight of the dead bodies the police had removed. Consumed with grief, he listened to soft music Don played. Susan offered him a drink which he accepted. Robert's death had placed a different focus on everything. He no longer saw life as the adventure it was at the beginning of the summer. He could never be that carefree again.

Only minutes before he'd spoken to Ahmad and had agreed to fly to Palm Springs to meet with him after the funerals of Robert and old Buck. Buck wanted these funerals behind him as soon as possible, and welcomed the recuperative powers the desert could bring him. Before Robert's death, he was going to tell Ahmad that he was leaving him. After Robert's death, he wasn't so sure. He felt he needed the protection from the world that Ahmad could offer him. There remained the problem of Shelley which he planned to deal with later in the evening.

Buck looked over at Susan. "You know, don't you, that that bullet was meant for me? Who would want to kill Robert? If Gene's the killer, he loved Robert and hardly wanted him dead. Robert stopped my bullet. Don't you see: I'm alive because Robert is dead!"

"Stop it!" she said. "You can't go on feeling that way." She kneeled before him, taking his hand in hers and kissing it.

Don got up from a nearby chair and came and sat with Buck on the sofa, placing his strong arm around him and holding him tight. Don kissed him on the cheek. "Robert is gone, but we're here for you now."

He leaned into Don's chest for the comfort it offered him. At his feet Susan continued to kiss and massage his hand. He took comfort in the warmth they provided.

Lars came into the room and called Susan to the phone. Getting up, she kissed Buck on the forehead.

When she'd gone, Don held him closer and whispered in his ear. "I'll always be your loving man. I'm not Robert. I'll never replace him. No one ever can. But I'll spend the rest of my life helping you forget him."

Buck reached up and rubbed Don's cheek. "Thanks for being here."

Susan came back into the room. "This is an awful time to bring it up. But Robert's funeral is in the morning. You're his sole heir. They want to know what you want to put on the stone."

Rising from the sofa and gently easing himself from Don's protective embrace, Buck stood on unsteady feet. "Is that it?" he asked. "Has it come to this? Reduce a man's life to something you can write on a damn stone?" He took a few steps but didn't seem to know which way to turn.

At the bay window, he pulled open the draperies and looked out at the water with the city in the background. It looked so peaceful tonight even though a killer stalked it. Was it Gene? He turned to Susan. "Tell them, ROBERT DANTE, 1950-1977. HE GAVE THE GREATEST GIFT OF ALL—AN UNFINISHED LIFE."

***

Back at Desire, Buck headed down the long corridor to where Shelley was kept. "We've been unable to get Sister Rose on the phone," Lars said, walking by his side. "Her staff said she's retired for the night and is taking no calls from anyone."

"Shit!" Buck said. "I wanted to come clean with her—tell her I have Shelley here. It's only fair that I do that."

"Do you want me to send my men over there?" Lars said.

"Let her sleep. It's the middle of the night. This thing with Shelley can wait until morning."

Leaving Lars, Buck headed alone into Shelley's darkened suite. At first he saw no sign of life. The boy may have been asleep. At a sudden movement, he whirled around to confront Shelley—still clad in his briefs—emerging from the bathroom.

There was a smile on his face when he saw it was Buck. He rushed to Buck's arms and planted kisses all over his face. "Thank God you're back. I was going out of my mind."

Buck backed away. "It's the problem with your mind that you're here in the first place."

"My mind is okay—just fine. I'm coming to my senses."

"I hope so," Buck went over to sit before the vegetation that gave the impression of being outdoors even though they were underground. "I've come to tell you something. I deliberately left the door open. You're free to go. I had no right to bring you here. All you have to do is walk out that door. A limousine is waiting to take you anywhere you want to go."

"What if I told you I'm not going to Paradise Shores?" Shelley came over to Buck and kneeled at his feet. "My place is here with you."

"You're just a kid. You don't know what you're saying."

"I know perfectly well what I'm saying," Shelley said.

"What about that young man I encountered in St. Moritz? You didn't want to have a God damn thing to do with me."

"That was then. I'm different."

"You're different all right," Buck said. "You seem like a completely different person from the Shelley I left in Palm Springs. I can't put my finger on it. But it's like..."

"Like what?"

"I don't know," Buck said. "What matters is that in the past few hours major shit has come down."

"Can I help you?" Shelley asked.

"Right now I need to help myself. I'm going to go away to join Ahmad at Palm Springs. I don't know when I'm coming back."

"You're leaving me?" Shelley got up and moved away from Buck.

"I've come to my senses," Buck said. "I had this obsession about you. It wasn't love. Why don't you walk out that door and never come back to Desire again? I can at least let you grow up."

"You're kicking me out?" Shelley said.

"God damn it!" Buck said, rising from his chair. "I brought you here by force. You can bring kidnapping charges against me."

"I'll never bring charges against you or harm you in any way." He moved toward Buck, coming only inches from his face. "I love you. I want to be with you. You can do what you want with me. I'm not afraid."

Buck turned his back to Shelley, staring again at the vegetation. "I'm not going to do anything to you."

"You want to send me to Paradise Shores? How do you know I'll be safe there? Are you going to let Calder Martin get at me? Do you think I'll be safe with Calder Martin? Do you think Rose will protect me?"

"I don't know." Buck stumbled and felt dizzy. "I don't know anything. I've lost someone I cared for, and I didn't even know what I had until it was too late." He moved to the bed where he fell down upon it. He didn't want to break down in front of Shelley but he couldn't help himself. He started crying. He felt hands on his back, loving and comforting him.

"Please go away," he said to Shelley. He turned over and looked into the boy's face. Shelley too was crying. "I should never have had a relationship with you," Buck said. "It was wrong."

"I know who I am and I know what I want." Shelley snuggled close to Buck. "I want to be here with you."

Buck forced himself to get up from the bed. "The part of my heart that's still beating isn't beating for you."

Shelley lay on the bed, looking shocked. He jumped up from the bed and reached for a robe. "Okay, so you won't be here for me. No one in this whole fucking world's ever been there for me when I needed someone."

"If you ever need me, and this is a solemn promise, I'll come to you at any time," Buck said.

"Do you really mean that?" Shelley asked. "Is that something I can really count on?"

"I mean it," Buck said.

Shelley looked at Buck one more time, then turned and passed through the open door.

When he was gone, Buck didn't want to leave the room. He would spend the night here. He fell back on the bed and cried real tears until he felt he could cry no more. Eventually he cried himself to sleep.

He didn't know what time it was. But he felt hands on him. It was Lars, awakening him. He turned over sleepily and in a groggy voice asked, "What is it?"

"It's Shelley. He's at Paradise Shores. He wants you to come over right away before he calls the police."

Buck sat up in bed and searched Lars' face. Buck's eyes opened wide as if fully coming awake. "Oh, my God!"

***

Purple around his eyes from lack of sleep, sweat dripping from his forehead, Gene steered his boat into the open sea, staring dull-eyed at the blackness ahead. He was going to take the boat as far as it could go.

She was with him, but in a coma. He'd slipped back into Paradise Shores and removed her body from her bed. Rose's face was a study in horror, but he tried not to see that—only the beauty that had been there.

He loved her, and wanted her to go on the journey with him. He'd smuggled her body out of her darkened house and had carried it to his car. Then he'd driven to the marina. Covered in a blanket, she lay on the deck of his boat, accompanying him on their final voyage.

Images of death almost obliterated the open sea before him. He didn't want to think of that. He wanted to remember happier days when he was part of the university class of '71. Buck, Robert, Barry, Leroy, Pamela, and Susan—all of them thought then that the whole future of humankind rested on their shoulders.

He took a sharp turn to the left, heading north. He couldn't be sure. Not that it mattered. The empty sea stretched before them.

A burning in him felt like a slash of sunlight cutting into a sleepy eye. His insides were hot and hollow, his brain groggy.

Looking back at that death-dealing carnival in Okeechobee seemed like a distant dream, more fantasy than reality.

His body was filled with a drumming fever, with a delirium, and he sailed with a rhythm all his own, having nothing to do with all the other ships or boats at sea.

To die was the easiest thing to do, far easier than living. He stood quietly, welcoming the sea breezes cooling his body and taming the fires that burned within.

He'd had none of the answers in life and had tried to find them in others, only to be misled and brutalized.

He was crying but they were tears of joy. He wasn't alone for the final journey. She was with him. She'd accompany him where he was going. God would forgive both of them. With her by his side, he would be admitted to heaven so much quicker than if he'd made the journey on his own.

He was almost out of fuel. He checked the hand grenade in his pocket. Abandoning the wheel, he walked over to the deck and picked up her near lifeless body. Gently he removed her gown. Placing her back on the deck, he removed all his clothing. He wanted them to enter the water nude like a symbol of rebirth, appearing naked like Adam and Eve in a different world from the one they'd left behind on the mainland.

Picking her up, he planted a kiss on her lips, ignoring the grotesqueness of her face eaten away with acid. Instead of that hideous mask, he chose to remember when he'd first seen her—all bright and radiant at her temple. A golden light had shined down on her then. The same golden light returned. The moon was lighting the sky with a brilliance he'd never known before.

He lowered her body into the water and drifted into the sea with her. He let her go only momentarily when he removed the plug from the grenade. He hurled it toward his boat. Reaching for her, he watched the boat explode in flames, momentarily chasing away the darkness of the sea.

She'd drifted a few feet from him, but he quickly recaptured her. He would swim out into the sea with her, carrying her along, until his body could go no more. Then they would enter their watery grave but would find immediate redemption and rescue by God.

The moon had seemed to follow him all through the night, lighting his way and shining a golden light upon him.

As he found himself gasping for breath, his load growing heavier, he did something he hadn't done all night. Fearing that the golden lumination of the moon was waning, he looked directly at it for the first time tonight.

It was a Blood Moon.

Epilogue
1997

The sun rose over Paradise Shores. It held out the promise of a spectacular day. He'd been in California for weeks, and was glad to be back in Okeechobee. In spite of where he wandered, this was still his city, and he wanted to be here in lieu of all other places.

Buck reached out for Shelley but the bed was empty. From the bathroom he heard noises of Shelley showering. Gradually his awakening eyes took in the bedroom. It was Rose's old bedroom. Shelley had never changed the rose motif—in fact, the entire house was just as Rose left it on that night she mysteriously disappeared twenty years ago.

Slowly he got out of bed. He stood nude in front of a floor length mirror. His body had held up well over the years but he winced at the slight tire he was developing around his midriff. He'd have to work even harder at his private gym to get rid of it. In spite of the graying at the temples, his hair was still blond. He reached for his robe. Now that he was forty-seven years old, he didn't parade around nude as he had in the past.

"Good morning, love of my life."

At the sound of the voice, Buck turned around and stared at Shelley, emerging fully nude from the bathroom except for a towel draped around his neck.

"Welcome back home," he said to Shelley. "We've been away a long time."

"I like California better anyway," Shelley said, moving toward him. "When I'm back here, they always demand that I go preach at the temple."

Buck met him halfway at the bottom of the bed, reaching for him and kissing him. As Buck ran his hands over his friend's body, he found it as velvety smooth as ever. In spite of the passage of time, Shelley's body was perfection itself. Even though he was thirty-four years old, he still looked twenty. It was amazing. Buck always called him "the timeless wonder."

After releasing Shelley, Buck headed for the bathroom. When he emerged later after showering and dressing, he spotted Shelley at his desk by the bay window overlooking the rose garden.

"Giving 'em hell today?" Buck asked, coming up behind Shelley and kissing his ear.

Shelley reached up and ran his hand through Buck's hair. "Last night was very special. God, do you know how to make a guy feel good."

"I should," Buck said, straightening up and going over to check the morning paper. "I've had twenty years of practice. After all that time, if I don't know what turns you on, I never will."

"It was just as good as the first time," Shelley said.

"You remember the first time?" Buck asked.

"I'll never forget it. You'd kidnapped me."

Buck glanced quickly at the headlines. There was a ring at the door. He got up from the chaise longue and went over to let in the butler with the morning coffee. He noted a long white rose on the breakfast tray. Thanking the butler, he told him that they'd be having lunch today at Desire so there was no need to prepare anything.

Pouring coffee for both Shelley and himself, Buck settled back in his chair to read the paper. He'd long ago reacquired the *Examiner* and he still had the *News*. On Sunday he published a joint edition of both papers. Suddenly, something Shelley had said struck a strident note in his brain. He looked over at the young man who was still busily writing at his desk.

"That wasn't the first time," he said to Shelley.

Distracted, Shelley didn't seem to pay him much attention. "What's that, love?"

"I said that wasn't the first time. When I kidnapped you and made love to you, it wasn't the first time. Hell, we'd had an affair. *An affair.*" Buck was raising his voice.

He caught Shelley's attention. He got up and walked over to Buck, planting a kiss on top of his head. "And what a glorious affair it was."

Buck grabbed Shelley's arm and forced his face down to confront his own. "That's not the only time you've said something enigmatic like that. You don't even seem to remember the intimate things between us that happened when we first met."

Shelley pulled away. A look of fright came on his face. Freeing himself from Buck's grasp, he got up and looked away. "Don't get up," he said to Buck. "Don't look at me. The time has come for me to tell you something, and I don't want to be facing you when I tell you this. Do you promise to stay where you are until I've finished?"

"Of course," Buck said. "You've got me really scared."

"You've always suspected me, ever since you kidnapped me. You even told me you found my body slightly different. Around you I'm so unguarded, so filled with love, that I've slipped up and said things. Like I did this morning. I mean, about that time at Desire being our first time."

"I know," Buck said. "You've never been the same after you came back from Switzerland. I've always loved you but it took a long time to adjust to you. It was like I was loving a different person."

"You were," Shelley said.

"What do you mean?"

"You were loving a different person."

"You're Shelley, aren't you?"

"I'm not Shelley. Shelley left you twenty years ago. I'm Fred."

"Fred!" Buck bolted from his seat and whirled around to confront Shelley...or was it Fred?"

"Shelley's dead. He was killed in Palm Springs in 1977. It was an accident. He was injected with some substance that was supposed to knock him out for hours. It knocked him out all right. It killed him."

A sound not quite like a scream escaped from Buck's throat. "This is no game. You're telling me the truth."

"I can prove it. Shelley's nude body is preserved in a block of ice in Orange County in California. Rose had his body frozen in the hope that future advances in medicine might know how to bring him back to life. She wanted to give him that one hope. It was all she could do at that point. She wanted him to finish his life one day, even if it were in another century."

"Who are you? The man I've been making love to for twenty years?"

"I'm his twin," Fred said.

"I didn't know he had a twin."

"I know you didn't. Rose knew. I was her adopted son too."

Buck started to cry. He couldn't help himself.

Fred moved toward him, taking him in his arms. "Does that mean you'll stop loving me?"

Buck pulled him close, kissing his neck. "I'll never stop loving you. You belong to me. I've held you in my arms for twenty years loving you night after night. Somewhere along the way I must have stopped loving Shelley and started loving you."

"I'm glad I told you. All these years I've had to be Shelley. I took over his role. I've inherited everything. I've become Shelley. Calder Martin knew I wasn't Shelley but he's dead. Rose knew...but."

"She left us. She'll...Fred."

There was a ring at the door. Fred went to open it.

It was Lars. "Your car is waiting. You don't have much time to get to the temple. Traffic's bad this morning. Hi, Buck."

"Good morning, Lars."

"Your car is ready too," Lars said to Buck.

"I need a few minutes alone with Shelley, and then I'll be right down. I want you to go with me this morning."

"See you downstairs." Lars turned and left.

When the door closed, Buck walked over to Fred and kissed him on the lips. "I don't know if I'll ever get over the news you just told me. I'm trembling all over. But let's keep it our little secret."

"I hope when I get back around noon, we don't have to talk of it any more," Fred said.

"I don't want to talk about it. Let's pretend this conversation never happened and go on as before."

"That's what I want too," Fred said.

Buck held him close, then kissed him tenderly. "You're going to be late. What's your sermon about this morning?"

"I'm ranting against same-sex marriages."

Buck winced and blew him a kiss. "That's a subject you know a hell of a lot about."

Fred moved toward the door but hesitated. "I've always loved you since that first time. I've never been with any other man in my whole life. You were the first and you'll be the last. That's how it's going to be with us."

"Just go on being Shelley. It's best this way. I can't get used to a Fred."

"I am Shelley. I've assumed his role. There's no turning back now. This house. Everything. All the money. The temple. Everything Rose had. Everything Shelley had. It's all mine now. There are times late at night that I think I really am Shelley."

"And so you are. I've called you Shelley too long to call you anything else."

"Please go on calling me that and loving me." A frown crossed his brow. "And don't forget: the President is coming today."

"How could I forget a thing like that? He's got Camp David. What does he need with our humble Desire?"

"At least we'll get to see your son."

"I know," Buck said. "That's the only reason I can tolerate these presidential visits."

Fred turned and left, leaving Buck alone in the room. He would try not to think or dwell on what Fred had just told him. He'd learned over the years to blot out many things. That's how he'd come to deal with pain and loss. He planned to go on an inspection of his homes this morning, stopping off finally at the old Brooke mansion of his grandfather's.

He didn't spend much time any more at his old homes, but he still wanted to go by them whenever he could. If for no reason, the memories.

Before he did that, he had another stop to make. Lars understood and knew where Buck must go, but he always kept it a secret from Shelley.

***

In the back seat of the limousine, Lars put his arm around Buck as if he sensed acute distress. "You've always been here for me for years and years," Buck said, "and I'm damn grateful. Sometimes, though, I wonder what kind of life it's been for you."

"It's been a life of service devoted to a man I love," Lars said, reaching over to hold his hand. "I wouldn't change a thing."

"We've been through a lot," Buck said.

The familiar scenery passed before him, scenes vaguely remembered when he'd biked through the neighborhood as a boy. He wanted to think of anything today but what Shelley had told him back in their bedroom at Paradise Shores. He shared most secrets with Lars, but this was one he didn't want to divulge.

"We've got to get back to the coast soon," Lars said. "The natives are getting restless. You've got projects to make decisions about. The big but fading names are calling. Are you going to get back to them?"

"Who, for example?" Buck said, sitting up.

"Costner, Madonna, Cruise."

"I'll call Cruise this afternoon when we get to Desire. Hold Madonna for next week. As for Costner, I never got the message."

"All the biggest names in Hollywood at the millennium will be into grandparents' roles," Lars said. "There are just so many grandpa and grandma roles."

"Tell me about it," Buck said. He sighed. "With my beautiful son, I don't think I'll ever be a grandfather. There will be no Buck Brooke V."

"You said you wouldn't name your son Buck Brooke IV."

Buck smiled. "I know, and then I went and did it anyway."

"Are you looking forward to seeing him this afternoon?" Lars asked.

"I always look forward to seeing him. He's my son. I wish he were with us all the time. I'm only sorry he always shows up with the President. A Republican president at that, and I'm a lifelong Democrat."

"Your son loves the President, and the President is certainly crazy about him. They don't go anywhere without each other."

"I should never have let this thing develop between them in the first place," Buck said. "He was only fourteen at the time. I should have had the jerk arrested and charged with child molestation."

"Now, now," Lars cautioned him, rubbing Buck's hand. "All your son had to do was to remind you of your involvement with Shelley at that age. That ended the argument."

"I know."

"Young Buck was only a child then," Lars said. "But he's certainly at the age of consent now, and he's still with the President."

"I have this feeling that it's like a time bomb waiting to go off." He squeezed Lars's hand. "My son, an intern at the White House. The President of the United States. What a story this would make."

"The President has really concealed his tracks," Lars said. "I think the American public thinks of him as a womanizer more than anything else."

"We've concealed the President's tracks," Buck corrected him. "If I recall, and I do, it's cost me a lot of money. I don't know how long I can succeed in buying people off."

"It will all come out eventually. Hopefully he'll be out of office then."

"I don't want my son hurt." Buck closed his eyes and settled back into the upholstery. He knew that young Buck might not even be his son. He looked like him but in some ways he looked like Don Bossdum too. He'd never wanted to have tests done. He didn't want to know who the father is.

Don and Susan would be waiting for him at Desire when he arrived with his son and the President. As always, Jill and Sandy would see that everything was perfect. Regardless of where he went, Jill and Sandy were always with him, flying around the world, looking after him and anticipating his wishes before he did.

Susan was no longer publisher of the *News*. She'd become his own media director. At times he felt she ran the show more than he did.

So many of the others had gone from his life. He missed Uncle Milty something dreadful. Buck was at his bedside the morning he died. Hazel was long gone too. But at least she'd become mayor of something—not Okeechobee but his newly created Sun City. She didn't turn out to be a good mayor, but at least she got to hold the office.

Coming back to Okeechobee always brought back a memory of Gene. He wondered if Gene were still alive. He liked to think he was. He could never be sure. Gene was never found. He'd just disappeared from the face of the world, the way Sister Rose had gone. Rose had been officially declared dead after seven years. As her sole heir, Shelley had assumed control of her empire.

Before she'd flown to the Middle East twenty years ago to make that propaganda film, she'd drawn up a final will and testament, requesting that "Mr. and Mrs. Buck Brooke III" become the guardians of Shelley until he reached legal age. When Buck learned of this provision, he was shocked.

Rose in life always managed to shock him. So it came as no surprise that she would shock him in death. He closed his eyes and relived the night she'd disappeared. Shelley had been the first to discover Calder Martin's dead body. But Buck didn't want to dwell on that this morning. The day was too beautiful, too perfect to think of the horrors of the past.

Of all the people who had passed through his life, the one he remembered almost every hour of every waking day was Ahmad. After an unpromising beginning, theirs had grown into a great love affair. He never knew how much he loved Ahmad until Uncle Milty had called him on November 8, 1984 with the news that Ahmad's private plane had mysteriously exploded over the skies of southern Morocco. There were no survivors. Buck's scream on that dreadful afternoon still echoed within his own head. It was a scream from his heart.

Two weeks later there had been another call from Uncle Milty. "I've heard from Ahmad's people," he'd told Buck. "He's left you everything." Until the day he had a fatal stroke, Uncle Milty had spent his days trying to figure out exactly what Ahmad had left him in various parts of the world. It was a fortune so vast that its total value seemed to fluctuate wildly day by day.

Ironically, inherited wealth didn't matter in the end for Buck. He'd made his own money—not as a publisher, but as a producer of films. He'd had no preparation for such a role, but as Uncle Milty had told him, "All you need is money." Buck had had his flops—some colossal—but he was known more for his successes.

Ever since Susan read to him Gene's final request to take care of Jill and Sandy, Buck had virtually adopted them. They ended up, however, taking care of him more than he took care of them. They'd become indispensable to his life. He'd even been the best man at their wedding. They never spoke of Gene.

At the cemetery, Lars walked with Buck toward the grave site. Lars always stopped fifty feet away and let Buck have his private moment. Buck carried white roses and placed them on the grave. This morning was no different from countless others. He laid the flowers on the grave and looked up at Robert's tombstone. He kneeled and closed his eyes in silent prayer.

"I love you, Robert," he said to the wind. He looked at the empty graveside beside Robert's tomb, knowing that he would one day join him there. They'd sleep side by side.

Lars came up behind him and reached down for him. Buck took one final look at Robert's grave, and walked with Lars down the flower-lined path to the mausoleum of old Buck. The chauffeur carried flowers for his grave too. Buck took the flowers from the driver and placed them on his grandfather's tomb. "You started it all, sir. There's a Buck Brooke IV," Buck whispered to the silent grave. "And he's winging in now on the presidential plane."

"And we can just make it to meet the President," Lars warned him. "Not to mention be there to greet your son."

At the Okeechobee airport, where crowds had gathered, Buck was escorted to the head of the reception line, taking a position in front of the newly elected mayor. After all, Buck was the official host.

The Secret Service were the first off the plane, followed by both of the President's daughters, neither of whom had improved with age. As was his duty, a chore he'd performed so many times before, Buck kissed each woman on the cheek and welcomed them home. Even as he kissed them, his attention was focused on the ramp where his son stood in the breeze. The wind whipped his golden hair. He was a beautiful, charming boy. A young Robert. A young Shelley. Buck couldn't wait in line. He ran to the ramp and embraced his son. "I love you, guy," he whispered in his ear.

"I love you too, dad, and I've missed you something awful."

He hugged the boy again and kissed his cheek. "Don't stay away so long."

"We've been busy," his son said, squeezing his arm. "We've got an entire world to run."

"I know that must keep you busy, and I bet you make all the more important decisions," Buck said.

His son looked a bit miffed. "Don't you tease me. You'd be surprised at some of the decisions I've made. More than you think."

The Secret Service asked them to stand back behind the line. A band was playing "Hail to the Chief."

Down the ramp bounded the President of the United States. Buck was amazed at how handsome and youthful he still looked. Except for a few telltale wrinkles under his eyes, time seemed to have stood still for the President.

In front of the cameras, the President ignored Buck Brooke IV as if he didn't know him. His face lit up as he extended his hand to Buck III.

"Glad to be back in Okeechobee," the President said.

"Welcome home, Mr. President," Buck said, extending his hand in front of the cameras to greet Barry Collins.

Darwin Porter / 512

The Georgia Literary Association

Rhinestone Country (isbn 0-9668030-3-5)

A homo-erotic interpretation of the Country-Western music industry and closeted lives south of the Mason-Dixon line, sweeping across the racial and sexual landscapes of the Deep South.

Hollywood's Silent Closet (isbn 0-9668030-2-7)

A steamy, loosely historical account of the pansexual intrigues of Hollywood between 1919 and 1926, compiled from eyewitness interviews with men who flourished in its midst. Pre-Talkie Hollywood had a lot to be silent about. A "brilliant primer" (*Gay London Times*) for the *Who's Who* of early filmmaking.

Midnight in Savannah (isbn 0-9668030-1-9)

A gay-themed novel loosely incorporating Carson McCullers, Pamela Harriman, Libby Holman, the City of Savannah, and references to Georgia's most famous murder.

Razzle-Dazzle (isbn 0-1-877978-96-5)

In this "über-campy" romp, Porter re-defines the word bitch. There's something here for everyone: Sadists, size queens, romance readers, thrill seekers, gossipmongers, defenders of the paparazzi, bedmates of Cuban men, and anyone who ever hated Jesse Helms.

Butterflies in Heat (isbn 0-877978-95-7)

A scorching cult classic, and one of the best-selling gay novels of all time. It created the original character of *Midnight Cowboy*, blond god Numie Chase, a hustler with flesh to sell. Decadent and corrupt, this novel of malevolence, vendetta, and evil holds morbid fascination. "How does Darwin Porter's garden grow? Only in the moonlight, and only at midnight, when vegetation in any color but green bursts forth to devour the latest offerings."

And coming soon:
The Secret Life of Humphrey Bogart
(details you never imagined about the early life of America's most famous movie star),
and
Goin' South, a story about evil, greed, violence, vengeance, and homophobia in a small Georgia town. The *Gentleman's Agreement* of the post-millennium New South.

Distributed in the US by Bookazine and Ingram; in the UK by Turnaround Books, and in Australia by Bulldog.

Imaginative entertainment *for the 21st-century sensibility*